THE CROWNLESS QUEEN

CASSIDY CLARKE

~Dedication~

Dear reader,

I fought tooth and nail to write the "right" version of this story. The "realistic" version of this story. The "best" version of this story.
This isn't that story.
This is the funniest version of the story. The most self-indulgent version of the story. The most romantic version of the story.
It's my favorite *version of the story. And that's what makes it the best one.*
So here's to the ones who fight their hardest to be something they aren't…and are brave enough to decide the real version of themselves is pretty good, actually.
Maybe even the best.

Content Warnings

THE CROWNLESS QUEEN includes content that may be triggering to some readers, including:

Death

Amnesia

Blood/Gore/Body horror

Religious terminology/rituals

Grief

Possession

Illness outbreak/Medical environments

Food descriptions

Mild language

Violence

Misogyny

Mentions of physical and emotional abuse

Hallucinations

Manipulation

Drowning

Panic attacks

Harm and death of non-domesticated animals

Light spice (fade-to-black only)

Please read safely.

CHAPTER 1

SOREN

The second they stepped onto the shores of the island kingdom of Arborius, Soren Atlas nearly turned around and walked right back onto the pirate ship they'd hired to sail them here.

Not because she'd lost her nerve—because it was so damned *crowded* and *bright* and *loud,* and her head had yet to stop pounding after she'd smacked it on the deck of the ship this morning. She and Anima had done their best to shift control of their shared body carefully, deciding together that it would be best if Soren didn't show up with a gold eye, but their body had dumped them on the deck anyway.

After the fit had concluded, Captain Patch had been kind enough to tell her she could win a trophy with that impeccable impression of a fish flopping itself to death on a dock. And even now that her legs had agreed to do their job again, they stuck to the end of the gangplank like someone had coated her boots in tar.

But she didn't have time for the indulgence of dawdling.

So step off she did, shrugging her heavy satchel onto her shoulder—then protesting when Elias immediately lifted it off, slinging it over his own arm as he came around from behind her.

"I've got it. Ah—hey," her battlemate and perpetual fussbudget of a fiancé said sternly, holding the pack out of her reach when she tried to snatch it back. "If you saw someone bringing their sick fiancée to a physician for help, and they made their fiancée carry her own bag, what would you think of them?"

She crossed her arms, grumbling under her breath.

He cupped one hand around his ear, leaning down. "I didn't catch that. Try again, but less pouty?"

She pinched his ear, earning a satisfying hiss of pain before releasing him. "I'd think they were a prime example of an asshole."

He raised one eyebrow. "Point taken?"

"Point taken." Not that she had to be happy about it.

"Good." He adjusted the strap on the satchel, patted it once, then held his hand out to her. "Then let's go."

The dock spokes jutting into Arborius's harbor were heavily guarded for a kingdom committed to peace. Leather-armored rangers strolled up and down the spokes jutting into the sea, armed with knives and leather-bound logbooks they marked carefully with feather quills as they chatted with captains, assessed their cargo, and met with passengers pleading for aid.

Elias did not plead, and for that she was grateful—maybe she didn't look as bad off as she felt. Instead, he spun a short and unfortunate fib about her *stomach problems* that—while making her want to kick him soundly in the shin—seemed to convince the ranger examining Patch's ship.

That, and the clothes Patch's crew had donated to help them blend in better. Even with Arborius's alleged neutrality, neither of them had felt comfortable making their outlandish case in their bloodstained Nyxian uniforms, even if those were the only clothes they had besides a spare article or two jammed into their bags.

The crew's work—both their outfits and the staging of the ship—seemed to do the trick. The ranger finished his assessment with a smile, at least, which she assumed boded well.

"Head straight down this dock, turn left, and head for the building with the green roof," the ranger ordered, ripping out a page from his logbook and handing it to Elias. "They'll assess her and do what they can. Once you've finished there, make your way back to your ship."

Alarm fluttered in her stomach. "Patients are being seen out here? Why not in the city?"

The ranger narrowed his eyes at her, that polite grin losing its luster. She plastered a wan, feeble smile across her face. "I visited before, with my father…he had the same illness, gods rest his soul. He came for treatment often, and we were always taken to the infirmary in Elderwood, so I thought—"

"We've adjusted in recent years," the ranger interrupted—not unkindly. "Makes things more efficient…and easier on those who might struggle to make it to the city proper. You'll receive the same quality of care here as you would in Elderwood, swear on my life. And if you require more intensive treatment, you'll be escorted there with the next group."

We don't have time to wait, Ani whispered in the back of her mind. *If they try to treat us here, it could take hours before we're sent on to Elderwood.*

Soren had never been in a particular rush when it came to her health; most things she brushed off until they found ways to demand her attention. Infected splinters that rendered her fingers puffed-up and clumsy. Toothaches that eventually stopped her from chewing on one side of her mouth. Colds that simmered into clotted lung when she wouldn't put her training on hold to rest and recover.

But if ever there was a time to learn that lesson, it was now.

Besides, she couldn't fault Ani that urgency. Not after what they'd left behind in the shambles of Andromeda.

They say the wolves reclaimed the city. Some kind of unholy corruption…man and beast alike slavering for blood, tearing each other to shreds in the street.

Those whispers had dogged them the entire journey from Andromeda to Sirena; everywhere they'd gone, news of Andromeda's collapse had followed on their heels.

But the loss that cut unhealing notches into Ani's heart and pumped panic into their shared veins…that went deeper than Soren's ache for the city that raised her.

Not deeper than other griefs Soren carried with her from the overrun capital…but deep, all the same. Ani had lost her friend.

Kriss Lupin had never been what Soren would call a *friend.* They'd been sisters-in-arms, at best, and even that bond had never quite taken. They'd been a tad too alike; feral and orphaned, angry at something they couldn't fight, and their separate rages had rubbed each other wrong instead of establishing a kinship.

Ani and Kriss…it had been an odd friendship, to be sure, but one Ani had needed in the wake of separating from her brother's suffocating grip.

And Tenebrae had killed Kriss for it.

Elias squeezed her wrist, winding her back into the present; she leaned her shoulder against his before beaming at the ranger. "Of course. I understand. Oh, but wait—darling, you didn't tell him about your rash!"

Elias blinked. "I…what?"

She rested her hand on his bicep and squeezed, offering the ranger another hackneyed smile. "He's shy about it, poor thing, but it needs looking at. It started here—" she put her hand over his stomach, then trailed it downward as she kept speaking, "—and then it just kept creeping down and down until—"

A strong, fire-scarred hand caught hers in an iron grip, halting her demonstration at Elias's waistband. "She's *joking,*" Elias hissed through a false grin at the ranger, who'd started scribbling in his logbook again. "The green roof, you said?"

"That's right." Soren nearly burst into giggles at the genuine concern on the ranger's face. "Sir, if you're in need of an examination, there's no shame in—"

"Thank you for your help! It's appreciated." Elias's lips stretched so far in an attempt to fake pleasantry that they started to pale at the edges. He twisted her aside, keeping a firm grip on her hand as he steered her back toward the ship—then, as soon as they were out of earshot, he muttered, "You are *awful*."

"What, was I supposed to sit through you describing my *troublesome bowels* to that poor man without teaching you a lesson?"

"I *panicked*, all right?"

"You had the entire trip to come up with something!"

"And I spent most of it heaving over the side," he reminded her. Like she could have forgotten. "You can imagine why stomach issues might have been at the forefront of my mind!"

Can you fight about this later? Ani groaned. *Preferably* after *we get separated?*

"You're no fun," she sighed—then pointed to her head when Elias shot her a questioning look. "Sorry. Goddess."

"Right." They retreated several paces down the docks before Elias halted, glancing at the Starsinger, then back toward the forest towering beyond the outpost. The great wooden gates stood unyielding, taller by two than most buildings situated along the shoreline. "So. That didn't work."

Soren huffed. "I told you we should've used my name. I'm a future *queen*, for gods' sakes."

"And *I* still don't think using their dead niece's name would get us an audience. A sound ass-kick back onto our ship, maybe."

"But at least they'd have to look at us long enough to find our asses."

Elias blinked. "Pardon?"

She palmed her face. "It would get their *attention*, jackass. We're not going to find that relic by sitting in their spare infirmary for hours."

Even if the idea of using her born name to announce herself so publicly had her shaking in her shoes. But historically, playing the *Princess Soleil Atlas* card won her some kind of spotlight, however brief. The truth might put some pep into due process's step.

And speed was what they needed. Especially now that Nyx had fallen. Now that the God of Chaos had made a marionette of her elder sister and stolen the throne of Atlas, leaving her parents' fate unknown.

Now that both of her brothers had given themselves over to crueler gods, as well.

The urgency of her own predicament wasn't enough to stop her thoughts from running down fear-cobbled streets, chased by worries about what harm Tenebrae, Tempest, and Occassio could be dealing to her remaining family. What costs her loved ones would pay while she pursued this mad, last-ditch hope that Arborius held the cure for an ailment unlike any they'd seen before…a hope whose fulfillment or failure would determine if they had any chance at all of *also* dragging her brothers back from the brink.

A pursuit that put her half an ocean away from them, when they might need her most. And until she confronted the god and goddess in their bodies, until she knew for certain they'd hung on, like she had…

Then she was all Atlas had left. A queen not just in the making…but by her brothers' choices, by her sister's, a queen already *made*.

Her mouth dried out. Despite the sun shining high in the sky, the air carried the gentlest nip of cold…but that wasn't why goosebumps chose that moment to prickle her arms beneath her tunic sleeves.

Speaking her name and title on these shores felt like a step she couldn't take back. A commitment she would have to carry out to its conclusion, regardless of what unseen consequences might arise.

Even if claiming that ill-fitting crown felt like digging her brothers' empty graves.

But a queen wouldn't sit on the docks and wait to be summoned. A queen would demand an audience. A queen would use the power gifted to her by the accident of birth.

You don't have to do this, Ani said softly. *We can use my name. I can take over, perform a couple miracles, and maybe—*

Thanks for the offer, Goddess Great, Soren interrupted—not sarcastically. That Ani was willing to take the burden of this choice off her shoulders…it meant more than she could say. *But this is my family. I should be the one to speak to them.*

It's my kingdom.

It's my family, she said again. One point in their favor: her aunt and uncle, Queen Genevieve and King-Consort Cypress Olivander—plus her gaggle of cousins—held power here in Arborius. *Besides, if you make a scene out here, in front of all these people…we'll end up stuck for hours anyway while they all beg a miracle from you. And we're not strong enough to pull off that kind of play, anyway.*

Their shared heart twisted as they observed the groups of people struggling off the various ships docked alongside the *Starsinger.* Some were clearly ill, dull of eye and short of breath; others nursed wounds that bore infection or went too deep to fully stop bleeding despite stitches on the surface. Some even had to be carried off the ships by loved ones who wore worry like a heavy cloak around tense shoulders, its collar framing clenched jaws and eyes circled with bedside-vigil bruising.

In those frantic, hopeful faces, she couldn't help but see herself. Couldn't help remembering when this had been her exact plan: to travel to Arborius and return with a cure for Elias's Viper wound, the death sentence dealt him by an Atlas hand.

And in the people being carried off those ships…in their slack, lifeless features, their ravaged bodies, their pained mutters and groans…she couldn't help but see Elias's festering wound, the poison devouring his strength bit by bit, a slow crawl to an inevitable pyre.

His beautiful face, slack and somber in death. His spine breaking with a snap she still heard in the shadows of sleep, when the world quieted too much to drown the echoes out. *I was going to ask you to marry me.*

Nausea stomped down on her stomach, throat burning with the memory of her ragged screams over his broken body. She fussed with her sleeves, pulling them down to her fingertips—maybe they would hide the shakes rattling her knuckles.

Elias's hand settled over hers from behind, and she clung to it with all her might, drawing it around her waist and pinning it over her heart, allowing the weight to settle her racing pulse.

"This could have been us," she whispered, gazing unseeingly across the docks. "These people, they could have been *you.*"

"And thanks to you, it wasn't me," he murmured into her ear, kissing the corner of her jaw, then nuzzling his nose into her curls. "We're going to be all right—both of us. But we need to get you to that relic."

Anima's relic. The one thing that could separate her from the goddess her body played host to, before that body gave out on them both.

She clung to his hand for several more seconds…soaking in the warmth, the steadiness, the strength. Letting her body ease into shape against his. Forcing herself to breathe in time with his strong, even heartbeat thudding against her back.

And despite the fear cording his muscles in palpable anticipation, his arms stiff as suture thread, he did not rush her to the next step…he simply held her. Letting her shore up her courage, shielded by his ever-present shadow.

But she couldn't hide there forever. Queens needed to learn to stand by themselves…*as* themselves.

"Plan B," she muttered. "Let's tell them who I am."

CHAPTER 2

SOREN

She'd been right: introducing herself by her real name definitely bought her plenty of attention.

Rather, it bought her plenty of stares every time she tried it—and soon after, the realization that not one of these people was going to believe her.

Not the kindly older ranger with a perfectly groomed silver beard and mustache they tried first, who promptly diagnosed her with severe delirium and delusions of grandeur before telling Elias to rush her to the green-roofed infirmary straight away. Not the girl barely brushing her teenage years who greeted them at the infirmary's front desk—she didn't even know who Soleil Atlas *was*—nor the stern medimancer who came to see what the fuss was about.

In fact, the latter had shamed them for using a dead child's name to try and skip ahead in the queue ("Gods rest her soul," she'd been kind enough to add—Soren didn't bother telling her that the gods were generally the cause of her lack of rest these days) and told them that they could either wait their turn quietly like decent people or try their luck on some other island.

A staunch, stubborn lash of *put-them-in-their-place* she might have respected, if not for the part where it hammered the final nail into hope's coffin.

Which left them in the exact place they'd been trying to avoid: sitting on one of at least twenty wooden benches gathered in the plain room where they made those who weren't actively dying wait to be seen, hoping there was *someone* in this building important enough to get them where they needed to be.

And willing to listen to a story that, admittedly, only someone very gullible would believe.

After approximately five minutes of silent stewing, Soren said, "Plan C, then. Maybe if you stabbed me, they would—"

"No."

"New rule. I've decided you're required to give every one of my plans at least thirty seconds of thought before you say no."

Elias stroked his chin with his fingers, considering for exactly thirty seconds before saying, "*Definitely* no."

She groaned. "We don't have time for this. They'd probably take us back faster if I was actively bleeding."

He made some noncommittal noise, rubbing his hand down her arm. "Just…hold off on that. I'm thinking."

"Thank you for your sacrifice. I know thinking's hard for you."

"You're welcome."

She slapped her hand over his forehead—no fever, but one had to be brewing in there with all those gears turning full throttle. "Does it hurt? Should I call that grouchy healer back?"

He rolled his eyes toward her hand, but didn't push her off. "Sass isn't helping."

"It's helping *me*."

When he only responded with a grunt, pinching the bridge of his nose and bowing over, resting his elbows on his knees…she paused. Lowered her hand. Looked at him—*really* looked at him.

"Hey." She smoothed the pad of her thumb over the divot between his brows. "You're wrinkling again."

At that, his lips finally tilted into something closer to a smile. He took her hand, rubbing his thumb over her knuckles, gazing just past her as he pressed a kiss to her palm. "Graying, too, I think. That fit this morning took at least ten years off my life."

"That was Ani's fault." She carded her fingers through his hair with her other hand, checking for signs of silver.

"Sure."

"I'm not dying," she said—so forcefully she surprised even herself. "So quit acting like a griefstruck old widower and start thinking of better plans, or I'll go out and pay Patch extra to try the stabbing thing."

"I'll do it for free," chirped the man himself—when she looked up, she found the pirate doing his best to take up the entire broad doorway, his shoulders straining with the effort of spanning the space with his arms. His fur-lined vest hung open, showing off his heavily inked torso, and he'd pulled his hair up into a neat knot atop his head. Chips of color sparkled along the base of that bun, an arrangement of hairpins she'd envied more than once on their trip here. He'd also cuffed his gray linen pants and traded boots for sandals; he looked more Atlas than she'd ever seen him.

"Anything to report?" he asked.

"Only that if you keep stretching yourself out like that, you're going to dislocate a shoulder," she said; when he pushed himself to stand straight, crossing his arms and giving her a frank assessment with his eyes, she sighed and added, "They're remarkably blasé about people claiming to be long-dead royals."

"And we didn't think claiming goddesshood would go much better," Elias muttered.

"And to be fair, the girl who was in here claiming she was Mortem born into a mortal body *did* start vomiting blood directly after, so…" Soren shrugged. "Can't blame them, I guess."

Patch's sunburned nose wrinkled. "Gorgeous. Well, me and mine need to be shoving off—Elowyn's just finished replenishing her supplies. I've never seen the girl giddier, and I'd let her stay overnight if I could, but the weather's turning out there."

Soren craned her neck around him to peek outside—the sunlight hadn't waned, at least not to her eye. But far be it from her to argue with a seasoned sailor. Maybe that hint of cold in the air promised an oncoming storm.

"We understand." Elias stood up, offering his hand—Patch took it and planted a kiss on his knuckles, grinning at Elias's flustered scowl before switching his attention to Soren.

"You get yourself well, Princess," he ordered. "I expect to see you back on my ship someday. We'll make a proper Atlas sailor of you yet."

"Yes, Captain." She offered her hand, and this time he did shake it. When he held out his arm in silent invitation, she obliged, grateful for an embrace that didn't treat her like sunbaked porcelain, a pretty thing poised to shatter. He smelled of salt and sun and sweat, and for only a moment, her heart panged with such consuming envy she had to catch her breath.

What she would give for the freedom to waltz back to that ship and sail off to the next horizon, caring nothing for kingdom or kin or chaos encroaching on the world.

But queens didn't run from trouble. Especially trouble they were partly responsible for.

She was about to pull away when he tugged her closer, his breath tickling her inner ear: "Wait for my signal. When you hear it, run for that gate like a bard caught in a priestess's bed."

A beat of confusion—then, giddy understanding. "What are you plotting, pirate?"

"Why, Princess, I have no idea what you mean. That delirium's getting worse—you really should get seen to." And with a wink and a loose salute, Captain Patch ducked back out of the infirmary doors, leaving them hanging open behind him like dropped jaws.

"I love him," she declared.

"I'd like him a lot more if his ship didn't want me dead," Elias grumbled. "What did he say to you?"

"Nothing really. Though, we might want to step outside for a few minutes. I could use a little air...and there's a signal we need to listen for."

Elias's shoulders fully slumped. "Oh, I'm going to hate this, aren't I?"

"Well, that's nothing new."

"Is it too late to try the stabbing plan?"

"Oh, *now* he likes my ideas! Maybe if you'd gone along with it in the first place—"

The second the sole of her boot slapped against the sea-smoothed wood just past the infirmary's threshold, a concussive *BOOM* shook the boards, rattling her teeth in her skull.

The effect was immediate—most people ducked or dropped entirely, covering their heads with their arms and shielding their ill or injured companions with their own bodies. Others—mostly rangers, and a handful of cure-seekers who had the look of soldiers, hunters, and other rough-and-tumble types of work—braced themselves through the initial blast before taking off running toward its source.

That source happened to be a sturdy ship boasting the name *Starsinger* on its scarred hull, one of its cannons smoking…a ship now rapidly fleeing the docks for the open sea beyond.

"Mutiny!" Patch's cry rose above the clamor as he sprinted back toward his ship…purposely flinging out his arms and legs, tripping or shoving those heading in the same direction under the guise of frantic fury. "That's *my* damned ship—*my* damned crew! Come back, bastards—this is *mutiny!*"

"Is that the signal, do you think?" Elias asked dryly. "Or should we wait for something less subtle?"

She elbowed him in the ribs. "Just *run*, jackass!"

And run they did, hand-in-hand and heart-in-throat—in the same direction as Patch at first, then they veered, splitting from the crowd and hurtling down the main bridge from the docks to the mainland, where that hulking gate stood guard between them and their mission.

Between her and survival.

They had barely gone a dozen paces when a warm, thick substance coated her tongue, the familiar tang of iron tying her chest tight with dread.

And with pain.

But they couldn't stop. Not this close—not with the crowd's hysteria subsiding behind them, Patch's distraction losing its grip on their attention. It wouldn't be long before the rangers gathered themselves and noticed two people racing in the wrong direction.

So instead, she kept running.

Almost there.

Almost there.

Almost…

There.

As one, she and Elias skidded to a halt at the end of the bridge, him breathing so hard that curls of smoke huffed from his nostrils, and her…

Well, she was breathing, a little. That was enough for now.

Because they'd reached the Gates of Arborius.

Even from far back, they'd been a sight to behold…now they altered her understanding of the word *massive.*

The gates were the culmination of the immense walls that encircled Arborius's one and only city of Elderwood: they towered over fifty feet high, built entirely of famous Arborian darkwood, gleaming like sable coins in the sunlight. This close, she could see every curve and knot in the wood—every notch and dip, every fleck of decadent amber and vein of lustrous bronze buried in its ebony core.

Fifty feet high, decorated in swoops of rich emerald and gold filigree…and not a foothold, handle, or crank to be seen.

And if she wasn't mistaken, she could hear the clatter of bootsteps ascending the guard towers to either side of the main gates—which meant the clatter of crossbows being primed wouldn't be far behind.

"Elias," she wheezed. "Archers."

"I know. I'm thinking." He tugged her flush against him, wrapping himself bodily around her—forging a suit of armor from his own limbs, ready to take any arrows that dove from the archery slits in the towers.

No smartass jokes about his mental prowess this time. She didn't have the breath for it.

Instead, she turned inward. *Ani. Can you get us in?*

I have an idea, but it would—

Then you need to take over.

Resistance balked on the far side of the wall separating them inside her body. *But we—*

I know. Physical strain was one thing. Another full melding of their souls, throwing the whole of her power atop this failing body's bones…

What if it broke them?

What if it did something worse?

Ani huddled in the darkness, quivering like a cornered mouse.

But the time for playing it safe was over.

So Soren let her soul brush up against Ani's trembling presence—one soul that swam in saltwater and burned with starfire, the other sweet as nectar and honey. And at that gentle touch, Ani lost all grip on her composure.

Please don't die, she sobbed. *Not because of me. Please don't die.*

I have no plans to die today. Or any day, if I'm being honest. Been there, done that, you know?

It's not a joke.

I know. Especially not now, when something bigger actually *depended* on her survival.

She wasn't just Atlas's Heir—she was the only one left to fight for them. If things didn't go right...there was no one left to pick up her sword. To carry on in her stead.

The reason she could not afford to fall...and the reason it was so hard to believe she would not.

Finn's tired smile and half-mad eyes gleamed in her memory. *I think you might be the only person left in the world who still trusts me. So do me a favor, little sister...trust me.*

Kallias, gone without goodbyes, only a piece of paper to replace the man she'd forgotten until it was too late—the man she still needed to teach her how to do right by their home. *Your rule will be like nothing Atlas ever seen...a queenship to reshape the world. Wherever I go next, know that I'll be watching...know that I'll be the proudest bastard Mortem's wretched hand ever took. (Don't tell Elias I called her wretched.)*

Jericho's face, contorted by Tenebrae's vile grin. *Turns out all I had to do was slip a noose over the necks of your parents and she gave right up.*

Enna's glittering tears clustered like stars on her lashes. *I'm staying, sweetheart.*

Her whole family had already fallen...what would make her any different?

Elias's arm tightened around her. "Soren—what's that look for? What are you thinking?"

She tilted her head back, searching his gaze...and saw only worry. Only faith.

Only love.

That was her answer.

She *would* be different—because she had already fallen. Fallen over and over and over, and each time, she had risen again.

Because she had made this man a vow. *If we fall, we fall together. Together or not at all.*

She had first sworn that to him with vengeance seething in the grit of her teeth, not much caring who she swore it to, so long as they could hold a sword.

But in the years since, they had sworn it again, and again, and again—and had kept it, again and again and again.

Had broken it, once. And it had nearly broken them both.

Gods and relics and this mortal body be damned, she had not come this far to break her vow to him again. Not before they had the chance to swear some new ones.

She caught his hand and held it against her heart. His brows furrowed over his ebony gaze, but he didn't pull away. "I don't like that look."

Her throat tightened.

Gods, he was so beautiful. What right did he have to be so beautiful and ridiculous and *good?* What right did he have to make her love him so gods-damned much?

Why did he have to make all of this so *hard?*

"Don't burn me," she whispered, and now his brows mashed together, his mouth screwing up in denial. She reached up and smoothed out those creases between his brows. "If this doesn't work, if I don't make it out…don't burn me, okay? Bury me in a locked coffin, if you have to, but—"

"I'm not *burying* you," he spat. "Or burning you. I'm not talking about this—"

"Elias." Her voice broke. "We have to switch—we don't have time. Just promise. Please?"

Those dark lashes of his fluttered shut, kissing the tops of his cheeks. For a long moment, he held that pose: eyes closed, lips thin, brow dragged down with the weight of his pain.

A pain her heart echoed, a plea that rang across the chasm that kept yawning open between them. A chasm they kept trying to cross, only for it to widen itself just before they could finally reach each other.

She eased her hands over his cheeks, running her thumbs over his trimmed beard. The strands tickled and scraped, a tingling soreness spreading across her palms, but that soft pain was the least of her worries.

"You are going to come back to me," he said—then, harsher: *"Tell me you're coming back."*

It might have been the dirtiest lie she'd ever spoken. It might have been the truest thing she'd ever said. But it didn't matter which—not when Elias Loch challenged her like that.

"I'm coming back," she promised. Or lied. Or hoped.

Whatever it was, he sealed it with a kiss—a real one, a fierce collision of his lips and hers that shook every numb and listless part of her to vivid, voracious life.

Not yet, those pieces screamed into the creeping cold. *Not yet.*

One last rallying din against the dark.

Then she pulled away from him. And she turned her focus inward.

Let's do this, Goddess Great.

Alarm flared from Ani's side of the wall. *Soren, wait…*

The longer we wait, the weaker I get. So let's just go. On the count of three.

Soren—

One…

I am not counting down to your—

Two…

Soren, what if—

Three!

Pain.

A swarm of wasps crawling through their veins, stingers dragging like a plow tilling soil, venom seeping into their blood like tainted groundwater.

A spile hammering into their bones, dripping marrow like maple sap.

A chain wrapping around their heart and *tugging*, yanking it against their chest wall with a heavy *thud*…then holding it there. Refusing to let it beat again.

Please. Soren couldn't tell if it was her or Ani begging. *Please keep beating.*

It was never easy, removing herself entirely from control of their body…in fact, it took every ounce of her willpower to force herself to let go, especially after the fit they'd had this morning. Every instinct screamed to cling to control however she could, even if it hurt. Even if it harmed.

Even if it killed.

But they *didn't have time* for fear to force its will upon sense.

So she ducked out. And in a blink, her body was no longer hers to command.

CHAPTER 3

ANIMA

L ight.

Light dappling the spread of mushrooms and moss coating the darkwood gates, greens and browns and golds reminding Anima why she had chosen them as her favorite colors. Light gleaming off Soren's engagement ring, the sun skipping gleefully from facet to facet. Light playing over a plop of blood that shed from her nose and splashed on the earth between her wavering feet.

Soren? Ani couldn't breathe, couldn't move—not until she knew. *Soren, tell me you're—*

I'm here.

Two words more precious than any offering ever laid on her altar. And with them came every sensation that she'd come to know as *Soren*—a reckless collision of passion and bravery and love, so much *love* that it took Ani's breath away. The kind of love that fought tooth and nail for those under its claim.

A love so ferocious and unfailing that, upon realizing some portion of it—no matter how new—laid claim to *her* as well, she began to cry again. *Oh, thank the old gods.*

Well, it's definitely not thanks to the new ones, teased the princess.

Ani's eyes burned.

Oh gods, no, Ani—it was a joke. Relax. I'm okay—we're both okay.

They were most definitely *not*. But with a host of rangers closing in, they couldn't afford to believe anything less.

Ani pushed Elias aside. "Back up," she ordered—when he obeyed, she reached one hand toward the apex of the gate, extending it like someone asking for help standing up. "I'm home," she sang to the trees beyond. "Will you let me in?"

Beneath their feet, the ground trembled.

Above their heads, shadow blocked out the sun.

And behind them, a chorus of gasps and screams went up as one of the Arborian darkwood trees—five or six times taller than the gates themselves—*bent* itself in a long, gradual arc, bark and dust and evergreen needles raining down on their heads. It stretched with a lazy groan, unfurling its topmost branches until they settled lightly on the ground at their feet.

Bowing before the Goddess of Life.

Something whistled above their heads—a crossbow bolt gone awry. Instead of one of their hearts or throats, it buried itself in the bent darkwood's bark.

With a cheerful "Thanks!" to the tree, she leapt into its branches like a little girl accepting the offer of a piggyback ride; Elias stared, mouth agape, even as the pounding of pursuing footsteps finally began to head their way.

She reached one hand out to Elias. "Are you coming, or would you rather get arrested?"

"Um," he said.

Don't baby him, Soren complained. *Tell him to get his ass up here before I kick it up here.*

"It's not actually a choice, Elias," Ani said gently.

You never listen to me.

"Right." He took her hand, and she helped him onto the tree's waiting bough...

And with a dizzying *whoosh*, the tree lifted them into the sky.

"This is worse than the ship," Elias yelped, clinging to the darkwood trunk, the bark smoking beneath his fingertips. He screwed his eyes so tightly shut that, even in the midst of Ani's boundless glee, she briefly worried he'd never be able to open them again. "This is so much worse than—"

Ani's giggly whoop echoed through the trees, cutting off the rest of his cry. In sharp contrast to the fire-touched priest beside her, she barely kept her hand pressed to the trunk, not so much as a filament of vine or bit of bark to keep her from falling.

She needed none. No tree had ever let her slip between its branching fingers before.

Soren did not offer the same trust. The order to *hang on to something for gods' sakes* swelled against the wall between the two of them, begging to be freed—but like Elias's mortal terror, Ani's joy swept it aside.

It couldn't be contained. It infected both sides of the wall, catching in Soren's spirit; and despite her friend's mortal fear, the next thrill was theirs to share.

"How high are we?" Elias asked, eyes still shut.

"It's hard to tell. Maybe, mm…three hundred feet?"

Elias's knuckles paled. Matchstick flames leapt from his fingertips. *"Get me down."*

"I thought you liked heights!"

"I *do*," Elias said—as he shook in every limb, refusing to look up or down or *anywhere*, about to catch the tree on fire with his smoking hands. "As long as my feet are on the ground."

"You should at least take a peek. Who knows when you'll get a view like this again?"

She wasn't lying—the view *was* spectacular. The darkwood trees—all gentle giants built from blackened bark and needles so green she suddenly wasn't sure she'd truly *seen* green before in this life, varying in height but all of them taller than any palace or castle she'd ever visited, spread out like a verdant carpet over the sprawling island. Here and there, deciduous trees interrupted the evergreens with hints of other colors: firebrand orange and wedding-band gold, cherry-tart red and mottled-toad brown.

Dew sparkling in the topmost branches sprinkled the forest with stars, and the sky beyond…

Blue at first, then white—a layer of cotton that darkened to thunderous gray on the horizon. A storm, just as the pirate captain had warned.

Beautiful. And yet…

Those tortoiseshell patches of autumn colors splashed across the island's spring-toned face rang a tiny silver bell in the back of their shared head—a dusty little trinket labeled *Soren's Good Sense.*

The princess distracted herself from that good sense by entertaining the possibility that fall came early to Arborius, the same way winter arrived unreasonably early in Nyx and always overstayed its welcome. But Ani had a sensible bell of her own, one less gently used, corroded with age—and in every small silence between Soren's chimes of warning, it rang thrice.

A bell that knew better.

A bell that knew the seasons *never* stepped a toe out of line here…not in the kingdom grown by Life herself.

"Hold on," she said, unnecessarily—Elias had only tightened his grip since she'd last looked. "I'll bring us down."

CHAPTER 4

ELIAS

If he'd set about stoking bitterness's flame rather than shoving its throbbing coals beneath a layer of cold, stifling ash, Elias Loch might've complained about the irony of the massive gates swinging open mere seconds after Anima's arboreal puppet had deposited them on the ground. If he'd had time to consider his own state, he might've lamented how his kneecaps were near collapse themselves, and his stomach—still a bit seasick—was still making up its mind on whether it was going to empty itself onto the worn dirt trail Ani had directed them to before handing control back to Soren.

But thanks to the boot-beats of pursuing rangers growing louder with every second, bitterness had no space to breathe; instead, he could only be grateful when the dizziness finally abated, leaving room for dogged determination to direct his steps in a straight line.

A similar but subtly different determination burned in Soren's eyes as they pushed on through the trees—the only glimmer of her he could see past the gleaming gold of goddesshood in her gaze. The proof Anima was firmly in control now.

Gods willing—or at least, Anima willing—for the *last* gods-damned time.

No sooner had the thought crossed his mind than trouble forded into their path. As if irony enjoyed listening in on his hopes and arranging its timing accordingly.

Mottled in shadow, several paces downwind, four figures slipped on soundless feet from the evergreens, blocking their way in a half-moon arrangement—two standing on the trail, two others flanking on either side.

These damned rangers were *quick*.

Elias and Anima skidded to a halt. But more footsteps still pounded behind them, closing in. Voices shouting for them to halt. Bowstrings groaning in bloodthirsty anticipation.

Forget getting an audience with the Olivanders. They'd be lucky if they lived to see the sunset after this, neutral kingdom or not.

Anima hissed a curse—one so filthy he knew for a *fact* she'd learned it from Soren.

Elias set his back to Soren's, slipping his smallest finger around hers. "You with me, smartass?"

"She's listening," Ani breathed.

A smaller miracle than the one they chased now, but a miracle all the same.

"Pack tactics," he murmured for his battlemate's ears, tightening the crook of his finger when a reluctant quiver twitched through hers. "Can you two make it?"

Six words, and the plan took shape between them. A strategy neither he nor Soren had ever liked, despite understanding its necessity, because it required a battlemate pair to break the most sacred piece of their vows.

But thanks to Mortem's blessing, he could not be killed by arrow or blade—and if she didn't reach the relic in time, she might be killed without any weapon at all.

In the pause, he monitored the conversation happening behind that golden façade…a crinkle to their freckled nose. A scrunch to their lips. Grinding teeth.

"She says you're a jackass—sorry. But she can make it," Anima whispered. He couldn't tell who was trembling harder, him or her. "*We* can make it."

"I know you can," he lied, grateful the goddess didn't know how to read him half as well as Soren…hoping his battlemate wouldn't snitch on him. "You know the way, right? Just get her there…I'll be right behind you."

The conversation behind her eyes shifted, a torrent of snow set to avalanche. To sweep his conviction off its feet.

"What, smartass?" he prompted.

"She says…" Ani's swallow strained against her throat. "Walk us there?"

He grabbed her hand and squeezed it tight. "Every step."

The pursuing footsteps churned to a halt behind them—trapping Elias, Anima, and Soren between opposing ranger forces, all with arrows nocked and aimed.

"On my mark," he breathed, barely moving his lips, afraid even the dribble of sweat down his temple might be enough movement to draw their fire.

When Ani nodded, Elias hauled in a breath. Said a silent prayer.

And with a sharp, practiced exhale, he set the closest rangers' beautiful darkwood bows ablaze.

He nearly whooped the same way Ani had in the tree when the rangers leapt apart, leaving a seam in their ranks—and Ani *tore* through that seam faster than his father used to rip the stitches out of his own wounds, muttering about how he'd heal faster without them.

A peculiarity he only understood now that he shared the same blessing.

While the rangers were still screaming curses, dropping their bows and stomping them into the dirt to smother the flames, he drew his scythes, dove through the gap he'd made in their little blockade, and ran backwards down the path.

Pack tactics: strategies for battlemate pairs to use when they found themselves surrounded. To every pair's displeasure, most of them required one battlemate to be the distraction while the other escaped ahead of them, but the logic was sound. Split the pair, split the enemy's focus—and, if they were lucky, they could quickly regroup and win themselves a more defensible position.

He and Soren had taken turns playing the distraction many times, but never like this. Never without the goal of reuniting and facing their enemy together…and never relying on someone else to play his battlemate's part.

But he'd had plenty of practice fighting alone over these terrible, torturous months apart from her. He'd happily do it now if it meant he *never* had to do it again.

The path seemed happy to play along—every backward step met solid, smooth ground. The wind was less willing; when the rangers without burning bows got ahold of themselves and started shooting, arrows cutting through the air with a whistling hiss, the wind tilted its hand to guide them straight toward Elias's heart.

One of his scythes sliced through the first arrow. His next swing knocked the second out of the air.

And the ground chose that moment to betray him.

His heel clipped a divot in the path, throwing his balance; the third arrow sank into his left lung, his next breath seizing in a cough that expelled a plume of smoke.

A cry of dismay went up—not from behind him, but from somewhere in the ranger ranks. Something about how she'd given the order to *disarm* him, not *kill* him.

Life had gotten very strange indeed, when he wished they'd aim to kill instead. Almost as strange as a soldier tearing fresh stitches out of gaping wounds.

If they pierced his lung or heart, it could only slow him. But if they deadened a nerve in his arm and made him drop his blade, pyromancy couldn't summon it back into his palm.

Yanking the arrow from his chest would be nothing but a painful waste of time; so he forced himself to endure, wheezing around it as he struck arrow after arrow from the air, refusing to let even one whiz past him. Not one would find its mark in Soren's back.

Blood bubbled around the shaft of the arrow in his chest, a sickening sign of a deflating lung; but with a pop of searing heat, that blood curdled and clotted, scalded by his superheated skin. The arrow itself blackened and cracked before flaking into soot; a moment later, his lung inflated with a full breath.

For half a heartbeat, the constant hail of arrows halted. The silence stank of confusion—a loss of nerve. The pause gave Elias time to gain some ground, to think—and his gaze caught on the dry brush scattered at the edges of the path. On a dead tree emerging from the desiccated thicket, its trunk already half-sundered, only standing thanks to the support of a generous neighbor's branches.

Worth a shot.

Instead of extinguishing his blades, he tightened his grip until every groove of the hilts stamped deep into his palm—until he could feel the eternal heat purring in the core of the Artemisian steel. It flickered like a candle, soft and simple, ready to answer his call. Ready to fade or flare by his will alone.

The fire in his core did not burn half so gentle. It shivered, roiled, thrashing angrily against its bonds. Destruction only barely restrained.

Well, he was about to loosen its leash.

He jammed his blades into their sheathes before skidding sideways, changing direction so fast his head spun, sprinting toward the dead tree.

The bone-dry, brittle-barked tree just waiting for something to take up residence in its lifeless wood.

Nesting rodents. Hungry insects.

Or fire.

Bowstrings snapped. Arrows whistled. Two found their marks in his arm and hip—before he could really comprehend the sensation as *pain*, they burned away, leaving only dim throbbing where he ought to feel raging agony.

He collided with the tree, its spiky bark scraping his hand bloody as he caught himself and dropped down beside the split in the tree's trunk. Splinters gnashed on his fingertips as he drove his hand into the heart of the tree's husk; he squeezed his eyes shut and reached into his own heart, rattling his ribcage. Waking the beast.

And with a roar that resonated from muscles to marrow, his phoenix-gifted fire tore free of its mortal cage, erupting from his palm and igniting the tree from the inside out.

Elias yanked his hand free; with another muttered prayer, he twisted on his heel, landing a solid kick on the weak seam in the trunk.

With a groaning cry and a chorus of cracks louder than a snapped bone, the tree crashed across the path. Its hollow, half-rotted trunk split open, air flooding into the cavity—

Colliding with the fire he'd set in its heart.

More screams. Stronger curses. Orders to run and soak their cloaks in the river so they could beat out the flames; orders for the others to circle around and get after him.

But they wouldn't find him. He was already running, chasing a different flame through the trees; a glimmer of red curls catching the sun, the only trace of his battlemate running for her life.

CHAPTER 5

ANIMA

Ani barely kept from weeping as they stumbled as fast as their ravaged body could manage through the Elderwood Forest.

Her home.

She knew most of the trees by name, though not all—many she had coaxed from seed to sprout to sapling herself, lovingly persuading them to grow tall and strong and steady. Back then, they had been so small, so sparse—now they were grandparents with many *greats* preceding the title, several generations spanning a single forest. The only mortal beings that had known her in every life; that had cast shade on every one of her faces.

And she could marvel at none of them. Not properly. Not until she could look upon them with her own eyes; not until she could touch them with her own hands.

Not until they could finally stop *running*, iron and salt swamping every sense, dampening the perfume of pollen and river water and green, growing things with the odor of violence and fear and a body desperately trying to die.

Meanwhile, Soren tussled with her own memories—memories of these same places that sifted between the torn-down ruins of the wall between them with reckless abandon. Flashes of summer picnics and giggling children and affectionate calls from parents not to wander too far.

Are you all right? Ani whispered.

No, Soren panted back. *But this isn't the time!*

As if driving her point home, their next stride landed with a *crack,* like a branch breaking beneath their heel—but the sound came from inside their skull, not under their boot. A rush of dizzying heat and dazzling stars crowded behind their eyes, gushing out through their nose—Ani slapped their hand over the torrent, then peeled it away, staring at their blood-slicked fingers. Blood that poured faster from their nose with every aching, bone-shaking stride.

Wonderful, huffed the princess as Ani shoved their sleeve against their nose to sop up the blood. Mere moments later, their arm began to tremble, muscles aching with effort.

The price for Ani using her magic to call the darkwood to their aid.

But they couldn't stop. Elias might have been death-blessed, but he was only one man—and judging by the snapping strings and stomping boots coming ever closer, he was losing ground.

The last half-mile to the relic was a blur of blood and sweat and crippling exhaustion, the clamor of battle ebbing and flowing at their back, until all at once the ground graded up into a slope. And when they stumbled up that slope, spitting blood and wheezing…

There it was.

Her tree—her home. The Arboretum Absolute.

It had been a century or two, at least, since she'd visited last, but she still knew it at first sight: the gargantuan tree stood apart from its fellow sentries, a circle of empty space surrounding it. Dead grass unfurled from roots as broad around as an ordinary oak's trunk, death flattening the brush twenty—thirty— Sancta help her, *fifty* feet around their quarry. The trunk stretched at least a hundred feet before branches even *began* to show, and they clustered so thickly together that she couldn't hope to get some idea of where the tree *stopped.*

Compared to its girth and staggering height, the door built into its bark— a beautiful piece of sable wood, gilded hinges, and etchings of flowers in full bloom—seemed the perfect size for a mouse. Maybe a bird, if they didn't mind taking refuge so close to the ground.

Almost exactly as she remembered it. But that circle of dead grass…that set her warning bell chiming again.

This was *her* home. Death should not have been able to tiptoe so close to its roots.

You grew this? Soren breathed to Ani.

I did. Ani could barely form the thought, overcome by memory. By worry. *The first of this forest.*

We have to climb that?

Yes. The relic was kept in the shrine at the very top. A choice she regretted now.

Soren was quiet for a beat. *Has anyone ever told you you're an overachiever?*

Ani giggled—inwardly and outwardly. *Actually, no.*

Well, consider it said. Another moment of silence they didn't have to spare. *Welcome home, Goddess Great.*

No tears. Not now. Not yet.

With one last bracing breath, they stepped forward together.

As soon as their sole settled on the ground—half over the border between dead grass and lush forest floor—a horrific ripping sound rent through the clearing.

Ani shrieked; she staggered back, but their legs failed, dropping them on their seat as—

As one of those roots tore itself free, clods of dirt the size of carriage wheels falling and bursting apart on the ground, scattering buried rocks and clumps of grass and hairy clusters of smaller roots.

CHAPTER 6

SOREN

*S*o, Soren said, dimly aware of their fingers digging into the crisp grass as they watched the root slowly sway above them like a squid's tentacle, its bark groaning and showering splinters as it moved, *when were you going to tell me your tree doesn't like visitors?*

"This isn't normal! I mean, there are defenses in place, but they shouldn't have activated for *me*, and not until we got to the door, I don't—" Ani's voice quivered as she beheld the work of her hands. "It's never done this before!"

Of course it hadn't. *So what do we do? I thought you said it would let you—*

"It *would* let me in. Maybe it just doesn't know it's me."

It's a tree, Soren reminded her. *It doesn't* know *anything!*

"It's not just *a* tree," Ani said. "It's *my* tree. I'm going to try again."

Ani, I don't know if—

But Ani had already shoved them back up, walking toward the tree. And Soren didn't even try to stop her…mostly because it didn't matter. If they didn't make it to the tree, she was dead; if they got crushed trying to make it to the tree, she was also dead. No use arguing about it.

Grass snapped like brittle bones as they inched forward. The root froze in the air, quivering, rigid—a hunting hound catching scent of its prey.

"Shh." Ani reached their hands out as if pressed to invisible glass. Another step. More snapping and breaking and *one of the dead met Soren's eyes and gave her a cruel, bony smile.*

Shivers erupted from the center of Soren's very being, swarming outward like a beehive broken open. She didn't think she'd ever stop hating that sound.

You're talking to a tree, Soren hissed.

"You know me, little one," Ani cooed, ignoring Soren's disbelief; more bark dust showered down as the root coiled toward them, its inflexible skin breaking to allow it to move. To seek. To hunt. "You remember me."

The root stopped again. This time, it lowered slightly, almost like an acknowledgment.

You're talking to a tree, Soren said—dumbfounded this time.

Because it was *working.*

Shh, Ani thought. *Let me concentrate.*

They'd crossed halfway through the clearing now. Step by cautious step, Ani growing bolder with every inch, they approached the sanctuary of one of the most powerful magics that had ever been recorded…armed with nothing but a sword Soren couldn't lift and magic Ani couldn't use without weakening them.

"I won't hurt you." The door was only five paces away now. Four. Three. "You know me—you know I would never hurt you."

The entire tree gave a shudder that shook the earth.

"I'm Annelisa." Ani said her mortal name like a secret, in a whisper even the wind couldn't carry. "Do you remember me?"

And with a soft sigh that almost sounded like an echo—almost sounded like *Annelisa*—the door swung gently open.

The root dove back into the ground. Like it had never emerged at all.

See? Ani asked—Soren didn't appreciate the smug tone. *Told you.*

Can we cover the I-told-you-sos after we get the relic, maybe?

I only had the one, anyway.

"Halt!"

They wrenched around, pain cracking through every limb; a ranger stood halfway down the hill, arrow primed on her string, sighting her shot without sparing the bestial tree a glance. As if somehow, the behavior that had startled its maker didn't give this mortal a moment of pause.

To the woman's left, Elias had been forced to his knees; one of the other archers held a hunting knife to his neck.

"Stay where you are," shouted the lead ranger, "or we will not hesitate to draw blood. Too many of you take *neutral* to mean *passive*."

It had to be exhaustion. Blood loss. The hysteria of terror. But when she saw her battlemate roll his eyes, looking almost *bored* by the threat, Soren wanted to laugh.

She couldn't remember the last time either of them had the luxury of fearing death.

Meeting her gaze, Elias dipped his chin against the edge of the blade like a dare. Clenched his fists against his knees. Mouthed, *You're coming back.*

With a mighty effort, Soren nodded back to him, forcing a smile. *I'm coming back.*

And together, she and Ani stepped into the yawning maw of the tree.

A bowstring snapped. An arrow flew. Elias shouted her name.

The door shut all on its own behind them.

CHAPTER 7

ANIMA

A cape of shadow swept around them as the door wedged shut, stranding them in a sea of nothingness.

Rot and mold hung heavy in the air, damp and oppressive, blotting out any lingering hint of evergreen needles and river water. Ani made the mistake of breathing deeply through their mouth; their tongue curled back, trying to scrape the taste off with their teeth.

What is that? Soren gagged as Ani tugged their shirt collar up and covered their mouth and nose, the fuzz tickling their nostrils with the threat of an oncoming sneeze. *It smells like something died.*

"Something did." More than one something—Ani's skin crawled as her senses brushed up against patches of *wrong* in the dark. Large forms with no life in them; no life except for small and wriggling scraps of it. Maggots worming their way deeper into decaying flesh.

That's disgusting.

"We need to find the stairs," Ani whispered. "They should be straight out from the door."

Once, entering her tree had been a relief, not a terror. Once, she would have danced over the plush moss rug and sang her hellos to the tree—and to the birds that roosted in hollows up and down the walls, who would have sung their hellos back. Once, she would have kicked off her shoes and sprinted to the spiral staircase, sprucing up the flowering vines woven around the banister as she took the steps two at a time, her short legs burning with exertion and energy as she tore for the chamber at the top.

But not now. Not blind and weak and trying not to step on anything unpleasant.

Or dangerous.

Don't you have lights in here? Soren growled.

"Somewhere. But they're activated by magic."

Soren stayed quiet as they cautiously slid forward another pace or two. *Might be worth the risk.*

"Or it might send us into a fit," Ani countered, "and we'll have done all this for nothing."

They both thought for a moment, weighing the options on either side of their head like a scale weighing out coins.

Together, lighter and deeper tones blending in their shared head, they said, "Blind it is." And they started moving again.

Despite their mutual agreement, Ani's magic scratched beneath her skin, yowling to be let out; it scraped and snarled and whimpered in pathetic plea.

Not yet, she tried to soothe it, but it only begged harder, recognizing the one place it could always roam without collar or leash.

Her magic rarely rebelled against her, but she couldn't blame it for this tantrum. She wasn't much happier about her sanctuary now serving as a tomb. The Arborians outside hadn't struck her as lackadaisical caretakers, but for it to have fallen this far into desolation and disrepair…

Somewhere in the dark, something skittered across the floor.

Soren's swordswoman reflexes tugged the tendons in their wrist like marionette strings, twitching their fingers toward the sheath hanging from her belt. *What was that?*

Why would I know any better than you?

It's your tree!

I can't see either, Soren! Ani swung their other hand in an arc out in front of her—then froze as it plunged wrist-deep into something sticky. Something soft and clinging and strangely thready, like silk fiber gathered but left unwoven.

Please, Soren's calm tone belied the slow sinking of their stomach, *please please please tell me that isn't what I think it is.*

The floor buzzed under their boots as that skittering repeated, closer now.

Ani loved all creatures; big and small and strangely shaped, scaled and furred and feathered, they were all endearing in their own way. She'd often hosted mice and rats here during the bitter cold of winter; she'd happily allowed snakes twice her size to sun themselves on her windowsills, scratching their scales as they basked against the sun-warmed stained glass. Most mornings, she'd woken to find the ceiling of her bedroom had been swallowed by a colony of fruit bats, their sleepy chirps waking her with the sun.

But one particular creature defied even her open-minded adoration. One creature she could never bring herself to *hold*, let alone house.

A primal whimper was the only answer she could muster for Soren as she tried—and failed—to extract her hand from the silken shackle wrapped around her wrist.

Light, Soren breathed in their head.

We can't.

Bristle-stiff hairs brushed against their ankle, and Soren took that whimper and tore it into a cry: "Ani, *light!* Now!"

Ani staggered back until their shoulders collided with the wall of the tree. And at the same time Soren punched through the wall between them just enough to heft her sword, Ani drove their heel against the wood and screamed a word in a language long lost to time.

With a joyful, whooping thrill, her magic burst free; green light poured from beneath their bootheel, flooding into the seams that had cracked through the wooden walls after all these centuries.

Stretch marks. Growing pains. Marks of the tree's expansion in her absence.

Proof that up until recently, it *had* been well-cared for. Thriving, even.

For only a half-beat of her heart, confusion overtook fear.

Then the light flared.

As it barreled upward, that glow of power branching out through the dark, the color shifted. Verdant emerald paled to starlight white, and when it streaked across the ceiling to light up the globe-thistle-shaped glass fixture secured in the center…

Soren's too-loud burst of hysterical laughter, followed by a deadpan sigh of, *Oh, I should have let you kill me, Ani*, confirmed all her worst fears.

Because crawling slowly toward them, its crick-legged, chink-filled body standing easily over ten feet, was a spider.

A twitching, foamy-fanged, red-eyed *spider.*

Its host of lidless eyes gazed at them, a milky sheen coating each one like poorly painted marbles. The frothing venom gathered at its mandibles, tinted blackish-green, dripped in gobs of poisoned lather; every undulation of its rows of legs brought it closer to them, its fangs chattering together like it had caught some kind of chill. Its chitinous shell clicked ominously as it moved.

Soren dragged their eyes from the spider, eyeing their caught hand instead. *I need to cut us free if we're going to have a chance. I can barely swing this thing with two hands, let alone one.*

Let alone in the state she was in now.

Ani forced their gaze back to the spider. *I think sudden movements might be a poor choice.*

Staying stuck is a poorer choice!

The spider crept closer; visceral fear skated over their skin, and Ani couldn't resist drawing back, cringing into the wall—then biting down a gasp when she glanced past their stuck hand.

As they'd feared, they were caught in a web—a web the likes of which Ani had never seen. It spanned over half the circular chamber; the fireplace, the long pink chaise, the birchwood table, the shelves of cookbooks and plant pots…all of them were swathed in spider silk, silvery drapes cast over every piece of her old life like burial shrouds. Beneath those silvered palls, she counted three odd lumps that didn't match her memory of her foyer's arrangement.

At least now they knew where the dead things were—and what had rendered them so.

I'm going to cut us out.

No! Ani made the mistake of looking into the spider's eyes; they drowned her in malice, in a pool of clouded blood. *Let me try—*

The spider lunged.

A tandem scream tore from their throat, and that probably saved them—their joint focus on swinging the sword, their shared adrenaline, allowed it to complete its arc and chop into the webbing, slackening the hold on their hand.

They rolled underneath the pouncing spider, not pausing to look back; instead, they scrabbled toward the staircase, Soren doing her best impression of Elias's prayers (though her versions were sprinkled with far more expletives) while occasionally getting interrupted by Ani's screams of *hurry hurry hurry!*

Falling plates. Broken porcelain.

Something bit into their calf.

Deep into their calf.

Their chest-first impact on the floor flattened the breath out of them, killing their scream; they rolled onto their back, wrenching their leg free from the spider's jaws and swinging Soren's sword.

The spider reared back; the blow fell short, glancing off one of its legs. Panting through the throbbing, feverish pain, they released the sword with one hand and dragged themselves back. Splinters stabbed into their palm, but neither of them flinched.

Do you know if it has any weaknesses? Soren demanded.

Ani's mind raced. "Um, shoes? Really heavy books?"

Now's not the time to be smart!

"I've never seen one the size of a—"

The spider jerked toward them again, then skittered back, almost like a fencing feint; they gave up on their pursuit of the stairs, gripping the sword two-handed again, glancing down at their leg. Blood flowed over the edges of the wounds like a cluster of waterfalls—far faster than it ought to be.

Gonna guess the venom stops clotting, Soren muttered. Their head swam; Ani forced her own thoughts through the fog, helping Soren keep their grip on the sword.

One lucky blow—that was all they needed.

"Go for the head," she choked. "That's everything's weakness, right?"

Soren glanced at the many-eyed head. Then down at its feet.

Should've let you kill me, she muttered again.

Then she lunged for the spider's legs.

Ani's protesting scream drowned out the spider's clicks—and the awful shriek of steel against chiton as Soren sliced through its front legs.

The spider collapsed in a frontward somersault; dark, brackish blood spewed over the floor, soaking their clothes and seeping into their shoes.

With a feral shout, Soren shoved their body into the gap left by the spider's amputated limbs, thrusting the sword up beneath its gaping maw.

More blood, mixed with venom, poured out—oddly cold. Ani gagged as Soren yanked the sword out and stumbled back, favoring their bitten leg, watching through squinted eyes as the spider twitched—sagged—twitched again, then finally crumpled into a pile of limbs, its still-shuddering legs akimbo.

That, Soren said, *was the grossest thing I have* ever *had to do.*

Then she dropped the sword.

Soren never *dropped* her sword.

"Soren!" Panic sparked, and Ani quickly took over their hands as Soren faded back, scooping the blade back up—or trying to. Even hefting it up to their shoulder felt nearly impossible. "Come on—come on, the stairs—"

With this leg?

She had a point. The last dregs of their strength were leaving them, draining away with every drop of their venom-laced blood. And just the effort of pushing through to handle the sword—not even to fully take control—had faded Soren like a crumpling flower, her spirit shrinking back on her side of the wall.

"Hold on." Ani couldn't heal the wound, not with poison in it, but she could do *something.* "Just—hold on. I can fix this."

With mighty effort, Ani shoved the sword back in its sheath; once she had both hands, she let their knees hit the floor, crawling over to the massive spread of webbing.

She still remembered the steps to treat a poisoned wound; make a tourniquet, halt the blood flow, keep the poison trapped in the affected limb. Not a cure—but better than nothing.

Too many minutes later, Ani dragged them up to their feet, testing their weight on the leg now wrapped snugly in spidersilk. It hurt, and hot blood still seeped through—but it held. Their knee didn't buckle.

It might be enough to get them to the top.

"Soren?" she panted. "Still with me?"

With you, Soren answered. *Mostly.*

Mostly didn't assuage the mounting terror stirring her blood. "I'm going to get us to the top. But you have to walk with me, okay?"

A vague sound of affirmation was the only response she got.

So close. *So close.*

"Soren," she snapped. "You did not come this far to quit on me because of a spider bite, so wake up and *walk with me*!"

Their head jerked forward like a sleeper jolted from a nightmare, Soren sucking in a breath; she flexed their fingers around the hilt of her sword, loosening Ani's white-knuckled grip on it.

I'm with you, she croaked. *I am. Let's…let's get up this damned staircase.*

"Stay awake."

I'm trying. I'm trying, Ani. I swear.

That was what scared her the most. Because Soren's *try* usually held more ferocity than another's *solemn promise*, and this felt less like trying and more like failing.

But she couldn't very well say that to a woman who'd fought gods and monsters and her own traitorous body just for this last-ditch shot at survival. So instead, she limped to the spiral staircase that spun up through the circle cut into the ceiling, setting their uninjured leg to the first step to test it.

It creaked and moaned and complained about the weight of their toes, but it held.

Thank the old gods.

Ani. Soren swallowed hard. *There will probably be more…things…up there. Keep the sword out.*

Ani hesitated. "I don't know if it's a good idea."

Why not?

In answer, Ani let her imagination paint a picture with her fears: a picture of them tripping and tumbling, Ani's inexperience with handling a sword ending with them speared through the heart by their own blade.

Soren's laughter didn't match Ani's scowl. *Ani, even you're not that klutzy.*

This time, she shared a memory: a memory of her doing that very thing in one of her other lives. She remembered little from the years she lived in other hosts, but she remembered that…it might have been Orchid. No, it *had* to have been Orchid, because that was the lifetime she'd inherited a bodyguard along with the body.

She couldn't remember his name. Or what he looked like. Or *why* she'd kept a bodyguard on, despite having no need for one. But she remembered how the color had utterly fled his face when he saw her splayed on the ground, a kitchen knife driven into her chest—and how he'd sworn the premature white hairs in his beard were *her* doing when she calmly asked him to remove the blade so she could heal properly.

A funny little twinge twisted in her chest, right where that dagger had gone in.

She hadn't thought about that in a long time.

Huh. Soren didn't sound amused anymore. *All right, well…just be ready to grab it, I guess.*

Each stair wailed in protest as they eased onto it, wood buckling slightly wherever they stepped; cold adrenaline spiked up their legs every time, muscles squeezing together in anticipation of a fall. Each jolt wrung dizzying pain from their bite wound, spurts of heat and blood colliding with ice and fear.

But they kept climbing. Step by precarious step, stair by wasting stair, they kept climbing.

Some stretches they climbed faster, when they ascended through dark rooms filled with a chorus of hisses or scampering feet; others they stopped to breathe in, collapsing on their backside and staring down into the spiral of decaying wood below them, neither willing to point out how lucky they were none of the steps had snapped yet.

How much farther? Soren asked. Every cord of muscle in their chest strummed with screaming pain, cutting that breath short—instead of a proper exhale, their lungs expelled it in a harsh, blood-clotted cough.

Ani bent into the cough, digging their fingers into the soft wood to stop their trembling; gentle caps bumped her fingertips as tiny mushrooms sprouted in the makeshift substrate.

No. She tore her hands away, balling them together and bunching them up in their shirt. No more magic—no growing, no healing, no calling to the beast carcasses in the foyer to come and carry them the rest of the way. Not until Soren was safely separated from her.

"Not far," she lied, refusing to look up and count the remaining floors. Knowing there were too many. Knowing it didn't matter, because they had to keep going anyway. "Just a few more stairs."

Are you lying to me?

Ani didn't answer. Even though the silence answered for her.

She stood up instead. Gripped the banister instead.

On the next step up, their leg plunged straight through the wood.

And when they crashed into the steps below and above, those gave, too.

Fortunately, Soren had picked up on a couple things, having shared this body with her for so long. So when terror struck Ani stupid and screaming, her entire portion of their mind emptying to make room for the might of her fear, Soren threw out their hands and called to the life yet lingering in the tree.

Soren's intent took shape as a mental shriek, arrowing out in the form of green tendrils of magic: *Catch us!*

Friction seared their wrist as something thick and ropey twisted around it, yanking upward; both of them cried out in shared pain and dismay as their shoulder ripped right out of its socket. When the second vine shot out and caught their other wrist, though, they were ready—they grabbed on and tugged back, lessening the force as the vine wrenched them to a halt, dangling over the hollow abyss they'd just wasted most of their strength scaling.

"Well," Ani choked, "that could have been worse."

Soren didn't answer.

The sweat pooling in their armpits and coating their arms cooled as they dangled there, as did the pain in their leg—some slight relief. But Ani couldn't focus on anything beyond that heavy silence. She prodded at it mentally, her best attempt to nudge something with no real form. "Soren?"

A flicker of *something*—no words, no voice, but something.

Something that weighed less and less on their body the longer Ani sat there, breathless, waiting for an answer that might never come.

That Soren might not be strong enough to give.

She spared one look at the vines—and one thought for their wounds.

No more magic. But if they kept trying to climb at this pace, in this state, Soren would die before they even found the top.

"Don't worry," she whispered to her friend's flagging spirit. "I'll get you there."

She'd promised Elias. And as long as she lived in this body, a promise to that particular boy would always burn in her veins like a blood-oath.

It felt like they hung there for hours while Ani took a page from the spider's book, weaving a host of vines into a web of her own, pulling together a makeshift hammock beneath them. Then she lengthened the vines around their wrists, lowering their body into the hammock. Once their weight settled and the hammock held, she released those two vines and called down sturdier ones to anchor into the hammock—woody, bark-coated ones that wouldn't snap while hauling her and Soren's weight.

She gripped one of the vines and shifted onto their hip, trying to spread their weight out without putting pressure on their dislocated shoulder…or their bitten leg.

Difficult, since the injured limbs were on opposite sides of their body.

Gritting their teeth against a groan of pain, their neck crawling with the intense desire to climb out of their own skin, Ani croaked, "Take us up."

The vines obeyed; like guardsmen hoisting a drawbridge closed, her biomantic ropes dragged her and Soren up through the tree's hollow center. They hung directly parallel to the staircase, so as they rose, Ani was able to spot more missing and weak steps; more places they eventually would have fallen had they tried to climb again.

She'd made the right call—at least, the best call she could under the circumstances.

Time would tell how steeply they would pay for it.

Though she could still sense Soren's presence beside hers, it dimmed with every smooth pull of the vines; a candle nearing the end of its wick, close to flickering out.

"Hold on," she whispered, clutching the vine tighter. "Just hold on."

And at long, long last…they arrived.

The door to the shrine, unlike the rest of her home, stood exactly as she remembered it: a solid piece of gnarled wood, the splinters only barely smoothed from its surface, no knob or handle or latch to be seen. The craterous knot in the center also remained…and the inscription carved into its core.

Heart throbbing in their throat, Ani brushed their thumb over the inscription, mouthing the words to herself.

May you find the miracle you seek.

Swallowing, she pressed their palm against the text.

Green light leaked through the gaps in their fingers, blinding them for a moment. And then…

The door opened without a hitch.

With a sob of relief, Ani burst into the room, pure fervor guiding her steps, nothing standing in the way of her—

Of her—

Their boots clapped hard against the ground as she came to a halt, not understanding what she was seeing.

Not *wanting* to understand what she was seeing.

"No," she breathed. Then, voice shredding into a hysterical scream, she shrieked, "*No!*"

Because the one thing that could separate her and Soren from this single body was exactly where it ought to be, exactly where she'd left it: it sat upon a wooden pedestal, kept in a simple ceramic pot. Painted daisies and leaves dotted its cream surface, its rim gilded with golden paint.

The pot sat in perfect condition. But the bloom…

"No," she moaned, rushing to it and framing the space around its head with their hands, afraid the slightest touch might result in utter catastrophe. "Please, please—"

She knew why her tree had driven everyone away.

An ice shard that never melted: an impossibility.

A feather plucked from a deathless phoenix: a rarity.

A mirror with no reflection: a curse.

She and Tenebrae alone had chosen humble vessels to carry their magic. His boyhood music box, its pins plinking out a lullaby composed by their musically inclined mother when he was born, and…

And for her, a daisy.

A common flower, a choice that Brae had argued severely against. He'd wanted her to pick something rare or grow something entirely new—something that spoke to the majesty and might of the new pantheon they'd created. *Something miraculous,* he'd said.

Fear had kept her eyes on the flower in her hands, not the sketch-covered music box in his. It had kept her retort about his choices locked up tighter than those wound-up gears.

What fear hadn't done, just that one time, was stop her from making that choice for herself. Because of all the living things she grew, she loved daisies the absolute most.

But the bloom in this pot looked nothing like a daisy. Nothing like the flower she'd grown so carefully, each petal drawn out by hand, encouraging it in whispers as it took form and flourished for her.

The bloom on the pedestal wasn't flourishing.

The bloom on the pedestal was *dead*.

Gnarled, swamp-green growths swelled through its crooked stem, ballooning out in grotesque lumps; it slumped over, bent like a broken neck, its head dangling bonelessly at the end. The petals, yellowed and dried to a crisp, barely clung to the withered center. And when she tried in vain hope to bask it in verdant light, begging it to spring back to health…

Nothing. It just sat there, sickened beyond saving.

Not sickened.

Blighted.

Another cry—this one a roar, ancient anger shaking Ani to her toes; shaking the tree down to its roots. And this body only knew one way to meet its anger.

She spun, fists dashing at the air like she sparred with an invisible opponent. Graceless, arcing swings, fingers folded all kinds of wrong; if she'd actually struck something, her knuckles would have split like logs under a woodcutter's axe.

Ani. She almost didn't hear Soren's breathless whisper over her own tantrum, driving their blistered, aching heels into the floor with a reckoning scream. *Ani, stop.*

"No! No, I can…" Ani dashed at their streaming nose, their stinging eyes, and raked in a harsh breath. "I can do this. Just give me a minute to think."

You tried. So quiet. A quiet Soren was never a good sign. *We both tried. It's okay.*

No, it wasn't. It wasn't okay. It was *wrong*. It was *unfair*. It was—it was—

Kriss's snarl—formed in defense of Ani, frozen in death—flashed behind her eyes.

Pale cheeks dappled in blood, pale hair torn from its skull-tight braids, pale lips breathing their last.

Anger cooled. And in its place…

Wrath.

Not the human sort. The divine sort.

No more dead friends.

She'd sworn it, and she'd meant it, and she'd keep it.

Ani grabbed Soren's engagement ring.

Soren's attention piqued; the change flickered through their shared mind, a drooping tulip raising its head after a late-spring rain. *What are you—?*

Ani worked the ring off, concentration crinkling up their nose; when the ring popped off their fingertip, she tucked it into their left palm, pushing until it hurt. "Hold that."

Ani, I can't—

"Hold it, or I will *drop it*, and I will *kick it*, and you will never see it again, do you understand?" Seething fury—seething fear—stoked Ani into a frenzy, and she paced back toward the door, hand extended, ready to make good on her wild threats. "I will kick it so hard your rotting *ancestors* feel it. I'll wreck the damned thing if I feel your fingers so much as twitch, so *help me* I will, Soren!"

Only silence answered her at first. No other force took command of their hand.

Ani held the ring over the broken, plunging staircase. "You still think you can test the gods? Because I'll—"

Their fingers tightened around the ring—not Ani's choice.

"I thought not." Embarrassingly, her voice quivered—she cleared their throat as she pulled back from the staircase, afraid to look away from their closed fist. "Keep holding on. I'm going to figure this out."

Their throat sprouted a lump of its own, choking off their air. She cleared it with a fierce cough, returning to the bloom's pedestal.

Their fingertips met only smooth, icy granite when she swept them across the pedestal's surface; when she lifted them, only dust and dirt particles filled in their fingerprints. No evidence of tampering. But past it, reclining somewhere in the curtained-off alcove between two wooden columns…

Rot. Ruin. *Wrong.*

Chills scampered over their skin like mice fleeing a flooding den. She arched their feet in their boots, tiptoeing painfully past the pedestal.

The mauve curtains draped from the ceiling had once cordoned off a private reading area. Lapisian silk, gifted by Occassio for some birthday when they weren't in the middle of a spat or seven. And considering Lapisian silk sold for a hundred gold per foot back then, costing well into the thousands for an entire bolt, it easily made the most expensive gift her sister had ever given her.

Ani didn't like expensive things, or gifts given out of guilt, or mauve. But Cassi had tried. And to her sister, finery, status, presents luxurious enough to spoil…those meant something to her, even if they meant nothing to Ani.

Love, in its own way.

Now, those curtains hung tattered and dull, tarnished by dust. And that could have been an explanation for Ani's thudding heart and quivering insides…

But the bare, bruised foot sticking out from under the left curtain seemed the more likely culprit.

Old bruises. The nauseating tint of rot to the skin warned her back before the stench of death could hit her in earnest, but she was still close enough to see what she needed to see.

A mangled set of toes. Thorns sprouting from beneath the toenails. A bulging ankle that looked like the kneecap had actually slipped all the way down the leg until it could go no further.

Bravery could have coaxed her into tugging the curtain aside. Into facing what her brother had done in its entirety. Anger could have been her valiant shield held up against guilt as she took in the face of the unfortunate saboteur he'd sent to do the job.

But she'd always had a better handle on mercy.

Whoever that corpse had been, their family had to be grieving hard enough for their disappearance without knowing what awful task they'd died for. So she left the curtain closed, swallowing something—another sob, another scream, who knew—as she stumbled back to the relic.

No doubt left. This was a targeted attack. An intentional blow leveled against her by her brother.

Another punishment.

Maybe the bloom had been corrupted…but the magic inside, he couldn't have blighted that, could he? That magic was *hers*.

He couldn't take one more thing from her.

He wouldn't.

She wouldn't *let him*.

The magic had to be untouched. If she could just extract it from the bloom's core, unwinding it from the corrupted bits without letting them collide…

Ani exhaled sharply, forcing all her fear out in one breath, and wrapped their fingers between two tumorous growths in the stem—

It snapped.

Before she could fully close their fingers around it, before she could even begin to call to the magic inside…

The stem just *snapped*.

Hope crumbled, collapsing into a yawning pit in their stomach.

The stem followed suit. It crumbled to nothing—crumbled to *dust*—in their hand, and no matter how she begged, it wouldn't stop breaking, wouldn't stop fading—

Until she was left with nothing but a dried-out daisy in the hollow of their palm, half its petals releasing their brittle grip on the flower's center. Until she stood in a dusting of her own failures, grains sifting through the corroded gaps in the floorboards.

Ani fell to their knees.

"Soren," she sobbed.

I know, Ani.

Death had a smell and a presence…and a sound. A breathy, hollow rattle that scraped through a person's voice as they passed—a rattle that scraped through Soren's voice now.

Whatever Soren knew, Ani didn't. All she knew was that they'd made it—against all odds, they'd made it—and she'd still *failed*.

She stared at that withered, useless flower in their hands. Stared as her tears finally overflowed, pouring in streams down their cheeks, droplets plopping into their palms like they might yet water the daisy back to life.

A punishment.

Not just a punishment from Brae. Maybe a god older and more patient had finally decided to rebuke Ani for her hubris. For the role she played in trying to usurp him.

Her sister had always taught her that Sancta was not an unjust god; Mora had believed wholeheartedly that Sancta was loving and merciful, never unwilling to forgive a sorry soul.

Mercy. Redemption. Teachings that had vanished from public knowledge during Emperor Solomon's reign, but Mora had sworn rested at the very heart of Sanctan faith.

Redemption. A chance to put right what one had done wrong.

But no one could look at this and call it *mercy*. Because she had reached out for redemption—had crossed kingdoms and oceans for the chance to grasp it—and been denied at the doorstep.

"Sancta," she whispered, lips trembling and tasting of salt, "this can't be where it ends."

The air shivered, strummed by the name of a forgotten god.

"I know I don't deserve mercy. I haven't earned redemption." Her voice broke; two more petals fell, leaving one lonely petal clinging for its life. "I have harmed more than I have helped. I have broken more than I have fixed. But please...please..."

She bowed their head over the bloom and whispered her prayer over it.

"Let me try." The only plea she could put words to. "I don't deserve it, but she does. For the girl whose soul is twined with mine—for the boy waiting outside, praying that she lives—just let me *try* to make this right."

A goddess, kneeling at her own altar.

A force of nature, bent before her own failings.

A lost little girl, begging for the god she'd defied to *just let her try*.

The light in the room brightened—not much, not enough to make her squint, but enough to catch her attention.

A warm breeze rolled over them from behind, stirring their curls.

And in the palm of their open hand, the petals began to tremble.

Wonder halted the flow of her tears; she forgot to blink as the petals drifted back up to the daisy's center. One by one, they burrowed themselves back into their appointed places.

And when they settled, they spread.

Hysteria didn't loosen its clutches on Ani's heart, but it did switch tack—disbelieving laughter replaced mournful sobs as her bloom slowly softened, its petals paling from withered yellow to brilliant white, its center brightening from lifeless brown to vivid gold.

And in its center, a perfect pebble of rich green light took form. A pebble that pulsed like a small heart, an unimaginable power barely contained.

"There you are," she whimpered through her laughter, petting it gently with their fingertip. "*There you are.*"

It's beautiful.

Ani swallowed hard, trying not to whimper again at the sound of Soren's voice. "It is. Are you ready?"

I can honestly tell you I have been ready to have you out of my head since the second I knew you were in it.

She laughed. Sniffled. "Keep holding on."

Never letting go. Their fist tightened around the ring; Soren's fear tightened around their chest. Not fear for herself. *Be careful, Ani.*

Ani had to wipe away fresh tears with their wrist, blowing out a long, slow breath. "I will."

She set the flower back in its pot. Plucked that pearl of magic from its center and held it up to eye level, watching it swirl.

The power of creation pinched between their fingers.

Not *their* fingers—Soren's.

Maybe she couldn't redeem every mistake. But she could redeem this one.

"I will do everything in my power to heal what we broke," she whispered. "I swear it."

And it started here.

It started with her friend.

Because leaving her with her body torn to shipwreck shards…that didn't feel like healing.

She pressed that pearl to Soren's heart. And as the pain of all their injuries burned away, evaporated by the deluge of song and light and imagination and *color* that hummed with pristine potential, she whispered, *Goodbye, Soren.*

See you soon, Goddess Great.

And with one last breath of mortal air—a final goodbye to the body that had housed her unhappily for all these months—the Goddess of Life performed her best miracle yet.

CHAPTER 8

ELIAS

This was not the first time Elias had knelt in a waste of soot and ash, fingertips rooted in pyre-dust, bargaining with Mortem for the safe return of his battlemate.

But unlike the shock-sundered aftermath of his first battlemate's pyre, he had reason to believe against all odds that his prayer would be answered this time.

And unlike that night, he did not kneel alone.

To either side of him, Arborian archers took up arms, longbows trained on the entrance to Anima's tree; behind him, another kept her arrow flush to his neck, the steel nipping playfully at the branding seared into his skin.

And to his ever-growing disbelief, their leader sat off to the side, watching the tree with pursed lips…braiding strands of grass between her nimble fingers. Every so often, she raised a thatch of grass to her mouth and gave a warbling whistle; each time, a matching whistle answered her from deeper in the forest, and her nose crinkled in self-satisfaction before she tossed it aside and began to weave another.

An attempt to confuse him, maybe…or a way of communicating with reinforcements further in the woods.

Whatever it was and whatever that meant for him, he didn't care right now. All he needed to be all right was for Soren to walk back out that door.

The archer at his back shuffled, her arrowpoint taking the opportunity to nuzzle deeper into his skin. The hairs on the back of his neck stiffened.

All he needed was for Soren to walk back out that door…but still. He preferred sooner over later.

"Captain," one of the archers at his side ventured, "should someone go and see what's holding up—"

"Shh! Wait, please." Another thatch of grass—another whistle, this one sliding smoothly from low to high, a trill breaking out right at the end. She paused, waiting, head tilted to one side—when the identical call finally answered, she said, "Arrow-tipped jaybird. Go on."

"It's been over an hour," the archer said. The stone in his stomach flipped over. That long already? "Should someone go see what's keeping the reinforcements?"

Another soldier might've been flattered—even with him sorely outnumbered, they still felt the need to bolster their ranks. But he'd always preferred underestimation.

Well, maybe if you hadn't lit the forest on fire, snarked a voice in his head. It sounded suspiciously like his battlemate.

He hung his head, brow nearly brushing the grass as he forced all his anxiety out in a harsh, hard breath.

Flame gushed out with it, scorching a circle in the already-burned grass beneath him.

"Sorry! Pits, hang on," he swore as bows wailed under the strain of their strings, the archers shouting warnings or—in two cases—letting out embarrassingly shrill shrieks. He smothered the flame with his knee. "That was an accident! I'm still—"

An arrow buried its entire head in his shoulder muscle.

He turned to glance at the feathered fletching. Then looked up to the archer who'd fired it, her arm still bent from the draw, her face screaming that she was praying her hardest for preserved life.

"It didn't work before," he said slowly, "when you shot me in the *heart.* What made you think the shoulder would be better?"

The archer blinked at him. Swallowed. "Um. I don't rightly know." She looked at her bow, then at his shoulder, brow furrowing in consternation. "This doesn't usually happen."

If his muscle hadn't been throbbing with agony while his magic worked to expel the arrow—this one tipped in steel, not sharpened wood—he might've laughed.

A call burst from somewhere back toward the hill, this one human, not avian: "Good response time, troops! Aim and composure left something to be desired, but we can discuss that at a later date."

The leader of the archer troupe brightened, standing from her cross-legged sit without using her hands, as her fingers were still twisted up in grass. "See? Patience pays its due." She nodded to the men who crested the hill, joining them in the shadow of the Arboretum Absolute. "Sage. Wolf."

Well. Patience must have owed them a grave-deep debt. Because they hadn't summoned more Arborian archers to bolster their ranks.

They'd summoned a pair of princes.

The first, at least, aligned with Elias's expectations of Soren's family—starting with the glazed wooden circlet of chiseled vines and leaves that crowned his deep brown, auburn-cast hairline, held in place by two braids that wrapped around either side of his head to meet in the back. Marking his status without any doubt.

Beyond that, he wore a similar uniform to the archers—deep brown hunting leathers—but with that hint of royal flair no prince seemed to be able to resist. The leather gleamed with gold detailing, pleated and tooled with beautiful designs, runes and botanical art combined in an artful dance. Above the leathers, the thick velvet cloak cast over his shoulders was fastened at his neck with a golden leaf clasp.

It was difficult to tell if his rich golden-brown complexion carried the russet freckling common in the Atlas bloodline, or if the spray of sun flecks and shadow dapples were playing tricks on Elias's eyes. But the prince's stare—brown as bitter chocolate, teeming with muted anger—carried a keen edge that reminded Elias uncomfortably of Finnick Atlas.

But it was the other prince—one who bore no resemblance to the Atlas family at all—who set Elias thoroughly on edge. Because he wore raiment Elias might have once considered the telltale uniform of an enemy.

Layered robes in myriad shades of green and brown. A resin-coated darkwood medallion strung around his neck that winked wickedly at Elias each time it swung through a beam of sunlight. Amber eyes that gleamed with disdain when he looked from the tree to Elias. No bow or quiver on his back; instead, he'd strapped a bandolier of hunting knives across his chest, along with a small leather pouch. Wooden hair clips carved in the shape of oak leaves held his shoulder-length hair back, showing off snowbright braids cutting through the onyx. Like an aeromancer had run their fingers over his scalp and shocked the strands white.

Not just a prince of Arborius. The medallion, the robes…those made him a priest of Anima.

"Wolf," the lead ranger said again, "I apologize for calling you away, but as it involves the Arboretum…"

"It's no trouble." Wolf regarded Elias without blinking. "This is one of them?"

"It is. I thought you two might want to hear the story they spread when they made port."

"I know how this looks," Elias promised, "and sounds. But my battlemate—"

"Save your breath," Prince Sage interrupted as he and his brother halted in front of Elias. His voice flowed haughty and amused at the top, but underneath, it utterly *boiled* with calm, carefully contained rage. "A very concerned healer down by the docks already spilled your dung heap of a tale all over my best boots. Now, I don't know where you and your battlemate have been for the past decade, but there are two things you should know."

"Firstly," said Prince Wolf, his leather gloves creaking as his fingers flexed, "neutral or not, we do not take kindly to anyone *forcibly* entering our forest, let alone trying for the Arboretum Absolute."

"And secondly," Prince Sage added, dropping to one knee and forcing Elias's chin up to meet his gaze, "Princess Soleil Marina Atlas was murdered over a decade ago, to the great agony of the Olivander family. I don't care to hear any other version of that tale—the first was tragic enough. Whatever affliction has convinced you to use her name as some kind of *manipulation*…we have no cure for that, nor any other condition you've come here seeking help for. We help those who need it, enemy or friend, but we have nothing for someone who would use the name of a dead child that way. Now, if you'll be kind enough to point me in the direction of your missing battlemate…"

"Happily," said Elias, jerking his chin against Sage's hand, nodding toward the tree. "But I'm guessing you won't find it so easy to catch up with her."

Prince Wolf rocked back a step, finally blinking. "The tree let her in?"

Prince Sage raised a hand sharply—to silence him or Wolf, he couldn't tell. "I will give you one chance to tell us where your partner is hiding, take her back to the docks, get back on whatever ship brought you here, and let her die in peace. If you choose to commit to this charade, we will be forced to—"

"Prince Sage," interrupted the lead ranger—she bent to hover between him and Sage, looking decidedly sheepish. "I'm afraid he's telling the truth…about the tree, at least. It let the girl in."

"It can't have." Prince Wolf turned away, fully losing interest in Elias, taking a single step toward the tree. "It would never let anyone in but—"

At first, when the world disappeared in a detonation of green and gold light, that was all Elias knew: light.

Soft, but all-consuming. Beautiful, but blinding.

He could think of no other word for it but *glory*.

And then the silence.

Not the peaceful kind. The unnerving kind that resonated through the skull, buzzing deep in the eardrum like a bass note struck on a pianoforte. The kind where you knew you should be hearing *something*, that the noise had to be truly cataclysmic, but it struck so hard that the ear couldn't recognize it as *sound* at all.

The rangers all dropped their weapons and covered their ears, including Sage—he looked to be shouting, but no sound scaled past the force barreling into them. Only the lead ranger held her stance, something wild pacing behind her eyes as she sighted down her arrow. She didn't flinch or fold—not even when a scarlet droplet trailed from her ear down the side of her neck.

It would have been in his best interest to take advantage of their distraction; to cover his ears and run. Instead, he gritted his teeth against the pressure throbbing in his eardrums, ignoring the blood that began to drip like candle wax down the side of his jaw as he drew his scythes.

He wouldn't face this unarmed, whatever *this* turned out to be. If it got him riddled with arrows—again—then so be it.

The halo of jaded power slowly receded, pulsing inward like a puddle-ring rippling in reverse, until the only thing left glowing was the door.

Or rather, the empty hole where the door had once stood.

He couldn't see the door itself—he had a bad feeling that it had burst into splinters, scattered about the clearing like punched-out teeth. And he had a worse feeling that whatever had done it wasn't far behind.

Movement at the door proved him right: a hunched, many-limbed body curling jointed legs around the edges of the hole, pulling itself through the opening in rigid lurches.

Core terror dimmed his flaming blades from ferocious orange and scarlet to simmering, subdued blue.

A spider.

A spider that looked to have crawled straight from the pits of Infera.

It spanned at least fifteen feet across, its carapace catching the dappled light like dull black leather. Its front two legs were cut short at the top joints; the stumps waggled uselessly in the air, flanking the dried ashen-green foam stuck to the bristles near its fangs. Toward the underside of its mouth, that spittle darkened to an ichorous black substance, and its eyes…

Its eyes glowed with the same green light that had exploded from the tree.

"I knew I shouldn't have gotten out of bed today," Wolf muttered behind him.

The Prince sounded…lopsided, some words louder than others. No matter how hard Elias listened, he couldn't straighten Wolf's voice out—the ringing deep in his ears wouldn't abate.

With a curse he could barely hear, he shook his scythes, forcing away fear and pulling his spine straight, fueling the fire back to a healthy color. He'd fought corrupted wolves; had fought corrupted *friends*. This was—

Something pale and human-shaped shifted on the spider's back, out of tune with its jittering, automatic movements.

When the spider emerged fully into the clearing, the sun glinting off the dull copper curls of its prisoner, fear switched its sights to her.

"Soren!" he shouted, getting right up to the edge of the clearing. None of the Arborians stopped him. "Don't shoot, don't—*Soren!*"

"It's okay!" He nearly collapsed in relief at the sound of her voice, stringent with terror and pain as it was. "I think—I think Ani gave it a command, but it's dead, I killed it—"

"You *think* or you *know*?"

No answer that time.

Once the spider staggered closer, the picture came into full focus: while the creature still crawled, death had definitely had its way with it. Its eyes didn't track his movement as he stepped over the border of the clearing; the blackened substance was definitely blood, tainted and tacky around its death-wound. Tendrils of green magic looped around its jointed limbs, puppeting it through the motions of life—forcing it to carry its passengers safely to the edge of the clearing before collapsing into a rickety cluster of legs and hair and wasted venom.

Passengers. Plural. Because his battlemate sat astride its back, cloakless and bloodied...but cradled in her lap, silent and still and *small,* was an unfamiliar, unconscious girl.

CHAPTER 9

ELIAS

"Bows down," came Sage's soft order from behind him. "Everyone, back up—secure the perimeter. I don't want as much as a mouse to scrabble past your bootheels, you understand?" A pause, then: "Medwenna—thought you said only one girl went into the tree."

"Only one did," came the lead ranger's voice. Her tone struck him wrong—like awe, almost, but beaten out of shape until it became something unnerving. "But her eyes were gold then."

"Gold?" demanded Prince Wolf, but Elias didn't wait to hear the rest; he extinguished his blades in their sheaths and dragged himself up onto the back of the spider carcass, steadying Soren with a hand to her shoulder and steadying the girl's limp body with the other. When his weight shifted the spider's corpse, the stranger's arm slid, dragging her whole body over the edge with it—he quickly pushed her back toward Soren, who hauled her further into her lap.

Everything about Soren's posture screamed *don't get close*—she hunched over the girl like a wolf defending its kill, watching his every movement with rapt attention. Like he might try and take the girl away.

Dark hair hung long and loose past this stranger's waist. She had a pert, pretty nose; her lips were parted and petal-pink, pinker than most could achieve without some kind of cosmetics, a soft flush that also blossomed beneath her chestnut skin.

Soren had wrapped her cloak around the girl, who wore no other clothing to speak of; but she was considerably shorter than Soren, and slimmer, so the cloak covered everything but her bare feet and calves. Despite the thick material, she shivered like she'd just been pulled from an ice floe.

Blood flowed down one of the girl's ankles, fingerpaint strokes dealt to a canvas in generous handfuls; when he traced the path of that garish work, he found flesh torn open like a split wineskin, the wound's edges fizzed with yellowish flecks of foam.

Nausea dug its fingertips into his stomach and flipped it completely upside down.

He'd never seen a wound like that before—infected, laced with poison, or otherwise. And considering he'd had to cut necrotic flesh from the borders of his own Viper wound, gagging back sobs and sick while he did so, he really thought he'd make it his whole life without seeing anything worse.

He could barely choke out the words. "Is this…?"

In any other circumstance, the look Soren gave him—like he had just beaten out every other kingdom's contestants for the *world's biggest idiot* competition—would have been cause for a wrestling match. But compared to her absent stares and sickly smiles, he was so happy to see her *glaring* again that he almost shed a few tears himself.

"No," she said, "of course it's not. I went into a tree and happened across some stranger with no clothes. Yes, it's Ani, now will you just tell me she's alive and stop looking at me like I'm insane, please?"

"I always look at you like you're insane."

A sniffle. A laugh. Her lips, nearly white with shocky pallor, barely twitched. "Well, it's really bothering me right now."

"Then I'll stop." Jamming the toe of his boot into one of the chinks in the spider's carapace, he put his weight on his palms, bending over and pressing his ear to Anima's chest. But his ears were still ringing too loudly to hear a heartbeat.

Above his head, he could sense Soren's distress mounting, tangible terror leaking into the air. But before she could career off the edge into full-blown hysteria, Anima's chest rose and fell beneath his ear—a shallow breath.

"She's alive," he said—then surged up to catch Soren again as she sagged forward, dread melting into relief as she pressed a kiss to Anima's brow.

"Good," she seethed. "Because when she wakes up, I'm going to kill her for being so *stupid*."

Far be it from him to argue with that.

He lifted his hand toward Soren's face, inch by cautious inch. "Can I check those cuts?"

She blinked. Swallowed. Nodded. "You're being weird. Am I acting weird?"

Elias wiped that trail of blood off her chin with his thumb, checking for any obvious injuries beneath—no cuts, no bruises, no signs of a cracked or broken jaw. A lot of blood for a split lip, but he'd take it. "A little. You're probably in shock."

"That sounds right." Her voice was thin as a polish rag, buffing her words until he could barely make them out at all. She drifted forward, head bent toward his shoulder—he leaned in to let her settle there, and she sighed into his sleeve. "You smell awful."

He'd scuff her skull for that later. "I think that's the spider, smartass."

Something crunched below—a curse followed before Sage appeared next to him, one boot braced on a leg joint, the other planting itself on the spider's back so he could lean in. "Well, I can confidently say this is the oddest examination table I've ever used, but it'll do in a pinch."

Elias twisted on his seat and spread his arms out, shielding Soren and the girl in her lap. "What are you doing?"

Sage put his hands up—empty of weapons. "You came for healing, didn't you?"

"You just threatened to let her die, didn't you?"

"Not my best first impression, I'll ken to that." His eyes traced practiced patterns across Soren's wounds before returning to Elias. "I give you my word— not a hair on her head will see harm from me. We'll deal with your infractions later."

They'd come here to beg their help—he couldn't smack it aside when they offered it freely. Even if he really would prefer to do exactly that.

"Touch her without her permission, and this forest burns," he warned, shifting back around; Soren's forehead immediately sank against his shoulder again, like she didn't have the strength to hold it up. He braced the back of her neck, kissing muttered reassurances into her hair; but he kept his glare on the prince.

Sage turned his attention to Soren, all that heartsick anger evaporating like snowmelt in springtime sun; he leaned in and smiled at her with all the kindness in the world as he prompted, "Can you tell me your name, lass?"

Soren's head jerked up. She stared at the prince. "Sage?"

"No, that's *my* name," the prince teased…but his jaw flexed, a muscle leaping beneath his beard. "And I'd love to know how you—"

Sage's cautious question cut off into a low, startled grunt—Soren had thrown herself out of Elias's arms to wrap her arms around Sage instead, her face buried in his armored shoulder.

"Hi," she choked. "Sorry. I know this is weird for you. Just…hi."

"Hello to you, too," the prince said, firmly but gently extricating himself from her arms. "Might feel less topsy when I know who you are. *Can* you tell me your name?"

Soren mimicked his suspicious squint as she wrapped her arms around herself now, a slight curl to her lips. A smile, but one that might twist into a snarl at any provocation. "Not if it's going to get arrows shot at us again."

Sage coughed—snorted—then coughed again, raising his fist to his mouth. "Fair enough. But you can't convince me you thought that charade was going to work."

"You're one to talk about charades. Aren't you the one who tried to teach Finn and I how to lie properly? Or have you forgotten about the tadpole incident?"

The prince *spluttered*, his eyes widening. "I—now hold your—no one *knew*—"

Soren pointed to herself, finger to beating heart. "Someone did."

Sage stared her down for several seconds too long. Then he bent closer, one hand out—

Elias put himself back in the prince's way, thrusting his own hand out like a shield, the other arm guarding Soren's front. He bled a bit of fire into his hands…just enough to set the air wavering with warning. "That's close enough."

"Elias." Soren gathered a handful of his shirt and tugged. "It's all right. Let him."

"Sage," Wolf hissed. "What're you doing?"

Sage just waved the other prince off as Elias reluctantly moved aside; his eyes were glued to Soren's face, probing, confused. His thumb brushed over her temple, testing her curls, seeking something Elias couldn't identify.

"You do look like them." All arrogance and anger were gone—in their place, grief-touched wonder softened the edges of his lilting brogue. "Gods, you look like *her*."

There was a question carried in his voice…one Soren seemed to understand, because she reached up and tugged her sleeve aside, baring her fire-scarred shoulder. The ranger's eyes settled on those withered folds of pinkish, ruined flesh, and the bump in his throat strained against his skin.

"It is…a long story, Sage." Soren said—she didn't seem worried about hiding the grief clouding her green gaze in silver mist. "The longest gods-damned story you'll hear in your life."

Concern flitted through Sage's eyes, but only briefly. "And I want to hear it, lass—all of it. Something tells me I might even be able to stay awake through the whole thing. But no use telling it twice—save your breath for now." Sage extended his arm—then paused, glancing at Elias, then back at her. "Better make sure you're well enough to move. Do you want him to stay or go?"

"Oh, he stays." She threw a weary grin at Elias. "I don't know how much you know about battlemates, but—"

Sage rolled his eyes. "I've treated a few pairs in my time, gods help me. Never have been able to get any of 'em to separate. Almost lost a finger the one time I tried." He raised a crooked finger in demonstration—then hovered it in front of Soren's nose, moving it side to side. "Follow my finger for me…good. Did you hit your head?"

"No." A quick, definitive denial.

"May I check for myself?" Sage asked; he shifted to and fro, searching Soren's face, but her gaze darted downward. Her fingers danced nervously across the unconscious girl's forehead, gathering loose strands of hair back from her brow.

"I want Elias to do it."

"Heard." Sage looked to Elias. "Guessing that's you?"

"The spider, actually," he deadpanned.

"If all the holes in your hide hadn't come from my rangers, we'd be having a word about backtalking to healers." Sage tapped his own temple. "Don't leave one inch of that skull unchecked. You know what you're looking for?"

A kernel of heated temper popped on the tip of his tongue, a cluster of bitter words that burned when he swallowed. But even though they blistered his throat on the way down, he didn't cough them up. "I do."

"Bless Nyx for that—whoever's training you all, they make my job a little easier. Let me know what you find. I'm going to grab my bag."

"You brought a medical bag to come arrest us?"

The prince smiled, almost rueful. He scratched the back of his neck. "Yeah, well…hope makes us do funny things."

Even after Sage's admission, Elias didn't let his arms fall until he heard the prince's boots hit the ground. And only then did he turn to Soren and splay his fingers toward her head; when she dipped closer, eyes fixed on Ani's face, he set himself to the task of probing her skull for any hidden wounds. Once he felt confident that she didn't have any brain matter leaking out of her skull, he slid his hand beneath her chin and pulled it up, leaning back to hold her gaze. Better to keep her talking. "So. Are you going to tell me what this tadpole incident was?"

"Oh, you know…a bucketful of tadpoles, an empty tub in one of the guest rooms, a bored prince and princess, a dare from their older cousin…"

"Oh, gods."

She grinned. "That's what Mama thought—she kept telling Papa that Anima struck us with a plague."

As soon as she spoke Anima's name, she looked back down to her, eyes welling with new tears.

"What happened in there?" he asked softly.

"I woke up and found her like this." Anger and terror lit a green fire in her eyes, driftwood flames burning away the haze. "I told her to be careful, she promised, I don't know what she—"

"Soren," he interrupted. "Breathe. You're not breathing."

She tried—but it stopped short, shoved back out by an agitated sob. "I told her to *be careful.*"

Heart wrenching at the helpless distress that broke her voice, he pulled her in by her chin, pressing his brow to hers. "C'mon, with me—breathe."

He drew in a slow inhale through his nose, then exhaled through his mouth; Soren copied him, though her inhale crackled in her nostrils. When she exhaled, it smelled of blood.

Something warm and wet pooled in the crease between his hand and her cheek—a crimson-tinted tear. But at least her breathing began to calm.

She clearly didn't have full grip of her senses, she was covered in what he had to guess was a mixture of the spider's blood and her own, and her pant leg had been yanked up to make room for a makeshift bandage that looked eerily like a spider's web…but she was *alive*.

"Let's get you two off this thing." He turned to check for any waiting threats behind them—and found Prince Wolf standing a short distance away, frozen, staring at the spider's corpse like his mind had wandered somewhere else and he had yet to coax it back. "Your Highness, I could use some help getting your goddess down from here."

With a sleepwalker's waking lurch, Prince Wolf shook himself all over and broke into a jog, cautiously tracking the tree's roots out of the corner of his eye.

"I'll take her," Prince Wolf said as he reached the spider, holding his arms out. "You take care of your battlemate."

In one smooth movement, Elias hauled Anima over the side of the spider, handed her off to Prince Wolf, and turned back to Soren, fumbling to tear the leg of her pants open wider. "Keep talking to me. What's the damage?"

"My leg," she said immediately, clarity dawning in her gaze. "This damned thing—" she stomped her other foot down on the spider, "—bit me. And my shoulder got yanked out." She rotated the shoulder in question, doubt rippling across her bloodied face. "But it doesn't hurt so much anymore."

Shock. Had to be. "All right. I'll take a look."

"Can we get down first?"

He held out his arms, a silent invitation; she dragged herself into his reach, and he pulled into his arms, careful not to knock her leg around too much. He leapt down from the spider's back; Soren grunted when he landed, like the impact jolted her, but she didn't voice any complaints.

Wolf had already set Anima on the grass, Sage hovering over her leg; when Elias and Soren approached, Sage looked up, jaw set with grim uncertainty. "If she is who you claim her to be, then she ought to be healing on her own."

"It's slow when she gets a new body," Soren croaked, looking between both princes like she was trying to get her bearings. Her grip on his shoulder tightened. "It has to settle first."

"How slowly?"

While Soren and Sage exchanged clipped questions and answers, Elias set Soren on the grass and started searching for other injuries. When he bent her leg to the side, his mouth went dry.

The webbing on the underside of her calf was *soaked* in blood.

When he touched the damp, fibrous sheath, his magic surged, a sudden thrum of power that warmed his own blood; it brought to mind how his cat arched her back when she recognized a threat, hissing and spitting, trying to scare it off.

Venom.

"I need to get this off." He reached up and squeezed Soren's knee; when she turned to look at him, he croaked, "You have a knife on you? Something small?"

Soren shook her head, but Wolf immediately jammed a hand down his boot; he rifled around for a moment before yanking out a small hunting dagger and offering it to Elias.

"Thanks." Elias glanced up at Soren apologetically. "This might hurt."

She curled her fingers into the grass, her brow crimping as she braced. "Ready."

As efficiently as he could, he sawed through the webbing, inwardly preparing for what he might find. He peeled the sopping bandage away, his stomach doing another backflip at just how *heavy* it hung her blood—

And froze.

Confusion forced his thoughts to click by at a slower pace, so it took a moment for him to process what he was seeing—why Soren's leg was mottled with sticky red stains, but no fresh blood. Why the skin was unmarred, no torn flesh or exposed muscle to be found. Why traces of that same yellowish foam muddled the blood, tinting it orange, but didn't lead to any source.

"What in the depths?" Soren hissed. Sage shot her a sharp look, then scooted toward them, craning his neck to look at her leg. Medwenna, the lead ranger, returned from whatever Sage had sent her off to do right then; she hovered over his head, frowning toward Soren's leg.

Then Soren cursed at the top of her voice, falling back onto the grass and covering her face. "Gods damn it, Ani!"

"What?" Elias snatched his hand back to avoid getting kicked. "What's the tantrum for, what?"

"She took them," Soren hissed, flinging herself back upright; she stumbled to her feet, but kept stumbling, her buckling knees throwing her back to the ground. Elias shot up to catch her, and she sagged into him, cursing and thumping her fist against her own hip. "She took *my wounds.*"

His gaze snapped back to Anima's leg; as he took in the tight, swollen skin and fast-flowing blood, he hitched Soren closer.

That wound had been dealt to *her*—and in her weakened state, not even able to stand without using him as a brace...

Gods knew what would have happened if Ani hadn't taken it.

"Here." He helped Soren sit, then went to join Wolf by Anima's side, easing his hands over her leg. Even to his hands—hands that could cradle hot coals without blistering—that feverish flesh burned to an uncomfortable degree.

He shut his eyes, trying to think back to Kallias—trying to focus on what he'd done to burn out the poison when the prince had been targeted in Artem, not the way Kallias had looked. But the image crept in anyway: how he'd found his friend sprawled out on a cave floor with blood-flushed cheeks, unable to breathe, his chest rising and falling only because Raquel forced it to do so.

How terrified he'd been to lose him.

How saving him that day had only been a temporary stay of that loss.

"Wait, don't!" Wolf snarled, *shoving* Elias's hand off of Anima's leg.

Elias raised his hands. "I'm not going to hurt her. She needs help, and I can—"

"I know what you can do, sanguimancer." Wolf's voice thinned, stretched between caution and a darker emotion Elias couldn't identify. "But—"

"What my brother is trying to say, in his own charming way," Sage laid a hand on Wolf's wrist in warning, "is that an untrained sanguimancer is liable to do more harm than healing."

"What's a sanguimancer?" Soren sat up again, scowling.

"I've done this before," Elias argued. "I saved Prince Kallias's life—"

Wolf's brogue rolled with scathing grit. "Even if that's true, you're lucky you didn't kill him faster. You could just as easily shove all that tainted blood straight to her heart and drop her dead!"

"She's the Goddess of Life. I don't think she *can* drop dead."

"She shouldn't be able to be wounded, either."

"Will you two cut it out?" Soren groaned. "Look, whatever sandmancy is—"

"Sanguimancy," he, Wolf, and Medwenna all corrected.

"Blood magic," Medwenna explained further. "It's extremely rare, only estimated to present in roughly—"

"Hold off on that for now, Medwenna," Sage said—not unkindly.

"But she asked."

"She stopped listening after *magic*," Elias promised. "Maybe after *blood*."

Soren flashed a particular finger at him. "If it can help her, why would we wait? Have you got some other Mortem-blessed wielder lying around?"

Sage and Wolf looked at each other; Wolf shifted on his feet, eyes darting back and forth.

"Wolf," Soren prodded, driving a rod of warning through his name this time. "If this is some stuck-up anti-Mortem attitude—"

"Our father is better suited for this," Wolf interrupted. "That's all I will say without his blessing, but I swear on my ma's grave, I would not risk the Goddess's well-being on prejudice." He frowned at Elias. "I did not mean to give the impression that I hold your faith against you. I don't."

He didn't believe that for one second. But with Soren's glare drilling *please get along* holes in his skull, he dipped his head anyway.

Soren scooted on her backside over to Anima's prone form, ignoring his protests to hold still. She set her knuckles against Anima's brow. "Gods, she's burning up."

Sage, still wearing a frown deeper than a Nyxian snowdrift, looked over his shoulder into the woods. "We should get you all back to Elderwood, fast as we can."

Soren cast a helpless look at Wolf. "You're sure Uncle Cy can help?"

Wolf's glare softened; when he set his gaze on Anima, it lingered, troubled thoughts running a maze behind his eyes.

"I am," he said firmly. "But we need to get you both to our infirmary. Are you able to stand?"

Soren shook her head at the same time Elias did—then scowled at him. He shrugged. "What? You can't."

A resigned sigh from Wolf. "Then I'll carry the Goddess. Medwenna, if you can hold the cloak while I...?"

"I've got it," Elias said quickly. He and Anima might barely be allies, but she'd taken this suffering from his battlemate's body—it didn't feel right to leave her entirely in the hands of strangers.

Between his grip on the cloak and Sage bracing Anima's injured leg, they managed to get Anima safely transferred into Wolf's arms, the cloak securely tucked around her. Her head lolled to the side as Wolf stood, but he caught it quickly, his broad hand spanning the side of her head as he tucked her carefully against his shoulder.

"Thank you," Wolf said; that bitter, grinding tone from earlier had vanished again, swallowed by quiet composure and an almost sheepish bend to his scowl.

Elias merely nodded. There wasn't much else to do—or say.

He let Wolf get a few paces ahead before he helped Soren to her feet, wrapping his arm tightly around her waist; she tossed her arm over his shoulders, leaning her sweat-damp temple against his sleeve.

Together, he and his battlemate wordlessly followed the princes, the ranger, and the goddess into the woods, leaving the cursed tree and its corrupted inhabitants behind.

CHAPTER 10

ANIMA

"Her fever is rising."

Water lapping against ceramic. Soft splashing—the spatter from a wrung towel.

"Da, how close…?"

"Close." Strained, steeped in focus—she didn't know that voice, nor the one that came before. Nor the hands settled on her leg, one on her knee, one on her ankle—another on her forehead, someone's fingerprints probing her skin, cool and smooth as lakeside pebbles.

She arched into that beautifully cold touch on her head, a low moan scraping her throat; after a pause, a swallow, a shaken breath, it palmed the stray hair from her sweaty brow. "I thought she would begin healing herself by now."

"It has been centuries since Anima took a host. Your guess is as good as anyone's. Besides, if it's true that she took this other girl's wounds…" The cycle repeated: water drizzling into a bowl, the squelch of squeezed-out cloth. "I've never heard of a miracle like that. Even if she is who you believe her to be, this is new to all of us…maybe even to her."

Silence.

"Bring me more water and rags," the first voice requested after that pause overstayed its welcome. "It's going to be a long night, but I'll do all I can."

"Thanks, Da."

She wished they'd stop talking. It made it so difficult to slip back into the pain-muffling sanctuary of sleep…to ignore the heat gnawing on her leg like a dog worrying a bone with its teeth.

Not just heat. Not just fever.

Fire.

Fire.

Her eyes flew open to Death's grave-dark glare, gold as the fastenings on the finest coffin. Final as the click of its ruby-crusted lock.

Her sister Mora dug soot-stained nails into her leg—agony blistered, bubbled, *boiled* in her veins, a scream catching in her chest and dragging her back into an anguished arch.

"Mora," she sobbed as she crashed back down, thrashing her arms backward, clawing for any kind of purchase above her head—that cool, calming touch had vanished, fleeing from the wildfire consuming her from the inside out. "Put the fire out—Mora, *please* put the fire out!"

Her hand found nothing to grip—instead, it plunged into something pale as sunbaked earth. Fine as spider-silk.

Paler. Finer.

She swallowed a gag as she pulled back a fistful of white dust. Dust piled in scattered mounds all around her.

Mounds of pyre-waste. Mounds of ash. Mounds of bone and skin and hair reduced to powder so fine the breeze carried off portions like a pallbearer, bodies scattered across the barren deathbed of a city scorched for its sins.

Or for hers.

"You did this." Her eldest sister's voice bore neither seed nor sprout of the quiet malice growing like a weed behind her eyes. "This is *your fault.*"

"I know," she sobbed, no breath, no voice—smoke and death-dust clouded her lungs. "I kn—*I know! I know I know no no no no—*"

Confessions climbed to cries for mercy as fire floundered—festered. It blackened her bones, abraded her veins, stripped away her life layer by curling layer. Like a sheaf of paper carelessly fed to the hearth.

"I'm *sorry.*" Pain wracked every fiber of this body; she could not judge the scope of it beyond its disintegrating parts. She did not know it; she could not gain any kind of understanding of it being hers. "Please—please, I was trying to fix it, I'm trying, I'm—"

"A monster." Spittle peppered Ani's face, freckling new blisters into her skin as she cringed back from her sister, trembling in body and spirit alike. "You *steal* life—you *corrupt* it. How dare you claim to be its preserver, its protector? Its *creator?*"

A hiccupping breath popped and burned in her lungs. "I'm a—"

A monster.

I'm a monster.

I'm a—

"Shhh."

A cool breeze stirred her hair; a damp, comforting caress bathed her forehead and cheeks, smothering the flames. Wiping her tears.

"I know it hurts," murmured the voice above her…smooth and dark and kind. "But you have to breathe. Can you do that for me?"

Come on, Ani, pleaded someone else—someone whose voice she knew almost as well as her own. *Breathe for us.*

At the next pass of dew-laden cloth over her forehead, she obeyed, suddenly brave.

If it stoked the fire, so be it. Soren needed her to breathe.

"Good." The murmured praise warmed her insides in a different way…the drowsy sort, not the dying sort. "Keep breathing, Goddess." Then, aside: "I'm going to give her something for the pain. It might keep her asleep for a spell, but she needs the rest."

Her name is Ani. Soren again. *Not Goddess.*

"My name is Ani," she mumbled in agreement—well, she tried. Instead, it came out in a senseless slur of sound that didn't make *any* of those words.

And before she could try again, something sweeter than syrup drizzled over her tongue, soaking her senses in honey and spice. Hints of chamomile and turmeric floated over the back of her tongue.

For one moment, something bright and lovely broke the darkness effusing her eyes…trails of starlight combing through an ebony sky.

Then the stars went out, and she slipped into a softer, safer sleep.

CHAPTER 11

ELIAS

E*lias.*

Cold sweat. Coal and smoke coating his tongue in acrid powder. His taste buds curdling, blistering, until ashen numb burned all sensation away.

Elias.

Saccharine rose petals and sour blood. Splintered wood stabbing beneath broken nails.

Screaming.

Elias.

He couldn't scream loud enough—no one could hear him over the pyreside songs, sorrowful dirges drowning out his pleas for someone to realize they were burning him alive—

Elias Loch!

Elias started awake, choking for breath—he immediately covered his mouth, checking to make sure Soren hadn't woken.

Darkness still shrouded the room, but the graying shadows gave away dawn's impending entrance. On the cot across the room, his battlemate lay curled on her side, her snores muffled by the collar of the thick sleep shirt he'd let her steal; she'd pulled the collar up over her nose and tugged the sleeves down over her fingers. Not only that, but she'd rolled herself up in every single blanket like a cocoon. He could only tell she was there at all thanks to the tufts of curly hair sticking out from beneath her makeshift cowl.

He tried to stand, but something halted the movement.

Cursing silently, he squinted at his feet…and his heart melted.

He'd been wrong—Soren hadn't taken all the blankets. Sometime after he'd fallen asleep, she'd thrown one of them over his lap and tucked the hem under his feet.

His best friend couldn't remember the difference between left and right without checking her hands to see which one made an *L*, but even heartsick and worried and worn to the bone, she remembered he hated to sleep with his feet uncovered.

Gods, he loved her.

After unwrapping his feet and pushing the blanket aside—he would have added it to Soren's pile, but he doubted she'd appreciate waking up to a blanket that smelled like sweaty feet—he stood up and scrubbed a hand over his face, grimacing at the tacky chill of fresh sweat.

One piece of his dream hadn't been imagined, then. The powdery film of charcoal still lingered on his tongue, too, like he'd really been breathing in the fumes from burning coals. And the voice—

Elias Loch.

Adrenaline spiked him through the heart; he whipped around, seeking any shadow out of place, but found nothing.

We don't have much time, Phoenix Priest. The voice carried the chill of the grave—and the muted fury of sizzling embers. *Are you listening?*

He swallowed hard—then regretted it when that chalky film spread to his throat. *Mortem?*

No answer. But now that he'd woken fully, he could sense her—Death lurked in the rafters, attention rapt, her keen eyes boring into his back.

She hadn't spoken to him since they'd fled Nyx. Since she'd ordered him away from Soren's side to protect her temple and the acolytes who guarded it.

If it had taken something that dire for her to seek him out before, he couldn't imagine they were about to have a low-stakes conversation. And if he'd been a betting man, he would've gone all in on it involving Anima.

Mainly because, when Wolf had returned to change the Goddess's bandages a couple hours earlier, Elias had jumped to assist him. Worse, once the prince had gone on his way, he'd continued watching Anima for any signs of distress until he'd finally dozed off himself.

Mortem had every right to be pissed. Had someone told him mere days ago that he would have been able to sleep comfortably with Anima in the room, let alone that he would *deprive* himself of sleep to ensure her safety, he would have tracked down Occassio's relic just to walk through time and punch some sense back into his future self.

Still. It wasn't like he'd been the one to cleanse her blood and save the life of her new body. Even if he'd been the first to offer.

Unfortunately, *semantics* didn't hold much weight with the Goddess of Death.

Damn me to the pits.

He paused. Winced. *I didn't mean that.*

Thank you for the clarification. Mortem's voice took on a hint of wry humor that burned away with her next words: *Anima must be dealt with.*

He glanced at the sleeping goddess. *She's* been *dealt with. She has a body now—one that belongs to her, not a host. She won't hurt anyone else.*

A sigh came from somewhere above his head; a wave of heat followed it, but not the scorching heat of his dream. More like the nipping warning a bonfire gave when you held your hands too close to its heart. The shadows wavered before him, a heat haze in the shape of a feminine form.

"That is not enough," she said. No longer a murmur in his head. "We have to remove her as a threat."

Remove her. That…made no sense. "She's the Goddess of Life."

"And you are gifted with the magic of Death." Mortem's shadow rippled again. "Her magic hasn't settled yet—in this body, she is vulnerable. We won't get another chance."

An order he would have happily followed…had it been given any earlier.

Looking at Anima now—fast asleep, dressed in a linen nightgown two sizes too big, strands of hair stuck to the broken-fever sweat coating her cheek— shame and irritation clashed together like cymbals struck against his ribcage.

Watching her giggle and gossip with Soren over these past weeks—then watching her battle the spider's venom in her new, untested body—had made it hard to remember the immense power hiding inside this dainty stranger. Tree- bowing, death-defying, world-breaking power.

A power that had drained his half-feral battlemate of her famously boundless energy. A power that had left her barely able to lift her own eyelids, let alone a sword. Let alone a crown.

Looking at the wounded girl on that bed, her small frame absolutely swallowed by the thick quilt, her mouth puckered with agony even in sleep…pain she'd shouldered for *Soren's* sake…

The infuriated, all-devouring grudge he'd been holding against her for all these months suddenly seemed absolutely ridiculous.

"That isn't my decision to make," he rasped.

"Make it regardless." Unyielding iron shored up the command. "You have little time before she returns to her full strength, now that she's taken her relic back."

The hairs on his nape bristled. "You didn't tell me to stop her from taking it."

"Would you have followed that order?"

Because his mother hadn't raised him foolish, he held his silence.

Another sigh. "I wouldn't ask you to sacrifice your partner. But Soren is free from my sister now—you have nothing to lose by ending her."

"But nothing to gain, either!" Soren stirred, frowning in her sleep; he lowered his voice to a hiss. "She is an *ally* in this fight, not an enemy."

"It is only a matter of time before she returns to Tenebrae." The cold certainty in Mortem's voice belied the spike in temperature around him. "And when she does, we will be well and truly outnumbered. She is more powerful than all the rest of us—whichever side of the board she falls on, that is the side that wins. Better to remove her from it entirely."

Discomfort wormed deep in his belly. "Goddess, Anima has proven herself more than once. She has had multiple chances to rid herself of my battlemate, and she chose to protect her instead. When she faced Tenebrae in Nyx—"

"Do not mistake a guilty conscience for staying power. Anima has always had a soft heart—that did not stop her from pledging herself to Tenebrae's cause. Her fear of death rules her above all else. Her relic has been here for centuries— unlike the rest of us, she could have remade her body at any point. Do you think it's a coincidence she only did so *now*, when Tenebrae is so close to having everything he needs?"

For a moment, doubt snuck in—but he buried it with a firm, "My battlemate has shared a mind and body with Anima. If she says she stands with us, then I trust her judgement."

Mortem's presence flared dangerously, from bonfire to deadly blaze. "I did not take you for a fool, Elias Loch."

She might as well have slapped him across the mouth with a blistering hand.

"Your devotion to your battlemate is admirable," she continued, though her dismissive tone suggested she found it anything but. "However, the reason you trust her judgement is the exact reason I doubt it. She has been under my sister's thrall for some time now—there is no way of knowing how her mind has been warped by her influence. You feared it yourself for a time."

"And those fears were unfounded," he retorted. "Anima went into that cursed tree for her—created a new body for her. Took on a *poisoned wound* for her. She is only in this state at all because she chose to spare my battlemate that suffering!"

A suffering he knew too intimately. The scar on his shoulder still burned from time to time, and not with the magic Mortem had gifted him.

"She has proven herself to be a friend," he finished. "She is *Soren's* friend. And I will not betray that. I will not see harm come to her."

All at once, the sweltering heat collapsed, cold air barreling in to fill the empty space. The chill that seized him in the silence went right to his bones.

He couldn't remember the last time he'd felt cold.

"You will not?" The question was terrifyingly soft.

Fear ached in his knees, urging him to lower himself before her and beg for forgiveness. But lying to her felt worse than defying her. So he answered, just as softly as she'd asked, "I will not, Goddess. Until and unless she stands in our way."

Sweat poured down his back as the silence stretched on; he could have sworn the shadows themselves crept closer to eavesdrop, their abstract forms lengthening as the sun climbed groggily into the sky.

Finally, Mortem murmured: "Tread carefully. Risking your own life in the name of blind loyalty is one thing…risking thousands of lives over it is another. That girl's love for you is not worth the world."

Anger sparked down his tongue like flint striking steel. "*That girl* is going to be my wife—and my queen. And I don't recall you frowning upon my *blind loyalty* when I devoted it to you."

The placid chill of an autumn morning delved sharply into the numbing bite of a snow-covered grave. The hearth in his chest cowered to coals as Mortem's visage grew, stretched…loomed over him like a sunset shadow, all ghostly limbs and smoldering soul-stuff, a silhouette wearing embers as eyes.

"*Tread carefully.*" Not a warning now; an order. A commandment passed from deity to devotee.

A commandment teasing its potential to become a threat.

Now he knelt; now he bowed his head. The seam in his once-broken spine ached beneath the weight. "Forgive me."

The shadow of Death crept closer, its edge dusting the tips of his feet. All feeling fled his toes.

"For the trespass of temper, or for placing your fealty to your battlemate over your oaths to your goddess?" asked Mortem.

A dangerous question.

"My temper was a trespass," he allowed, "but I owe no power in this world more fealty than I owe her."

A more dangerous answer.

"I will leave you with this." The way she said it, it sounded more like *You had better remember this.* "Your battlemate is not the one who answers your prayers—and my sister is not the one who granted you your power. When you took on the mantle of Phoenix Priest, you made oaths to me, as well—to carry out my will on my behalf. The moment Anima turns against you, I expect you to turn in kind."

He bowed his head. "Yes, Goddess."

For the first time since he'd entered her service as a boy of eight, he didn't dare test the resolve behind that oath.

"Be careful where you choose to wander here." Her ethereal presence wavered before his eyes…almost like a shiver. "The dead do not rest easy on Arborius."

And with a bellow of heat not unlike an oven door falling open, the Goddess of Death disappeared, taking the shadows with her.

67

CHAPTER 12

SOREN

For how often Elias—and many, many others—groaned about her inability to shut her mouth, Soren had always been oddly vulnerable to stage fright.

There was a difference between talking when no one was listening and talking when no one *else* was talking, and that difference was enough to reduce her brasher, better self to this: a girl whose blade-beaten hands trembled like a damned leaf, her comb repeatedly fumbling into the porcelain sink of the infirmary washroom as she tried to yank it through her damp curls.

The ninth time it happened, she picked it up and threw it with all her might. With a wobbling *twang*, the metal comb buried itself tines-deep in the wall.

No pain blistered behind the throw. But its absence almost ached worse than its presence.

Gone, just like she'd wanted.

But it hadn't left alone.

While it would be appropriately dramatic to say she would rather be *anywhere* doing *anything* other than preparing to meet her Arborian family for the first time in a decade, the truth was, there was only one place she really *wanted* to be: at Ani's bedside.

Feverish and restless, Ani had finally settled after the second-longest night of Soren's life. The Goddess of Life now looked life*less*, her parted lips leeched of color, all blush drained from her cheeks—but Sage had told her over and over that was actually a good thing. It meant the fever had finally broken…that the venom had been properly flushed from Anima's brand-new bloodpaths.

Whatever her uncle Cypress had done, it had worked. And thanks to their mutual fatigue in the infirmary yesterday, he hadn't shown any sign of recognition upon seeing her, saving her from having to navigate another reunion in her own bone-weary state.

All reassurances aside, she'd feel a lot better once Ani actually opened her damned eyes. Even with the poison gone, she had yet to stir…except for the screams that she was *sorry*. The gasping, breathless sobs that it was *her fault*.

I'm a monster, she'd shrieked, staring at Soren with unseeing eyes, heedless to Soren's attempts to bring her back to her senses. *I'm a monster.*

And worst of all…

The terrified pleas for someone to *put the fire out.*

The fire's long out, kid.

Soren braced her hands on either side of the sink, bending against its strength, bowing her head and squeezing her eyes shut until a headache bloomed through her temples.

Every twisting knife of memory—every rebound of her brother's shaken promise at the Saltwater Ball—thrust her further into her head. And each time it ached afresh, remembering that no one here was going to call her *Soleil* once she reintroduced herself…or *kid*, or *killer*, or any of the other things she might've answered to if they were wielded by the right voice.

Do me a favor, little sister—trust me.

She should've caught the lie, the mask. Finn never called her *little sister.*

And now, here she was…an ocean away from him, trying to play his kind of game alone. Without him to feed her the lines when she forgot them. Without a goddess at her back, a goddess nothing like the one who was playing a different game with Finn's body now.

And despite all of that, despite the demands of duty chafing against her innermost parts, she hadn't wanted to move from her hunchbacked vigil in the chair at Ani's bedside. Any amount of distance from the goddess felt…wrong.

Not just wrong, but dangerous.

Which was *ridiculous* and *silly*, because she'd chosen it…had fought so hard to get the goddess out of her that she'd breached the borders of *impossible* to do it.

She'd wanted this. She'd *needed* this.

And now the silence in her head was making her miserable.

Miserable enough that she'd planted herself in that chair and refused to leave all night, even when Elias had tried to tug her away to eat and sleep and bathe off the blood and venom; she'd held Ani's hand through the worst of the pain, and when some medimancer had imperiously told her she needed to leave and let the goddess rest, she'd given her a glare that Elias had described as *pits-damned terrifying, Soren, never make that face again.*

You should've seen me when you were dead was all she'd said in return.

He hadn't tried to make her leave again after that; it was Sage who'd finally chased her off to sleep in the cot across the room from Ani, as far as she'd dared go. And that was only because he'd reminded her she had a meeting with the remaining Olivanders in the morning *that really can't wait, so stitch that scowl up, sourpuss, and get geared up with something better than the tadpole tale, will you? My ma will ream me ragged if she hears that.*

As if that kind of pressure would help her sleep more soundly.

But even though she'd rather spend another day doing her best gargoyle impression in the chair by Ani's bed, Sage was right—she had a duty to fulfill, because she'd finally arrived on the cusp of her first task as Atlas's Heir:

Convincing her aunt and uncle their story was true…and procuring a treatise of alliance. *Without* the considerable advantage of an actual goddess's support.

She drummed her fingers on the sink's porcelain lip, staring herself down in the mirror—hating how it took a few blinks to recognize those eyes as her own. Hating how her skin seized when she found green staring back instead of gold. Hating how this body still felt…stretched. Used. Like it didn't fit right over just one soul anymore.

Hating that Kallias and Finn would soon have to suffer the same *unprecedented* affliction.

But at least she'd gone first—at least when her brothers finally shucked the god and goddess out of their bodies, it would be a *well*-precedented affliction. When it came time for their turns, she'd feel at home in her own skin again…and she'd know how to help them come back from it, too.

Something to strive for, anyway.

Gripping the comb until its remaining teeth chewed at her palm, she gave it her best tug.

The comb didn't budge. But her shoulder did.

Pain ripped through the joint, half cramping, half tearing—a sensation that froze her in place, staring at nothing as she tried to comprehend the fact that she was about to have to explain how a *comb* had dislocated her shoulder.

But her fears were unfounded. When she rolled her shoulder, it obeyed—even though it clicked once or twice every rotation. Like it was chuckling at her.

Just sore. Not a fit.

"Very funny," she muttered to her shoulder, clinging to the sink one-handed and bracing her foot against the wall as she pulled fruitlessly at the comb. "You ought to do shows."

Her rude, stuck-up shoulder ignored her. As did the comb, which didn't seem keen on coming out of the wall anytime soon.

Fine. She'd have to chalk up her hair as a loss. But at least she'd felt strong enough to step into the shower on her own this morning, though Elias had asked to sit on the nearby stepstool in case she got weak or dizzy. Afterward, he'd given her space to get ready without waiting for her to request it; and all this time, he hadn't peeked inside to see if she was all right (code for *still alive and not possessed*) or to interrupt her (frankly atrocious) rendition of a bawdy bar tune to work out the catch in her throat.

An Atlas bar tune. She didn't know where she'd learned it, but she'd woken with its melody stuck in her craw, and she hadn't been able to loosen it without singing it herself, feeling her way around the lyrics with her long-forgotten Atlas drawl.

She didn't hit every note right; her Nyxian accent stretched a few vowels the wrong direction and clipped a couple consonants short here and there. But it was a start, and a start would have to do.

"Elias," she called—then waited through the noisy *wham-clank-clatter-curse* that followed from outside the washroom. "Did you just fall?"

"No," he said, definitely from a floor-ish direction. "Just dropped my book."

Funny; she definitely hadn't heard a *flutter-thump-curse* in there anywhere. But she decided to let him have it. "Is it going to bother you if I lean full Atlas for this?"

A pause. "No," he said again…this time from a less floor-ish direction. "Not if you think it will make your aunt more likely to listen. Why would it bother me?"

Her chest bubbled with warmth like she'd downed a bottle of champagne in one swallow. "Just didn't want to startle you when I started sounding all strange…and extra attractive."

"You always sound strange."

"And attractive?"

"No comment."

She pouted. "You could stand to tell me I'm pretty every so often, you know. I wouldn't complain."

His sigh could've blown a sailboat all the way back to Atlas. "Soren, if I said something every time I thought about how attractive you are, you'd never get a word in edgewise, and I'm pretty sure you don't want that."

Well, that made it hard to keep this guilt game up. "I *might*."

"But then you wouldn't be able to distract yourself from how nervous you are." A page flipped. "Like you're doing now."

She tossed her head back after rinsing her flushed face, towing her curls over the top of her head and scrubbing the water out of her eyes. "I'm not nervous."

Depths-damned terrified, definitely. Using all her strength to keep her smartass remarks from rattling against her teeth, for sure. But she'd left *nervous* behind about three seconds after she'd woken up on that cot and seen it was daybreak—and Ani was still unconscious.

When she opened the door to grab the bag of cosmetics Medwenna—the odd but kind ranger from the woods—had brought her, a russet-brown hand appeared, blocking her reach. "What're you looking for?"

"Kohl pencil. I left it—"

"You're sure you're not nervous?"

She bristled, pushing his hand—he didn't give. "Do Mortem's pits smell like sulfur?"

He rolled his eyes. "Well, you've got to be *something*, because you already put that stuff on—and now it's all over your face."

Pits. Someone needed to invent waterproof kohl. "Maybe I just felt like redoing it."

"Or maybe you're not paying attention at all," he countered.

She couldn't muster another clever quip; all her retorts were spent. And she didn't want to say anything else floating through her head, because he'd only argue. Or worry. Or look at her like he'd looked at her when he'd climbed up on the dead spider's back, when shock had shattered and scattered her mind into a mosaic of glass and stone.

Some memories of that ordeal could have drawn blood with their sharp edges; others were completely impassable, blunted by a barrier she couldn't climb or clear away.

So instead, she shut the door, turning back to the mirror. She squinted at her own reflection until the muddled four-leaf-clover-shaped freckle at the apex of her nose came into focus—and the black streaks smeared down her cheeks. "Everybody in the world is going to die if I can't give a good speech. You'd be nervous, too."

"Soren, you don't have to give a good speech. You just have to tell them the truth—that Tenebrae is after true godhood, he's willing to break the world open to do it, and it's in every kingdom's best interest to stand against him, neutrality or none."

Truth isn't always enough.

She rubbed the ruined kohl off of her face with her washcloth, watching the inky remains trickle down the drain. Unable to scrounge up any words no matter how deep she dug.

"Tell me what you're really afraid of." Elias's hushed challenge floated through the doorjamb.

Truth might not be a satisfactory weapon for this battle, but it certainly knew how to come when called—and it seemed it had learned that trick under the firm tutelage of her battlemate. Because at his command, an answer crawled off her tongue, flipping over to show him its belly: "I'm afraid they won't believe me."

"No, that's what you *think* you should be afraid of. What's actually scaring you?"

Damn him. She hated when he was annoying and right and *annoying about being right.*

She pressed her full weight into her palms and pushed against the counter, letting the cloying aroma of sweetpea soap scrub her aching mind clean.

"Finn's the one who can play a part," she croaked, reaching out to mindlessly crank the faucet's handle back and forth. "Kallias is the one who knows the rules of all this…the politics. But they left, and it's down to me, and I'm…"

I'm going to fail them.

Truth. Not a fear, but a certainty—a dreadful understanding that cowed her like armies and bounty hunters and goddesses never had. A weightless terror that threatened to melt her down and rinse the remains into the basin beneath her hands.

I'm going to fail.

"I don't know how to lead a kingdom," she groaned instead, leaning back in to redo the kohl around her eye. "I barely know how to lead *you* when Jakob makes us do Midnight Mayhem."

One of the training exercises for battlemate pairs—one battlemate blindfolded and forced through a maze, the other guiding them with nothing but their voice. She and Elias were the only pair that consistently failed, because they ended up bickering too much…and had a bad habit of running each other into walls.

She was walking into this blind. And even if Elias had wanted to, he couldn't guide her around these obstacles. She had to fumble her way through on her own.

"You know more than you think you do," he promised. "You had a good example."

Her scoff knocked her pencil awry; she cursed under her breath, filling in the line until it looked straight again. "Yeah, when I was *nine*."

A pause. "I was thinking about Ravenna."

The kohl pencil cracked between her fingers.

She'd believed herself to be orphaned, motherless, before. So this grief *should* have felt familiar—it should have sifted into shape along the path of old scars, aching like old wounds sometimes did.

This grief was not familiar.

This was not *grief.*

"Atlas needs an *Atlas* queen," she muttered. Gods knew if he could even hear her through the door.

Silence shuffled its feet outside the door, hesitant to be broken; when silence held its tongue like that, it meant Elias had opinions. None she wanted to hear.

But silence wasn't waiting when she wrenched the door open. A pair of midnight-dark eyes greeted her instead, one expectant brow arched like the scythes strapped to his back.

"They need whatever help they can get," he said, reaching without looking to yank her comb out of the wall; when she turned and leaned her head back, he started guiding the comb through her curls, teasing out the tangles with its narrow teeth. Once the clumps came undone, one of the many pockets of tension sewn into her body loosened; another gave way when Elias set aside the comb and rested his hands lightly over her hips, his fingers settling into their dips as he stamped a kiss into her hair. "If you ask me, they couldn't ask for a better queen. Your aunt will hear you—you're her family."

Maybe he was right—maybe they couldn't ask for a better *queen*. But had she been given the chance to pick, she wouldn't have chosen *herself* first out of the lineup of Atlas royals…or second. And she could only avoid the humiliation of last pick because Jericho had chosen Vaughn's life over the lives of the Atlas people…and Nyx's people, too.

But something about Elias's faith defied a retort. She couldn't blame Mortem for favoring him above her other worshippers; his faith had been tested and found unbreakable, the kind that made the impossible become possible, the lost become found.

His belief sustained her, even against her will. So she slid her hands over his and pulled them up to wrap around her middle, his palms holding her heartbeat. "Do I have any kohl on my face?"

He took her chin and turned her head toward him, studying her face with a careful frown. "No—wait. Yes. Here." He tugged his sleeve down over his thumb, scrubbing away the offending mark…then paused, his frown deepening. "Your pulse just—"

She clapped a hand over her chest. "You can hear my heart beating?" That was going to get embarrassing in extremely short order. "Since when?"

He shrugged. "Not all the time. It's sanguimancy—what we were talking about in the woods. Blood magic. I haven't really…" He trailed off, splaying his fingers over her heart, a frown taking shape in his voice. "Gods, it's *pounding* now. Are you okay?"

Flushing from the hollow of her throat to the roots of her hair, she pushed his hand away, shielding her heart awkwardly. "Stop listening to it! That's weird."

He blinked. Then grinned. "Oh."

"*Stop*," she whined. "Go back to being grim. That was better."

He chuckled, but didn't tease her further… a mercy she didn't deserve, after so many years tormenting him exactly the same way. "Sanguimancy doesn't come as naturally to me as other things. I used it once, to heal Kal when he got poisoned in Artem, but I don't think I—what? What's that look for, what?"

She gaped at him, her jaw falling so far she felt it pop. "I'm sorry. Repeat that. There's a magic that can heal poisons?"

Elias held up one hand in a *What?* gesture. "Yes. Why?"

"Why?" Oh, if he could hear her heartbeat, it had to be roaring in his ears right now. "You didn't think maybe that would've been relevant to bring up, oh, I don't know—when you were *dying from poison*?"

"They're still extremely rare!" he protested. "Cypress was the only one Kenna knew of, and he was in Arborius, anyway. Felt like a wild wolf chase that wasn't worth bringing up."

She covered her face with her hands. Considered screaming. Thought better of it. "When my legs stop trying to make a praying woman out of me every time I walk, you'd better be ready to run for your gods-damned life, because I'm gonna *kill you*."

A pat on her head. "Sure you are."

"*Stop*," she groaned, pushing him off—then crossing her arms tightly over her chest. "Yes, congratulations, you drive me wild, Elias Loch. Are you happy now?"

His grin could've bridged the gap between here and Sirena. "Yes."

"I hate you."

"Do not." He gripped her by her hips again, harder, and closed the distance between them himself, pressing flush against her as he bent to steal another kiss…

"Hello?" A knock resounded at the main chamber door that separated the washroom from the infirmary halls. "Anyone home? Look, if you're dead again, lass, I'm going to be pissed you even bothered showing up."

Thanks to that kiss, she was the furthest from *dead* she'd been since that temple in Atlas when she'd agreed to play host to the Goddess of Life.

"We're coming," she called, biting back a grin as Elias cursed princes and their poor timing, patting out the pyromantic heat now coursing through his tattoos. "My battlemate's taking his sweet time getting decent."

"Oh, I see. The Heir's too good to open her own doors?"

"*The Heir* is still getting over scaling a million-foot-tall gate, running through the woods, and kicking a goddess out of her body!"

When Elias finally crossed the room to let Sage in, her cousin swept inside with all the confidence he'd ever carried—if not more. His boyhood conceit had aged into a commanding presence now, though a hint of a dangerous smirk livened the corners of his mouth.

A fetid, foul thing flooded her throat as she took him in; its fumes burned behind her eyes as she fought to smile back at Sage, who had done nothing wrong.

He'd committed no crime besides looking a bit too much like her brothers. One more than the other.

She should have braced better for this; Sage was the original Trickster Prince, after all, though tamer and taller and not entirely easier to read. Him the figure sketched in full color, Finn the shadow he'd cast on the world.

A shadow set free, left to fester into something darker, dangerous.

A shadow that kept secrets, not promises.

Sage crossed his arms, smiling easily at her. "That nap didn't do you any favors. You still look like a half-molted chick that fell out of its tree."

"Yeah, well, the last ten years didn't do you any, either—you still don't have any manners." She glanced at the bundle he cradled to his chest. "What's that?"

"My manners." He tossed the bundle to Elias, who caught it one-handed. "Fresh clothes for the pair of you, courtesy of Ma and Wolf. They'll not be a perfect fit, but they'll cover your kits well enough."

Her throat tightened. "You told Aunt Gen?"

"Are you sure you remember me? I'm not touching that convseration with a ten-foot pole. No, I *stole* these, and then I ran out of there like my arse was on fire."

Elias narrowed his eyes at the bundle, then looked at Sage skeptically. "Won't they recognize their own clothes?"

"I'm hoping Wolf chooses today to be a bit extra dull—and that my ma will be too busy experiencing a full-tilt miracle to pay attention." He jerked his chin at Soren. "If you saw the dead come back to life, lad, would you stop to notice what the dead decided to don for the occasion?"

All emotion fled Elias's features.

Sage grimaced. "Oh, gods, that's a bad face. What'd I say wrong?"

"Don't worry about it," Soren said quickly, getting up to give her cousin a proper hug—and to give Elias a moment to come back from wherever Sage's words had sent him. "Thank you. We'll change and be out in a moment."

Sage nodded…then cleared a curse from his throat as he hugged her back, crushing her to his chest. "Gods, lass…I always wondered how you would've turned out. It's turning my head sideways to hear you all grown up. Finn must have wept himself withered when he saw you."

Another pain, another loss, another fall. But she laughed through it. "Actually, he caught me climbing out a window. Then he told me he'd come in planning to hate me."

Sage frowned thoughtfully. "Eh, well…could've gone either way with that kid."

Once he left, shutting the door to give them their privacy, Soren turned back to Elias. "How's it look?"

Without a word, he withdrew one piece from the ensemble and held it up, letting her take in its full measure—and her heart took a running leap, plunging straight down to her toes.

Wherever Sage had pinched this piece from, it must have contained keepsakes from her aunt's younger years. She couldn't think of another reason for her aunt to have kept an Atlas-blue waistcoat, the Sun Kingdom's crest stitched in thick golden thread between the shoulders, the same thread unfurling across the lapels in tidal waves of embroidery.

"Full Atlas," she and Elias said at once—and to his credit, when he smiled at her, it only showed half the resignation she'd expected from him.

So with a sigh full of his missing half, she cracked her knuckles and spread her arms wide. "All right, lover. Help me look queenly?"

He drew her close by the back of her head, planting one of those tender kisses between her eyebrows. "Believe me, that's an easy ask."

CHAPTER 13

SOREN

Thankfully, though their trip to the infirmary's common area revealed a curving staircase built in the center of the circular space, they happened to be only two floors up. Sage led them down the stairs and across the slick wooden floor, crossing the massive woven rug in its center without care for where he set his mud-crusted boots, nodding to every person they passed. The rug itself was dyed deep blue, cut through with white, gold, and black—with a start, she recognized it as Nyxian-made, an artistic rendering of the boundary between day and night.

All sorts of people milled in and out of the common area: medimancers and physicians hurrying to their next tasks, patients guided by caretakers or walking alone, and couriers delivering flowers, food, and extra bedclothes to various rooms. A grotto cut into the far wall appeared to be a pub of sorts, where patrons trudged in with haggard faces and emerged with brown paper bags and tired smiles.

Busy, but not chaotic. Even the most rushed individuals moved with order and purpose, never looking lost or unsure or overcome.

"Don't worry," Sage said to Soren as she cast a horrified look between the couriers and the winding steps. "The steps are mostly for show—we have a few lifts that carry people up and down. Artemisian in design, but we added a little biomantic flair to it. Remind me to show you later."

She probably would've been more capable of being impressed if the now-familiar pains in her legs had improved after her first night sans goddess; instead, soreness raised its voice to chorus with those bruise-like aches. Like her body believed they'd run the entire way from Nyx to here…then dove headfirst down that unending flight of stairs.

It made sense. Even at her best, yesterday would have left her stamina in tatters.

Sage strode to the door attendant, gesturing to her as he spoke; while she waited, a warm presence brushed against her side like a hot summer wind. Elias wrapped his arm around her shoulders and nuzzled his brow to hers, smiling as he gazed into her eyes. "Have I mentioned yet that you look beautiful?"

She snorted, pinching his bearded chin. "Only thirteen times since we left the room."

His dark, dark gaze trailed downward; he fussed with the sleeve of her waistcoat, then tipped his head to the side, teasing her earlobe with his lips. A shiver played piano down her spine as he rasped, "And have I mentioned yet that I wish to all the gods we didn't have to leave that room at all?"

Her cheeks pinked. "*Elias Loch.*"

He chuckled. "There goes your heart again."

She smacked him in the chest—the impact sent tingles through her fingers, painful at first, then numb.

"I've arranged for a courier to be sent if your friend wakes," Sage called as he came back—then paused, frowning as he reached out and felt Soren's cheeks. "Did you spike a fever on us, lass?"

She opened her mouth to reassure him—then caught the teasing glint in his eye and shoved his wrists away instead. "Remember when I said I was happy to see you? I take it back."

"It was only a matter of time. And speaking of time, I hope you're hungry—the family ought to be in the middle of breakfast about now."

"Without you?"

He rolled his eyes, raising his hands and bending his fingers in quotation marks as he said, "Apparently I've been uninvited on account of 'repeated incidents of poor conduct.'"

"Such as…?"

"*Such as* nothing. I'm innocent."

Doubtful. *Highly* doubtful.

The notion of what exactly Sage could have done to get himself banished from a family meal packed with *seven* mischief-makers—well, six, to be fair to

Wolf—well, seven, to be fair to her aunt—kept her so preoccupied that it wasn't until they left the infirmary, Sage and Elias flanking her on either side, that she realized they had just exited a tree.

Not a building. Not a tower. A *tree*, somehow tall and thick enough to have had its innards carved out without killing the tree itself. High above their heads, about where she'd expect to see clouds begin, boughs filled with evergreen needles waved like hundreds of hands greeting them; proof that life still poured through its limbs, flowing sinuous and languid beneath its bark.

And it was not alone.

The city was not, in fact, a city—not the sort she knew, built from dead wood and manmade brick and chiseled stone.

This city grew from the very ground it stood on. This city *lived*.

A host of roots made up every foundation, each one's girth broader than the span of Elias's shoulders; they plunged so deep into the soil that to try and uproot them would have been worse than a fool's errand. And clearly, no one had tried—the long, lush grass growing between their finger-like grip and the thick moss coating their bark proved that.

Some trees bent in a gentle curve—their trunks trained over generations according to the inhabitants' liking, Sage explained on the way—while others stood straight as rods. Rope bridges hung suspended between most of the tree-towers, connected to iron balconies built into the trunks—and across those bridges, people milled in clusters, their voices floating down like bursts of fallen leaves.

A forest grown to house a kingdom.

The streets of Arborius were winding paths of wooden planks occasionally branching off from the main road to curl out of sight, leading other places she couldn't see. Along those streets grew thriving, well-tended patches of wildflowers, flourishing ferns, and bushes brimming with mouth-wateringly plump, colorful berries.

"I thought the whole thing about Arborians living in trees was a mean joke," Elias confessed, and Sage laughed in earnest—a harsh cackle that grated on childhood memories of pranks played on and with her.

"We take *family tree* a bit seriously here. Most of these trees house many generations of the same family…as new additions are born or new people marry in, they just carve further up into the tree. Some families are so vast they've had to connect multiple together—those are the ones you see with the bent trunks. Even with multiple biomancers going at it, training a darkwood trunk takes a year at least. It's a stubborn wood."

"I don't remember it being this beautiful," Soren admitted.

Sage patted her shoulder. "You were small still when you visited last. I'm not surprised."

He might have been even less surprised had he known exactly how many things she had forgotten over the years…and how long it had taken her to remember.

As they made their way, many people offered Sage a smile or a raised hand of acknowledgement, and paid little attention to her. But Elias, many eyed with discomfort. In fact, a few outright skirted around them, crushing daisies and carrot flowers beneath their heels to stay out of his path.

"What's their problem?" she hissed to Sage.

"Mortem-blessed…they carry an air about them." Sage shrugged. "Death walks beside him. Folks can sense it, even if they don't know what they're sensing. You've just been around him too long to notice."

"Wonderful," Elias muttered, tugging uncomfortably at his eyepatch, avoiding the gazes of those approaching them.

"Should I step on their toes?" Soren offered. "Trip them while they're looking down their noses?"

Elias coughed out a laugh. "I don't think that will help."

"What does Sage know, anyway? They're probably just intimidated by your handsomeness."

Sage tossed his braid over his shoulder with a sharp sniff. "If that was it, they'd be dodging *me* like squirrels in a panther pen."

"What's a panther?" they chorused.

"Big cat. Forget it. Look, lad, I'll not feed you fibs—your magic might earn you a sour sneer or two here. Mortem's not our favored friend. But no one will act on that prejudice unless they want to take a turn about one of our detention cells."

Elias frowned, a glimmer of curiosity in his eye. "An issue for some—but not you?"

"You ask me, no god or goddess's blessings should be frowned upon. Magic is magic—you could choose to build a cookfire for a starving man or burn my perfect arse to a crisp. Just like I could heal a wound and cleanse it of infection…or tear it all the way open to let the elements in." Sage held up his fingers, wiggling them—familiar beads of verdant light took form at his fingertips, dripping off and dissolving in the air. "For the most part, our people are fierce believers of the same. But, well…when you candle a clutch of eggs, you're always going to find a dud or two." Before Soren could ask what *that* meant, her cousin gestured ahead. "That's the one we want."

To her surprise, the tree he pointed them to was not the tallest or broadest—not by a long shot. Still enormous, but if someone had asked her to guess which tree served as Arborius's palace, it was far from the first she would have guessed.

Sage was still talking, Elias listening with rapt attention…but only half the conversation filtered past Soren's ear to wade through her mind. She'd drifted too far into her own worries.

Reunions had become an unavoidable necessity as of late; dying twice would do that to you. This one felt different. Riskier, in some ways, than any of the others.

Her kingdom—every kingdom—relied on her convincing *this* kingdom to break their neutrality.

Every god and goddess now walked the earth, either in body or by proxy. Two stood against them—two stood apart. Only Ani had declared herself for their cause—for her *friends*.

One could argue Mortem and Tempest had staked their sides clearly; that opposition was opposition, the enemy of their enemy was their friend, and all those seemingly sensible things people said to make themselves feel better about their odds.

But Tempest had taken Kallias. That made him an enemy. Not allied with Tenebrae, but still an enemy.

And as for Mortem…

She glanced out of the corner of her eye at Elias. At the feather hanging around his neck. At the patch hiding his goddess eye. At the cauterized scars trailing from his ears to his neck, where he'd clawed himself open trying to drown out Tenebrae's corruptive music box.

Time would tell which side Mortem would land on.

Their entrance into the Olivander family tree passed in a flurry of activity, blurred by her distracted thoughts. But she did register a few details: the foyer had the same sleek wooden floors as the infirmary, cushioned by plush rosemary-green rugs. Though Sage led them straight down the hall to the waiting lift, she caught whiffs of woodsmoke and spices from the kitchen that made her mouth water; and while most of the doors down the hall were shut, she did get a glimpse of the living area she and her cousins and siblings had once claimed as their playroom.

Its petal-toned array of furniture, muraled walls, and cheerful garden boxes in every window had hardly changed. Some of the flowers were different— probably replacements grown by her aunt as her tastes had shifted—but everything else…

Finn's ghost still sprawled on the floor, tossing cards in a pile as Sage taught him how to stack a deck in or against someone's favor; a mirage of Kallias and Jericho rippled against the far wall, laughing as Wolf and Brook engaged them in a debate over which flower would best represent Atlas.

Soleil was there, too…she knelt by the fireplace without fear, giggling as Sparrow introduced her to her namesake creature, the tiny bird fluffing its feathers out as she stroked its fragile wing.

"Soren?"

She looked up to see Elias waiting at the end of the hall, a frown just beginning to take form; Sage held the door open to the lift, also watching her. But his gaze was warm, understanding.

"I'll happily give you a tour down memory lane later," he promised. "If Sparrow doesn't hog you, that is."

She snorted, finally easing onto the lift; it creaked, but held steady. "Scared to stand up to your little sister?"

Sage signaled to the biomancers running the lift; with a jerk, the tough, woody vines drew upward, suspending the lift in midair. As they rose, he pointed at Soren warningly. "I know a trap when I smell it, lass. Trying to get me in trouble with my kid sister already?"

"She stirs up trouble when she's nervous." Elias settled his hand over her shoulder again, massaging the muscle lightly; she bit back a groan of relief as he slowly undid the knot forming there. He knew where she carried her stress. "Gets the attention off her."

She scowled up at him. He smiled innocently back.

Once they exited the lift, Sage led them to a room she didn't recognize. Not small, but its excessive furnishing fooled the eye.

Two armchairs. A curve-backed chaise. A full couch that looked so soft she just knew it could swallow her whole if she sat on it. Each one was upholstered in fabric the same shade as the spindles of goldenrod cast generously across the dark purple wallpaper: all blooms, no stems.

A long, low table bisected the room, lined with place settings on either side; a row of assorted candles stood at attention down the middle, already lit.

None of the furniture sat empty. And this time, she could put a name to every single gods-damned face before even one turned her way.

In one armchair sat Queen Genevieve Atlas-Olivander—*Aunt Gen*. Soren could hardly see her skin for freckles; her burnished red hair hung in loose, gentle curls, threaded with swirls of white. She did not wear a gown; actually, she looked as though she'd just come in from gardening, the knees of her roughspun green trousers damp and crusted with dirt stains, the sleeves of her cream-colored linen shirt rolled up to reveal suntanned arms that contrasted with her pale hands. She was laughing at a joke that had been told before they entered the room; not a rare occurrence, judging by the feathered corners of her squint and smile.

Her uncle, King Cypress Olivander, sat in the other armchair—his arm and her aunt's both hung off their chairs, their hands twined in the thin seam of space between them. He was chortling, too, eyes bright as new coins; now that she'd slept enough to actually take in the sight of him, she realized his dark brown skin carried no lines at all. His grin beamed in defiance of his age, too, though his black locks had grayed some. He wore simple clothes, himself—brownish trousers and a scarlet sweater paired with leather boots. Gold earrings lined his ears from lobe to apex, some studs, some dangling botanical charms.

The gold hoop in his nose, she remembered…specifically, she remembered yanking it out as a very small child. He must have gotten it re-pierced.

Despite the eight-year age gap between him and her aunt, the two of them could not have acted more perfectly paired. When her aunt leaned in to say something, her uncle had already turned his head to listen—when her aunt's smirk suggested the beginnings of a joke, her uncle had already begun to chuckle. And no matter what, their hands never separated.

On the two pinioned cushions sat a boy and girl who could be no more than a year apart in age. The boy, black-haired like his father and freckled like his mother, his brown eyes focused on the stack of waffles on his plate; the girl, brown-skinned and smiling her father's smile, her dark auburn hair done in locks like his.

Oak and Juniper—six and five, respectively, last she'd seen them. That made them sixteen and fifteen now, give or take a few months.

On the couch were two women—one was around Soren's age, her golden-brown skin glowing with a rosy blush, the morning sun catching on streaks of honey-wheat gold buried in her flowing chestnut hair. The daisies tucked into the pocket of her soft pink tunic caught the corner of Soren's memory first, erasing all doubt over which cousin it was—Sparrow, who'd insisted on crowning her in flowers every time she came to visit, who whistled to birds and giggled when they came to sit on her shoulders, who swore up and down and sideways that she could speak to the fish in the ocean and ask them to warn her of any approaching sharks.

That meant the woman beside her had to be Brook, who was the only one dressed like she had somewhere else to be—her russet-and-brown hunting leathers clung to her form, emphasizing the folds of her stomach and the breadth of her thighs, a hunting knife resting in the dip of her hip. Her coarse hair was the same color as darkwood bark, just a shade shy of true black; she kept one side shaved, the rest flipped over her head, a couple sections braided among the waves. Scars crisscrossed the backs of her hands, striping her rich hickory skin; though, judging by the thinness, Soren guessed they were gardening scars. She'd seen the same marks on her mother's…on Ravenna's hands after she came back from tending her private rose garden in the castle greenhouse.

Roses that had likely died with her.

And then there was Wolf, smiling up at the chattering girl perched on the arm of the chaise beside him—a girl she could only assume to be Nutmeg.

The youngest member of the Arborian royal family was only two when Soren last saw her—a cherub-cheeked toddler with chestnut hair like Sparrow and hazel eyes like Brook who'd once trailed eternally on Soren's heels, a precocious little girl determined to keep up with her elder cousin.

So it didn't surprise her that, out of all of them, Nutmeg was the first to jump to her feet at their arrival; she also looked like she'd just come in from working outdoors. Sunburn pinked the tip of her nose and the apples of her cheeks, and clusters of burrs clung to both her braids. She watched them with her head tilted like the curious bird that currently stood on her wrist, happily pecking seeds from the pile in her palm. When she ran her finger down its feathered head, it chirruped happily.

When Sage crossed the room to give Wolf a back-slapping hug, the eldest of her cousins accepted it with a grunt and a mutter in his brother's ear…but his gaze stayed on her. Though he carried many traits from his father, those amber eyes had clearly been inherited from his mother. Not Genevieve, but the late Queen Calla Olivander, Cypress's first wife.

He smiled—trying to comfort her, maybe. But she couldn't pretend she didn't see the troubled thoughts hiding behind it. Or how he kept glancing at the door behind them, one foot tapping idly at the floor, glassy gaze the only sign of the sleepless vigil he'd kept over Ani most of the night.

"All right, family," Sage announced with a quick one-two clap, pivoting and spreading his arms out toward her. "I'm going to need your full attention, because we have something to settle this morning."

"I thought we agreed we'd stop inviting him to breakfast," Oak grumbled through a mouthful of waffle.

Juniper sat back, her locks sweeping across her back like a curtain. "*I* didn't invite him."

"Rescinding invitations to standing events only works if you change the place and time." Sage bowed to snatch a waffle off his little brother's plate—then dodged the retaliatory swipe of Oak's fork toward his ankle. "Where else would you all be eating breakfast?"

"We should switch to the patio," Brook suggested to Sparrow.

"Enough," chided Genevieve…in a voice so similar to her sister Adriata's that Soren's heart tried to flee up and out, lodging at an odd angle in her throat. "He's brought guests. Behave."

"*Handsome* guests," Sparrow agreed, flashing a winning smile at Elias. He ducked his head with a muffled cough, the most telltale sign of embarrassment he ever showed.

That nostalgia-tinted fondness for her cousin banked a smidgen.

"That's not *behaving*," Brook laughed, slapping Sparrow's bicep.

Chewing his stolen waffle, Sage toed aside a couple empty plates before stepping up onto the table, summoning a chorus of groans from the others; he ignored them, gesturing toward Soren as he swallowed. "I will give you five seconds to guess who our lovely guest here is."

"We're not doing that," said Brook and Sparrow together.

"Someone you paid handsomely to play whatever game this is," Genevieve guessed.

"Feels weird to guess when she's right there," Juniper protested. "Can we write it down?"

"I'm so sorry about him," sighed Cypress, one hand braced to his brow. "If he paid you to play along—wait, weren't you in the infirmary last night? *Sage Samuel Olivander—*"

"This is going about as well as I thought it would," Elias muttered above her head.

A sharp sniffle cut through the rising din of voices, silencing them—and drawing every eye back to her.

"Sorry," she rambled thickly, clearing her throat and wiping at her eyes. "I'm—I'm not usually—" A laugh. Another sniffle. "Gods, I think I missed you all."

"Olivanders," Sage said, gently this time, "I would like to present to you…Princess Soren Marina Atlas, formerly Princess Soleil Marina Atlas. She's come a long way to ask for our help…and I, for one, am damned pleased to see her again."

For a long, long, long moment, no one moved. No one spoke. No one breathed.

Until Nutmeg *leapt* up on the chaise, her bird companion bolting with a shrill cry; she bobbled unsteadily on the cushion as she shoved her finger toward Wolf, shouting, "*I knew it!* I knew it, I *knew* it, you all owe me *so much gold!*"

"We don't owe you anything!" Oak protested, also leaping to his feet—the plate flipped, his last syrup-doused waffle smearing across the cushion. "You bet she was alive, but you bet she'd show up somewhere two years from now. I bet it would be last year, so I'm closer!"

"I only got to join the pool last year, that's not fair, it's *ageist*—"

"Actually, Oak, you bet they'd find her *bones* last year," Brook corrected, raising her voice over Nutmeg's whining. "*I* said they'd find her alive—"

"You did not!" Juniper and Sparrow argued in chorus—then Sparrow added, "You said dead! You and Wolf both did, but Wolf—"

"*Wolf* has been out of the running for five years," the prince in question sighed, dropping back onto the chaise, pinching the bridge of his nose like he'd sprouted a sudden headache. "Let's not talk about this in front of—"

"You took *bets?*" Soren squawked. "On whether I was *dead?*"

Cypress, to his credit, looked mortified—well, mostly in shock, but mortified too. "You did *not.*"

"We did," Sage said shamelessly. "And actually, only one of us hit the full parlay, because the lad with her is Nyxian. She got raised there, not lost in Atlas somewhere."

Silence fell again as they all glanced at each other, brows drawn, seeking the winner.

"Well," said Queen Genevieve, grinning slyly, "seems like you all owe *me* some coin, my loves."

Another chorus of groans and protests crashed through the room, Cypress's the loudest of all—but Soren heard none of them clearly, because Sparrow crossed the room in two graceful leaps and smothered her in a pine-scented hug.

"Hi," she sobbed into Soren's shoulder.

"Hi to you, too." Tears flooded in too fast for her to force them back. Maybe this wasn't a thing worth crying over, but she was so tired still, and so relieved they hadn't challenged her…and this was the first time she'd reunited with family since her memories came back.

The first time she'd experienced it as it *should* be. Joy, not anger. Celebration, not suspicion.

Sparrow—fourth-born out of seven, a biomancer who shared her birthday with Finn, a magical talent with Jericho, and a love of the ocean with Soleil and Kallias—only embraced her for a solid second and a half before whipping to face Elias, a snarl creeping across her face. "I take back the *handsome* comment until I know exactly *who* this is and *why* Nyx had you in the first place."

"Sparrow, it's okay." Soren thrust an arm between them. "This is my battlemate, Captain Elias Loch. Elias, this is my cousin, Princess Sparrow."

"Pleasure to meet you," croaked Elias.

Sparrow narrowed her eyes, holding her mistrustful stance.

"I'm also marrying him," Soren added. "If that helps."

It appeared to. After that, the older cousins—and Nutmeg—all took turns embracing her. And Elias, even though he accepted each with an awkward pat and a wide-eyed look her way.

Juniper and Oak didn't join; they retreated toward the back of the room, awkwardly huddling together, trying and failing to look like they weren't watching her. Too young when she'd died to really remember her; too old now to be excited just for excitement's sake.

Wolf's parting hug was quick, but warm—it accompanied a kiss on the head he used to disguise his whisper that he was off to sit with Anima. Once he slipped out, Brook held her face and demanded to know if she was all right—then demanded to know how she'd managed to steal their mother's engagement outfit from the family keepsake trunk without being seen. And while Soren was still ratting Sage out for that, resulting in a wrestling match between the two that promised broken dishes were soon at hand, her aunt came and knelt before her.

A queen. On her knees. Holding Soren's hands in hers as she gazed up at her, silvery tears bringing out the green cast to her gaze.

"Oh, sweet girl," she whispered. "I can't believe you're here."

"Me either, Aunt Gen."

Her aunt stood, teasing a curl away from Soren's brow. "I prayed to Anima for this every day since the fire. I prayed she would give you back to your family—to your mother." She clutched Soren's hands to her chest. "How is she? How is Addie?"

With the jingling of coins changing hands in the background, Soren swallowed down the dread that welled up in her throat. "We need to talk, Aunt Gen. You and I, as..." Another swallow. A deep breath. "As queen and queen-to-be."

Genevieve's beaming joy dimmed at once. "Something's wrong."

"Yes."

Now her aunt's hands explored her damaged places—her hollow cheekbones, her frail hands, the gnarled scars marring her knuckles. "What do you need from us?"

"More than can be said here," she hedged.

"It's political shite, Ma," Sage added, coming to stand at her side—and slapping some coin into her hand, which was almost enough to make Soren laugh. "Astrid's already waiting on us."

Astrid. She didn't know that name, but judging by the slope of Genevieve's brow, it held a clue about what was coming.

Her aunt beckoned to her uncle. "Cypress, Brook—come with me. Sage, if you wouldn't mind showing Captain Loch to a guest room—"

Soren grabbed Elias's wrist, anchoring him to her side. "He stays with me."

Her aunt hesitated. "If this is an Atlas matter, it may be better kept to family."

She drew what steel she could in her voice. "Let me be clear—as my battlemate, not just my fiancé, Captain Loch carries more of my trust than anyone in this world...with my safety, with *everything*. Where I go, he goes...or neither of us does."

"We go together," Elias agreed quietly. "Together or not at all."

To Soren's surprise, it was her uncle who stepped forward, offering a hand—after a brief pause, Elias took it, giving it a firm shake.

"Your tattoos," said Cypress, "and the scythes. Artemisian?"

"They are. My mother was born there, and I just returned from my own...pilgrimage."

"Hm." A grin broke through her uncle's thick beard. "You and I will have plenty to talk about, then—I was born there as well."

Soren blinked. She hadn't known that—though thinking about it now, she should have assumed, given what Elias had told her about *sanguimancy* being a Mortem-blessed magic. The magic her uncle had used to save Ani.

"My late wife was Arborius's heir. Our marriage was arranged as well." Cypress added, without pain in his tone—only love, shrouded in a hint of fond sadness. "We can discuss it later. For now, come—tell us what brought you all this way, and what we can do to help."

CHAPTER 14

SOREN

The journey to her aunt's office went quickly; and, to her pleasant surprise, her aunt and uncle spent much of it getting to know Elias.

It would have been wonderful to indulge in it; to let her shoulders sink into their usual slouch, to let her mind sink into the familiar cadence of familial banter about Artemisian fare and weapons from foreign kingdoms and about Elias's cousin's bakery, *The Sugar Spinner.*

It would have…if she wasn't sweating so badly she worried she was about to slide right out of her shoes.

Every echoing slap of sole against wood rippled through her stomach a moment later, a current of nerves bouncing off its hollow walls. If the ocean of anxious perspiration clasped between her palms got any deeper, she'd have to give it a name. Maybe draw a map in case a very tiny boat wanted to take a trip.

Finn should be here to play the part. Kallias should be here to teach her the rules she had to follow.

Her mother should be here instead of her. Either of them.

She was the last damned person who ought to be leading the charge onto this battlefield of barters and bargains—but she was. Because she was alive.

Her, and no one else.

This was her burden to bear—this was the price of her survival.

Play the part. Follow the rules.

Survive the fight.

A queen doesn't abandon her people.

The next thing she could really focus on outside of her own head and the specters of her brothers and mothers haunting the walls of her skull were the way-too-damned-*official* walls of her aunt's office instead. Everything came roaring back with a bolt of pain through her too-straight spine when she took a seat at a low table in the center of the room, papers stacked before her and a glass of water being poured for her by Elias, who kept his gaze carefully fixed on his task. And a woman she didn't recognize—blonde and impeccably dressed and smiling at Soren like they were old friends—was sitting across from her, already talking.

"I hope you know how grateful I am to see you all right," said the stranger, taking a sip of her own water; when she set the glass back down, a crescent of crimson lipstick decorated its rim.

Too red to be blood. Too red to be blood.

With great effort, she drew the tension out of her battle-ready body as the blonde woman continued, "We never officially met, as my time in Atlas came after the fire, but I consider your family as part of mine. And I want to say—"

"I'm sorry," Soren interrupted, scrambling for manners, for decorum, gods why hadn't she paid better attention in meetings before— "but could you remind me of your name?"

"No need to remind you—I hadn't gotten that far." The blonde woman extended her hand, her cream-colored bell sleeve trailing over the round table's surface. "I'm Lady Astrid Thorne. I trained as a diplomat under my parents in Atlas and spent quite a bit of time with your family. Prince Finnick in particular remained a close friend after I returned home."

Would hearing his name ever *not* make her feel like someone dumped a jar of glass shards and rusty nails in her stomach, then shook it up like the world's most macabre snowglobe?

"A pleasure to meet you." She reached out to shake Astrid's hand, feeling as if that glass had filled up her mouth, too—every word stung. "I am...I am grateful to hear he had a friend."

A sliver of grief pierced through the pleasantry in Astrid's blue eyes; a grief that mirrored her own so perfectly that she immediately decided she liked this woman. "I cannot tell you how deeply it pains me to hear of his fate."

A quick peek at Sage revealed where Astrid had heard the story; her cousin just nodded for her to go on, his sheepish smile out of sync with the grief in his gaze.

"Me too." The response flopped like a helpless fish, manners dying on the deck of her inexperience. She cleared her throat, sitting up straight.

Posture, tone, decorum. Follow the rules. Play the part.

Genevieve and Cypress, seated to the right of Astrid, exchanged swift looks; Genevieve leaned forward, finding Soren's gaze across the table. "What's happened to Finn?"

By now, she could tell the story in its entirety almost without thought, without pause. Even during the harrowing and horrible parts, she shoved through as if shouldering through locked doors, not pausing long enough to let it touch her.

So when Genevieve collapsed into Cypress's arms, an anguished sob halting Soren's story in its tracks, she merely waited…fidgeting, finding other things to look at, whatever it took to keep her own emotions from taking their place at the table.

"I survived—I believe Kallias and Finn can, too," she said firmly. "And my parents still live."

Gen caught her breath, wiping away the tears she'd shed for her niece and nephews. "You're sure?"

"Yes." Even if they only had Tenebrae's word for it, she couldn't consider the alternative. "But we also know they are Tenebrae's hostages—and I fear if we don't act quickly, they'll become his examples."

"We?" Astrid prompted; but when Soren looked at her, she found no chink in the woman's polished exterior. No trace of confusion. Only patient expectation.

She made a mental note to pinch Sage for being such a blabbermouth.

"I don't plan to let the suffering of my family or my kingdoms go unanswered." She folded her tremoring hands in her lap. "And I've come to request that Arborius support us in that answer."

Yes, good—that sounded right, the confidence, the challenge.

Astrid glanced at Genevieve, who took a swift breath to compose herself; then the diplomat looked back to Soren, not one of her coiffed curls shifting out of place. "To be clear, you are requesting military support."

Sweat trickled down the back of her neck. "Yes."

Astrid picked up the stack of papers in front of her, shuffling them before giving the stack a sharp tap on the table to level it out. "Give us a moment."

That was it? *Give us a moment?*

"Of course," she said, plastering a smile she hoped looked *something* like Finn's perfect mask over her face.

Give us a moment. Was that good? Was that bad? Had she been too demanding, too meek—?

Elias's hand slid over hers, his fingers curling into the gaps between hers. A silent reminder to breathe.

She did her best. Still, it felt like days before two women across the table turned back to them. Genevieve's red-rimmed eyes no longer revealed anything—no emotion, no sign of whether she'd swung in their favor or against.

Trepidation tickled Soren like the tendrils of an anemone, peppering stinging kisses along her throat.

Astrid set the papers down, taking up her fountain pen and uncapping it with a graceful twist of her fingers. "Princes Wolf and Sage brought your tale to me themselves—they vouched for your story, even the less believable bits. So as we move forward, I want to make it clear this is not a debate of whether we believe what has happened to you. You have been through unimaginable pain and trials beyond the natural, Princess, and I am sorry for your suffering."

A pinch in her chest. To be *believed*—too simple a thing to push her so near to shedding tears.

"That said…as you know, Arborius has been neutral since its founding, and not just as a matter of tradition. It is essential in many ways to our kingdom's culture. We are healers, and at most, we are hunters."

"I am aware of that," she said, careful not to shred the words through clenched teeth, "but this is not a conflict of kingdom against kingdom."

"Which is why we are considering it at all." Soren had to appreciate the frankness—and the indication, seemingly, that their request had not been immediately refused. "We are not naïve. We understand this threat outweighs tradition. But there are practical concerns. The rangers are skilled, but not in warfare. At best, we will bring numbers, but not expertise. Without the Atlas army at your command, and the Nyxian army largely scattered, you will need soldiers and leaders who are intimate with that sort of combat."

Soren glanced sideways at Elias; his stony expression would reveal nothing to the others, but she could read other things: his hand in his pocket, wrapped around his prayer beads. The faint lines sketched in the corners of his mouth. His measured eye contact.

The point was valid—he thought so, and she unfortunately agreed. But that didn't change anything.

"My battlemate and I are happy to provide training to those who need it," she said. "While circumstances prevented a traditional ascension, my battlemate was granted the rank of Captain by Queen Ravenna herself—had things been different, he would have received command of a company in addition to his title. He's well-equipped to teach inexperienced fighters."

"That will help," Genevieve acquiesced—but the dip of her auburn brow pumped Soren's stomach full of uneasy nostalgia.

She knew that expression…not on her aunt's face, but on Adriata's. And it never preceded a positive outcome.

"This gap in experience is why we would like to hear what support you've already garnered on this front." Genevieve shuffled through her pile of papers, licking a finger before plucking a sheet free and sliding it to Soren. "With Atlas under another's thrall and Nyx presumably unable to offer organized support, that leaves us with Lapis, Artem, and Tallis. Have they already agreed to bolster your numbers?"

Hollow ringing drowned out every damned thought in her head.

"Artem stands with us," Elias jumped in quickly. "Last we heard, Empress Idris is in Sanctaviv, gathering support from their reserve barracks there."

Astrid wrote something down, nodding to herself. "When was this?" she asked—when Elias told her, her head bounced right back up, her golden brows arching. "That long? You've received no further contact?"

Soren's heart sank.

"I would imagine it's been difficult to get word to anyone," Elias said. "Mount Igniquit was claimed by Tenebrae worshippers. I would guess they've been working to intercept any outgoing communication…and even if they haven't, we haven't lingered long anywhere since we left."

"You mentioned Lapis visited Atlas for an alliance—did that come to fruition?" Genevieve asked.

"No," Soren admitted. "Finn warned Queen Esha of trouble in Atlas and sent her back. He told her not to answer any summons unless it came by Kallias's hand, and…"

"I understand." Genevieve's gentle words saved her from having to say it, but not from the lump in her throat; it didn't stop tension from twitching in Elias's hand, either. "Tallis?"

"They didn't seem keen on an alliance during my encounter with them." Something about being bound and drugged and gagged by mercenaries had left a poor taste in her mouth about that entire kingdom in general.

Genevieve and Astrid shared a long, long look.

"So," Astrid said slowly, "you have come to us…and no one else."

Play the part. "I think we can agree the prospects are a bit thin. But if Arborius will help—"

"You heard Astrid." Sage wore a troubled frown of his own, his fingers dancing an agitated jig across the stack of papers before him. "I'm not sending my rangers into a slaughter as front-line fodder."

"We will try to reach Empress Idris," Astrid said before Soren could open her mouth. "Our messenger birds could succeed where other methods of communication have failed. In the meantime…" With a graceful flourish, she slid a piece of paper toward Soren's extended hand, the ink still wet. "That leaves us with Lapis and Tallis unaligned in this conflict…and I believe there is one that will make a better partner for us."

Rotten lemon and spoiled sugar coated her tongue as she picked up the paper, scanning the fresh script, careful not to smear the words.

"You want me to ally with Tallis," she said flatly. "The kingdom that tried to kidnap me."

Astrid smiled apologetically. "I understand your hesitation, but keep in mind that your survival is an anomaly—it's never happened before. Tallis feels particular animosity towards the gods, and the fate of divine hosts is a large motivator behind that. You were a walking sore spot."

"It's no excuse for the way they treated us in their custody." Sometimes she could still feel Arthur's rough-palmed hand roaming over her. Like he'd left handprints behind only she could see.

Ani had been in control at the time. But it was Soren's body he'd touched.

"You're right," Genevieve agreed. "But Lapis is still recovering from its own civil conflict, not to mention brewing a new one that could boil over any day. Tallis, however, engaged in warfare only twelve years ago; that conflict may have ended, but experience and training live on past the signing of a treaty. Their army will be far better prepared to take on a threat of this nature…and in this case, though we disagree heartily with it, their venom toward the gods will be an asset to us."

"Will they fight alongside Anima?" Elias demanded. "And gods-blessed warriors?"

"Under most circumstances, the answer would be no," Astrid admitted. "However, as discussed, this is bigger than tradition. I have worked closely with Tallisian emissaries before, and I've spent considerable time with both their prince and princess— and I consulted with Captain Reydis-Harald this morning. We believe that if we craft the offer carefully, they would be willing to consider it."

"Captain—?"

"Medwenna," Sage supplied. "You met her at the Arboretum. She's lived here for a handful of years, but she grew up in Tallis."

Soren stared down at the piece of paper; the jumble of letters finally arranged themselves into words, and she forced herself to pay careful attention to each.

A treatise of alliance. A stipulation of terms. Very little of which she could even understand, let alone assess.

Play the part. Play the part.

She didn't need to know everything now—Tallis was weeks away from here, even by ship. By the time any official emissaries arrived, she would be practiced enough in this jargon to pass herself off as a capable Heir. If Genevieve and Astrid penned the treatise and helped present her cause, surely Tallis would at least consider it.

"Will we be reaching out directly to King Denali?"

"Actually, we'll be making our case to Prince Everin first," Astrid said. "Not only is he favored to inherit the throne of Tallis, but he commands his father's armies. His support could mean the difference between acceptance or denial."

Genevieve's lips pinched. "We also have ties to him already—we arranged an engagement between him and Brook some time ago."

She blinked. "Brook? *Your* Brook?"

"We only have the one," Sage said—not sounding particularly happy about it.

"Provided you can convince them helping you reclaim Atlas is to their benefit," Genevieve warned her son into silence with a look, "I believe they would be amicable to extending the terms of our standing arrangement."

"It's also worth remembering that Tallis is rumored to possess a god-killer," Elias murmured reluctantly. "If we're to have any hope of defeating Tenebrae…"

Soren's heart sank even further. "Do you know anything about that, Aunt Gen?"

"I don't." Genevieve's eyes narrowed. "But I'm sure Captain Reydis-Harald would be willing to share what she knows."

"Willing?" Sage snorted. "You'd make her whole rotting year."

"Remember too that the agreement we write up today isn't set in stone." Astrid stood and circled the table, pointing to a section of the document Soren hadn't gotten to yet. Purplish ink smudged the diplomat's fingertips, matching the script on the treatise. "This lays out the basics, but it's expected that a more detailed draft will be drawn out upon initial approval. You can add more specific stipulations later on."

Soren dug her fingertips into her temples, staring down at the treatise.

"Princess Soren." Astrid covered her hand with hers like they were old friends, her eyes twin pools of depthless cerulean.

Soren had never seen blue like that. Not even in the Atlas ocean. Nor had she realized just how badly she needed to feel someone holding her hand right now.

"We understand it's a lot to throw at you…forgive us if we haven't paid enough mind to the fact that you are recovering from an incredible ordeal, nor to the fact that, for the majority of your life, you were not raised as an Heir. I am happy to explain anything that you aren't familiar with." Aquamarine memories glimmered in her gaze. "And as a very intelligent young prince once told a work-addicted diplomat-in-training…there are actually very few things in life that can't wait until the next morning."

For that kindness alone—for a memory of Finn from someone who'd known him, the *real* him—Soren covered Astrid's hand with hers.

"My kingdom and my family, they come first," she said. "And if this is what it takes to free my parents and my people, then of course I'll do it. Whatever you think it will require. But I want it made *very* clear there will be additions made at a later date."

"Of course. For the moment, I'll finalize this for initial presentation." Astrid picked up the treatise and added to Genevieve, "Should I send word to Prince Everin?"

"If you would, please. Come back after you're done, Lady Thorne—we'll have more details to work out." After Astrid bowed and left the room, Sage hot on her heels, Genevieve turned back to Soren, offering a much softer smile. "Astrid is our best—you couldn't be in better hands. Nothing would get done around this kingdom if not for her."

She'd expect nothing less from one of Finn's peers. He wasn't the type to gravitate toward lazy, lackluster friends.

"She and Sage make a fantastic pair," her aunt added. "I didn't see it at first—Astrid is no-nonsense, I'm sure you can tell, and Sage…" A fond grin. "Well, my son is all nonsense. But opposites do attract sometimes."

Ah. That explained Sage's blabbermouth behavior.

Elias's elbow bumped hers; she smiled at him sidelong. "I've seen that myself."

"You would have—your parents were like that." Genevieve chuckled, picking up her mug of steaming *something* and sipping at it; the sight of the steam floating up from the ceramic mug made Soren suddenly aware of her cold fingers. As she tugged her sweater sleeves down to cover her fingertips below the table, her aunt added, "My sister's a spitfire. Our mother used to joke she never actually gave birth to Addie—a sunbeam just happened to shine into an empty cradle and decided it wanted to stay. She was all fire…all light."

Another sip, so slow it felt mocking. Maybe she didn't realize that Soren had leaned forward, sweater-clad fingers clinging to the edge of the table, desperate for more.

Desperate to remember how her birth mother had been before the fire, before the war. Desperate for any hope that Adriata might become that woman again.

Desperate to know she might not be entirely motherless.

"She was always the darling of Atlas. But your father—gods save that man, what a scoundrel. A sweetheart, but a scoundrel. Our mother tried to talk Addie out of that marriage from the day she picked him to the day before the ceremony, but in the end…I don't know if I've seen a man more changed by love." Genevieve's smile softened with nostalgia. With sadness, too. "I miss them both every day."

"What happened between you two?" All she knew was that the two sisters hadn't spoken since her funeral.

"That's a story for another time. Astrid should be back any—" A knock at the door. "—Well, Astrid's here now, it seems. Come in!"

Gods, the diplomat was quick.

Disappointment tried to bend her into a slouch, but she sat tall in defiance of its weight as she searched for something more to say. She didn't want to leave any important question unasked. "How long it will take for the missive to arrive in Tallis?"

In the end, it might have been better if she hadn't asked. Because if she'd kept her mouth shut, she might have heard the extra set of footsteps behind her. Or heard Elias's sudden cough, a call for her attention.

Instead, she only realized her mistake when a new voice, drawling and smug and *Tallisian*, spoke up: "Oh, I can't imagine it'll take long at all. Arborian messenger birds have been known to dodge lightning strikes."

At first, she thought she had to be imagining the accent—but then she saw the newcomer's face. The Arborian crest burned into the wooden ring he wore on his left hand. The duo of hand-carved throwing hatchets crossed over his back, the handles jutting out above his shoulders like protruding bones.

Oh, gods.

"Prince Everin," Genevieve said, "this is my niece, Princess Soren Atlas. She has quite the story to share, and I believe you'll find it interesting."

CHAPTER 15

SOREN

Prince Everin Arden. Of gods-damned Tallis.

Not sequestered in his mountaintop castle, awaiting her summons to war—but right *here*. Now.

He swaggered into the room like he owned it, breezed past her, and took her aunt's hand, kissing her knuckles politely. "Good afternoon, Your Majesty."

"To you as well." Genevieve gestured to the seat next to Soren. "Please, sit."

Soren swallowed, diving past her growing headache to try and dredge up the energy for more diplomacy. More debates. More jargon about laws and traditions and what they'd expect her to give up to win a war far worse than the one she'd signed up to fight in.

Everin pulled out the seat, dropping into it with a thud that started an avalanche of paper, the stack of documents in front of Soren slumping over. He reached out a hand to her, brows raised. "Your Highness. A pleasure."

Follow the rules. Play the part.

Don't punch that cocky-ass grin off his face.

Holding onto her manners for dear life, she took his hand, forcing herself to politely kiss his knuckles instead of fracturing them with a handshake Jakob had once told her ought to be counted as a weapon. "Likewise."

The mountain prince's grin widened, which did not make it easier to resist the temptation to throw a punch; however, he took his hand back and sank into the chair, crossing his ankles as he took the mug Astrid offered him—missing the apologetic look she offered Soren. "Y'know, I did hear a rumor about the dead Atlas princess coming back to life. Thought it was just a tavern story, but here you sit—and since ghosts can't hold a candle to your beauty, I'm afraid I have a few apologies to make to the patron who told the tale."

It took all her self-control not to turn and look at Elias. Especially because she was reasonably sure she could smell smoke.

Everin tipped his head back to sip from his mug, his dirty blond hair falling from his face like bolts of silk; not remarkable in color, but far prettier in composition. His beard showed signs of careful trimming, accentuating the sharp planes of his broad cheekbones and strong jaw; he sat like they'd all come here to entertain him, his chin tipped up even after he finished drinking so he could look down at her. Arrogant, unbridled amusement glittered in eyes forged from iron and silver.

A man beaten into shape like a weapon, drawn in harsh lines and corded with lean muscle…and wielding an ego that had smacked her square in the face before he'd even started talking.

Yep. She could definitely smell smoke.

Play the part, play the part, play the part.

But which part to play? And how to play it?

What would *Finn* do?

She flashed the Prince her best approximation of a banal smile, lifting her glass of water to give her hand something to do. "I *have* been told I have an otherworldly presence."

Technically, Elias had told her that she was a fire-beast freed from the pits of Infera specifically to punish him. But the implication was the same.

"Trust me—if they heard the screams of the phantoms that dwell in our mountain passes, they wouldn't dare make the comparison." Everin didn't break eye contact as he took his next sip. "I met you once. I don't know if you remember."

"I'm afraid not." She'd met his sister, Princess Raini, once or twice during her childhood in Atlas; but no matter how carefully she combed through her memory, picking apart every fleck of sand and flake of snow, she couldn't find a trace of the Tallisian prince. "But I hope you won't take that personally—up until recently, I had a hard time remembering many things."

"Here's a hint: you weren't going by the name *Atlas* then."

Her glass rattled, and she tightened her grip to steady it. "We met in Nyx?"

"Briefly. I spent more time with your sister Ember; it was about five years ago, when my father started looking to arrange a marriage match for me. From what she told me, you were preparing to enter the barracks for the first time…which would more than explain why you don't recall. You had bigger things to worry about." He looked askance at the sheath hanging from her belt. "To claim the name Atlas now…I have to imagine that's a fascinating story, all right."

A story she told him in sparse detail—much sparser than she'd told her Arborian family. Luckily, Gen didn't bring up the details she withheld; her aunt let her tell her own story, as much or as little as she liked.

That, at least, she had to be grateful for.

By the end, that cool amusement had heated. His iron-gray gaze simmered with repressed hatred as he rubbed the back of his neck…a casual gesture to disguise the way his thumbnail picked at the handle of one of his axes. A warrior's habit she recognized; she kept running her thumb over the empty space on her belt.

"The gods walk the earth," he said flatly. "All of them?"

"Except Mortem, but—"

"Mortem has other ways of establishing her presence." Everin rocked to his feet, pushing the chair aside; its wooden feet shrieked as he shoved it. He began pacing, shoulders flexing like a mountain lion on patrol.

Soren risked a look toward Elias; he gave an infinitesimal shake of his head.

"*All* of them," Everin muttered again under his breath—then cursed, pacing the other direction.

"Not all of them are enemies." Soren ignored the warning look Genevieve shot her. "Anima has chosen to fight beside us. When the three of us arrived here—"

Everin careened around to face her so fast that she jolted back in her chair. "One of the goddesses is here? In the flesh?"

Soren glared at him, only just stopping herself from baring her teeth. "She is a friend—*my* friend."

Now Everin looked at her like she'd grown two heads—and tried to convince him he was imagining the second one. "You're not flogging serious. You do know how they claim their hosts, yeah? They kill—"

"I know exactly how it happens," she hissed, "because *I* was the one she claimed."

She didn't give a damn about the Tallisians being faithless—pits, up until the gods had decided to show up and start sticking their noses directly into her business, she'd thought the Tallisians had it exactly right. And had he only held a grudge against the other four, she might've *still* let it slide, because she also didn't give a damn about them. Tempest, Occassio, Tenebrae, Mortem…the four of them had taken her brothers. Her sister. One had a death grip around Elias's neck, and Soren really did prefer hers to be the only hands with that privilege.

But unfortunately, she *did* give a damn about Anima. And potential alliance or none, she wasn't going to let this bastard go off and settle a centuries-old score by beating retribution into her friend's fragile new body.

Incredulous laughter filled the room; Everin bent into it, guffawing with all his might.

…Then again, just one little punch couldn't hurt. She'd done worse to Elias, and he'd still agreed to a far more intimate thing than alliance with her.

When no one joined the prince in uproarious laughter, he looked up. Still grinning, a malicious cut of teeth with no emotion behind it, he said, "Not a bad story. But no one survives playing host to a goddess, Princess."

"Well, then, it seems I'm going by *No One* these days, too." She looked to Astrid. "Could you make a note of that for me? It's getting a little hard to keep track."

Astrid's lips twitched. She scribbled something down on her paper.

Everin's head cocked to one side; a precursor to more mocking, she thought, until a curious tinge darkened his eyes.

"Let's say I believe you," he said, with a *let's say you're not dumping a pile of wolfshit in my lap* heavily implied. "How did you survive when no one else has?"

She'd had vows to keep to her battlemate. Tenebrae had broken the rules by threatening her into consent. Anima had refused to burn her out. Elias had told her he wanted to marry her, and she would've fought all five gods bare-handed and broken-ankled just to come back and smack him upside the head for not saying so sooner.

"A number of things," she hedged, "but none of them would have done the job had Anima not chosen to help me instead of hurt me. She's the reason I survived. And even then, it was…a close call."

Now the Prince took in her bruised knuckles and empty sword belt with dawning understanding—dawning *interest*. "And where is Anima now, if she no longer resides in you, Princess?"

"The Goddess's business is not ours," Genevieve interrupted firmly. "We called you here to discuss whether you and your father might be willing to make adjustments to our prior arrangement."

At that, Everin stilled. "Adjustments of what sort?"

"With the Chaos God on the throne of Atlas, as well as wreaking havoc in Nyx, there is no doubt he will continue his assault throughout the continent," Astrid said grimly. "We can expect he will come for us—Tallis for your *rumored* weapon, and us for the last of the godly relics."

No mention that Anima had already claimed it. This diplomat was good.

"Anima's bloom," Everin guessed; Astrid nodded in agreement. "He has the others?"

"Only his own," Elias explained. "The others have been claimed by their respective gods or goddesses. While the physical objects might not be in his possession, it's the magic they're really after, so—"

"I get the gist." Everin turned back to Genevieve, hiking a thumb over his shoulder. "Does the royal family keep a lecturer on retainer now? Because we both know there's a more suitable candidate wandering around here somewhere."

"That is Captain Elias Loch," Soren ground out. "My battlemate."

"Oh, right. Nyxians fight their wars with the buddy system." Everin gave Elias a lazy salute. "Cute. My boyhood school had the same policy."

"We would like to make a new offer in light of this threat," Genevieve said, effectively drawing attention away before Elias's flaring tattoos could cause a stir. Astrid slid the paper across the table; Everin swept it up, his smirk flattening into a serious line as he looked it over.

His gray eyes shot up to Soren around the middle of the document, then looked back down. She couldn't read the thoughts locked behind those iron gates.

"Our arrangement would extend to include Atlas," he said, stretching each word out like he was testing them for a trap, "and Princess Soren would offer what she can as Heir, to be established at a later date…in exchange for military support in reclaiming Atlas and publicly declaring our opposition against Tenebrae. The God of Chaos."

He didn't need to be quite that deprecating about it. Plenty of other people had heard their series of increasingly foolhardy plans and hadn't taken *that* tone.

"You would be bolstering our ranger reserves," Astrid explained, "as well as any additional allies Princess Soren can provide. We felt it best to leave you the room to make your own requests of Atlas in exchange for your aid."

When she said it, it almost made sense.

Everin turned to her, holding the treatise like he'd caught a snake by the head; like if he loosened his grip, it would strike with venomous fangs. "And can she provide?"

Soren held his gaze, wishing to the gods she could mimic Finn's snakelike smirk. Then he'd know whose bite he really needed to fear. "*She* can."

"Has Princess Brook given her approval? This would affect aspects of our arrangement, surely."

"She has." Astrid handed him another paper, this one older, faintly discolored at the edges. "I gathered her signature before I came to find you."

Everin frowned down at the second treatise—then at the one in his left hand—then back at the second one.

"I'd like to take the day to look these over," he said. "And of course, I can't make any binding agreements without my father's blessing. But if what you've told me is true, and there is a war against the gods brewing…" A feral, catlike grin. A lion coiled to pounce. "Personally, you'd have to chain me to the tip of Mount Argentum to keep me out of it. But the Atlas piece…" His gaze found her. Assessing—and finding something lacking, if his next words were any indication, "That will require further discussion. And not the sort my father will be keen to have in writing."

Sudden wetness on her fingers drew her attention to her hand; she'd started shaking again, hard enough to toss a wave over the lip of her glass.

Not out of fear of this swollen-headed prince, but of what she saw in his eyes: the satisfaction of a predator who had spotted a limping piece of prey. The lazy confidence of a hunter already assured in his prize.

Gods, she felt sick.

"I'm afraid I missed breakfast this morning," she croaked, catching Astrid's concerned look at her spill, "and I'm starting to feel a bit out of sorts. Prince Everin, I hope you'll forgive my abrupt exit, but since the goddess left me…"

"Please—you owe no explanations. Don't mistake my skepticism for scorn. To survive what you have…well, if my people were to hear of it, they'd hail you as a legend. I certainly do." Everin shuffled both papers together in one hand, using the other to take hers, bowing his head—but not kissing her knuckles.

Maybe that was meant as a slight—a sign of disrespect. But something about the way he did it made her think otherwise; he waited until she pushed herself back from the table, then came to stand in front of her, playing out the motions of kissing her hand without actually touching his lips to it. And when she caught his gaze, he gave her a coy smile and a nod. Like he understood something she wasn't saying.

Maybe he had to remind himself to use his courtly manners, too. Or maybe Elias had caught fire behind her, and the prince was trying to avoid getting his suggestive eyebrows singed off.

"I look forward to our potential friendship, Princess," he added. "All jokes aside, you have…a storied face. I look forward to hearing the tale of your survival in its entirety."

She smiled tightly at him. "I'm sure I'll be seeing you soon, Prince Everin."

"As soon as you like." With a wink, he released her hand, going back to his seat at the table and jumping into conversation with her aunt once again…leaving her feeling like she'd been thoroughly dismissed from her own meeting.

CHAPTER 16

SOREN

By the time she turned away from the table, Elias already had the door open—the knob glowed orange and gold underneath his clenched fingers, his fist curling tighter every second. His uncovered eye was nailed to the back of Everin's head.

"Elias," she muttered as she slipped past, fixing her gaze ahead, "the knob is melting."

She didn't look back to watch his response, but she heard his near-silent curse…and the quiet *hiss* of molten metal being doused.

That drew her to look back, but an ink-stained hand caught her shoulder. "Keep going," Astrid said under her breath. "I handled it."

After several minutes of tense silence through the halls, Soren finally whispered, "Is it safe yet?"

"Not quite." A few more paces, then Astrid sighed, stopping by a large window. Its sill boasted sizable boxes of colorful crocuses and violets. The slender diplomat hauled those off, brushing traces of soil and scattered petals to the floor before she hopped up on the sill, crossing one leg over the other and twining her fingers over her propped knee. "All right. Thoughts?"

"He's an *ass*," she and Elias blurted at the same time.

Astrid's mouth twitched with smothered amusement; then she sighed and plucked her spectacles off the bridge of her nose, folding them and tucking them into her pocket. "He certainly has his moments. But having worked with him and his men for many years during their visits here, as well as Brook's to Tallis, I promise that isn't his only trait. Nor his most prominent."

"You're right." Soren crossed her sore arms. "He's also an arrogant bastard."

Some of that pretty politeness fell away from Astrid's face. "Look, I didn't say he was perfect—I said he's your best shot. And he is." The diplomat mirrored Soren's pose. "Princess, now that we're alone, I'd like to speak frankly: without the assurance of a war-ready force at our side and additional training for the ranger reserves, Queen Genevieve will not grant you the assistance you're seeking. She will not send our rangers to their certain death."

Soren stared at her, all feeling abandoning her fingers. "She won't do *anything?*"

"She would, of course, grant you and the rest of your family asylum—"

"The rest of my family is *gone!*"

That outburst echoed through the empty hall, bouncing off wood and glass: *gone, gone, gone, gone.*

It echoed in her heart, too. *Gone. Gone. Gone.*

"Or they soon will be," Soren added softly. She tried not to think about their drowning dungeon—tried not to remember Elias's feverish eyes gazing back at her, his clammy forehead pressed to hers through metal bars. Tried not to remember *I chased you all the way here—now I'm asking you to walk me home.* "It's her *sister.* How can she just refuse to help?"

Had it been *her* younger sister, Auralee, locked in a cage the ocean swallowed every night, she would have given anything to reach her. Anything.

She curled her left hand into a fist, trying not to think about the note folded in her pocket. Trying not to look at Elias, though she could sense him at her back. The air around him boiled with held-in fury.

"I know it doesn't make sense to you," Astrid said softly. "But the same way Adriata is devoted wholeheartedly to her war, to her vengeance, Genevieve is devoted to peace. That she is considering your proposition at *all* proves how deeply she loves her sister. Many have come to her—and the Arborian queens of the past—offering far less risky alliances, and all have been turned away. Even if you think it heartless, I hope you will hear that and understand."

She could never understand abandoning family. But she held her tongue.

"That said," Astrid continued, "I won't lie to you. Everin is an arrogant, pompous man—and he *can* be unbearable, you should hear Sage and Wolf talk about him behind closed doors—but his actions speak louder than his words."

Unlikely, unless his *actions* included picking up an out-of-tune trumpet and blowing all his hot air into it.

Astrid seemed to pick up on her skepticism, because she added, "Everin and his men never sit idle when they arrive, though they have every excuse to do so. They deliver supplies, they bring food to the medimancers and physicians, they help convert infirmary floors into quarantine spaces when required…they've been indispensable on many occasions. And his…*confidence*, shall we say, is why his people are so doggedly loyal to him. I would greatly encourage you to give him more chances to show you what he has to offer as an ally. Brook has never offered any complaints, and Medwenna speaks very highly of him. She's known him and his men since they were children."

This diplomat was damned good at her job. Soren's flaring temper had already cooled some…if only because they didn't *actually* have the option to reject the one ally they'd been offered.

Play the part. Follow the rules.

"That's twice you've mentioned his men." Elias's weight shifted to favor his right side—the one bearing his Viper scar. "There are Tallisian troops occupying Arborius?"

"Not quite." Astrid's lips quirked. "He had some nerve, poking fun at you for the battlemate system. Everin actually took a page from Nyx's book some time ago when he saw how devoted your battlemate pairs were…and how deadly that devotion made them. He took it upon himself to experiment with fighting in a triad. I'm sure you'll meet the other two before long."

Two more Everins. Great.

She and Elias exchanged glances once again.

"Fine," they said together—then, despite her knuckles still begging for her to let them stamp a set of dents into Everin's chin, Soren added, "I'll try."

Not a lie. She would try—try not to break his face if he taunted her battlemate again. That was *her* job.

"Take the day to settle your thoughts about this," Astrid urged, sliding off the windowsill. "We won't hear from Everin until he makes up his own mind about you—and even then, like he said, this alliance will rely on his father's blessing. You have time to win him over."

She didn't know that she could play nice for the span of another meeting, let alone several. But she did her best to seem appropriately convinced, dipping her head to Astrid and muttering her assent.

"What he said about his father not being keen to seal this arrangement in writing…" Elias ventured. "Does that mean what I'm afraid it means?"

For the first time, Astrid smiled with a hint of trepidation. "I will confirm with him…but yes, I would assume he means for you to travel to Tallis to plead your case yourself."

That notion refused to sink into Soren's head. It smacked against her skull like a bird flying headfirst into crystalline glass, a smear of bloody feathers and nonsense.

"No," she said flatly.

"Your Highness—"

"We *just* arrived here. Tallis is weeks—*weeks* away. We don't have time for a journey like that." Something ice-cold and awful took off through her veins. "My parents—my brothers—"

"Princess," Astrid interrupted, firm but not unsympathetic, "we must think about your kingdom in its entirety—and even though it may not feel like it, this *is* how you help your family. A single soul cannot siege a city."

Well, she'd *tried* doubling up on souls. But her body hadn't cared much for that tactic.

"Take the day," Astrid urged again. "Get some food, get some rest. Even one of the matters we discussed would leave most people in your position overwhelmed. We'll meet again in the morning."

She swallowed down that icy hysteria. Managed a halfhearted nod.

Even after Astrid left, neither of them dared speak freely—so the tension kept building with every turn down a new hall. When they entered the lift, she almost turned around to tell Elias that if he didn't say something, his head was going to explode, and she didn't feel like cleaning molten brains off the walls—but when she did turn, the expression on his face was so severe that for once, she didn't dare tease him.

Once they reached the infirmary and stopped outside Ani's sickroom, he guided her in first before turning around to close the door. No Wolf, but Ani slept still—her bandages looked fresh, no sign of the soiled ones. Maybe Wolf had left to discard them.

She shut her eyes, bracing herself.

The door clicked shut.

"*What* in Mortem's smoking, blistered pits was that?" Elias thundered, rounding on her with a flare of fiery light through his tattoos, staring at her in open fury.

She put her hands up. "I don't know."

"They cornered us—they didn't even warn us he was here!"

"I know."

Elias dropped to his seat on the floor, knees cocked; he ran his hands over his haggard face. "Did you see his face when he found out Atlas is vulnerable? And Nyx?"

"Like a hound on a scent."

"Exactly. We can't trust him—we don't know what he'll demand in exchange for his help. We have to try something else."

"You heard Astrid—he's our best chance. And without him, we get nothing."

Elias stabbed his finger toward the door. "Nothing might be better than that!"

"You know it's not!" Soren threw up her hands in helpless fury of her own. "I can handle one puffed-up prince."

"He's not arrogant without cause. You've *heard* the stories about him—"

"What do you want me to say?" Sore, seething, she dropped down on her seat in front of Elias, splaying her fingers out toward him. "That I'm willing to trade my people's lives so I don't have to risk bartering with him? That I'm more afraid of him than I am of Tenebrae? I'm not!"

"I want them to help us without making you give him a damned thing! I've seen what happens when someone sacrifices too much for their kingdom. I saw what it did to—"

He broke off—swore—reached up and ripped off his eyepatch. He bent his head, roughly rubbing his eyes. His next breath wavered as he exhaled.

Chest aching, Soren leaned forward and rested her hand on his knee. "Elias."

"They're your family," he muttered, not looking up. "It's not right."

"I know."

"I'm not angry at you."

"I know."

Now he lifted his head; anger cooled into anguish, rage put out by unshed tears.

"Kal would kill me for putting his kingdom in that bastard's hand," he croaked, dragging his fingers back through his hair. "I mean it. I think he would actually have killed me."

Soren swallowed the lump in her throat; it refused to budge. "Well, Kal's not here. It's just us—just me and you. Do you think we can do this?"

"I don't like—"

"I know you don't like it." She held his gaze, afraid that blinking would somehow show how little confidence she had about this herself. "Do you believe we can do this?"

He stared at her for too long. Long enough that she had to start wondering what she'd do if he said *no*. If he demanded they give up and go elsewhere for help.

Because as Genevieve and Astrid had pointed out, they had no *elsewhere* left to go.

If he asked her to forsake this mission…she didn't know if she could. Not even for him.

She didn't like that feeling. That choice.

Luckily, she didn't have to make it; instead, his hand slid over hers, his thumb brushing her knuckles. "Of course I do."

"Then let's do it," she whispered. "You and me—and when it's all over, if he's really that unbearable, I'll say goodbye to him with a solid kick in the crotch."

Finally, he smiled—or at least, he smiled just enough that *she* could tell what it was. Other people might have looked at it and seen a grimace, but that was just Elias—his lips didn't always bend the right way. She'd once teased him that she needed to teach him how to smile properly…and he'd proceeded to flash her a smile so pretty it nearly blinded her.

He could have dazzled the twilight stars into dimming their glow, if he'd wanted to. He just rarely wanted to.

"I'd like to see that," he murmured.

"After we're done saving the world," she promised. "I'll even get some new steel-toed boots for the occasion."

"Feels like a step down, as far as difficulty goes."

"Well, some things you do for the accomplishment, like killing gods." She smirked at him. "Other things you do for the joy of it, like kicking princes until they cry."

"Finally, a plan I like." He lifted her hand and pretended to kiss it, putting on ridiculously puckered lips—as she giggled, he looked up and finally gave her a warm, tired smile. "I'm proud of you, you know. You handled yourself brilliantly in there."

"You think so?"

"Mm-hm. Every inch a queen." He shook his head. "They gave you nothing—no warning, no time—and you stayed on your feet. Took the hits and threw them back."

"I felt like I got pushed out on the skating pond with my skates untied."

"You didn't look it."

"But I felt it." She stared down at her shoes, tapping the tips together. "Gods, Elias, I don't know what I'm doing."

"You're doing exactly what you set out to do." He caught the tops of her boots in his hands to halt their clicking, giving her an earnest look over her knees. "Saving your people—both peoples. I don't like what they're making you do, and I definitely don't like that prince being involved, but none of that is because I don't trust you. Just…promise me that if it goes too far, if they ask for too much, you'll trust yourself—and trust me. Trust that we can find a different way."

How could she trust that? Neither of them had ever done this before—neither of them had tested their showmanship skills, not even on a lower-stakes stage. On the one occasion her parents had finagled her into her school's Saltwater Festival pageant, she'd torn off the itchy sleeves of her costume before she'd ever taken the stage, then forgotten two of her four simple lines. Finn had been swift to fill in the gaps, his improvisation saving her from dissolving into a puddle of embarrassed tears under the spotlight's judgmental glare.

She would've given up her sword hand to have him here to slip her the right lines now. To teach her sleight of hand and sleight of heart, stealing alliances and armies until they were spoiled for choice.

Actually, she would've given all that and more just to have him *here* at all.

"Food and rest," Elias reminded her. "Everything will look better after that."

When she nodded her agreement, he gripped the footboard and dragged himself up, then hauled her up after him, steadying her when her stiff legs wobbled. Stiff from sitting all day, but no pain—a sensation she might never stop marveling over. One she swore to herself she'd never take for granted again.

"Food and rest," she agreed. Then back to the battlefield.

Elias glanced at her wobbling legs—though he seemed to make a valiant effort not to—before he offered, "Rest first? I know you didn't get much last night."

That was true, and Prince Everin had certainly sapped the life out of her. Or was it all the showmanship and playing the part of the royal that had her aching and unsteady?

Gods, did Finn suffer from any of these afflictions when he whipped his masks on and off? Or was her body rejecting rulership as fiercely as it had playing host to a goddess?

"All right," she relented. "Can we make a deal?"

"Depends."

"I'll sleep, but will you..." She gathered fistfuls of his shirt, flexing and loosening her grip. "Will you sit with Ani? Please?"

The answer came far faster than she expected, with an earnest willingness that warmed her middle. "Of course I will."

"If she so much as *blinks*—"

"I will shake you so hard your nose will snap straight," he promised—earning a grind of her heel against his toes.

She dragged her feet to the extra cot...literally. The scrape of her calloused heels against the wood made her ears itch, but the blanket—one of her aunt's handmade quilts—welcomed her like a hug.

Elias dropped into the chair and propped his heels on the frame of Anima's sickbed, reaching down to untie his boots; a moment later, he threw his socks across the room, chuckling at her gasp of delight.

"You're my favorite," she said as she tugged one sock on.

"I know."

She pulled on the other sock. "Even though you're annoying."

"I know."

"I love you."

She couldn't see his face; he'd turned to watch Anima, just like he'd promised. But his voice flickered with warmth as he said, "You're starting to grow on me, too."

"Say it back."

"Say please."

She threw a pillow—then immediately regretted it. Even though it whacked an incensed, satisfying "Ow!" from her battlemate, it also left her down a pillow, and her body ached desperately for every scrap of softness she could shove underneath it.

"Say it back," she whined—then added, "and please give me back my pillow."

"I love you *too*, you menace." He tossed the pillow back. "Luckily for you, because otherwise I'd be keeping that damned pillow."

She laughed. Or she meant to.

But to her horror, it came out as a messy, shredded sob.

Elias spun in his seat so fast that when he stood, the chair kept spinning on one leg before clattering sadly to the floor. "What's the matter? What hurts?"

"Nothing," she sobbed.

"You don't have to be brave about—"

"No, you're not hearing me." Blotches of heat patched her cheeks, her skin sticky with tears, and she couldn't even care, because— "Elias, I threw something. And it *didn't hurt.*"

It hadn't fallen short of its target. It hadn't nearly wrenched her shoulder out of place. It hadn't left her clawing for every breath or stanching a bleed in her nose or convulsing violently on the floor.

It had flown steady and sure, hitting its target true.

A pillow. Just a bundle of cloth and feather stuffing. Hardly a weapon to write ballads and legends about.

But she'd thrown it. It had made Elias say *ow.*

And she didn't feel silly for crying about it, not one bit. Because as realization dawned in her battlemate's midnight gaze, his own tears followed; a dawn that brought a torrent of beautiful, cleansing rain.

A rain that washed them both of any lingering dread as he joined her on the cot, and they held each other, and wept, and poked fun at each other for the ridiculous faces they made while weeping. And for the first time since a night long ago…a snow-smothered night spent breathing incense smoke and researching poisonwork by candlelight…

They both slept without fear that one would not wake the next morning.

CHAPTER 17

ANIMA

On the last night of her first life, Ani had shared a room with her sister for the first time in decades.

Neither had felt safe sleeping alone, not with what Tenebrae planned to do the next day—and knowing that Tempest and Mortem still hoped to foil his plans however they could. Neither she nor Cassi had known for certain how far Nature and Death would go; neither of them trusted that their siblings would pull their punches, so to speak, if they thought removing Time and Life from the equation would tip the scales in their favor.

So they'd huddled together in a cheap, drafty room in some backwater hostel, knowing Tempest and Mortem would look for Cassi in the ornate inns built on the north side of New Sanctaviv. That chilly, frightening night, Ani had laughed so much she'd almost broken a rib—had smiled so much that her cheeks still ached the next morning. Cassi had relaxed out of the cut-crystal rigor she so often held herself in, enough to grin and giggle with her as they gossiped about the scandals in their individual kingdoms and shared stories about their friends that left them both muffling their laughter in their pillows to avoid waking their sleeping neighbors.

She'd fallen asleep still smiling. But the next morning, she'd woken to silence—to a cold, empty space on the bed beside her and the most awful weight sitting on her chest. Like that night was the last she'd ever have with her sister.

Waking up in the Arborian infirmary without Soren felt exactly the same.

She dozed with her eyes still shut, listening to the rustling branches and bickering birds somewhere outside, wondering why Soren hadn't yet greeted her with an amused, *Rise and shine, lazybones* or *Good morning, Goddess Great.*

Uncurling their muscles in a long, lazy stretch, she cast a thought like a skipping stone across their mind: *Be still, my heart. Surely the Princess of the Sun Kingdom isn't dozing the day away?*

Her teasing barb found purchase in *nothing.*

No sense of humor wielded like raised fists, ready to throw quick jabs back into her more vulnerable parts. No mental eye-roll or imagined middle-fingered salute. No sea salt or starshine.

What happened? Did we have a fit? She inched further through her mental space, searching blindly, distress climbing the ladder to terror in record time when she only encountered more emptiness.

There was no door, no wall, no curtain—no separation between the partitions of their mind, because there was nothing to *separate.*

"Soren!" Ani shrieked, flinging herself to her knees with a jerk, blankets and sheets bundling around her in rumpled layers. "Soren, where are you, *where are you*—"

"Goddess, wait!" called a male voice—which she immediately dismissed, because she didn't care *who* he was. His wasn't the voice she was searching for.

And until she found Soren, she couldn't *wait.* Not for anything.

She shoved herself out of bed, her bare feet landing with a heavy thump, the way they always did when Soren's tall, broad-hipped, strong-and-soft body made contact with the floor…

Except they didn't.

Even as Soren had lost weight and muscle in her body's fight to survive Ani's possession, that thump had greeted them every morning, a reminder she still had the strength to stand. But this time, that impact came quiet and wispy—when she tried to straighten up, her knees wobbled like a newborn filly who hadn't learned how to use her legs just yet.

And before she could sort out that strangeness, agony lanced her leg open like a sharpened scalpel.

The pain caught her so off guard that she couldn't muffle her cry, nor stop herself from buckling into the pair of arms that appeared to catch her. Not Elias's arms, not burn-pocked and tattooed, but scarred and lean with hunter's muscle.

Despite their rough composition, the hands that curled beneath her elbows cradled them with gentleness…not a tender sort of gentle, but a cautious sort that dreaded its own strength. That avoided touching fragile things for fear they might shatter.

Ani's breath thinned and quickened, confusion and fear puddling like oil and water as she turned her head to take in her surroundings.

The soothing smell of fresh-cut wood and fresh-washed sheets; the darkwood-paneled walls dominated by shelves and cupboards stuffed with jars, their labels marked with names and dates. Most of the names she recognized from her own days as a healer and medicine-maker, all familiar poultices and tinctures and syrups.

In the two windows at the foot of the room, hammered metal garden boxes overflowed with living herbs, also carefully labeled. Some had been recently cut; others flourished at full height, waiting for there to be need of them. Crawling plants poured over the tops of the cupboards and to either side of the shelves, their pots positioned at the very edge to allow them to tumble over.

All of it looking almost distorted and nightmarish—not because of the arrangement itself, but because she had somehow lost several inches of height.

"Goddess," said another voice, this one feminine—but still not Soren. "Can you hear me?"

Ani twisted to see two individuals standing at the foot of the bed; behind them were three chairs shoved against the wall, like they'd been sitting together while they waited on her and Soren's awakening.

One she recognized from Soren's memories—Sage, the second-eldest Arborian prince—and the other she didn't.

The woman stood with her hands behind her back, watching Ani patiently. Each strand of her sleek, beautifully coiffed golden hair fell just so, one curl artfully sweeping over her high forehead; her straight nose and square face didn't have a single freckle, dimple, or blemish, her pale skin pinking perfectly at the apples of her cheeks. Despite her rigidly perfect appearance, she smiled at Ani with genuine warmth.

"You're safe," she added. "Captain Loch and Princess Soren brought you home, with help from Prince Sage and Prince Wolf."

Wolf. That name had always come first on the list of Soren's Arborian cousins.

Ani looked up—and up, and *up*—until she found a muscle hopping in a clenched jaw. A frown etching faint lines into a handsome face. A pair of topazine eyes that caught the light like hardened amber.

Prince Wolf Olivander, gazing down at her without blinking.

"Oh," she said, a bit breathless. "Thank you."

"Would you like to sit?" Wolf asked.

"I'm fine."

He glanced down at her hands, still braced against his inner arms. "You're shaking."

She nodded, suddenly dizzied. "I should sit."

She couldn't quite tell whether his lips twitched in the direction of a smile or a stronger frown.

Ani clung to his arms as he lowered her back onto the bed, the mattress creaking beneath her; the pain bled out of her leg in slow spurts, relief loosing a sigh from her lungs.

She smiled up at Wolf. "Thank you."

He cleared his throat, bowing his head as he released her.

Ani smoothed her hands back over her hair, suddenly self-conscious—and mortification flooded her as she encountered a beautifully woven, horrifically complex tangle matted from the base of her skull past her neck.

Wait.

Past her neck. Her hair hung *past her neck.*

She patted further down, that dizziness tunneling into her head like a mole digging a new den.

Too long. How long had she been asleep?

"Soren?" she stammered out—part call, part question.

"Still breathing." Sage clapped Wolf on the shoulder, who gave him a sideways look of reproach. "And walking under her own power, which is more than I expected this soon."

"Thanks to you, Goddess," Wolf added. "If you hadn't taken her wounds…our medimancers say she wouldn't have survived the ordeal."

With a rush of aching pain, a cluster of memories struck Ani like a stone to the forehead—the tree, the spider, the stairs, the relic.

She looked down, lifting her hands to her face—familiar hands. Hands she hadn't seen in nearly a thousand years.

Without meaning to, she found herself on her feet again; Wolf moved toward her, but Sage flung an arm across his chest. "Let her."

For the first time in a *thousand years,* Annelisa Medeis turned to the windows to find her own reflection staring back at her.

Her first reflection. Her born reflection.

Heat rushed to her eyes and nose, bursting out in a torrent of tears.

Ani covered her face and wept into her hands.

Hers. Not stolen. Not broken.

All *hers.*

Delicate hands settled over her shoulders. "I know this is a lot to take in at once," said the woman, still calm, still gentle. "Take your time. We are in no rush."

"Actually," said Sage, "I do have a prior engagement…"

Ani peeked out just in time to see the woman turn and level him with such a cool glare that Ani was fairly certain Sage *actually* bit his tongue, folding his arms over his chest and stepping back one pace.

Ani didn't even know this woman, but once she had that permission, she fell into her arms, unable to quiet her sobs—and the woman let her, giving her a warm hug.

"Would you like us to give you a moment?" Wolf offered.

Maple syrup. That was what his voice reminded her of—dark and flowing. Rich and smooth.

Something about hearing a voice like that with her own ears felt…different. Not wrong, not like the room and the angles and the floor—just different.

And that *different* distracted her just enough to sniffle and lift her head from the stranger's shoulder, wiping her cheeks with a messy laugh. "No. That's all right. I'm so sorry, I don't even know your name and I've already stained your beautiful shirt."

The woman waved a hand in dismissal, like she got wept on by goddesses every day. "Well, we can fix that. I'm Lady Astrid Thorne, diplomat and liaison of the Olivander family. This is Second Prince Sage Olivander, commander of our ranger reserves and medimancer units, and First Prince Wolf Olivander, who presides over your temples here and oversees the upkeep of the island. And what may we call you?"

Anima smiled uncertainly, rubbing her own arms, trying not to start when her fingers encountered tender skin instead of hidden muscle. "You already know my name."

"But I don't know what you prefer to be called. I prefer Astrid, though Lady Thorne is fine if you're more comfortable being formal."

"I call her lots of other things," Sage offered, "if you need more options."

Ani giggled, wiping at the leftover tears lingering on her chin. "I prefer Ani."

"Ani." Astrid grinned at her, folding her hands behind her back again. "See? Not strangers anymore. Though you may wish otherwise when you get to know these two better."

"I can't imagine so." Ani dipped her head, a little discombobulated by the weight of her thick tresses. Soren's cropped hair was much lighter. "It's good to meet you both."

Sage gave her a two-fingered salute, clicking his tongue in time with a wink. Wolf gave a low, graceful bow. "Goddess."

"Ani," she and Astrid corrected at the same time, Astrid with particular emphasis.

Wolf's mouth twitched again—Ani expected him to scowl, but instead, he looked up at her and offered the smallest of smiles. "Ani," he corrected himself. "Apologies. It will take some getting used to. I've been in your service for most of my life. To see you standing before me…" A quick, quiet exhale. "Forgive me."

Ani tipped her head, curious. "You've done nothing that requires forgiveness, Prince Wolf."

Now he smiled fully, but it struck her as…wry. Maybe even scornful. "You are very kind to say so."

"He tripped me yesterday, actually," Sage sniffed. "It was right rude, if you ask me. No apology to speak of."

Wolf shut his eyes. Let out a longsuffering sigh. "You tripped *over* me. It's not the same thing."

"Boys," scolded Astrid, and both princes straightened a bit, clearing their throats and looking askance. "Ani, I am sorry to do this when you're still recovering, but I'm afraid it can't wait now that you've woken." Astrid sat on the edge of the bed, gesturing for Ani to sit as well. "Depending on what you choose, we will need to begin the process immediately."

Ani's brows came together; she sat down beside Astrid, secretly grateful to get off her new, uncertain legs. "What process?"

Astrid cleared her throat, crossing her ankles and folding her hands elegantly in her lap. On her left hand, a square-cut emerald sparkled, set in a wooden band. "It is customary, so Prince Wolf tells me, that when you return to Arborius—regardless of your physical form's identity—we offer your throne back to you."

All feeling fled from Ani's fingers.

"What?" she squeaked.

"Each lifetime you return to Arborius," Wolf explained, pulling a chair around and settling himself in it, "the royal family is obliged to offer their own abdication. This is your kingdom; you grew it. It's yours to rule, if you so choose."

"He's right," Astrid said when Ani snapped back around to look at her. "As the First Queen, you're within your rights to take your throne back. If that is your desire, I can begin—"

"*No.*" She hadn't meant to sound quite so aghast, but she couldn't help it—the denial came from the very depths of her. "Rotting bones, no. Of course it should stay with the Olivanders—I couldn't—"

This wasn't sounding very goddess-like. She cleared her throat, taking in a deep breath through her nose, steadying her hands in her lap.

"Arborius should stay as it is," she said firmly. "I came because I wished to repair what I broke, not to break anything further. The crown stays with the Olivanders."

To her surprise, neither Wolf nor Sage slumped in relief—instead, Sage wrinkled his nose, grumbling under his breath as Wolf silently held out a hand. After a moment of digging in his pocket, Sage pulled out a coin and dropped it in Wolf's palm; without a word or a shift in expression, Wolf pocketed the coin, bowing to her once again. "We are honored by your trust."

Ani looked to Astrid for help; smiling, she patted Ani's hand and said, "In all your previous lives, you've also declined to take the throne back. Every single one. But it's still tradition to offer—and should the offer be accepted, there is an expectation to follow through."

It didn't matter, really, but it did reassure her that she'd made the same decision previously. She cleared her throat, nodding in what she hoped was a confident acknowledgment. "Can you tell me anything else about Soren's condition?"

"I'm sure she'll tell you herself when she returns. She and her battlemate are getting themselves a meal."

"For now, let's talk about *your* condition." Sage plopped down on Ani's other side, jostling the bed, smiling down at her like they were old friends. "Our best medimancer saw to your immediate injuries—that'd be me, of course— and our father cleaned that nasty venom out of your veins, but you've yet to start healing faster than natural. Soren says that's typical when you, ah…borrow someone else's shell?"

"Sage," growled Wolf. "She's not a hermit crab."

"Well, apologies for not knowing the proper *terminology*, Your Holiness—"

"Not the time for bickering." Astrid reached over to poke the prince's shoulder—then gentled when she spoke to Ani again. "We expect your recovery will go much faster now that you've woken. And Princess Soren is doing very well, all things considered."

"Do…do you think she'll be able to fight again?"

"Don't even have to think." Sage patted her knee reassuringly. "If she was any other patient, I'd have already told her she was clear to report back to her barracks. But I wouldn't be so sure if you hadn't…well, whatever you did, you did good. Seems you took the brunt for her."

His confidence soothed the prickling panic needling her skin. But she still couldn't stand the idea of sitting in this room with no one for company but her own thoughts, even for a short time. She'd gotten so used to never being alone that even having her mind to herself suddenly felt…scary.

"Will you take me to see her?" she begged.

Sage sighed. "I'm afraid I can't—whoa, catch that falling face, love! I can't take you, but someone will. Alas, I owe my wife a home-cooked meal and my illustrious company; I've been spending too much time with my mistress lately, and the old crone's starting to get suspicious."

Before Ani could gather her thoughts about that—or pick up her dropped jaw—Sage stood up, squeezed Ani's shoulder, then grabbed Astrid by the chin and stole a passionate, blush-inspiring kiss before striding out, whistling cheerily.

"I'm his wife," Astrid assured her with a roll of her eyes—and a pleased smile that belied her annoyance. "His mistress lives in the stables, and trust me, she much prefers sugar cubes and hay over the delicious veal I requested."

"Oh." Ani tried not to sound too relieved. "That makes more sense."

"Sage usually requires a little translation for newcomers, so don't feel left out." Astrid stood as well, pausing to give Wolf a quick peck on the cheek. "Wolf will take you to find Soren. I'm sure you'll find him a much more palatable guide."

The diplomat's graceful departure left Ani gazing awkwardly at Wolf— who, in turn, seemed determined to look anywhere *but* at her.

"There's a change of clothes on the nightstand," he said; when Ani looked, she found a pile of neatly folded fabric. "I can summon a medimancer if you think you'll need assistance…"

A blush claimed her cheeks, and she hastily shook her head. "I'll manage."

"Princess Juniper's the closest to your size, from what we could judge, but we can find you something else if we miscalculated. And once you're feeling well enough, my sisters—or whoever you choose—can help you find clothes that better suit."

"That's very kind. Will you thank Princess Juniper for me?"

"Of course." Wolf cleared his throat—stood in silence for a moment, as if waiting for something—then abruptly said, "I'll wait in the hall," and practically fled the room.

Palatable guide, indeed.

She frowned down at the clothes, wriggling her fingers, reacquainting herself with the way they bent and curled.

Whatever she'd done to make this prince so jackrabbit-jumpy, it could wait. Right now, all that mattered was getting to her friend.

Ani grabbed the pile of clothes, silently praying they would fit.

And that the flustered heat in her cheeks would fade by the time she left this room.

CHAPTER 18

ANIMA

Becoming someone new never failed to remind Ani just how much she loved being alive.

Dust motes sailed on rays of early afternoon sunshine, bobbing up and down through gold-and-rose seas as she and Wolf descended the long staircase down to the ground floor of the infirmary. Windows lined the wall on the way down, each cradling garden boxes on their sills or dangling hanging plants from their egresses; she trailed her fingers through their leaves as she limped down each step, clinging to the cane Wolf had procured for her, silently chanting reminders to herself to take them one at a time. Soren's long legs had been able to eat up the distance easily; her new ones, not so much.

She'd needed a medimancer's help to get dressed, after all. Her arms had wailed in agony with every attempt to lift them above her head, and afterward, her legs had followed suit. She'd been outfitted with a cane to ease the journey.

Wolf had offered to take her down in something called a *lift*, but she'd refused, though she had taken a moment to marvel at the Arborartemic feat of invention. Even though her body still bobbled off-balance with every step, she craved movement—the burning strain in her muscles thrilled her.

The screaming pain in her bandaged leg, not so much. But beggars couldn't be choosers.

The broad staircase had been designed to allow more than one person to fit on each step; a wooden rail bisected it down the center, making it possible for two streams of people to climb up or down without any collisions. Yet, despite there being ample room for both of them, Wolf made an effort to stay ahead of her—every time she began to catch up, he lengthened his stride, going from one step at a time to two.

"Prince Wolf?" she panted, coming to a halt on the next step—she leaned heavily on her cane and braced one hand on her knee, scrunching her fingertips into the soft ochre fabric of her skirt. Even though it had been borrowed from one of Wolf's teenaged sisters, it was still too long and wide—she'd had to knot some makeshift hikes in the skirt and cinch a corset belt made of tooled golden-brown leather around the high waistband to keep it from slumping. She'd also had to cuff the sleeves of her dusty purple blouse, but she didn't mind. They were beautiful clothes…and they meant she didn't have to walk around in a nightgown in public.

Wolf paused and rested his hand on the rail; he turned to look over his shoulder at her, studying her with guarded eyes and a slight frown. "Are you in pain?"

"Some. I just need a moment."

He stepped up one stair, his hand hovering uncertainly between them. "We should take the lift."

"No, no—I can manage." They were already halfway there, anyway. "I want to remember how it feels."

Now his brow knotted. "How what feels?"

"Walking on my own legs. And the pain—how a wound feels when it won't heal on its own." With two quick huffs, she forced herself to straighten, limping the rest of the way to join him on the stair. She bent her head back to look at his face, offering a beaming smile. Maybe he just needed a little friendliness to offer some in return.

He stared at her like she'd grown rabbit ears. "You *want* to feel pain?"

Her hope wilted. "Oh, well, I don't…it's not…I know it sounds strange." Now that he'd given her that look, anyway. "It's just—it means—"

"You don't have to explain yourself to me, Goddess."

Good, because she was doing a poor job.

"It's so different here than I remember," she blurted instead.

"Oh?" Neutral—or politely disinterested. She couldn't tell which.

"We didn't have lifts when I was here before—well, not that I remember, anyway. It's all a little fuzzy between lives."

He shifted an inch closer to the rail—an inch further from her. "It's a recent addition. We installed them during my late mother's reign."

Ani fumbled her smile, forgetting to hold it steady against the old grief dusting his voice.

Come on, Ani, think! Say something! Anything!

"Oh," she said lamely.

Anything but that!

"A brilliant addition," she added hastily. "I'm happy to see how Arborius has flourished."

"We are honored that you think so, Goddess."

"Ani."

He dipped his head, a silent apology—then, without another word, started walking again. Two steps at a time. Never looking back.

Which left her dawdling behind him on the staircase, a pebble-tough lump forming in her throat, a quailing flush of rejection fluttering beneath her breastbone.

For someone who supposedly served her fervently enough to have been placed in charge of her former home—a worshipper so devout, he'd been set above all the others—he'd been acting cold as a river rock underfoot since she'd woken up.

What she could've possibly done wrong in the ten collective minutes she'd spent conscious in this body, she couldn't begin to guess. But she'd clearly done *something*.

With a quiet huff to herself, followed by an inhale that sent a torrent of lilac and mint and lemon sweeping over her senses, she tried to match his pace again—

And clipped the back of her heel on the second step's edge.

Her injured leg didn't have the strength to catch her balance; instead, she pitched nose-first down the staircase, a panicked whimper fleeing her mouth before it could get smashed against her teeth—

All at once, something halted her fall; lilac and mint and lemon drowned in a rush of evergreen and woodsmoke.

"Careful," Wolf scolded; with one arm under her knees and the other around her waist, he lifted her fully away from the steps, twisting back around without letting her clip the railing or the wall. He set her down gently on the stair in front of him instead—so gently that her feet made no noise as they settled back on solid wood.

Maybe she'd injured her head, too—these waves of dizziness were growing in strength and frequency. "Sorry. Um, thank you—thank you, also."

"Are you sure you should be out of bed?" he asked—passably polite, but still gruff, his voice like rough-cut wood around the edges.

Now her cheeks could have set the tree on fire. "I tripped, that's all." She pointed her chin up, taking the next step more carefully. "I'm not going back until I see Soren myself."

He didn't resume walking until she'd gotten five steps ahead—yet it only took him two strides to place himself beside her again.

"Here." He held out his arm to her.

She glanced at it, then looked up at him, uncertain. "You don't need to…"

He narrowed his eyes at her. "Humor me."

Fine. She wrapped her arm through his. "Surely you have more important things to do."

A quiet cough. She would've called it a laugh if she didn't know better. "Trust me, Goddess—it's not even close."

Rotting bones, these hot flashes were going to be the end of her.

"For the moment, I have been relieved of my daily duties," he added.

That seemed like odd timing. "Why?"

"Until your magic settles, as Soren put it…you're vulnerable. My parents have decided to post a guard beside you to ensure your protection, and the Reapers can manage better without me than our rangers can without Sage."

"Reapers?" The term struck her as vaguely familiar, but only just.

"Those who assist me in maintaining and safeguarding your temples around the island…and the Arboretum, before its defenses began to act up." A light shrug. "I can't be in two places at once, so my daily duties are being carried out by a handful of the other Reapers for the time being."

A seed of mortification sprouted in her chest and spread, weaving roots through her ribs. Her lungs. Her stomach.

Her cheeks didn't flush this time—they didn't bother. A rush of blood to skin couldn't properly show off the embarrassment thriving within the greenhouse of her body.

Her brand-new, beautiful, useless body that couldn't heal itself and save her from this abrasive, itching instinct to hide until everybody forgot she was even there.

No wonder he could barely stand to be around her. He'd been forced out of his rank, his routine, his whole rotting *life* to play guard for a goddess who, to the best of anyone's knowledge, couldn't actually *die*.

Why were these people so determined to turn her into a burden?

"That is not necessary," she insisted. "I don't require protection."

"I could not—" An abrupt halt—of both his words and his feet. He cleared his throat and started guiding her down again, step by cautious step. "I didn't make the call, Goddess. The Queen did. I'm sure she'd be happy to discuss it with you if you're against it, but in the meantime, I have my orders. I would appreciate it if you would let me fulfill them."

I have my orders. A dutiful answer for a prince who'd only ever known peace.

At least now that he was busy assessing the stairs ahead, he wouldn't see how deathly embarrassed she was.

Some goddess, tripping over your own feet. She drove the cane down more sharply on the next step—not as satisfying as stomping her foot, but better than nothing. *Some goddess, needing a babysitter in your own kingdom.*

By the time they reached the door to the pub on the second floor of the infirmary, she hadn't come up with anything more clever to say, or a topic of conversation that might better suit Wolf—nor had she come up with the courage to outright ask him if she should request a different guard.

"I'll wait out here." Wolf gave a graceful bow after releasing her arm. "If you come out and I'm not in sight, find anyone wearing a uniform and ask them. They'll know where to find me."

She stared at the door, suddenly unable to move.

All that effort and embarrassment to march down here…and she couldn't take the final step over the threshold.

"What's wrong?" Wolf's voice sharpened; he bent to catch her attention, studying her face with an intensity that made it difficult to remember what, exactly, was wrong.

As did the thunderous growl through the timbre of his voice when he cursed, lifting her wrist and pressing his thumb to it, testing her pulse.

"You're shaking again," he muttered, distracted; a cluster of white strands escaped from one of his braids, drifting over his eyes.

Compared to his avoidance on the walk here, the force of his full attention struck her like a slap. Ani looked down at her wrist, slightly alarmed by how small his long fingers made it look.

And terrified he'd notice how fast her pulse was fluttering beneath those fingers, hasty as a hummingbird who'd mistaken coffee for nectar.

"It's nothing," she tried feebly. Passersby kept pausing to look at them, clearly startled to see their prince hunched over an injured girl half his height. A couple squinted a bit too closely at her face, then gave a dismissive shake of their heads as they walked away.

At first, she didn't understand why—until she caught one of them looking between her and something past her shoulder.

That *something* was a six-foot-tall portrait of herself mounted on the wall to her left. Her first and current self, tawny freckles and round cheeks and all, gowned in a dress made entirely of flowers. A garden in full bloom.

Oh, wonderful.

"If it was nothing, you wouldn't be—" Another cut-off retort. Another quiet curse. The prince shifted on his feet, hashmark creases cutting into the bridge of his nose…like the barest beginnings of a flinch. Like he was the one trying to walk on a stitched-up leg.

"You don't have to be brave." The words charged out like an oncoming army, fierce and rushed, like they'd had to force their way through an invisible barricade. "Pain doesn't make us weak—mortal or goddess."

"I'm not—"

"You are," he interrupted—and though mortification quickly followed that infraction, he added, "I know the look on your face. You're hurting."

How to explain that this pain had nothing to do with her leg? How to explain to this stranger that somehow, Soren had gone from a terrifying enemy to a very vocal headache to someone who knew her better her own family…a family Ani had wrecked worlds for, stolen immortality for, usurped a true god for.

And now that her survival didn't depend on Ani's help, she could very well be about to tell Ani to make herself scarce.

"It's not that," she said softly. "The leg, I mean, it's…"

Ani shut her eyes, breathing in deeply through her nose.

Evergreen and woodsmoke. Fry oil and cooking spice. Hints of vinegar and sugar, tangy and sweet—some kind of homemade sauce.

Water flooded her mouth. A famished, audible rumble invaded her stomach, appetite weeding out the anxiety doing its best to choke out her courage.

Something about hunger paired with the proximity of food had a knack for kicking fear several rungs lower on the ladder of priority.

Raising her chin and patting his hand, Ani said, "I'll feel better with a meal in my stomach, I'm sure. But your concern is appreciated—and if anything goes poorly because I insisted on leaving my bed, I will make certain you are not blamed for it."

Wolf drew back, taking his hands away—he put them in his pockets, but not fast enough for her to miss how he clenched them. "It's not blame I'm concerned about."

"Wolf." This silly dance could go both ways—if he insisted on *Goddess*, she could insist on *Wolf*. "May I be honest with you?"

He rocked back on his heels like he'd been kicked in the chest. But he immediately said, "Of course."

"I haven't eaten since we got off our ship. Are you familiar with the term *hangry*?" She'd only just learned it herself, when Soren had to explain why Elias had gotten especially cranky after seasickness had purged his stomach.

"I'm familiar with the affliction, yes."

"Well, I don't have that. I get sungry."

A slow blink. "Sungry."

She nodded with all seriousness. "*Sad* and hungry. If I don't get a bite of whatever smells that good in there—" she pointed to the pub door, "—then I'm going to start crying. I won't mean to, it'll just happen. Do you want to see a goddess cry?"

His throat strained. "Oh, ah, I don't—"

"I didn't think so." She took a step back, reaching for the door—when her palm collided with it, the wood murmured welcoming words, sharing a hint as to what waited beyond. Hushed conversation, heavy boots, a warm hearth. Soup spills and fresh herbs and laughter reverberating through the eaves. "I will see you in an hour."

Wolf's gaze lingered on her face. Then her leg, though the bandage was hidden beneath her skirt. Then her face again.

In that moment, she changed her mind—his disinterest was far less unnerving than his pinpoint focus.

Not unpleasant. Just unnerving.

"On second thought," he said, "I would be grateful if you would allow me to join you. I have grieved my cousin for a decade, and…it would be nice to get to know her again."

She…was not sure that was the reason he'd changed his mind at all. But she could hardly argue. "You don't need my permission—but I'll give it, if it will put your mind at ease. Please, join us."

Wolf offered his arm again. With a gusty breath she prayed was not as noisy as it felt, she took it, allowing him to escort her inside.

The pub welcomed her with open arms, an embrace filled with fireborne warmth and cooksmoke. Large, irregular stones paved the floor, smooth to step on but abstract in their shape; she could have spent an hour picking through them like a cloud-watcher, pointing out hearts and animals and other shapes you could see if you bent at just the right angle. Hooded lanterns hung from the eaves, flickering cheerily with false flame; round wooden tables served as the hedges that framed out a maddening maze, pub workers weaving between them at a harrowing pace.

But there was a method to this madness; as she watched the servers dodge and spin and tell each other which path to take with nothing but looks and pointed nods, it became clear that they each knew their way backwards and forwards through that maze. That they could have walked through it blindfolded without spilling a drink on the canvas aprons boasting the pub's name—*The Oaken Barrel*—or setting a plate in front of the wrong patron.

Wolf bent to murmur in her ear. "Are you still certain you're up for this?"

No.

But it was too late, anyway. A shrill cry cut across the controlled chaos, one that had only shouted her name like *that* inside their shared head:

"*Ani?*"

A fire-crowned form shot up from one of the tables; the man beside her caught her by the belt loop, his head tipping in a concerned bend. She shooed him off, garden-green gaze aimed toward Ani like a cocked spear set to soar.

This was a bad idea.

Ani flinched from the fury in Soren's face, reaching back for the doorknob, but it was too late. The long-legged princess devoured the distance between them in three forceful strides—

And enveloped Ani in a hug so tight it crushed all her broken pieces back into a whole.

"What in the *pits* are you doing up?" Soren seethed. "Hours of sitting at your bedside like a lovesick hound, and right after I get dragged out, you decide it's time to rejoin the living? If I wasn't so damned glad to see you, I'd throttle—are you crying?"

"No." Yes. "I'm so happy you're all right."

Soren pulled back to hold Ani's face in her hands, her thumbs pressing into Ani's cheeks as if testing for tears. "Only thanks to you. Now tell me which of my cousins' asses I'm kicking for letting you out of bed. You look worse than Elias when someone takes Mortem's name in vain."

Ani reached up to cup her own cheeks. Despite the warmth of the pub, her fingers encountered cool, clammy skin. "That bad?"

"She's lying." Russet-brown hands slid over Soren's hips. Elias peered around her, frowning. "You look much worse."

Ani sidled back, putting space between her and Soren, hoping he would see the peace offering for what it was. "I'm sorry, I know you probably don't want to see me, and I understand, I really do—I understand, but I just needed to see her, and—"

Wordlessly, he flung his arm out…and snagged the back of a nearby chair. Dragged it to their table. Dusted off its floral-patterned cushion.

"Come sit with us," he said, coming back and offering both arms—one to Ani, one to Soren. "You're shaking."

Gratitude swelled in her throat, replacing the lump of fear and shame. Warming her chest with something other than embarrassment.

"Thank you," she whispered, letting him lead her to the offered seat— she thought Wolf might have muttered something, but she couldn't catch it. Soren ducked under Elias's other arm, hugging hers around his waist—but over his shoulder, she pinned her eyes on Wolf, seemingly noticing him for the first time.

"So *you're* the bastard who let her out of bed," she scoffed. "I should have known."

"Don't be upset with him," Ani protested. "I decided, not him."

"I'll be upset with whoever I please, thank you." Snorting, Soren dropped onto the bench and pulled one leg up by the knee, grimacing as she guided it down—then she did the same to the other, carefully arranging herself in a cross-legged pose. "Sit your ass down, Wolf. I'll kick it later."

Heat flashed up the column of Ani's spine as Wolf circled to her side, his broad hand clasping the back of the chair beside the one Elias had pulled out for her; Ani braced for the shrieking of wooden feet against stone pavers, but instead…

Instead, Wolf lifted the entire thing with two fingers curled under its headrest, setting it down at an angle, facing in such a way that he could keep all three of them in his eyeline when they sat.

She had the strangest urge to grab her hair and draw it across her face like a set of drapes.

"If it helps my case at all," he said to Soren, "I did tell her she ought to go back to bed. Repeatedly."

Soren's eyes looked ready to fall straight out of her sockets and plink around on her plate. "Wolf Olivander, defying the desires of his goddess? And you didn't drop dead on the spot?"

Wolf laughed—not a painful-sounding snort or a halfhearted smile. A full-chested roll of laughter. "I will throw you over my shoulder and dunk you in the river, lass," he threatened, reaching over the table and ruffling Soren's already-mussed curls. "I don't care how Nyxian you got, you're still my little cousin, and I'm not afraid to remind you."

"I'm shaking in my boots," Soren drawled.

When she bantered that way—spoke that way—it made things seem so much lighter. So much easier.

It made Ani almost miss, at the right angles, just how sick her friend had become.

Soren's body had wasted away more than Ani had even realized; they'd done their best to eat extra helpings to combat the massive amount of energy being used to keep their body functioning, but they'd only managed to slow the deterioration of muscle and mass, not stop it. Her collarbones jutted against her freckled skin, peeking from beneath the slumped collar of her soft cotton shirt; its deep blue shade only washed more color from her friend's once-sunkissed skin. Though she sat straight—or at least, no more slumped than her usual cocky slouch—her eyelids kept drifting downward, as if fatigue dangled from her eyelashes, coaxing them to close.

But when she reached across the table and clasped Ani's hand, her grip held as strong as her focus—removed from Wolf, riveted on Ani instead. "You shouldn't have taken my wounds."

Ani and Elias locked eyes across the table. The angle of his body—turned outward on the bench to face Soren, every muscle coiled to spring despite being at rest—told her everything she needed to know about what would have happened had Soren been forced to fight the spider's venom herself.

"I needed to." There was no question about that. "If I hadn't, you would have…I would have had to…Soren, it was all my—"

"Hey." Soren pulled her other hand free from Elias's grip, covering Ani's instead; with a smirk, the princess ordered, "Relax. You're forgiven, Goddess Great."

Ani burst into sobs.

Wolf went stock-still. Soren exchanged looks with Elias; then, with a sigh, she lifted her other arm and hip-bumped Elias to force him to make room for Ani on the bench. "All right, come here."

Still blubbering, Ani circled to the other side of the table and clumsily slid onto the bench, wrapping her arms around Soren and hiding her face in her sleeve. Seconds later, Soren's shoulder was soaked and sticky, flooded by a goddess's tears.

She almost expected Soren to flinch away—though Soren was a very physical person, she'd often grimaced when other people invaded their space without permission. But when Ani curled up under Soren's arm, there was no tension. No recoiling.

Just warmth. Just a calm, easy familiarity. An *"Oh, I know you. Welcome back."*

Soren settled her arm around Ani's narrow shoulders, chuckling as Ani started crying harder. "Gods, Ani, how would you have reacted if I *died?*"

"I don't *kno-ow,*" Ani whimpered, muffled by Soren's shoulder. "I don't want to think about that."

Soren ran her fingers through Ani's hair; tiny tugs of pain told Ani she'd started unraveling the nest of tangles in the back. "Hey…you did it. We both made it. What's there to cry about?"

Ani hiccupped. "I thought—"

"I know what you thought, and you were wrong." Soren gently scraped some loose strands of hair from where they'd stuck to Ani's wet cheeks. "Thank you. You saved me."

The two of them gazed at each other for a moment, silent—but that silence spoke plenty. Like they could still hear each other's thoughts, even with their minds split apart.

"You only needed saving because of me," Ani whispered finally. A truth she would tuck behind her heart for safekeeping. Being forgiven did not give her the right to forget. "But you're welcome."

An argument gathered on Soren's face like a stormcloud set to burst. But before she could do more than open her mouth, Elias swooped in. "So, is this…I mean, did you come up with this body yourself? Or is this—"

Relieved, Ani twisted to face him. "This is how I looked in my first life."

A low hum. "Your real face."

She nodded, ducking her head, suddenly shy again. It was harder to hold his gaze without Soren's help—nevermind Wolf's, for Sancta's sake.

"I figured. You look a lot like Mortem." When Soren elbowed him, hissing a wordless scolding, Elias quickly added, "No offense—I sensed some bad blood there."

Shyness wilted into sorrow. "You're not the first to say it."

She and Mora had always looked alike, wearing their mother's sleek brown hair and springtime sprays of freckles, while Braeden and Peter had shared their father's onyx curls and dimpled grins; as always, Cassi landed somewhere in the middle, a collision of both their parents that made her look most like whichever set of siblings she happened to be standing next to.

At least, that was what she'd been told. Her father had died before she was born, and their mother had died only a couple of years after, leaving her with scant memories of the latter and scarce stories about the former.

"Will you leave her alone?" Soren's tone dripped reproach—on *her* behalf. "Ani, let me know if you want me to punch him. I won't mind."

"*I* mind," Elias protested.

Soren drove a hard poke into the center of his forehead. "Then maybe use that mind to *think* before you dive into someone's sordid history with their sister."

"Do you even know what that word *means*?"

"Which one?"

"*Sordid.*"

"That's my name, don't wear it out."

"It's *not* your—it's not even that *close*—"

They continued to bicker, even after one of the servers presented them with a platter of toasted sandwiches and bowls of mashed potatoes. The golden-brown bread stuffed with heaps of sauce-glazed meat couldn't fully distract her from their verbal sparring match; she watched even while she ate, relishing the zing of the reddish-brown sauce tingling on her tongue and the dark notes of smoke buried in the meat. Exchanging hesitant smiles with Wolf whenever their eyes met, hoping she didn't have a ring of sauce around her mouth.

She could have cried from happiness, though the sauce burned her chapped lips. Though the buttery richness of the mashed potatoes and the peppery bite of the gravy on the side made her so thirsty she downed her glass of water in two gulps.

This was life: delicious food and conversation filled with more laughter than words. The sugary singe of a perfectly seasoned sauce. The ache in her head and leg and stomach, the edges of pain dulled by contentment. The occasional brush of Soren's shoulder against Elias's. The love warming Elias's gaze like a fresh-lit hearth as he pretended to scowl at her teasing.

The way her face lit up like Mortem's flames whenever she risked a glance at the eldest Olivander and found him already watching her.

Pain and pleasure. Lies and truth. Sugar and spice. Annoyance and affection…and apple pie, which one of the attendants brought after a subtle wave from Wolf that Ani would not have interpreted as a summons for dessert, but vowed to commit to memory *immediately*.

By the time she polished the last gob of pie off the plate with her fingertip and popped it in her mouth, the food sat heavy in her stomach. But she didn't mind—the discomfort of a too-full stomach beat the discomfort of an empty one any day.

Empty bellies reminded her too much of her girlhood. Of a plate piled with mismatched scraps while her siblings went without, refusing to let her share no matter how much she begged. Of Cassi poking a new hole in her belt every other week when Peter wasn't around to fuss.

"Ani?"

She looked up, still clutching the spoon, to find Soren watching her with furrowed, frustrated brows.

"What is it?"

"I can't tell what you're thinking." Soren's mouth bent, her green eyes tainted with sadness. "I kind of hate it."

"I hate it too," Ani said softly.

Just like she hated the look Wolf and Elias exchanged, a diagonal toss of assessing thoughts that clacked like a shaken bag of seeds.

"Maybe you should get some rest," Elias suggested. "Both of you."

Shared mind or not, she didn't need to look at Soren to know the answer to that.

"Not yet," they said together.

"Captain Loch is right," Wolf argued, a bit too fast—like he'd been waiting to suggest the same thing himself. "Goddess, I don't mean to be obstinate—"

"Yes he does," Soren interrupted. "Wolf, how dare you argue with a goddess to her face? She oughta smite you. Ani, you oughta smight him."

"I will not be smiting anyone," Ani mumbled.

"If it's a smiting you're spoiling for, lass, I'm sure Sage would be happy to give you the opportunity," Wolf chuckled. What was this, all this *laughter* and *banter* suddenly coming so easily? What had she done wrong on the way here? "None of us are fool enough to get in the sparring ring with him anymore."

"I'll take a rain check," Soren said breezily, pushing his hand off. "Maybe once I'm done negotiating with Prince Prettyface. Thanks for the *warning*, by the way."

Wolf sighed heavily, scratching his beard. "I can't read my mother's mind, and you very well know that. I didn't think she'd suggest allying with *Tallis*, of all the rotting…"

"*Tallis?*" Horror wrung the word out of Ani in a breathless squeak. "The Queen wants to ally with the *Tallisians?*"

Abruptly, the atmosphere around their table shifted from shared laughter to shared purpose. Ani's spine straightened in response to Soren's suddenly perfect posture; Elias moved too, dropping his hands and shifting one leg over the bench, facing Soren fully.

"Right," Soren murmured, her lips barely moving, "Ani, we've got a new problem. Their pits-damned prince is here."

Oh.

Oh, Sancta trod on her rotting *bones*.

"He's here for *me?*" How was that possible? They'd only just gotten here, they'd only *just*—

"No, no—he's not here *for* you. But he does know you're here, just…" Soren held up one hand, kneading her temple with the other. Her curls, though clean and combed, were a rumpled mess; they all bunched toward one side of her head. "My aunt wants us to strike an alliance."

"And they happened to have a Tallisian prince in stock for just such an occasion." A tiny flame sprung out of Elias's fingertip; he pinched it against his thumb, extinguishing it.

Urgency burned just as hot in Ani's fingers. She set aside her spoon, the warmth of food and friends all but forgotten. "But they're your family. And *Tallis* is…"

"I know. My family wants to help, it's just…complicated. *Politically.*" Soren rubbed the bridge of her nose. "We've only had the one conversation. I needed some food in me before I fell over…and I didn't want to leave you too long, either."

Because she'd been hurt, recovering? Or because she'd been left vulnerable while a Tallisian stalked the paths of *her* home? *Her* old kingdom?

A chill seeped under her skin; when she shivered, Wolf looked askance at her, a curtain of shadowed thought falling over his gaze.

"You were never left unguarded," he promised, as if her skull had gone transparent—as if he'd read her thoughts straight through it.

"All right, what's your problem with them?" Soren crossed her arms on the table, jerking her chin at Wolf. "I mean, I know why *I* have a problem, but—"

"Heathens," Ani, Wolf, and Elias all muttered under their breath at once: Ani with a nauseated pang through her chest, Wolf with a roll of his eyes, Elias with a lifted-lip sneer.

Soren sighed, muttering, "I oughta have known" before picking up her entire remaining chunk of sandwich and shoving it fully into her mouth.

"Faithlessness on its own is not a danger." Wolf traced circles over the table's grooves with his fingernail. As Ani followed that concentric circle, his nails caught her attention—pared down further than comfortable, nearly past the quick. "But in Tallis, faithlessness is…a religion of its own, in a way. A crusade. And not a benevolent one."

"In the same way Artem has waged holy wars in the past," Elias said quietly, the first time she'd heard him sound scathing toward Artem, "Tallis wages blasphemous ones."

"Nothing holy about war," rumbled an unfamiliar voice—followed by an extra chair slamming down on all four feet at the end of the table, a leonine form slinging into it with effortless grace. "You Nyxians oughta know that as well as we do."

That *voice.*

In a panic, Ani tried to dive into the safety of the back closet of their mind, tried to slam the door and let Soren take this fight…

But there was no back closet. No door. No Soren.

No place to hide from the Tallisian that slung one arm over the back of his chair, the pelt of a great cat thrown over his shoulders…a pelt skinned from something wild and once-living, not one of the false-fur ones many Nyxians liked to wear.

A shiver of sickness crawled up her throat. She swallowed it down.

Not Arthur Rath, the mercenary who'd harassed and harmed her and Soren, but a Tallisian still—because only Tallisians still carried that particular bite in their bark, a grindstone grit that mimicked the slip of a shoe over loose pebbles. A sandpaper purr that thrust her a thousand years into the past…straight back to a city long-dead, a crucible long conquered.

The ghost of Old Sanctaviv haunted her from the malice pressed between the suspicious furrows of the man's brows.

Maybe it made her a coward. Maybe it proved that despite all she'd done to separate herself from the girl who quailed before her brother's faintest hint of displeasure, the core of her hadn't changed shape at all. But when she skimmed over that malicious intent, she thrust her chair back a screeching inch or two, her spirit curling in on itself like a rotting root steeped in tepid water.

The man's lip curled, revealing a vicious cut of teeth and tongue—a grin showing off canines that shaped themselves as fangs in her misty vision. "A little ghost told me we had a goddess playing house somewhere around here. Hoped we'd run into each other…old family friends and all. Thought it'd be nice to catch up."

Another screech of chair against floor. When she looked down, she found Wolf's hand curled around the edge of her seat, angling her chair behind his.

Angling *himself* in front of her, the pub's chandeliers washing his sleek black hair in golden waves of light.

All the while, his gaze never left the Tallisian stranger, who crossed his arms and sulked like Wolf had ruined his favorite game.

A moment later, Ani came back to her senses. Remembered the last time she let someone take a blow for her; remembered *pale cheeks dappled in blood, pale hair torn from its skull-tight braids, pale lips breathing their last.*

She put her palm to the arm Wolf had braced against the table—though her hand was too small to cover the breadth of it, her fingers bridged the paths of old scars like unmapped forest trails. Some raised, some rough; some like wounds dealt into the topography by floods or rockslides, others hammered into his flesh by way of repetition. Armor scrapes. Quiver-strap callouses.

If he took a blow to spare her, when she would heal and he would not…

She couldn't bear that.

She raised her chin and shifted her chair out of Wolf's shadow, forcing herself to unlock her limbs from the rigor of blinding fear. To face this heathen and his hate without a human shield.

But Wolf reached his other hand over, pinning her hand over his bicep. Not a confinement; a subtle warning and request. "Don't you have better places to be, Everin?"

Calm. Friendly. But an autumnal frost beneath his skin began to spread, weaving a root-killing web just below the surface…an aching, unexpected cold that cooled the frightened, fevered heat in her trembling hands.

Prince Everin. Prince of Heathens—Blood of the Emperor.

She knew his name. They *all* knew the names of every king to come from that hate-tainted bloodline, past and current…and future.

Wolf glanced down at her out of the corner of his eye. His placid expression shifted for just a moment…a pebble dropped into a serene pool, spreading ripples that narrowed his eyes and creased the bridge of his nose.

"Not really. I actually came to extend an invitation to Princess Soren, here—oh, apologies. I should clarify." Everin smacked the heel of his hand to his forehead with a humorless grin, his glittering eyes never splitting from Ani's. "I mean your *victim*—the poor woman you tried to kill. I know it's hard to remember the names of us mortals. Especially the ones you use and toss aside like—"

"Hey." Soren palmed her butterknife. "You're the one speaking about me like I'm not here."

Everin's gaze dropped to the knife. "Not the most conventional weapon, dinnerware."

"It does the job."

A slow, sinuous shift of muscle. "And the job is…?"

"Enough." Wolf's voice dropped so low it could have underscored a rumble of thunder. "Make your invitation and go. Your grudge has no place here. As long as the Goddess is on this island, our laws apply…no violence. No bloodshed."

"Oh, relax, Wolf," Everin drawled; when Wolf did not, he reached behind his back and drew out an axe with a bellowing sigh, setting it across his knees and scooping up Elias's unused napkin, swiping it lazily over the flat of the blade. "She's *immortal*, you zealot. Even if I used each axe to cut her into a different piece, *which I'm not going to do*," he added when Soren spun the butterknife, Elias lit the tip of his finger on fire again, and Wolf's shoulders rippled like the rising hackles of his namesake, "the pieces would either crawl back together, or she'd find some other body to steal. I just wanted to get a look—never seen a goddess in the flesh before."

The back of her neck tingled, her own hairline bristling as Wolf's fingertips stamped into her hand, the most careful pressure…a restrained but firm request to move further behind him, one she somehow heard like he'd spoken it.

A funny, fluttery feeling spread through her chest.

Maybe it made her a coward…or maybe it made her human. Maybe it meant nothing but that this new skin of hers understood mortality in a way her spirit never could.

But she obeyed that silent command. And only once she'd tucked herself into the safety of his shadow did Wolf finally ease from his rigor.

"Out," he said flatly. "Or else I'll have Medwenna lock you up overnight for the second time this week. And we both know how pleased she'll be about *that*…nevermind what Brook will have to say."

"Fine, fine." Hands raised, axe handle circled with his thumb and forefinger, Everin stood, flashing a challenge at Soren through his smile. "Finished reviewing the treatise. Interesting stuff." Ani almost hoped he would clarify, but instead he announced, "We leave in the morning for home—me and my men. If it's an alliance you want, you'll be on our ship tomorrow."

Soren's jaw dropped. She thrust herself out of her chair, rocking on her heels—a surge of muscle Ani recognized as her holding herself back from starting a fight. "*Tomorrow?*"

"That's what I said—sorry, you do still speak our language, yeah? Do I need to try Old Sanctan?"

"Oh, the mountain man can speak dead languages now?"

"He certainly can," said Everin in flawless Old Sanctan—so flawless Ani's eardrums spasmed, an inner-ear itch she couldn't scratch.

Soren's eye twitched; in contrast, Elias didn't blink as he stood and positioned himself at her side. The smell of smoke—incense, not wood—filtered between the mouthwatering aromas that now turned her stomach as Soren protested, "That's too soon. I haven't had time to consider—"

Everin cracked his neck, lazily swinging his axe in a low arc, heedless of the fact that he currently stood in the center of a busy pub. "You're the ones who insisted it was urgent."

"I didn't mean—"

"My ship. Tomorrow. Either you're on it or you aren't, but if you aren't, consider your request denied." Everin backed up without turning, flicking her a wink that chilled her to the bone. "Be seeing you, Anima. Maybe we can have a chat when your guard dog's not around."

Wolf's gaze tracked Everin's path between tables and booths until the door shut behind him. Then, without turning, he said: "Are you all right?"

No.

Soren slammed back down into her seat, calling down curses that stung Ani's ears—Elias, for once, didn't flinch at her profanity, his and his battlemate wielding their fury as a matched set. Soren's blazed in her eyes; Elias's blazed in his ink, limpid red and orange flooding from beneath his sleeves to pour down his wrists, cresting over his knuckles.

"That went better than I thought," Wolf sighed.

"How badly did you *think* it would go?" Ani choked.

He blinked at her—then down at her hand, still pinned to his arm. He released her like he'd accidentally slammed his palm down on a hot stove. "Worse."

She ripped her hand away with equal urgency, balling it up and coughing into it. "Soren, you don't have to—"

"Of course I have to," Soren seethed.

"I don't like it," Elias said immediately. "He's backing you into a corner on purpose—trying to get the upper hand before we even get there."

"I know." With a whooshing sigh, Soren dropped her forehead into her hands, scraping her fingernails back into her hair. "But we *can't* refuse."

"Like the pits we can't."

"We *can't*," Soren repeated. "We refuse them, Arborius refuses us. We go back to Atlas empty-handed. We die. End of story."

"There's a few steps in the middle you skipped, I think," Ani mumbled.

"I didn't think you'd want all the gory details."

"This is good, even if it doesn't feel that way," Wolf interjected. "He's giving you a personal escort—it shows good favor from the go. His methods leave something to be desired, but it means you've passed the first hurdle."

"And our odds of passing the next?" Elias asked.

"That, I can't say. But ignorance may be bliss, here—to know your odds in certainty can affect how hard you fight. If defeat is inevitable, you won't try...the same with success. Better to fight as if against the impossible."

Soren balled her hand into a fist, staring at it emptily. "I think I'd prefer to know my odds. Even if they're not in my favor."

Wolf smiled, but it got lost somewhere between his lips and his eyes. "Trust me…you wouldn't."

Elias's fingers flexed, his thumb rubbing circles around his prayer beads—they clacked like chattering teeth, but slower. A tic that told her the priest was walking far down the winding avenues of his own mind.

Ani folded her arms on the table and buried her chin in them, hiding her frown as she probed Elias's expression for any chinks in his unreadable armor. But she might as well have been staring at the closed cover of a leatherbound book, waiting for the words inside to simmer to the surface; the Phoenix Priest was not a story so easily read.

As if she'd spoken his title rather than thought it, his gaze found hers, his fingers halting their rotation. Though the patch over his eye shielded his flaming iris from view, his other eye burned into her just as well. "What?"

"Nothing." Ani quickly averted her gaze. "Just…spacing out. Tired."

"Huh," Soren deadpanned, "weird. Why could that be?"

Ani pouted, burying her face up to her nose in her crossed arms now. "I feel fine. It's late, that's all."

Elias glanced at the grandfather clock in the corner of the pub. "It's only half past seven."

"That's…that's late for me."

"Did you take a piece of my stubborn ass with you when you left, too?" Soren demanded. "Ani, you're exhausted. You created a *living human body* two days ago. That's impossible. You do know you did the impossible?"

"Women do it all the time," Ani mumbled.

"In nine months, sure. And they come out this big." Soren held her hands about eight inches apart; Elias silently reached over and adjusted her hands, spreading the gap closer to twenty inches.

Soren blinked at her hands. "Oh. Really?"

Elias gave her a look. "Soren, you've held babies before."

"Well, my point still stands." Soren pointed to Anima. "You're a freak of nature, and you're amazing, and if you don't get your tiny ass back to bed, I'll make Elias haul you over his shoulder and carry you there."

"I'm not tiny!"

Soren put her thumb and forefinger about two inches apart in front of Ani's face, mouthing, "*Tiny.*"

Elias didn't reach over to adjust her accuracy this time. Ani shot him a look of betrayal, and he shrugged one shoulder. "Nothing wrong with being small."

"I could fit you in my shirt pocket," Soren said.

"My mother's pretty short, and she's the toughest lady I know."

"If you stepped in a puddle, you'd have to tread water."

"Elowyn, that healer on Patch's ship, she's short." Elias started counting off on his fingers, ignoring Soren's jabs and Ani's growing pout. "Samhain, you met her. My twin sisters are—"

"You could wear a thimble as a helm." Soren twisted a curl idly around the tip of her finger. "Make your bed with a handkerchief. Hey, if you need a sleepsack, I could let you borrow one of my socks for—"

"All right, I get it!" Ani burst out, throwing her hands up.

Wolf coughed—or was that a masked chuckle?

She shot him a look of reproach—and in return, he finally smiled in earnest.

And she knew in her heart of hearts that even Sancta's fabled lantern, which legends whispered had been used to set the sun aflame at the beginning of time, couldn't have been more beautiful than that smile.

"Well, *I'm* tired, even if you're not." Soren curled her fingers around the edge of the table as she stood; from Ani's angle, she could see Elias's bracing hand against the small of Soren's back, a subtle support cloaked in shadow.

Emotion dug a hollow place in her chest; a hole to drop her heart in.

She'd taken all the suffering she could, all the weakness she could—but those small habits, those little wounds, those would take longer. Those had to close on their own.

Soren leaned into her eyeline, catching her gaze. "Hey—cut that out."

Ani forced a smile. "Cut what out?"

"The wallowing. Blaming yourself."

"I thought you couldn't hear my thoughts anymore."

"Don't have to." Soren pulled her in by her hair, planting a kiss on her forehead. "You're wearing them all over your face. I'm going to be fine."

Ani's chin quivered; she forced it to still with a harsh swallow, begging the tears building in her eyes to stay put until she could get back to her infirmary bed and lose her composure in private. "I know."

"Say it." Soren's hand fell to her shoulder. "Say I'm going to be fine."

Not an order. A plea for someone to agree with her. To look at her and see no lingering brokenness, no jagged cracks that couldn't be mended by magic.

"You're going to be fine," Ani whispered.

Soren put on a smirk. "Thank you. Now work on believing it, and maybe we'll get somewhere."

Ani stitched a smile of her own together, but she'd never been skilled at sewing. "So…we leave tomorrow?"

Soren nodded—but Elias and Wolf traded looks again before Elias said, "Anima…it might be best if you stay behind."

Stay behind.

A doll left in her dollhouse, waiting for her playmates to return and find use for her again. A treasure trapped in a locked chest, too precious to fulfill the purpose for which she'd been designed.

"I'm not staying behind," she protested at the same time Soren scoffed, "Elias, she's not staying behind!"

"I'm not being an ass about it, I swear on my father's grave," said the death-touched man, raising his hands in surrender before the weapon was ever pointed at him. "You really think it's the best idea to take a goddess into the *one* kingdom that may have a way to kill her? I doubt King Denali will feel more favorable about an alliance if we walk in with one of their most hated enemies. And even if we could convince him…" His throat strained as he swallowed. "We don't have time. *Kal* doesn't have time."

Bitter dregs of some powdery emotion coated her throat. "Oh."

"No." Soren's gaze, almost panicky, flitted to Ani. "We're doing this together—we *have* to do it together. I'm not leaving you behind."

She would've been lying if she'd said the thought of separating from Soren—not just in soul, but in body, in distance—didn't spray caustic terror through her. A terror that gnawed and scraped and soured her insides until this body felt more ruined and wasted than the last.

But Elias, as he too often did, had made a very sensible point.

"Soren," she whispered, "it's all right. He's…he's not wrong. I should stay."

A shimmer flitted through an ocean of green—a memory whose path she could trace from one eye to the other, a shooting star that took all the light in Soren's gaze with it when it died.

"I am not leaving you here," she said again, soft like an echo. Like a dream.

Pale cheeks dappled in blood, pale hair torn from its skull-tight braids, pale lips breathing their last.

Starshine tears infused with a mother's love, a goodbye spoken in a language with no words, one last whisper from a woman who would bid her final farewell to the stars before the dawn rose on her death.

Ani got up. Went to her friend. Took her hands in hers—and nearly forgot whose hands were whose. The branching lines of Soren's palms, the peaks of her knuckles, the valleys between her fingers—she knew them like her own.

Maybe, frighteningly, *better* than her own.

"I will go with you," she said, "if you ask me to. But Elias is right—the moment I set foot in that kingdom, I ruin your chances of saving yours. And I can't stomach that. Can you?"

Soren's silence—and the mist that coated her gaze as she stared down at their hands—answered for her.

"I can do more good here." The truth, she hoped. "You can do more good there."

"The Goddess still holds much sway here," Wolf volunteered. "Even if things go poorly in Tallis, she…ahem. You, Anima. You may gain ground with my mother where others would not."

"And you would support that?" The prince didn't strike her as the war-waging type.

"For family?" He didn't blink. "Without question."

She really needed to get these heart palpitations seen to. By *anyone* but him.

"Then it's settled," Ani said, though nothing felt *settled* at all. "I'll stay."

Soren's nod said she agreed. But the white-knuckled grip she held on Ani's hands…that said something else.

Something neither of them could say out loud without dooming what little family Soren had left…those *Ani's* family had taken from her.

CHAPTER 19

ELIAS

The dead do not rest easy in Arborius.
Nor did those who belonged to Death…and had defied its command.

A song. A scythe. A voice that itched in the lightless places no one could scratch, in his eardrums and bone marrow and the winding tunnel of his smoke-sore throat.

"You talk too much," he heard someone say. "It itches."

Steel against steel. Blow for blow. Hand to hand.

Hands—her hands, his hands, his scythes dripping in sin unforgivable, its dark scarlet shade painting the steel and his hands and her.

Her.

Her green eyes bound to his by betrayal, blown wide to the whites. Green only so stark because the pupils had narrowed in pinpoint pain.

Green to black to gold.

Gold and scarlet and death.

"Finish it," she hissed, smoke trailing from her parted lips. "Finish her."

Soren's face. Anima's eyes.

Mortem's voice.

"Finish her."

A flicker of tidal blue and sun-drenched copper over his shoulder. A skybright smile dimmed to a stormdark scowl. An enemy turned brother turned enemy again. A circle he couldn't bring himself to close.

"Finish him."

"Wait." He arched his neck against the growing pressure to turn around and face that enemy. That pressure wrenched his shoulder, his wrist...his blades, which slid silently from their sheath of slit-open skin, hungering for new blood. For blue and copper. "Wait—"

Burning like starfire, Soren's fingers dug past his skin, finding purchase in his skull.

"Finish them all," she breathed in his ear.

Mortem was right; the dead did not rest easy in Arborius. And if the dead did not rest easy, those who had defied Death in a double portion did not rest at all—nor did those who had danced under Chaos's thrall.

Elias had been all three at one time or another—the dead, the defier, and the dancer.

And now that Anima had awakened, he felt as if he'd become all three at once.

What he'd said back in the pub was true—every reason why it was foolhardy to bring Anima with them on their mission to Tallis. But it was what he *hadn't* said that haunted him now...that mangled his dreams with death and bloodshed and the itching impulse to kill anything that winked a golden eye his way.

That, with his goddess's mandate burning in his ears...it was best if the Goddess of Life was anywhere Elias Loch was *not*.

Because the alternative...

Scythes sliding silently from their sheath of slit-open skin, hungering for new blood.

"Finish her."

Soren, Wolf, Ani, they'd all had their eyes on the Tallisian prince in that pub...but perhaps they should have been watching him, instead.

He dragged himself out of bed and cupped his hands before him, sheltering them close to his chest. When he called for it, a globe of fire surged to life in his palms, orange and red with hints of blue.

No chaos. No corruption.

A relief...but disquieting too, somehow.

For these last few weeks, he'd peered at every unusual sensation or emotion with unease tantamount to paranoia; every restless night, every innocuous muscle spasm, every song stuck in his head. Chaos had never made itself known in him...no sign that it had lingered at all.

But if this wasn't chaos, he didn't know what else to call it.

Finish her.

He ground his palms together to smother the fire, his throat tightening. His tongue swelled with unspent screams, but he bit down until it bled them out, panic slumping into an exhaustion that struck bone-deep…

…Until a horrifyingly loud gurgle drove him up from the bed, adrenaline burning through his fingers—and through the bedsheets—until he realized it had only been Soren's stomach, complaining loud enough that his mind had mistaken it for a beast.

He tore his fingers out of the sheets, cursing as he patted out the tiny fires eating holes in them. His mother used to call down Mortem's curses on moths for doing the very same, running her fingers through the linens and counting the meals moths had made out of them with mounting fury. It was, perhaps, the angriest he'd ever seen her.

"What is the use of a creature who harms what has helped it?" she would seethe, shaking out the sheets and tossing them over their clothesline, the yard dappled in sunspots shining through the offending holes.

He didn't want to be a moth.

He didn't want to be a murderer.

When he'd first looked into the face of his battlemate and seen gold instead of green, he'd only hesitated long enough to whisper his goodbyes before wrapping his hands around her throat.

Then, Anima was merely the presence that had snuffed out his best friend's life.

Now, she was the woman who'd sacrificed family, power, and pain to save his wife.

Well—soon-to-be wife. But it felt good to think it. To practice.

To pray.

"I know you're an early riser, but this is getting absurd."

He looked up at Soren, no longer buried in blankets; instead, she gazed back at him patiently, one knee cocked up like she was prepared to leap after him if he tried to run. Her sleepshirt rode up her midriff, baring her scar from Ursa.

The scar now marked with tally lines of twisted skin twice as thick, one to each side. Lines that matched the exact breadth of his own blades.

"Elias." He didn't deserve the love with which she breathed his name. The simple trust with which she held out one hand to him, wiggling her fingers. "Come back to bed, lover. You look like the pits."

Felt like it, too. But the idea of forcing himself back to sleep sent a pang of dread tunneling from the dagger scar over his navel to the seam in his once-broken spine.

When he kept his silence—and his distance—Soren frowned. "Nightmare?"

Embers flared in his fingertips. He curled his hands into such tight fists that his nails nearly broke skin. "Something like that."

Soren flopped onto her back, blowing out a long breath, staring at the ceiling—then she sat up, gripping her wrist with her opposite hand and dragging her arms up into a stretch that popped each of her vertebrae in succession. "All right, jackass, get a shirt on."

He did so quickly, afraid to take his eyes off of her too long—but when she released her stretch and turned to face him, arms swinging, brow raised, he found no hidden pain flattened between her lips or tunneled between her laugh lines. "Where are we going?"

"You'll see. Boots on, too."

"For what?"

The gleam in her eyes needed no light to shine through the dark. "Training."

With one word, she swept that strung-out tension in his muscles away.

As always, Soren knew him better than he knew himself—knew he needed to move. To breathe. To sweat out the heat that ebbed and flowed like the ocean Kallias had introduced him to back when they were *Eli Dorian* and *Your Highness,* when he'd stammered out an Atlas-accented lie about coming from a town so far inland that he'd never seen the sea.

"Don't be afraid," the prince had laughed when the first wave chased him back from the water to the dry side of the shore, seeking safety in the border between sugar and sludge.

He'd expected mockery from the First Prince, a man as born to raging seas as Elias had been to blinding blizzards.

Instead, Kallias had grinned as he sank ankle-deep in the sopping wet sand, beckoning Elias back as the wave made its retreat. *"They aren't strong enough to knock you down, not this shallow. I won't let them take you."*

The ragged, patched-up black canvas pack he'd lugged from Nyx mocked him from where he'd shoved it under the nightstand.

Kal's letter was still safely hidden in its pocket, its twine still tied in a complicated sailor's knot he kept pretending he didn't know how to untie. Even when Soren had pointed out he could simply cut it off.

Yes. He needed to get out of this room.

More than that, he needed to remember that a duel with his battlemate wouldn't end with her bleeding or blistered or whispering breathless forgiveness before he'd even pulled his blades back out of her stomach.

He needed to *not* imagine those blades buried in a different body altogether—or golden eyes, not green, watching him with the same baffled betrayal before the light winked out of them forever.

Normally he'd ask another question or ten before blindly following his battlemate when she had *this* kind of mischief in her gaze, but...

Not tonight.

"Lead the way."

Arborian darkwood struck nearly as hard as steel.

But *nearly* wasn't *equally*, and though the impact of the practice weapons against the stuffed manikin almost satisfied the restless itching under his skin…

Almost wouldn't chase away the restless discomfort left behind by his nightmares.

"What'd that poor guy ever do to you?"

Muscles still quivering with the aftershocks of his last blow, he turned—and promptly dropped his practice weapon, storming across the room in three strides. "What in Mortem's tarry, sorrow-scorched pits are you *doing?*"

Soren looked down at him, vague annoyance flitting over her features like a butterfly seeking a blooming perch; except she had already found one. She balanced precariously on one of the wooden dowels driven into the display hung heavy with blunt-edged steel weapons, heedlessly running her fingers over them rather than doing silly things like, oh, *keeping her balance* ten feet off the ground. "You didn't answer my question. And watch your language."

"He called me a sour name." He reached out to her, but she kicked his hand away. "Will you get down from there and use a stepstool like a normal person?"

Her fingers danced across hilt and blade; her eyes danced with teasing mirth. "But I'm already up here."

That realization drove its knuckles into the battered flesh of his heart, reversing its rhythm.

She *was* already up there. With no help from him.

She'd climbed the weapons rack—a sturdy structure, certainly, but those dowels and hooks were hardly ideal hand and footholds. They required balance—focus— strength.

Strength.

And she'd climbed it so quietly, so effortlessly, he hadn't even heard her do it. Nor was she trembling now, or gasping for breath; she wasn't bleeding or wheezing or losing control of her own limbs.

She stood still and steady and strong. And as she stared down at him, hands lowering to wrap around two dowels, her irritation softened into worry. "Elias?"

It wasn't until he tried to speak, and couldn't—until she scrambled down to the bottom row of dowels and thumbed away what he'd thought was a drop of sweat rolling from beneath his eye—that he realized he'd lost his composure.

"Will you please get down?" He sucked in a shaky breath, wiping fiercely at his damp cheeks. "So I can—"

Her heels struck the ground before he even finished. And before he could ask if it was all right, she reached out herself and cupped his face in her hands, kissing him softly. Featherlight. Like she thought he might bruise if she got closer, took more.

He'd endured far worse than bruises to gain the privilege of kissing this woman.

He slid his hand behind her neck, tugging her closer, taking ground until he could taste the spearmint and springwater lingering on her lips. He'd never liked the taste of mint, but gods, did she wear it well.

"Mmph," she mumbled against his lips, tapping his chin twice with her fingertips—he pulled back immediately, and she traced those fingers over his jaw, probing gaze locking with his. Her smirk knotted up at the corner. "What're the waterworks for?"

"I missed this." A confession he held no shame over. "I missed *you.*"

Those green eyes took on their own saltwater glint. "I missed me, too." Another kiss, to each corner of his mouth—another to the bow of his upper lip—another to his chin. Teasing him. Maddening him. Lighting a different kind of fire in his core. And then...

Then the world went out from under him.

The floor struck a match in his skull, light flaring in front of his eyes; the impact drove every sip of air from his lungs, leaving him stunned and blind and—

Laughing.

Laughing in spite of it, laughing with no breath, laughing as he scrambled to his feet and chased his battlemate back to the weapons rack. Laughing as she pounced back up, catching one of the hooks and pulling herself toward one of the practice swords, restored muscles shifting like a well-oiled pully system; laughing as he gripped her by the hips and wrestled her straight off the wall, her shrieks of playful protest drowning out the chorusing birds outside.

"You're going to regret that, smartass!"

"I regret *nothing,* jackass!"

And in a flurry of lighthearted blows and wriggling limbs, they fell apart only to surge back together, thrown punches punctuated by giggles and threats; they dropped into their old dance with a sort of stuttered ease, muscle memory faded with time. But though they did not know each other's gaps and guards like they used to—though they had gained new and painful weaknesses, new and different patterns, new and exciting strengths—this first lesson felt like the promise of more. Like a vow.

And if there was one thing Elias did without falter, it was keep his vows.

CHAPTER 20

SOREN

She might've felt a little worse about arriving late and sweat-soaked to meet the Tallisians if she hadn't walked into the Olivander tree's common room to find Everin pressed facefirst against the floor, his arm bent at a rough angle across his back by a man she didn't recognize; another stood above them both, counting at a volume that suggested he didn't have an *inside voice*.

She slung on an overcoat gifted to her by Sparrow and did up the buttons one by one, pausing between each, testing for a tremble in her fingers. When none came, she dropped to one knee and took up her loose bootlaces, shrugging off Elias's warning tap on her back.

As she pulled the bowknot tight, the hooting commotion from the center of the room slowly dwindled…replaced by the march of three sets of footsteps approaching her from the front.

Deep breath in, through her nose; slow breath out through her mouth.

She could not treat them like enemies, no matter how badly her body ached to lunge at them, weapon out—no matter how tightly her back muscles clenched in a choregraphed twist when she heard a huff of laughter above her head, a few inches too close for comfort.

"Sorry for being late." She squeezed her voice into a pleasant shape as she looked up.

"Looks like you had something better to do," snickered Everin, eyeing her training-tossed hair with a knowing squint.

"I had paperwork to finish off," she lied. "Fell asleep at the desk."

"Paperwork?" His eyes flicked to her battlemate. "Thought your name was Elias."

How *dare* he be quicker at throwing innuendos than her? "It's his middle name—a family name, if you must know. His Grandfather Paperwork invented boredom."

A smile climbed her mouth like an ivy vine as two sets of laughter rewarded her: one deep and rich, the bass drumbeat of a bonfire song, the other cackling like a startled bird.

As for Everin, he didn't laugh—but his squint shuddered into curious amusement. "Allow me to introduce my friends." Not his soldiers, not his guards—his friends, who peeled away from their positions at his back, coming to stand beside him instead. "Princess, meet Matthias Bane and Kessen Drake."

The bold, brassy laugh had come from Matthias—a burly man with biceps the size of her head and a grin warmer than the heart of a hearth. He wore no coat, leaving his thick middle and muscular arms and shoulders on full display. When she offered her hand, he shook it instead of kissing it, his grip strong but restrained; when he stood straight again, the beads of various metals threaded in his rich brown braids—black, silver, gold, and something redder than copper—clacked against each other.

"It is a great honor to meet you, Your Highness," he said with such genuine admiration she couldn't muster the appropriate amount of skepticism. "If either of these muttonheads gives you any trouble, you just say the word, and I'll have them out the nearest window."

"Muttonheads?" Her mouth struggled to shape the strange word; it didn't fit easily in either of her accents.

"Mutton's another word for sheep."

"Oh, like the…" She held her hands up to the sides of her head, miming out horns.

Matthias chuckled, mirroring her gesture. "Yes, like that."

"Oh, that explains so much!" She covered her mouth in mock pity, dropping her voice to a whisper. "No wonder your prince's head is so swollen, with all that skull-bashing going on."

Matthias craned his neck to look at the other two. "Can we keep her?"

"No." Everin wasn't smiling anymore.

"Hey!" The other man took up the prince's dropped grin, pointing between his head and Soren's—he was closer to her age, sporting a bright shock of copper hair and an even brighter red beard. "Redhead!"

"Um…yes?"

"Fantastic." He gave a satisfied clap. "Kessen Drake—but since you're my sister now, you can call me Kess."

Her core tensed, bracing for grief; she tugged until it loosened into a laugh. "Oh, is that how it works in Tallis?"

"It is now."

"Forgive me," Matthias leaned around Soren to reach for Elias, "but I'm going to pretend I didn't catch your name, since Everin was an ass about it. Matthias Bane."

"Elias Loch." Elias clasped his offered hand, the annoyed twitch in his temple settling. He glanced at Matthias's beaded hair—then blinked, jaw dropping. "Those red beads—those can't be what I think they are."

"Sanguine iron." Matthias's grin broadened at her battlemate's impressed whistle. "You've got a good eye. Not surprised, with those weapons you wear. Artemisian?"

"They are."

"Never seen a set like that. Custom-made?"

"Self-forged."

It was Matthias's turn to drop his jaw. "You're kidding."

"He doesn't kid," Soren sighed. "Trust me, I've tried to teach him."

"Well, these two *only* know how to kid." Matthias knuckled Kessen's head, ignoring the boy's protests, then shoved Everin's shoulder with a friendly irreverence that suggested titles and blood and heirship meant about as much to them as they meant to her and Elias. "I reckon that'll make for a perfect balance."

Everin tugged Matthias to his side with an arm wrapped around his shoulders. "What did I say about making me look bad in front of the lady?"

"That it would be the easiest flogging thing I ever did?"

"I hope you three aren't picking fights already." Medwenna, the ranger who'd caught Elias their first day on Arborian shores, announced her arrival by breezing in and tossing a bundle of thick fabric at Matthias and Everin, knocking twin *oofs* from their chests, followed by grumbled complaints. "I apologize for them, Princess. They've been away from royal trappings too long to remember how to wear them. Might take a moment to find the right fit."

Kessen lit up, catching the bundle Medwenna threw at him before throwing his arms around her; though the archeress stood tall, the lanky boy still claimed at least a head on her. "Everin said you were tagging in, but I didn't think he was serious!"

"When have I ever lied to you?" Everin demanded. "Tell me even one time!"

As Kessen began to count off instances on his fingers—ranging from *that time you said you'd leave the last chicken leg for me* on his left pinky to *when you promised I wouldn't lose my finger* on the middle finger of his right hand, which came right after the stub where his pointer finger ought to be—Soren sidled to Medwenna, placing her back to the bickering duo. "My family didn't mention they were sending an Arborian representative with us."

"Strictly speaking, I'm not being sent…nor am I *representing* anyone." Medwenna glanced sideways at Everin, then back to her bag. "I didn't leave Tallis by choice—I was exiled."

That felt like a lot to drop on a near-stranger, but in all honesty, she preferred it over small talk. "Are you sure it's safe for you to come along?"

"Oh, absolutely not." Medwenna never looked up from her pack as she tied it shut, then undid it and tied it again. "But I told Sage I thought it best if I went along, and he agreed. We don't trust Everin to lead you true when it comes to this alliance."

Alarm rang through her chest. "Genevieve said you and Everin were friends."

"Oh, we're better than. I know every inch of that man's head like my own—I trust him with my life. With more." A sharp tug unraveled the bag's ties again; Medwenna mindlessly set to retying them, watching Everin and his men as they elbowed and argued and sparred with insults as dull-edged as the weapons she and Elias had played with that morning. "Which is exactly why I know he'll lead you astray if it serves him best. That's not to say he will—it's just to say he may. But he'll keep his paws to the path if I'm around."

Because she could stop him from veering off? Or because she could catch him after he already had?

"If it isn't safe, don't feel that you have to accompany us. I've had my own run-ins with people like him." Hunters, scoundrels…princes, fools. "I know how they lay their traps."

"This is bigger than safe, Princess. I'm grateful…and I trust your capability. But my presence will help, and my absence will hurt. Besides…" A hungry, excitable gleam in the archeress's gaze. "You still haven't told me your version of the story—the true version, not rumors or theories. Being the first to know your piece of history, that's enough reason to go."

"A story is worth risking your life?"

"Not a story. *History*. Besides…" A secret gleamed in her smile. "There's just something about a lost princess story, don't you think?"

"I heard the *H* word." Everin swooped in like an eagle, bending Medwenna back by the shoulders to smirk down at her. "Don't use up all your breath before we get on the water."

"You're interested in history?" She couldn't think of anything duller.

Medwenna blushed. "I was a historian in my birth kingdom."

"She was *the* historian," Everin corrected—where he ordinarily teemed with conceit, a bacteria allowed to flourish where it oughtn't, this bragging glowed with a sweeter sort of pride. "The youngest Grand Historian in the history of Tallis."

"Enough bragging, you." Medwenna swatted his wrist, still not looking up. "Get your things, get our boys—we're wasting daylight as it is."

Everin rolled his eyes—but he did do as she said, walking off with a whistle and a twirl of his finger in the air. His men jumped to grab their bags without question or complaint.

Maybe it would be good having Medwenna along, after all.

CHAPTER 21

ANIMA

On the last day before her first death, it took Ani an hour to finish saying goodbye to her brother.

Peter hadn't been half as reluctant to leave as Ani had been to let him; he hadn't even set foot on his ship yet, but as he gave each of them halfhearted hugs and distracted smiles, his gaze stayed ever-trained on the horizon. The rest of them were bundled in thick coats and scarves and furs, but not Peter—even the bitter cold of Braeden's kingdom couldn't persuade him to put on anything thicker than a lightweight, long-sleeved tunic. The air never even fogged when he breathed.

"Why do I feel like I'm never going to see you again?" she'd cried into his shoulder, and he'd laughed before sweeping her into a much heartier embrace.

"Most goodbyes aren't forever," he'd reminded her. *"You know you're welcome in Atlas anytime."*

"But why do you have to rush home?"

"Because someone is waiting for me, and I've already been away too long."

The next day, the carriage she'd boarded to carry her to port had crashed, mangling her body until death took her. And after that, Peter never rushed through their goodbyes again.

So it was no wonder this awful knot in her belly refused to loosen as she watched Soren and Elias prepare to disembark from the docks at the Arborian seaside for the next leg of their mission.

Without her.

Ani had treated a handful of amputees in her time who suffered pain in a part of their body that no longer existed; even when the wound healed, the limb lingered, tormenting the body with its dying screams. And she felt their pain now like it was her own.

There was no longer any doubt she had leaned too long on Soren's support. Without it, everything tipped off-balance, an absence that pressed in like a presence...like a haunting. A vital piece stripped away from the whole.

But Soren was not a piece of anything. She herself was a whole, and the fear tingling in Ani's fingertips was nothing but her body panicking over the loss of something she'd never possessed in the first place.

They needed this. Both of them. No matter how many times she had to dig her teeth into her tongue to stop herself from pleading to be allowed to go along.

Her people needed their goddess. Soren's kingdom needed its Heir...and allies. And Ani could not give Atlas either.

So when Soren strode back down the gangplank, her thumb wedged beneath the strap of her bag and her brows already mashed into a concerned jumble of wrinkles, Ani forced a sunny smile. "I hope Sage gave you plenty of that tea I asked for—I don't think he fully grasps how severe Elias's seasickness is."

"That's so cute," Soren scoffed.

"What?"

"You trying to pretend you're not two blinks away from bawling. You really think I spent all that time in the same body as you and still can't tell when you're upset?" Soren shut one eye and tapped over the lid; a demonstration or a mocking wink, Ani couldn't tell. "You used up so many of my tears, I have to save what's left for special occasions."

A lump formed in her throat. She coughed to break it up. "Like what?"

"Like when Elias tries to bore me to death with recitations from his holy book." Soren hesitated. Her lips turned down. "Or when I have to say goodbye to my friend."

That did it. The burning in her eyes overflowed, hot tears bubbling down her cheeks. "I know you have to go—"

"And I know you have to stay."

The silence strained between them, desperate to be broken. Soren's rich amber boots—new ones gifted by her family, cobbled with soles made to grip stone and soil alike—toed at the wooden planks keeping them aloft over the encroaching ocean.

It didn't help that this goodbye—whether final or not—had to happen beside a roaring sea. That it had to be uttered so close to a creaking ship, its sails buffeted by the wind, the sailcloth tugging at its restraints as if eager to be on its way.

To sweep her in its tailwinds, a silent reminder of her place, her fate:

To be the one left behind.

"It won't be a long trip," Soren ventured at last. "A handful of weeks to reach Tallis, sure, but once we get there—"

"You have no idea what's going to happen once you get there."

"Yes, I do. I'm going to invite them to help us kill a god—which Sage says is basically everyone's dream there, no offense—and if that's not enough to do the job, I'll remind King Denali that if Tenebrae wins, Tallis isn't exactly going to avoid his wrath." Soren wiggled her fingers and brows, baring her teeth in false foreboding. "Can't imagine His Almighty Bastardness will ignore the one kingdom that might have a weapon that can hurt him. Honestly, I'm surprised they weren't the first to go."

"We have a…complicated history with that kingdom. Particularly their royal line."

Soren sighed with all the patience of a seven-year-old forced to wait for dessert until after dinner. "Complicated how?"

"You remember what I told you about Sanctaviv…about the Emperor?" When Soren tipped her hand side to side in a noncommittal gesture, Ani pinched the bridge of her nose. "Soren, you need to start paying attention to these things when I—"

"You're starting to sound like Elias," Soren warned. "You're going to make me pull out my emergency tears already?"

"This is important. The Tallisian royal family is directly descended from the Emperor—the man whose reign ended because *we* overthrew him."

"So?"

"*So*, Tallisian kings—" and princes, if she had to guess, "—they have long memories. I would avoid mentioning your…association…with me as much as possible. And I wouldn't hope for an imminent threat to sway them. Brae knows better than to strike blindly at a people who have spent as many centuries hating the gods as we have spent *being* gods. He won't risk going up against that kind of malice. Not without all of us at his side."

"But he will risk it eventually."

"Only when it's no longer a risk." Only when the five of them united could crush what remained of Emperor Solomon's abominable craving for ownership and control. "But—"

"An eventuality is all I need," Soren interrupted, glancing over her shoulder to the ship; her thumbnail flicked at the strap over her shoulder, drawing Ani's attention to the chewed, uneven edges. Soren normally gnawed on her lip in times of stress, not her nails. "They're waiting for me. Just…promise me you'll be careful. Stick close to my family. I don't want to come back and find out you let the whole goddess thing go back to your head, I just got it out."

Ani fidgeted, looking askance in the direction of Elderwood proper. "That might be difficult when your cousin still won't look me in the eye."

"Who, Wolf?" Sage asked—Ani hadn't even realized he'd approached from behind. He passed them both with an armful of burlap sacks, a jumbled aroma of herbs wafting by with him. Good news for Elias's stomach. "He's probably just sweet on you, lass. I wouldn't worry about it."

"He's what?" Soren and Ani asked at once—though Soren sounded more disbelieving than confused.

"Sweet on you." When she continued to stare blankly, Sage hemmed and hawed, hefting all the bags against one arm so he could scratch the back of his neck. "It just means…look, he's …ah, forget it. I can't save him from tripping over himself every time." He pointed at Soren, then at his own chest. "You, though…you're pulling up what I'm planting, yeah?"

Soren let out a gusty groan. "Why would you tell me that right when I have to *leave*? That's so rude!"

"I'll tell you everything you missed when you get back!" Sage hollered as he strode away.

"But what does that *mean*?" Ani asked desperately—but Sage had already skipped up the gangplank, whistling merrily the whole way.

Maybe *some* members of this family could do with a bit more respect for the gods, after all.

"It means go easy on Wolf." Soren enveloped her in a hug—then squeezed tighter before adding, wickedness dancing in every word, "Or don't. I never have with Elias."

"You've never what with Elias?" asked the man in question; Ani reluctantly pulled away from Soren just for the death-touched soldier to swoop in and take her place, crowning his fiancée in a kiss before trying to take the bag off her shoulder.

"Ah!" Soren yanked the strap back up. "I'm fine, jackass. I can carry it myself. Get going, I'll meet you up there."

Elias pinched Soren's chin and kissed her slow and languorous, nipping at her bottom lip as he pulled away. "Smartass."

"I think he likes you," said Ani when Elias strode away, not doing very well at smothering his own smirk as he mounted the gangplank. In fact, he was so distracted it took three whole idle rocks of the boat for him to go, as Peter would've called it, *green around the gills*.

Soren studied the back of her hand, seesawing it back and forth to let her ring catch the light. "You think? It's so hard to tell. I mean, he *did* give me this expensive ring, and he made this whole speech about wanting to spend the rest of his life with me, but what does that mean, you know?"

"Men," Ani giggled. "The great puzzles of our time."

"Honestly." Soren took her hands again and squeezed. "I meant what I said yesterday…no more wallowing, no more *sorry*, no more calling yourself names. That's what he wants—he wants you too ashamed and scared of making another mistake to make *anything*, good or bad. Keep that leg wound clean until it starts to heal. If I come back and you're down to one leg, I'll be pissed you took my chance to get one of those Arborartemic ones, with the fancy gears in the wood—"

"Soren." Ani squeezed her hands back. "I love you, too."

Soren blinked her own tears away, giving her one last embrace…one of those bone-cracking, soul-healing ones she didn't think her friend understood was a talent many lacked. "I will see you again. *Soon.*"

With her next heartbeat, an extra pearl of warmth tumbled into her veins, borne by blood from her chest to her hand—as it went, it grew in size and brilliance, a glowing marble shining beneath her skin as it sailed the streams of her flesh-and-bone body, bobbing to a halt in the center of her palm.

And from that bud of light bloomed a hibiscus. A flower of oceanside castles and the princesses born in them—the first flower she'd ever grown in Soren's body.

"I will see you again," she promised, taking that flower and threading it behind her friend's ear. "On my word as a goddess, I will see you again."

Soren reached up without looking away from Ani, fingertips hesitantly fussing with the lush pink petals, pollen shedding on her thumb as she brushed over the stamen.

"Show-off," she croaked.

"You never appreciate my miracles."

"Well, when my body was the one performing them…"

"Will you get going?" Because if this goodbye lasted any longer, she'd forget *why* it would be foolish to sneak herself into one of the crates or barrels bound for that ship. Why she, a goddess born over a millennia ago, still needed to fear the keen-eyed prince watching from the prow.

A long-dead emperor smiled at her when she locked eyes with Everin Arden. An emperor whose laws had condemned her eldest sister to the stake for saving a man's life—a mortal evil whose ghost still sought to stand tall against the gods.

As Soren finally tore herself away, her body swaying with the ship as she boarded it like she'd been born on its pristine planks, a presence behind Ani drew her gaze over her shoulder.

Wolf stood behind her, but he didn't look at her—he watched his cousin instead. "You wish she wasn't going."

Not a question, but she answered anyway: "Yes. But I can't make her choices for her."

Not anymore.

"No, I suppose not." His gaze lowered to her as hers rose to meet it—his chin nearly touching his chest, her head bent almost all the way back. "But you can wish her well on the journey—and wish again for her safe return."

Wishes are for children. We are gods. We wish for nothing—we create it.

A gem-tough lump formed in her throat, faceted and sharp, as she watched Soren make herself at home on the ship. As the sun caught on her hair and the pale pink promise tucked within.

"I can wish," she agreed in a whisper.

Just in case the wind might yet carry her words across an ocean. Just in case her brother heard her lesser prayer.

CHAPTER 22

ANIMA

This new body, though fashioned exactly after her first, did not take to sleep as well as she would've liked.

She'd never been especially prone to nightmares, not even as a little girl. But the first night after Soren and Elias left, the darkest parts of her imagination swept her into a ghoulish dance. One that turned her in circles around the dusty dancefloor of her lonely mind from dusk to dawn.

Waking in her sickroom proved to be a blessing, though she'd almost protested when Wolf had led her back to it the night before. He'd promised her that after one last night of observation, they'd find her more permanent quarters; but after a night of strident terrors clawing at the walls of her mind, it was a relief to open her eyes to something familiar, if only just.

As if fashioned with some sort of sixth sense, Wolf was waiting when she finally opened her sickroom door, looking as if he'd also been up for hours; a stiff *good morning* and a brief glance at her face later, he said, "I'd like to show you something, if you'll allow me."

Anything seemed better than wallowing in the awkwardness still flourishing between them. "Lead the way."

For a prince, Wolf had such a well-practiced bow—spine unbent, dipping gracefully at the waist, gaze sweeping downward as he went—that she almost forgot she didn't like getting bowed to.

The walk was neither long nor difficult; even her injured leg barely protested as she followed Wolf. They kept to one of the paved trails, where her cane never caught or sank; just when the pain started to mount from an ache to a throb, he stopped.

"Here," he said.

Ani wasn't sure what *here* was supposed to be. They'd come to a halt some distance from Elderwood proper, where civilization thinned and forest thickened; a copse of willow trees lined up before them, their swaying branches reminding her of the giggling maidens who used to toss their hair and bat their eyelashes at her older siblings.

"It's beautiful," she offered.

One of Wolf's brows tilted. "This is just the entrance."

Her middle absolutely *squirmed* with embarrassment. "Oh."

"We have to receive permission before we can enter." Wolf covered his mouth with his fist, cleared his throat, and called, "Guardian, I seek guidance from she who grew this glen."

That's a lot of Gs, Ani thought—then waited for the laugh. Then had to swallow, hard, when she remembered no one was there to hear her joke.

Why had she agreed to let Soren go without her?

"You may enter."

The rumbling voice came from nowhere. Like the rocks or the ground or the trees themselves had spontaneously gained sentience. But when the willow branches parted of their own accord, swept aside like stage curtains, they revealed the source.

An armored and helmed figure greeted them; she could make out nothing but ice-blue eyes peering out from the slit in the metal, keen but kind, deeply creased at the corners. He did not bow when he looked at Ani; instead, he dropped to one knee, inclining his head.

"The shrine will always be open to its maker," said the Guardian. "Welcome back, milady."

She fumbled for something to say. "You're quicker to recognize me than most."

Wolf coughed again behind her; maybe he was catching a cold?

The Guardian did not raise his head. "You will understand, I think, when you enter." He stood, holding out one gloved and gauntleted hand to her. "Allow me to escort you. I see you are injured."

"It's temporary."

"All pain is, milady." With that, he guided her past the flirtatious willows, Wolf falling into step behind her.

And indeed, as soon as she set foot inside, she understood *exactly* why this Guardian had recognized her at first sight.

They had not stepped through a gap in the forest, but through a door—the willows were so thickly knit together she hadn't realized they guarded a structure behind them. Though she still walked on grass, this glen was circled in walls of stone ten feet tall and at least a foot thick, decorated in tapestries of ivy and climbing hydrangea. Wood framed the glass-paned, steepled roof; the rain promised by this morning's heavy dew had started to fall, pattering against the frosted windows above her head.

Except for the very center, where a hole had been cut into the glass; there, the rain fell freely, showering the centerpiece of this secret shrine: a stone fountain, its basin filled nearly to the brim with rainwater and lilypads. Frogsong harmonized with the rainstorm's melody; when she approached, the singers disappeared into the water with two burbling *plops*. A duck bobbed along on the other side of the basin, busily tousling its feathers clean with its bill.

But it was the figure standing in the center of that fountain that made sense of the Guardian's familiarity.

Hand-chiseled. Lovingly preserved. Wearing her patina of age and weathering with a gracious smile and proud shoulders. Hands outstretched, though Ani couldn't tell if they were reaching to give or to take. A circlet of blooming flowers sat upon her brow.

Releasing the Guardian's hand, she drifted ahead, her head going floaty and weightless as she traced the lettering on the bronze plaque affixed to the fountain's lip.

"The Crownless Queen," she murmured, barely aware of her lips shaping the words.

"Carved after your disappearance from your first life." Wolf stood with his hands folded behind him, squinting up at the statue's head. "Legend holds that you never wore a crown, not once during the whole of your reign. And on the rare occasions when your advisors insisted, *you* insisted on growing your own."

"I remember." Her first life was always the clearest in her memory, despite so much time stretching between then and now. "The metal ones pinched, the wooden ones itched...the jeweled ones were too heavy."

"Hm." No inflection. "I come here for quiet and clarity when the rest of the city is too loud. When my crown begins to itch." He glanced at her out of the corner of his eye. "When I can't sleep so well."

She batted her braid off her shoulder; it slapped against her spine instead. "I see why. It really is beautiful—I'm glad you showed it to me."

"And that you didn't stop at the door?"

A giggle, shrill and abrupt, bubbled up out of nowhere; she cut it off in the middle by clamping her fingers over her mouth, laughing into her fingers instead.

"That too," she agreed once she could trust herself *not* to make another horrendously ungraceful sound.

Wolf looked down at her. And maybe it was just the way the stormcloud shadows shaped themselves around his mouth, but she could've sworn he smiled.

"I wish we could stay, but I'm afraid I've already kept you too long," he confessed—maybe. It was hard to tell when everything he said sounded like a confession. "My mother has a request for you."

Aching to stay—but also aching to be useful—Ani had no trouble arranging an eager smile in return. "Whatever it is, I'll be happy to help."

CHAPTER 23

ANIMA

S he had spoken much, much too soon.

When Wolf had broken the Queen's news that the people had caught wind of her presence in the kingdom, and that if she did not present herself, she might find herself discovered (cornered, rather) at a less opportune time…she'd considered slinking back into her borrowed room, hiding under her bed, and refusing to come out, relying on the kind little mice scurrying under the floorboards to carry her sustenance and stories.

But unfortunately, goddesses didn't have the privilege of hiding.

She had chosen the path of worship. So worship she must allow.

Upon her arrival at the largest temple in Elderwood, the line to greet the Goddess of Life had coiled in concentric circles through the short, stout tree's singular chamber, hollowed widely into a near-perfect circle. There were several windows wedged into the trunk, each positioned to provide optimal sunlight to the garden boxes and clinging ivy and hedge sculptures inside.

That light had also revealed that the line trickled out the front entrance…and from what she could tell, it wound so far down the street that the businesses located nearby had closed down for the day, knowing anyone who might have patronized their establishments couldn't reach them anyway.

So she'd spent these past several hours being put on a pedestal—literally. The stone altar rose in layers like a wedding cake; with the kind of poise only an imposter's terror could inspire, she'd sunk gracefully into a cross-legged pose on the patch of grass and wildflowers in the center of the altar's crowning circle after panting and limping her way up the tiered steps, leg screaming in protest.

And she hadn't moved since.

Not when a trio of women came in with their arms overflowing with cut flower bouquets, painstakingly arranging each of them in glass vases on the altar's lowest ring. Not when a harried, impatient, sweat-soaked man herded a flock of at least thirty children to the front of the line and conducted them through singing a hymn she vaguely recognized by its tune, though the lyrics had changed since her time. Not even when three dozen men carried in a mature maple tree, its extensive root system biomantically gathered into a many-stranded knot at its base.

She stayed seated through it all. Not just because she didn't like heights or how dizzy they made her, but also because her legs had fallen deeply asleep over an hour ago, and she genuinely feared that if she tried to stand, she'd fold at the knees and tumble straight into the thorny rosebushes brought in by one of the first visitors that morning.

The only redeemable parts of the day were the miracles she got to perform.

Small ones, hardly anything of merit—she'd expended most of her strength to create this body in the first place, and even if she hadn't, her magic would take time to settle properly. Even so, she'd been able to do a few little things: healing a newborn baby's cleft lip, repairing a ranger's broken arm, and bringing an older man's dead orchid back to life. He'd confessed it had belonged to his late wife, her favorite of her many plants—according to him, "the damned thing" seemed determined to die with her, no matter how carefully he tried to care for it. Ani had spent the next ten minutes scribbling down instructions for care and giggling as he shared tale after tale of his gardening misadventures.

That encounter had almost made this whole rotten day worth it. Even though the people waiting behind him had grown restless, to the point that the guards had started to come and escort the man away before Ani had commanded them to leave him be, she would have happily sat and listened for hours longer.

Her absolute favorite, though, was the little girl who toddled up to the altar carrying an *absurdly* fluffy, lop-eared rabbit nearly as long as the girl was tall.

The little girl had looked at Ani with full-hearted, earnest faith, presented the rabbit, and told her how Bear (the rabbit) had hurt his paw when *someone* (said with an imperious, wrathful glare toward the older boy standing behind her) had stepped on it.

Healing Bear's bruised paw was one of the greater joys she'd experienced in recent memory—as was getting to snuggle him afterward before sending him back down to the little girl, his furry form cradled with care by one of the rangers.

But that had been two, maybe three hours ago now, and despair was creeping inward far faster than the sun was creeping downward.

A hushed throat-clearing climbed the pedestal, barely an echo by the time it reached her ears: "Goddess?"

Ani blinked, surprised to find Wolf standing at the altar…and to realize the temple was now empty besides the two of them. The door still sat propped open; sunset spilled through the doorway and the windows, silhouette smudging the prince's finer details as he knelt, gesturing toward the tiered dais. "May I?"

May he…what? Kneel there? Look her in the eye for once?

"Of course." She did her best to sound confident. Like she had any clue what she was giving permission for.

Wolf rose and stepped over the last cluster of offerings, balancing on the first rung of the dais. He didn't even watch his step—he just walked, his feet never plunging into a reservoir or trampling over a flower. Like he'd climbed this precarious display a thousand times; like he would have known the path to her blind or backwards or sleeping.

When he reached the second-to-last rung—which, while smaller than the former rungs, still stuck out at least two feet out from the very top platform—he knelt once more. Both knees, this time.

Her heart wedged firmly in her throat as he extended his hand, fingers curled in a loose fist.

"Forgive the delay." A request as crisp and quiet as an autumn leaf drifting down to rest amongst its fallen friends. "I felt it would be wrong to go out of turn when there were so many others with more urgent needs." He glanced at the maple tree from the corner of his eye, and the corner of his mouth bent downward. "Or better gifts."

Rot chew through my bones. If he deemed the tree a worthy gift, who knew what he might have brought to try and match it? "I'm happy to accept your offering—or your needs. Whichever you've brought."

With a nod and a throat-clearing, he settled his hand in her palm.

Wolf's fingertips carried the gentle chill of steeped peppermint tea; soothing, but not what she'd expected to find in that particular vessel. To find an autumn breeze hiding in a warm-blooded hand felt just as strange as taking a sip of steaming tea and tasting winter within.

Then, with a series of clinks not unlike a handful of marbles being returned to their bag, Wolf dropped a pile of pebbles into her palm.

Each a different color and shape, all of them the special kind of smooth only achieved through the sculpting of a fast-flowing river. They glimmered in the setting sun; not crystal-cut and harsh-edged like Cassi's favored treasures, but still containing a subtle twinkle buried in their dull outer shell.

Just like the ones she used to infuse with life as a child, giggling to herself as they performed a spritely jig across the kitchen floor.

Just like the ones Mora had snatched away, only returning them after Ani promised not to make them dance anymore.

"Why did you bring these?" she breathed, sifting through them with her smallest finger, admiring the subtle hues of purple and blue and reddish-pink. One of them, pearl-white and perfect for skipping, still had a damp speckle of river water drying on its underside.

"What's a daisy worth when I can grow them with half a thought?" He pinched his fingers together in the air; a daisy sprouted between his fingertips, unfurling into a flawless bloom. With a tired scowl, he released it, letting it drift to the floor. "I'm fond of rocks. Pretty as a plant, but terrible tough. You won't see these wither if you stick 'em in the sun too long."

She looked down at the cluster in her palm.

"I know they aren't half as grand as…" Wolf faltered, staring around the room with a hard swallow. "Well, any of this. I hope you don't take offense— none was intended—"

"No!" Sancta swallow her in shadow, she couldn't get anything right today; first her slight outside the Crownless Queen's shrine, and now this. She closed her fist firmly around the pebbles, embracing them against her heart. "Wolf—I mean Prince—I mean—no. I love them."

Now it was his turn to stare. "You do?"

"I do." Ani tucked the pebbles into her pocket before she gripped her own ankles, grimacing as she forced her legs to uncross; the numbness in them dissolved into painful, fuzzy prickles.

She couldn't stand until feeling came back to her legs. So instead, she scooted forward on her seat, heedless of the grass staining her skirt or the stone skinning her palms, until she sat face to face with Wolf.

Amber and honey. Fresh snow and midnight silk. A neutral mask that could have hidden devotion or indifference or displeasure.

Ani grew a daisy of her own and tucked it behind his ear.

"It's the intent behind the gift that determines its worth," she told him. "And daisies are my favorite."

His silent stare didn't waver or wane.

"Though I'm fond of rocks, too," she added, grinning. "They're much better dancers than flowers. The roots get in the way."

"Ah," he said. "Good."

Her heart sank, and she squeezed her kneecaps, forcing some of the nerves out of her fingers. "Prince Wolf, is there something I—"

"Forgive me," he repeated abruptly; he thrust himself to his feet, offering his hand when she didn't follow suit. "You've been here all day long—you must be tired. I sent everyone else on home."

She stared at the offered hand, hesitating. "If they were waiting all day, I don't want to disappoint—"

"I believe the only ones left were those who already got one audience with you and wanted to seek another." Finally, he smiled—a coy, careful thing, like they were sharing a secret. "I can't blame them, but I'm aware that even goddesses have their limits."

Ani blushed. "Was it that obvious?"

"Hardly. You were very gracious."

That amused tone wasn't exactly convincing. Nor was that reluctant smile. But she took his hand, relieved that when he pulled her to her feet, her knee did not fail its one and only task of keeping her upright.

She looked askance at the offerings—particularly the tree. "I have no idea where I'm going to put that."

Wolf huffed—she couldn't tell if it was a laugh or a scoff. Maybe a sigh. Depths, it could have been a cough for all she knew. "I did tell them they were overdoing it a little, but they insisted—nothing less for the Goddess of Life."

"Do I need to…" She gestured to the hoard, but Wolf shook his head, running a hand through his hair.

"No, don't worry about it. The other Reapers and I will take care of cataloguing them, then move them once you decide where you'd like to take up more permanent residence." He paused. "Which can be anywhere you like. There are a few younger trees in the city that are empty, but if that doesn't suit, anyone here would be happy to give up their own—"

"Prince Wolf," Ani interrupted, "can you do me a favor?"

His brow furrowed. "Anything."

"Please assume that I have no desire to take anything from your people. Even this—" she gestured to the ungodly pile, "—is too much, but I know it makes them happy. I will not be asking anyone to give up their home, their things, their crowns, or anything else. I do not require it…nor do I deserve it."

And even if she had, she wouldn't have taken it, because what kind of awful person took someone's safe place away for something as silly as status? How could she justify banishing generations of a family from their ancestral home just so she could feel important?

"Please," she repeated. "I want my presence here to be a blessing, not a burden."

Wolf looked as though he wanted to say something, but instead he dipped his head. "As you wish. For now, I'll escort you back…unless you'd like to stop for a meal first." He offered his arm to her. "Can't have you getting *sungry* on me."

The joke—followed by a *wink*, of all things—startled a giggle out of her. "No, we certainly—"

The smell hit her first.

Sour milk and rancid, rotted herbs. Molded wood and the fetid fluids of a body still fighting an inevitable decay. Living death. Spoiled blood. Flesh peeling away from flesh.

Wolf let go of her arm and spun precariously on his layer of the altar, making a wall of his own back. Ani nearly gagged as the stench from below layered over her tongue like soil in a garden bed, sowing seeds of malice and mayhem in the rows of her tastebuds.

Blight.

She knew it in her blood and bones and the unknowable places where her magic lived and grew. She knew it without sight, without sound, with nothing but that teaspoon of essence seasoning her tongue.

But sound still came. And it brought horror and helplessness clasped in its shaking, feeble fingers: "*Help me.*"

She hooked her hands over Wolf's shoulder, pulling herself up to look past him; her legs, half-numb and half-hurt, quivered as she stretched them to their furthest extremes.

An older woman stumbled toward the altar—one hand out, gut-wrenching coughs cutting her pleas into pieces. Despite the wrinkles molded into her sun-pocked skin and the slight hunch to her back, her arms were shapely and strong; likely from swinging the axe lashed to her belt. The long-handled blade clipped the floor as she fell to one knee, spitting sparks that somersaulted just short of the altar's base.

With the woman's next retching cough, another sickening swill of rot and illness and *fear* swept over Ani's senses; without thinking, she dropped back down to her soles and gripped Wolf by his cloak, towing him up and back.

Now she shielded *him* from the sickness wafting off this woman in waves.

When she looked up at Ani, it was with pitted eyes; black sclera, eerie green irises, pupils hazed in cobweb-silver mist.

"Help." Purple-black spittle foamed at the corners of her lips; when she bared her teeth in an agonized snarl, her gums flashed dark, too. "Something…something in the woods. Goddess, *please.*"

And before Ani could even get the breath to say yes, of course she would help…before she could even step one layer down the altar…

A rattling breath. A slump of strong shoulders. A too-familiar dimming of the eyes.

The woman fell face-first at the foot of the altar, and she did not get up again.

And where she fell, where that blackish ichor dribbled from her mouth into the watering trenches in the altar…the lush, lovingly cultivated plants began to wither. To droop.

To die.

"Go," Ani croaked; when Wolf only stared at the woman's body, his pupils blown wide, she shoved him back and screamed: "*Go!*"

The world spun around her like a kaleidoscope, vivid greens and dying purple-grays and the colorful array of offerings tumbling across her vision as he swept her into his arms and plunged down the altar, clearing the diseased plants and toxic water without even grazing his heels on the stone shelves.

He didn't look back as they fled; not even when Ani reached over his shoulder, thrust out her hand, and yanked back her fist like tugging an invisible rope. The temple door slammed shut in their wake, the tendrils of vines she'd summoned to close it already beginning to twitch and shudder.

"No," she choked. "No, no, rotting *bones*..."

She'd thought the corruption they'd encountered in the Arboretum Absolute had been cleansed by the miraculous restoration of her relic. But as the tree-temple began to shudder, patches of decay punching dents in the shell of its bark, she could practically hear Brae's delighted laughter buried in the creaking of sickened wood.

The Blight had been a blow against her, she'd thought when they'd claimed her relic—his last-ditch effort to kill her closest ally and leave her with no one in the world to turn to but him.

She'd been wrong.

This wasn't a blow; this wasn't a weapon aimed with precision, set to strike at her heart.

This was a conquering. A punishment. A reminder of what her oldest brother could do—what he *would* do—to put their family back together.

The relic wasn't the target. It was the trap.

When Tenebrae had poisoned her relic, he hadn't done it to kill her friend.

He'd done it to kill Ani's *kingdom*.

CHAPTER 24

ELIAS

He owed Sage Olivander his pits-damned life.

The tea Ani had requested on his behalf could've tasted like rotten eggs and roof runoff for all he cared. The way it caught his unsteady stomach and set it back on its feet, shooing the nausea as easily as his mother used to shoo them out of her workshop when she'd been struck with inspiration, he'd actually considered falling at the Arborian prince's feet and swearing fealty to him when they returned to the island. To garner that much awe from a holy man said plenty about the tea's potency…and how terrible that seasickness had been.

He felt well enough, in fact, that after the others had vacated the cabin their sixth day into sailing, he knelt on the ship floor without fear of the position worsening his vertigo. And when he folded his hands atop his and Soren's rumpled, musty quilt, for the first time in many, many weeks…he could pray without wringing the trembling out of them first.

Or at least, he started to, before the cabin door crashed back open, followed by a groaning gag. "*Ugh.* Can't you do that somewhere else? Your zealotry's going to infect the room."

He glared over his shoulder at Everin, who crinkled his nose and waved his hand in front of his face as if to fend off faith's fetid odor. The golden-haired prince had already found an excuse to shuck off his shirt, despite the cool morning; it was slung through his iron-buckled belt like a dishtowel.

"Can't you do *that* somewhere else?" Elias retorted. "Your narcissism is bringing my nausea back."

"Sorry, was that supposed to be a comeback? My dead mother could hit with meaner mitts than that, stones keep her bones." Everin swaggered over, planting himself cross-legged on the bed; heedless of Elias's vestments spread out just so, he picked up the holy book bound in cracked black leather, thumbed through it with his tongue pinned between his teeth, then tossed it into Elias's lap. "So. Phoenix Priest, huh? I never understood that one."

After a solid two days of debate, he and Soren had decided it would be better to be honest about what he was. Better to control how it came out than risk it being revealed against his will.

He'd expected at least one axe to find purchase in his deathless skin. But the Tallisians had merely muttered or grunted their understanding as they took in his golden eye…and each forked over some coin to Medwenna, who'd looked quite pleased with herself.

"You wouldn't understand any of it." He shut the book and tucked it away. *We need him to save Kal. We need him to save Kal.* "Get off my bed."

"It's my ship." The prince smirked salaciously. "They're all my beds. But I am perfectly happy to let you all borrow them…especially that pretty ghost of yours. She can haunt me belowdecks any day."

I need him to get out of my face.

Only imagining all that gilded-lily hair going up in flames kept his manners grooved enough to grip. "I heartily encourage you to offer her that exact invitation. I'd love to hear what she says."

"You didn't answer my question." Everin scooped up Elias's prayer beads with one finger, twirling them idly; when Elias tried to snatch them back, the prince leaned out of reach.

His gut swirled. "You didn't ask one. Please give me those."

"I didn't? I meant to." Everin slid the beads over his neck with every irreverence a faithless man might—spinning the beads around their tether as if they were wood and string, nothing more. "What's a man wriggling under Death's heel doing with a once-dead princess on his arm? I'd think she'd want to steer clear of that whole thing."

"She didn't actually die." It'd been a near thing, definitely, but between the two of them…well, he'd gotten a good bit nearer. "I'll only ask nicely one more time: give me my beads."

The prince made an impressed *hmm* sound, his eyes skimming Elias's glowing tattoos with cold, violent glee. "Thought Princess told you to play nice."

Deep breaths. He couldn't actually start a fight after all these years of telling Soren that brawling didn't solve anything. "Thought you didn't want my zealotry to infect you."

Everin blinked—then laughed. "Well, damn. Can't argue with myself, can I?" With a flick of his fingers, he shot the beads at Elias's face; they stung his palm when he caught them. "There you go, hotshot. Don't say I never gave you anything."

Before he could fully leash his temper—or remind the prince to *get the pits off his bed*—Everin's gaze snapped to the door. He *sprang* off the bed, pitching himself against the wall instead…just as a set of footsteps halted outside.

"Relax," he ordered with a roll of his eyes when Elias spun, digging around for the dagger in his boot. "It's just Medwenna."

Sure enough, the voice that floated in was touched by an Arborian brogue, but still clearly rooted in the mountain kingdom. "*Just Medwenna* asked your meddling arse to *fetch* Captain Loch, not harass him, which you blatantly ignored. So you'd better shape up that attitude and have a smile on for me when I get in there."

Medwenna cracked the door open and peeked her head in, her golden-brown hair knotted messily at the top of her head. She didn't blink at the sight of Elias on his knees, or the prince sprawled shirtless against the wall. "You're not already picking a fight, are you?"

"What? Of course not," scoffed the prince. "I wouldn't—"

"After I specifically asked you not to?"

"I wouldn't dare—"

Medwenna narrowed her eyes. "I also specifically requested a smile."

Everin put on a grin so big it should have broken his jaw. "Better?"

"Much." Medwenna eyed the beads and book in Elias's lap. "Now apologize to him."

That mocking grin shrank to a sheepish grimace. "I was just asking a question or two."

"You were not, and don't you think you can lie to me. We've barely left port—no harassing Captain Loch, no harassing the Princess, no harassing—"

"It might be faster if you give me a list of the people I *can* harass."

"Nobody."

"That's unreasonable."

"Matthias and Kessen."

"That's a given."

Medwenna made a face Elias recognized from back in his boyhood…a face he'd seen plenty of times just before a weary teacher sat some troublemaking student next to *his* desk in an attempt to bore them into behaving.

"Fine," the man groaned, shoving his hands in his pockets and making for the door—but Medwenna splayed a hand, blocking his way.

"*I promise…*" she prompted.

Everin threw his head back with a groan. "Winnie…"

"Go on. *I promise I will not harass our guests.*"

Everin sighed. Scowled. Slumped.

"I promise I will not harass our guests," he grumbled. "May I go now?"

"I didn't hear an apology."

"Kings don't apologize—current or future."

The archeress crinkled up her nose, but waved him off. "We're not done talking about this."

"Yeah, yeah." Everin pressed a chaste kiss to her head. "You're sounding more and more like Will every day, you grouch."

"Then it'd do you well to remember he only got grouchier when you didn't listen to me, so fall in line." She swatted Everin's back as he left, smiling apologetically at Elias. "Captain Loch, as I'm sure he forgot to tell you, I have need of you topside, if you please."

"Is everything all right?"

Medwenna worried her lip with her teeth. "I'm afraid your battlemate's picked a fight she can't win."

CHAPTER 25

SOREN

As always, sailing came with its pros and cons.

The pros: Sage's herb sachets, steeped into tea, had done wonders for Elias's shaky, sea-tossed stomach. Twenty minutes after his first cup, he'd been able to separate himself from the ship's railing; now, nearly a week into their voyage, the crew had begun to joke he had steadier sea legs than the Heir of Atlas did.

She played grouchy about it, if only because it made Elias grin with a pride she hadn't seen since he'd placed first in their mountaintop training games his first year, ranking over far more established recruits in terms of endurance. Jakob had joked Elias was the only man a mountain ever moved for. Elias had made some pious comment about faith being the right tool for the job.

But the sailors were wrong—because if mountains moved for the faithful, then ships steadied for the salt-blooded. And her body finally seemed to remember the first nine years of its raising, taught to walk while tottering on sandy shores and swaying on sailboats captained by her parents or eldest sister and brother. Her steps shifted with the ship like she'd been born to it.

After all, she had been.

Still, the cons remained…one of which being that by her sixth day cooped up in a wooden box floating on a massive body of water, she could no longer keep boredom at bay by marveling at the view. Mostly because the view stopped changing pretty damn fast.

So maybe she should've kept her mouth shut when the Tallisian trio decided to pass the time by sparring. Maybe she should've sat quietly on the sun-warmed deck and kept right on tying a series of sailor's knots, feeling her way through the loops and coils until smoke-stained instructions from her father fused with muscle memory gave her the correct knot. Maybe she shouldn't have started loudly critiquing Kessen on his nervous, bobbling stance or pointing out Matthias's tendency to favor his right ankle.

But she didn't. And she didn't. And she did. So it didn't take long for Prince Everin to pause his low-toned talk with Medwenna off to the side of the ship to call, "Princess, if you're going to run your mouth, you'd better be able to cross the finish line."

She tossed her rope aside and leaned her weight back on her palms, sapping the deck's heat into her perpetually cold fingers. Golden brilliance lit the backs of her eyelids as she shut them, turning her face to the sun. "Plainer words, Prince."

"Either close your fists or close your mouth."

Medwenna hissed a scolding under her breath. Matthias hummed deep in his chest…a warning or a chuckle, she couldn't tell.

Aged, wave-beaten wood scraped her knuckles as she folded her fingers into fists. "You first."

When she popped one eye open, she was just in time to see Everin halt Matthias and Kessen with a swift snap of his fingers. The two froze, Kessen mid-kick toward Matthias's weak ankle, Matthias gripping Kessen's fist and bending it to the side.

"I've heard a thing or two about battlemate pairs," he said as his men fumbled back to baseline, flanking him. "Haven't had the privilege of seeing them fight myself, not up close. Don't suppose you and your lover would do us the honor?"

Nausea and hunger could exist in tandem. Long hours spent on guard duty, the hot and sweaty recovery after a brutal training session…many things had taught her that lesson firsthand. But being handed the chance to show off what she and her battlemate could do—what they could *be* when they fought together as one—had never turned her stomach like this.

Nor had she ever wanted it so gods-damned much.

"Would I love the chance to tattoo my knuckles on each of your pretty faces? Sure." She leaned back, pretending to bask again. Pretending her heart wasn't battering her chest at a dozen beats per breath. "But my battlemate's not as easy to bait."

"She called me pretty," Kessen gloated. "Matt, did you hear that? I'm *pretty.*"

"She called all of us pretty," Matthias corrected. "And I don't think she meant it nicely."

"Still—"

"Not easily baited, you say?" Everin's palms rasped together, a grin breaking through his beard. "We'll see about that."

"Ev," Medwenna warned as the prince strode toward the door to the lower cabins, "just fetch him—don't pick a fight."

The prince flashed her a thumbs-up over his head without turning around, whistling jovially as he vanished from view.

A beat of silence.

"One gold says he comes back with his nose broken," said Kessen.

"Holy men are packed with patience." Matthias stroked his beard sagely, eyes narrowed. "One gold he comes back alone."

Oh, this was a bet she could win. "One gold that—"

"Uh-uh!" Kessen wagged his finger at her. "You're not allowed in on the game. No betting *against* battlemates *about* their battlemates. Even I know better than that."

She scowled. "That's unfair."

"Yeah—'cause you'd win."

Matthias crossed the deck to offer her his hand; she took it, letting him haul her to her feet with one smooth pull. The sun glinted off the beads wound through his beard, gleaming like bared teeth, a predator cloaked in shadow—but his smile was friendly. "You know your stuff. I've been needling Kess about his balance since he first toddled into the training hall."

"I didn't toddle," Kessen grumbled; with the next sideways pitch of the ship, he stumbled, righting himself with a cough into his fist. "Tell you what—you go stand on a rocking chair and tell me if you can hold a proper stance. Seriously. I'd love to see it."

"You can either make excuses or make progress—" When Kessen mouthed along with Matthias's words, rolling his eyes, Matthias slapped him upside the head with a scowl, "and I'm hearing an awful lot of excuses."

Kessen's eyes narrowed. He shoved his loose linen sleeves up to his elbows, cuffing them clumsily. "Fists up, old man, I'll show you *progress.*"

As they began to circle each other again, Kessen bobbing like…well, a bobber, one of the little round things her father kept on his fishing line to let him know when he had a bite, she turned her head to the side, listening for any sign of Elias's approach. Maybe if he held his patience long enough, two-thirds of this *triad* would whittle their energy down before she even had to throw a punch.

Medwenna suddenly huffed, taking off in the direction of the cabin.

"Where are you going?" Soren called after her.

"It's been too long," she called back. "He's causing trouble."

A couple minutes later, the patter of bootsteps announced Everin's hasty exit before he made it; Medwenna and Elias emerged shortly after, the latter with both hands hooked around his prayer beads in a death grip, knuckles pale. He hadn't been wearing them around his neck lately, reserving that space for the cord housing his battlemate braids and Mortem's relic…but he wore them now.

And if looks could kill, Elias's glare would've decorated Everin's back with two midnight daggers.

She swallowed a laugh, driving her fist into her chest to get it all the way down as Elias sulked over to her. "Aw, you made a new friend!" she cooed.

"Very funny." He dropped to his seat beside her. "I heard you're picking fights."

"Our hosts want to see what battlemate brawls look like up close."

Elias cast a dull smile toward the Tallisian trio. "Do they, now?"

"Seems so."

"Why didn't you just say so?" Elias called to Everin. "If I'd known you wanted your ass kicked so badly…"

Matthias hooted with laughter; Kessen, on the other hand, tossed all humor aside. He took a menacing step, his stride sinking into a something so close to a stalk that instinct pushed her weight onto her other hip, dipping her in front of Elias. "Speak to him like that again, and we'll see who—"

"Easy, kid." Everin threw out a lazy arm in front of the overzealous soldier. But nothing lazy lurked in his smile as he bared his teeth their way. "Let's settle this like proper soldiers, shall we?"

He held up a hand—from somewhere behind her and Elias, a small white object flew through the air, landing perfectly in his palm. He closed his fingers around it, tossing a wink over their heads. "What would we do without you, Winnie?"

"Die," the historian said cheerily, strolling over to a patch of shade with a book tucked under her arm.

Everin grimaced, a wordless *true enough*. He took the chalk, bent until the tip dragged against the deck, and began walking in a slow circle.

"Only three rules." Matthias unbuckled his weapons belt and tossed it; Medwenna caught it without looking up from her book, setting it aside just in time to catch Kessen's. "No magic, no blades, no broken bones."

"No ruptured organs," Medwenna added.

"Four rules." Matthias raised another finger.

"No broken cartilage, either." Medwenna flipped a page. "Noses are cartilage, not bone."

Kessen's disappointed *aww* suggested he'd been looking forward to breaking a bit of cartilage himself. And she didn't think he'd planned on aiming for *her* nose.

It was getting harder not to like him.

Matthias's thumb went up. "Fine. Five rules."

Medwenna worried her lip as she read, fingertip skimming the page. "And maybe—"

"No, no, no more." Matthias closed his fingers into a fist and shoved it into his pocket. "If we add more than five, we might as well fence instead."

"We know our manners," Soren promised; at least, Elias did, and he'd probably let her copy his work if she forgot. "Five rules is plenty."

Elias shot her a look that strongly suggested he thought she was full of it. But for once, that might play to their advantage.

With a flourish and a dramatic bend backwards to crack his back, Everin completed the chalk circle; he whistled and threw it toward Medwenna.

It flew right over her shoulder. Not one golden-brown hair twitched.

Everin frowned. "You missed."

"I don't catch on command." Medwenna licked her thumb and turned another page. The sun tried to cover the title with its glare, but as Soren squinted, a helpful cloud came by to offer its shadow: *Borrowed Time: A History of Divine Hosts.* "Particularly not when you whistle. I'm not a hunting hound."

Everin threw his hands out to his sides, turning toward Matthias, who shrugged and put his own hands up. A silent *not my problem, don't ask me.* "How else am I supposed to get your attention?"

"Try my name, perhaps? I'm getting quite good at responding to it."

"Not when you're *reading.*"

"That sounds like you," Soren said to Elias, who elbowed her in the ribs. "Ow!"

"Friendly fire," Matthias and Kessen yelled as one, followed by a high-five…which missed entirely, thrusting Kessen's hand deep into Matthias's beaded locks, a leather bracelet around Kessen's wrist snagging on some of the beads.

While the two of them tugged at hair and arms and snapped at each other to *just hold still,* she hauled herself to her feet and began to stretch, tuning out the noise…listening instead to the adrenaline swishing through her blood, filtered from heart to vein to muscle.

Ready, it whispered to her.

Ready to fight. Ready to win.

Bone and muscle and blood, all in agreement. But her mind quailed; her heart quivered.

A sparring session with her battlemate was one thing. But putting on a show for a prince and his pair of friends, that was another.

Stage fright.

This body had answered to another for so long, it didn't quite feel like hers yet. Like her childhood bedroom in Port Atlas's palace…something that should have been home, should have been safe, and wasn't.

But if she never tried, she'd never know.

A chorus of mocking wolf whistles from the Tallisians gripped her by the wrist and unspooled her from the deeper trenches of her body—she opened her eyes to find Elias clutching his shirt and cloak, cheeks and tattoos aflame, one with bloodied heat and the other with molten magic.

"Didn't know the War Wolf could shed its coat," laughed Kessen.

"Those pretty tattoos going to keep you warm tonight?" Everin's gaze glittered. "Your bunkmate might decide find a new bed to share when she sees us mop the deck with you."

"His bunkmate would sooner die." She shrugged off her jacket—and a wave chose that particular moment to barrel into the side of the ship, shattering into sea-mist, coating her in a frigid cape of damp that swept through her skull and cleared away the cobwebs.

That clarity tunneled down and out. Tingling goosebumps. Eager fists. Dancing heels that sent her trotting into the center of the circle, facing Everin down.

Prince of Heathens, Ani had muttered under her breath when he showed up in the pub. *Blood of the Emperor.*

In Nyx, they knew him as the Pride of Tallis. Lion-Tamer. Stone-Breaker.

People claimed he could cleave a boulder in two with one swing of his axe. That he could read a battlefield and turn its tide with a single command. That if one had to choose between Prince Everin Arden and a hunger-maddened bear, one would be better off with the bear.

But she also remembered a lesson from Finn: anyone who needed that many names to bolster their legend had paid for that renown, not earned it. Their titles and triumphs came from a commissioned gossip-monger's pen, not whispers from the people.

The man standing before her was just that: a man. As were the two who shuffled in to flank him, staggering themselves almost like a staircase: Kessen edged out in front of Everin, Matthias a step or two behind.

Elias's shoulder—clothed again, damn those Tallisians—brushed hers as he fell in beside her. Neither in front, neither behind. Equal footing. Equal danger.

"All right, smartass." His eyes gleamed—just as hungry for this as her. A craving straight to the core. "Remember, no broken bones."

"What if it's an accident?"

"Not one person on this boat would believe that. I don't care how big those green eyes get."

"On my mark," Medwenna called, hand up; for a moment, the world blurred, Soren's focus captured entirely by those three raised fingers.

"What do you say, Princess?" Everin leaned in, speaking so low she didn't think even Elias heard him. "Like those rules?"

She matched his stance—and his whisper. "What say you and I play by Nyxian rules?"

His brow rose. "I'm listening."

One of Medwenna's fingers bent.

"You break it, you take it," she breathed. "Up to you how hard you hit, but you better be ready to take it in kind."

The second finger went down.

Everin's teeth gleamed in the sun. *Hungry.* "You're on."

The third finger bent, and before Medwenna's lips finished forming the *three*, Kessen broke formation and cut between her and Everin.

Soren threw her hands up with a stuttering surge, signals mixing in her brain—but she sorted them out just fast enough to bat away his attempt to jam the feeling out of her shoulder. When he immediately followed it with a wide swing, knuckles careening toward her face, she ducked—

Bone on bone. A crack that thrilled from her crooked nose to her aching toes.

Kessen staggered back, cradling the jaw Elias had just struck—but she couldn't stay still long enough to see what he did next.

They were down a shadow. Only Everin remained behind Kessen.

She dropped from her crouch to hit the deck on all fours, shoving herself sharply backward, right between Elias's spread legs—wood scraped her knees, stinging like she'd knelt on a wasp nest, but she didn't slow. Instead, she somersaulted just in time to drive her heels into Matthias's shins.

He'd used Kessen's brash assault to slip behind Elias. Remarkably quiet, for such a husky man—but that quiet didn't hold under Soren's bruising blows, broken by mild cursing as he jogged backward, putting distance between them while she bobbed back to her feet.

"Throwing a body as a distraction…not so effective when your opponent's got two sets of eyes," she panted.

"Maybe." Matthias winked. "But we've got three bodies."

Before she could regret gloating, her vision went dark.

Elias's back collided with hers; by the time she figured out that someone had yanked the hood of Elias's cloak back and hooked it over her eyes, that same someone swept her ankles out from under her.

Her teeth cracked together as her jaw slammed into the deck; buzzing pain sang through her gums as she staggered back up, freed but dizzied, seeking her battlemate's back.

She bumped against something solid. Panic plunged steeply into relief as she fumbled for his elbow to steady herself…

And almost choked when she encountered cold mountain stone instead of hearthfire heat.

"What's the one thing you can always count on a battlemate pair to do, Kess?" called Everin, a taunt that blustered through her curls like a playful hair-tousle—or an arrow that barely missed a deadly mark.

"Go back to back, sir!" Kessen barked, an abrasive bite that hadn't been there before.

"And how do you put down a battlemate pair?" Everin's arms formed steel bars around her, lifting her feet clean off the deck before she could bolt.

"You force them apart," Matthias answered this time. "And you *keep* them apart."

Everin set her down only to spin her out, almost like they'd shifted from a duel to a dance. The world did a somersault, a nauseous twirl that set her at the back of the boat…with three Tallisians forming a corrugated wall between her and Elias.

Scorch-black eyes met hers over Everin's shoulder. *You all right?*

She dipped her stinging chin, rubbing the splintered scrape. Her fingertips came away streaked with blood.

"Bad news," she told them, rotating her jaw to try and pop the tension. It felt like one of the planks had jammed itself into the hinge. "We can still fight just fine apart."

"Oh, sure. But it's not about the fight." Everin squared his stance, hands open, fingers loosely bent. He faced her while the other two turned to face Elias, Matthias turned in slightly toward her battlemate's right side. His weaker side.

"Go on, then," she ground out, falling into her own ready pose: hands up and open, knees bent. "Please enlighten me about the training that's saved my life a hundred times over."

"When you get between battlemates, they forget about everything else." Everin swatted one hand, dismissive. "Their duty, their orders—stakes, their whole damned kingdom—it all goes *poof.*" He mimed out a dissipating cloud with his fingers. "It's all about getting back to their partner."

Maybe if Elias had actually been listening to the prince's little speech, they wouldn't have so neatly proven him right. But instead, he feinted toward Kessen, who reeled back; by the time Kessen had regained his balance, Elias had already cut into Matthias's space, delivering blow after brutal blow to the Second's side.

Not *too* brutal—she heard no snapping ribs or strangled gasps. But where Elias had once sparred like a man who'd rather be doing anything else, dancing in and peppering punches in all the right places before dancing back out…now he drove in without mercy, a streak of russet and onyx winnowing from one opponent to the other, juggling two opponents with a decadent grace she couldn't manage against one.

Damned Death Goddess.

Everin settled on his heels, watching her now—content, it seemed, to stay right where he was. To wait on her.

Fine. He thought he could bait her—the barracks' best heckler three years running? She didn't think so. They'd given her a *trophy,* damn it. She'd *perfected* this craft.

"So you thought adding a third distraction would help?" She tsked. "Must be nice having a spare. Which one is it? Do they know?"

Nailed it. His perfect grin flipped belly-up, rotting into a snarl. "Watch it."

"Ooh, touchy!" She threw her hands up in mock surrender, backing up a pace, toeing the empty space behind her. "You know the first thing *I* learned in the barracks? If you can't take a punch, don't throw a punch."

"Oh, I can take the hit, Princess." He cracked his knuckles, taking the pace she'd retreated…edging between her and Kessen. *Got him.* "But you're not hitting the target you think."

"So you haven't told him?" She looked over the two other Tallisians with a pitying hum. "It's got to be the kid, right? He's got *new puppy* written all over him. What put your last hunting dog down?"

One day, perhaps even very soon, she'd learn to keep her mouth shut. Or she'd figure out how to box up her meanest thoughts and bury them like the world's worst chest of pirate plunder.

But for today, consequences came in the form of breathtaking pain crunching through her sternum.

"*Hey!*" Elias shouted as she backpedaled, her back striking the railing around the deck—and her heart striking her toes when the momentum carried her heels off the deck, sea spray licking her nape as she started to tumble over the edge.

Someone caught her wrist, hauling her back onto the deck. She gripped the railing, coughing to unstick her lungs from the back of her chest, not even able to find the words to thank Medwenna for the swift rescue.

"What are you—get your hand off me, Drake, I'll burn the prints off your fingers, I swear by my own wretched pyre—*hey, that's enough!*"

Back and heart throbbing, she flipped around just as Elias barreled between her and Everin—though the prince hadn't pursued—and thrust one hand out in warning, the other reaching for her.

"You all right?" he asked.

"I'll live."

"That's not an answer, smartass."

"How is that *not an answer*, jackass?"

"Not my fault you grew out of your sea legs," Everin taunted. When she blinked away the sunspots of pain dappling the deck, she found both Matthias and Kessen standing at Everin's sides once more. But the way they held his arms, their backs facing her and Elias…they weren't defending him. In fact, Matthias had his arm barred across Everin's chest, whispering urgently in his ear. "You think you can run your mouth about my men and—"

"You've been running *your* mouth about me and my battlemate since the second your scabby, silt-stuffed carcass marched into my aunt's office. Forgive me for assuming it was fair game!"

Everin shoved a finger toward her; not a kind one. Kessen cringed, and Elias immediately took a step forward, tattoos catching fire—she shot one hand out and hauled him to a stop.

"Don't," she hissed. "Not worth it."

"Aw, good guard dog," Everin cooed to Elias, silver eyes alight with livid, reckless fire of his own. "Do you come running when she whistles, too? Whine at the door until she lets you up on the bed?"

People had told her many, many times over the course of her life that she had a quicker draw on her temper than her dagger. That if she always let anger be the executor of her actions, she'd land herself in the heart of a funeral pyre before she got her first white hair.

Been there, done that, she would've told them now. *Crawled right back out.*

Pyres and grave dirt and ruby-red roses, they didn't frighten her anymore. Not when her battlemate wore their scent like cologne, coating her skin with the essence of death when he traveled the map of her body by hand; not when she'd clawed herself free from them, soot-bruised and thorn-bitten, again and again and again.

Not when her mother had gone ahead of her, lining the path from life to death with wishing stars.

Which was a very long-winded, elegant excuse for why she let go of Elias and immediately punched Prince Everin Arden, the only hope for her kingdom's survival, square in his own crooked nose.

CHAPTER 26

SOREN

"I don't see what all the fuss is about," Soren grumbled. "The way I see it, we're even."

"Will you stop talking?" Everin groaned; he sat on the edge of his bunk, hunched over his knees, stanching his bloody nose while Medwenna set about preparing a numbing salve. "Gods, my ears are still ringing. Who taught you how to hit?"

Pride tingled in her toes; she wriggled them to get the energy out, pouting at the bruised prince. It was hard to tell which went deeper: the blow to his face, or the blow to his ego. "Poor thing. Not used to getting your pretty face bashed in?"

Everin grinned at her through bloodied teeth, though those teeth mashed into a grimace as he angled his head this way and that. "Not especially. They usually aim somewhere lower. Shoot straight, Princess—how much pretty did I lose?"

"Frustratingly little." Ani might have repaired her wasted muscles to the best of her ability, but it had been a good while since she'd had to aim a solid punch at anything. Ani usually put a stop to it when she tried.

"Tallisian bones, baby." The prince knocked on his own cheekbone with a chuckle. "This jawline's tougher than titanium."

"I'll have to test that next time."

"There is no next time," Elias and Medwenna chorused.

"You tried to do it first," she grumbled at her battlemate.

"'Course I tried. He disrespected you."

"He disrespected *you*."

He grunted, which was as close as she'd get to him conceding the point. Even if Everin had stopped at nearly shoving her off the ship, she would've earned the right to throw that punch—honestly, the fact that she'd restrained herself that long at all should've earned her an *atta girl* and a shoulder pat from her battlemate.

Not that Elias had ever *atta girled* anyone in his life. But a girl could dream.

"I should've let you," Soren mumbled as Elias set his palm over her sternum, then prodded the edges of the bruised, swollen area with his fingertips. Tiny pulses of pain lit up under every pressure point. "Maybe he would've broken your nose back, and then we could've matched."

"As fun as that would've been, I think I'm all right." Elias kissed her between the eyes before handing her a cold, wet cloth. "Nothing broken—just a nasty contusion. Keep that on there."

"Yeah, yeah." She set the cloth to her chest and simply breathed, letting every curse and complaint from Everin's side of the cabin soothe her sore temper.

"I'm very sorry about this," Medwenna offered as Elias ducked out from their bunk, narrowly avoiding the upper frame. The ranger sat on her knees beside Everin, the prince facing her with his eyes shut and his legs crossed. Her thumbs gleamed with some waxy, honey-like substance—she applied it to Everin's nose in careful sweeps, starting at the bridge and coating out toward his cheekbones. Despite his cavalier attitude, he'd gone silent now, the furrow between his brows easing with every coat of the numbing salve. "And so is he. Right, Everin?"

Everin grumbled something incoherent.

A loud *crash* followed almost immediately—Soren jumped so hard her skull clipped the top bunk's supports, she and Elias both swearing in chorus as they spun to seek out the culprit: a silver tin that seemed to have leapt off the bedside table of its own accord, its lid still whirling like a top, its bounty of wrapped candies scattered across the floor.

Silence. Then Medwenna said, "Will's not happy with you."

"Well, what else is new?" Everin took Medwenna's wrists and pried her hands away from his face, glaring at the offending tin. "Keep it to yourself, Will. If you wanted to keep nagging me, maybe you shouldn't have died."

Elias looked at the tin. Then looked at her.

Madman, they agreed with one shared nod.

"I don't think we've made Will's acquaintance," Soren said carefully. "Is he a very tiny person? Is he hiding in the tin?"

Medwenna's fond, fragile smile pinched her in the ribs. "Not exactly."

Soren sat forward. "I'm not following."

"No one invited you to," said Everin, followed by a mopey *ow* when Medwenna knuckled the top of his head.

"You, get. I don't have the patience to keep treating your stings every time you stick your tongue in the wasp's nest."

"Fine. But if Will keeps causing trouble, tell him he can throw things at me outside." Tossing two middle fingers toward the empty corner of the room—and the candy carnage still strewn across the floor—Everin shouldered his way through the door.

"You too, Elias," Soren said—then widened her own eyes back at him when he gave her an *Are you insane?* look.

"Please?" She fluttered her eyelashes at him. "I could use a little quiet."

His left eye twitched. But without another word—or another layered glare—he followed Everin out onto the deck.

Hopefully neither of them would come back with new wounds to nurse.

"No, but really," Soren asked as soon as the door closed, "how can you *stand* that guy?"

Medwenna's silence suggested she actually offered serious consideration to the question. "By owning a good pair of shoes. They make it easier not to trip over the common sense he keeps tossing away."

To make a joke when all Soren wanted to do was stew…that was so unfair. "I'm serious. You've been so kind, and he…and he's just…I don't get it."

"Everin was my late husband's best friend."

Soren's breath faltered.

"So I'm making an ass of myself, is what you're saying," she mumbled.

"No," Medwenna chuckled, coming to sit beside Soren. She held up the salve jar in silent offer; Soren took it, rubbing it over the bruise while Medwenna tipped her head back and forth, as if weighing a thought with an imaginary scale. "Not at all. I'm hardly ignorant of his faults, Princess. We all grew up together…Everin, Will, me, and Matthias."

The salve was warm, sapping up the heat of her fingers; moments later, the pain went dull and dozy. Barely there at all. "Not Kessen?"

"Ah…no. He came later." Medwenna's gaze went glassy. "Those boys were inseparable. When William and I got engaged, Matthias and Everin held a duel to see who would get to marry us. Everin won. You should've heard the ridiculous things he slipped into our vows." A pause. A darker swirl of emotion muddying her pretty face. "And when Will was hurt, and we realized the physicians couldn't do a thing to save him…Everin's the one that helped us escape."

"Escape?"

"Use of magic is illegal in Tallis. Even traveling to other kingdoms for magical assistance is forbidden…if you're caught trying, you're imprisoned at best, executed at worst."

Soren grimaced. "How'd he get you out?"

"He snuck us out on one of his visits to Arborius. We stowed away successfully, but there was only so much the physician on board could do, and it was a long journey. Too long." Medwenna fussed with her ring finger, eyes still fixed ahead. "Will passed one day, three hours, and twenty-eight minutes before we made port. Everin helped me count."

When Elias had died in her arms, the last thing on her mind had been counting the time past his last breath. But shock struck everyone differently… sometimes, it even struck the same person differently at different times.

She tugged her mint-green cardigan more tightly around her shoulders— the color didn't suit her, but Jira had worn it beautifully. It was one of the many items she'd stolen from her first battlemate when she'd died, unwilling to watch even one more piece of her friend disappear when her parents came to claim her effects. And by some stroke of luck, she'd seen this old thing in one of the tipped-over laundry hampers that had been abandoned by castlefolk in the chaos of Andromeda's fall; Elias had almost lost his mind when she'd wasted precious time triple-knotting it around her waist, her own shirt in bloody tatters from his scythes.

"But you went to Arborius still?" she prompted, blinking until the imprint of that night scrubbed off her eyes.

Distractions—those would keep her focused. Keep her sane.

"I had no choice. Everin got us out, but we all knew there would be no hiding what happened…even if Will had lived, we would've both been fugitives from our kingdom. Only Arborius's neutrality protected me."

"What killed him?" Too personal by ten counts, but morbid curiosity numbed out propriety. "A battle?"

"No." A wry smile; a damp, unsteady sigh. "No, that I think I could have borne better. It came from nowhere…he was meant to meet Matthias and Everin at this pub they used to visit every couple nights, but he never arrived. When they came looking for him and realized I sent him off hours before…" Medwenna's eyes clenched shut, and the story broke, emerging in abrupt spurts of empty fact. A recitation with no emotion. "Whoever did it left him in the street. Everin found him. Matthias came and got me. It was the worst night of my life."

Gods.

She couldn't picture death in any other context but war—she'd lost her grandparents to illness, but she'd been too young for that to stick. Every other loss, whether the blow came by weapon or deity or sacrifice, came sculpted in warfare's image. "What happened? Who…?"

"We don't know. No one ever caught them…not for lack of trying. Will gave them what he could, and Everin pulled every inquisitor off their other scents to track that one. Him, Matthias, they *scoured* that city—neither of them shut their eyes for three days straight. I had to drag them by the ears to the infirmary so Will could scold some sense into them before they ended up in beds next to him."

"You really expect me to believe the Heir to Tallis's throne couldn't find the person behind one murder?"

"Oh, no, I apologize—I wasn't clear. They never found the person who *did* it." Medwenna swiveled to sit against the wall beside her, staring at the upper bunk's support planks. She couldn't tell if the gleam in her eyes was a trick of the light or a trick of tears. "None of us had to guess who was *behind* it."

"Who, then?"

Medwenna kept staring upward. "King Denali never liked that the former Grand Historian chose me as his successor. I was the youngest who ever served, as Everin mentioned, but I also the first woman. And Denali...did not care for the way I conducted myself." A light tremble in her voice. "He had his own ideas to make me fall in line. And when none of them succeeded, he changed tack to punishment."

A sick, angry pang rippled through her center. "Bastard."

"Yes. But I'm letting myself wander, so answer your question...Everin did right by my Will." Medwenna locked her gaze on Soren's directly for the first time since she'd met her—before, she'd always looked just a bit below or just a bit above, never head-on. "And he's continued to do right by me. He risked more than you'd think, getting us out...and suffered consequences he still won't tell me about. For that alone, I'll stand with him wherever and whenever he asks." A wry little smile. "And even when he doesn't."

She couldn't fault her for that...nor could she entirely fault Everin. Honestly, she didn't even know why his teasing had her hackles up in the first place. She'd taken and thrown out far worse during her time in the barracks. Had thrown worse out there on the deck, too—had invited him to do the same before the match had even started.

"So why the thing with the candies?" she asked after a long pause.

"Oh." Medwenna's quiet emotion broke into an awkward, stilted laugh; she smoothed a hand over her honey-wheat hair, smiling at the candies with strange fondness. "Tallisians have...unique beliefs about death, compared to the other kingdoms. No one can pin down the exact origins of the story, but our mythos doesn't leave space for Mortem...nor her purported realms, Infera or Arcaea. We believe our dead come back to guide us when we pass on...and sometimes they wait right beside us."

Soren gripped the sheets beneath her, suddenly wishing her fingers didn't feel so cold. Too late, she remembered the salve—uncurling her fingers again took several seconds, the skin bound to the fabric like she'd drizzled them in syrup. She reached instead for the damp towel Elias had left her. "Tallisians believe in ghosts?"

"Of a sort. You can imagine why those myths might have been twisted in other kingdoms." Medwenna slid from the bed to kneel beside the scattered candies. As she plucked them from the floor and dropped them back into their tin, each landing with a soft *plink*, she added, "Will was the first of us to go...and he said before he went that he didn't intend to see the next life without us." The ranger's shoulders trembled beneath her powder-pink shirt, and her voice shrank when she murmured, "Without *me*. He promised he'd let me see it first."

"See…what, exactly?" If they didn't believe in Arcaea or Infera, what else was there?

"I don't know. No one does." Medwenna looked over her shoulder, the reverent shine in her eyes not at all unlike Elias's when he spoke about Mortem. "It's the one piece of existence that will never be history…something that only exists in the future, and never in the past. Can you imagine that? A place untouched by the past?"

A place with no memory. A place with no ash or graves or grief—a place with nothing to dust or repair or remember.

"It sounds terrifying," she admitted. "But I haven't had the best experience with that…not having a past."

"And I can hardly heap any blame on you for that. But for a woman whose life's work is built on the bones of the past…" Her fingers tapped against the tin, an anticipatory tune. "I can't picture it, a place with no bones to give it shape. He promised to let me go first."

The historian was repeating herself now, but she decided not to mention it. Elias had endless patience for her flighty mind when she told him the same story a dozen times; she could afford Medwenna the same generosity.

"So now he's just…waiting." She shot a furtive glance at the tin. "Here. With us."

"Well, so we like to think." That glassy haze of distant passion vanished with Medwenna's next blink, and she stood with a quick throat-clearing, setting the tin back in its place. "When odd little things happen—things falling off shelves, strange sounds, whispers on the wind, that sort—we believe it's Will offering his opinion, when he can." Patting the top of the tin, she turned back to Soren with a dry smile. "And he wasn't pleased when Everin wouldn't apologize to you, so it seems he likes you."

Being liked by a ghost was a new one, but hey, victories were victories. "I think I would have liked him, too, then."

"It's a good thing to have, a haunting." Medwenna pressed a kiss to her thumb, then brushed it over the top of the tin. "People love to whisper tall tales that turn ghosts into something dreadful…something made of teeth and claws and terror. Another kind of monster. But what could be monstrous about loving someone so much, even death can't snatch you from their side?"

A lump formed so fast in her throat, she nearly choked on it. "That, I do believe in."

All at once, Medwenna's fond smile vanished. "You should warn your battlemate."

Those quiet, abruptly cold words stiffened her clean fingers; the towel dropped into her lap, and she sat forward, heart racing. "Warn him about what?"

"The dead in Tallis are different…whatever power he commands over that realm, he won't find it half so pliable there." Medwenna tugged a lock of her hair over her shoulder, the motion not unlike gathering a length of rope. "Hauntings shape themselves by our beliefs. If he believes they are to be feared, they will become something frightful. An open mind is encouraged."

"I'll speak with him about it." But if her mind could only open a crack to the idea of ghosts being real—and capable of throwing candy tins—she doubted he'd even turn the knob. "I'm glad you're here, Medwenna…but I'm sorry you have to wait to be with him again."

The ranger shrugged, releasing her hair to fuss with her empty ring finger instead. "In some ways, it's a comfort. Death can come for me when it wishes. I have just as many people I love waiting for me in death as I have standing beside me in life." And indeed, the smile she gave Soren—or almost gave her, since her eyes were fixed just over Soren's shoulder—was painted with a sheen of peace. "I imagine you must feel the same."

The furious, ice-cold thing taking up residence behind Soren's heart, frozen tines stretching painfully through her ribs, didn't feel like peace at all. And though she couldn't see it, only feel it…in this moment, she imagined it to glow faintly green.

"Right," she lied.

As Medwenna excused herself to go and make sure Everin hadn't picked another fight, that frostbitten creature drove icicles into her center, spearing her aching organs. And with every shock of cold, her fingers wandered closer to her pack…to where she could practically hear Kallias's words leaking from their binding, ink pouring from paper, script taking on the voice he hadn't been brave enough to use for his goodbyes.

No. She wouldn't call it that, a *goodbye.* He might've intended it that way, but she didn't have to play along.

According to Medwenna, this haunting would shape itself according to what she believed. So as long as she *didn't* believe it—as long as she took that goodbye and sculpted it herself, an alchemy of intent that could turn dried ink to wet clay—she could mold it into something else.

An *I won't give up.* An *I'll hold on until you get back.*

Shame tinted that arctic mass from green to blue.

What was she *doing,* picking fights, drawing blood from the one person that might convince King Denali to give them the army they so desperately needed? What did his taunts matter when her brothers were still out there, fighting for their lives, waiting for her to come home?

They'd waited ten years the first time. She wouldn't keep them waiting again.

I know you will survive this, Kallias had told her in his letter. *This, and anything else the gods throw at you. I'm not much of a gambler (unlike Finn, apparently—what's that about?) but I'm betting it all on you. Take back your throne. Take back our kingdom.*

A hollow-boned hand squeezing hers. Night-dusted shadows circling smiling brown eyes. *Do me a favor, little sister—trust me.*

"I'm coming, Kal," she whispered, pulling her hand away from the pack. "I'm coming, Finn. Just hang on."

As much of a prayer as she could muster. And even if she could have come up with something better, the door opened again just as she finished.

Prince Everin leaned partway into the cabin, his other half angled back out like he wanted to run. He rocked back and forth on his heel, shoulders hunched, avoiding her gaze…the most uncomfortable she'd seen him.

"It's just that Kessen already feels like the odd one out," he said to the ceiling, as if finishing a conversation that had been interrupted. "You're sharp, nailing him that fast, but he doesn't need some stranger picking that scab. And Medwenna—"

"Can we just agree we were both asking for it and call it even?"

"Deal." Everin's shoulders loosened in relief. He slapped the doorframe twice, shaking his head with a click of his tongue. "Some swing, Princess."

And when the door shut once more behind him, she found herself smiling down at her sore knuckles.

CHAPTER 27

ANIMA

It only took three weeks from the moment Ani watched the blighted woman fall dead at the altar.

Three measly weeks in this millennium she'd lived—a fleck of leaf litter hidden underneath an expanse of terrestrial refuse, a carpet woven by centuries of autumns.

Three weeks for decay to rot through Arborius's defenses.

Not defenses of military might; those were few and far between, and weapons would do nothing against corruption made corporeal. This defense guarded against traveling illnesses, the sort that hopped from person to person through breath or touch; its name rumbled through the city, and she could've sworn the very roots of the darkwoods quivered at its harsh, solemn ring:

Quarantine.

She hadn't seen a city go from bustling to barren in so short a time since Old Sanctaviv's demise. But this was not a ruin; this was a rescue.

The tree-bridges were cordoned off, dire warnings posted at every exit and entrance in every building. Schools were vacated, children rejoicing at the cancellation of examinations and assignments while their parents shared worried looks, but no words, over their heads. The bravest of pages ferried necessary goods between buildings, outfitted with scarves to guard their noses and mouths and thick leather gloves to protect their hands.

And even so, it was not enough.

For one week, the first patient—the one who'd died at Ani's altar—remained the only victim. Long enough that they'd begun to venture into conversation about the possibility of a one-off, that the quarantine might have come down at just the right time.

On the eighth day, the second victim arrived. And then the third.

By the two-week mark, they were both dead. And more patients joined them one after the other, no one sure where they'd encountered the foreign contagion, no one able to point to a cause before chaos stole their senses.

Three weeks for the infirmary to pack with patients. Three weeks for her kingdom to turn septic, not one piece of it spared this rancid infection.

All her fault. Always her fault.

On the first morning of the fourth week, half the washbins lining the infirmary halls were overflowing with tar-stained rags. And before the sun had risen, it had been *all* the washbins—but Ani had snuck out of her sickroom while ebony pitch still soaked the sky, tying her hair into a sleek knot at the top of her head and stealing the pair of spectacles she found resting on the nightstand. After jamming them on her face—and getting used to the sudden shift in her vision—she went down the lift, praying her *bodyguard* wouldn't show up too early for his duties.

Luckily, no star-streaked hair caught her eye. Humming with the giddy satisfaction of a successful escape, she borrowed a linen half-apron from a storeroom on the lower infirmary floor before marching to the nearest medimancer and asking where she could be of most use.

The elderly man hadn't recognized her or questioned her; instead, he'd handed her a pair of skintight gloves and one of the full washbasins before directing her toward the laundry with a knobby finger.

And that was where she'd been for the last several hours—elbow-deep in hot, sudsy water, raking stained cloths over waterboards and rinsing them until the water came out clear three times over. The constant motion had knocked several strands loose from her bun, and steam had frayed them into an impossible mess, but she hadn't had time to clean her hands and put herself back together; every time she got to the bottom of one basin, three more appeared, carried in by sweating couriers who scrubbed their hands red before running back to the upper levels.

No one looked at her twice; no one dropped to their knees or kissed her soap-sopped boots or thanked her endlessly for deigning to put her hand to such a lowly task. Some couriers smiled at her, exhausted as they were, when they dropped their burdens beside her station; a couple medimancers thanked her when they came to fetch the clean rags, hefting the baskets against their hips and hurrying back to their patients. But these were simple manners, not groveling; what she deserved for lending a helpful hand and nothing more.

Wordless camaraderie connected them, threads spun into this infirmary's well-knit web. Every shared nod and spark of silent understanding put her on surer footing; she marched across the laundry like she'd seen Soren march to conquer battlefields in her memory, her heels taking to the slippery tile like her friend's took to snow and sand.

This was *her* battlefield. And if washrags and soap suds were to be her weapons, she would wield them like none had before or since.

Nevermind that if Brae could have seen her now, prune-fingered and poor-postured and nursing more than one chipped nail, he'd have fallen into fits.

Goddesses do not do their own busywork, he'd fumed when he'd caught her washing a stain from her own shirt one day. *What will they think if they see their deity doing the work of a laundress, Anima?*

They will know I am one of them.

The memory hit nearly as hard as his slap had; it struck her head aside just as well.

A sting lanced her skin like a scalpel; not her cheek, but her palm.

When she lifted her hand from the water, it ran red.

She'd lost her grip on the washrag; preyed upon by memory, she hadn't halted her rhythmic scrubbing in time. A pale weal stretched down the heel of her hand, much deeper than it ought to have been—the waterboard had slit through her gloves and several layers of water-softened skin.

You are not one of them. You are better…you must be better.

She set her jaw against the surge of shame, but her hands moved regardless—to grab one of the clean cloths and wrap it around her palm, hiding the wound before anyone saw it.

You must be better.

By the time she'd emptied out the tainted washbasin, cleaned it, rolled it back, and filled it to the brim once more—all one-handed—the pain had subsided. Picking at the tail of the towel, she unwound it from her palm; her breath whooshed out when she found the skin intact, only a pinkish stain to suggest she'd ever been cut at all.

Her magic was finally settling. And thank Sancta for it—she'd be needing it sooner than later.

Before she could plunge her freshly gloved hands into the near-boiling water once more, another full washbin slammed down just shy of her toes—and she leaped so far out of her skin that she nearly hit her head on the laundry's ceiling.

"Easy! Only me," laughed the woman who'd set the bin down, batting aside her golden-brown hair as she laced her fingers together and stretched forward. "You're buzzing like the beehive I bumped into this morning."

"Princess Sparrow." Ani's muscles all unknotted at once, and she slumped against the basin, bracing a hand to her chest as she tried to steady her sprinting heart. "Rotting roots, you scared me!"

"Sorry, love." Her warm, sheepish smile proved it. "I didn't realize you were here—Wolf's been tearing the tree apart looking for you."

"I guessed as much." She fought a grimace. "I suppose this is the part where you tell me I have to go back to my room for my own safety?"

"You ask me, you're doing more good down here than you would be up there. I don't answer to my big brother." A sly little-sister smile. "If he asks me—for the *fifth* time—I'll tell him I saw you heading to the top floor. That oughta take him some time to scout out."

Gratitude thrummed in her heart. She clasped the princess's hand. "You're a blessing."

Sparrow's cheeks pinked. "Ach, hardly. I just think a woman ought to be able to do her work in peace. If I had a bairn-sitter trailing me every which way while I kept my bees, I'd be hiding in the laundry, too." Blinking, Sparrow peered closer at her—then frowned as she tapped the spectacles Ani had stolen. Borrowed. "Did you take his glasses?"

Mortification swarmed underneath Ani's skin. "These are *Wolf's* glasses?"

Of course they were his glasses—who else had been near her room recently that wore them?

"Well, no wonder he can't find you," giggled Sparrow—then, when Ani made a distressed noise in the back of her throat, the princess plucked the spectacles off the bridge of her nose. "Oh, it's fine—here, I'll take them and hand them off to him. Unless you need them?"

"They were just part of my disguise to get down here." Ani couldn't see, but it *felt* like every inch of her had gone ruby-red. "I didn't know they were his, I swear it on my first and future bones."

Sparrow frowned, looking down at the glasses—then at Ani's fingers. "It must be very strange, to have lived in so many bodies. I can only just make myself at home in one."

"It can be…disorienting." Like when she'd borrowed a pair of earrings from one of the other Arborian princesses, forgetting she hadn't pierced her ears in this body yet. Or when she gripped a pen a certain way because in a previous life, she'd only had three fingers on her dominant hand. Or when her right arm sometimes lifted of its own accord, reaching out to a shade of memory tethered to her side…and found only emptiness.

She hated that one most of all. It never failed to rip open some hidden split in her chest, a geyser of grief flooding every inner orifice until she was left drowning on dry land.

Grief without memory was useless. She couldn't process a loss she couldn't remember; she couldn't heal a wound without knowing the weapon.

"Maybe you should take a break." Whatever Sparrow had seen in Ani's face, it must not have been pleasant, because her eager smile had bent into a more sympathetic shape. "I'll handle Wolf—though you know you could issue him any command you like. He'd follow it without question."

"I would hate to leave them short a pair of hands..."

"Don't trouble yourself," said a different voice—Astrid breezed in through the door, dressed in a cornflower-blue linen dress and one of the aprons Ani had also stolen. Borrowed. "I've got enough hands to make up for you and one extra."

Ani gave a cursory glance over her midsection, just in case. "I'm afraid I only see two."

"She means me," chirped the girl that skipped in after Astrid—Nutmeg, the youngest Arborian princess. Ani hadn't seen anything of her since they'd arrived; according to Wolf, the girl had her own studies to see to most of the day, and in the evenings, they could rarely drag her away from the stables long enough to stuff down supper and sleep before she started it all again the next day.

She would've expected a girl Nutmeg's age to cringe and moan at the mess before them; instead, she eyed the bins with the gleam of conquest in her mossy gaze, carelessly tying her hair back with a cherry-red ribbon.

"I'm Nutmeg," she added, sticking out her hand to Ani—then wincing and dropping into a curtsy. Then lowering her hand, because she'd kept it stuck out toward Anima when she'd curtsied. "Sorry. Ma says my manners are more scrambled than my da likes his eggs. Would you like a curtsy or a handshake?"

"A handshake, absolutely," Ani laughed. "But I've had my hands in vats full of this swill for a while, so maybe later, Princess Nutmeg."

"Fair 'nough. You can call me Meg—everyone does, unless I'm in trouble."

"And how often are you in trouble?"

The girl grinned without shame—looking so astonishingly like Soren Ani had to bite her lip on another laugh. "Never. That's why they call me Meg. Are you hiding from my big brother?"

"Um..."

"Meg," Astrid interjected, "why don't you change out of your riding boots before we get started?" Then, when Meg scurried to do as she was asked: "Well? *Are* you hiding from Wolf?"

"Of course not," Ani said at the same time Sparrow said, "Of course she is! He's driving the poor lass up a tree."

"We can hardly blame him for being concerned." Before Ani's guilt could settle too deep, the diplomat squeezed her shoulder. "But I will speak to him about giving you space, if you wish. I know his intention is not to make you uncomfortable."

"He isn't." Uncomfortable wasn't the right word. "It's only that...if I can help, why wouldn't I? Besides, Sage said light exercise would do me good—he even suggested helping with patients."

"Sage suggested she assist with *mostly healthy* patients," said that very prince—Sage stood in the doorway, looking and sounding rather cross. Had all the Arborian siblings suddenly been struck with the urge to visit the laundry? "Not the patients in *quarantine* with a *deadly, mysterious illness.*"

Ani's cheeks burned. "I'm not helping directly. It's just laundry."

Sage groaned, hammering his forehead with his own fist. "Laundry soiled with a contagion, and you with a compromised immune system, besides! Get your arse back upstairs, Goddess. I see you sniffing around the quarantine area again, you're on bed rest for a week, clear? Meg, you can stay, but I want you gloved up in the next ten seconds or…what? What're you two looking at?"

Astrid and Meg were both glaring at him, the former with her hands on her hips, the latter with her nose scrunched into a flurry of crinkles.

"I'd change your tone if I were you," warned Astrid. "You're speaking to the Goddess of Life."

"I don't care if she's the bloody Goddess of Smiting Mouthy Princes. I'm not going to be the one who tells Wolf I let his goddess go spelunking in a laundry barrel teeming with sick. He's tearing the tree limb from limb looking for you, by the way."

"So I've been told." Ani stripped off her gloves, skimming the boil-off of disappointment from her voice before she added, "I'm due for a break, anyhow— and I should let Wolf know he didn't manage to misplace a whole goddess."

"It would make him a right terrible bairn-sitter. I mean bodyguard," Sage corrected hastily when Astrid jammed her toes into his shin. "Last I saw, he was— oh, shite. Incoming."

"I *heard* that." Wolf's grumble entered the room ahead of him—Sage ducked out of the doorway just in time for Wolf to duck through it, cane in hand.

Not Ani's cane; that, she'd been able to leave behind in her room this morning, her leg finally willing to bear her weight. This one was taller, fit for his frame; the head was carved precisely to match the grip of his palm, and the shaft boasted intricately carved flowering vines.

The eldest prince barely batted an eye when he caught and held Ani's gaze. "I've been—"

"I *know.*" So much for skimming disappointment aside. She stomped from the laundry, tossing her gloves in the nearest wastebasket.

Wolf hurried after her, hot on her heels. "Forgive me, Goddess. I only meant to—"

Like a bursting bud, her temper blossomed out of her control. She spun around, propping her fists against her hips. "Why do you keep *doing that?*"

"Doing what?"

"Asking for forgiveness. You have done nothing wrong—"

"Nothing wrong?" There it was again, that ghostly guilt, the stiff shoulders, the consternation painting his brow in shadowed creases. "Goddess, I—I cannot say that I am not grateful for your discretion and your mercy, but you of *all* people know…"

All at once, his words ran out, a gushing river suddenly dammed—he stared at her, first with frustration, then confusion, then…

Dawning understanding. And behind that understanding…anger.

"You…*don't* know," he said. "You have no idea what I'm talking about, do you?"

She could only stare at him.

When he took a step back from her, the thud of his cane echoed through the empty hallway—echoed through her chest, where her brand-new heart had already started skipping beats. "I thought you were being kind, but you—you *actually* don't know what I'm on about."

She'd made a mistake. She didn't know how, but she knew she had—because now he looked at her with faith crumbling from his amber gaze. A crumbling that revealed something dangerous behind it.

Perhaps she'd reached her limit for *fear* today. Or maybe fear relied on an instinct greater than logic, an instinct that had been put to sleep by the soft clatter of pebbles she carried in her pocket.

But that anger…it did not scare her. It set her at ease.

The unbreakable calm, the undiluted devotion, the endless patience…all of it had set her on edge, because it hadn't felt real. It hadn't felt true. But that anger? That rang with an honest pitch.

So when she said, "I don't. But I'll hear it, if you want to tell me," she did not quail. She did not flinch.

Not even when he started laughing.

"So you're telling me—wait," he said, like she'd tried to speak, like *he* wasn't the one interrupting himself. "Wait. You mean to say that…all those years, all those prayers…" Another laugh, this one so brittle she could've broken it with a feather. "You weren't even *listening?*"

Oh.

Oh, no.

She'd never thrust herself into the archives of her *own* past with such fervor; she'd never torn memory from mind like papers from a desk drawer, ripping apart what little she clung to from the in-between place for a trace, a scrap, a *whisper* of him—any paper-thin sheaf of prayer that had fallen from his lips.

Nothing.

She remembered *nothing* this man had ever asked of her.

"Yes," she whispered—then, at his disbelieving scoff, she pushed more force into her voice. "Yes, Wolf, I listened. I always listened. That's not—it's complicated."

"If you had listened, you would know—"

"Do you remember what I told you?" She didn't remember deciding to take his free hand—she just blinked and found herself holding it, found him staring down at her.

She cleared her throat, ignoring how that stare burned her cheeks.

"When I take a host," she said softly. "I forget things. When I'm not in a body, I know much more—" she knew *everything*, so much it would break her if she tried to hold even a portion of it, a price she freely paid each time she bound herself to mortality, "—but here, as a human, I just…" A helpless shrug. A fluttering gesture toward her head. "Human minds can only hold so much. I only remember so much of living as Soren because this mind is new—it has enough room. But that doesn't mean I never listened—it doesn't mean I didn't hear you. I am…I am *so sorry*—"

Then a thought struck her.

"Wait." She dropped his hand, planting hers on her hips again. An indignance of her own began to well, condensing on the walls of her chest like a greenhouse meant to grow bitter and thorny things. "Is *that* why you've been so stiff and strange with me? Because your prayers were *mean?*"

His throat bobbed. When he spoke again, his voice strained beneath the weight of his words: "My mother used up her last words praying to you. Do you remember *them?*"

Another grief with no tether, a thorn with no stem. A misty visage of dimpled smiles and kind brown eyes and dark freckles; a loving, lilted lullaby cooed over her cradle.

She pretended, sometimes, that the mother she'd lost before her second birthday was still imprinted perfectly on the surface of her mind. But Unlike Cassi, she'd never been a good pretender. The face she saw when she pictured her mother was an approximation…an educated guess built with Braeden's smile, Mora's eyes, Peter's freckles, Cassi's songs.

So despite sharing the loss, she did not share the grief—but it didn't stop her heart from aching, rubbed raw by the devastation he now wore in plain sight. "Wolf…"

"That's a no, then."

"I listened." She didn't know why she was desperate. She didn't know why she was *defending* herself, like she'd had some control over this, like she'd done something to cause that gutted look on his face. The look that gutted her in return. "Wolf, I swear to you, I listened—"

But he did not.

He did not listen—not to her apologies, not to her promises.

With a final breathless laugh…one molded over with spores of an anger so old it crumbled when it touched new air…he dashed his hand beneath his eye, then tucked it into his pocket like it had suddenly gone cold.

And without another word, he turned and stormed from the hallway, leaving her to grapple with his accusations alone.

CHAPTER 28

SOREN

Medwenna could not be still.

Soren's knees itched just watching her; the historian kept starting to pace along the bustling harborside of Craghaven, then stopping. Fiddling with her thin hood, then tucking her fingers away in her pockets. Removing the hood entirely, glancing around for a second or two, then throwing it back on.

After her fifth repetition, Soren carefully inched over and squeezed her shoulder—and Medwenna swung a fist she'd already had clenched and ready.

The impact rattled Soren's hand from wrist to knuckles as she caught the ranger's thrown punch; she met Medwenna's startled-doe eyes over their hands, and the historian squeaked out, "I'm so sorry. I'm afraid—"

"Yeah, I can tell." Soren brought Medwenna's hand down before releasing it. "And so can everyone in this harbor. You need to relax."

Embarrassment powdered Medwenna's cheeks in rose-gold. "Relaxing is…not a primary skill of mine."

Soren resisted the urge to glance at Elias, who stood ever-vigilant at her shoulder; she wasn't sure he'd blinked since they'd departed the ship. "Reminds me of someone else I know."

"Any suggestions, Your Highness?"

"Deep breath in first." When the ranger obeyed, she continued, "Good. Now out, slowly. Controlling it's the key. Breathe in, breathe out…control what you can."

The mantra rolled off her tongue, practiced, heedless of the pain that would come after.

A crunching in her heart; a slicing, a bleeding. Broken glass underfoot.

Another innocent habit honed into a weapon by her mother's memory.

"Why're you so on edge?" Pain warped her voice. "You're being escorted by their golden prince—you're probably safer than I am right now."

Medwenna's throat bobbed.

Soren blinked. "Or…not?"

"Not nearly." Medwenna's tawny hair spilled from her hood as she shot an uncomfortable look over her shoulder—at the castle crowning the crags beyond. "Not many here would dare cross Everin, but…*not many* isn't the same as *none.*"

"You're an Arborian citizen now," Matthias reminded her as he piled his pack—and Medwenna's, and Everin's—onto his back. "Denali's men can't lay hands on you without causing a ruckus with them. Or going through months and months of fiddly paperwork, which I'm sure Lady Thorne would clumsily *misplace* until they eventually gave up."

"There are other paths he and his walk to hunt," Medwenna muttered under her breath. "And plenty of dens where they can bury their kills."

Matthias, to her surprise, rolled his eyes; but tired knowing warmed his voice as he said, "And Everin Arden could walk those paths barefoot in the middle of a snowsquall, eyes closed and ears plugged, without so much as stubbing his runty toe. Anyone numbskulled enough to risk a hunt on *you,* we both know he'll sniff them out well before you snap the snare."

Rose-gold darkened to rose-red as Medwenna tucked her braid back into her hood. "You hush, Matthias Bane, you're going to stir up trouble."

"I flogging hope so." His fixed his eyes on the ranger as she turned aside to check the crowd for Everin's inevitable return from meeting with the dockmaster. "Stones know *someone* has to."

Soren glanced over her shoulder to find Elias already waiting to catch her gaze.

What's that about? his bent brows and creased mouth said.

Not a clue, she replied with a one-shouldered shrug. Far be it from her to try and peel apart the layers of meaning slapped over Matthias's words.

Even if she'd been equal to the task, her buzzing nerves kept distracting her, dragging her focus back to the city built into the mountain beyond.

Not built into the mountain the way Artem's crown city, Igniquit, was; where Igniquit's cityscape sat heavy in the mountain's belly with tunnels branching out like ever-growing veins, Craghaven climbed the stone cliffs like one of the sleek-furred mountain cats she'd seen here and there while patrolling the Nyxian side of the border. The buildings clung to the rock with steel claws, metal supports driven deep into the granite to hold them steady; her stomach took a sharp dive toward her toes as she realized the moving specks miles up the peaks were *people*, not a trick of the sunlight making her vision swim.

"What's the look?" Elias wrapped his arms around her waist and followed her gaze, his chin settling on her shoulder.

"It's just…" Nauseating. Knee-quaking. "Higher than I expected."

"I didn't think getting your memories back would make you afraid of heights."

Had she not been relieved to hear him making light of her Atlas heritage, she would have made light of his jaw…by punching a tooth or two right out of it. "Is this payback for making fun of you for being seasick?"

He nodded against her shoulder. "Yes."

"Wow. Really? Not even going to lie about it? What would…" She glanced around, suddenly aware of their potentially hostile audience. Not a smart plan to invoke the name of a goddess in the open, even in jest. "…Her Sootiness think of that vengeful streak?"

"You've been calling her names since the day I met you. Take a guess."

"Well, why didn't you *tell* me my actions would have consequences?"

"I did." He paused. "And have. Every single day. For five years."

"Almost six."

"You're making my point for me."

"Point taken, then. But you didn't tell me *today*."

"Fair." He kissed her neck before turning to gaze up at the peaks again, frowning. "Hey, Soren?"

She reached up to scratch lightly at the hinge of his jaw, his stubble prickling her fingertips. "Yes, lover?"

"I don't know if you've heard, but your actions have consequences."

She palmed his forehead and shoved him off of her as he laughed; he reeled back, meeting her scowl with a smile that was all innocence. "What? You wanted me to tell you!"

"As soon as we get up to that castle, I'm finding a parapet and shoving you off."

He darted in and pinched her ribs, too fast for her to dodge; before she could throw a blow in return, he caught a fistful of her jacket and pulled her in for a sweet kiss on the corner of her mouth, ignoring how her face scrunched up. "Not if I feed you to a bear first."

"Will you two quit flirting and keep up?" Kessen hollered—her and Elias turned their heads as one to find the redheaded soldier standing with Matthias and

Medwenna several paces ahead. Everin had also returned, glaring at them over the milling sailors and travelers.

"You're on a bit of a tight schedule, if I recall," he called, voice scalding. "Or did you forget when you got lost in each other's eyes?"

She should've taken the time to muster a scathing retort *before* that reminder of duty set her feet to the docks. Because all humor died when they took their first step out of the harbor…a literal first step of what had to be hundreds of thousands from the base of the mountain to its peak.

Her knees twinged just looking up at the gauntlet set before them…and her heart followed suit with the unwanted realization that, if not for Ani working her miracle, she would never have been able to make it to this meeting with King Denali at all.

But because of that miracle, when she set her boot to the steps, she was able to take them two at a time, scrunching her face up against tears as she reveled in the strain. Not a deadly, devouring weakness; just the stretching burn of muscles doing their job.

Intoxicating glee swept through her, a headier buzz than any liquor—in fact, it turned her so tipsy with joy that she bumped Kessen with her hip as she passed, meeting his open-mouthed stare with a wink tossed over her shoulder. "Last one up's a limping deer in wolf country!"

"That's awful, Soren," Elias sighed, pinching his nose as Medwenna warned, "Kessen, go carefully, please!"—but Kessen had already taken off, high-kneeing his way up the steps with the reckless stamina of a boy who'd learned to climb before he could crawl.

That stamina got him four or five flights ahead before she finally gave up, folding herself in half, staring at the cut stone under her soles to center herself.

And to keep herself from looking back.

Even with her eyes glued to the ground, the lack of substance to the air told her enough about how high up they were. And if that hadn't done the trick, the cold would have—the seaside humidity had frozen in her hair, weaving a fragile coat of frost and salt.

A strange itch tickled the back of her leg. Unthinking, tunneled into the blur of exertion and thin air, she bent down to scratch it away.

And the second she put pressure on it, that itch sank its teeth in and *twisted*.

Her knee collided with the stone, but the hot burst of bruising blood beneath the skin wasn't what drove the breath from her in useless bursts. Nor was it the understanding that she'd just broken down on the world's tallest staircase, several miles of carved rock between her and kinder ground.

It was that *twist*—a loop that pulled tighter and tighter, her muscle tied in a better sailor's knot than the snip of rope still nestled in her pocket.

"No," she growled at the ground, bearing her weight on her fingertips, easing herself slowly to her knees. "*No.*" A prayer to her muscles, to her body and all its battered scaffolding, begging it to hold steady. "No more fits. We're healed—she healed us. No more."

But that knot didn't loosen. It climbed; it *pulled*, plaiting more muscle into the braid until it stretched from the top of her ankle to the center of her thigh.

Darkness stifled the world around the edges. Like earmuffs. Like a kiss on the temple. Like falling asleep with a fever.

She'd pushed too far, defied herself to death—soon her nose would burst with blood and her body would try to rip itself apart and what if she didn't come back, what if the light went out and she couldn't find her way home?

Scared, strangled, unable to breathe, she clung on to the step for dear life. *Don't pass out. Don't pass out, don't pass out,* do not *pass out…*

Until a man's voice, decorated in boyish panic, lifted one of the muffs to talk in her ear: "…Know. I don't know. I got to the top and didn't see anyone, so I came back down. I just got here!"

"You didn't see anything?" Elias. "No one talked to her? Touched her?"

"How many times does he have to tell you the same story?" Tumbling gravel, acerbic grit—Prince Everin. "The kid didn't do anything. Lay off."

The image of herself stuck kneeling in front of *him* spooled the last of the woolen darkness in; she blinked color and light back into the world, met with her hands still gripping the stair like one might grip the edge of a cliff. Or the rope on a lifeboat.

"Elias," she muttered, and there he was.

"Talk to me."

"I think…I feel like…" The lump in her throat wouldn't budge no matter how hard she swallowed.

His own throat bobbed as he bent around her, fear glittering star-bright as he raked his gaze over her. "Is it a fit?"

It didn't matter that she'd feared the same. That she'd just been praying to her body to hold itself together; praying Ani's medimancy hadn't been the caulk sticking all her failing pieces together.

Her fears living in her own head was one thing. But when someone else gave voice to them, it gave them substance—it gave them possibility.

"Of course not," she snapped. "It's just a cramp, jackass. Don't make a scene."

He jerked back, brows pinching together; his huff of breath turned to frigid fog. "You just collapsed on a staircase that goes to the pits-damned sky, but I'm out of turn for *making a scene?*"

Hot blood spilled through her cheeks, tingling in the tip of her nose—but not dripping out. "Sorry. Just help me up."

His palm pressed against the small of her back, but his warmth couldn't reach through the wool coat buttoned around her. The unforgiving fabric shrank with every breath, stifling and scratchy—she swallowed and slid her finger beneath the collar, trying to pop it without her battlemate noticing. But the smaller button holding it shut evaded her fingertips.

Panic cracked open like a spring seedling in her throat.

Not a fit. Not a fit.

Elias might've said her name again. Might've said it more than once. But she couldn't tell, not with her heart drumming bass-deep in her ears.

Four fingers shoved into her collar now, clawing, ripping—seeking freedom through sheer force. But the button wouldn't give.

Elias's shout of alarm came too late to warn her—she looked up just in time to see a flash of silver plunge down toward her throat, lean edge gleaming, hungry for blood as it winnowed toward her jugular—

And sliced neatly through her high collar.

Her hands flew to her throat as the split pieces of fabric flopped to either side, ripped fibers and frayed thread turning her stomach strangely. Possibly because if the dagger had aimed half an inch deeper, her *flesh* would've peeled away instead.

Everin loomed above her, impassive as the mountain they stood on. Gave her a lazy blink as he sheathed the dagger.

"Better?" he asked.

Worse. Much, much worse.

An Heir bearing portents of war and treatises of alliance couldn't afford to be seen like this—brought to her knees by a muscle cramp. Strangled by her own coat.

Defeated before even crossing the castle threshold.

She dug her fingertips into the stone, hating its refusal to let her bury herself in it; hating that it let everyone see how her knuckles had gone white; hating how breathless she sounded when she said, "Unnecessary. You gave my battlemate a heart attack."

Everin gave Elias a cursory once-over. "Seems fine to me."

Fine was a hilarious way to describe her battlemate, who was glaring at Everin with his jaw barely holding on to its hinges, thin curls of smoke twirling from his gloved fingertips like wool whizzing into a spinning wheel.

She patted Elias's shoulder; he turned his head toward her without taking his gaze off of Everin. "Seems like overkill, using a dagger to undo a button."

"*Seems like overkill,*" the prince parroted, "ripping out your own throat to undo a button."

A casual swipe of her hand over her neck revealed raised scratch marks.

"Oops." Hopefully her affected shrug looked relaxed; to her, it felt like her shoulder jilted in its socket. "I'm so damned cold, I can barely feel my own ass out here. Is it still there?"

She peered back over her shoulder—stomach tossing as she judged the height they'd ascended, the harbor far below.

"It's still there," Medwenna said helpfully. "Frostbite can definitely relieve a person of an extremity or two, but I've never come across a case of—"

"Medwenna," Everin said, "sarcasm."

"Oh." The ranger's frown whittled her focus to a pinpoint when she aimed it at Soren. "Are you still struggling to breathe?"

She gave the sensible plan—*telling the truth*—a second or two of good, solid consideration before firmly dismissing it in favor of *covering her possibly frozen but still present ass.* "Nope. All good. This mountain air is no joke, huh? I haven't been this high up in so long, I nearly forgot."

Everin's eyeroll screamed his disbelief so loudly, her ears started to ring. "She's checking to make sure you don't have altitude sickness, Princess, not poking at your pride. Suck it up and shoot straight. I'm not dragging your senseless hide up these steps if you drop again."

Her palms prickled, but she did her best charade of Finn's diplomatic smile. "And I appreciate the concern on my behalf. But it's passed—I'm fine to go on."

"Soren…" Elias murmured in her ear.

She slapped the back of her hand against his chest. "I said I'm fine."

His chest rumbled beneath her knuckles. A growl, a groan—some frustrated sound he didn't fully give voice to. But he didn't argue; he settled for cradling her hands as she stood, fingers flexing around them, unsaid words trapped between his gloves and hers.

But those words would have to wait their turn. At least until they were out of Everin's earshot—him and his triad.

Matthias had started off with Medwenna again, the two intently debating the possibility of someone's backside freezing off. But Kessen hung back, slinging guilty looks at her like a handful of skipping rocks.

"Sorry," he mumbled, rubbing the back of his neck as they began to climb again. "My mom always says I'm an awful show-off. Grew up with three big sisters, so I can't really help it."

She snorted. "You call that showing off? Two more paces and I would've had you."

Scoffing, he swiveled to one side, the telltale sign of an impending hip check—then seemed to think better of it, flicking her elbow instead. "Oh, *please.* You were a mile behind me!"

"Kessen!" At Medwenna's scolding call, he went stiff as a soldier who'd just mouthed off to the wrong general. "Stunted stones, let the poor lass breathe, will you?"

"Coming!" Kessen pointed between them both and mouthed something that looked like *knee trash*—or, more likely, *rematch*—before trotting ahead to join his own people.

Giving Elias an opportunity to get a handful of those unspoken words out.

"It's good you stopped." Elias hooked a finger through her sword belt and tugged her closer. "If it *had* been a fit and you'd kept climbing, you'd be in bad shape. You made the right call."

No, she'd panicked—she'd misread her own damned body's cues. Had mistaken a cramp for one of the body-wrecking fits of spasms that had plagued her and Ani for weeks.

And Prince Everin had watched it all. Was still watching from a few stairs up, his mouth set off-kilter, refusing to claim a smile or a frown.

"We can take a pause, if you need," he said, in the plainest tone she'd ever heard him take. "These stairs are no joke—most folks don't take them all in one go."

Oh, *pits* no.

His preening, his ego, his temper—she could go toe to toe with any one of them. But his *pity*? That would kill whatever pieces of pride she had left.

"I just need to stretch this out." She forced her ankle flat to the stone, straightening her leg until the muscle seized—screamed—then finally fully loosened.

A solution in a matter of seconds. A solution she might have employed immediately, had she not fallen into complete hysteria first.

"Sure." She didn't like the lilt in Everin's voice, but he just spun his finger in a cyclone motion as he turned on his ankle. "Sun's dying fast. We'd better chase it while we can."

CHAPTER 29

ELIAS

Thanks to their escort, gaining entrance to Castle Craghaven took nearly no time at all.

Not a word passed between Everin and the host of guards patrolling the castle's grim, heavyset face: at least half a dozen at the doors, and a full dozen lined in measured spans across the parapet. The windows were paned in perfect shadow, but as the sun shooed the dove-gray clouds away, it betrayed what might await behind the dark façade: winks of steel that suggested a crossbow or other distance weapon had already taken aim.

The most heavily guarded fortress in the six kingdoms, if hearsay could be believed. Even Lapis, for all the paranoia its queen steeped herself in, could not compare.

Cavernous did not quite cover the interior of the castle's entryway; the sun painted its soaring sandstone walls in light so warm it stung his eyes like the borders of a bonfire flame. A lush crimson rug rolled down the hall like a lolling tongue, welcoming them into the maw of the beast.

It irked him beyond reason to see Mortem's signature color displayed so boldly in this godless fortress. But like Medwenna, who kept her head down as Everin ushered them all into the bright, open-air loggia beyond, he focused on putting one foot in front of the other.

Not on the bloodred rug. Not on the statues of crowned men posed with their hands and heads held high in conquest, their fists filled with implements of holy status.

Blooming flowers. Lightning bolts. Crystal balls. Even chaos bore some scorn here, the conquering hero's hand overflowing with spiny vines or disturbingly well-carved eyeballs or cloudy white crystal dripping like water through its fingers, all carved from types of rock or gemstone he had no names for.

But more than anything, more than all the others…

Onyx skulls. Garnet flames. Incense sticks and rose petals.

It only made sense for the Kingdom of Heathens to fear the Goddess of Death most of all.

"Elias," Soren hissed in his ear, "cool your heels. You're kicking up smoke."

Damn it. There went another pair of socks—and if he was very unlucky, possibly the pair of boots.

As casually as he could, he fell off to the side, leaning into the grainy sandstone; it scraped pleasantly against his blade callouses, not unlike his housecat slinking her spine along his outstretched hand. Muscle memory guided his thumb over its grit as he lifted his boot, peering at the sole; no scalding, thankfully, but if he pressed hard enough, the softened material gave a bit.

"Sorry," he muttered. "Just…"

"I know." Her gaze flitted back down the hall. "You going to be okay here?"

The question could have mocked, if she'd wished it to. So he trusted the genuine concern in it; and loved her for it, too. Loved her for not making light of how deeply unsettled this all made him. Loved her for the way she assessed him with her sideways seaside gaze, washing away any pretense before he could get a good grip on it.

"It's for Kal." He twisted the lock on grief's cage, jamming it so hard it might never come undone. "I'll manage."

She set one hand over his heart, fingers playing a rhythmless tune against his chestplate. The armor had seemed like a good call for this particular entrance.

For a time, she didn't speak; she just stared at her own hand, fingers slowly tapping to a stop like a storm running dry, raindrops plinking out a funeral dirge for the clouds that created them.

"I have your back," she said under her breath. "I know I haven't been here, but…I'm still your blade. I'm still your army. You know that, right?"

The childlike uncertainty in her voice took his heart, still only partly mended, and snapped it in half over its knee. "Of course I do." He traced a knuckle lightly down the path of her jaw, and she shut her eyes, leaning in. "Where'd that come from?"

"Nowhere." She turned her head to kiss his palm. "Just…been meaning to say it for a while, is all."

Instead of answering, he kissed her, needing to feel the shape of that promise still lingering on her lips. "You know there's no one else alive I'd trust at my back, right? Only you."

Sunbright smiles. Tempestuous glares. "Maybe I'm not your friend, but you are mine. And I don't leave my friends to suffer beneath their burdens alone."

No one else alive, anyway.

Soren didn't answer; instead, she stepped in when he tried to step out, fisting his shirt in her hand, holding his gaze.

"I know I let you down," she whispered. "In the temple. When I said yes."

Golden eyes. Shy, wilting smiles. "That's not very kind."

He teased his thumb down the bow of her lip, because where even the *idea* of touching her in these intimate places had once paralyzed him in the tantalizing gap between terror and need, the idea of *not* having her like this now made him feel a scary kind of reckless. "Soren…"

"Don't tell me I'm wrong."

"Now, or ever? Because one I can manage, and the other…"

She flicked his bicep. "I'm trying to be serious."

And he was trying just as hard *not* to have this conversation. "While I wish we had time to bask in that little miracle, we actually do need to catch up to the others."

Scoffing, she skittered ahead, sticking her tongue out; he blew her a kiss, and she spun with another huff that almost, almost sounded like the girl he'd first met on a snowy, sparkling winter day; a girl who'd pointed at a lonely ring on the back shelf of his mother's booth and demanded he retrieve it for her.

It had taken him too many years. Too many snowy, sparkling winter days. Too many nights gazing at her sleeping face, her empty hand, and imagining how he might finally find the courage to risk everything for an answer. Wondering if that night would be the night his hope for a *yes* might outweigh his dread of a *no.*

I let you down.

But that ring now glimmered like a single star perched on her right hand; a star that carried his every prayer and wish in its silver setting. And he followed it into the heart of the Kingdom of Heathens without looking back.

Even though his spine crawled with maggot-worm wriggles and death-throe shivers, convinced the lifeless eyes of those blasphemous edifices were fixed on his back, searching for just the right chink to stab a blade through.

CHAPTER 30

SOREN

The next handful of hours tumbled past without truly touching her awareness, only a handful of moments standing out clearly:

Getting separated from Elias against her will, Matthias promising to stay by his side while she dealt with *Heir business*. A page stopping Everin in the hall and informing him Princess Raini was away visiting extended family and was not expected back for some time, ignoring her presence entirely. Everin, whose coiled muscles had relaxed after that news, introducing her to one of the ministers who served his father, a snivelly man bathed in cologne; the overpowering stench of strong lavender kept stoking Soren's headache long after the minister left her in the capable hands of the royal dressers to be given something *more suitable* for meeting with the King.

She couldn't guess at what hadn't been suitable about her clothes, unless the King would find the mud on her boots offensive. But the dressers, unlike the minister, handled her with gruff, respectful camaraderie. Though every dart of their needles and eyes suggested a lack of care for anything but pure efficiency, they chatted just enough to keep her mind hovering at the edge of her fears, never plunging all the way back in until one of the dressers put a hand to her back and turned her to face herself in the mirror.

Fear was not the right word for what she felt when she took in the stranger smiling in the glass, lips taut, fists curled.

They'd dressed her in Atlas colors from head to toe.

Vivid aquamarines, stunning sky-blues, and depths-dark navy came together to form an ensemble worthy of a queen: a gown with chiffon skirts that billowed delicately around her like clouds afloat on a summer breeze, never entirely still, not looking entirely real. The armored corset gave her some peace of mind, but even its boning was tinted blue. The gold jacquard jacket they slipped over her shoulders tugged mercilessly at a loose thread in her middle, nearly unraveling her; she brushed her hand over the scratchy texture, flecking a bit of loose gilding off with her thumbnail.

Finn had a jacket sewn from similar fabric, maroon instead of gold. She vaguely recalled opening her eyes in the Atlas infirmary, blood loss and pain-dulling tinctures playing havoc with her head, and seeing it draped over the arm of the chair he'd shoved right up to the edge of the bed, his hands folded under his chin, staring sightlessly at her sheets.

I know it won't be you, he'd murmured into his folded fingers, rocking in place, tapping his foot—unable to be still, just like her. *But will you forgive me if I pretend, just for a minute? I'll go back to grieving you after. I just want to pretend…call it a game, yeah? Play one more game with me.*

She mentally planted her boot atop that memory and ground it down to dust.

This wasn't a game. This wasn't pretend. She didn't have half the imagination her brother did; if there was something to grieve, she'd grieve it. Until then, for the sake of her resolve, she couldn't start thinking that she might be too late. That this silly show might all come to nothing.

She could not play this game with him. But she could play it for him.

"Is it to your liking, Princess?" One of the women leaned in to tug on her misbehaving curls. Soren opened her mouth, ready to tell her to back off—only for that open mouth to drop entirely when the woman's fussing resulted in her curls meekly slipping into place, as if by some unknown magic.

"Tell me your secrets," she commanded, and the woman laughed like she wasn't serious.

"Good eyes, years of practice. Curls like yours, they smell fear, I swear on the stones the earth grew from. You have to show them who's boss."

Soren admired herself in the mirror, her fingers reaching toward a curl, ready to pinch—then thought better of it, lowering her hand before she could ruin this woman's work. Not that it had looked much like work. "I like it very much."

And she did. The colors, the shape, the comfort of having armor wrapped around her middle rather than simple cloth—she liked it all. The little girl she'd once been even marveled as the skirt floated over the floor, promising a truly impressive twirl when she found the time and space to test it.

But the woman she was growing into stared back at her without regard for twirling skirts or armored garments. That woman took in her bent posture and straightened it until her spine ached; she took in the shades of Atlas blue and reminded herself why they were here. *Who* they'd come here for.

"Is there anything else we can fetch for you, Princess?"

She regarded her empty head, no crown to be seen, and muttered, "No. It will have to do."

After that, more pomp and circumstance floated by on small talk's shallow current, a never-ending stream of pretty smiles and practiced words until someone finally whisked her away, explaining she would be joining the prince for a meal before his father summoned them to the throne room.

The silence held as they scaled the heights of Castle Craghaven. Atlas's palace was more of a glorified manor, a host of rooms connected by halls like a walled-in maze; this castle, so heavily fortified on the outside, seemed uncomfortably open inside. If a space had no need of walls, there were none—the open-air loggias that led from one yawning chamber to the next should have been covered in snow or blown leaves, but only pristine white or gray stone met them each time her escort flung open the next set of doors or simply walked through the rounded archways.

Just as the castle seemed to defy dirt and debris, it defied the chill that *had* to be near-unbearable this high up in the mountains—each time she braced herself for buffeting winds and knife-sharp cold, she met only the faintest hint of frost and river and stone.

"It's hard to explain," the guard escorting her said when she finally let curiosity nudge her into asking about it. Hedging, she thought at first—then she took in his bent brows and thoughtful frown.

Gods knew if anyone asked her how Atlas's palace floors stayed relatively sand-free, she wouldn't be able to give an adequate explanation. Maybe he'd never bothered to ask about it himself.

Soren only knew they'd arrived because a hum of voices echoed back to them from the final set of doors—much shorter than the archways and grand entrances they'd gone through up until now—and when she slipped through, she found the space beyond furnished with the same strange simplicity. It smelled of dust and honey, the latter owed to the mead splashing over the lips of stone tankards, its amber tide soaking into the wooden tables as a surprising number of people traded small talk and laughter and an occasional argument. All were dressed in fine clothes, just like her—and seemed at least somewhat uncomfortable, just like her. But she knew the look of nobles when she saw them; these must be the rest of Denali's ministers, a bevy of lords—and *only* lords—he surrounded himself with in order to appear delegatory.

At least, that was what Ravenna had told her.

Another shard of grief she had to crush under her heel. Another thorn to pluck from her heart.

It might have been easier to distract herself if she hadn't been seated at the head of the only empty table, forced to awkwardly fiddle with her napkin ring and pretend she didn't notice the way people kept stealing awestruck glances at her, their mutters rising in pitch with every look.

Little Soleil Atlas, alive. Can you imagine?

Right next door to us, all this time…

Poor girl got her life stolen twice.

It has to be a lie—the gods don't leave survivors.

One word came to her more than any other, carried by so many voices she couldn't hope to block them all out:

Miracle.

She's a miracle.

She wanted to stand up on the table, introduce herself, and see if anyone had any urgent questions for the *miracle* in the room. But instead, she took the nervy energy sparking in her hand and put it toward a less showy pursuit: bending her flimsy fork nearly in half.

"Princess!"

Flicking the tines of the fork with her thumbnail, she swallowed a sigh as she swiveled toward the foyer entrance—

And promptly dropped the fork entirely, its tinkling cry of abandonment ringing out over the suddenly silent room.

No one looked her way now. Something else—*someone* else—had captured the whole of their attention. Including hers.

She swallowed, mouth suddenly bone-dry, as Kessen entered the foyer, his eager wave suggesting he didn't notice the stares—nor did he care.

Probably because they were directed toward the man he was escorting.

When people whispered about Elias Loch, both on and off the battlefield, they often called him a war-wolf: loyal, clever, lethal. Calm on the hunt, but feral when someone drew blood from his packmates. A creature that would lash out without mercy when cornered, dealing wounds that went too deep to mend.

But today, they would not compare her battlemate to any ordinary beast. To any simple creature of the natural world.

Today, and for many days after, they would whisper about when the shadow of death darkened the Tallisian king's door…and how, at the sight of him, the Heir of Atlas dropped her jaw so hard it hit the floor and left a dent in her chin.

Shimmering black velvet clung to him like a second skin; though the sleeves sheathed his arms from shoulder to wrist, arrowing out to a point that ended just shy of his center knuckle, the draped neckline exposed a swath of his muscular chest, which—oh gods *damn her*, had they *oiled his chest?*

Heat blistered through her face like she'd laid out in the sun for hours. She swiped her thumb under her lip to check for drool; none had made an escape yet, but she couldn't count on that. Especially not if he kept walking like he owned the room, chin high, gaze glittering with disdain.

This was an attack. A dirty, underhanded, absolutely beautiful attack she needed to thank someone for. Immediately.

The one mercy her battlemate offered: despite his attempt at a show of cold dismissal of those who glared his way, he couldn't seem to keep his gaze in one spot. Attention made him uncomfortable, and this…well, this was a *lot* of attention. But gods help her, she couldn't even blame them for staring.

"Hello, you," she purred as he reached the table, slinging one arm over the back of her chair. "Come here often?"

He rolled his visible eye, bending neatly at the waist to give her a chaste kiss on the cheek. "First time, actually. My battlemate dragged me into it."

"Hmm." She strummed the string on his eyepatch, then pinched one side of the split in his shirt, running her fingers down the seam, admiring the down-soft texture of Nyxian velvet. "You look beautiful."

His bashful blink told her all she needed to know. "Don't tease me, all right? I didn't pick it."

"I'm not teasing!" Maybe she needed to start complimenting him more. "Elias, honestly. They couldn't have picked anything better. Depths, if there weren't so many people here, I'd already have it off you."

"I'm still here." Kessen leaned between them with a petulant scowl. "You do know that, right? You know I'm still here?"

Soren blinked at him. "Who are you, again?"

"*Now* she's teasing," Elias chuckled as Kessen dropped into the chair at her right, putting on an impressive pout; Elias grabbed the chair on her left and waited while she scooched her chair over, making room for him beside her at the head.

She hadn't even taken the smoky smudge of kohl lining his eye into account yet.

"You look a bit pirate, lover," she murmured in his ear, biting her lip on a grin when he let out a dismayed groan.

"I knew it reminded me of something." He rubbed at the kohl with his thumb.

Soren barely kept her shriek in, seizing his hand in both of hers before he could do too much damage. "Stop! You'll ruin it!"

"That's the plan, yes."

She clung tighter when he tried to uncurl his fingers. "I won't let you take this from me."

He frowned, peering closely at her face, not unlike the way he prodded unfamiliar paths for hazardous obstacles. "Really? This actually does it for you?"

"I'm considering working it into our marriage vows."

"You two are so flogging weird," Kessen muttered, the last word garbled as he shoved an entire bread roll in his mouth, cheeks bulging as he attempted to chew. "Anf uhully I'm the weird one, sho you know it'sh true."

"Quit talking with your mouth full." Everin slapped Kessen upside the head as he rounded the table, snagging the chair at the other end and dragging it out. Its feet shrieked unpleasantly against the floor, and several of the other guests turned to glare before realizing who'd committed the gaffe. They quickly dropped their gazes back to their own plates.

Kessen swallowed—with considerable difficulty—and thumped his chest, coughing out, "I only choked the one time."

"It's not about that. It's plain bad manners." Everin looked up at Matthias as the last member of the triad took his seat, nodding politely to her and Elias. "Matt, you see this kid? Get your house in order."

Matt scoffed. "My house? I didn't see *my* ugly mug in any of the portraits." Everin grumbled under his breath, flapping his hand to mimic a talking mouth as Matthias added, "It's your castle. You deal with it."

"Glad you could join us, Colonel Bane," she called across the table.

He flashed her a winning smile. "Good evening, Princess. You look radiant—you as well, Captain."

"Thank you," the two of them said together—for some reason, Matthias's compliments didn't seem to rile Elias the way Everin's did. He even smiled back at Matthias before engaging him in a conversation about ores and smelting that quickly sprouted feathers and flew straight over her head.

She turned her attention to Kessen instead, who'd already cleaned half his plate and was eyeing the platters lining the table's center as if plotting the best plan of attack. "I once fit a dozen miniature cupcakes in my mouth at one time."

"Flog off," he scoffed. "No you did not."

"Yes I absolutely *did*, and I'll thank you not to accuse me of lying about such serious matters."

Interest dug a thoughtful furrow in the boy's unwrinkled brow. "This sounds like a challenge to me."

"Then get your ears cleaned out." Everin threw a napkin at Kessen's face with impressive accuracy. "I meant what I said last time: the next time you stop breathing, I'm going to let that be that. Let nature take its course and all."

"If she can do it—"

Everin stabbed his fork toward Soren. "*She* has survived an assassination, a war, and a divine possession. *You* almost cracked your skull coming down the stairs too fast about five minutes ago. You are not the same." His silver gaze darted behind her, glinting like a coin flipped into a wishing well, and he added, "Kess, switch sides."

Kessen frowned. "But I—"

"Now."

Kessen took his turn grumbling, kicking his chair back so hard it started to tip over—he whirled just in time to set it right, a blush crawling up his neck as he gathered his plate and hurried to the other side of the table.

"Sorry I'm late." Medwenna slid gracefully into Kessen's abandoned seat at Everin's right; over her shoulder, two—no, *four* Tallisian guards looked to their prince, waiting for his nod of dismissal before they peeled off in various directions, filtering across the other tables to find seats.

If she hadn't believed what Astrid had told her before about Everin's sway over this kingdom, that proved it: for an exiled woman to not only enter the heart of the castle, but to enter *protected,* and without one word of protest from those gathered?

He didn't just hold power here. He had it in a chokehold.

"Shame on you for your tardiness," Everin swiveled in his chair to face Medwenna, tapping his fork against his porcelain plate. "You'd better have a good excuse."

Soren didn't quite know what constituted a good excuse. But at the very least, the prince didn't open his big, punchable mouth even once while Medwenna gave the excuse she had, a story that began with struggling to do up the buttons on her sunshine-yellow silk gown and somehow ended up with her walking the interior gardens for a couple hours, hunting down a particular variety of Tallisian tea leaf she'd been pining after.

If someone had asked her to list Everin's chief personality traits, *patience* wouldn't have come close to making the list. But for this, he seemed to have all the time in the world.

At least, until a man in a different uniform—not the gray-on-gray ensemble of the castle guards, but pure white, not a mark or stain marring it— bent to murmur in his ear. The snow-bright armor worn snugly over his ivory gambeson made no sound when he moved, even when the plates scraped against each other; the light reflected from it in stunning shards of rainbow, chips of beauty cast across the tablecloth like beads tumbling from a broken necklace.

"I want that armor," she whispered to Elias. "Can you make me that armor?"

"No one can make you that armor," he muttered back, eyeing the set with a look nearly as covetous. "It's iridescent iron—only one vein ever found, and they mined it dry a century ago. The sets that were made, they're usually passed through family lines, melted down and reforged to fit—*aaand* you stopped listening. Soren? Hello?"

She jumped at the sound of her name, trawling her attention back to him instead of that whatever-he'd-called-it armor. "I'm listening! Just because I'm not looking—"

"What's that armor called?"

Damn it. "Well, I haven't had a chance to ask its name, but if you give me a minute to introduce myself…"

Elias rolled his eyes. "I don't know why I bother."

The sudden shift of Everin's chair stopped the argument in its tracks; he didn't look alarmed, necessarily, but tension rode the line of his arm as he casually reached over and braced it on the back of Medwenna's chair, turning it to face away from the entrance—to the throne room proper, not back into the hall. "Head down, Winnie, if you don't mind."

The color drained so swiftly from Medwenna's face, Soren tugged her plate back a few inches just in case the ranger fainted across the narrow table. She didn't need anyone swooning into her first meal in weeks that hadn't been cooked in a ship's galley.

A moment later, that door opened to admit two guards and a page. The latter strode to the center of the room, clapped his hands twice, and called out, "My lords, you may enter as desired. As for our guests of honor, I ask that you grant His Majesty a moment to consult with his court before making your entrance. Prince Everin, he asks that you join him now as well."

"I figured, Oskar." Everin hauled himself up with a heavy sigh, bending into his exhale…bending down to Medwenna, to whom he murmured, "Stick by Matt. He's got his orders if things go bad. I've got people already inside, too. No one can touch you."

Medwenna nodded, her smile wafer-thin. "Thank you."

Everin squeezed her shoulder, then cleared his throat, stretching his hands to the ceiling and letting out a pronounced yawn. "All right, then—let's get this over with." He flashed Soren a wink. "Hope you've got your speech ready, Princess."

Her dinner spoiled in her stomach.

She'd lain awake most nights on the ship doing exactly that—reciting her proposal in her head, changing a word here and there, testing out the fit until everything felt foolproof.

But staring at that door, she suddenly couldn't remember a single word she'd ever spoken. With the exception of *Get me out of here right now before I embarrass myself.*

Once the room cleared but for their borrowed entourage, she stood up, her knees suddenly numb. Elias took her hand as they approached the door, pressing a kiss to the knuckle below her engagement ring. "Ready for another grand entrance?"

She snorted so hard one of the guards at the inner door jumped, nearly fumbling his crossbow. Tallis's finest, clearly. "When you're supposed to be dead twice over, you can't really have any other kind of entrance."

He chuckled through that wolfish grin—the one that had struck her so starry-eyed the first time she'd seen it in the sparring circle, he'd become the first new recruit to put her on the ground. And in fewer than three blows, no less. "Then we'll put on quite the show walking in together."

She snorted again—laughter this time.

"Pardon me," interrupted one of the guards, her ruddy complexion paling, "but what do you mean, you're *both* supposed to be dead?"

Soren raised her hand. "Got assassinated, then hosted a goddess in my body."

"Got poisoned by an Atlas viper. Then had my spine snapped by a necromancer." Elias shrugged. "Healed up pretty well, all things considered."

Both guards looked ill. Neither offered further questions.

A few minutes later, the page who'd fetched Everin came back out, shutting the door behind him and halting before her with a bow; when she remembered to offer her hand, he took it, shaking it instead of kissing it. Polite, but not cold.

"I apologize for your delayed welcome, Princess Soren," he said. "It is a great honor to meet you in person."

"Have tales about me really spread so fast?" She prayed her inexperience with finer points of diplomacy wouldn't mangle her manners.

"Many here at the castle have been eager to make your acquaintance for far longer than we've known of your latest exploits." A warm smile. "We've heard much about you from your sister. Princess Yvonne is a well-loved visitor in these halls."

That explained his easy greeting—why he hadn't met her with the wide eyes and dropped jaw of a man meeting a decade-dead royal. Yvonne had made her own excursions out this way plenty of times; Ravenna had even credited her oldest daughter's friendship with Princess Raini for holding Tallis back from accepting a marriage alliance through Prince Kallias's hand when Atlas offered it.

These people knew her as the Third Princess of Nyx, not as the Heir of Atlas.

The *Second* Princess, now that Yvonne was…

"The pleasure's mine," she whispered; good that her manners stayed in this room while her mind fled elsewhere, to the sister who might yet not have any idea she'd ascended from princess to queen. Who might not know yet that she'd been orphaned all over again.

Gods, she envied her that ignorance.

Heat bled slowly through her side, creeping toward her back when the page opened the door for her—Elias's hand, poised to catch her if she stumbled.

She reached behind her and caught that hand, forcing his fingers to relax as she wound hers through them.

His resigned sigh smelled like kicked embers. But he didn't argue, out loud or otherwise—he just squeezed her hand once. Then again, a bit tighter, when she ran her thumb over the back of his empty ring finger.

Old habits died hard, some said—and so had the two of them. It would take time.

The quiet struck her first as she entered the throne room: every snuffle, every footstep, every rustle of clothing stuck out, because no one seemed willing to whisper or gossip or giggle. The lords lined the walls in double-file; walls that were more like waterfalls, streams gushing from a gap between the seams of the stone walls and the stalactite-toothed ceiling. They tumbled into a basin shaped like an upside-down U, a self-contained river that followed along one wall, curved behind the dais, and hugged the opposite side.

Seven long, broad steps separated the flat of the dais from the floor. On the middle step sat Everin, one knee cocked up, eyes glazed with boredom thicker than cinnamon bun icing; and at the top of the dais, King Denali Arden watched from his throne like a lion lounging across a stone slab.

His lazy slouch mirrored his son's exactly, his golden-furred cape draped over the arm of his throne. He did not share the silver sight of his son, but there was nothing plain about the way his pale blue gaze seized her and did not let go. Sweat trickled down her back as he studied her from head to toe and up again; not the demeanor of a king measuring up a potential equal.

That look measured her in a way that diminished, that doubted; it shrank her soul until her own skin felt like a poorer fit than ever.

But she did not have time nor the skill to tailor it; so she pinned all the shrunken and sagging places with a fist pressed to her heart, a pressure to force her pieces back together.

Follow the rules. Play the part.

"Thank you for accepting our request for an audience so quickly." And thank the gods her voice rang out without a hitch, so clean and confident she nearly didn't recognize it. "As I'm sure you've been informed, the situation does not leave much time for due process."

"He has," said Everin, "but best you share the story yourself. Tales told second or thirdhand are not always favorable."

Luckily, telling the tale was the easiest part. By now, it was merely a matter of removing or adjusting certain details, and she'd practiced that plenty in the days leading up to this.

It was the hush afterward that her heart bucked against, counting the seconds the Tallisian king absorbed her recital and request in perfect silence. It was the impassive looks traded between him and his son, unyielding as the stone they stood or sat upon, that tightened her sweat-slick hand around Elias's, her fingers trying to slip out of his grip with every twitch.

"You," said King Denali—the first word he'd spoken. But he wasn't looking at her anymore—he was eyeing Elias in a way that set her hackles on end. "You're to be king of Atlas by marriage, then, yes?"

Elias's turn to squeeze her hand. "Yes, Your Majesty. King-Consort."

A grin split open across the King's face. A cringe flexed through her muscles; she shrugged it off as he mused, "A Nyxian man on the throne of Atlas, after a decade of bloodshed. Imagine that. Not the most conventional way to win your war, boy, but a clever one."

"This has nothing to do with the war between my kingdoms," Soren cut in. "We are well beyond that conflict and have been for some time. I speak for both now."

The King did not even spare her a second look. "Tell me…Captain Loch, you said? Should we find ourselves in a position to offer aid, to which kingdom would we be providing a treatise?"

Elias blinked, then looked to Soren, his teeth worrying the inside of his cheek. "As Princess Soren has told you," he said slowly, loudly, like the King might not have heard, "she is the Heir of Atlas and Second Princess of Nyx. She comes with the blessing of Queen Yvonne—" A tiny fib, one her sister would know to play along with if it reached her ears, "—and also has the support of Queen Genevieve Olivander. Both can confirm our—"

"Father, if I may?" Everin interrupted, finally rising. When Denali extended a hand, offering his son the floor, Everin turned back toward her. "Princess Soren, you've requested aid in ousting a pretender god from this world—a summons we as a kingdom cannot ignore. It is our highest calling…and has been from the very inception of our bloodline."

At that, the lords broke their silence; some nodded, others clenched fists, and some even murmured their assent. A rousing that cleared the fog from the eyes of figureheads.

"This isn't a matter of whether we wage this war." Everin reached up and freed one of his axes from its sheath, holding it before him like a scepter. He caught and held her gaze. "It is a matter of whom we wage it beside."

Whom. Pretentious ass. Had he practiced that with Medwenna beforehand?

"So when you propose alliance," Everin continued, "what are your terms? What do you request we give? What do you offer in return? And why should we fight beside you to free Atlas rather than claiming it for ourselves?"

Had she and Elias not guessed this would come up, she might have lost herself in the horror that drove a chill past flesh and bone, ice clustering in her core; had one of Everin's fingers not bent twice, a twitch that could have meant nothing, she might have thought them betrayed.

Instead, she took two steps—one forward, one to the right. Putting herself slightly in front of Elias; forcing herself into the King's eyeline.

Everin's finger stopped twitching.

"We request numbers," she said, "and individuals willing and able to prepare less experienced reserves in Arborius for heavy combat. We offer the chance for you to do what you have wanted to do for generations: rid this world of the gods." All but one or two, anyway. "You have seen how fiercely Atlas fights for its causes; and while your conflict with Artem remains at a standstill, from what I've heard, that is not a situation you are entirely pleased with. Should war come to visit your kingdom again, you will be glad to have us as allies."

"Name the number," Everin prompted.

This, she could name without thinking. "Three battalions, at minimum. But the more the merrier."

Everin didn't blink. Maybe he'd already done the math, too. "Anything else?"

"We also request that, should you agree to ally with us, you come armed with every weapon in your arsenal." Heavy, careful emphasis on *every*. "We request that you retrieve the god-killer."

A clipped guffaw from the King. He relaxed back into his slouch, what little interest he'd shown guttering out. "*That* little myth is still making its way around the kingdoms, is it? What other fairytales did your parents bore you to sleep with, girl?"

Tension spidered up her back, spinning its web between her shoulders. "I have heard it from many mouths—" Ugh, that sounded clumsy, but it was too late to rephrase now, "—and I would deem most, if not all, trustworthy on the matter. My brothers' bodies have been taken by Tempest and Occassio, as mine was by Anima—their survival is paramount."

"Oh, I see." King Denali let out a sigh, soaking it in utterly saccharine sadness. "Poor girl. I don't mean to be cruel, but your survival, while wondrous…it is hardly the norm." He *chuckled* as he shook his head. "I hate to say it, but your brothers are dead. That you did not precede them…well, I commend you for it. The gods never leave survivors."

Until right that second—watching the King laugh once more as he helped himself to a glass of amber liquid—it hadn't occurred to her that the slump in his spine and the glassiness of his gaze suggested anything other than perpetual boredom. That his disinterest was a thing she could break with the right turn of phrase.

It hadn't occurred to her that the King of Tallis, who held the fate of both her peoples and both her families in his hands, had shown up to this negotiation already unwilling to entertain the idea that her survival could be replicated. That he had so little intention of hearing otherwise that he'd shown up already drunk.

Drunk.

She hadn't gotten a wink of sleep, had hardly eaten, her appetite and exhaustion driven out of her by fear for her family; she'd clawed through training and battle and bloodshed, devastation and possession and her own damned humanity, had left friendly shores and her friend behind on them, endured his damned son for weeks aboard a ship, all to stand before him and lay down her pride at his feet, to *plead* for his help, and he…

Girl, he'd called her. Not *Your Highness*. Not *Princess*. Not even *Officer*, the only one of her titles she'd actually gods-damned earned.

And he *still wouldn't look at her.*

Her hand slid into the folds of her borrowed dress.

And when the butterknife she'd stolen from their table sailed into the seam between the throne's cushion and frame, barely an inch shy of his left eye, she couldn't help but think how utterly appropriate it would be when she got killed for making a point.

Her wrist got yanked into someone's iron grip before it could even fall back to her side; Elias shouldered his way between her and whoever had grabbed her, but she thrust out her other hand, warning him to stop.

Never looking away from the throne. From the man who treated her family's fate like a *joke*.

King Denali's eyes darted from her hand to her face, shock morphing into fury faster than a flame twirling up a dry wick.

That was fine. She didn't fear fire anymore.

"Do not laugh at me," she said quietly. "My people are dying. My family is in chains, both human and divine. My mother is dead. *Do not laugh at me.*"

"You are certainly possessed by *something*," thundered Denali, yanking the knife from his throne as he rocked to his feet—not entirely steady, which only dumped oil on her temper, "if you think you think you can threaten me, command me, and disrespect me in my own castle, girl."

"Apologies." Her purr rumbled through the backs of her gritted teeth. "I didn't realize the Mountain King could be so easily cowed by a bit of loose silverware."

Denali lurched down the steps, fist raised. "If you think you've tasted death already—"

"Father!" Everin thrust into the King's path, catching him with an arm across his chest—he met his father's wrathful look with an easygoing grin, chuckling like he'd just told a lovely little joke. "Forgive her…and me. I may have put the princess up to a little mischief, that's all." He met Soren's gaze—his smile grew, but the narrowing of his eyes sent a different message. "She's been a good sport, but I'd hate to see her suffer any real consequence on my behalf. I didn't believe her when she said she could strike a target true with any weapon I set in her hand—a mistake I won't make again."

Play the part. Play the part.

But she couldn't unstick her face from whatever truth it showed. No matter how she tugged, her lips wouldn't stretch into a sheepish smile; nothing could cool the reckless, righteous anger pumping like poison through her veins.

If he mocked her again—*her*, whose mettle had been tested against death and found death wanting, for whom the word *miracle* had lost all meaning—she didn't think she'd mind the consequences of what she'd do next.

But then she remembered the man at her back. The man who would do his damnedest not to let those consequences fall on her—and in doing so, might be the one to take them instead.

She was not a miracle of her own making. Too many had sacrificed themselves to make each of her survivals possible. And though death only kept the loosest of grips on her battlemate now, she didn't trust it enough to test it—not in a kingdom that claimed it could kill the unkillable, even if its own damned *King* refused to believe as much.

So she smiled sweetly at the King of Tallis, tasting honey, smelling smoke. "Your son swore to me your sense of humor would prevail."

The King squinted, liquor muddying the shifting emotions in his eyes; then, with a forced chuckle, he clapped a hand over his son's wrist. "Be careful of agreeing to such schemes. My boy picks the riskiest peaks to climb, and he doesn't always see where the footholds stop."

She couldn't tell which of them that threat was truly meant for—if not both. But at the very least, the castle guard released her wrist, returning to his place at the back of the room.

"I do not make light of your troubles," King Denali went on, condescension thinly veiled by false compassion. "And judging by where you came from, I can guess *exactly* who handed you the notion that such a weapon may exist here. But I fear you are only the latest of many to find false hope in a lie—a fable certain fools like to dress up as fact."

Everin's fingers flexed.

"I see," she said. *I see your sycophantic sharkshit.* "Regardless, my other requests stand. Tenebrae will not be content to stop with us—he will come for you, and soon. Frankly, knowing your history, I wonder if he hasn't already begun."

This time, the collective shiver that ran through the listening lords carried a concern that ranged from uneasiness to outright paranoia, some immediately turning from side to side to search their neighbors' faces. Like golden eyes might make themselves manifest at the mere suggestion of divine presence in this hall of heathens.

The difference between those who'd been told which foes to fear and those who had come face-to-face with them. When you'd only heard stories of wolves, you searched for fangs in every mouth.

Not every set of teeth was eager to bite. But fear made wolves of everyone.

"Let him come."

It had been a while since she'd heard idiocy so pure from someone who wasn't her. So it took her a couple moments to realize King Denali wasn't testing her gullibility with a "joke" of his own—she even looked to Elias to double-check, but his disbelieving stare confirmed it.

"Your Majesty?" Not her best retort, but he'd struck her so dumbfounded, it was a miracle she'd even remembered his proper title.

"Let the God of Chaos come—let him and his bring their war to our mountain. It will be their downfall." The King stepped back up to his dais, snatching up his glass; he drained it, slamming it down so hard on the arm of the throne that the base shattered, leaving him holding a ring of jagged glass. He marveled at it, turning it from side to side before looking down his nose at her. "I am flattered you traveled so far to beg this of us; and I will not lie to you, the prospect is intriguing. Every Tallisian king has dreamt of such an opportunity…to draw blood on one of those so-called *gods*." His fingertips danced on the broken glass, nails clinking in maddening repetition. "But intrigue does not feed and clothe an entire army. You offer nothing, yet ask for everything; and as you've said, the fight will one day come to our door regardless. Why waste time trying to fish Atlas out from trouble of their own making when we could use that time to prepare for the coming assault?"

A waste. Her kingdom, her family—a *waste.* "That is not what I—"

"I have heard your plea. You have heard my answer. You are a princess of two kingdoms without an army to show for either one. Tallis will not commit itself to a hopeless cause." A girl, the first Soren had seen in this room, scurried up the dais with a new glass, this one sloshing with wine darker than old blood; Denali traded the broken glass for the new one, ignoring how the girl flinched as he shoved the ring of shards into her hand. Droplets of spilled scarlet—both wine and blood—melded as they trickled down her wrist. "But by all means, stay the night before making your way home. Everin, you'll see to their lodging."

Panic pushed a protest out of her before she could even script it out. "But I—"

"Your Majesty—" Elias stammered at the same time, but Denali was through paying attention to anything save his wine glass—and she had already used the one projectile in her arsenal.

Before she could muster up both the breath to shout and the words to make sure she didn't waste it, they were escorted out.

With no army. No alliance. Not even a promise of consideration.

She had failed.

CHAPTER 31

ANIMA

For four days, Ani had no shadow.

Not for lack of trying—though Wolf himself did not appear at her door, nor did she see him around the infirmary, she had a run-in or two with a pair of Reapers he'd sent to do his job for him. The first time, they'd given her the most awful excuse for his absence and their resulting presence…that he had a *mild illness* and would be *indisposed for a bit*.

She'd almost crumbled…almost sought him out right then. In a land struggling under the burden of Blight, her mind didn't hear *mild illness*…it heard *rotting bloodpaths* and *spilling ichor*. The sort that destroyed offerings and turned water toxic.

But the Reapers insisted it was nothing. And considering it couldn't be nothing *and* something severe enough to keep him confined to his chambers, she had to assume the entire story was an excuse to give her the silent treatment.

Luckily, she had learned something from Soren about being petty. And if the prince was going to give her the silent treatment—and feign sickness, of all things—she wasn't going to give him the satisfaction of hearing about her daily doings from others.

After the fifth day dodging those Reapers—a long day spent working with blighted patients, the number of which had finally stabilized after Arborius's well-oiled quarantine efforts, holding steady at roughly a hundred individuals in the throes of fever and agony, their organs shifting where they ought not to be, their skin literally crawling with pitch-dark veins spreading just beneath the surface—Ani wanted nothing more than to sleep.

But instead of rest, the memory of that affliction curled around her mind…bloodpaths that looked far more like thorny brambles. One patient couldn't close her eyes because the thorns had sprouted between her lashes; nor could she cry, though the sobs ripping fistfuls of breath from her lungs should have brought on a deluge. Instead, she stared endlessly at the ceiling, her lids held open by sticky scraps of gauze while medimancers and physicians took shifts standing vigil, dripping false tears into her eyes to prevent additional pain.

Another had perished early that morning—the first of Ani's personal losses, and not likely to be the last—with his teeth overgrown and curving backwards until they cut into the roof of his mouth. When they'd taken him away and investigated his insides to track the source of his demise, they'd found his liver had shoved itself into his chest cavity; one kidney had been found in his stomach, half-digested despite the gaping hole in the organ wall; and one of his ribs had grown, curving into a grotesque spiral until it finally pierced through his heart.

She had covered his sewn-up body with a blanket, whispering sorrowful apologies to the shroud for his needless suffering. Gripping the edge of the examination table to stop her shakes. Dazed by visions of *pale cheeks dappled in blood, pale hair torn from its skull-tight braids, pale lips breathing their last* like she'd breathed in a huff of anesthetic vapors.

And then she had moved on to the next patient.

It was the way of things in infirmaries, at least during outbreaks like this one. No time to weep, no time to grieve…no time to stop. Instead, you pretended to forget their faces—knowing you'd dream over and over of what you could have done differently—and moved to the next, tying on the same smile you'd greeted the last patient with.

It had been…*so* long since she'd worked in an infirmary ward. These couple days had aged her a hundred years.

That was how she returned to the rooms set aside for medimancers and physicians who worked for days at a time: heartsore, skinsore, and desperate for the creaky cot she'd been sleeping in since her argument with Wolf. But when she flopped facefirst onto the bed, a soul-weary groan towed out of her like darkwood roots ripped from the ground, she didn't find herself smothered by musty cotton and goose down.

Instead, paper crinkled under her face, her lips pressed to the flap of an envelope. When she pulled back, she found a juniper-green envelope half-crushed into the pillow, its silver wax seal separated and smooshed into the paper.

"Rotting roots," she muttered, tearing it open and squinting through the shadows in the windowless room to make out the small, elegant script:

You are cordially invited to join the Arborian royal family for supper.
No rush and no obligations—come when you can, eat what you like, go when you must.

She studied the clock on the wall—six chimes past noon—then looked down at her pillow, the head-shaped indentation in its middle practically cooing sweet nothings in her ear.

An ear that still rang with the wails of her dead patient's son when she'd broken the news to him.

She had so little appetite. But dinner and conversation had to be better than nightmares and death…and maybe she'd get the chance to apologize to Wolf, who hadn't shown his face since accusing her of being an absent goddess.

She hadn't expected to notice *his* absence, let alone that it might pinch in ways she wasn't familiar with. The reliability of his presence had become an odd comfort; without it, everything felt like that first morning she'd opened her eyes in her new body…off-kilter, out of place, setting her ill at ease.

If this helped her regain her balance, she wouldn't mind putting off sleep another hour or two.

She spent the first hour making herself presentable for dinner in royal company.

The sleeves of her pale pink gown hugged her arms, sheer as mosquito netting; beaded flowers and elegant vines dangled down the skirt and climbed the sleeves and bodice, the thick applique crusted over the gown like sparkling frost on early spring petals. The hem of the heavy tulle skirt danced across the floor, silent as it dusted the surface of the shimmering opalescent tile that led her to the dining hall. She'd even washed and fixed her hair, tying the frontmost sections back and pinning them in place with a rose-gold comb.

She did try to put on a pair of heels, but the balls of her feet ached too deeply from standing and walking all day long. Luckily, her skirt covered the soft slippers she'd chosen instead.

The setting sun aimed spotlights at the chips of color embedded in the floor, and those spotlights bounced back—they fractured into thousands of rainbow dewdrops condensing on the ceiling and walls, a rain refusing to fall. If she hadn't been sweating badly enough to must up the dining hall if she dallied much longer, she could've spent an hour craning her neck back to stare at them. Pieces of a discarded daydream scattered to the skies.

Cassi would've loved it. She would've dismissed the idea of dinner altogether and laid flat on the floor, flashing the cheap rhinestones lacquered on her nails to add new performers to the intangible ensemble.

But her empty stomach wouldn't allow her to indulge. Instead, she approached the arched doorway at the end of the hall; the guards stationed on either side didn't wait for her to offer an explanation or flash her invitation before they hastily seized the wrought-iron handles, bowing their heads nearly to their chests as they hauled the two halves of the door apart.

Their swift action made her stomach drop. The sight of people scrambling before her was…tedious? Uncomfortable? What would Mora have called it?

Disconcerting.

"The Goddess of Life, Anima—" announced the guard to her left—but her name dropped off sharply at the end, and when she peeked to the side, she found him staring across at his fellow guard…stalled by what appeared to be panic. The other guard shrugged wildly—then caught Ani peeking and froze, pretending to cough into one hand and swat a fly with the other.

"Is there a problem?" Ani prompted.

The guard who'd started to announce her jumped as if she'd screamed in his face. "It's customary to announce a family name. I apologize…I don't know yours."

Because they had so rarely given it after coming into their power…and *never* gave it after their ascension. Few would have connected the name *Medeis* with the gods.

"I have no family." She'd never told a lie that tasted so much like a truth. "You did it perfectly. May I enter?"

The guard went redder than the one fine dress Mora had kept from their mother's things, nodding as Ani swept into the room.

Anticipation soared as she gathered the faces around the table…and crashed into disappointment, pure and sickening as a mouthful of sassafras syrup, when she realized Wolf was not among them.

She also realized she was *grossly* overdressed—even the slippers were too much. Most of them wore sweaters and soft leisure pants, none wore shoes, and Sage looked halfway asleep even as he opened his mouth in silent request— followed by Astrid feeding him a grape. The blonde diplomat, at least, had worn a gown as well; though simpler in design, the rich turquoise silk set her eyes off beautifully, flattering the golden tone of her skin. The neckline was modest, cut in a shallow, wide *V*, flowing seamlessly into off-the-shoulder sleeves. The expensive fabric rustled as she shifted toward Ani. "I'm glad you came. Please, sit."

Cassi would have killed for that dress, or even a bolt of the silk…not after they'd taken on the mantle of godhood, but before, when she'd been a talented tailoress working in one of the upper-crust modistes in Sanctaviv proper. For all her elder siblings had sacrificed to keep them from sinking into absolute squalor, Cassi always brought back the heaviest coinpurse…even though Peter and

Braeden came home caked in mud and bruises, muscles too sore and stringy to lift their own plates for supper, and Cassi came home with nothing worse than needle-nipped fingers and strained eyes from staring too closely at her stitching.

And, every so often, a stiff neck from staring constantly over her own shoulder.

"Ani." Astrid's voice prodded her back into the present. "Is something the matter?"

"No." She gave herself a mental shake, straightening her posture and playing her best game of graceful goddess yet in this body. She arranged her seat on the bench like she rode sidesaddle, plucking at her skirts until they lay smoothly over her knees. "It was just a long day in the infirmary. I…I lost a patient."

The demeanor of each Olivander banked sharply sober…except for Sage, who just nodded, handing Ani an empty plate. "Fill that up. If I can still see porcelain when you're done making a plate, you're not done."

The spread lining the entire dining table didn't resemble the sophisticated feasts she'd indulged in at other palaces across her many lives; every dish on the table looked distinctly homemade, served in hand-thrown cookware that bore a different pair of initials on each handle. *CO*, *SpO*, and *OO*.

The food itself was just as rustic: mashed potatoes smothered in fresh gravy, roasted chicken with the skin still on and the bones still inside—she refused to let that turn her stomach—crusty bread that steamed every time someone reached over to rip another hunk from its whole, a medley of vegetables that smelled fresh-picked and home-grown, and at the very end, a chocolate cake messily frosted and dotted unevenly with raspberries.

Once her plate was full, Ani slid into her own seat. "Will Prince Wolf be joining us?"

Every single one of them—even Nutmeg—fell silent, exchanging a flurry of looks.

"I'm afraid he hasn't felt well for the past few days." Astrid dabbed her painted lips with her napkin. "Nothing serious, but with this Blight going around, he and the Queen agreed he shouldn't take risks. He told me he sent his regrets, and replacements…did either arrive?"

"It seems not." Those poor replacements. They'd been chasing her like a wild goose for days. "Is there anything we can do? I'm happy to lend my—"

"No," Sage interrupted hastily. "Thank you, Goddess, but Wolf is a mighty grouch when he's unwell. Better to leave him be. He'll be right as rain in no time."

That did not assuage her concern. Or her frustration.

For a time, the conversation took smoother trails. The cousins badgered her for every detail she knew of Soren and Elias's relationship—their meeting, their friendship, their romance. The proposal (the proper one, not the deathbed one) especially captured Nutmeg, who clasped her hands to her chest and sighed longingly…Astrid, too, though her smile seemed more sad than sappy.

Out of nowhere, Nutmeg's attention winged to an adjacent—but far less simple—subject.

"What about you?" she asked eagerly.

Ani swallowed her next bite sideways, choking it heavily down. "What about me?"

"You've had so many lives—you must have the best love stories." The little girl's gaze gleamed with unbroken dreams. "Tell us one!"

Now she might choke for a different reason. "Oh. Um…I hate to disappoint, but I'm afraid I don't have *any*, let alone many."

"Don't be shy," Brook urged. "You're in safe company. None of it leaves this room."

"It's not that." She fussed with a lock of her hair, studying the pattern in the tablecloth. "As I told Prince Wolf—"

"You and *Wolf* were talking about love stories?" Sparrow's eyes were wider than a midday summer sun.

"No, no." Coffin crush her, this discussion was catching root rot faster than an overwatered houseplant. "He asked a different question, but the answer was the same. I—I don't remember. I don't keep much from my previous lives when I take a new host. And from what I do remember, I don't believe I ever, um…dabbled."

"Oh, you should've said!" Sparrow's gaze lit up. "I can't believe Wolf didn't tell you—Arborius has fabulously kept records of you and your hosts, specifically. Your journals are shelved in the shrine—Brook and I have read them all!"

Ani's hands lost all feeling. Her fork clattered to the table. "My—"

"She's right," Brook chuckled. "And so are you, mostly—you don't have many stories. But you *were* married once."

Had she not already been sitting, she would have fallen.

"Who…?" The breathless whisper barely found her own ears.

"You were living as an Arborian woman…Orchid Viviane. She was born with an incurable illness. The physicians and medimancers gave her five years, even with intensive care—but thanks to the innovation of her medimancer mother, Orchid lived much longer than anyone expected." Brook paused to take a sip of water. "She lived until she was just a couple years shy of thirty, when her condition took a sharp downturn. Knowing she had only a handful of days to decide the direction of her demise, she chose to offer her body to the Goddess—er, to you—guessing your power could do what the medimancers could not."

Sparrow held her fork up like a lecturer's baton, picking up where her sister left off. "Now, Orchid was born into a family that immigrated to Arborius a generation or two earlier, and they had enemies abroad with long memories. That, along with her condition, encouraged her parents to bring a bodyguard on staff for her…a man named Alder Finch."

A bodyguard.

A set of stairs. A dagger in her heart. A sprinkling of white in a young man's beard, an affliction he claimed had been caused by her own clumsiness.

"According to your journals, Alder's devotion to Orchid did not end with her death. He refused to be dismissed, and he served as—"

"Sparrow." Sage's voice carried, despite being much softer than his excitable sister's. "Let's give her a moment."

Sparrow frowned at him, then looked to Ani—and her face dropped. "Oh. I'm…my apologies, Goddess. That was thoughtless of me."

"No apology owed." She hoped her numb lips obeyed her command to smile. "Your memory is commendable, to remember all that just from reading it. Both of you."

Sancta strike her down, she was just *saying* things—none of which reflected the questions Sparrow's story had seeded in her mind.

She stood up, nearly stumbling as she swung herself back over the bench. "Forgive me, but I've spent much time in Prince Wolf's company these past few days, and I fear I'm beginning to feel a bit unwell myself."

"Ani, we're happy to talk about something else," Astrid offered, but Ani put her hand out, shaking her head. Hoping nothing else was shaking.

"It's not that, honest," she lied. "I'll join you all for dessert later on, if I can."

If they raised more protests, she didn't hear them…not over the echo of *You were married once* droning in her head over and over. A bell tolling without the help of a tender.

In the moment, all that drove her steps was the need to flee—to get away from those pitying looks and intimate stories about her life handed down by a stranger.

But the closer she drew to her room…the more her steps slowed.

If she holed up in her room for the night, she'd just keep *thinking* about this. That bell would continue to ring until every nook and cranny in her mind pealed with the sound, unable to tell if it tolled a wedding song or a funeral dirge.

She'd just keep searching fruitlessly for a name she'd never heard, dreamed, or held until now.

Whoever he was, he'd never been *hers*—he'd loved and been loved by an entirely different woman. There was no sense in grieving something she'd never known.

But sometimes the body didn't care for the mind's good sense. And judging by the confusing tangle of emotion constricting every beat of her heart, a coil of snakes nesting in her chest, her body planned to do what it pleased with this information.

She needed a distraction. She needed something else, *anything* else, to worry about.

Which was how she ended up stopping the first member of the Olivander family's staff she saw, asking after the location of Prince Wolf's chambers.

CHAPTER 32

ANIMA

Prince Wolf did not reside in the same portion of the tree as the rest of his family.

By the time she climbed to the second-highest floor, she was bent nearly in half, wheezing like a lung infection had slipped in between the ground floor and this one. But somehow, she still had breath left to lose when she looked up from the landing to find a singular door waiting for her, so tangled in ivy vines she could barely see the wood beneath, let alone find the knob.

Surely he couldn't leave his door this overgrown on purpose. Not unless he never received guests.

Or he'd purposely trained these plants to prevent an easy entrance.

When she eventually did free the knob—after painstakingly unraveling the vines around it, mouthing silent curses as she crooked her finger around each stem and guided it free—she stuck her hand in first, rapping her fist on the inner wall.

"Ma? Is that you?"

Not the same strong, syrup-smooth voice she'd grown used to—a low, muttered mimicry, robbed of the intensity that had struck her silly and stammering more than once since they'd met.

"It's Ani," she ventured, sliding past the seam in the door. "May I come in?"

She heard no response. That pesky weed of concern dropped seeds and spread, the sprouts fanning out their prickly leaves until her whole center stung with worry.

Wolf's chamber was a home in its own right, and from what she could see—which was very little, as the only light came from the dwindling sunset—she stood in its foyer.

"Prince Wolf?" Shucking off her slippers by habit, she explored her surroundings with the tips of her toes until she found the edge of a macrame rug; then she set her shoes down, counting herself through a ten-second breath to calm her nerves before she hiked up her skirts and carefully pushed further in

Beyond the short, narrow corridor connecting the foyer to the rest of the space, it opened up like a yawning mouth. And in the light of the lanterns, the flames within fluttering soft as moth wings…

Ani almost forgot entirely what she'd come here to do.

This chamber was not particularly grand, nor particularly clean. The polish had worn away from the well-trodden floors in stretches that suggested frequent pacing; some boards bucking upward, others sinking, all of them ready to creak complaints at the slightest provocation. And she could already sense several uninvited visitors of the eight-legged variety crocheting their crafts far above her head.

But none of that could cast an unhomely shadow over the stunning kitchen to her left, outfitted with butcher-block countertops, midnight-blue porcelain backsplash with plush moss growing in the caulk between tiles, and trailing plants tumbling from the tops of every cupboard and the edges of every shelf. Some hung brown and withered, long dead; others were thriving, new growth peeking out from the old; and others sat between the two, leaves jaundiced from overwatering or crisp from the drought of neglect, but not quite beyond saving.

The wood-burning stove belched heat from its blazing belly, but judging by the fact that her soles stung like she'd shuffled barefoot onto a sheet of ice, it wasn't enough to heat the whole chamber. Ingredients were scattered haphazardly across the island in the center, its rounded bulk formed from a severed tree stump, roots and all, the top sanded and coated in resin, the sides still crusted in bark.

Those abandoned ingredients tweaked one of her ribs wrong—not a full pang of dread, but the beginnings of one.

Someone had started cooking, clearly. But between stoking the cookfire and actually setting pot to stove, something had gone wrong.

And as she dragged her gaze away from the kitchen, she quickly found out what that *something* was.

This home flowed seamlessly between three distinct areas, bordered only by their contents—the kitchen, what appeared to be a study, and the living area. In the center of the chamber proper, another tree—not a darkwood, not a stump, but the skeletal form of a mature cork oak—served as the support for the second floor. Its massive limbs shrugged up beneath the upper level of the chamber; a staircase wound around the trunk, its banister arcing gracefully toward the opening above…

And half-concealed in the shadow of the staircase, propped up on a long leather chaise with a wool blanket puddled on the floor beside him, was Wolf.

For a moment, her heart ceased to beat. Fear branched through her, a vision of a man's decimated innards, a woman's thorn-crusted eyes.

Had she been wrong? *Was* he blighted, after all?

It took several moments standing there to assure herself that this was different by far than anything she'd encountered in the infirmary. But regardless, it didn't look *mild* like everyone had claimed.

With one glance, she could tell he wasn't fully lucid—whether thanks to pain or fever, she couldn't be sure this far away. But when she stepped closer, he cringed back, gaze leaping to her like she'd materialized from thin air. Like she hadn't announced her presence more than once.

"What are you doing here?" Venomous. Lacking breath. He sank his nails into the chaise's cushion, clinging to it the way Braeden had clung to her after she'd crawled out of her own grave, choking on dirt: like letting go would cost him something precious. Something he'd lost once already.

"I came to see how you were faring. I knocked, but you—"

"Get out." A weighted wheeze. A shaking finger pointed toward the door.

She took another step toward him instead. "I only want to help. I know you're angry with me, but if you just—"

He twisted, burying his face in the back of the chaise, his shout no less startling for being muffled: *"Get out!"*

Sick to her stomach—sick to her heart—she stared at him a moment longer, indecision curling and uncurling her fists in the layers of appliqued silk.

"No."

Wolf looked back over his shoulder, bloodshot eyes widening. "What?"

"No." She plucked a hair tether from the end table beside the chaise, ignoring his weak protest; she tied up her hair as she talked, calm conviction soothing the hurt and embarrassment from her bones. "You need a healer. I can heal. I'm staying."

At the beginning and end of everything—when one wiped away the cobwebs of lies and legends and a litany of stories her brother had told her about who and what she was—she was a healer. And she had treated patients far more frightening than the irritable man before her.

"I do not…" Wolf's teeth chattered, halting his speech; after a second, he palmed either side of his jaw like it might stabilize the shivers. "I do not want you here. I do not want your help. I want—"

"And *I* want to be sleeping off the forty-eight hours I just spent watching the bodies of quarantined patients tear themselves apart," she snapped, striding into the kitchen and turning on the faucet; the cool water did nothing to douse her fuming temper. "I want to be stuffing my face full of chocolate cake. I want to be doing a lot of things, none of which are being yelled at for trying to help you, but guess what? Neither of us is getting what we want, because I'm here instead of my bed, and you're getting seen to whether you like it or not." When she walked back, drying her hands and tossing the rag away as she halted at his side, she added, "Is that *understood*, Your Highness?"

An owlish blink. A perplexed frown fiddling with his lips. "You're yelling at me."

She huffed, crossing her arms, the sparkly bits on her dress scraping her skin. "Well, you yelled at me first. So we're even, aren't we?"

"I yelled at you twice." Factual that time—maybe even a bit guilty.

"I get one more, then, so don't make me use it."

When she plopped down on the foot of the chaise, his pain-drunk eyes followed, trailing lazily from her bare feet to her dress. "You look lovely."

There was no way in Sancta's shining sky she was going to let him see her blush right now; she tamped down that tingling heat with a pert *hmph*. "Flattery will not get you out of this. Now tell me where it hurts."

His lips bent sideways, like a fractured bone. "It would be faster to tell you where it doesn't."

Not the answer she'd been hoping for. "I don't want to do it fast. I want to do it right."

Wolf licked his lips—a sight that fully distracted her at the task at hand until he rasped, "The worst of it is in my head…light makes it worse. Everything else is just sore from the fever."

A migraine and body aches. Less worrisome than she'd feared at first. But the fever still concerned her.

"Here." She offered her hands. "Squeeze my fingers for me."

He shifted onto his back with a grimace and a low groan, fastening his hands around hers. Though the left exerted far less pressure than the right, his left arm shook from the effort.

Weakness on one side—rare in migraines, but she'd seen it before. Now the sudden appearance of his cane made sense…a mobility aid he needed during a flare of this condition, but not at baseline. "Good. Hold still."

She went back to the kitchen, snatching a stool from its corner; she huffed and puffed as she carried it back, but she got it there without dragging its feet on the floor. That definitely wouldn't have helped his headache.

The entire time, Wolf did not look away from her; instead of glaring, his tired face now clouded with confusion, his jaw ticking as he watched her struggle with the stool. "I could—"

"No."

"You don't have to—"

"Shush, you."

A halfhearted growl was his only reply.

Only once she'd perched on the stool, her hands glowing green as she circled her palms over Wolf's temples, did she dare ask: "Why did you hide up here instead of seeing a medimancer?"

"I think…" He squinted into space, thoughts churning behind his gaze, like he was turning stones over in his memory. "I don't know. I thought I just needed to lie down."

She made a noncommittal noise, unsure if she believed him. And unsure if it mattered enough to press. "Has this happened before?"

"Yes." Another drowsy blink. "Many times."

Not the Blight. Not the Blight.

Not my fault.

"How have you not been diagnosed, then? Treated? Someone must have—"

"I have been." His eyelids floated closed, his forehead contorting in pain; throat tightening, she pulled harder at the threads of agony pulsing venom-green in his head, willing them to loosen their grip. "My ma…my late ma, not Genevieve, she had the same…" A quiet cough. "Illness."

Late. That word deadened her limbs so swiftly, she almost worried her veins had emptied entirely, all the blood draining to her toes. "The illness that killed her?"

When he dipped his chin, the light pouring from her palms stuttered, dimmed, died; she clapped them once to rattle her power loose again, forcing blood back into her fingers.

"I'm older now," he mumbled—when she gave him an inquiring look, he swallowed thickly, his hand crushing a fistful of the chaise's leather upholstery. "I'm older than she was when she died."

Unlike her, he said the word *died* without pausing—like its shape formed just as comfortably in his mouth as his own name.

And it left her at a loss for words in its wake.

I'm sorry would only comfort her—it would only give her the reassurance that she'd offered basic manners. It wouldn't do a thing to soothe him.

"I lost my mother when I was two," she said instead. "I don't remember her much, if at all…sometimes I think I do. I pretend I do."

When she dared to find his face, she found him watching her, unblinking. The canyon-deep languor-lines in his forehead smoothed as she idly twirled a line of magic around her finger, unwinding the tangle of pain and pressure under his skull.

"I was six," he said. "I wish I didn't remember her."

"You don't mean that."

His lip curled. "I don't say things I don't mean."

His foul mood wasn't only a result of the pain, then. She glanced over her shoulder—then back at him—then over her shoulder again.

The stove fire hadn't died yet. It could be saved, if she hurried.

"Keep this on your forehead." With a gentle but firm shove of the damp cloth into his hand, she hopped to her feet and crossed back into the kitchen.

After she stoked the stove back to life, hunted down the cubby where Wolf kept his pans, and set one to a burner with a *clang*, she looked over her shoulder just in time to catch him hauling himself upright. "What are you—?"

"*Lie down*," she barked at him—the harshest she'd ever spoken in this body.

Wolf folded back down immediately, pressing the cloth to his forehead with a mutinous frown. "What are you doing?"

A quick inventory of the ingredients—a loaf of bread with a slice half-cut through, a daub of butter, a cantaloupe-sized wheel of bright orange cheese, a glass bottle of cream, tomatoes larger than her fist, and a handful of other items—gave her an educated guess of what he'd been planning for his meal. "I'm going to make you dinner."

"Why?" A puzzled curiosity that didn't come from sickness-slowed, fever-fuzzed thoughts.

"You didn't join us tonight. If you weren't feeling well earlier today either, I'm hazarding a guess you missed lunch." She smiled over her shoulder. "I have a secondary diagnosis for you."

Such awful dread claimed his face that she immediately felt guilty for the joke. "And what would that be?"

She neatly dodged his terror, focusing on stirring the medley of butter, onions, and garlic beginning to brown in the pan. "I believe you've contracted a severe case of *hanger*."

For too many beats of her nervous heart, only the wooden spoon scraping the bottom of the pan broke the silence, whirling the delicate aromatics to prevent them from scalding.

Then, laughter.

A mere apparition of the rich, gut-deep laughter she'd heard from him only once or twice…and dreamed about more than once or twice. But it was still laughter, breathless and bleary though it might be, and that still felt like a victory.

He didn't speak again after that, and neither did she—but it wasn't a silence born of tempers driven to the brink or resentment so complete it tied tongues and smothered breath. This quiet reminded her of waterfall pools and spring rain; of nature singing lullabies outside her treetop window.

Peaceful. Companionable.

That quiet reigned with a loose fist as she bustled around the kitchen, leaving room for her to hum. If she didn't busy her voice some way, she'd end up chattering his ear off as she stirred and roasted and buttered and flipped.

Wolf didn't seem to suffer from the same restlessness; in fact, she'd begun to worry he'd fallen asleep by the time she drizzled a touch of olive oil over the final result and carried it to the chaise. But when she lit the lamp and crouched down to check him, she found him just…watching through weighted eyelids, fighting slumber as he eyed the plate in her hands.

"Tomato soup," she said, tipping the platter slightly to show him. "And a toasted cheese sandwich. I saw what you had out and took a guess."

"Good guess," he mumbled, pulling himself upright. When she set the tray on his lap, he lifted the spoon with stiff fingers, sipping cautiously at the soup—then more enthusiastically, his eyes widening. "I didn't think goddesses could cook."

Nothing satisfied her more than being on the receiving end of that look— admiration she'd earned with the work of her hands, not with her magic or miracles.

"Not all of us can." She took her seat at the foot of the chaise, leaning back and hugging her knees to her chest. "My sister Cassi can bake, but unless you're aiming to cleanse your house with fire, don't let her anywhere near a stovetop. Not even with a teakettle."

"I would've tapped Mortem for the kitchen-killer," he chuckled around his next slurp of soup—then, after a bite of the golden-brown sandwich she'd sprinkled in grated sea salt: "Anima raise me from my grave and make me dance a jig, that is bloody *fantastic*."

She bit her lip on a smile. "I try not to raise anyone from their graves— though I can make other things dance a mean jig."

Wolf looked up from his meal, his cheeks rounded with a hearty mouthful—and his eyes even rounder with mortified realization.

"My apologies," he mumbled after swallowing, pressing the heel of his hand to his brow, grinding at it with a grimace. "I am…not in possession of my sharpest senses."

"You're hardly the first to curse by my name," she laughed, "nor was that anywhere close to the filthiest I've heard. You should've heard what Soren came up with those first couple weeks we shared a body."

"I could be addled as an adder that bit its own tail, and it wouldn't excuse shouting at you." His throat bobbed as he swallowed, looking almost painful. "Tonight, or…or in the infirmary."

"No, it wouldn't." A bead of sweat dribbled from his temple; she plucked the cool cloth from his other hand and wrapped her fingers in it, dabbing the sweat from his jaw. "But if we're tallying our sins tonight, Prince Wolf, I promise you that mine will outweigh yours by the thousands."

A warm hand closed around hers.

What does it feel like, getting struck by lightning? she'd asked Tempest once.

Like the first breath after drowning, he'd told her, with the nostalgia of someone discussing an old friend. *Like coming back to life.*

That was how it felt when Wolf held her hand: like the first breath after drowning. Like a ray of sunlight through crumbling grave dirt.

"What dances for you?" he murmured.

No one. Nothing. Not anymore.

"Pebbles," she murmured back. "Wax dolls. Dead things that deserve one last dance."

His gaze drifted, wandering over her shoulder—slipping into deeper delirium, she thought at first, until he lifted his chin a notch. "Desk. Left side."

Reluctance held her still…not in defiance of his direction, but because his hand on hers had utterly paralyzed her.

His mouth quirked upward. "Trust me."

And despite the strangeness that had settled between them from the moment they'd met, she found that she did.

Wolf's desk, to her surprise, was not made of darkwood—she ran her fingers over the sleek birch surface, thumbing the pen scratches, her nail flaking raw splinters from beneath its varnish.

An image swirled to life in her head, golden pollen-dust twirling into a memory: she stood so impossibly tall, towering far above the brush and far below the first layer of darkwood branches, warmed by the squirrel hibernating in her heart chamber.

Trees did not feel the way humans did, but they still *felt*. It just took some extra translation.

But the desk itself wasn't what Wolf had sent her to see. And when she found the object sitting to the side on the desk…

Oh, gods.

She was going to cry. She didn't know why, and it was going to be embarrassing, and she couldn't do a thing to stop it—all because of this rounded jar made of pink glass, capped in some pearlescent material.

A jar half-full of pebbles.

The glass gave each of them a rosy cast, but when she unscrewed the lid and shook out a small palmful, a whole host of colors doled out among them: a spectrum of reds, blues, pinks, purples, grays, blacks, whites, and greens.

Emotion wrapped its hands around her throat, throttling out any attempt to speak. So instead she took the jar back to Wolf, knelt at his side, set the jar down…

And blew gently onto the pile of pebbles in her hand.

One by one, each nub of rock began to shiver—they tremored together, stacking in a rough approximation of limbs and torsos, necks and heads, until two tiny figures formed in her palm.

When she murmured a request in one's "ear," it offered its hand to its companion; when the other took it, they swept into a dance.

Surprisingly steady, for what they were. And with perfect ballroom form, no less.

Wolf watched the waltz as if mesmerized, sunlit-maple gaze glistering with fever.

"I used to make things dance, too," he murmured. "Before it started to hurt."

"What danced for you?"

Wolf reached out, and for a heart-hammering moment, she thought he might be about to take her hand again; instead, he lightly pinched her palm between his thumb and forefinger, tipping it at a gentle angle so he could better view the stone dancers.

After an entire minute wiled away without an answer, she let the rocks settle—let them rest.

"Wolf," she whispered, "why do you have these on your desk?"

He kept staring at the pile of pebbles. Kept tracing the heel of her hand with his thumb, featherlight…almost timid.

"The way you smiled at me, in the temple," he said. "I wanted you to smile at me like that again."

Tenebrae had always said it wasn't godly to gasp. So she didn't want to imagine what he'd think of the incredibly undignified, giddy squeak that came out of her next. "They're for *me*?"

A warm chuckle; a tired wink that might have been an accident. Wolf released her hand to tap at the corner of her cheek. "There it is." He gave a slow shake of his head…if she didn't know better, she'd call it *fond*. "People were lining up to shower you in gold and gems…in bloody *trees*. And you didn't smile at any one of them like that. Only that man with the orchid, the little girl with that monstrous rabbit—and at me, when I handed you a pocketful of pebbles." His grin turned topsy-turvy, flipping her heart just as off-kilter. "Been picking them up here and there ever since."

His eyelids lulled, a dip that dumped ice over her heart. His hand slid from hers—she had to catch it to stop it from banging into the tray and spilling still-warm remnants of soup.

She clung to his heavy hand, staring down at it.

Rotted roots, what was she *doing*? Blushing over the ramblings of a man half-senseless with a fever she could feel from a pace away? Squealing like a schoolgirl over an offering?

He was sick, suffering, muttering in the language of dreams and delirium. None of this should be spinning her head like a tuft of dandelion fuzz lost in the wind.

He'd paid attention in the temple…he'd taken note of which offerings had pleased her, and he'd acted accordingly. A worshipper seeking her favor, that was all.

Even if he hadn't looked at her like a worshipper then. Even if he was *still* looking at her differently, with no trace of that alienating awe. And unlike all these days they'd spent in each other's company, tonight, he let her hold his hand…he didn't try to put space between them.

But he was not himself. And if he came back to his senses and remembered his rage over his forgotten prayers…

She didn't know if she could bear that now.

Not after he'd held her hand. Not after he'd called her *lovely*.

It was her turn to step away. Her turn to set herself apart.

"You should sleep," she whispered, settling his hand against his chest, patting it awkwardly. "I'll make you something for the fever before I go."

"No need," he yawned, sounding groggier than before—but more peaceful, too. Like someone living through a beautiful dream instead of a restless night. "In the study, the small chest on the floor…there should be a vial left. Look for the purple label."

She'd never retrieved or popped a cork from a vial so fast in her entire life. Nor had she trembled so badly while helping her patient swallow it, even though Wolf gave her the mercy of shutting his eyes, letting her work without his unnerving focus pinned on her.

"Good," she whispered when the vial was empty; he hadn't even screwed his nose up in complaint at its taste, another indicator this wasn't the first time he'd suffered an episode like this.

Or, she realized with a pang, the first time he'd expected to go through it alone.

"I don't know," he'd told her when she'd asked why he hadn't gone for help. *"I thought I just needed to lie down."*

When she looked around Wolf's chambers—the stocked chest in his study, the pillow under his head that didn't match the chaise at all, and the leaves she'd tracked in after freeing the overgrown doorknob—it wasn't hard to recognize his excuse as a lie.

A man who had a bed pillow stashed in the living area of his home, a chest filled with tinctures to mitigate pain and fever and nausea, and an unturnable doorknob…that man wasn't one who couldn't recognize an oncoming flare of chronic illness.

That was a man who didn't want anyone else to suffer alongside him.

"You're glowing," Wolf said suddenly.

She snorted. "How delirious are you, exactly? On a scale of one to hallucinating."

"Six." His head lolled to one side, his woozy smile lolling to the other. "You have fireflies in your hair."

When she reached up to prod her hair, fluttering wings and tickle-tipped feet kissed her fingertips: heart racing, she gently plucked one out, lowering her cupped palm to eye level.

A kernel of phosphorescent light blinked dozily in her palm: a pinch of fairytale magic bottled up in an insect's body. A wishing star with wings.

She towed a hand through her hair, ruffling the fireflies out; when she asked them to roost in the rafters, they obeyed, twinkling in the shadowy parts of the ceiling instead.

It was suddenly very difficult to swallow. To smile. To blink without shedding a tear.

"Rest, Wolf," she whispered, gathering his thick blanket from the floor and spreading it over him—tucking it under his feet, a habit left over from Soren's body.

When she turned to go, arrow-calloused fingers brushed hers. Not grasping, but...reaching.

"Ani," Wolf murmured, voice muzzy with sleep, "don't leave."

Ani had only experienced this feeling secondhand through Soren—but at the sound of her name on Wolf's lips, she absolutely *melted*.

He'd never said her name before.

He could have followed that whisper with the harshest of heathen curses; he could have flung every insult crafted by human tongues in her face, and not one of them would have been a mighty enough force to move her from his side.

So when he did none of those things—when his hand only hovered, waiting—she took it without fear. Held it without hesitation.

"I won't," she murmured.

He fell asleep still holding her hand; still smiling, if only just, slumber loosening its corners until his lips parted just enough for her to hear his gentle breaths.

It frightened her, terribly, just how very fast her heart was beating. Just how difficult it was to breathe.

Just how little she wanted to be anywhere else but here.

CHAPTER 33

ELIAS

He did not mean to fall asleep.

Not in a den of heathens. Not after such a sound rejection from a heretical king.

But sleep had not come so easily for so very long. And even in the wake of a defeat, even with half-baked ideas of where they could go and what they could try next swarming his mind until it felt like he'd shoved a wasp nest through his ear, there was a certain magic to resting beside his battlemate that let sleep prowl up to him on padded feet. He never knew it was there until he was blinking awake, sunlight stinging his eyes…

Except this was not sunlight.

Too hot, too wild—it swirled around him in a frenzy, crackling like crunching leaves, curling its fingers into his clothes and not letting go. Never letting go.

Those fingers were flames, utterly rabid, chewing through his shirt and clawing for his skin.

"Why are you hurting me?" His shout crumbled into a cough; he buried his mouth and nose in the crook of his elbow, squinting through tears and smoke.

End her.

"End who?"

Golden eyes. A shy smile. *"That's not very kind."*

Had to end her. Had to kill her, had to spare her, had to *wrap his hands around his battlemate's throat and* save her *end her* get her back *end her* help her—

The fire burned black. An inferno of shadow.

His scythes appeared in his hands.

End her.

Mortem's charred command, no allowance for mercy or defiance: *"We have to remove her as a threat."*

Gold sputtering, dying, dissolving into tears that weighed on auburn lashes. Sword-scuffed hands wrapping around his wrists, both of them soaked to the wrists in her blood.

"Elias, wake up."

Tears dripped from his chin; blood dripped from his hands. "No."

"Elias, wake up."

If he woke up, he'd have to face this, have to watch her die by his hand, and what came after would make madmen look upon him with pity. "Don't make me. Please don't make me."

"Eli. Get up."

He screwed his eyes shut, blood salting his tongue as he bit down hard on his trembling lip. "I can't. I can't..."

A strong hand against his cheek. Still slick with blood—but not Soren's. It was too wide, too warm; the callouses were all wrong, the sword grip entirely different.

"Eli."

He opened his eyes to Kallias: blue-eyed, battered, bruised and bleeding and barely awake.

But smiling. Still smiling, even with swollen lips and a broken cheekbone and—

And a scythe stabbed right through his heart.

"No," he moaned. "Gods, why did I...I didn't mean to—"

Kallias held his face in both hands.

"End them," his friend begged with his dying breath. With gold pouring from his pupil, polluting blue-green waters.

"Get out of him!"

"End them," said Kallias's body—but it was not Kallias at all. A storm spoke through his lips; a god glared through his eyes. *"End them all."*

And Kallias's hands wrenched Elias's head sharply to the side, a crack like lightning splintering down his neck.

He woke already sitting up; already digging his nails into his temples, trying to pry invisible hands from his face. Panic ignited, setting every gasp on fire—he couldn't get enough air. He couldn't—

The sound of his neck breaking rang through every bone again, loud enough that his head went light and wobbly; if Soren hadn't chosen that moment to drive her heel into his haunch, nearly booting him right off the bed, he might've dropped into a dead faint.

"Elias, get up," she moaned into the pillow. "Get the door."

All the breath left him in a single gust, taking the built-up heat with it. And without that...

Gods, he was *freezing.*

Another knock—not a breaking neck, after all—drove into the door, three sets of three beats exactly the same amount of time apart. At his battlemate's wordless whine, he finally shook his senses awake, praying he didn't look as frenzied as he felt when he finally tugged on his trousers and padded to the door.

When he opened it, he came across Medwenna, frozen mid-knock—she frowned at him, then finished her final two beats on the doorframe instead before folding her hands behind her back. She didn't bat an eye at his shirtless state. "Prince Everin is waiting to escort us back to the docks. He's going to get passage booked back to Arborius for us."

"Already?" They hadn't even gotten a full night of sleep.

Medwenna shrugged helplessly, avoiding his gaze as she toed the floorboards of the inn Everin had brought them to the night before. "I tried to convince him to let us linger for a bit, but he says his father's eager to have the matter behind him—and he's eager to see me safely off." A conflicted bend of her lips—not a smile, not a wince. "We're fortunate no one has brought my presence to Denali's attention."

Why she'd risked being present at all still made no sense to him—she could have hidden anywhere in the city and avoided the King's notice. But she didn't strike him as someone who left potentialities unexplored; if she had not taken that path, she had her reasons. "Understood. I'll get her up."

"Dress warmly—it smells like snow out here." Medwenna set her finger alongside her nose, tapping the bridge lightly. "Never done me wrong yet."

Privately, he doubted anyone could have peered at the plump buttermilk clouds and *not* known a blizzard was on its way.

When he crawled back into bed, Soren cracked one eye open. Her hand wandered tentatively from beneath the blankets, searching until it collided with his wrist. She tugged at him with an impressive yawn. "Please tell me she was just here to say we could sleep as long as we wanted."

"I wish." He bundled her in his arms, blankets and all, and pulled her across his lap. "They want us out."

"Mm." She didn't sound surprised. "Is it because I threw a knife at their king?"

"They didn't specify, but…" He shrugged, teasing the curl that always claimed its place right in the center of her forehead. "Seems like a safe guess."

Soren wriggled around to cuddle into his side, giving a mighty yawn before burying her face in his shoulder. "You smell sleepy."

He snorted. "I *smell* sleepy?"

"Mmhm." She gave a deep, exaggerated sniff, laughing when he pushed her away by her forehead. "Like blankets."

"Odd, considering a certain someone stole them all from me."

"I think that's an exaggeration." She withdrew into her blanket cocoon like a turtle pulling its head into its shell.

"Yeah, I bet you do." He rolled back layer after layer of blanket until he found his battlemate's face; her cheeks were rosy and warm, her gaze hazy with sleep, and the smile she flashed at him…

His heart melted down to dross, dripping straight through his ribcage.

"Marry me," he said.

"Oh, my," she deadpanned, fanning herself with her hand—the hand with quite the visible diamond perched on one finger. "I'll need time to consider…I mean, this is all so sudden…"

He lowered her back on the bed, crawling over her, bracing all his weight on his palms as he leaned down to kiss her ridiculous mouth. "What if I said please?"

"Are you free this afternoon?"

A chuckle chased away the last of the chills left behind by his nightmare. He kissed the imprint the pillow had left behind on her flushed cheek, then patted it, forcing himself up and off the bed. "On your feet, smartass. Medwenna didn't make it sound like we could take our time."

Five minutes and a full bag later, he turned to strip the bed linens for the innkeepers only to find Soren had stopped halfway through packing her own bag. She stared down into it like it contained an endless abyss.

"Soren?" he prompted.

Her stricken gaze rose to meet his. "Huh?"

Rather than try to articulate it, he gestured between her and her bag, then crossed his arms, waiting.

"Nothing."

"Try again."

She thrust the bag from her lap, rolling off the bed and striding off to the bathing room. "Nothing. Just got distracted."

Well, that was obviously a load of wolfshit, but she shut the door before he could find a way to tell her so that didn't end with him getting punched.

The bag remained open, gaping like a bleeding wound waiting to be stanched.

He looked at the bag. Then at the door. Then at the bag.

Sated curiosity, his mother had always told him, was not worth the wounds it often dealt. To pay a price without knowing what you were paying for was a leap of foolishness, not faith.

He offered a silent apology to her as he eased onto the bare mattress, peering into the depths of the bag.

But when his vision caught on the crinkled, tearstained sheaf of paper a moment later, unfolded just enough for familiar handwriting to spill out, he remembered why he always, *always* listened to his mother.

His battlemate's gutted look made all the sense in the world now—he probably wore one to match as he stared at Kallias's fancy penmanship, his eyes irresistibly drawn to the shape of his own name.

Take care of Elias. He grieves as hard as he loves, and—

Ripping his eyes from that paper ripped something out of his chest, too.

He snatched up the pack and yanked on the drawstring to close it—too hard. The cord snapped, and all tension in the bag's sides sagged out, spilling the contents with what had to be the most calamitous series of clatters he'd heard in his life.

He would never, never, *never* ignore his mother's advice again. He'd swear it on any grave or pyre or altar he had to.

"Are you messing with my bag?" came his battlemate's cross voice from the bathing room.

"When have I ever messed with your things?" he asked, messing with her things until he could fit them all into his arms. "I don't know where in the pits they've been. They might be contaminated."

"With what? Cooties?"

"Reckless idiocy. I hear it's catching." And he proved it by shoving everything back into her bag—along with the broken drawstring—and setting it by the door just as she left the bathing room, a damp cloth in her hand, her eyes a bit red.

"It's not where I left it," she pointed out unnecessarily.

"Well, no." Gods damn him, this was why he never lied. "What's your point?"

She gave him a look. Not a word spoken.

"I might have touched your things," he confessed.

"*No,*" she gasped.

"I was just trying to close it, but, ah…" He held up the bag, and it lolled open once more, baring her scrambled belongings. And the broken string. "It didn't go so well."

"That old thing's been trying to die for a while," she sighed, catching it one-handed when he lobbed it at her. She dug around in it, tongue poking out the corner of her mouth, until she tugged out a leather tie with a triumphant "Aha!"

While she did her repairs, he gathered the rest of their things; once she had a makeshift tie around the bag, he offered her his hand. "Walk with me?"

"Anywhere and everywhere." She took his hand, something he would never take for granted again. Something he had sworn not to, after all they had endured—after Artem, after—

Elias grieves as hard as he loves.

He tightened his hold on her hand—and didn't let go for anything.

CHAPTER 34

ELIAS

Medwenna did not take them to the harbor.

They seemed to be wending in that direction when they started—the journey down the steps was easier than the way up, if more dizzying, but he'd climbed taller mountains than this. So while they descended, he tracked their path.

Casually, at first—second nature, nothing more. But when they reached the bottom and Medwenna swerved northeast, not southwest toward the harbor, a touch of suspicion came to visit.

He let Medwenna and his battlemate continue their conversation—or rather, the conversation Medwenna was carrying out quite well with only a grunt or *hmm* from Soren, who watched her own boots—but he gave Soren's fingers two quick, sharp squeezes. When she looked up, curiosity warming the sour-milk splash of fear across her complexion, he made a motion like clicking open a compass—a gesture they'd seen Patch perform a thousand times on their journey to Arborius.

Soren stared at his palm, eyes narrowing; she looked up for the first time since they'd set shoe to stair, marking their path with her darting gaze.

"Isn't the harbor the other way?" she asked as they descended steep stone-lined streets, swerving to avoid getting crushed by hardy workhorses with hooves the size of Elias's head or the carts they hauled.

"It's a shortcut," Medwenna promised—which made no sense, as the stairs led straight down to the water, and the winding streets would've required a map and a sled to navigate if they didn't have her as a guide.

He and Soren exchanged looks, then slowed as one.

"A shortcut that leads further from the water?" Soren's voice tiptoed more carefully around the accusation than he would've expected.

"Oh, well, I—" Medwenna tripped over her words—then actually tripped. Soren lunged and caught her arm, pulling her up; the ranger laughed nervously, dusting off her knees like she didn't realize she'd never hit the ground. "Sorry. My mother used to say—"

"Medwenna," Soren interrupted again, an edge of warning creeping in, "why are you taking us away from the harbor?"

Medwenna hesitated, tongue hovering between her teeth. "Ah. Well…"

"Forgive her," said Everin as he stepped out from a nearby alley. As usual, Kessen and Matthias flanked him; however, unlike usual, he wasn't clothed like a hunter who'd gotten halfway dressed before getting bored and leaving off the rest. He actually wore a coat, its buttons done up to the collar; the hood slumped back over his shoulders, but the sleeves cuffed at his wrists, and his tapping foot rang out with every strike against the stone. Steel-toed—maybe steel-soled, too. "I called in a favor."

Pulse thudding in his ears—his own, Soren's, and a whole host of others that threatened to deafen him—Elias stepped back, Soren following a half-beat later. Noting Matthias's keen eye on his scythes, he released Soren's hand to grip her hip instead, tugging her closer to his side…and getting his fingers around the spare dagger she kept sheathed there just in case he ever found himself disarmed.

She shifted her stance to allow him a better grip, affecting a yawn at the same time—just a bored princess struggling to keep her attention and her feet in one place. "If you wanted to see me again, you could've just waited a minute or two. The natural light down at the harbor's so much better for my complexion."

"Are you sure?" Everin arched a brow. Winked. "I think the shadows suit you."

Elias started to draw the dagger. Soren reached behind her back to pinch his wrist.

"Prince Everin," Matthias said, with a pronounced patience that suggested he wanted to use a title closer to Elias and Soren's favorite nicknames, "now's not the time for flirting. Especially not with an engaged woman. Especially not when you are *also*—"

"You are *no* fun." Everin rolled his eyes—then turning to the side, beckoning them toward the dead-end alley. "All right, everybody in. We need to have a more private chat."

"No thanks," he and Soren chorused together.

"I'm not in the habit of getting murdered in shady alleys," Soren added. "I prefer larger-scale deaths. A mass assassination, godly possession, that sort of thing."

Everin had the nerve to look offended. "You think *I'd* try to murder you? During the *day*, no less? I've got people to do that, it's beneath me. You should be flattered I'm seeing to this matter myself."

"What matter?" Elias pushed through gritted teeth.

Everin widened his eyes in exasperation, gesturing to the alley once more in exaggerated, lagging motions. "The one we need to chat more privately about, zealot. What's the matter? Need to pray about it first?"

"Already did. Mortem says your time grows short," he deadpanned. "I'd say you have minutes, at best."

Irritation chafed through his blade hand like a dog's teeth grinding over bone when Everin threw his head back and guffawed, as if the Goddess of Death marking the hour of his last breath was a joke.

"I'm sure she'd be thrilled," Everin chortled as he took Medwenna's hand, teasingly kissing her knuckles as he guided her into the alleyway. She rolled her eyes as she spun into the shade.

He didn't trust Everin or his men, and he didn't exactly have unshakeable faith in Medwenna—the woman was still mostly a stranger, and they only had Sage's secondhand word that she could be trusted with their lives.

But for Soren, that seemed to be enough—she reached behind her to pry his fingers off the spare dagger, stepping forward herself. "If you insist on the dramatics, fine. But stick one finger out of place, and I'll bite it off."

"You mean cut it?" Kessen ventured.

"No." She bared her teeth in a grin. "I mean *bite it.*"

Kessen gulped audibly. Even the typical bustle of a central city couldn't bury it.

Once they were all bundled into the alley—empty but for the snow blown up against its walls and a metal barrel at the back, a shoddy fire greeting them with a flickering wave—Everin kicked back against the dead-end wall, rasping a hand over his well-groomed stubble. "Well, congratulations: you're now privy to one of this kingdom's worst-kept secrets."

"Which is?" Elias muttered.

"My father's an ass." He jerked his chin at them. "Go on, you can say it— he's an ass."

"And we hate him," Kessen added helpfully.

"Right, almost forgot that part." Everin rolled his eyes. "And we hate him, also."

Elias and Soren's gazes collided again; the surprise and suspicion twisting his stomach into clumsy braids shimmered over her eyes like sunlight on water. The shadow and the light.

"This feels like a trap," Soren said. "You do realize that, right? You realize this feels like the world's most obvious trap."

"That would require planning, which again…beneath me." The arrogance in Everin's smirk could've rivaled the gods-damned ocean in scale. He cast a hand back through his blond hair; a gesture so like Kallias that he had to wrestle his temper down.

He fixed his eyes on the embers in the heart of the fire, timing his breathing to their pulses. "Get to the point, if you please."

"You're right," Everin said to Soren—such a frank confession that she stepped back a pace, her furrowed brow doubling in depth. "Sitting on our beautiful backsides and waiting for the Chaos God to bring war to our door—once he's taken out the rest of you and maybe added more of his siblings to his ranks, no less—is foolhardy and prideful. Not that I'm against those particular virtues—"

"He's the chief executor of them, usually," said Matthias.

"—shut your trap, Matt—but you stand no chance without us, and we stand no chance without you." Everin's smirk crept toward a full-blown grin. "And neither of us stands a chance without the god-killer."

"Which your father refused to give us and claims is just a myth," Elias reminded him.

"It exists. But the King doesn't have it."

Every eye in the alley turned to Medwenna, whose fists were clenched together in front of her; she shook them up and down like she was rattling a jar of marbles, her cheeks flushed in excitement. Or cold. Difficult to tell.

"Could you explain—"

Soren didn't even get the chance to finish before Medwenna burst into a full-blown ramble.

"King Denali doesn't *have* the god-killer. No one does." Medwenna paced as she spoke, her hands taking the position of someone holding a book, her finger tracing the invisible page. Her eyes rolled toward the sky as if the text was scrawled on the inside of her skull. "It was sealed away centuries ago. Thieves of a more pious persuasion kept trying to nick it, so one of the old kings finally had enough— he spirited the weapon away to one of our smaller mountains and had it spelled with old magic to keep it safe. The mountain repels the holy."

He knew the weight of Soren's gaze on him like he knew the weight of his own weapon in his hand. But he kept his eyes and body facing Medwenna. "How do you know that's the truth of its whereabouts?"

"Only those who lived the histories know the truth for certain," Medwenna admitted. "But the ruling king at the time wrote about it—he claimed to have carried the weapon to its resting place himself. And he told the story firsthand to his Grand Historian." At his blank look, Medwenna added, "Tallisian history is kept orally and in writing. Each king is given a blank journal to keep when they take the throne, and our Grand Historian undergoes quite the gauntlet of memorization in order to take the title. You must—"

"Winnie," Everin said, "keep your feet on the path, if you can. We can talk about the details later."

"Of course." Medwenna cleared her throat, flipping invisible pages backwards. "What was I…the god-killer. The weapon was sealed away, and no one has retrieved it since. Some have tried—*many* tried before memory of its location was allowed to fade into fables, quite intentionally…but none who enter the mountain have left with their quarry." Her eyes shone. "Quite the spooky notion, if you ask me. Not a living soul knows what might have been put in place to protect it. All we can gather from the stories is that there will be trials demanded of those who wish to claim the god-killer, designed to oppose gods-blessed in particular. I personally have a theory that there are five trials, one for each god or goddess, but—"

"You just have all that bobbing around in your head?" Soren demanded. "I can't even remember what I had for breakfast this morning."

"You didn't," Elias reminded her. "Neither of us did."

Medwenna blushed. "To make a long story short, we have every reason to believe the god-killer is still there."

"That's all well and good, but what does that mean for us?" So far, all he'd heard was that the god-killer was being kept somewhere even more impenetrable than the most well-guarded castle in the kingdoms, and to claim it, they'd need to conquer a round of trials more complex than the ones he'd nearly failed in Artem. Not exactly an improvement on their predicament.

"We've got a plan." Everin tipped his chin up toward Medwenna, who nodded eagerly. "Get inside, get the god-killer, get back out, and get that nasty bastard off your throne, Princess—and off this mortal coil, if you catch my meaning."

"As I've said before," Matthias sighed, "that turn of phrase is really only for when you're not making your point *glaringly obvious.*"

Everin thrust a threatening finger his way. "I will put you in the stocks. We have time."

"That's not a plan," Soren protested. "That's a to-do list, at best."

Which still made for a better plan than Soren usually trotted off with to commit her schemes, all of which robbed years off of his life and added premature gray to his hair, but he kept his mouth shut.

"Well, there's more to it." Everin scratched the inside of his ear with his little finger. "That's just the big picture. Best to break up your goals into manageable pieces, right, Matt?"

"*Now* you want to quote my seasoned wisdom?"

Everin rolled his eyes. "You're three months older than me, you gnat."

"Thought planning was beneath you," Elias grumbled.

"Oh, Winnie did all the planning. I just did what I always do—nod and go along with it." A fond grin at the ranger, who had already gone back to pacing, muttering to herself. "When you're a powerful person without a good head on your shoulders, you let the smart people do the talking for you."

"The plan is in motion," Medwenna added distractedly. "Retrieving you two was the first step. Next, getting out of the city without being seen—any of us, but particularly you two and myself."

Elias balked as the Tallisians all nodded like that was that, breaking the circle and heading for the alley mouth. "What about the ship?"

"We've already sent decoys ahead," Medwenna assured him, cheerful once more. "The ship should be departing any minute."

That left him at a loss. So he did what he always did when they had to rely on instinct over thought: he looked to Soren.

Who had already started following the Tallisians, rolling her pack more snugly over her shoulder, pulling him along by the tips of his fingers.

"We don't have a better plan," she said when he made an uncertain sound in the back of his throat. "Not that I'm thrilled about the whole *repels the holy* thing, considering your persuasion, but it's probably just something they say to keep people from trying. And if it's not…what's the harm, right? We can't get in, fine— we'll leave then."

"Right. Great. We'll try to get into the mountain…that never lets people back out."

"It's not *not letting* people out, it's a *mountain*," she scoffed, as if she hadn't nearly been killed by a sentient tree not too long ago. "I think we can outsmart a giant rock."

Reluctance twisted his wrist, his hand fidgeting in hers. "Soren…"

"Do you have a better plan, jackass? Besides going back to Arborius or trying for Lapis? Because we both know it's no use. Better this than waiting around for Tenebrae to get sick of playing house."

"No, smartass, I don't." He tugged her to a sharp halt. "I just want to make sure you're really thinking about this—what it means if we don't come back out. For your family *and* for Atlas."

No one left to save her parents.

No one left to save her brothers.

No one left to save her people.

And, perhaps the most alarming of all outside of their own selfish hearts…

No one left to inherit Atlas's throne.

Her eyes rivaled a crypt for hollow pits and shadowed nooks. But she gave a stiff bob of her head. "So we make sure we come back out."

And with a final heft of her pack, like its weight grew heavier with every passing second, she strode off in pursuit of the Tallisians. A group of strangers dangling the key to salvation before them…and near-certain death in pursuit of it.

He had a terrible feeling about this. A sensation like rot eroding through his stomach, burning from the inside out.

But he'd made a vow. If this was where she wanted to go…

He had no choice but to walk her there.

CHAPTER 35

ANIMA

Ani crept out of Wolf's room before the sun rose, sleepless thoughts bobbing through her brain like a dandelion seed batted about by an errant summer breeze.

She tried to go to the infirmary and lose herself in the constant cycle of caring for patients—tried to cart away ichor-stained rags and heal warped bones without letting her mind wander to thoughts of Wolf. But in the inky suds floating on the surface of the washbasin, she saw his gaze swallowed by the glossy black of pain-blown pupils; in those corkscrew bones, she saw him crumbled in a heap on his chaise, moans muffled by his beaten-in pillow.

In the sheet-covered corpses, she heard his rasping confession: *My late ma had the same illness.*

She held out all morning—a morning where Wolf *still* didn't report for his duties—before throwing in the towel and setting off on a different mission.

Outside the stale, sickened air of the quarantine ward, she could finally breathe her deepest; when she reached the bottom of the steps leading up to one of the infirmary's entrances, a patch of grass caught her sore feet, coaxing a relieved groan out of her chest. She shucked off her stained, laceless shoes and sweat-damp socks, tucking them against the bottom stair before plunging into the thicket.

The plush grass swallowed her feet well past the ankles, but she didn't mind. It tickled, yes, but it also cooled and cushioned—and she needed nature to carry and lead her.

Following it between bramble thickets and poison ivy patches, she asked it to spread the word to every stalk woven into its carpet of roots: if any of them knew the prettiest paths to walk, she wanted to be led that way.

Not the most reliable informant, grass; by the time the whispers made it through millions of blades, they'd often jumbled into an incoherent heap. Trees were better, but they rarely tattled, even to her; they took people's secrets quite seriously.

So when the whispers that came to her took a moment to make sense, she didn't think much of it at first.

Anima. Rustling undergrowth. Creaking branches. *Anima.*

"It's me, I can hear you," she promised, kneeling down to cup her ear against the grass. "Go on, little ones."

Hurts.

She frowned. "What hurts?"

Grass didn't feel pain. Trees did, sometimes flowers, but never grass.

Hurts.

"I don't underst—"

The ground *writhed* under her feet.

Earthworms wriggled up from the soil, squirming between her toes; isopods and flightless beetles scurried over her feet, mandibles working like mad; mice and voles dashed from the branches of bushes skirting the path, burrowing into the cuffs of her borrowed pants or scrambling up to hide in the pockets of her apron.

Another quake through the world's skin, and the grass drooped—the grass *changed.*

Withering. Wasting.

Wailing.

Hurts. Hurts.

Ani fell to her knees, weaving her fingers into the grass. Warmth buzzed in her veins like the channels of a beehive, and she shoved it out, out, out—

Pain split her fingertips open; her torrent of magic slammed to a halt, so concentrated her fingers began to glow green.

She tried again to shove it out; again, the magic refused to obey.

Her power wouldn't go into the ground.

"What's happening?" she breathed, gathering a fistful of grass. The strands were darkening, wilting, but...

Not dying. That was why her magic wouldn't go into it—the grass wasn't dead. There was no room for *more* life inside a living thing.

Help. The grass *grew*, pushing her palm like a dog begging to be petted. *Help.*

"I'm trying—"

And like any dog might when pushed to its limits, when she tried once more to thrust her magic into its roots, the grass lashed out.

The blades stiffened. Lengthened. Sharpened. And before she could pull away—

Dozens of needles *shoved* through her hand, drowning out her screams with their own.

HELP US.

Ani ripped her hand free of the grass-turned-thorns, staggering backward—but the path back wasn't safe, either. Like thousands of nails hammered wrong-side-up into the earth, every step pierced her soles; she had to *tear* her feet free, hot blood pouring out of the punctures as she spun this way and that, trying to find a safe place to tread.

Panic whimpered in her throat, but she couldn't scream; if someone came to help, they might trip onto this pincushion path, too.

She jammed her feet into some of the narrow gaps where only soil lived, places where the forest creatures had crawled out of the ground to escape; one of the mice in her pocket squeaked when her toes curled into a mound of dirt, collapsing the mouth of its burrow.

"Sorry," she squeaked back. "No choice."

The mouse peered up at her, tiny nose wriggling—then bolted along with its fellow forest-dwellers as the undergrowth began to rustle. To crack.

Something was coming.

And she had nowhere to run.

The grass *bowed* before it, this creature slithering amongst the undergrowth; and as the creature went, it took the undergrowth with it, roots and branches snared by greedy fingerling vines. They clawed fallen branches and dead leaves and animal bones into a flowing train of decay at its back—and at its head, bark and stem and bone began to take a new shape.

Ani's heart stopped.

For five eternal seconds, the Goddess of Life might as well have been dead. Her heart did not beat. Her lungs did not breathe. Her blood did not flow.

But the caricature before her did all those things and more.

It *smiled* at her, this force skinned in debris and destruction; chips of bone and stone made for teeth too sharp to be human, its eyes pitted pools of shimmering pebbles. Its hair flowed with dried grasses and ivy chains and willow strands; its hands were marked out in strips of bark, the seams held together so tightly by gods-knew-what that she couldn't see what demarcated its form beneath.

Ani stared into a monstrous mimicry of a human face.

Its eyes skimmed over her head; a moment later, buds broke open across its brow. A flower crown braided together of its own accord, blossoming in haphazard blooms of splattered, misshapen petals. Unnatural colors tainted the flowers, spoiled greens and bruised purples and withered grays; thorns circled each one like high collars, forcing the blooms to keep their heads up—or be speared through.

The monster tipped its head to the side; its base vines undulated erratically, carrying it closer. It reached out a hand; its fingers scraped Ani's cheek, trailing sap and splinters across the soft curve of her jaw.

Ani's lungs quivered. She tried to twist aside, but those bark-covered fingers dug in, wrenching her head back around.

"Mouses and hawks." A twig snapped as its smile widened. Its voice warbled up and down in pitch…a mockingbird call. "Butterflies and birds. Why did you make me a bird, butterfly?"

Was it babbling, or had fear scrambled her brains *that* badly? "I can't…I-I didn't make you."

"You remember," it said matter-of-factly. "Houseflies don't, goldfishes don't—but butterflies remember. *You* remember."

Sappy, acrid air skated over her tongue when she finally made herself breathe. "Where did you come from?"

Its hands dragged from her chin down her neck, then parted to scour her arms, carelessly clawing furrows into her flesh; she bit down on her throbbing lip, refusing to scream again as it took her hands in its misshapen talons. Spindly, thick protrusions…not unlike roots.

Like it had rooted and grown and ripped itself out of the soil.

"Right here." It tightened its grip, a careless crush of bone and cartilage that added another octave to the scream building in her throat. Her heart quailed away from its touch, scrabbling down her ribs like a ladder, dropping deep into her stomach. "You remember."

"I don't—"

"It hurts." Pebbles tumbled in its gaze; its irises changed like chameleon scales, a shimmering shift from jade to pewter to obsidian. One rolled down its cheek, pearly blue. "It still hurts."

"What hurts?" Her bloodied feet stuck to the dirt as she slid backward, prey animal instinct warring with good human sense. "I didn't hurt you—*you* hurt *me*!"

The cornered animal wanted to run. The sensible human knew better to try when even the ground could grow teeth.

The monster let her put that inch between them, but its smile festered into a rot-flecked frown. "You are a butterfly," it repeated, suddenly angry; her heart took another flying leap, lodging in her throat. "You *remember*!"

A demand it punctuated with a shove to her shoulders, tackling her to the spear-tipped ground.

A splintered hand muffled her agonized wail as a host of six-inch long thorns twisted into her body; she arched her back, but that only forced the brunt of the pain into her shoulders and haunches.

Squinting through tears of agony, she watched as the monster hovered over her, bone-teeth bared, dripping sap like rabid spittle. Its shape warped, bone and wood shifting. Human, then canine, then deer-like—then back to human.

"You made me," it declared, spitting leaf litter in her eyes. "You hurt me. You forget. I remember. I *remember.*"

A warped howl rang through the woods, *from* the woods; the forest sang with predatory glee as the monster disintegrated, burying Ani in a pile of waste and ruin and blood.

And with her body stuck full of thorns, throat swollen with unshed tears, the butterfly remembered.

It hurts. It still hurts.

Thorns thrust through her skin, seeking the soft places inside her.

Thorns thrust through a daisy's bloated stem, impossible to extricate.

You made me. You remember.

The last thing she remembered from inside her tree: a torrent of magic exploding outward as she held her bloom to her heart, the power of creation freed from its binding.

And Blight had followed.

You made me.

She tore herself out of the ground, throwing herself into the safety of soil, watering it with her blood. Tried to scream.

She had no breath to scream.

"What are you?" she choked.

A harmony of crooning wind and creaking trees was the only answer. But the hairs on the back of her neck refused to lie flat.

Prey instinct.

She was not safe yet.

So like prey, Ani ran.

CHAPTER 36

ANIMA

The trees sated themselves on her blood.

Warm as mulled cider, spiced with panic, every drop drained another ounce of will from her body; as the roots glutted themselves on ichorous rain, singing with power bled from her very veins, the world forgot it was autumn.

Dead, dry leaves turned soft and supple, waving like verdant flags in the frosty breeze; where the darkwoods reigned, evergreen and ever-growing, their canopies stretched out foot by foot. The more she fed them, the further they reached.

The leaking wouldn't stop.

Healing. She should have been healing.

Why wasn't she healing?

Why did she feel so *cold*?

Her teeth chattered madly as she stumbled through tangles of undergrowth, yanking her torn cardigan tightly around her wound-riddled body. It hurt too much to run. But if she stopped...

"Heal," she whispered, shoving her hand over as many punctures as she could; her magic glowed, then sputtered. "Come on, *heal.*"

Another sputter—then it steadied. A softer, sweeter warmth took the place of the hot blood trickling from every wound.

A furious howl. Something hooked into her sides, flaying flesh from her ribs; she doubled up, slamming to one knee with a sickening *crunch.*

Her kneecap, she believed at first—believed it hard enough that even though the pain that followed seemed dull, lackluster in comparison to the sound, she couldn't bring herself to try and rise.

"It hurts, it hurts," warned the mockingbird monster. It rose in a rippling, featureless wall of refuse thrown down by the trees, dragging its hooks out of her skin: thorn-pocked vines that whizzed back into the shadows when it reared over her. "I am *hurt.*"

Sobbing, swallowing her own sick, Ani hobbled back to her feet. Pain did swim through her knee, but it held when she put weight on it.

Something it couldn't have done if it had shattered like a stomped-on plate like she'd feared.

So she dared sneak one glance at the ground.

A deer skull leered up at her from beneath a carpet of overgrown moss; the brittle bone had collapsed inward when she'd fallen on it.

Rapid glances pulled out more bones hidden amidst the soil and sod...animal, all of them, except for a single human femur. But considering it stuck out from the decayed carcass of a massive grizzly, she'd say whoever it belonged to had probably gotten the lucky end of the deal.

These creatures hadn't decided to lie down and die here by coincidence; if the clods of soil and root clinging to their carcasses were anything to go by, they'd been buried up until recently. Maybe a flood had turned the ground over; maybe an earthquake had sifted the soil aside. Maybe it didn't matter.

Because the Goddess of Life knew how to dance with the dead. And she now stood in the center of a boneyard.

If she could just get some distance between her and this monster, she could call her own ranks to war. She could put lifeless soldiers of dust and decay between them, and she could run, she could find—

"Anima?"

Oh, thank *Sancta.*

"*Anima!*" Wolf shouted again; too far away to see, just close enough to hear "Goddess, I know you're out here."

Ani towed in gasp after gasp of forest air until her lungs finally inflated enough for speech; she opened her mouth, shoving all her will into turning that breath into a voice. "Wol—"

Woody claws covered her mouth, splinters catching on her split lip.

The monster's many-layered hiss of warning writhed like maggots in Ani's ear. A beetle scrabbled out from under a flake in one of its fingers, lurching on rickety legs as it clambered onto Ani's upper lip.

Ani could muster nothing but a sob of frustration—and a gag as the beetle crept up her cheek, making it all the way into the wisps of hair at her temples before it collapsed, twitched twice, and succumbed to the Blight that had birthed it.

"I know I'm likely the last sorry sod you want to see," the prince added, voice thick with a frustrated shame that pierced her heart, "but I want to offer an apology, if you'll—"

"Leave me alone!" the monster called—a flawless mimicry of Ani's own voice.

Temper sparked, lighting a wick of anger in her chest.

"If you choose not to hear it, I understand. But I…you shouldn't be out here alone." Though he sounded stronger than the other night, a whistling wheeze blew out every time he ended a sentence. "And while I take responsibility for my part in your lack of escort, I—"

"Leave me alone." A breeze twirled around Ani, leaves crinkling, branches creaking. "You hurt me. Leave me alone."

Ani's heart lodged in her throat—then free-fell into the dust when the grass began to gossip about Wolf's parting steps.

No, no, no—don't leave me here!

Focus, barked a different voice—an echo permanently stamped on Ani's spirit.

It didn't surprise her, that her anger spoke with Soren's voice.

Fix your feet. Help me breathe.

Ani squared her stance the way Soren had taught her, toes sifting into the fallow dirt. And despite the wet-wood odor that soured her sinuses, she breathed deep. Breathed slow.

Breathed until she could feel the earth breathing with her.

Earth did not live, not the way most defined life—it did not have a beating heart or veins humming with blood. It had no mind to think or soul to dream. It had no sinew or bone, no muscles or marrow.

But from the earth sprang all things green and growing; forests and gardens, weeds and wildflowers, crops and poisons. And though they had no lungs, these things still breathed.

Ani inhaled; tuber-like roots nosed from the dirt, slithering up her legs.

Ani exhaled; branches above her head bent to reach for her, twigs extended like grasping fingers.

Take me away from it, she whispered to the darkwood looming over them. *Take me into the sky.*

But trees kept secrets. And this Blight, it seemed, had taken some of them into its confidences.

The roots twined around her ankles froze; shuddered; withered. They peeled away from her skin, curling backward over themselves.

The earth caught its breath.

Ani did, too.

"Do not leave," seethed the monster. Its screams rose to a deafening pitch as the branches ripped back into the sky, the darkwood groaning when shards of bark rained from above. "Do not *leave me alone!*"

When the Blight lunged, Ani closed her eyes and prayed her body would remember how to heal…and if it did not, that her eldest sister would remember her own teachings on mercy.

Bone splintered. Wind roared. Pain—

The pain did not come.

She waited and waited for the shock to fade, for agony to let her know where the damage had been dealt—but it never did.

She peeked one eye open.

The dervish of dirt and bone and bark that seemed intent on hunting her now drifted several feet away, claiming a wolf-like shape; its features reassembled in a rictus of canine bloodlust as it dodged blows from the beast that had cornered it.

A beast constructed from dug-up bone.

Ani's heart hammered as the massive bear skeleton reared up on its back legs, easily twice her height; sickly green light wove between its ribs, filling the chinks in its spine, banding bones together like makeshift tendons and muscles. It roared in the monster's face before dropping back to all fours—

Revealing Wolf several feet behind.

Ani nearly sobbed.

He hadn't left after all; he'd circled around to the other side of the clearing, his steps so soundless even a force of chaos—a thing trained to sniff out and shatter silence—hadn't noticed.

But he hadn't drawn his bow, nor his knives; his bandolier hung heavy with blades, every sheath still occupied. His cane lay at his feet.

He held nothing in his extended hand…yet sweat gleamed on his forehead, bright as a broken fever. Emotion danced over his face in perfect tandem with the flecks of green magic; at first, that smoothing of his furrowed forehead made no sense to her, the easing of his labored breaths not typical of a man in deadly peril.

But when he maneuvered his fingers like a practiced puppeteer, and the bear's skeleton swiped its claws in nearly the same gesture, she found that emotion's name.

Relief.

A mortal faced with an impossibility made of corruption and malice and ill-bred magics should not look like that. Especially a man as ill as Wolf.

Unless he wasn't ill at all.

Unless that lie masked an even more unbearable truth.

But one didn't have time to question such things while they were still happening.

Wolf gestured, a severe cut of his hand barking a silent order to *run;* and even though every step riddled her body with bursts of pain and heat, she obeyed.

Wolf didn't look away from the collision of bone-beast and Blight; even when she failed to stagger to a stop in time, crashing into his side, he just caught her by the waist and tucked her behind him.

"You're not healing?" he demanded, arm out, defending her front.

"Not quickly enough." Lying was useless; her saffron-green tunic showed the blood too well.

"Can you run, if I make you a path?"

Run—and leave him behind.

"No," she whispered.

If he said anything else, the chittering snarl of the bone-bear drowned it out; it had driven the Blight back several paces, its claws jammed up with chips of stone and wood, its teeth stained with smears of inky, spoiled ichor.

She took a tottering step back. "Y-You're a necromancer."

His "illness," his mother's death…her fault, after all.

He ripped a strip of cloth from his own shirt with his teeth. "We need to get pressure on your wounds."

"But you're—and it's—Wolf, *you're a—*"

"Come *here*, woman," he grunted—he had the nerve to sound exasperated. "Before you bleed yourself dizzy. That bear won't keep it busy long."

"What did you just call—?"

A nauseating *crunch* dragged their attention back; the Blight recoiled from the pile of broken bones that had once been a bear, folding into a dust storm of dangerous intent. It set its balled-up fists to hips shaped only by wind and intangible shadow, cheeks flushed with ruddy clay. And its eyes found Ani, even with Wolf interposed between them.

"I am hurt," it chirruped—no longer her voice, but a chitter of plant-stuff only she could understand. Yet even that foreign language rang with wintry calm that dropped Ani's stomach to her toes. "I will fix it."

A shiver shot through her spine, lodging like an arrow in her heart.

The Blight sank to the ground—*into* the ground. And where it dispersed, chunks of debris flinging across the forest floor…

Those pieces took root and *grew*.

No longer stone. No longer bark. No longer branch and bone and rancid blood.

Roots erupted from the soil, crooked like arachnid limbs; they skittered and swarmed up the trunks of the nearby darkwoods, wrapping them up with the tight, unbreakable grip of reunited lovers.

One spasmodic *squeeze*, and the darkwood trunks dented in.

Arborian darkwoods, prized for their stone-tough trunks, tested for authenticity by dragging a sharp-edged diamond along the surface and checking to see if it left a scratch behind…

Dented. By *roots*.

"Run," Ani breathed.

Wolf swept an arm under her knees; she folded with a yelp, and he bolted.

A deafening snap. A cataclysmic groan that fissured her skull with pressure pain.

She and the forest screamed as one when the first darkwood fell.

A small one, just barely born by this forest's standards. Its fifty-foot height was not nearly enough to damage another of its brethren; it collapsed into one of the elder trees nearby, not even tall enough to brush the elder tree's first row of branches.

But the corrupted roots weren't content with one piece of prey.

Wolf bounded through the thickest parts of the forest as if nothing lay before him but open land, sweat clumping the hair on his brow. He didn't waste the time it would take to look over his shoulder—but Ani did.

He didn't see when the next darkwood began to fall, a slow but inevitable drift to its deathbed—but Ani did.

He didn't watch as the Blight culled tree by tree without mercy. But Ani did.

The trees she had planted one by one—the first great miracle she'd performed for *herself* since they'd taken on the mantle of godhood—she watched as they were strangled. Severed. Sent toppling to their demise with nothing to break their fall.

Screaming for their goddess to save them.

She tried. She reached back for them, pouring every drop of blessed power into her hands, commanding the murderous roots to wither away.

But the trees kept dying. One by one by one.

Helplessness—hopelessness—dragged her hand back down. Her magic shivered. Shrank. Spluttered out.

She hid her face in Wolf's shoulder.

And when the forest's screaming began anew, its goddess covered her ears.

CHAPTER 37

ANIMA

D*rip. Drip. Drip.*

Blood raining from her back, plump droplets plunging into the basin below; dewdrop tears pouring from the Crownless Queen's statuesque face as she bore witness to her own future failings.

A shame she and Ani shared.

Drip. Drip. Drip.

Why Wolf had chosen to retreat *here*, not the city proper, she didn't know—and hadn't asked. But she guessed it had something to do with the shrine's Guardian: a man who, after a couple blinks, she recognized as the same one who'd carried a dead orchid into her temple and asked her to help him heal it.

After towing the door open—wearing no helmet this time, revealing silver-streaked raven hair—the kind, unyielding man asked no probing questions.

He asked only what Ani needed. And when Wolf answered, "Privacy and discretion," the Guardian gave them both.

A cold breeze skated over the water's surface, carrying the chill to Ani's inflamed back; and though the shiver that wracked her limbs hurt in a different way, it at least swept away some of the heated itch spreading over her skin.

Like a doting mother, wherever the cold peppered her with kisses, the pain lessened; but it couldn't keep up with Wolf's penetrating gaze.

As if filled to the brim with wound-flushing alcohol, whichever hurt he set his attention to burned white-hot before he ever probed it. And each time, she bore down on her lower lip with her teeth, scuffing her fingers raw on the chalky edge of the fountain and refusing to whimper or complain.

Because if he tried to ask her forgiveness for this, she might just scream her head off instead.

She adjusted herself on the edge of the fountain, lessening the pressure on her hip, and stared down into the water—her bloodied, muddied face reflected in the clouded pool.

Drip. Drip. Two tears of her own joining the rain.

"I know," Wolf muttered over her shoulder, so low she could barely hear him. "Mine's not a bedside manner to envy. I'm sor—"

"Don't." Her voice broke. "Don't say it."

His palm—warm now, no trace of grave-deep chill webbed beneath the skin—settled briefly between her shoulder blades.

"I am sorry," he murmured, breath warm on her neck, "that you're in pain. I am not taking the blame."

Her throat *ached.* She drew her cardigan—now worn backward, baring her back while shielding her front—flush to her shame-steeped chest. "You should have told me the truth."

The pressure on her back didn't change, but he pulled back regardless. A distance established by wariness, not withdrawal. "About my magic?"

"About *your* suffering." She wiped a tear. Then another. They fell faster than she could keep up with. "That I caused it—that it's my fault."

He didn't condescend to her by claiming otherwise. He just said, after a weighty sigh, "Fault implies intention—and I don't believe you had any intention to harm me. All of us know better."

"All of—?" Understanding tore a new hole in her heart. "The Reapers. *All* of you are—?"

"Yes." His fingers spread over her back, braced against the curl of her ribs toward her spine; a moment later, he pressed a dripping cloth to another cluster of wounds. "It's Arborius's best-kept secret—to the best of our knowledge, we are the only kingdom to offer asylum to those blessed with necromancy."

"Because of you?"

"Because of *you.*"

Shock numbed her wounds enough for her to peek over her shoulder; he met her gaze without blinking. "*Me?*"

"It was a few centuries back. Do you recall anything about a host named Venetia?"

"I think so." The name sounded familiar, at least. Like finding a favorite coat she'd outgrown in the back of her wardrobe.

"She was the first you took after every kingdom declared necromancy illegal. A practitioner came to the island begging asylum, and you befriended her. Between the two of you and whoever was queen at the time, you worked to quietly find and ferry necromancers on the run to the island to live out their lives without the fear of bounty hunters." Like a skirt caught in a bramble patch, her skin snagged painfully as Wolf extracted a thorn; when he tossed it aside, her breath tumbled out in a gush. "Through centuries of research and experimentation, we've found ways to treat the negative effects of the condition…not cure it, not yet, but we've been able to provide relief. My mother was our first necromancer queen. Besides you, naturally."

"Your mother…" She hesitated.

"Ask." A neutral invitation.

"I've never heard of a necromancer being able to have children."

"Nor can they be twice-blessed," he agreed, squeezing out the cloth, then soaking it again. "But that she was. Blessed with medimancy and necromancy. My father says she was a miracle in that way." A twist of wry, almost rueful humor touched his voice at the same time the cloth touched her back. "They theorize that combination is why she was able to bear a child—and why I was born twice-blessed, too."

"And it was her magic that…" She couldn't bring herself to say it.

"In a way." He hesitated. "Thanks to Arborius's unique ecosystem, living here is enough to increase a necromancer's life expectancy by a fair amount. Still fewer years than most, if more than we'd be favored with elsewhere…but my mother was a unique case. She used her magic more frequently than we recommend to keep it from turning on her while she was pregnant with me, afraid it would sap my life if she didn't oversate it. And afterward, it had grown used to the excess. The kind of sustenance she needed was unsustainable. Even here."

Her mind scrambled for the most benign detail she could comment on. "What do you mean, unique ecosystem?"

"Well, Arborius being all forest, we're privy to a constant cycle of life and death. Our magic rarely lacks for energy to consume, barring some…unforeseen circumstances." Wolf cleared his throat. "My episode the other night was the first in some time, and more severe than most. I haven't had cause to repress my magic in quite a while, but with my cousin's arrival, then so many falling ill—"

"You didn't want Soren to know?"

"Her tale didn't exactly suggest a favorable view of such magic." A soft curse. "If Jericho had just *told* us…gods, we must've found a hundred ways to hint over the years. I think Brook even asked her plain to her face when she snuck her husband out here for a proper assessment, but she didn't tip over."

Ani trailed her fingers in the water, scrubbing some mud away; a strange heaviness still wrapped around her shoulders, snugging them tight. She waited to see if Wolf would say more; when he did not, she ventured a change of subject. "Are my wounds healing yet?"

"Slowly but surely."

An aching, swollen clot of tension formed in the center of her forehead, right beneath her wrinkled brow. She rubbed it, heedless of the water dribbling down the bridge of her nose. "That thing…it kept saying I *made* it." She scrubbed at her cheeks now, then her arms. "And I'm afraid I know why."

"Something to do with the Blight?"

Ani shook her head. "I'm afraid it *is* the Blight."

Used by her brother to taint her relic, then freed by her use of that relic; and when it left, it took a piece of creation with it.

At least, she could come up with no other explanation for how a corrupted magic might have made itself a body. Or how it could have dealt *her* body wounds that seemed so reluctant to heal.

In the weighty silence that followed, even the gentle rumble of stone against stone was enough to startle them both; the shrine's Guardian poked his head through the open door, clearing his throat. "Your Highness, there are worshippers approaching the shrine. Shall I send them away?"

"No. I'll be taking the Goddess to the medimancers to have these seen to properly—she just needed a moment of quiet." Wolf dipped his head. "Thank you for your discretion, as always."

She pinned up her smile—it took all her will to hold it up, and even then, it sagged in strange places. "Yes, thank you."

The Guardian bowed low. "Anything you ask of me, milady, it will be done. Always."

Absurdly, that made her want to cry again. "How—how is your orchid?"

"Exactly as I remember." He straightened, brushing a hand down his uniform. "You have a remarkable memory…you must have performed a thousand miracles that day."

"You tell remarkable stories." And that miracle had been a pleasure to perform. "If it ever requires another sprucing up—"

"I shall refer to the instructions you left me," the Guardian chuckled. "We must be cautious of becoming too reliant on miracles, milady…and those who perform them."

A stinging rush swept over Ani's face. "You think the gods unreliable?"

Wrinkles feathered around his jaybird-blue eyes. "I think you are offering miracles to others while bleeding through your clothes."

Her dizzied mind could not follow the thread—like silk coated in oil, it slipped again and again through her fingers. Before she could catch it, Wolf helped her stand, guiding her toward the open door.

He didn't bid the Guardian farewell—nor did the Guardian speak again. But Ani's mind stayed behind, still chasing that dastardly thread in circles, trying to tie the Guardian's words into something that made sense.

CHAPTER 38

ANIMA

When Wolf called a family meeting, they did not gather in Genevieve's office; instead, they crowded into the card room on the ground floor of the Olivander tree. The four eldest Olivander siblings, who each beelined for particular pieces of furniture like they'd been assigned seats; their parents, who shared the chaise before the hearth, both shifting their gazes between Wolf and each other; and Lady Astrid Thorne, who walked in like she'd called this meeting herself.

Whoever formulated her cosmetics for her, Ani needed to ask for a referral. She rarely wore them herself, but if those creams and powders could mask the chronic exhaustion and pallid complexion of long, sleepless stints in the infirmary—stints Astrid had been pulling nearly as often as her—it might be worth clogging a few pores.

"Say it again, but slower," said Sage as he fell into the old, overstuffed armchair. "Or write it down, maybe. Might make more sense to me if you do it like a storybook. How are you at illustrations?"

"You ask them to repeat themselves, then don't let them get a word in edgewise," Astrid scolded, perching on the chair's arm and swatting her husband on the shoulder with a small, well-loved notebook bound in aquamarine leather. Its cover had begun to curl back at the edges, so many other papers and clips shoved between the pages that it seemed bloated with use.

"I'm not ribbing them, love," Sage protested—then, when she aimed an infinitesimally raised eyebrow his way, he added, "Maybe about the writing part. But I do think a sketch would be helpful. I can barely hear straight after all those trees falling." He nailed Ani with a longsuffering stare. "What's that rotting ridiculous…*if a tree falls in the forest and no one is around, does it make a sound?* The answer is *yes, obviously*, you daft—"

"Sage," Wolf sighed, "are you going to let me speak or not?"

"Are you going to start making sense?" Sage spread his arms. "I thought the Blight was an *illness*. Now you're telling me it's—"

"It's not an illness," Ani interrupted—then covered her mouth. "Sorry, I didn't—"

"Oh, go on, dear," Genevieve urged. "Trust me, interruptions are the only way you'll be heard in this house."

"Unless you're me," Astrid said.

"Unless you're her," all four Olivander siblings agreed before Sage added, "Privilege of being the prettiest face in the room. Used to be mine till she showed up."

Another eyebrow twitch from Astrid.

"Until I asked her to court me and she was just foolish enough to say yes," Sage corrected himself.

"And happy to be a fool for you." Astrid dusted his hair with a handful of affectionate kisses. "Now let Ani speak."

"It isn't an illness." She couldn't look at Wolf for some reason, even though she ached to. The slumbering heat under her skin promised to become a full-fledged flush if she tried. "It's…more of a corruption. An infection might be a better comparison, or a poison, or—"

"A parasite," Wolf muttered.

Humor dipped below the horizon line in Sage's gaze; in its place, understanding dawned. "It's feeding. Like your, ah…condition, Wolf, it—"

"She knows." Wolf's eyes cut to her—and cut that face-flush free. "No use dancing it."

"Thank the *gods*," Sparrow and Sage groaned together. Even Genevieve's shoulders slackened like they'd shed a weight.

Astrid alone gave no reaction beyond measuring Wolf with her gaze. "Like necromancy feeds on life, Blight feeds on chaos. And if the host does not provide enough from the outside, it feeds from the host itself."

"I haven't seen it do this before," Ani confessed. "It's a corrupted form of medimancy, not biomancy. It's always infected people or animals."

"Let's not take what it has *always* done into account. I worry too narrow of a view might risk much in terms of our response." Astrid eased herself off her perch, making a new one of her husband's lap; Ani might have blushed if Astrid hadn't somehow managed to make even that look business-like. She crossed one leg over the other, flipping her journal open and jotting a note; Sage laid his head on her shoulder, tracking her pen with slow, weary blinks. "I hesitate to put the amalgamation of two divine magics in a box of any sort, let alone try to label that box."

Ani blinked. "Pardon?"

"Not a good strategy to tell something impossible what it's allowed to be," Sage nuzzled into his wife's shoulder to hide his yawn, if poorly. "Better we assume it can than it can't. Better to prepare for the worst."

That last one, she understood.

"You said it spoke to you?" Brook, who'd stretched out in the padded alcove of the bay window situated between two bookshelves, eyed her with hawkish brows mashed together.

"In the way that things speak to me."

Their flurry of swapped looks rang a little alarm bell in her head. Not *Good Sense* or *Impending Doom*, but a far more oft-rung bell that told her she'd said or done something strange.

"I understand things others wouldn't," she explained hastily. "Plants, trees…animals."

"I *told you* all I wasn't fibbing," Sparrow said crossly; she sat on the floor at her parents' feet with a snoozing cat in her lap, a mouse peeking out from her collar, and a lizard with tiny spikes along its chin clinging to her shoulder. She scratched its head, and Ani could have sworn it mimicked the cat's contented purr. "They all have words of a sort—even the bees."

"Great," Sage grumbled. "Now you've gotten her started."

"This is serious." Cypress's scolding hushed his entire family in one go. "No matter what we *think* this abomination is, we *know* it is on the hunt. Our quarantine protocols won't be sufficient."

"No." Sage's voice lost strength as his neck did; his head fell against his wife's shoulder, and he squeezed his eyes shut, pinching the bridge of his nose. "We'll need to overlap—quarantine and assault practices."

"Some of those will contradict," Brook warned.

"Not all that many." Sparrow scratched behind her feline companion's ears. "Most of those will be finer points; we can iron them out in the morning."

"For now, our top priority is locking down Elderwood." Genevieve pinched the bridge of her nose, a perfect mimicry of her second-eldest son. "We'll need to ferry additional supplies to the dockside infirmaries."

"I'll handle that with the Reapers." Wolf balled up his fists and pocketed them. "We can use our talents to transport supplies without risking infection passing on."

One blessing, that bone could not carry Blight with it.

"I'll help," Ani volunteered.

"You will not," Wolf said, at the same time Sage said, "Much appreciated, lass."

The two brothers stopped, staring at each other in consternation. Sage sat up straight. "You got any good reasons I ought to refuse the boons of a goddess?"

"I've got five, but if you want to see them, it's best we step out," Wolf said flatly. Sage's eyes narrowed—so did Astrid's.

"Boys," Genevieve warned, and the two tossed their gazes to opposite sides of the room—but neither relaxed. "Unless you have a good reason, Wolf, I'm not quite keen on telling a goddess what she can and can't do in her own kingdom."

"That thing hunted her. It came after *her*." His glare burrowed into her chest like he'd fired it with his bow, a blame that withered her resolve. "If anyone ought to stay within the city limits, it's her."

Instead of blood, instead of indignance, desperation poured from that wound. "*I* am aware of what it did. I am aware that this is my fault. That's why I must help."

Wolf gave a confused, fluttering blink. "Goddess, you misunderstand—"

"I *will* help," she cut across him, what Soren might have called a *parry*—a refusal to let him take the ground she'd reclaimed. "But you are right that I am a target…and that may make it more dangerous for any who accompany me." She directed her attention to Sage and Astrid. "If you could recommend where I can be the most help—and the least harm—I would be happy to follow your lead." Next, she looked to Genevieve. "And I must insist Prince Wolf be dismissed from his duties as my escort."

Sparrow winced, drawing in a hissing breath through her teeth. Wolf's swift inhale was much softer, but the tumble of emotions across his eyes rang through her like the brutal howl of his namesake.

She didn't understand those emotions. But it confused her that none of them looked like *anger*…not anger, nor blame, nor relief.

"Wolf?" prompted Genevieve. "Is this your wish as well?"

"Over my dead, dancing corpse."

Not one of the Olivanders looked surprised. Sage didn't even stir from his heavy-lidded doze. But Ani's blood churned, sweeping through her veins like whitewater rapids.

She crossed her arms over her chest. A wall to keep her widlly beating heart in check. "As *you* pointed out, if it's me it's after, my proximity will put you in danger."

"So you wish to dismiss your guard at the exact moment you need one?"

"I am a goddess—"

"It made you *bleed!*"

Wolf's passionate outburst brought on a different kind of silence than Cypress's low scolding; instead of turning aside, all the gathered Olivanders stared wide-eyed at the eldest prince.

Prickling pains throbbed in Ani's back. The ghosts of newly healed holes in her flesh.

"And you think I would rather see *you* bleed?" she whispered into that silence.

Wolf raked a hand through his hair. Looked to Sage, who glanced away with his lips rounded in a false whistle; looked to Genevieve, whose knowing green gaze held her son's until he looked away.

"If she must help," Wolf said stiffly, "then the guard remains. It is not up for debate."

"I am inclined to agree," Astrid spoke up, smiling her apology when betrayal parted Ani's lips in silent protest. "It presents the least risk to all parties. Compromise is not always the best path, but here, I think both of you could stand to give ground. Wolf, we will not forbid Ani from lending her talents if she wishes to; and as for you, Ani, there is a very thin line between selflessness and senselessness. I respect your desire to reduce casualties, but if this creature can slow your healing, I worry about what might happen if it corners you again. I would ask you to allow Wolf to accompany you as long as he is willing and capable—and yes," she added when Wolf opened his mouth, "I also suggest you stay within Elderwood proper."

"But I—"

"Not just for your well-being," Brook said; the Heir had taken all this in with few words, much like her father, but hundreds of thoughts rustled like wind-tousled grass in her gaze. "Our people will look to you as an example. They will see you as a comfort. If you buck quarantine, they'll question why they must follow it…or worse, be inspired to action at the cost of their own well-being alongside you."

Why were they treating her as if her *well-being* abided by mortal rules? Didn't they understand how much more *fragile* they were? How pointless, how *silly* it was to set a human shield in front of a—

Pale cheeks dappled in blood, pale hair torn from its skull-tight braids, pale lips breathing their last.

"I must rest," she choked, each word lodging more firmly in her throat than the last. "I trust your understanding of this kingdom—do as you see fit." Then, to Wolf: "I suppose you'll want to escort me."

His jaw worked, but no emotion swayed his expression this time. "You suppose right."

"Stay here for the night, at least," Genevieve added swiftly. "We've had a guest room ready for a while. Better not to walk back to the infirmary in the dark."

Ani established her silence with a sharp nod; she stewed in it all the while they walked through the dimly lit halls, empty of the palacefolk she'd seen here and there during the day. Very few, compared to Atlas—mostly cleaners and launderers, and only a handful of each. For the most part, the Olivanders seemed to keep their home themselves.

Wolf endured that silence nearly three minutes before he broke it. "I would ordinarily consider this a moment to offer an apology, but you don't seem fond of them."

She didn't answer. Because if she did, he'd hear the tears in her tone, and then there'd be no dodging one of those gratuitous apologies.

"It was *not* your fault," he said, a bit faster than usual, his cadence strung out with nerves. "I never meant to heap that blame on your head, but I…I hear now how it sounded. If you're insisting on putting yourself in danger because you believe you are responsible—"

"I don't *believe* it." She dashed the back of her hand across her grief-dewed cheeks, under her running nose. "I know it."

Another swift inhale, like she'd kicked him instead of corrected him.

Then his fingers closed around her wrist. "Ani. Look at me."

Ani. Don't leave.

Just like the night before, his plea snared her like barbed wire around a bird's wing, crushing her hopes of flying away.

His hand left her wrist. Found her shoulder. Coaxed her to turn around with such cruel, irrestible gentleness.

She could hardly see his face in the low lamplight—and what she could see vanished quickly beneath another surge of tears. So instead she focused on the shooting stars in his hair, the sort Soren called *wishing stars,* and wished that the shadows would disguise the dewdrops rolling down her cheeks.

But only her imagination fancied those pearly streaks as stars, not the sipping of his life by insatiable magic, silvery scars dealt as it savored every taste. Her wishes fell on deaf ears as the rough pad of a calloused thumb scraped away her next tear.

"What are these for?" A helpless, baffled whisper.

She shook her head.

"Because of me?"

Her chin quivered.

A hushed curse. "I swear on my useless bones, if you can't stand my company a moment more, I'll bite my wretched tongue from here on out—or I can appoint someone else to serve as your guard. But I cannot…I cannot see you unprotected."

The shadows flickered as he moved—as he knelt and took her hands in his. He tipped his head back to find her misty eyes.

"If my presence is truly such a trial, I'll find someone else," he swore. "Before the night's out. Just say the word and I'll make myself scarce."

Absurdly, a broken giggle bubbled up through the swill of withheld sobs. She rolled her eyes toward the ceiling to keep more tears from falling; a trick Soren had taught her. "Oh, don't be ridiculous. You have to know your *presence* is not the problem."

Apparently, he did not have to know anything of the sort—when she looked back down, the baffled creases carved into his forehead had only deepened.

"I want you to be safe," he said. "That is all I want. I did not realize you would think it so terrible a thing."

"The wanting is not the terrible thing." Tremulous fear rippled through her heart, tightening her fingers around his. "It's what comes after."

"And what comes after?"

Pale cheeks dappled in blood, pale hair torn from its skull-tight braids, pale lips breathing their last.

Her hand lifted without intention on her part. She tilted Wolf's chin with her fingertips, coaxing his bowed head upward until the sparse light finally caught his wide, searching eyes.

"When someone aims for a goddess," she whispered, "they do not strike lightly. And what might harm me will do far worse to you."

Confusion thickened again, at first…then cleared abruptly with a startled blink. "You're afraid for *me?*"

"You said you want me to be safe—is it really so hard to believe that I might want the same for you?"

He rubbed his neck with one hand, looking askance—then stood with a lurch and a cough. "I'll show you your room. My sisters chose it, so I'm sure it will be to your liking—they've got a good sense for this sort of thing—"

She let her empty hands fall. "Wolf—"

"—It's the *only* thing they have a good sense for, actually—"

"*Wolf.*"

His boot scuffed against the floor, halfway through turning away from her.

"Yes, Goddess?" Enunciating every syllable of her title, like he was reminding her of it. Or reminding himself.

"I appreciate your concern," as ill-placed as it might have been, "and I am willing to accept your escort."

A loosening of his bunched shoulders. "Thank—"

"All I ask of you," she interrupted, "is a promise."

His shoulders straightened again, guarded, braced. "Ask it."

"Promise me you will be a support, not a shield." It felt like she'd swallowed a marble; she couldn't work the hard bead of emotion down her throat. "People put themselves in harm's way for me before. I can't allow it. I can't *bear* it."

Wolf was silent for a beat—then lowered his head. "You have my word."

His word did not give her the reassurance she'd hoped. But he could give her nothing else, so she merely nodded in return, letting him lead her through these shadowed corridors.

Praying, in her own way, that those shadows had not covered any deceit in that solemn oath.

CHAPTER 39

SOREN

The Sanctum of the Faithless—or as Medwenna called it, the *Sanctum Infidelium*—was only a day's journey by foot.

And she was grateful. Because another day of having to dodge the snowballs Everin, Matthias, and Kessen kept lobbing at each other was liable to wreck her nerves—and her knees.

Though watching Elias get a faceful of slush from Kessen gave her a much-needed laugh. One that warped into screams of terror as her battlemate armed himself and came after her, wielding his skills as the most formidable snowball-flinger in their company.

It was the one "morale-boosting" activity in the Nyxian barracks where people across companies fought for the right to pick Elias the Pious first…and he never let them down. She still leapt out of her skin on occasion when his fingers brushed past the nape of her neck, her body recalling the half-dozen times he had snuck up behind her like a gods-damned specter of death and dropped a round of ice down her shirt.

When the clamor died down, however—all of them soaking wet and shivering like a shorn wolf in an ice bath—Medwenna's idle whistling turned out to be even less bearable than the soaring weapons of warfare. And the woman *would not stop whistling*. Tunes, at first—Arborian and Tallisian alike, some of which the Triad purposely sang as off-pitch as possible. Then, when she ran out of melodies, Medwenna shifted to teaching them bird calls.

As they set up camp for the night, the ranger—unlike the rest of their travel-worn troop—seemed perfectly content. She settled cross-legged on the ground near the fire Elias and Everin were working to stoke, her cloak tossed aside despite the chill growing steeper with every minute; she held a twist of grass she'd woven earlier to mimic each call as she taught it to them.

"Medwenna," Soren interrupted at call one-hundred-and-seven, "I appreciate the lesson, but I'm a bit worried it'll attract bigger things with bigger teeth if they think a million birds live in these trees."

Soren almost felt guilty when Medwenna's eager smile banked sharply into a sheepish bend. "Oh—I'm sorry, of course. Forgive me. I didn't mean to bother."

All three Tallisian heads popped up, each wearing a look of warning more severe than the last.

"Not a bother at all," Soren lied hastily, since she wasn't in the mood to die tonight.

Three thumbs-ups flashed her way before the men went back to their work.

Everin—who was currently in the middle of his fifth attempt to set a pile of kindling alight—tossed the flint and steel to Elias, whistling as he sauntered back to them. He dropped to his seat beside Medwenna, one hand out; she handed him her makeshift whistle, and he pressed it to his lips. An unfamiliar warble fluttered through the blades; a heartbeat later, an answering warble came from somewhere above their heads.

Everin pointed upward. "Which one was that?"

"Arrow-tipped jaybird." Medwenna took the grass back, mimicking another call. She lowered it, pausing—then beaming when the answering call came. "What about that one?"

"Silver shrike." Everin smirked up at Soren, giving Medwenna's braid a playful tug. "Calls are a handy thing to know as a hunter, and my apprentice here knows them all." He paused. "Honestly, she knows everything about everything. I think if she ever had to say *I don't know*, she'd keel over and die."

"Well? Would you?" Soren asked.

Medwenna shrugged modestly. "I wouldn't know. I haven't had to yet."

She'd never envied anyone quite so much.

"Everin!" called Kessen, wearing a distinct tone all sisters knew by ear—the tone of a tattletale about to let loose. "The zealot's using his magic!"

"Ah-ah-ah! What did I say?" Everin leaned around Medwenna, flicking his fingers toward Elias as if they too could spit sparks. "None of *this*."

Elias spread his arms, unused flint and steel in one hand, perfect tinder-igniting flame in the other. "What's the difference?"

"One's natural as rivers and rocks, and the other makes me want to kick your teeth in."

"That's not the magic," Soren corrected. "It's just his face—been like that as long as I've known him."

Elias closed his fingers to extinguish the flame in his palm, flashing her a particular finger. She flashed hers back; he dropped the flint and steel just to double up. Rather than drop all her tentpoles to retaliate, she settled for sticking her tongue out.

Kessen frowned, looking between them. "Aren't you two getting married?"

"As soon as humanly possible," Elias confirmed.

Soren crossed the site, piling the tentpoles at Elias's feet before taking his arm and nuzzling her cheek into his shoulder. "Aren't we adorable?"

"Terrifying, actually," Kessen mumbled.

"At least you say what you really feel." Matthias's gaze slid to Everin. "Keep things honest. That's rare these days."

"Sure is, Matty." Everin knuckled Medwenna's hair before striding back to the fire, plucking the fallen flint and steel from the dirt as he went.

"Here's what my prince is trying to tell you." Matthias followed Everin, stealing the flint and steel, ignoring his spread-armed protest. The beads in his long braids clattered as he knelt by the kindling, looking up to Elias without malice. "Tell me this, zealot—let's say you walk the same road home every single day. You know this road from beginning to end; you know its bumps, its pits, its curves, its obstacles." The flint and steel struck, frightening a spark out; it arced into the pile of tinder like a shooting star, but only a drizzle of smoke emerged from its landing site. "And the more you walk it, the easier it becomes, until you could map it out in your sleep." Another strike of flint; another spark; another star. This one caught; the tinder began to crackle, flame hoisting itself up to trace a gentle, tentative caress across the firewood.

"But let's say you discover a shortcut." Matthias stole a twig from the tinder pile, holding it up to demonstrate the flagrant bead of flame at its end. He touched it to the other side of the tinder pile; it caught immediately, snatching fistfuls of that little fire in greedy gasps. "And you think, *well, it gets me where I need to go so much faster—why would I ever go the long way again?*"

Matthias flipped his hand, driving the twig down into the dirt like a blade into a back; the fire smothered, the scorched end crumbling into charcoal dust.

"But one day, that shortcut vanishes," he said. "Doesn't matter why. Maybe a rockslide buried it. Maybe a sinkhole swallowed it up." A pointed look. "Maybe it actually belongs to someone else, and they decide not to let you trespass on their path anymore. But for whatever reason, you putter on back to the main road…and you can't find your way for anything. You trip on every stone, you tumble into every ditch…the path you used to know like the back of your hand now takes you twice as long to cross, because you've fallen out of practice. You put blind faith into something that didn't belong to you."

"And if it goes away…" Everin arched a brow, running his finger through the air, tracing Elias head to toe. "Where does that leave you, zealot?"

Zealot wasn't all that different from *Pious*, but it still made her want to punch Everin's pretty teeth from his gums. Though maybe that had more to do with the way his lip curled when he said it, sounding out the two syllables like throwing two punches in rapid succession. One to send his head spinning, the other to knock him fully to the ground.

"Say the word," she murmured in Elias's ear, "and I'll use my diplomatic immunity to give him a black eye."

"You don't have diplomatic immunity," he muttered back.

"I'm pretty sure I do."

"I'm *absolutely* sure you don't."

Soren scowled. "I don't like how he talks to you."

"I'll manage." He kissed her forehead, then twisted to hide his words in her hair, laughter buried underneath: "It's not the first time I've had a cocky royal calling me names."

She drove her fist into his stomach—not hard, but enough that he grunted upon impact.

"You have a very weird relationship." Kessen sat at the campfire, putting his palms out as it slowly grew under Matthias's watchful guidance. "It's…fun. Did anyone pack marshmallows?"

Soren gasped, diving to steal the spot beside Kessen, grievances and parables forgotten. "You have s'mores here?"

Kessen caught the bag of marshmallows that Everin tossed him, but nearly fumbled the thin, long stick Matthias threw after—he had to snatch it back just as it leaned into the edge of the fire, blowing on his fingertips before frowning at Soren. "What's a s'more?"

Soren pointed at the makeshift skewer. "Marshmallow, chocolate, molasses biscuit?"

"Oh! We call them mallow melts, but yeah, same difference." Kessen offered her the skewer, reaching simultaneously for another, which felt like a poor choice—and proved itself to be when Everin tossed another, and Kessen fully missed it, the stick crashing into the campfire. The logs collapsed in a cloud of sparks and smoke.

Everin applauded loudly, startling a cluster of birds from the nearby treetop: some of the arrow-tipped jaybirds he'd greeted earlier. "Good catch."

"Leave off him," Medwenna scolded. She hunted down a stick herself, joining the half-circle around the fire and handing Kessen the twig while Elias reached into the bonfire and rearranged the logs. "That was hardly a fair toss."

"It's as fair as any other!"

Medwenna's laughter echoed off the snow-coated trees, their evergreen boughs shivering in the wind. "Sure enough. Tell that to the poor bird you nearly speared, throwing it that high over the kid's head."

"All right, all right, settle down," Matthias sighed, the snow creaking as he settled himself by the bonfire. "If we kick up a fuss after the sun sets, the spirits will do the same to our dreams."

Elias frowned, dropping to his seat on her left; when she offered him her skewer, topped with the plumpest marshmallow in the bag, he took it and hovered his palm over it. A wavering haze of heat ribboned from his palm; the marshmallow's sugary surface swelled and bubbled, caramelizing beautifully as he rotated it. "What do you mean, spirits?"

She didn't hear Matthias's answer, too busy trying to stop her mouth from watering as she watched the marshmallow turn the most flawless shade of golden-brown she'd ever seen. But Elias's sharp intake of breath pulled her back; his eyes had widened to the whites, skimming the growing shadows around them like something might emerge any second.

"Most spirits are spooks at worst," Matthias continued—ah. They were back to the ghost thing. "Mischief-makers on occasion. But the wanderers…those you ought to be careful of. Especially you, Elias."

Her hackles rose immediately. "Why him?"

"He's the scion of Mortem," Medwenna cut in. "Death calls to death. We believe wandering spirits have no tether to life. This leaves them…aimless. Lost and alone."

Right. Medwenna had brought this up on the ship, but she'd forgotten to warn Elias…bigger things on her mind, after all. Confronting Denali had felt more dangerous than spooky stories.

"They're desperate to go anywhere else." Matthias shrugged. "They might follow you, thinking you offer an opportunity for some kind of rest. And with your…" he paused, saying the next word like he was trying to tiptoe over broken glass, "*abilities,* that might disturb your peace more than most."

"But they can't actually hurt anyone," Soren verified.

"No, not that we know of." Matthias tipped his head. "But overactive nerves are their own kind of harm. Just try not to let your thoughts wander to death…and maybe keep your prayers to yourself for the evening."

Elias's eyes glazed with some thought she almost recognized as he avoided Matthias's gaze. He handed her the skewer, melted marshmallow sagging from it, then tucked his arm around her middle, resting his chin on her shoulder.

"I wish I *could* help them," he said quietly. "I can't imagine it's pleasant, being trapped between life and death."

Trapped.

Unable to die; unable to live. Unable to speak or move or scream of their own accord.

Nausea carved the craving for sugar right off her tongue. "It isn't."

Five sets of eyes found her face—then leapt away, one by one. Kessen even coughed awkwardly into his elbow. But Medwenna reached past Elias to lay a hand on Soren's knee.

"You are not a ghost," she said softly. "You never died. Your spirit and your body remain tethered." A faint lift of her lips. "You will not be haunting anyone anytime soon."

She smiled back at the archeress—alarmed, if only slightly, by how close those words brought her to tears. And she tried not to look too closely at Elias, who'd reached up to scratch at the back of his neck, staring unseeingly into the fire.

Whose last breath still echoed deep in her ears in moments of quiet. Whose lifeless gaze still found her sometimes in sleep.

Who had slumped in her arms, broken in ways she couldn't fix, when Vaughn snapped the tether that bound his spirit and body.

"No more ghost stories," she decided out loud.

Nobody argued. And when they retired one by one to their bedrolls, no one said a word as Elias went to the dying fire and brought it back to life with an errant wave of his hand, light startling the shadows back to their own beds.

Tonight was not the night to pretend they were all too old to be afraid of the dark.

CHAPTER 40

ANIMA

A quarter of the island lay dead by the next dawn.

And while Ani could scrounge up plenty of gratitude that it hadn't been worse, that the casualties were mostly arboreal, not human…grief insisted on having its way with her, too.

So silly to be sitting in a patch of dirt, staring out at the corpse-littered forest, watering the empty soil with her tears; but knowing how silly it was to be hurting over this didn't make the hurting stop.

She dragged her nails through the dirt, gathering a handful of carnage. Clods of soil and strips of bark dribbled between her fingers as she lifted them, fresh tears bathing her cheeks.

Where trees died, so did creatures. The carcasses of squirrels and birds thrown from their nests or crushed beneath their homes had been gently called away by the Reapers; she'd thanked them as they guided the dead to proper graves, occasionally threading her own magic into the weave. After all, she'd insisted on lending a hand…even if she did fear her power might call the Blight back.

The living, stalking, *talking* Blight.

But surely now that it had killed this portion of the forest, it wouldn't return—chaos had no need to return to the scene of its crimes. It had already wrung every drop of discord out of this place.

Though if it returned, it might find some scraps baiting the path between her and Wolf.

The return of his constant presence *had* actually proven to be a comfort; she no longer felt the urge to peek over her shoulder everywhere she walked, because she knew exactly what she'd find.

And for all her fear that it would set him in harm's way, it was…nice, to have a protector.

Familiar, in a way.

But there were still things she needed to see to alone. So when it came time for him to see to the Reapers and lead their daily prayers, she made excuses about the awkwardness of being prayed to in person—and made promises to stay within the Olivander tree for an hour or two—until he finally agreed to go on his own.

And once she was alone, she knew exactly where to make her first stop.

"You want me to teach you how to shoot a bow?"

Sage's incredulity stung; or maybe that was just the stench of manure cloying the warm air in the stables. She focused instead on the notes of sweet hay and molasses water underneath—and on the raised eyebrow of curiosity he offered instead of outright denial.

"My magic, it was…slow, during the attack." She followed him as he moved behind his horse, a sturdy mare with a sleek bay coat and a bright white blaze that poured from beneath her forelock to the apex of her muzzle. A placard above her stall deemed her *Missy*—short for *Mistress,* if his and Astrid's joking exchange during their first meeting was anything to go by. "I am not used to being defenseless, and I…I don't like the idea of relying on others to be my shield."

Wolf had made her the promise she'd asked for. But promises didn't always stand strong when danger came to call.

He won't touch you again.

Pale cheeks dappled in blood, pale hair torn from its skull-tight braids, pale lips breathing their last…

Sage's reticent hum blended with Missy's nicker as he continued brushing burrs from her coat, a harmony that tickled Ani's ears; the prince frowned at her before setting the brush aside, folding his arms on the slope of the mare's back.

"Wish I could lend a hand," he said, "but I'm afraid my day's full up here. I've been neglecting this one in favor of my wife, and she needs a good see-to. Besides, I'd look like a right hypocrite if I went out now—I just issued the order this morning for everyone without permission otherwise to stay out of the trees.

Not sure how you snuck out here without Wolf's help, yourself—and don't tell me," he added when she opened her mouth. "I don't want to know."

In truth, the sneaking out had been very simple with Wolf otherwise occupied. Even under orders, most people weren't eager to tell a goddess *no*.

As if Ani's thoughts had written themselves out in her eyes, Sage added, "Actually, I'm sure Wolf would be happy to give you a lesson or two, if he's not driven you so far up a tree you never want to set eyes on his face again. He's the best below me—Sparrow could give him a sprint for his supper, but she's probably elbow-deep in her beehives right about now. Gods know I've never set a curfew she didn't break."

"I thought Wolf was a priest, not a ranger." And a necromancer, but she needed a day or two more of reckoning before she'd feel comfortable bringing *that* up in casual conversation.

"Aye, he is. But you don't get into this family without inheriting *some* ability with a bow." Sage's eyes twinkled. "We actually tossed two other siblings out for having poor aim."

She mustered an awkward laugh. "Right."

"In all seriousness, Wolf's one of our best hunters…though he's not doing a great job of demonstrating just now."

"Huh?"

Sage sighed. "Speak of the spook…" Without turning his head, he called over his shoulder, "I can *hear* you skulking about out there, Wolf! Get out here before you scare the horses. You're making me look like a tale-teller in front of Ani here."

Sure enough, Wolf stepped from the shadows of an empty stall, a rare emotion twitching in his temple: annoyance. Even walking with his cane again, she hadn't heard anything. "How do you do that?"

"You have a presence. Makes the horses shifty." Sage patted Missy's flank, then turned to dig his hand into the receptacle hanging from the wall: a glass lantern refashioned for sugar cube storage. He coaxed out two cubes and offered them to Missy. "You're a good girl, aren't you? Best scout we've got, yes you are."

Wolf's temple kept right on twitching as he turned his attention on her. But he still bowed. "Goddess."

Habit hooked her fingers together, a makeshift basket to catch any stray embarrassment blooming in her palms. "Prince Wolf."

"I thought you agreed to stay in the tree."

"Ani here has demanded archery lessons." Sage turned away from smattering Missy's muzzle in almost-smooches to slap his brother's shoulder. "I told her you'd be happy to help."

"I-I didn't demand—"

"Don't worry, we know," said Meg—like Wolf, Ani hadn't heard any hint of her approach until she popped her head over the stall door, draping her arms over it and dangling there. "We can take her to the targets, can't we?"

"You're already late for your studies." Wolf ruffled Meg's hair, annoyance easing into amusement with the next look he gave Ani. "*Someone* took her sweet time with her morning prayers. Would've sat there all day if one of the Reapers hadn't caught her snoring."

Meg groaned, throwing herself backward in a despairing arch; Sage lifted her lanky body up and over the stable door, setting her atop his shoulders instead. The ceilings were so tall the girl didn't even have to duck to avoid the rafters. "The books aren't going anywhere. When will I ever get the chance to learn from Anima herself again?"

She might have laughed, if one of Wolf's words hadn't caught her ear. "*You* were with the Reapers, Meg?"

"Oh, right!" Nutmeg brightened, shoving a hand in her pocket and rooting around. "Wolf *said* the jig was up. Wanna see a trick? Here, look." When Nutmeg swung downward and opened her palm, she revealed a small pile of bones, all yellowed with age; she cleared her throat authoritatively, then hovered her fingers over the bones.

Where most necromancers played to the puppetry of their craft, Nutmeg put on a different sort of performance; her fingers danced like she was plunking piano keys. With every "note," a small burst of green light popped in the pile, bouncing a bone out of place; the faster she played, the faster the bones found their places, until...

A skeletal mouse stood on its hind legs, its flexible tail flicking across Nutmeg's palm.

"Wolf said you liked to make things dance," giggled the girl, scratching the mouse's skull fondly; when she went back to playing, the mouse began to *jig*, necromantic power allowing it to kick and leap in ways living mice couldn't. "So do I."

A giggle of her own rose and fell in Ani's throat as she watched the mouse dance. As she watched the girl coming up with the choreography, mirth doing its own waltz through her innocent eyes, hazel leaning green as her magic went to work.

As she watched Wolf watch Nutmeg, too, smile soft, fingers pale-knuckled around his cane's head.

Not the only necromancer in the family, then.

"Amazing." She forced a laugh as the mouse affected a skirtless curtsy. "That takes talent, you know. Most people can't get the bones to do more than shuffle about."

"Wolf taught me." Pride puffed her chest and her smile. "And Sage."

Ani blinked at Sage, surprised. "Did you?"

"Medimancy can be helpful if you want to experiment with less conventional necromantic methods," Wolf explained.

Sage's smirk was nothing less than smug. "If you know exactly how the bones fit together, it's easy to fill in the funny spots so they can move the way you want."

Fair enough. She turned her attention back to Meg. "You sound…happy to have it."

"I love it." Nutmeg patted the mouse's head once more before releasing it back to rest, returning it to her pocket. Her round cheeks practically glowed, hale and rich with color; her satisfied sigh was deep and effortless. "You should see Da's face when I make a critter scurry over his shoes. You can hear him scream all the way to the sea."

She made a mental note to never tempt Nutmeg's mischievous wrath.

"If it's archery lessons you want," Wolf cut in, not quite meeting her gaze, "I suppose it wouldn't hurt. We can go now, if you like."

Nutmeg pumped her fist in the air. "Yes!"

"Not you." Sage patted her leg twice before lifting her off his shoulders, setting her down and knuckling her hair. "You're going straight home to study, else I'll get a reaming out from Ma for helping you play hooky again."

Nutmeg dropped her fist. "*Nooo.*"

"Not a negotiation." Wolf held the stall door open for the girl, unmoved by her moping and moaning. "Go on, get. You can bother Anima once you're done."

"I'm not bothered," Ani protested.

"It's fine, I know what he means." Nutmeg hugged each of her brothers, then threw her arms around Ani, squeezing her with a tightness that made it hard to swallow.

She so rarely received the gift of a good hug.

Once Nutmeg wrangled a promise that they would speak more at supper that night, the girl reluctantly tromped out of the stables; after she'd gone and Sage had returned to loudly whistling through his own work, Wolf beckoned with a tilt of his head. "Best we get to it."

CHAPTER 41

ANIMA

"Deep breath in. Steady yourself. If you let the wind take you, the arrow will suffer the same."

Breathing. An act so simple, it was the very first performed by all the world's creatures upon their birth. A task requiring so little thought it could be done during the deepest of slumbers.

An act rendered utterly impossible by Wolf's low voice rumbling in her ear.

It didn't help that they were the only two in the city's indoor archery range, the screened-in windows allowing the wind to travel through the stone walls with little hindrance. A choice made by necessity, Wolf had explained—if archers learned to shoot without paying consideration to the wind, they'd never shoot straight outside the range.

Now that she thought about it, she couldn't quite recall how she'd landed herself in this compromising position. Even hopping her memories like stepping-stones across a rushing river, the path fell short a stone before she reached the part where she convinced herself that having him mutter instructions this close to her face wouldn't be a disastrous distraction.

Nor did she feel entirely inclined to correct that mistake.

"I'm steady," she lied, thumbing the bow's arch with one hand, bouncing the string with the other.

"You're sideways." The small of her back tingled as he shifted behind her, like a lightning current ran between her skin and his; and, after asking permission and gaining it, his hands spanned the breadth of her hips, nearly sparking her soul out of her skin.

"Atta girl," he muttered as she followed his light-fingered nudges, cool and calm as a summer spring. He released one hip to smooth his palm up her spine, beneath the quiver; she bent according to his leading, and he hummed in satisfaction, dropping his hand back to her hip. "There. Perfect."

She was going to *wither and die.*

His grip tightened ever-so-slightly. "You've stopped breathing again."

She'd heard of *overcorrecting* before, but the wheeze that came out of her…that was just embarrassing. She coughed quickly to try and disguise it. "I'm not so practiced at focusing on so many things at once."

His throaty chuckle almost undid her. "Breathing oughtn't require your attention."

No, it really oughtn't, ought it? she nearly shouted back at him.

Another leftover Soren impulse, obviously.

This time, she shut her eyes and listened to the wind, its presence announced not by its own voice, but by the chittering host of leaves playing herald outside the windows.

Control what you can, Soren's voice whispered in her ear.

One breath all the way in.

One breath all the way out.

"Keep your eyes closed," Wolf murmured. "Feel the flats of your feet against the ground. Imagine you're rooted to that spot—nothing can sway you. Nothing can bend you."

One breath all the way in—

A whisper of memory floated through her mind like dandelion fuzz.

Arboreal giants kneeling in fealty. A rage that howled like wind, like wolves. "The unbowing bend the knee to me. You think I fear you?"

Cold hands lifted away from her hips to embrace her shoulders instead. "Breathe, Ani."

She hadn't realized she'd stopped.

One breath all the way in—one breath all the way out.

"Good. Eyes open."

At the same time her eyelids lifted, his hands did, too—he stepped around and away, retrieving his cane from where it leaned against the wall and backing off to the side. He watched her with an impassive frown, not giving any hint that their proximity had gotten him half as ruffled up.

Well, of course not, Ani. He's a grown man, and you're acting like a swooning schoolgirl about to play a game of Loves-Me-Not.

She cleared her throat, tossing her hair over one shoulder. A reclaiming of her senses—and her sanity—was paramount. Particularly considering she was carrying a quiverful of razor-edged projectiles. "Now what?"

His slight smile stoked the heat in her cheeks like a fire poker. "Nock, draw, aim, and shoot."

Get it together, she scolded her face, wishing she could pat her cheeks without giving herself away. *You've met handsomer men. You've been* worshipped *by handsomer men.*

If only she could bring even one of their faces to memory.

Four steps. Nothing mortifying could happen in the span of four steps. Any old fool could follow four steps.

Nock.

She reached back, plucking a feather-fletched arrow from her borrowed quiver. With one more shallow breath, she settled its notch to the string.

Draw.

Like magic, like a miracle, her fingers curled around the string with almost no thought on her part at all. And though the pressure should have chafed her fingertips, the string could have been silk for how softly it strafed her skin. As if the ghost of callouses formed on different hands haunted her grip now.

Aim.

She lifted the bow into position, her fingers fitting into the grip-grooves carved through the oiled wood. The textured cloth wrapped around the grip kept her sweaty fingers from slipping, but it did little to stave off their shaking.

Shoot.

One breath in.

Fresh wood and trampled greens outside. The dusty tickle of feather fletching just beneath her eye, a butterfly kiss to the apex of her cheek. A dash of evergreen and chicory; a sprinkle of maple sugar and bonfire smoke.

One breath out.

And with it went the arrow.

It sailed like a bird gliding on a southerly wind, swift and sure, only the faintest of wobbles to its flight as it struck its mark: a straw-stuffed target at the other end of the room.

She bounced on her tiptoes, ignoring the slice of pain that carved up her calf. "I hit it!"

"Hit it? You nearly landed a heart-shot!" Wolf's smile no longer seemed content with a small peek at the world; now he flashed her a full-fledged grin, the kind that crinkled up noses and ironed laugh lines into cheeks. "That's quite the showing for your first go."

Aaand there went her breath again.

Every time she got a good grip on it, that rotting smile stole it right from under her nose. Or out of her lungs, rather.

Wolf blinked; his smile hitched. "What?"

"What?" she echoed.

"You're looking at me."

"It's hardly the first time I've—"

"Not like that." He stepped closer. "What's the matter?"

"Nothing." *Everything. You. Is it getting hot in here?*

Another step with no sound, a hunter's prowl. It brought him too close, not even a foot between his boots and hers.

A sea of amber drowned her reclaimed sense—and sanity—as he peered into her eyes, searching, seeking. His fingertip traced over her temple, flipping a strand of hair aside. "Tell me what you've got running around in that head of yours, woman."

It struck her then, why that word—*woman*—had her swooning like a bluebell bathed in summertime sunlight.

Goddess or *girl*—those were the two words people used to praise her or put her down. One a refusal to treat her as human; one a refusal to treat her as an equal.

"You have a beautiful smile," she blurted out.

So of course, because she frightened away half the beautiful things that dared approach a deity, that smile turned to dust before her eyes. "That's...that's kind."

Every muscle in her body cringed inward; embarrassment had always been a painful affliction for her, one she carried in her soul rather than her skin. She jammed the end of the bow against the stone floor, balancing it with one hand on its top. "You say *kind* like you mean something else."

"I can't begin to imagine what you mean by that."

Her molars gritted together, a battle between her temper and her tired, tired heart—in a rare show of valiance, temper won. "Try."

Wolf cocked his head at her, a curious gesture not unlike the sort his namesake might put on. He drove his cane into the stone across from her borrowed bow. "I rarely receive compliments; I don't know what to do with them once they're handed to me. So while there's kindness in the gesture, that kindness often feels like a burden I can't put down."

She surprised herself by laughing. "You don't *do* anything with compliments, Wolf. Just let them be what they are."

His knuckles paled around the top of his cane. "They feel like pity."

That word knocked every last urge to laugh out of her. "You think I *pity* you?"

No words came; he just watched her, wary. Shifting like he might try to flee.

A hunter who watched her like prey. Like one wound from her could be enough to strike him down.

"Wolf." She closed that distance between them, letting the bow fall. Setting her hand over his. "Why would I pity you?"

His throat strained as he swallowed, his stare seeking another perch—any perch, it seemed, besides her face. "What else can you call this—a goddess agreeing to keep company with a priest who's used half his prayers to curse her name?"

"Is it not *you* taking pity on *me*—agreeing to teach a *goddess* how to shoot? A skill I should have no need to learn?"

It wasn't the right time to laugh again. But she nearly did anyway when his eyes widened well past the whites. "You think *I*—?"

"Have you considered that I might simply *enjoy* your company?"

This time, the laughter was his—an incredulous bark that startled a parcel of birds from one of the windowsills. "No one enjoys my company. I'm the wettest blanket this side of the sea—even my ma says so."

Ani crossed her arms over her simmering heart. "I've met wetter."

"Goddess, you've spent half your time on this island hiding from me."

"Because you—" Rot her ribs, because he *what*? What truth could she offer that wouldn't be *too* true, *too* telling? "Because my people need me. And I do everything in my power to answer my people's prayers. So you can imagine that it is not *easy* to face someone whose prayers I've forgotten—someone I've failed."

The *look* that claimed his face then—a softening of his stare, a parting of his lips, a swift and stark furrowing of his brow—she couldn't begin to pick out which emotions had come together to make it.

All she knew was that one moment, he was staring at her, speechless— and the next, he was cursing under his breath, dashing his thumb fiercely beneath his eyes as he turned away from her.

Coffin crush her, had she just made *him* cry?

"Wolf." Panic strummed her throat until her voice shook. "Wolf, I'm sorry, I wasn't trying to—"

"*You're* sorry?" The smile he flashed her—broken, but still beautiful, always beautiful—broke her heart alike. "You?"

"I don't know what that means." The question, the smile, the way he was looking at her.

"It means…" He drove his fist twice into his chest, huffing out a breath like he was trying to clean out something he'd smoked. "It means we should stop talking and get back to work. Before I say something you won't forgive me for."

That idea almost tantalized her. Almost spun a reckless dare on her tongue—*Say it. Say all the terrible things you've ever kept quiet, and let me do the same*— and wrecked everything in one fell swoop.

But that, she knew, was another impulse left behind by her braver, bolder friend.

Ani was not bold; Ani was not brave.

She picked up the bow and went back to her mark. And neither she nor Wolf said another word, terrible or otherwise, if it did not pertain to her shooting.

CHAPTER 42

SOREN

She couldn't feel her nose. The wind had stolen all sensation, the cheeky bastard, and made off with it with a shrieking laugh as it buffeted her body this way and that, trying to teeter her off this precarious pathway.

Pathway was generous. This stone imitation of a tightrope, more like. She could barely fit one boot at a time on the thin seam that separated unscalable climes from bottomless clefts.

"The Sanctum is strange that way!" Medwenna's chipper tone didn't translate well as it bounced off the rock; the echo came back ominous and shrill, like the faraway whistling of a war tune no one knew the words to. "You start at the top and work your way down."

If Soren ever did become a wandering spirit—a fate that felt closer and closer with every wobbling step—she'd spend her afterlife tracking down whichever king designed this *Sanctum* and throttle him for his commitment to showmanship.

Not that she'd expected the god-killer to be hidden down a path paved with golden bricks or anything, but come *on*. Matthias's boots were halfway over the edge even with his feet snugged against the mountainside.

She rubbed her numb nose, then immediately regretted it; she'd had to wipe it off on her sleeve so many times that the grips of her gloves burned against the inflamed skin.

Elias, on the other hand, barely seemed to realize they'd left dependable ground behind; he strode ahead on Everin's heels, effortlessly keeping up with a man who'd probably learned to hammer in a piton before he learned to walk. His hooded cloak, gloves, and boots rendered him in soot against the snow, a living shadow who'd lost its bearer.

And then there was Everin: no hood or gloves, golden hair gleaming like a handful of coins, whistling a jaunty tune to the wind as he took every curve at sickening speed. The idiot was practically *jogging*.

And as for her…well, she normally took to these things with the same variety of reckless idiocy. But even she knew better than to test the mettle of mountains.

"How much further?" The wind smothered her shout with a sharp gust to the face, like even nature itself had gotten tired of listening to her whining.

So tired, in fact, that its next gust barreled into her like a charging buck, blowing her balance off. And when she shifted to try and correct it—

The swish of a boot over snow.

The stomach-dropping absence of stone beneath her foot.

The sensation of all the breath leaving her lungs…like a silent scream.

Or something softer. Something relieved.

Muscle snagged and stretched painfully in her shoulder as a gloved hand seized her wrist, tugging her to a stop. She opened her eyes, and—oh, gods. Oh gods. Mistake.

She wanted to squeeze her eyes shut again, but it was too late to block out the sight of her own impending death: the patient cavern waiting with its mouth open for a snack to drop down its throat.

"I have an important question." Elias peered past her, studying the drop behind her like one might take in an unremarkable tapestry among a host of even less remarkable tapestries. An air of briefly interrupted boredom. "When exactly did you decide a heart attack would be the best thing for my health?"

Normally, that sort of teasing would've bolstered her. Not today. "Help me up."

"What's the magic word?"

Either the thin air was starting to get to her, or she was starting to hyperventilate. Either way, his face began to blur before her eyes. "Elias Loch, I will pull your skinny ass over with me *so fast*—"

He scowled at her. "Really? It would've been so much faster for you to just say please."

"Are you *kidding me* right now?"

"I *was*, but now I actually think I need to hear it."

Maybe she should've held back on accepting that ring. "Pull me up, *please*, you absolute raging *jack*—"

The last word cracked into a yelp as he yanked her up, catching her against his chest with a hand braced to her back. For a single dizzied moment, she thought he might drop her into a ballroom dip.

"And now for the thank you," he murmured, the tip of his nose brushing hers as he leaned in.

"Thank you," she breathed.

The Nyxian sky had nothing on the starswept darkness of his twinkling gaze. "You're welcome."

She darted in and nipped him sharply on the tip of his nose. As he reeled back, cursing mildly and mashing his glove against his face, she straightened her coat and strode ahead. "That'll teach you to make me use my manners."

"What manners?" he groaned; but he jogged after her anyway.

"Good news for you, Princess." Everin poked his head back around the next curve, his mouth canted grimly. The bastard hadn't even paused when she'd slipped. "We're here."

Here turned out to be…well, not that impressive. But even then, she nearly wept at the sight of the circular jut of stone held out from the peak like a platter offered to the sky; she dropped to her knees and pressed a kiss into the snow, snowflakes clinging to her lips as she pushed back to her feet and joined the others crowding around the peak.

"You good?" Kessen laughed.

"Shut up." She shuddered. "I'm never climbing a mountain again."

"Still better than the ocean." Everin stood at the front of the group, running his hands over the rock, prodding its chinks and pocks with his thumbs. As she watched, he leaned in and—honest to the gods—*licked* the stone.

"Everin, gross!" groaned Kessen.

Matthias put his face in his hand. "You have no idea where that's been."

"I think it's been *here*," Soren said, "considering it's a rock."

Medwenna came up and licked the stone as well, resulting in a louder chorus of dismayed cries; she thought she heard Elias gag behind her.

"Limestone," she said. "But definitely a trace of old magic."

"You can *taste* that?" Soren scrunched up her face, her tongue flinching back like they might ask her to taste it next.

"Mmhm. Hint of charcoal, squeeze of lemon…" Another lick, and Medwenna's eyes lit up. "Rosewater. This is it."

"Fantastic." Everin turned around with a dastardly grin, rubbing his hands together, his skin rasping like sandpaper. "So. Who's killing the priest?"

CHAPTER 43

ELIAS

A klaxon call shattered through his head, splintering down his spine.
Who's killing the priest?

Before he could blink—or remember that his current pact with the Goddess of Death sort of made the situation moot—Soren threw herself between him and the Tallisians like a growling guard dog, her sword already out of its sheath. Between her battle-ready stance and the cataclysmic blaze in her eyes, she cut a terrifying figure…

Which stood in sharp dissonance to her shrill cry of "*Pardon* me?"

To Everin's credit—what little Elias felt willing to offer, considering the prince had just given the order to end his life—he *did* look sheepish. "Look, it's—"

Medwenna gaped at Everin. "You said you told them!"

"I said I was *going* to tell them. And I was. I am. Now." Everin scratched his beard. "Most legends of the god-killer say that to gain entrance, you have to, you know… 'spill holy blood.'" He bent his fingers around the words. "A sacrifice to prove your intent, I guess."

"And you didn't think you should have mentioned that sooner?" Soren swept her sword out in an arc when the prince stepped closer; he leapt back, then put his hands on his hips, scowling at them like they'd just broken his favorite vase.

"What's the problem?" he demanded. "You're the flogging Phoenix Priest, yeah? No big thing. Just bleed out a bit, buy our way in, and get your goddess to do her dirty work before we go."

One of those words stuck out like a punched-out tooth. "Why *before?*"

"New magic doesn't exist in the Sanctum." Medwenna teased the end of her braid, gaze skimming over the peak's face. "Or at least, that's what the recorded legends and personal accounts claim. I usually consider a trait to be fact if I find it mentioned in at least three separate recordings, and this was mentioned in five."

Five accounts that agreed if one was to put an end to a god, one had to prove their hatred for their worshippers.

He stared at the circle of stone, an ache stretching against the extremes of his spine.

Not a platform. An altar.

"I don't like this." Soren's sword point dipped, but she didn't give ground. "I…I vote no."

"It's not a vote," Everin scoffed. "You want the god-killer? A little blood's not exactly the highest price to pay."

"I was a goddess's host." Soren turned just enough that he glimpsed a wildness in her eyes, a thread of unreason that hinted at a building craze. "That makes my blood holy too, right? We can use me."

"Sure we can." Everin rolled his eyes toward Matthias and hiked a thumb toward Soren. A silent *Get a load of this*. "But unless you said a pretty prayer this morning that put you in Mortem's pocket too, you're not coming back from that. Your boyfriend's the better bet."

Soren turned to Elias next, but he'd already started shaking his head. "You know the answer, smartass."

Her throat bobbed. She shut her eyes, nostrils flaring—when she opened them again, she wore calm like a cracked porcelain mask, the pieces barely clinging to her skin. "Who do you want to do it?"

He didn't need to look over his options. "You."

Every crack in her calm deepened by double, but she nodded. "Then let's get it over with."

They stepped together into the center of the circle; déjà vu clobbered him over the head, an echo of the countless times they'd crossed the boundaries of sparring circles to face each other down.

"Take it easy on me." He jokingly threw up his fists.

Soren snorted, rolling her eyes as she drew a dagger from her boot, palming it like a swarm of ants wrapped the hilt instead of leather. "Never have, never will."

Had it been anyone else who stepped into his breathing space, dagger poised to punch beneath his sternum, he already would have let his mortemancy off its leash. But as Soren set one hand against the back of his neck, a bracing grip that steadied the once-broken bone, he held that magic back by the collar. Refused to let even a drop of sepulchral ice leak into her body—only just healed, only just dragged back from the brink.

A death he could not save her from, even with all the gifts Mortem had granted him.

His throat strained like an overwound music box as he undid his cloak and handed it off to Matthias. "Be careful."

Soren coughed out a laugh, and her wrist rattled, the dagger nicking his thin shirt. "While stabbing you? Sure, I'll do my best." She hesitated. Mouthed her next words, silent but not lost to him: *They could be lying. You don't have to.*

Even without a coat or cloak, the cold didn't touch him; he could have been standing on Atlas's balmy beach, Kallias's laughter ringing in his ears instead of hers.

"You don't have to get in if you don't want to," the prince had chuckled while Elias dithered just out of reach of the waves. They pounced closer and closer with every gush, driving him further up the beach. "But they don't bite."

Kallias. If they didn't get this weapon—if they didn't get it fast—Kallias could be gone by the time they made it back. If he wasn't already.

Conviction set his jaw, and he steadied himself with a slow breath; he took her by the wrist, pulling in the hand that held the dagger, kissing her pale knuckles.

"We don't have time," he reminded her softly. "It's all right. I trust you."

Soren swallowed audibly, even over the mountain wind. She looked back down at his chest, wrist rotating this way and that—mentally aiming her blow.

"Besides," he added, a streak of reckless humor spearing through his pounding heart, "don't pretend you haven't dreamed of this moment since we met."

"Oh, sure. Every day." A breathless giggle. Another hard gulp. "Not quite how I pictured it, honestly."

"Then don't." He tightened his hold on her wrist. "Close your eyes. Don't watch."

Scythes buried to the hilts in her stomach. A crooked nose freckled in her own blood. Green eyes swimming in tears.

"Elias. Wake up."

He squeezed harder. "Close your eyes," he repeated—a rasp that he could barely hear himself.

Soren looked up at him. Crooked nose freckled in melting snowflakes. Green eyes swimming in tears.

And he knew in that moment that she wouldn't.

"Hey." He leaned down until he stood level with her, eye-to-eye. "Look at me, then. Look right here."

She bent her head to the side, giving him such a painfully fond look that it brought tears to his own eyes. "I have to look where I'm stabbing, jack—"

With a thrust of will unlike any he'd ever borne before, he hauled her wrist forward and plunged the dagger into his own heart.

CHAPTER 44

SOREN

A heartbeat that staggered like a drunk weaving down an icy street.

Blood that poured through her fingers like sand scooped from beneath the sea, more water than glass, viscous as the venom that once polluted it.

A panic so intense it barreled past what a person could even understand as fear; it settled as a numbness in her chest, absolute. All-consuming.

Jericho's face, frenzied but cold, as she jerked Elias's dagger out of his stomach. "Let her go to him."

Elias smiling through blood, head cradled in her lap, the light fading from his eyes. "I was going to ask you to marry me."

The sickening jut of severed spinal bone as she braced his broken neck, screaming and screaming and screaming and screaming—

Enna's tearstained cheeks. "It's all right, sweetheart."

Kallias's hastily scrawled goodbyes. "Take care of Elias. He grieves as hard as he loves."

Finn's gaze, glittering with clever lies. "Do me a favor, little sister. Trust me."

The tighter she clung to them, the faster they faded, like a beautiful dream filched by the waking world's greedy fingers.

But each time, the pair of hands that snatched her beloved few away belonged to those very same few. They stole themselves from her; they chose the paths that led to broken necks and queenless thrones, kingdoms down to their first and worst heir…sisters who couldn't call themselves that anymore.

Sacrifices that sculpted her into something new with every blow.

A wife without a husband. A daughter without a mother. A sister without siblings.

"Soren?"

That pained grunt called her back first; the smell of smoke joined it a heartbeat later, rousing her like smelling salts shoved under her nose.

Elias still stood before her; she still held the dagger, now soaked in blood. But beneath the rip in his shirt, only an ugly line of curdled, blackened blood remained; no open wound. Smoke still wafted from it, but even that was swept away by the howling wind.

Only a second had passed; a second of absence between the sickening give of Elias's flesh beneath her blade and now. She hadn't even exhaled the breath she'd taken before it happened.

Her lungs cramped as they finally deflated. She couldn't feel her hands. "Are you—"

"I'm fine." He lifted the hem of his shirt, baring his torso to the elements without a flinch; normally a sight that would have struck her stupid. Instead, she traced her finger down the wound, testing it for herself; though Elias's muscles spasmed under her touch, an instinctive flinch with no intention behind it, the scab seemed established enough. No fresh blood trickled out when she applied pressure.

"Are you two coming?" hollered Everin, voice almost tinny—when she turned, the world drifting past like a daydream, she saw the Tallisians had all disappeared…presumably into the mouth of a newborn cave, its jaws propped open for its victims to crawl inside.

"Give her a minute," Elias snapped. Then, softer, his hand against her jaw: "I'm sorry. Are you—?"

She pushed his hand off. "Considering I'm not the one who got *stabbed* to open a door, I think I'll live." Yes, good—sarcasm made a fantastic shield. "Let's not keep Prince Patience over there waiting, huh?"

He might have asked again. Might have called her name as she practically dove into the mountain's mouth, letting it swallow her…and any telltale tremors that might still be buzzing through her hands.

But she couldn't be sure, because she couldn't hear anything. Not with the goodbyes of the dead and the no-longer-dead and the *please-please-please-don't-be-dead* still crowding between her ears.

She wiped her battlemate's blood on her coat. And just as his hand found hers, the mountain sealed itself shut behind them with a grinding, ancient moan, smothering them in oblivion.

CHAPTER 45

ELIAS

From the time he was a little boy, Elias Loch had a fire burning in his chest.

Its name, the priests and priestesses had told him when he began his boyhood education in Mortem's temple, was purpose. A passion that stoked his soul.

Not many found their fervor in a house of death. For it to have found him there was a sign, they'd said; a sign he'd taken his first step on his destined path.

But whether that fire truly came from some divine purpose or divine power—whether it had always burned hot in his heart, or had only become fire in truth when he'd accepted Mortem's relic—it no longer mattered once the mountain closed itself up behind them.

Because the moment the light extinguished from this narrow corridor of chiseled stone, so too did that holy fire.

Every warm-blooded vein in his body froze over, a slurry of snowmelt slush replacing liquid flame; his gasp echoed out from him as utter *cold* pierced inward, violent shivers shaking him like his little sisters shook their joint coin bank, a futile attempt to jostle one last silver from its confines.

He'd forgotten.

Nyxian-born, taught to walk in snow nearly as deep as he was tall, and he'd still managed to forget what it meant to feel cold.

"Elias?" Soren's voice shoved through the shadow; her hand squeezed around his. "Gods, you're *freezing*. What happened?"

"Magic," he chattered out. "Like they said—not welcome here."

Which meant to pyromancy. No sanguimancy.

No mortemancy.

His cauterized wound chose that moment to give a restless, awful twinge.

A strange flicker sliced through the blackness several feet ahead—a moment later, a foot-long rod of buttery yellow light blinked to life, illuminating the grim furrow dug into Matthias's brow. "Do I have six bodies here?"

"One," Everin called.

"Two," Medwenna and Kessen said at the same time—then, after a heartbeat, Kessen grumbled, "Three."

"Four and five," Soren called, louder than the others—her voice echoed out before tumbling back, a hundred Sorens counting them off. "What's that light?"

"It's called a glamour rod—Lapisian invention. It'll only last a little while, but we've got more." Matthias's braids rattled as he walked a slow circle, passing Elias back his cloak. "I make six bodies, so that's all of us."

The light expanded and contracted across the tunnel, like the walls themselves were breathing; not a tunnel after all, but a chamber. Man-made, if the discarded hammers and rusted pickaxes littering the floor were anything to go by. Unforgiving stone made up the chamber's floor; more forgiving stone made up its walls, crevices lined with crystals that did them the favor of reflecting the strange light, tripling its reach.

Gold striped across porcelain. Elias's stomach lodged firmly in his throat.

"Seven bodies," he whispered.

The six of them all turned as one to the corner of the chamber; there, reclining with legs crossed and arms tangled behind its head, was a near-pristine skeleton. Its pearly grin, preserved by its closed-off tomb, almost seemed to widen when Elias looked into its hollow sockets.

A trick of the light—not a machination of necromantic power. But old traumas soured his blood with adrenaline anyway.

"At least this one's not walking," Soren joked weakly.

"Strange way to die," Everin mused, crouching beside the skeleton; he put a hand on its bony shoulder, jostling it like he meant to rouse it—then hacking when dust flew into his face. "Oh, tie me to the *stake*, it's in my *mouth*—"

Medwenna did an odd, tiptoed jig across the floor—he couldn't tell what she was avoiding, but she took a very precise path to the skeleton's side before dropping down and grabbing its head in both hands, bending it into the light.

Not a lick of fear or hesitation. He didn't know whether he should marvel or be very, very concerned about the company they'd agreed to keep.

Those concerns didn't linger long once he caught sight of the deep crack spidering through the skull.

"Not so strange after all," said the honey-eyed historian; she set the skeleton gently back in repose, then rummaged around it before holding up a fist-sized hunk of rock. A stalactite—far smaller than most, but apparently hardy enough to put a man to sleep with a concussion he'd never wake from. "Watch your heads."

He'd never *dreamed* he might find himself wishing for Finnick Atlas's company. But in a cave where the very stones stood against them, a sprinkle of foresight would've been a welcome boon. Even Occassio's maddening, malicious sort.

Not that it would have worked anyway, with whatever ancient rites had been used to seal this mountain from the sight of the gods.

"Well," said Matthias, gazing toward the opening in the wall ahead, "only one way to go. Who wants to lead?"

Soren strode forward and took the glamour rod; when she lifted it, glaring into the darkness like it had wronged her personally, even the light she carried seemed to shy away from her.

"My kingdom is counting on us," she said. "Let's not keep them waiting."

CHAPTER 46

SOREN

The journey through the Sanctum's uppermost corridors proved to be…uneventful.

Which was the nicer way of saying she was about to bash her own brain out of her skull just to alleviate the agony of unmitigated boredom.

She'd expected danger at every turn. Challenges meant to take her to and past her very limits. Traps set for those who carried the height of divine power in their pockets. A nip or two from a rat that scurried underfoot, at the *very* least.

Instead, for the first handful of hours—or days, if the ache of understimulation in her head made any suggestion—the only obstacles they encountered were each other's feet. Though the glamour rod had yet to begin dying out, it couldn't dispel every shadow. No matter where she set her stride, she always seemed to be tripping over someone else's ankle or getting her toes smashed by someone's heavy boot.

After kicking Elias's shin for the third time—an accident, she swore on her empty grave when Elias accused her of taking advantage of the situation—he moved to the middle of the pack, asking Medwenna some complicated question she didn't even try to understand. Within seconds, they were chattering like a flock of seagulls freshly fed by beachgoer's scraps, only using words she recognized every couple sentences or so.

So when Everin sidled up to her, she was almost grateful. Silence and shadows made it too easy for her mind to wander other places…to the people outside this mountain waiting for her. Relying on her.

And on the friend she'd left behind to fend for herself in Arborius.

Her private worries for Ani—and the aching emptiness where they'd once shared space in her head, a twining of souls that had nearly killed her—took their leave when Everin said, almost like they were already halfway through a conversation, "I'm sorry about your mother."

Never mind. She'd take boredom over *that*. "Thank you."

That was the polite response, wasn't it?

Gods, she didn't know—she didn't know *anything*. She'd been third in line for the crown of Nyx, for gods' sakes—nowhere near this kind of close-quarters politicking. In fact, she'd been kept away from it entirely on purpose.

"I'm sorry about yours," she wheedled off—then resisted the urge to smack herself. King Denali's consort had died over a decade ago, long before the attempted assassination of the Atlas family and the ensuing war. Returning the sentiment now—

"Thank you." A pause. Everin coughed into his fist. "I'm surprised you thought of that. She's been gone awhile."

"Enna spoke of her sometimes." Discomfort squirmed in her stomach, but she forced the strange truth out anyway: "She used to tell us stories of when she and the others were all friends. Your mother, the last Lapisian queen, Genevieve, my mother…" Her throat went dry. "Both my mothers, I guess."

"Mm." Everin's noncommittal grunt didn't help the growing flush in her cheeks. "It's got to be weird, huh? One foot in two places."

"You have no idea."

"Yeah, well…crowns are forged in one piece for a reason." He motioned like he was breaking a stick. "They don't split."

"Oh, they don't?" At least her sarcasm still held top form. "Thanks for reminding me."

"I don't envy you that mess," chuckled the prince. "Which says a lot, by the way, considering the state of my crown."

My crown. No question in that claim. "Your father's named you his Heir?"

"Not in writing. Hence the mess."

"But you want it?"

He looked at her as if she'd sprouted a third arm. "Who *wouldn't* want it?"

Of course. Who wouldn't want a heavy, uncomfortable headpiece that brought lifelong scrutiny and bone-crushing responsibility and the promise that, should danger come to your kingdom's door, you would be obligated to protect your kingdom's good over the good of those most precious to you?

"No idea," she lied through her smile. "We were born for it, right?"

"The problem with sharing a womb." Everin rolled his eyes. "My sister and I were both *born* for it. Stakes, four minutes and twenty-eight seconds say Raini was born for it first. But, like you saw—"

"Your father's an ass."

He snapped his fingers and tapped her on the temple. "You catch on quick, Princess."

She batted his hand aside. "Mm-mm. I don't know you like that."

Everin stepped a foot further away. "Heard. So, what exactly happened to Prince Pretty Face and Prince Parlor Tricks?"

"What exactly happened to your mother?" she shot back, not a lick of self-preservation showing up to stop it.

Silence fell behind and before them. Someone's blade stirred in its sheath; her money was on Elias.

But Everin didn't let that silence stay. In fact, his question-bent brow didn't even twitch as he said, "Artemesian border scuffle that went bad. And your brothers?"

The truth couldn't find its way from her heart to her head, let alone her tongue. "My brothers aren't dead."

"Right. A millennium of every single poor sap giving up the ghost after getting possessed, but all three of you will surely be the exception." Steel-gray eyes glittered like a gavel set to seal a death sentence. "Miracles aren't gifts, Princess— they're manipulations. If the gods don't have anything to gain from sparing your brothers—"

"Is he bothering you?" Medwenna's head poked over Soren's shoulder. "You look bothered. I can twist his ear 'round if you need."

"*I'm* going to come up there and twist the ear of the next person to invite the dead into the conversation," Matthias called from the rear. "Ghosts come when they're called, and your brothers will be no different."

"They're *not dead*," her and Elias snapped together.

Medwenna slowly receded from Soren's side, but her sheepishness lingered like an echo of its own. And maybe a whisper of pity.

Soren dropped back and found Elias's hand in the dark, pulling it over her heart, armoring herself against their arrowing doubt.

What would heretics know about miracles, anyway? She hadn't had a clue before Ani, and look at her now: a miracle made manifest, an impossibility dressed up like flesh and bone.

A hollow thrum sang through her soul. It hummed—it hurt.

She waited for it to fade…but it never did. In fact, it babbled louder and louder, talking over her thoughts until the feverish tint of madness began to color them, until—

Until she realized the others had begun growing restless, too—Medwenna sped up to walk with Everin, heads bent together, grim mutters exchanged;

Matthias shouldered his way forward to join the huddle, strong-arming Kessen out when the boy tried to follow.

"You hear that too?" Soren muttered out of the corner of her mouth.

"Running water," Elias confirmed lowly—his fingers flexed within hers. "A lot of it."

Exactly what they needed: a lot of water in a confined space that had a bad habit of closing its own doors. "I don't suppose you learned how to swim when we were in Atlas?"

His silence did not bode well. Nor did the look on Medwenna's face as she paused at the end of this tunnel, where the walls tapered to an uncomfortably narrow cleft in the stone.

"I hope you recall some of your seaside upbringing," said the historian. "How often did you try your hand at sailing?"

CHAPTER 47

ELIAS

If he hadn't regretted agreeing to this whole venture already, he did the moment he squeezed himself out of the terrifyingly tight passageway and came face to face with...

A lake.

There was no other word for it. They stood at the lip of a *lake*, its waves lapping gently at their toes. And worse than the expanse of water before them— and the ancient-looking ship tipped drunkenly on its side, its sail slumped over into the sand—was the realization that the slim slice of rock and silt underneath their feet was the only scrap of land to be seen in this chamber.

They were surrounded by choppy water, dove-gray and clouded by light spilling across its surface. The ceiling sparkled with strange stalactites; not lifeless rock, but otherworldly spires of stone that spiraled like corkscrews, their diamond shell gleaming with refracted moonlight.

"Occassio," Everin said without inflection. "Has to be."

Elias was inclined to agree, but he'd sooner dive headfirst into the center of that lake than say so. "Keep your senses sharp, then. Occassio's magic—"

"We know a thing or two about defending against mischief-makers, thanks." Everin bent to cuff up his pants nearly to the knee, then untied and kicked off his shoes, steadying himself on the slippery rock with both arms out. "Who's helping me drag this shoddy little sailboat into the water?"

"I'm on it!" Kessen bound after him like a faithful pup on a leash, shoes nowhere to be seen—Everin waggled one of his own boots at the boy, eyebrows raised, and Kessen turned around, a self-deprecating smile on his face as he retrieved his boots. Like this was some silly game.

"I have seen her warp far greater minds than yours into madness," Elias gritted out as he plodded to join them, leaving his boots on. He couldn't swim, anyway—taking them off wouldn't help him any if the water took *him*. Better he focused on keeping his balance in the first place. "She is not to be dismissed."

"She won't take me again."

The soft, almost dreamlike quality of his battlemate's voice pitted his stomach straight out of his middle—he turned back, expecting to see lavender glimmers or a silvery haze over her gaze, but only sea-bright green stared back at him. Soren's brow scrunched low over her eyes as she stared…not up at the haloed ceiling, but across the water, her head tilted to one side.

"I know her work," Soren continued, though the Tallisian men weren't listening; even Matthias, who seemed the most sensible of the three, had gone to supervise, shaking his head in disapproval as Everin leapt up on the hull, planting his fists on his hips and declaring himself *king of the gravyboat*. "This doesn't feel like her."

Honey and ink brushed up beside him; a fever chill trickled up his arm as Medwenna's shoulder grazed his Viper scar. She watched Soren in the same way he'd seen her pore through the pages of a history book the weight and size of a brick; like somewhere in its thin, tattering sheafs, pressed between records of royal lineage and long-winded coverage of succession law, she might find the answer to all they were searching for. "What does it feel like?"

But unlike the history books, Soren couldn't be cracked open and skimmed for secrets; she didn't give Medwenna an answer as she joined the Tallisians, shucking off her boots and handing them to Elias without so much as a look. She didn't even cuff her pants as she waded fearlessly into the water, curling her fingers inward when she trailed them over the boat's scarred base. The same motion he'd use to scratch a begging dog's belly.

He'd grown so used to uneasy feelings sloshing around in his middle that he'd almost gone numb to them. But without his fire to counter it, the frosty apprehension coating his bones made him wish for one of the atrociously patterned—and blessedly warm—sweaters Soren liked to knit him for special occasions.

"Toss me that rope," Soren called; a slapping sound suggested one of the Tallisians had obeyed, as did the sight of Soren backing deeper into the water with a frayed, knotted rope held loosely in one fist. She stood waist-deep in the fathomless depths, sleeves rolled to her elbows, baring the muscular forearms of a practiced swordswoman; as she spun her arm, expertly coiling the rope around her wrist and giving it a hardy yank, the heat swarming his blood broke the ice over his bones like a late spring thaw.

Gods, he was useless. How had he survived so long fighting the obvious slip of his eyes, terrified she might catch him lingering too long on a look that should have been cursory at most?

They were hunting a god-killing weapon, trapped in a mountain set up to murder those who worshipped the gods, and here he was—perhaps practicing the most intense course of faith in Mortem that one could—and all he could think about was his battlemate's gods-damned arms.

"You're staring," Medwenna said, helpful as ever.

"Not sure what I can do to help," he admitted. Part of the truth, at least.

Probably something more useful than watching—and thoroughly enjoying—his battlemate barking orders at the men climbing all over the boat. But he'd learned during his time in the army that everyone had their skills; like a set of armor, each solider filled in the gaps others left, and each piece served a different purpose than their comrades.

As strange as it still was to believe, the water was Soren's battlefield, her birthright. When she called for him, he would answer; but until then, he was happy to see her like this again: shoulders tilted back, chin held high, unafraid to argue with those of equal or higher rank when she thought a plan had not been properly put together.

"The tattoo on your neck," Medwenna said—so quietly he didn't quite hear her the first time. When he asked her to repeat it, she raised her voice above the sloshing waves and laughing curses from Kessen: "I said, the tattoo on your neck—it's an old rune. Sanctan."

A resonance buzzed through his head, that name striking a gong in the center of his skull. "Is it?"

Medwenna nodded; she reached back and rolled the collar of her shirt down, then tugged her braid aside to show him a smudge of ink on the base of her neck. Not a rune circled by moon phases, like his, but stamped beneath a skull circled in vines.

"It defies Anima's magic," she said, hushed as a snowbird's wingbeats in a blizzard. "If I was to die, a necromancer could not puppet my body."

The way Kenna had explained it to him, the symbols were a sort of old magic, something that existed before the gods. They could not negate the gods' magic, but they could offer some small protection against it—his allowed him to see through illusions, as did the one he'd given to Kallias. Finn had refused the same mark—a decision the haughty prince likely regretted now, if enough of him had survived to feel something as human as regret.

"I suppose Tallis never really believed them extinct like the rest of us," he croaked.

"Tallis never really believes anything." A wry smile. "It has saved and doomed us in many ways."

A triumphant shout went up from the direction of the boat, a four-part harmony that dipped into a three-part cacophony of curses as the Tallisians up top lost their balance; they half hopped, half tumbled down to the ground, where they helped Matthias and Soren finish hauling the boat upright and into the water.

"All right, lady and gentlemen," Soren called, tossing the rope up to Everin and slapping the hull as she sloshed back onto shore, "all aboard the *Huge Mistake.*"

"That's a terrible name," Elias muttered as he went to scale the hull. "That's all you could come up with?"

Soren silently pointed to the peeling paint at the back of the boat: faded red letters that spelled out *Huge Mistake,* complete with a doodle of a sad face at the end.

Good to know at least one of the arbiters of their potential doom had possessed a sense of humor.

"That's encouraging," he muttered.

"Don't be a wuss." As he clambered up, his battlemate slapped his backside much like she'd slapped the boat, bursting into laughter when he swatted her away—laughter that echoed ominously through the chamber, layering over itself until a hundred voices cackled at them. Mocked them.

"*Do* you know how to sail?" he asked as he landed on the deck, reaching down to help Soren climb up.

"I was taught." She swung herself over the edge, tapping her feet on the deck as if testing it before fully throwing her weight onto it. She blew strands of hair out of her eyes, studying the sails with a pensive frown. "Eleven years ago. With supervision. On a smaller boat. And Kallias did most of the—"

"This isn't sounding like a yes."

"It'll come back to me," she blustered, striding to the wheel. "Someone pull on that rope there."

Elias followed where she was pointing and tugged on the rope; the sail only sagged further down.

"I meant the other rope."

"Which other rope?"

"I—look, I need muscle memory, okay? Someone else take the wheel."

Everin cast her a skeptical look as he passed, heading toward the wheel himself. "Look, Princess, I'd just as soon die on dry land, so if you're going to sink us—"

The sail snapped open, catching a breeze that Elias couldn't feel at all. A breeze that hadn't been there a couple moments ago.

"See?" Soren's head popped back around the mast. "We're in good shape. Nothing to worry about. We'll be across in no time."

He had a very, very bad feeling about this.

CHAPTER 48

ELIAS

The movement beneath the water was only a trick of the light.

At least, that was what Everin kept promising, his fingers drumming faster on the wheel every time Elias announced he could see something flitting beneath the boat. And in fairness, the silvery-green streaks of light *did* seem to make a mad dash past the boat right when they were sailing beneath the brightest stalactites hanging from the ceiling. Like the light was playing tag with the fog floating near the lake's surface.

But he could've sworn one of those reflections *winked* as they swam by.

Regardless, the only sounds now were the creaking complaints of the boat—and of Kessen, who sat smack in the middle of the deck, pouting because he'd been banned from helping Soren after giving himself a nasty rope burn across his palm.

Soren, meanwhile, was a force of nature—she and the ship seemed locked in a feverish dance so precise that even a second wasted between steps could spell doom. She swung between the ropes and pulleys, the sails and the rudder, as if trading herself between partners; her feet found their marks without fail, steadying her against the dip and sway of the deck. She even hummed under her breath as she went, the breeze gathering her song into its arms and carrying it to his straining ears.

A shanty he recognized. Not from Atlas battlefields, but from skyless, sleepless Artemesian nights. From staring at a ceiling culled of its stalactites, hearthfire and shadow playing tag above his head as an enemy prince hummed himself to sleep a few short feet away.

Not a shanty. A seaside lullaby.

He watched Soren for a time, tracking her movements until the rhythm made sense, until he could follow the pattern—and when the opening came, he cut into the dance, stealing the rope she was reaching toward before she could begin her next twirl.

Not a stutter in her movements. She merely bent around him like a branch in the breeze, her hum rising in volume as her pace shifted; without a word, she left gaps in the rhythm for him to slip into, shifting it from a duet of sways and spins to a triplicate display, a braid corded with grace and trust and understanding.

"Do you remember where you heard that song?" he murmured, almost afraid to break her reverie as they spun around each other.

The hum halted sharply, like it had fallen on its heels—just as Soren did, sinking from her ballroom-bent feet to settle on her soles. But she threaded herself seamlessly back into the endless loop of tying and tugging and tasting the wind, popping her finger into her mouth before holding it up to test the direction of the breeze.

"Not exactly," she said. "I remember the tune, but not the words…I can't really place it. But it's stuck in my head. Not in the chaos way, just…" She shrugged, fiddling with a flap of torn sailcloth. "Can't get it out."

"Kallias hummed it to himself almost every night in Artem." He lifted his arm as she ducked under it, then leaned aside as she darted back in to adjust some moving piece he couldn't name. He couldn't tell if his throat burned from emotion or the hint of floral perfume steeped in the wafting fog. "He told me he used to sing it to you and Finn. I guess you two would get nightmares, and—"

"And we'd go hide in his room. Beg to spend the night in there." It was difficult to separate fondness from sorrow; both bruised her voice with heavy shades of gray. He couldn't tell which his battlemate lost herself in as she said, "I remember that part."

"So he taught you to sail?"

"Mmhm. Well, it was a group effort, but he led the charge. We were out on his little sailboat every morning he could drag me out of bed before classes."

"A mighty feat," he deadpanned.

"Get out of here." She rolled her eyes, gesturing for him to move; he ducked out just in time for her to slip back into her lonely rhythm, her humming grating a bit at the edges as she took it up again.

"Did you hear that?" Kessen asked suddenly.

"Hear what?" Matthias gave a cursory look over the edge of the boat; Elias did the same, but nothing caught his eye.

"I hear someone." Kessen sounded distracted…and not the way the excitable boy normally did. "You really don't hear that?"

"Very funny, Kess," Everin called. "Sit your ass down and quit—hey! *Kessen!*"

The shift from idle annoyance to barking command ripped Elias back from the edge just in time to see Kessen lunge *over* it, one arm extended, eyes wide with fervid desperation as he shouted an unfamiliar name. "Jules! *Jules!*"

Elias nearly had to dive across the length of the boat to catch the boy's coat; Matthias collided with them at the same time, and together they dragged a struggling, panting Kessen back onto the deck.

"What are you screaming at?" Matthias demanded; Kessen surged back up, and Matthias barred an arm over his chest, pinning him against the deck with a harsh *thud*. "Kessen! What's gotten into you?"

"I hear it too."

Soren.

His heart took its own plunge into icy waters; the groaning snap of old wood brought him to his feet before he even saw his battlemate.

His battlemate, balanced precariously on the side of the ship, eyes reflecting the eerie glow of moonlight and lakewater as she stared downward.

"Mama?" she muttered, brows drawn in like she was squinting against sunlight.

Horror struck him in the heart at the same time Medwenna cried, "She's going to jump!"

Soren's arms stayed limp at her sides; her bare foot hovered over the side of the boat, a step that would never find solid ground.

He lunged back to her, belting his arm around her waist and dragging her down, cursing when she hit the deck with a cry of pain; he pinned her by her biceps and knelt over her, using one leg to keep both of hers still.

She writhed like a wild animal, every muscle straining…straining back toward the edge of the boat, where her wild stare stayed fixed.

"Let me up," she said—almost sobbed. "Let me get to her, I can get to her!"

"Get to *who?*"

"Catch!" Medwenna again—a little late, as he looked up just in time for a thick coil of rope to slap him across the face. When he shook off the sting, she was already at work on Kessen, who continued to fight Matthias and scream at the top of his voice for *Jules*.

"Not Occassio," he yelled across the deck.

"No." Dread swam the currents of reflected light in Medwenna's eyes; she tore a strip of cloth from the hem of her shirt and tied it around her mouth and nose, blocking out the floral mist. "Anima—the dead alive again."

"What do we—"

Stars burst across his vision, red-rimmed and pulsing. Pain cracked through his chin, radiating up through the sides of his skull.

He knew this particular pain—knew the taste of those particular knuckles. Soren had just punched him.

"Elias!"

He tried to raise his head, but the blood whirlpooled in his brain; too dizzy to see anything but moonlit green blurs, he set his head back down, seeking his battlemate's movements in the shadows that dappled the deck. His lungs dragged in breath against his will, trying to replace what had been knocked out of him.

Freckled hands slapped down on the deck in front of his face, a mane of copper hair pooling beside them.

Relief set his breath free. She'd shaken out of it herself, and now—

Now...

Soren's hair wasn't that long. Not anymore.

The person in front of him sank down so he could see their face, lying almost nose-to-nose with him on the deck.

Pale green eyes misted in blue. A sad, strong smile. A hand held out to help him stand.

"Elias," said Kallias, his hand anchoring around Elias's, "you have to get up."

Emotion seized him by the throat so swiftly, he almost choked on his friend's name as he let himself get hauled to his feet; and the moment he found them, he surged forward to drag Kallias into the second-tightest embrace of his entire gods-damned life.

"Where in the pits did you come from?" His voice cracked so badly it hurt his throat; he swallowed hard, cursing himself as hot tears formed branching rivers down his face. "I thought—I mean, we thought—how are you *here*?"

Kallias shrugged sheepishly out of Elias's arms, scratching the back of his neck. "I guess a miracle worked out in my favor, for once." He held his hand back out to Elias. "This is a trap. We need to get you off this boat before you go much further—I can help you swim back."

"What about Sor..."

All the breath trailed out of his lungs as he turned to search for his battlemate.

The ship was empty—no Tallisians. No Soren.

"Where did they go?" He ran to the edge of the deck and looked over, but the strange silver-green light had vanished; only cloudy gray water waited below, lapping gently at the boat instead of slamming into it headfirst.

"She's all right—look." Kallias grabbed his arm and dragged it around, using it to point him in the direction of the shore they'd just left—Soren was already there, ruffling the water from her curls as she bickered with Everin.

None of them looked his way. Not even when he cupped his hands around his mouth and shouted their names.

"Elias, we don't have time," Kallias urged; the wind whipped his loose hair across his eyes, rays of sunlight dancing over sea-green waters. "The wind's picking up—we have to jump."

Jump. Into the water. With no idea how deep it went.

"I…" Gods, he couldn't catch his breath. His lungs were oddly…heavy. Burning. "I can't swim, remember?"

"That's what I'm here for."

"I don't know, Kal. We have to get the weapon."

A sunbright smile. A hand extended to help. His friend, back against all odds, ready to reclaim his kingdom.

"You've done enough," Kallias said. "You can rest now. Let someone else take that fight."

He could have wept…at the promise, at the offer, at the idea of letting the weight tumble off his own shoulders. To let someone else carry it the rest of the way.

They'd given enough. Lost enough. They needn't give any more.

He reached out his hand, ready to let Kallias lead him home.

Thunder *boomed*—not in the chamber, not in his ears, but in the quietest parts of himself. The soft pocket of darkness where instinct slept, roused by something grating against its hallowed walls.

Listen, rumbled that specter of absolute knowing. *Listen to what he's saying.*

Not an encouragement.

A warning.

"Eli!"

Kallias, ready to throw himself over the arena's railing, three guards barely managing to hold him back; Kallias screaming at the top of his lungs as he watched Elias give himself up to death, a king's unfaltering command roaring out of him like phoenix fire.

"Get up!"

"Give it up," Kallias coaxed, kindness never faltering. Hand never wavering. "It's all right, Elias."

Elias.

"Eli!"

Give it up.

"Get up!"

He set his hand in Kallias's…and twisted it at the wrist, anger unfurling through his cold chest as he shattered his friend's bones. Kallias shouted in pain, dropping to one knee; his fingers went limp, freeing Elias from his hold.

A tempestuous glare. Bared teeth—*serrated* teeth.

"What are you doing?" hissed the creature—yet another who dared wear Kallias like a costume, panting through his pain, sickening betrayal dampening his gaze. "What are you *doing?*"

Elias leaned down, looking his lost friend in the eye. And though his stomach ached with shame, begging him to fall for this cruelest of tricks, he swallowed back an apology he didn't owe.

"Kallias Atlas saved my life," he rasped. "He kept me fighting. He is my friend—and he calls me *Eli*."

A beastly sneer broke the familiarity of the facsimile's face. And even then, Elias could not bear to look as he hauled him—hauled *it*—up by its collar and thrust it overboard, its enraged scream gargling into nothing as it sank into the fog beneath the waves.

As the hallucination dissolved into waterlogged bones, a skeleton still baring its teeth as the depths swallowed it whole.

CHAPTER 49

SOREN

Her mother was drowning, and she couldn't reach her.

Memory could only propel her so far. Though every stroke she swam carried her forward, like oars pulling in perfect synchrony, the lake's cutting waves kept pushing her back.

There was no salt to buoy her like the sea back home. No paddleboard to carry her over the waves. No sister or brothers to lead the way.

Every time her head bobbed beneath the water, she surged back up to see Enna had floated further away.

"Mama!" she shouted. "Mama, swim this way!"

In the distant places at the back of her mind—places she abandoned in moments of terror—there was a voice screaming that this didn't make sense. That it couldn't be real.

That her mother had died, and she *knew* that, and she needed to swim back to the boat *now*.

But that was the thing about children and their parents: no child could really stop believing that their mother would always answer when they called. That even when death performed one of its most malicious thefts, their mother would come running when they needed her to save them. To soothe them. To make them safe again.

People spoke fondly of a child's infallible faith. Today, that faith kept her treading water, gasping in air that made her head swim with the scent of daisies.

She was gaining ground—she had to be. She could see the whites of Enna's eyes now as she panted and kicked through a cramp that tried to lock up her leg. The muscle screamed; she screamed back through her teeth.

Not again. She would not leave her here—not this time.

"Mama!" Rock and damp and dirt washed over her tongue; she spat the lake water out, but her next cry still bubbled in her throat: "Mama, *please!*"

"I can't move!" Enna's panicky call lit a fire in her chest; she blinked away fog and tears, sucking in a breath before cutting down into the water.

Beneath the lake's surface, fog of a different kind clouded her sight; she still couldn't find the bottom. But if she squinted, she could just make out the shadowy shape of Enna's legs kicking, the overwrought movements of an inexperienced swimmer trying to stay afloat. She'd only wear herself out like that.

As if the world itself listened in on her thoughts, that shadow grew, water closing up over it.

Her mother was sinking.

No. Anger surged, hot and painful, and she struck out against another cramp trying to slow her down. *No!*

Bubbles exploded in a column, whirling up from the shadow for a second, two, three…then halting.

All was still.

The urge to scream built in her throat. She swam faster, *faster,* but her body wasn't shaped to swim so long and hard; fatigue caught her by the ankles and wrists, every lagging stroke pulling her down instead of forward, breath aching to burst free…

Until arms snagged sharply around her waist, dragging her back up to the surface.

Her hands scraped against rough tile sides, and she scrabbled with all her might, clinging on and pulling herself above the surface with a hacking splutter.

A splutter that tasted like salt.

She coughed out Enna's name, but when she looked around, the lake had vanished—the boat, her drowning mother, the fog, all of it.

Seawater. Sunlight.

She looked down at her own hands, fingers splayed across squares of rich blue tile.

Not the lake. This was—

A splash exploded beside her; another head burst out from the water, a cross-looking expression half-hidden under dark auburn hair plastered over clever, irritable brown eyes.

"I'm feeling like we've done this before," Finn announced, dragging himself out of the pool—the swimming pool back in Atlas, back home. He plopped onto the edge, leaving his feet submerged, smirking down at her as he knocked water out of one ear. "Still trying to drown yourself, kid?"

She stared at him. Clung to the edge. Tried very hard to remember why looking at him made her feel like crying.

"Finn," she whispered.

"Oh good, she still remembers my name." He rolled his eyes. "Do you remember me teaching you how *not* to die in the water? Because I did. It was, like, the second actual conversation we had after you came home. Not counting the one right before your lover left a dent in my handsome head."

Something wasn't right. "I'm…I'm not supposed to be here."

Finn sighed, looking up at the ceiling for a long moment. "No, you're not." When he looked back down, his gaze gentled; he patted the tile next to him. "Come on out. The water's *not* fine."

For once, she didn't argue; she pulled herself out of the pool and sat beside him, shivering, staring down at her sopping clothes.

"So," he said, propping one leg up and resting his elbow on it, "where *are* you supposed to be, if not enjoying my sparkling company?"

"Tallis, I think." She snatched her hand out, trying to grasp more than that, but it scattered the memory like mist. "What are *you* doing here?"

"Looking for you." A one-shouldered shrug. "Didn't think I'd find you doing a shoddy impression of a whale, but—"

Against all odds, a laugh cracked out of her chest, and she elbowed him in the arm. "Excuse me?"

"What?" Finn put his hands up, laughing as he ducked out of her range. "Do you want me to tell you that you did a *good* impression of a whale? Because that's a lot ruder, if you ask me."

"I wasn't doing *any* impression of a whale."

"Could've fooled me, with all that flopping around." He dipped himself to and fro, clapping his arms together. "So graceful! So elegant!"

"That's a *seal*," she groaned through her laughter.

A dismissive wave of his hand. "Same thing."

"They're *so* not."

Finn pushed her this time; she had to catch herself on the edge with her heels and her hands. "Like you'd know. You were raised by wolves, remember?"

She stuck her tongue out. "At least the wolves taught me manners."

Finn chuckled, letting her take the round; they both sat in silence for a minute, watching the crystalline water. The warm, sun-kissed breeze wound in through the glass doors, thrown open to let in summer's glory; homesickness ran her through better than any sword as that breeze carried Atlas inside, practically dropping it in her lap. Warm sand and baking stone; fiddle music and gossiping neighbors; buttery dough and pastel taffies.

"You can't stay."

She looked at her brother, heart dropping onto the unforgiving tiles when she took in his solemn stare. "Why not?"

"Because this is just a dream." He leaned around her, looking somewhere over her shoulder. "You're still drowning. And we both know Elias is useless in the water, so I'm sorry to tell you, but you're going to have to save yourself this time around."

She didn't follow his line of sight—she didn't want to know what she'd see if she did.

"Then why'd you bring me here?" Temper flared, hot and sticky and awfully, annoyingly similar to devastation. "If I can't stay, why bother?"

He shrugged both shoulders this time, and suddenly...suddenly, he looked very, very tired. Tired enough that her temper sputtered into worry.

"I just miss you, is all," he said. "I wish you could be here." His mouth curled into a wretched smirk. "Well, no, I don't. It's all going to the depths here. You're better off where you are, trust me."

Do me a favor, little sister...trust me.

Tears coated her eyes; when she blinked them away, Finn was watching her, dry as a bone and frowning—the thoughtful frown that always preceded him proving he knew her entirely too well.

"There it is," he said quietly.

"What?"

"I was wondering when you'd remember I'm supposed to be dead."

"Don't give up," she said—when he laughed, she reached out and gripped his shirt, shaking him by the shoulder. "I'm serious. Don't give in to her. We're getting the god-killer, and we're—"

"Soren." He set his hand over hers. "I'm the last person you need to worry about right now. This has been fun and all, but I don't need saving. You need to wake up and save yourself."

"Why did you let her in?" Her heart and voice broke together, and she held on tighter, ignoring when he started to pull away. Ignoring how the tile began to disappear from underneath her. "I just got you back, both of you—you told me to *trust* you—"

"I did," he interrupted sharply. "I did tell you that. And I'm telling you again now. So *you* tell *me*—can you keep it up, kid? Just a little while longer?"

She stared up at him. He stared back, still holding her hand, not a lick of humor in his eyes now.

And somehow, when she nodded her silent *yes*...it wasn't a lie.

"Good." He curled his fingers under hers, prying them open. Making her let him go. "Then trust me—and *wake up*."

The warm breeze, her brother's face, the sunlight—all of it vanished. And when she opened her mouth to shout his name, a rush of cold and wet consumed her.

Water. It was everywhere, everything; it filled her lungs, pumped through her veins, stung her eyes as she forced them open, gathering her surroundings with a sudden burst of clarity.

You're still drowning.

Oh, gods. She was still *drowning.*

A trap. The lake was a trap, a trial, and she'd been gone before she could even see it.

This time, when she struck out toward the surface, she found it—and when she broke it, hacking up water, a rope splashed down in front of her only seconds later.

"Oh, thank the gods." Elias bent over the side of the boat, his voice muffled by the cloth wrapped around his nose and mouth. His eyes glimmered with powerful relief as he watched her swim for the rope. "I was about to go in after you."

"Like *the pits* you were," she coughed, forcing herself to sip in small breaths. The fog still floated over the lake's surface, though thinner than before, and she didn't know how much it would take to put her back under. "You would've sunk to the bottom before you even got close!"

"What was I supposed to do, sit up here and watch you drown?"

"I don't know, *maybe!*"

Elias groaned. "Are you really yelling at me for saving your life right now?"

"I'm not yelling!" she yelled. "It's a big cavern, I have to raise my—"

"Argue with me later, all right? Get your breath back. We need your help with the others."

"Convenient," she muttered, but it wasn't like she could protest—especially when she noticed the ship listing to the right.

Everin manned the wheel, but it clearly wasn't *him*; he gazed lifelessly across the water, lips moving silently as he kept spinning the wheel, aiming the bow directly at the ship-sinking rocks on that side of the cavern.

Medwenna knelt beside the mast, tying the final knot around Matthias's wrist; he and Kessen were lashed firmly to the wooden post, both struggling uselessly, both screaming—Kessen for *Jules*, Matthias for *Will*. But Everin didn't scream; he only stared, sights set, as if single-minded purpose had possessed him rather than panic.

Medwenna started toward him, her eyes taking on the same unbreakable focus.

"Everin," she called in a low voice, as if speaking to a wild beast. "Everin, you need to turn us west. We're sailing for the wall, do you see it?"

Everin's head idled an inch toward her. His hands stayed steady on the wheel.

"I know someone needs your help over there." Medwenna approached him with back bent and hands out, eyes not quite meeting his. "But we can't help anyone if we rake the ship to shreds, now, can we?"

"But I can see her," said the prince, one hand lifting from the wheel to point. Unlike her hands, which had yet to settle their shivers, his held true. "I can see her, and she's…"

"I know. I know you can." Medwenna stepped up behind the prince, nearly flush with his back…and fearlessly slid her hands over his eyes.

Soren knew the look of rage spreading through a body; she knew the look of a brawl about to break. And as Everin's body went taut, dangerous intent catching like fire along his limbs, Medwenna stretched up and whispered right into his ear.

Soren watched, not breathing, rattling off prayers to no one as Everin's hand rose from the wheel, curled into a fist…then fell back to his side.

Medwenna set her forehead against his temple, still whispering. And though Soren couldn't hear what she said, she could *see* the anger draining out of the Lion of Tallis, his head turning into Medwenna's embrace rather than away.

Everin's throat bobbed. His hand flexed on the wheel…

"Sorry, Mom," he whispered.

Then he released the wheel.

Soren jolted forward, almost tripping over a loose board in her haste; she caught herself on the wheel before she could sprawl on her face, letting memory that ran deeper than the mind guide her as she dragged the heavy hunk of wood around.

The ship righted itself with a sickening lurch, the bow pointed once again toward the opposite side of the chamber.

Gods, her heart was beating in her *throat*.

"Everyone with us?" she called, grateful beyond words that her voice didn't wobble.

"Sound off," Matthias spoke up groggily. "One."

"Two," Elias croaked.

"Three." Kessen's response came oddly quiet; the boy was staring at his hands. She decided to pretend she couldn't see the wet gleam in his eyes, or the hitched gait to his breathing.

"Four," she said instead.

"Five and six," Medwenna answered; she still had one hand on Everin's bearded cheek, and the prince didn't seem inclined to shake her off. He just stared off at nothing, brow furrowed deeply, his teeth anchored in his lower lip.

"Well," Soren said, "at least that's over."

Not even a second after the last word left her mouth, the wind picked up.

It swept over the surface of the lake, clearing away the fog—no. No, wait…not clearing it.

Gathering it.

The fog swirled together, thickening, darkening…rising. Elias cursed under his breath when it drifted up to the ceiling, roiling and writhing as the cavern slowly but surely went dark.

Moonlight gone, swallowed by a storm of dark mist, she couldn't find any of her companions—but she could sense their unease like static buried in an old shirt, waiting to burst when the shock finally came.

"I need to stop saying things like that," she said.

"You think?" Elias asked dryly.

Lightning cracked across the ceiling, offering just enough light for her to see the waves surging higher, fiercer…

Fed by the rain that broke out in droves, pelting against her like slivers of glass, a deluge unlike anything she'd ever seen.

The pieces came together in quick, horrifying succession, like the final pieces of a puzzle finding their proper position:

A storm had broken inside this mountain.

The water was rising at a terrifying pace.

And both sides of the cavern remained sealed, no exit to be seen.

This lake wanted them to drown—and it wasn't taking *no* for an answer.

CHAPTER 50

SOREN

"*Count the seconds after lightning strikes. See how long the thunder takes to chase it down. When you hear it, that'll tell you how far away the lightning is.*"

She didn't need to count—the storm didn't give her the chance. The thunder raced in on the lightning's heels, so loud her eardrums quivered.

The ghost of Kallias's hand settled on her shoulder; his voice rumbled in her ear, lower than the thunder's growling pitch. "*Sailing through storms is dangerous, but it's not a death sentence. Look at me—we're going to make it home. Say it back to me.*"

The ship's wheel creaked in complaint beneath her white-knuckled fingers; she forced them to loosen. Forced a deep breath in and out. Let the blood flow back through her fingers as she listened. As she counted.

Lightning first, then thunder. Further this time; not by much, two blinks instead of one, but still further.

She didn't need to look over her shoulder to know what waited behind her: three Tallisian soldiers who could climb mountains more easily than most could scale a ladder. An archeress suited to navigating the depths of mountains, forests, and the past alike. Elias, who never faltered even when their path led them through knee-deep snow or icy passes.

Not one sailor among them. Not one with saltwater and sunfire in their veins.

Only her. And her only halfway.

But if halfway was all they had, she'd stretch it as far as it could go.

"Everyone," her heart fumbled over its next beat at the sound of her own voice, "find something to hang on to!"

With the slight Atlas accent that had crept back into her diction since getting her memories back…any touch of command to her tone made no mystery of who her mother was.

The echo of Adriata Atlas lived in her lungs. A voice that had sung her shanties as lullabies and showered her in endless praise; a voice that had demanded the deaths of hundreds, thousands, of her heart kingdom's people.

It should have horrified her.

Instead, she straightened, steely resolve shoring up her spine.

That command was her birthright; the call of queens was hers to wield. And she would not forfeit that inheritance when she needed it most. Even if it hurt in strange ways to hear.

Even if it wove a phantom diadem into her knotted curls, a burden she nearly buckled beneath.

Lightning forked across the sky. Blue-edged silver. Bane of sailors.

One second.

Hail and rain lashed her skin, the sky weeping tears of stone.

Two seconds.

The current rolled beneath her heels.

Three seconds.

Seawater sprayed her face, and she closed her eyes, shielding them with her forearm.

"There." Kallias touched her shoulder, guiding her toward the shore…but he did not turn the wheel. He left it in her hands, resting his chin on her head, unflinching in the face of the storm. In fact, when he spoke next, she felt his smile against her hair. "Lightning rarely strikes the same place twice. Watch where it lands, then sail that way—fast as you can. You ready?"

In the same instant she opened her eyes, another bolt struck just off the starboard side of the ship.

"Go, Soleil!"

And with a roar aimed for the clouds themselves, she gods-damned *sailed.*

The wheel, the sails, the current—they all clashed in unlikely harmony, and the ship practically flew over the roiling waves. They careened toward the lightning's last target, water frothing over the sides of the ship like snapping jaws aiming for the unsteadier legs on this vessel.

Fear turned the locks on her knees and knuckles, freezing her to the wheel as that torrent aimed for her.

How many times had she pitted her body against forces great and small, and it had failed her regardless of which? How many times had she nursed bruises and sprains and swollen bumps after fits and falls, the evidence of Ani's invasive power devouring her inside out?

She'd been born with sea legs; she'd been raised in icy climes. These swells of storm surge should do nothing but lap at her ankles.

Just like a set of stairs should have done nothing but test the steadiness of her breath and her boots.

Instead, it had broken her. Put her on the ground. Made her beg to stand again, then spat on her bruised knuckles. Kicked her battered knees.

But Soren Atlas was done breaking.

Find your anchor.

She sank her heels into her brother's unshaking faith. Set her jaw against doubt's purring sneer.

And when the swell struck, it did not break her—it broke *against* her. Like a cresting wave colliding with a stalwart pier. Like a sled careening into a snowbank.

The frigid water soaked her to the skin, wringing a gasp out of her; but that was the only ground she'd give. Dripping lake water, clad in soaked wool and the memories of her brother guiding her home, she fit the grooves of her palm to the grooves in the wheel, breathing out the last of her doubt.

She'd wished for a battlefield. Here it was.

"Elias!" she barked. "Split them up—half to the left, half to the right. Stay against the sides. Balance it out."

"Where do you want me?" No hesitation in him, her fearless, fire-touched battlemate.

"Right behind me." She trawled in a breath so deep it inflated her lungs to the point of aching. "Those waves are about to get bigger."

She couldn't hear him move over the calamity breaking above her head. But she didn't need to.

She'd never been a woman of much faith. But what few and flimsy scraps she did have, she'd long since dedicated to Elias Loch.

He'd proved himself worthy of that faith a thousand times over. And when he fit his hands to the wheel beside hers, his heart thudding between her shoulder blades, he proved it yet again.

"Tell me the plan," he said.

She tightened her grip; her smallest finger brushed against his thumb. "Don't let me fall off this ship."

He slid his hands inward, arms flexing as he set himself against the squall. "Again, you mean?"

"Shut your mouth or I will kick your holy *ass*, Elias Loch!" Even if it was the last gods-damned thing she did before she died, so *help* her—

His laugh, wild with terror-born hysteria, struck the back of her head. And it was the last thing she heard before thunder sundered the world at the seams, roaring in the face of their corkboard ship as she set her sights on the opposite shore.

She could see it now: the faintest stripe of lighter water indicating a sand bar. The sliver of rocky shoreline just a few short yards beyond it.

They'd crash, sure—but if she crashed it just right, their sorry selves wouldn't join the sodden skeletons sleeping their afterlife away.

"Stop that," Elias said.

"Stop what?"

"You're not allowed to scheme in silence. Talk it through. What are we doing?"

She hesitated. "Promise me you won't yell at me?"

Elias groaned. "What did I say about leading with—"

This time, the grating crunch of rock against wood threw his voice away—and nearly threw the two of them off the side of the ship. Only Elias's ironworker's hands and his decision to crush her against the wheel saved them both.

If the imprint of the wheel hadn't been stamped into her ribs now, she might've complimented his *knuckle strength* or something equally ridiculous. As it was, she couldn't catch enough breath to make the joke worth it.

Especially because the ship was no longer moving. And considering she could no longer see the anchor resting on the deck, she was reasonably sure she knew why.

"What *now?*" Kessen's despairing cry hit her like an echo; she nearly giggled, that despair morphing into odd shapes as it tried to fit itself into her chest.

Gods, it never ended. Poor Kessen had no idea.

"Rocks," she groaned through laughter. "Of course there are rocks. Of-gods-damned-course the anchor got stuck on *rocks!*"

Somewhere between the first and second *rocks,* her laughter got lost on the way; a shrill screech took its place. She struck the wheel, pain crackling through the heel of her hand.

At least the throbbing was a good distraction.

"We're not moving!" Everin yelled—unnecessarily.

"You're kidding," she gasped, trying to twist around to glare at the prince; Elias stopped her, making her face the bow again. "Is *that* what an anchor does?"

"I don't appreciate the condescending tone, Princess!"

"I don't appreciate the unnecessary commentary, Prince!"

"Soren!" snapped Elias; one hand dropped from the wheel to snag her by the hip, holding her steady as the ship let out another death rattle. His fingers dug into her hipbone, almost bruising in their terror. "Eyes on the water, smartass. What's our move?"

Find your anchor.

She skimmed the distance between them and the shore.

"How much do you trust me?"

"You know the answer." Faith—it rang clarion-clear in his steady, swift retort.

She twisted to face him, back to the wheel, finding his eyes in the shrouded light of the storm. "I need to swim down and get the anchor loose."

His gaze flicked out over the water like a skipping stone. "Against those waves?"

"Yes."

He didn't even blink. "I'm coming with you."

"You can't swim."

"Then show me how."

"Elias—"

"You *heard* me." He seized her wrists, gathering them together, pressing her hands to his heart—over the braided tattoo stamped with their most precious vow. "I'll hold a rope or something, but if it's going to be a battle, then you'll have me at your back."

She wanted nothing *less* than for Elias to go into that water with her. But one look in his face told her he wouldn't be swayed; and if the roles had been reversed, she wouldn't have, either.

"You stay by the boat," she commanded, abandoning the wheel; it was useless, anyway. Her feet skidded on the slippery deck, but she caught herself, making it halfway before dropping on one knee and sliding up to the hull. She unwound the coil of spare rope looped through a metal hook, tossing the loose end to Elias. "Until you get the basics down, you need a safety net. Matthias, can you—"

The mountainous man had already slid to her side, taking hold of the other end of the rope. "Go carefully, Your Highness."

She gestured to the raging water. "I can't, but I appreciate the sentiment."

He grinned ruefully at her. "I'm really starting to like you."

"Hopefully I'll be back to keep up the streak." With a wink and a salute thrown one after the other, she dove back to her battlemate…then, after tying the rope securely around him, they both plunged into the water.

This time, no visions of her drowning mother or her tired brother greeted her; just grinning skeletons, watching in grotesque delight as she struck out for the stones that held their anchor fast. Its tine had lodged firmly into a gap between two smaller boulders; not large enough to impress, but not small enough for the momentum of the boat to yank the anchor free.

The back of her neck itched; she desperately wanted to look back and make sure Elias's shadow was still where it ought to be, bobbing beside the stranded boat. But the sooner she got this anchor unstuck, the safer he'd be.

She wrapped her hands around the anchor and tugged; of course, it didn't budge, because the gods and the world and whatever powers might yet be out there laughing at her misfortune couldn't make anything simple.

Whatever capricious being had been placed in charge of penning her life's path, would it really hurt them to give her an easy win once in a while? Or even once, *ever?*

Once, twice, thrice—four times she tugged at the anchor, the last time so severely that she nearly tore her own shoulders out of their sockets. Not one wiggle; not one inch of give.

Please, she screamed silently. *Please, just once.*

Breath spent, head spinning, she planted her feet against the boulders and pulled—

And in a rush of bubbles, the last dregs of her breath fleeing for the surface, she freed the anchor.

She clawed her way back up the rope so fast that when she broke the surface, gasping in breath for the second time, she nearly blacked out; luckily, *nearly* still allowed her to swim to her battlemate.

They tumbled back onto the boat like fish dragged up by a net, panting, exhausted, worn to the bone…but alive.

It seemed the storm had also run itself ragged; as she caught her breath and reached blindly for Elias, the pelting rain and hail beating against her face finally ceased.

Her hand collided with a soaking wet shirt, and she balled it in her fist, water bubbling between her fingers as she wrung the fabric out. "Elias?"

Only when his chest lifted beneath her hand—only when he coughed out, "Why would *anyone* do that for *fun?*" in the most innocently confused voice she'd ever heard—did she slump against the deck, letting all the tension bleed out of her body as a single, ugly cackle.

When the boat bumped against the shore—softly, so absurdly gentle that she burst into ragged laughter all over again—the other five all let out audible groans of relief. And when they all limped off the boat, Kessen dropping to his knees and kissing the stone floor without any regard for what algae might be growing on it, not one of them needed to hazard a guess about which god *that* trial had been made for.

CHAPTER 51

ANIMA

Sore-fingered and distractible after her archery lessons, her mind flitting from thought to thought like an errant butterfly, Ani only made it two days before she talked herself into going on an ill-advised, unaccompanied excursion.

To set foot in the woods this late at night was to tempt another attack by the Blight—the monster she had yet to see again since agreeing to remain within the darkwood walls surrounding Elderwood. The monster that haunted her waking hours until the sleeping ones fell fewer and fewer in number, every rustle of undergrowth or clatter of stone wrenching her heart halfway out of her chest before Wolf assured her it was nothing.

And even if she'd been willing to risk it, she'd promised Wolf she'd stay within the walls if he promised to get some real sleep in his own bed. She couldn't ask him to keep his promises, then turn around and break her own.

So she did not go to the woods. Instead, she armed herself with the lantern flickering on her bedside table and struck out for a different sanctuary.

It was too quiet in her borrowed room in the Olivander tree; and the sparse stack of romance novels she'd discovered on the nightstand were a bit too engrossing. She might wander so far into the embrace of those pages that she couldn't find her way out again, and another sleepless night was the last thing she needed.

There were other stories she'd waited too long to read.

It took longer to find the shrine's entrance than usual; either the Guardian had chosen to take shelter deeper in the city proper, or he didn't man his post in the evening hours. It made sense, of course—even the most stalwart of mortals could not use fealty to fend off exhaustion forever. But she still found it...and most importantly, she found it without being pursued by monster or man.

She brushed aside the shrine's protective curtain, expecting to see a shadowed alcove waiting—instead, she was pleasantly surprised by the gathering of lily pads on the pool's surface. Fist-sized globes of flameless light rested on about half of them, setting the entire shrine aglow. Most traditional Artemic blown glass got stained in vivid splashes of fiery color before being shipped out to other kingdoms, but the few here that had any staining at all were swirled with petal-pink and grass-green.

The pink winked at her, warming her heart like a well-timed inside joke. People often assumed her favorite color was green, and she couldn't blame them—she hadn't done much to challenge the assumption, and it was a fine enough color, but...the truth was, it had always been pink. As a girl, as a goddess...as whatever she could call herself now.

Then the misfortune of magic's manifestation had cast it as one of Occassio's signature colors. After a while, even wearing it had begun to feel shameful, like stealing a prized gown out of her sister's closet and parading around in it herself.

But here, floating placidly in this pool, watched over by the Crownless Queen's kind eyes...

Here, it felt safe to be a bit selfish.

"Beautiful, isn't it?"

Ani nearly jumped out of her skin as the shrine's Guardian stepped out from one of the branching corridors, a lantern in his hand. "Don't you ever rest?"

"Of course I do." The Guardian chuckled as he sat down on the circle of stones surrounding the pool. "My chambers are right down that path."

Mortification nearly set her hair aflame. "Rot take me, I'm so dense. I'm sorry, I didn't realize you—"

"Rest your head, milady. Plenty of folks do their praying at night. You're not the first here this evening, and you won't be the last." He set the lantern beside his left hip, then patted the stone beside his right. "Some miracles simply can't wait till morning."

That explained the ashen taste coating her tongue, the tingling in her hands as she sat and braced them on the fountain's stones. The residue left behind by fraught, fervent prayers.

These stones had been smoothed by generations of the faithful…eroded by brows bent to basin, tears saturated by someone's final dregs of hope, hands splayed in supplication to an unseeing statue.

"But then again," said the Guardian as she settled in, "I don't suppose you're here to pray."

"I'm afraid even a miracle won't help me." But the reminder of what was at stake might. "Am I still welcome to stay, even if I have no prayers to offer?"

He patted her hand this time. "There will never be a day where you are not welcome here."

"What about a night?"

He chortled again. "Well, a man does need his sleep. But funny enough, I trust you not to desecrate the place in my absence. What were you searching for?"

"The princesses mentioned I had journals stowed away here. I was hoping I might…"

"I see." With a heave and a discomfited grunt, he hauled himself up, cracking his back. "Let me fetch them—I've kept them in the back since the princesses returned them. I worry about thieves."

"Thank you."

Once the Guardian dropped off the vellum-wrapped parcel of journals, then returned to his chambers with a promise to give her space, she settled the parcel in her lap, playing with the string that tied it together—a string that, while paled by age, might have once been pink.

She tugged it loose, and the vellum wrapping fell away, revealing a pristine stack of cloth-bound books.

Each one a different color. Each one a different size. And…

Her throat ached as she swiped her thumb over the cover of the one on top. Each journal was stamped with a name embossed in gold foiling, none of them hers—and none of them the same.

Because she hadn't continued the entries after the first journal filled up in each life…or because she'd never lived long enough to finish one?

From the bottom up…*Isa.* Then *Lilibet.*

Lotus. Viola. Fearne. Venetia. Ansari.

And at the very top, the newest journal of all, though still carrying years of wear on its binding…

Orchid. A cream-colored tome with a pink silk ribbon marking someone's place.

The cover indented when she pressed down on it, plush but firm; it sprang back up as soon as she pulled her hand away.

She'd never seen nor held a journal like it. Yet it fit in her hands like a pot pushed onto a full display shelf, its bottom edge perfectly aligned; it felt as familiar as the hands themselves. Long-lost, but still hers.

It helped her feel less like a snoop as she cracked open the handwritten tome.

At the first curling letter scripted into its deckled pages, nerves chose her knucklebones as their new hive; she sucked in a deep breath, wishing she could borrow a plume of Sparrow's slumber-inducing beesmoke to put that buzz of terror to sleep.

Her name was Orchid, and she was very loved.

Her family went away to grieve before I woke up, but I see them in her memories. Her mother fought so hard to give her all the life she could. Her father held her hand through every treatment, every trial. Her older sister is the only one who supported her choice to let go. To let me in.

Her bodyguard is the only one who stayed the whole time. He's the only one who's still here now.

One of the things Mora told me that I can't forget: grief is an action, not an emotion. It's a thing that we do, and how we feel…that's different for everyone.

People grieve with sadness. With love. With relief. Anger. Despair.

Alder Finch grieves with devotion.

That name swung an axe into her heart.

He's in more of her memories than anyone else. He followed her everywhere. And now he's following me.

I did make sure that he realizes she's gone. I tried to be gentle. He assured me he understood.

I told him he could leave. He laughed. I don't know why.

Then he told me he has nowhere else to go.

All of that to say…it seems I have a bodyguard now.

This life is going to be a strange one. I can already tell.

What kind of mess did you leave for me, Orchid?

A frost-laden breeze barreled through the shrine's entrance, slamming into her with tidal force. She tucked her cloak in to trap her shivers, closing any gap that might let a draft in before she kept reading.

The next few entries were plain enough; they detailed the struggle to settle in her newest body, the relief when she finally connected to her magic, the little joys of getting reacquainted with mortal life.

Mostly mortal life.

The next entry that merited a pause began with penstrokes pressed so deep into the paper that they'd dented in the next page over:

Alder Finch will not let me dismiss him.

I do not need a bodyguard. I do not want a bodyguard. I have no desire or requirement for a mortal to follow me around and wait for something to try to kill me, especially because I cannot be killed.

But Alder Finch made a promise to Orchid Viviane that he would serve her all his days. His *days—not hers.*

"I had to let her choose to leave me," he said today. "Have mercy on a man with nothing else—this vow is all I have left of her."

What in the rotting world am I supposed to do with that, *exactly?*

When she raised her stinging eyes—had she forgotten to blink while reading?— she could only see a couple feet in any direction. Beyond the fuzzy-edged halo of light thrown out from the pool, sight-swallowing shadows had gathered as the night wore on, draped over the walls like silken shrouds.

Good. If anyone else suffering a sleepless night came out this way, maybe they'd fail to recognize her—even with her stone-faced edifice keeping silent vigil behind her.

The cold dragged in by the wind still lingered; though she'd shut it out of her cloak, it wound into the space between the tops of her boots and the cuffs of her pants. It nibbled at her toes until the feeling started to die, her socks proving to be a poor shield.

But she didn't want to go back to her room to read. Not when the next entry whispered rather than ranted, penned in script so small she could barely read her own self's shameful secret:

I may be a little in love with Alder Finch.

A shout lashed over the shrine, snapping her out of her reading reverie: "Behind you!"

The shrine's Guardian charged from the darkness with speed beyond his age, his sword pealing like a warning bell as he drew it. She didn't have time to heed his call before he vaulted onto the pool's stone border, blade belting out a high note when he swung it over Ani's head.

An unearthly shriek. A lessening of pressure around her shoulders; a pressure that had built so slowly, she hadn't even realized how cramped her shoulders had become.

A familiar howling scream that cut to the bone.

Cold fettered her at the ankles; not phantom after all, but physical. Slick vines soaked in some viscous liquid slithered over her bare skin.

The Guardian's blade made quick work of those slimy vestiges, freeing her ankles; before she knew it, he'd grabbed her by the hand and yanked her off the fountain. He thrust an arm across her front as what she'd thought were shadows peeled away from the walls, folding in on themselves in some places, ripping themselves to pieces in others.

She had been terrified to the very edges of her psyche too many times in the past several weeks. Horror should have struck her nearly dead; instead, it struck like a dagger gone dull.

The only reason she did not scream when the shadows stepped into the light, revealing a jumbled set of furious, almost-human features.

She reached past the Guardian's arm, loosing a shout that startled her with its strength: "*Stop!*"

The Blight jerked to a halt; darkwood bark shifted over its softer parts like chitinous armor, a current of frustration shuddering through it with a pitchy, chittering groan.

"You are not welcome here," she snarled. "Get *out.*"

The Blight observed her with a beastial curl of its lip. "I am here."

The closer the monster came, its tendrils whipping across the ground like tentacles, the harder it was to breathe. She kneaded her heart with the heel of her hand. "I made you—yes? That's what you told me—I made you."

"I am here." A ripple over its surface, a puddle struck by a pebble. "You made me. It hurts."

A quiver strummed her throat. "I-I can fix it. Just—just tell me where it hurts."

The monster halted.

Roots crawled in gasping surges across the floor, wandering aimlessly; when the monster drifted forward, the roots drifted too, the living train of a macabre gown.

"Everywhere," it moaned. "Get it out."

Too close, with the Guardian still imposed between them. Ani forced her way past his shielding arm and called to the fountain's stones; a handful answered her summons, tumbling into form as a shield that reached to her shoulders. "Stay back."

A low, humming growl—its eyes flashed like a wildcat's as its gaze snapped to the Guardian. Its jaw contorted into a muzzle, ichor dripping like saliva from its toothy maw. "*Hungry.*"

Her heart squeezed to a halt, constricted by fear's strangling grip. She didn't know what possessed her; only that it seared her veins as she thrust forward another step, hands out, magic thrumming through her palms. The light in the shrine shifted from soothing pink to sickly green. The stone shield thrust forward with her. "I said *stay back.*"

It recoiled like a kicked hound. "Hungry," it said again—more of a whine this time.

"There is nothing here for you."

Corruption fanned out like wings of shadow; it rose to its full height, still canine in features but somewhat human in bearing. "*Where?*"

"Away," she babbled. "Away from here—outside the walls."

It blinked. Licked its jowls with a leaf-like tongue.

"I am here," it said, almost dismissively. "I hunt *here.*"

And in a rush of hurricane-like wind, it swooped upward, shattering through the rounded portion of the shrine's ceiling. Showering them in glass rain.

The Guardian swept his arm out over her, shielding her with his cloak; then he flapped the cloth outward, scattering the glass away. "Well done, milady."

Well done? She was about to pass out or throw up—she couldn't tell which—and all she'd done was shout. She swallowed the sensation, casting her arm out the same way he had to dismiss the stones back to the fountain. "Thank you."

The Guardian's eyes widened; he sheathed his sword, hurrying to the fountain. "The journals."

Thankfully, though they'd landed in a scattered heap of ruffling pages when the stones had leapt to Ani's aid, all the journals seemed unscathed—a smudge of dirt here and there, and Orchid's ribbon bookmark had lost its place, but all intact.

Ani helped the Guardian gather them, even though her tremors kept loosening her grip. She had to pick up Venetia's journal three times; its magenta cover ended up muddied by the time she tucked it between Fearne and Viola's.

As they hurried, Ani croaked, "Do you think it's still close?"

"I could only understand some of what it said, but if it is like most creatures on the hunt, I fear it won't follow your orders. Even the best hunting hounds struggle to pull themselves off a scent on command." The Guardian drew his sword again; he glanced at Ani, then reached back beneath his cloak, retrieving a small dagger. He held it out to her. "I'll walk you back, but you ought to arm yourself—just in case. I'm afraid I'm not as agile as I once was."

Ani didn't care for such weapons—at least with a bow and arrow, she didn't have to see blood and death up close. But when she closed her fingers around this one's hilt, her hand steadied—and when she lifted it, studying the short but sleek blade, it didn't strain her sore arms.

"You wouldn't know it, watching you fight." Even Elias, whom she'd seen clear considerable obstacles, never landed with the same effortless grace as this Guardian. "What would it have been like if you were younger?"

His eyes twinkled. "Ach, I probably would've done a backflip. Just to show off."

Ani giggled; it loosened the last of her wound-up nerves, and she set a hand over her middle, forcing herself to feel her own breathing. Her own heartbeat.

"We need to warn the Olivanders that she's in the city," she said. "That the walls didn't keep her out."

The Guardian dipped his head. "Lead the way, milady."

This—this was the kind of faith that made it so easy to fall in love with goddesshood. The calm, unwavering sort that did not ferment into obsessive fervor or blind belief—the kind that looked at her and saw someone capable. Someone worthy.

The kind that bolstered her courage just enough to help her take that first step out of the shrine, arms laden with the stories of her many lives, hoping the monster would stay hidden long enough for her to figure out how to end its chaotic crusade being waged across her island.

But those hopes were dashed the moment they arrived in Elderwood proper.

Dashed by the sound of a woman's agonized screams.

CHAPTER 52

ANIMA

The city was so quiet, even Ani—who had never been any kind of hunter—could track the screams straight to the Olivander family's door.

The shrine's Guardian stayed outside, refusing to enter his sovereigns' home without permission, but made a promise to stand guard until she dismissed him. So Ani had placed her journals back in his arms and raced through the winding passages of the treetop palace alone, choking on her own heart, dread spreading like a poison through her veins until she finally found the source of the screams.

Genevieve and Cypress's room.

She should have knocked. She should have heeded the calls of the four or five rangers she'd passed on her mad dash through the tree; she should have let one of the two dozen palacefolk explain what had happened before throwing herself into it headlong.

But after every ragged scream, a prayer followed. A prayer intoned under harsh, heavy breaths; a prayer planted in the back of her head, growing louder and louder.

Behind that door, Wolf Olivander was praying for a miracle.

A miracle done in her name…or by her hand.

Her hand, which turned the knob without thought; without a care for propriety or politeness.

Wolf Olivander was praying in Anima's name—and Anima would answer.

Wolf's face was the first she found; not in the cramped collision of bodies around the bed, but pushed to the very back. He'd curled into the corner, almost like he was trying to hide himself in the shadows; his folded hands rested in the corner's seam, his bloodshot eyes stealing glimpses over his shoulder. His fingers wrung together, trapping sickly green tethers of magic between them.

Necromancy didn't always hunger for the dead; every so often, it reacted to the sick, too. The dying.

Sage, however, could not have gotten closer without kneeling directly on Genevieve herself; he kept his balance on all fours as he hovered over his mother, pinning her shoulders with both hands. His palms, eyes, and mouth all poured forth light, such a pale green it could have been white if not for the wavering hint of sour apple at its edges; she could even make out luminescence beating over his heart, though his shirt and vest mostly buried it.

Cypress knelt across from his secondborn son, hands pressed to his wife's wrist and jugular, his fingertips pulsing a plummy red. He, too, prayed—but to a different goddess. Prayers that scalded Ani's ears and made her mouth taste of soot.

Brook knelt at the head of the bed; no magic danced in her hands or beamed from her eyes. She simply held her mother's head in her lap, tears dripping ceaselessly from her chin.

And despite it all, Genevieve kept screaming.

Tattered, breathless screams that tore apart as she forced them through her teeth, her jaw spasming as she gritted down harder and harder.

Lockjaw—the Queen couldn't open her mouth.

Plump black veins cradled her jaw like loving hands. Every time Sage and Cypress's magic flared, they receded by a hair; every time the two men paused for a breath, the veins advanced again, gaining twice the ground they'd lost.

"How long?" Her own jaw barely loosened enough to let the question out.

"Slithered through the city less than an hour ago." Sage coughed into his fist, breathless, his magic sputtering; then he slapped his own chest, and the beam steadied. Genevieve twisted forward with a shriek, bestial, rabid—nothing like the kind, clever queen Ani knew. "Ma got in its way. Handful of others, too—most sickened, a couple dead."

"Show me."

Cypress and Sage switched, Sage holding Genevieve's wrist down while Cypress towed down his wife's tunic at the shoulder, admirably steady as he pointed to the culprit: a small, almost perfectly circular puncture in the soft skin beneath where the collarbone and shoulder met. A concave circle, the blighted skin collapsing inward; the inkstrokes of infection spidered out in all directions, weaving a web that spread further by the second.

A web that would soon wrap up Genevieve's entire body, primed for chaos to devour from the inside out.

A web spun by a creature she had unwittingly made.

"Give me the room, please." Sancta bless the confident command she'd learned in her first life, a gift from the physicians she'd trained under in her late youth. "I will do what I can."

If this failed, she didn't want them to watch Blight have its way with the Queen…least of all Wolf, who'd already lost one mother, who kept looking back at Genevieve with the wide-eyed terror of a child who'd turned around to find themselves suddenly alone in a crowd of strangers.

Finally, he turned out from the corner, but he kept his hands wrangled together. "Goddess, I can't—"

"Wolf," she murmured. "I'm listening. I heard you. I'm going to help her."

His mouth shut with an audible swallow. "I'll keep out of the way, but I want to stay with her."

"Me as well." Sage released Genevieve's wrist to wipe at the sweat beading along his hairline; the second he did, she lashed out, raking her nails down his face. He flinched back with a bark of annoyance rather than pain; he twisted her wrist back down, welts immediately beginning to puff up along his cheek. "You'll need the extra hands!"

Cypress shook his head, breathing heavily himself; he took Genevieve's wrist so Sage could move back, exertion shaking the King-Consort's hand like they'd just struck a deal. "The only thing that will take me from my wife's side is a set of pallbearers. I have faith in your miracles, Goddess, but I'm staying."

Faith. The word slapped her across the face.

When had she last worked a miracle without some ulterior motive? Without wanting to please or puppet or pressure someone else into loving her, into giving her something, into doing what she needed them to do?

Ani. Come on, enough stalling.

Ani shut her eyes. Balled her fist over her heart. Clung to that warm, teasing throb of light—one she carried everywhere she went.

Soren's last gift to her in their shared body: her fierce, anchoring love. A love Ani had done nothing to earn or deserve—a love the princess had given anyway.

He wants you too ashamed and scared of making another mistake to make anything, good or bad.

Her miracles had not always been selfless. She had restored life to the dead because it never failed to create unwaveringly devoted disciples; she had nursed acres of crops back to health because it bought her surges of worship. She had danced the dead into their graves because it gave her enough coin to buy beautiful things for her home; she had grown flowers for miles just to lead curious people to her altars.

Some of them prescribed by her brother's gentle manipulations; some of them machinations of her own mind. All of them to try and earn even a *mote* of the love she'd long ago learned only came from being needed. From making oneself irreplaceable.

Tears tried to form; she forced them back with a hard blink.

No, she had not always been selfless. But she had not always been selfish, either.

In this life, she had given a girl her body back, regardless of what it might do to her.

In this life, she had healed a rabbit's bruised paw, though his owner had given her neither offerings nor worship; in this life, she had coaxed a widower's orchid to bloom again, and he'd smiled as if she'd brought back the beloved wife he'd lost instead.

In this life, she'd stayed up an entire night to ease the pain of a prince who'd cursed her name, held his hand while he'd slept…and snuck away the next morning so he couldn't try to fall on his knees in front of her for it.

Knowing something was good to do and doing it anyway—that did not make her miracles manipulation. That did not make her a monster. It was what she would do afterward that would cast that lot one way or the other—if she used this magic to gain favor she did not otherwise have.

She took Brook's place at the head of the bed. Guided Genevieve's thrashing head into her lap. Clung to her temples as gently as she could while still holding her in place.

"Wolf," she said, "be ready to help hold her down."

She shut her eyes before she could see whether he listened, pulling in a deep breath through her nose until her lungs felt full. She held that breath in, begging it to last, begging it to see her through…

And she plunged her magic into Genevieve's blight-riddled body.

It had grown *so* fast—only an hour, Sage had said, but its roots were everywhere. Even though she gave that corrupted magic orders like a hound-handler, it could not have obeyed even if it wanted to; for every root she yanked out, two more grew in its place, thorned and twisted and clinging like burrs.

Those damned thorns. She couldn't get a good grip—couldn't pull them out.

She couldn't heal the Blight. But she could still work miracles—so she could get creative.

Distantly, she felt sweat dripping down her temples, already soaking her hair; she began to shake, an unending shiver that jammed her jaw shut just as tightly as Genevieve's.

Come on. She couldn't grit the words out through her clenched teeth. *Come out, come out, come out—*

You made me. You hurt me.

In a fit of stubborn rage, she wrapped her power around corruption's roots.

A parasite could not survive without a host. It would cling to Genevieve for its life, and it would win…

But she could give it someplace else to go.

This time, she did not try to pull the thorns out.

She pulled them in. Into *her.*

Darkness exploded through her head, a smoke bomb rupturing into clouds of not-quite-black, flinging shrapnel that pierced like—

Like *the thorny vine that burrowed itself into Kriss, through Kriss, latching into her body like a fanged snake's grip. Like Tenebrae's thorn-studded wrist, slitting deep into Kriss's throat, releasing a fount of blood that turned even Soren's strong stomach.*

A memory. A dream, because it should have hurt, but dreams didn't hurt and neither did she.

Why didn't she hurt?

Her head tumbled, tossed like *he tossed Kriss's body aside like nothing—nothing but a broken doll, discarded, already half-forgotten.*

Someone whispered her name. Or screamed it. Or *said, more softly than they'd ever heard Kriss speak, "The people who should have protected her—who should be protecting her—won't. So someone else has to, and I don't see anyone else lining up to volunteer."*

Blinding pain sliced a perfect line down her center, flaying her to the core; a voiceless scream gurgled in her throat. She doubled over with a violent retch, a glottal gasp.

She couldn't breathe. Her lungs folded up tight like a morning glory in the moonlight; tears spattered her skin like rain, like *pale cheeks dappled in blood, pale hair torn from its skull-tight braids, pale lips breathing their last—*

YOU HURT ME.

"Anima!"

Wolf.

The thorns latched on. Held on to her as tightly as she held on to them.

HUNGRY.

Hungry—and angry. Angry she'd taken them from their chosen meal…hungry for another one.

But she didn't let go. Not even when they tore her wide, wide open.

CHAPTER 53

ANIMA

When Annelisa Medeis was born, the earth stretched to make room for her. Braeden loved to start the story that way; every time he gathered her into his lap and set his chin atop her head, ready to recite the tale of her birth, he began with a showman's flourish and a storyteller's rasp.

He told her over and over of the earthquake: how the ground trembled alongside their mother as she fought to bring Ani into the world, mother and monolith laboring with all their might. How her first cry had struck the city into deafening silence. How the rock-rupturing quakes ceased when Ani's life began.

She had been born with such power that the world had to change to make room for it all. And when Mora reshaped it again, annihilating the city with a pious woman's prayer, Ani was the only one who kept her footing under the weight of their world-altering magic.

So she could only imagine what her siblings had endured as earth-breaking power made a new home in their mortal bodies. But if she did imagine…she had to imagine it had felt something like this.

Or perhaps the opposite of this.

This did not feel like an addition, an invasion—it felt like bleeding. Like emptying.

Like dying.

But she would not push it out. Not if doing so would push it back into the woman whose life rested in her hands.

Another scream from her; a frenzied command from someone else. "What are you waiting for? Knock her out!"

Panic wrenched a whimper out of her.

Not that—anything but that. If they sent her into the dark, how would she ever find her way out again?

"I'm trying. It's not taking."

"Then at least heal—"

"It's *not taking*. None of it, you get me?"

The silence stretched on for an eternity afterward.

That meant something—for an immortal to invoke eternity.

Had they left her here? Decided to let the Blight run its course?

Her voice clawed past the gag of pain to whimper, "Wolf?"

A bow-scuffed hand smoothed her forelock back from her brow. She could've sworn a pair of fear-chapped lips followed—but that might've been the dream again. "Right here, love."

Even need could not squeeze more than one breath through the vise around her throat. "T-too…quiet."

Not enough words.

"Quiet—not gone." It couldn't be the dream—not when the prickle of his beard against her brow burned like a rash of fire-ant bites. Dreams didn't hurt—they just pretended. "Never gone."

Not enough words to understand…yet he understood.

Tears burned behind her eyes. More bites. More blazes. "Hurts."

"I know. Da and Sage are going to help you sleep."

"No." No, no, no. "Let it hurt."

Another eternity. *Quiet, not gone.* Wolf was not a liar.

"What do you think?" Cypress. A solemn, probing question she did not understand.

Quiet, not gone. Quiet, not gone. She chanted it twice for every little eternity Wolf held his breath.

"Heed her." Quiet still—but the emotion in his voice wasn't. It screamed louder than it ought. "She knows what she's asking."

Let it hurt. Let it hurt. The dream didn't hurt—she did not want to dream.

Did not want to die.

"Ani." A warm hand on her head this time—a warm voice in her ear. Blazing bonfires and ice-nipped noses. Apple cider and maple toast. "I want to make sure you understand. We only want to help you sleep—nothing more. You will wake up again, and the pain will be less."

"No. P-Please." Gooseflesh erupted from her chest outward, a battle between fire and ice. A flush of heat ripping through her insides; a flash of cold numbing her outsides. A tearing in two that arched her spine up from the floor, her jaw breaking open in a voiceless scream.

Even her *tears* boiled; even her blood burned. Scalding rivers poured down her frostbitten cheeks, her trembling lips, her aching ears.

Wolf swore; not her name in vain, but Sage's, every syllable wrung out with desperation.

"If you can't keep your head cool, Wolf, I'll not let you sit here and spit soot in our ears," Sage snapped. "Be helpful or be scarce."

"She's bleeding from her rotting *eyes*, and you want me to be—"

"*She* is scared out of her wits, and you are *not helping*." Pressure around one wrist; pressure around the other. "I'd have already sent your useless arse out and handled this myself, but she's not babbling *my* name as she bleeds, now, is she?"

Quiet, not gone. Quiet, not gone.

Pressure around her fingers. Tentative. Tender.

"Ani." A painless tingle ran down her spine at that low, murmured plea…a low, murmured prayer. "What can I do?"

All those prayers…were you even listening?

The journey back to her body could have taken a moment. It could have taken another little eternity. It could have taken the rest of her everlasting, encyclic existence. And still she would have trekked onward, endless and endless, life after life after life, to answer just one of Wolf Olivander's precious prayers.

Whatever it took. Whatever it cost.

It cost her pain, to force herself to feel her fingers. It cost her strength, to bend knuckle and joint until those fingers curled, exerting the lightest of pressure. It cost her breath, to hold his hand and whisper, "Stay."

But everything it cost her, he gave back a hundredfold with his steady hand, with his unyielding vow: "All you ask, I will give, Goddess."

Goddess—not her name. But this once, she didn't mind so much. Not when he kissed it into her knuckles. Not when it strummed with faith unbroken. Faith unbreakable.

It shored up all the places chaos had torn her asunder. Reminded her deeper than skin, deeper than soul, why this Blight could not—*would not*—have its way with her.

Goddess.

She had made it; it could not unmake her.

She held on to his hand, to his faith…and she did not let go.

CHAPTER 54

SOREN

The entire time she'd known Elias, she had never—not once, not *ever*—seen him fall asleep without his feet tucked in.

But in the aftermath of their first two trials—Anima and Tempest, Medwenna murmured over the tiny cookfire they built in the first chamber they found with a hole in its ceiling—Elias didn't even take the time to hang his clothes out to dry. He simply flopped down as close to the fire as he could get, closed his eyes, and plunged straight into a sleep so deep she couldn't even rouse him with a kick to the back of his knee.

Or his back. Or his head. Or with a begrudgingly gentle pat on the shoulder after Medwenna expressed concern over all the kicking.

In the end, she'd given up; but she'd tugged the wet clothes off his upper half in an attempt to save him from hypothermia's stealthy approach. Everin, whose pack had managed to escape the ordeal without much water damage, was kind enough to donate a shirt to her cause.

(Kindness he conveniently managed to dig up after Medwenna nailed him with those sappy amber eyes, asking if he had anything to spare for the boy who'd helped her keep them all from drowning.)

In any case, wherever that kindness came from, Soren decided she could be grateful for it. Especially because she couldn't tear her gaze from her battlemate until his shivers finally eased, soothed by the thick gray sweater Everin had pulled from his pack.

Reasonably confident now that Elias wouldn't slip into shock or lose any important extremities to frostbite, she bundled herself up in her spare blanket and sank into a cross-legged sit. The small of her back ached—well, everything ached, but especially her back—so she turned Elias into her pillow, propping herself against his back to take the pressure off her own.

He shifted slightly—not further, but closer, pressing into her with a sleep-slurred mumble that could've been *Hey, smartass.*

She slid her fingers into Elias's damp hair, teasing the waterlogged tangles apart as she stared into the fire and tried very, very hard not to think.

If she focused on the piney scent of Everin's sweater and the starchy, slightly acrid smell coming off her fire-dried blanket, she could almost ignore the taste of lake grit between her teeth. The way her imagination took Elias's wet, snarled hair and suggested it might be clotted with blood. And how the firelight played tricks on her humming, fear-fevered brain, every flicker miming itself as a fork of lightning.

What she'd give to have Ani here. At least when they'd been stuck together, she'd had a built-in distraction always waiting in the back of her mind.

I hope you're doing better than us, Goddess Great, she prayed with a shiver, hoping the mountain couldn't tell where her thoughts wandered. *Because if you're doing worse, we're all done for.*

"Well." Everin sank down a couple feet to their left, blowing out a long breath as he prodded the fire with his axe; his hair stuck out every which way, fluffy and tousled from the rough toweling Medwenna had given his and Kessen's heads, their complaints rising with the smoke as she'd lectured him about the perils of clotted lung. "That was quite the party."

She tried to laugh, but the poor thing didn't even make it halfway out of her chest before it dried out and died, wheezing through her lips instead. She rubbed her blanket over the cold curls at her nape. "What kind of parties are you Tallisians throwing?"

"Oh, you know the old saying." He crossed his legs and arched his back, his spine popping. "It's not a Tallisian party unless you spot a ghost or two."

She glanced toward Matthias, waiting for his scolding—he'd been adamant about not inviting the dead into their sleeping space this whole journey. But this time, he kept his silence…and his unblinking vigil over the makeshift camp, dark eyes skimming the cave walls every few seconds.

Scarlet and ichor danced before her eyes, the flames mesmerizing a whisper out of her: "You saw your mother?"

"Mmm." He nodded, then cracked his neck. "Yours?"

With every snap from his bones, the pressure in her own joints pushed harder; she finally stretched her arms out and began popping her knuckles, relief loosening her lips enough for truth to squeeze out: "Yes."

"You dove in headfirst—I saw you." Everin blinked muzzily at the fire, a burgeoning yawn trembling at the corners of his lips. "Didn't even hesitate."

"So?"

"So, nothing."

The answer to *So?* was never actually nothing. "Spit it out, or it's going to bother me for days." She paused. "Or hours. Not feeling so confident at this point."

"Would help if you didn't dunk yourself into a sentient lake that wants you dead," he suggested helpfully.

"*Would help if you didn't bleh bleh bleh,*" she mocked—then covered her mouth, lips burning against her palm.

If she intended to prove herself as the future Queen of Atlas to the future King of Tallis, she was off to a spectacularly shameful start.

Everin's shoulders bobbed—at first she thought he might be coughing, proving Medwenna's clotted-lung fears right. But then he threw his head back, eyes crinkled shut, grinning like a fool.

Laughing.

And he wasn't alone—Matthias was chuckling into his hand, and Kessen's barking cackle echoed back from where he'd retreated to change back into his fire-baked clothes.

"Flog me running," Everin gasped, "you are *so* not what I thought you'd be."

"And what did you *think* I'd be?" Competent? Diplomatic? In possession of half a brain and perhaps even one or two queenly bones?

"*Boring,*" he said. "Boring as stones on a stage. I've met your families, and don't get me wrong—they're formidable. Emberlyn's got more blades than Matt does. Yvonne knows her way around inter-kingdom law almost well enough to give Medwenna a race for her rank. Everybody knows Kallias should've been first pick for Heir over Jericho, and Finnick…" A dramatic shudder. "That kid gives me the ghosts. Always did."

"Huh?"

"Finnick scared him witless," Matthias supplied—then ducked, dodging the still-drying boot Everin lobbed at his head.

"Anyway. Still never made it through a meeting with any of them without snoring." He gave her a grin that was all teeth, but not in a wolfish way—in a boyish way, the kind that didn't know how to make itself small yet. "You might be out of your flogging mind, but at least you're not pretending anymore. You make a terrible Heir."

Her own smile locked in place. "Well, I'm out of practice."

"Stay out of practice, Princess." Everin dropped onto his back, stretching out in a full-bodied yawn; his heels nearly plunged into the sparse fire, but he dragged them back just in time. "Trust me…this succession game? Not nearly as fun as it looks. If you don't pretend, then I don't have to, either. Would make for a nice break."

"I'm not pretending. I was still raised royal."

Everin popped one eye open, silver winking at her from the shadows. "You forget I've met your sisters—and they didn't keep many secrets about your temperament."

Oh, she'd teach him all about her *temperament.* "Whatever my former inclination, I am dedicated to my throne. Maybe your kingdom is lucky enough to have a spare, but mine no longer has that luxury."

"Well, maybe you'll get lucky—maybe there won't be a kingdom left to inherit by the time we get out of here."

Bastard.

She hadn't meant to say it out loud, but another laugh from Everin suggested she'd done it anyway.

"I wish," he said fervently. Then, without warning: "You dove in like it wasn't even a choice. Kess tried, too—so did Matt." He got quiet for a second, sucking on his teeth. "I didn't."

"That's why you have a pack full of dry clothes, so I wouldn't sound so disappointed."

"Not disappointed." He nudged one of the crackling logs, stirring sparks, breathing new life into the fire. "I saw my mother drowning, begging for me to save her…and I didn't jump."

It was suddenly hard to swallow.

When she didn't say anything, Everin scoffed under his breath, setting his axe aside and turning his palms out toward the fire. "Like I said—so, nothing."

Without the usual accompaniment that serenaded the moon into rising— no cricketsong, no dozy chirps from birds returning to their nests, not even an evening breeze to blow the darker thoughts out of their heads—the quiet thickened to an unbearable texture, suffocating her with the urge to say something, anything, to thin it. To break it.

"Medwenna didn't jump, either." She said it almost before it actually struck her; she twisted to find the historian, who looked half-asleep already though she had yet to rest her head on her own dry pack. "What did you see?"

"Will," she said without inflection. Almost dismissive. "My husband. Who else?"

What confused her more than the plain way Medwenna said it was the fact that it didn't seem forced. "Why didn't you fall for it?"

"*My* Will tried to convince me not to try for Arborius—to let him die— only so I wouldn't lose the comforts of my life in Tallis. My family. My position. The library." Her jaw cracked in an enormous yawn, muddling her next mumble: "He would never have brought me into danger with him. Least of all to save his own skin."

Across the fire, Matthias's mouth screwed up in a sheepish, guilty knot; Everin's head bobbed, a wordless agreement.

Her gaze slid toward Kessen. "And Jules is…?"

"Kessen's oldest sister," Matthias murmured under his breath, too low for the eternal echo in the Sanctum to catch. "Long story. Not ours to tell."

Again, silence insinuated itself among them. This time, though, she could find no way to break it without stirring up more spirits…either in memory or in the haunted eyes of her companions.

Luckily, Kessen had no such qualms.

"I don't know about you all, but I'm not sleeping a wink tonight," he announced loudly as he dropped cross-legged atop his bedroll. "Anyone want to play Risk or Ramble?"

Soren blinked at him. "Huh?"

"Don't mess with us," Everin scoffed. "I've never met a soldier who hasn't played a game of Risk or Ramble."

"Well, congratulations on your accomplishment." Still, she'd been thinking along the same lines as Kessen—sleep wouldn't be visiting her tonight, not with Enna's terrified face swimming in her memory. She tucked one knee up against her chest. "What're the rules?"

Kessen circled his finger in the air. "We go around the circle one by one. Pick someone else and ask if they want to Risk or Ramble—they pick Risk, you give them something to do."

"Usually embarrassing or unpleasant," Matthias cut in.

"And if they pick Ramble," said Everin, wiggling his brows, "you ask them any question you like, and they have to answer truthfully."

"Oh!" Soren slapped her forehead. "You mean Truth or Dare."

"Our name's better," Kessen snorted.

"Whatever you say. Sure, I'm game." She knit her fingers together and raised them above her head, stretching until the joints popped. "Any weird Tallisian rules I need to know?"

"Just one," Matthias said. "Kess, shake Winnie awake?"

"Medwenna has veto power for risks," Everin explained while Kessen crawled over to Medwenna's bedroll and gently tapped her on the temple until she roused with a groggy lift of her head. "That got established after the fifth broken arm between us."

"Oh, stakes," she moaned sleepily. "Not Risk or Ramble."

"It'll be fine—we'll go easy," Everin promised her.

"Speak for yourself." Nyxian games of Truth or Dare were all about one-upmanship, not going *easy*.

A sparkle of cunning played in Everin's eyes. He trawled his pack back into his lap, rifling through it without breaking eye contact with her. "All right, Princess—wanna make this interesting?"

"Always."

With a menacing chuckle, Everin lifted his hand—pinched between his thumb and forefinger was a small vial-shaped object. But instead of glass, it seemed to be forged in copper. *Old* copper, the sort that had traded its auburn lustre for dull splotches of blueish green. A lost treasure overgrown with algae.

It was Matt's turn to groan. "Not this stuff again."

"Shut your trap, Matt." Everin waggled the vial. "This is a special little prize I carry around in case of emergencies…you could call it a family heirloom. Sanctan confessional oil. One drop's enough to have you spilling your darkest secrets where anyone can see 'em."

Sure, and she was the depths-damned Emperor. "As if you'd just shove something like that in your bag and let it rattle around with your undershorts."

Kessen lost it with a loud "*Ha!*" and a hard smack against his knee; Matt's chortling joined a moment later, but Everin just gave a shrug and a grin. "Don't see why I shouldn't. Never know when you'll need to interrogate someone…or make sure a princess plays fair."

A wary knot tied itself in her sparse inhibitions, stopping her from reaching out for that vial.

This could all be a pile of sea-silt. This vial could hold nothing but some Tallisian liquor fancy or potent enough to only be sold in pathetic quantities…

Or it could be dangerous.

"Come on," Everin coaxed. "Not that different from liquor, is it? Unless your captain's got a stick the size of a log up his arse, I have to assume your version of the game still includes imbibing a truth-friendly substance or two."

"Or seven," Matthias grumbled. This time, he didn't even duck when Everin lobbed his other drying boot—instead, he caught it, tucking it behind his back. "If you think you're getting that back, you're mistaken, my friend."

"That's my second risk decided," Everin shot back. Then he dangled the vial toward Soren. "But to start off…how do you feel about taking a risk, Princess?"

The sparse portions of the vial that still held their shine reflected the flames back at her, framing her tarnished reflection in fire.

An omen if she'd ever seen one. Thank the gods Elias was asleep for this.

"You're on." She took the vial, lifted it to her lips, and—

"Whoa!" the entire Triad shouted, all three reaching out—she froze immediately, the lip of the vial not even brushing her lip yet.

"What?" she demanded.

"You don't drink it, you insane…" Everin rubbed his eyes, muttering for a moment before he explained, with a pronounced patience that suggested condescension, "It's *perfumed* oil. You rub it on your skin…only a drop, seriously. It's still just a game, and this is powerful stuff."

That caution made her feel just a smidge better. Even if it still set all her instincts bristling as she tipped the vial bit by bit, watching as a golden drop of viscous liquid beaded on its lip.

It caught the light, twinkling like a star just before it fell onto her hand.

As if her pores had slurped it through a straw, the oil soaked into her skin in mere moments. And when it did…

Well, nothing that exciting happened, actually. It tickled, maybe. Her cheeks felt a little warmer, but that could've been leftover embarrassment from almost drinking the stuff.

"My turn?" she asked; the men nodded, Medwenna reluctantly dragging herself back out of her bedroll to watch.

Perfect.

She held the vial back out to Everin. That smug sparkle in his stare dimmed; but she thought a glimmer of respect replaced it.

"Nyxian rules?" he guessed.

"Nyxian rules," she agreed.

"You're on." And with an expert flick of his wrist, he dabbed a drop of oil onto his own hand.

Several seconds of silence ensued…so many that Kessen started awkwardly humming to fill it up.

"Kess," Everin finally sighed.

"Huh?"

"It's *your* turn first. You called for the game."

"Oh." Kessen immediately flipped toward Matt. "Risk or Ramble, Matt?"

"Eh, give me a risk. Why not?"

"Just once," Medwenna mumbled, framing her face in with her hands and staring bleakly into space, "just *once* someone could pick Ramble."

Everin casually set his thumb to the knob of bone at the base of Medwenna's neck, massaging it in small circles. "I'll take a Ramble next, Winnie. Kess—easy, remember?"

Ah. That soothed her stinging pride. Go easy…not for her sake, but for Medwenna's.

Kessen looked decidedly put out. But he cocked up his knees, linking his arms loosely around them as he jerked his chin at Matt. "Take a risk—get the zealot's socks off his feet without getting kicked."

She clapped a hand over her mouth to muffle her cackle. "Oh, gods, good luck."

"Child's play." Matthias rose with a yawn. "She kicked him all over and he didn't even snore."

"Yeah, well, that's her. Everybody knows battlemates are weird like that."

"I don't think sleeping through getting beaten up is a battlemate thing, Kess."

"Lots of talk for a confident man," Everin whispered loudly to Medwenna, who giggled despite herself. "Let's see him prove it."

Soren held stock-still as Matthias calmly picked his way around their scattered belongings and bedrolls, coming to crouch beside her battlemate's feet.

"Princess?" Matthias gestured to Elias's boots. "May I?"

"It's your funeral." At least one degree of her bent nose's angle had come from trying to steal Elias's socks off his feet.

It would have been easy to wake Elias herself, if she'd really wanted to…she could have screamed or jabbed him right in his ticklish rib or simply kissed him until his body roused him to find out why he couldn't breathe. But even Soren, who held very little sacred, would never interfere with the sanctity of a fairly given dare.

Matthias would pass or fail this challenge by his own merit. And either way, she was about to be thoroughly entertained by it.

As Matthias set to his work, he picked up the tune Kessen had abandoned, humming under his breath like a lullaby as he started unraveling Elias's bootlaces.

She peeked over her shoulder; her battlemate's mouth had dug a troubled divot into his bearded cheek, but his eyelids stayed firmly shut. Even when Matthias pried one boot off…then, to her open-mouthed shock, managed to remove the hand-knit sock without disturbing Elias's rest.

An antsy buzz shook the banks of her veins, riling her blood; she had to dig her fingertips into the stone to keep herself from leaping up to study Matthias's technique. "There's no pits-damned *way*."

Matthias grinned through his bushy beard, his bassy hum steady as his hands as he went to work on the next boot. Kessen was mouthing lyrics to himself, but didn't seem focused enough on the song to actually sing them; instead, he was watching Matthias's work with rapt hope rapidly deteriorating into disappointment.

When the second sock came off, Matthias broke off to hiss a victorious cry while Kessen cursed him and his mother—who, according to Kessen's profanities, had been some type of unpleasant goat creature.

"All right," she laughed as Matthias tossed his spoils back to her, bowing before returning to his place. "That was impressive."

"Matt's never failed a risk," grumbled Kessen. "It's annoying."

"I keep telling you, you pull your punches on your risks." Matthias gestured toward Everin. "Risk or Ramble?"

"I'm nothing if not a man of my word." Everin flashed Medwenna a wink…which she didn't see, as she'd drawn one of her books out of her pack, sleepy gaze stumbling over line after line on those crinkled pages. But her head had drifted sideways, lolling toward Everin's shoulder…inches away from making a pillow out of him. "I'm up for a ramble."

Matthias leaned back against his pack, hands folded in his lap. Perfectly at ease but for the *tap, tap, tap* of his heel against the stone floor, he said, "Why'd you give the Princess the oil?"

Surprise settled over that competitive stir in her stomach.

Only the slight narrowing of Everin's eyes toward his Second suggested he might have been caught off guard by it, too. "That's all you've got?"

"You want me to do my worst?" She did not think she imagined the pointed look Matthias gave Medwenna.

Everin's throat bobbed. He shot an assessing look at her, then said: "Her family didn't keep secrets about the kind of woman she is. So I want know why she's trying to."

The bald-faced challenge rang through her like a solid slap to the face.

Play the part. Follow the rules.

She'd told him earlier: she wasn't pretending, wasn't keeping secrets. She'd been raised royal; this was just her learning how to carry the birthright she ought to have held all along.

"Your turn," Everin prompted, still looking at her. A teardrop-shaped shimmer on the back of his hand caught the light when he looped it around Medwenna's shoulder, coaxing her gently into leaning against his side. "Risk or Ramble?"

After what he'd just said, to pick a dare—normally her *only* pick in this game—would be cowardly.

And she'd be damned if she took the coward's way out in front of him.

"Ramble," she said. Then, because she couldn't help herself: "And please, do feel free to do your worst."

Kessen hummed nervously. Matthias's heel tapped harder against the rock. Elias stirred behind her, hand brushing the small of her back as he searched for her in sleep.

"One foot in two places," he said. "Crowns don't split. So—if you had your way, where would that crown go? On your head, or someone else's?"

That was his worst? That wasn't even a question. The answer was easy— she could have answered in her sleep, she could have answered after *bathing* in that silly snake oil, she could have told him that without any game involved at all, and—

"Anyone's head but mine."

And *what in Mortem's scorched, sordid pits had she just said?*

Everin's mouth curled up at one end. The loose rope at the end of the snare she'd snapped.

"And *now* we're getting somewhere," he murmured.

I didn't mean that.

I misunderstood the question.

It's mine. I want it. Of course I want it.

"I didn't—I m-misunder...I..."

Why couldn't she speak?

"Soren?" Oh, sure, *now* her battlemate decided to wake up. She could barely hear him shift onto his seat over the raging roar in her ears. "Why's everyone still awake?"

"Just a friendly game, zealot." Everin's smirk scribbled red around the edges of her vision. "Want to join?"

Soren kicked herself back from the fire, her back colliding with Elias's front—he tried to catch her as she surged to her feet, but she shook him off. "I don't know what was in that stuff, but that—that was—"

Underhanded. A dirty trick. You cheated.

She couldn't churn any of the accusations out past her tongue. And she was terrified she knew exactly why.

"Sounds to me like someone's trying to lie to herself." Everin didn't even blink when she stepped into his space; he just stared her down, no flinch, no sudden movements. "That's not going to fly, Princess—not for an Heir."

"I don't know what you mean by that."

"What I *mean* is, that crown of yours? You want nothing to do with it."

"That—I meant to say—" Her tongue tingled, clumsy and numb.

"Look, what you have to tell yourself to sleep at night doesn't mean stones to me," Everin drawled, shrugging Medwenna off when she set her hand on his shoulder, hissing for him to back down. "I'm not saying I wanted my crown right from the start. Truth is, for most of my life, I thought I wanted nothing to do with it either. But no matter what you *think*, there is going to be a moment where you *know*—and when that happens, you won't be able to pretend anymore. Even if you try. And liars don't make for strong allies."

I'm not pretending.

"I'm—"

A shakerful of pepper dusted her tongue. Tingles, at first.

"I," she snarled through gritted teeth, "am *not*—"

Pepper flakes transformed into iron teeth taking a bite of her flesh. Another snapped snare.

She was going to punch that satisfied grin right off his face—even if it had softened in the face of her incoherent scraps of an argument. Even if he looked a little like he wanted to take it back.

"Hey," he said slowly, "breathe, Princess. It's just a game—and it's your turn now, so do your worst. Ask me anything."

Like a boy who'd accidentally roughhoused too hard with a playmate. *Please don't cry! I'll let you push me back!*

The invisible teeth clamped down on her tongue disappeared like they'd never been there at all. But the riled-up rage pumping through her heart…

She didn't want to taunt him with truths. She wanted to throw fists. She wanted a *fight*, and…

And that would prove him right. Because queens didn't brawl—queens let others take the fight for them.

A slurry of sick, chain-linked emotions balled up in her throat, each exorably fused with the one that came ahead and behind.

"Let someone else have a turn." She dashed her knuckles under her nose, hating how it burned at the tip—hating that the redness would tell on the tears she'd managed to swallow. Gods, she hated how anger made her cry sometimes. "I'm done playing."

"Look, I didn't mean for it to come out like—"

However he'd meant for it to come out, she didn't stick around to find out. She struck out toward the shadows of the tunnel they'd scouted out as their exit, pressing her cold palms to her overflushed cheeks…and pretending she couldn't hear the soft, nearly soundless footsteps padding after her.

CHAPTER 55

ELIAS

"Soren!"

Whatever he'd missed during the brief time he'd been asleep, it had dealt some kind of blow to his battlemate—a blow that left her stumbling over every word, flushed and teary as she cut her way through the dark cavern like she strode through a curtain of impenetrable brambles instead of shadow.

He might have stayed to demand answers from Everin, had the prince not looked nearly as upset as Soren—had the prince not whirled on his own man and snapped "What *exactly* crawled into your craw and possessed you to do that?" while Matthias's gaze flitted about the cavern, avoiding Everin's at all cost.

A blow, but not one intentionally thrown.

"Soren." He finally caught up just past the next tunnel's opening, concern broiling as he watched her halt, swear, huff—pace, swear again, throw a loose punch into empty air. "You want to tell me what fight he just picked, or am I going to find out after we finish it?"

It wouldn't be the first time he'd leapt to his battlemate's defense without knowing the whole of the situation. Bar brawls, dare-fueled sparring matches, a trade of insults that flared into a trade of fists…half of which had been instigated by his battlemate, a fact he only discovered after putting himself staunchly in the wrong with her.

Not that he wouldn't have leapt anyway. He'd jump in the ring with her every time. But it'd be more likely to end in their favor if he could see the entire picture.

"Truth or dare." Curt; stinging with held-in tears. "He cheated."

"How do you cheat at truth or—"

She snapped toward him on one heel. "You don't believe me?"

"Whoa, smartass." Confused, he put his hands up. "That's not what I said."

"It doesn't matter how. He just—" She wiped at her nose like throwing a punch sideways, fast and fierce enough to have broken it if she'd aimed an inch higher. "He made me say something I didn't—I—I wasn't supposed to say."

"You only ever say things you're not supposed to—"

"This was *different*, jackass!"

"All right, all right!" Clearly it was *not*, but he didn't know what else to say. "Then what'd you say?"

Soren said all *kinds* of jaw-droppingly ridiculous things—usually on purpose, though mostly to him. He'd seen her embarrassed about a verbal stumble once or twice before, but rarely…and in moments with far higher stakes than a silly barracks game.

She hadn't been *this* worked up after the disastrous dinner with Denali.

Her teeth ground into her lower lip; she folded her arms over her chest, fathomless gaze fixed firmly on some empty shadow off to the side. Dapples of glow-rock light flitted over her furrowed brow like flakes of snow. "He poked at me about wanting my crown. Goaded me into saying I didn't want it."

Oh.

When he didn't speak, she coughed out a laugh with enough force to echo back down the tunnel. She scratched the back of her neck before cupping her hand against it, rolling it side to side until it cracked. "It's not a big deal, I just…I shouldn't have said it in front of him, not when we need that alliance. I didn't…" Teeth gritted, she cracked her neck the other way, grinding out, "I *didn't* mean it."

The hairs on the back of his neck lifted with a rippling shiver…like an enemy had just crept up behind him without his notice.

"Are you sure?"

"What?"

"Are you sure you didn't mean it?"

In the eerie light of glow-rocks above, her green eyes paled nearly to gray. "You *don't* believe me."

"I believe he made you say something you shouldn't have said. And if you want me too, I'll happily help you take it up with him." But saying something she *shouldn't have said* and saying something she *didn't mean*…those weren't the same. "Forget him for a minute. We'll figure that out later. Why'd you say you didn't want the crown if you didn't mean it?"

"Why does that matter?"

"Because if it's true—"

"It's *not*—"

"—Then we need to talk about this, smartass!"

She tore both hands through her hair, then splayed them out toward him. "*Why?*"

Because I hate how you let them treat you in that throne room.

Because you've told me a hundred times how little you envied Yvonne the title.

"Because I know damned well when you're lying to me," he said softly.

Flagrant frustration cooled into stone with her next blink.

"Look," she said flatly, "I get why you'd want that."

"Why *I*—"

"Oh, come on, jackass." She twirled in a circle with a scoff, as if seeking witnesses to his unreason in the unbreached dim beyond. "It's not like Atlas is your dream home. I can't blame you for wishing I'd abandon it, but I—"

"*Hey.* Stop that. I promised you I would go anywhere—even if that means sitting on Atlas's throne. But I'll be damned if I'm going to give up my home and my people just to lose you to a title you don't want."

"*Of course I want it!*" she snapped. "It's *mine*. My throne, my crown, my birthright. The one Nyx almost took from me—the one you *swore* you would support me in taking back, so what is this, Elias? Maybe you were the one who lied!"

It made all the sense in the world. Maybe it should have been true. Maybe she even believed it was.

But this was Soren. And while she'd always loved to fight him, and loved when he let her win . . . he couldn't give her this.

He loved her enough to stand against her. Even if that wasn't what she wanted. Even if that wasn't what she claimed to need from him.

"I know you," he said. The words buzzed in the space between them, like an echo trapped between two immoveable walls. "The whole of you. Better than anyone. And since you started talking about taking the crown, I haven't gods-damned recognized you."

Her arms crossed over her chest again. "I'm doing exactly what I—"

"You're not. You let Denali walk all over you. You let your aunt force you into this wild wolf chase instead of telling her you'd seen leeches with more backbone, and I've seen you call people cowards for *far* less. And you're out here chewing *my* head off for nothing because you don't want to piss off a prince whose ego barely fits inside this pits-scorched mountain. If I hadn't seen Ani's new body myself, I'd think she was still the one in charge here!"

Soren recoiled like he'd struck her. Her eyes widened—welled with hurt. "Elias."

He…he hadn't meant to say that.

"Soren," he whispered back, stepping into her space. She turned her head away, and he took her chin, gently guiding it back around. "I'm sorry. That was…"

Gods, he didn't know what that was.

"I'm sorry," he said again. "But I'm serious, too. I won't take this path with you if it's not what you want. So just tell me the *truth*."

"You *won't?*" He knew that nasty edge to her voice—the venom she loosed only at her most vulnerable. "What happened to your vows? What happened to *where you walk, I will follow?*"

He dropped his hand to take hers, a quiet claiming. When she didn't pull away, he twined their fingers together, palm to palm. "I've kept every vow I ever swore to you. I have been your blade. I have been your army. I have stood by your side and fallen at your feet. I have chased you across battlefields and borders and beyond death itself. But I'm not walking you home until you can tell me honestly where that is…and who you want to be when we get there."

Her green eyes gazed up into his. Furious still, at first…then, a blink. A frown. A hard swallow.

He expected a confession…the truth he had asked for.

"Why am I fighting with you?" she whispered. "I…I wasn't angry with you. I wasn't even…"

His hackles came up again. Dread swept his feet out from under him; he stepped out of her space to skim their surroundings, pulling one scythe partway out, wishing for the boon of bright blades right about now. But nothing stalked this tunnel except their own riled tempers.

Both spitting sparks of their own. Seeking each other's soft spots. Spoiling for a fight.

A familiar, frightful yearning skating over his bones.

End her.

End her.

End—

He dropped his scythe back into its sheath like it *had* caught fire. "No, no…"

"Kessen and Matthias were humming." Soren leapt back from him with a curse, pinning her hands beneath her arms like she feared they might gain a mind of their own. "Matthias made Everin pick that fight, Matthias never—"

"Cover your ears!" he barked, already grinding the heels of his hands against his, already three strides down the tunnel. Three strides further from her. "And stay away from me!"

She didn't argue. Not with those twinned scars in her stomach and a sourceless, sudden melody floating through the stale air like an errant breeze.

Not with the terror strangling him breathless as he burst back into the cavern and shouted, "Hands over your ears, *now!*"

Medwenna was the first to obey, but that was because she'd *already* had her hands over her ears—though she stood just to the side of the now-tussling Triad, within easy reach of them, she wouldn't peel her palms away from the sides of her head.

For his part, Kessen had one arm barred across Medwenna's front, bristling with protective intent; with the other, every time Everin and Matthias's brawling bodies stumbled too close, he shoved them out and away, lips moving with shouts Elias couldn't hear.

At Elias's order, Kessen's gaze snapped up to meet his; and with a rush of relief, Elias watched as he swiftly guided Medwenna down to her knees, dropped to one knee himself, and bent over her with his hands clamped over his ears. Putting his own back to his brawling brothers-in-arms.

A brawl that didn't slow or stop at his arrival; Everin and Matthias probably hadn't even heard him over their own shouting.

Something yanked his wrist down, freeing one of his ears.

"You take Matthias." Soren ordered, blowing past him after dropping his wrist; her sleeves were torn, two wads of cloth shoved into her ears. "I'll take Everin."

"Wait, are you—"

"Can't hear you, jackass!"

Damn it.

He barreled toward Matthias, plugging his own ears with his fingers again. Even provoked by chaos magic's croon, the two hadn't drawn weapons on each other; so he left his scythes in their sheathes, bowling into Matthias with all his strength instead.

Unfortunately, running into Matthias Bane felt a lot like running headfirst into a boulder.

Like a blanket tossed over his head, dizziness crashed down over him when he made impact…and Matthias didn't budge an inch. But at least it distracted the larger man enough to bring the brawl to a brief pause.

Brief, but just long enough for Soren to fling herself onto Everin's back, clinging with both legs and one arm while her free hand flailed for his ears, trying to stop chaos from seeping into the reckless prince's head.

"It's a trial!" she snapped when Everin spun, grasping for her, trying to rip her off his back; she dodged gracelessly before wrapping her arms tightly around his neck, shouting directly into his uncovered ear: "It's a *trial*, you ass! Stop fighting me and *cover your damned ears*!"

Everin's swipes slowed; stopped. Still heaving, but blinking like a man struck from sleepwalking, he put his hands over his ears.

Once Everin was out of the fight, it was easier to get Matthias's ears jammed up; Soren's sleeves were reduced to tatters, but within minutes, they'd all regained their senses. Matthias checked on Everin first, bumping foreheads with him and wiping away some of the blood he'd drawn; then he went to Soren, taking her hand and setting his brow against her knuckles.

"Forgive me," he said—or Elias thought, anyway. He wasn't bad at reading lips, but he was used to reading his battlemate's lips, not a near-stranger's. "I don't know what got into me."

"Trust me, I do." Soren patted his wrist. "It got into all of us—and if we don't get moving, it might get into us again. Let's find another place to camp."

"You think that's it?" Everin asked, loudly enough that Elias didn't have to read anything. "Third trial, just like that?"

Just like that was greatly underplaying the situation, seeing as Everin currently had blood dripping from the corner of his mouth and the beginnings of a black eye mottling his brow-bone. But considering how Nyx had fared under a full assault by Chaos, not merely a whisper of its presence in godless halls...

"I hope so," Elias rasped.

Because anything more might not be stymied by torn cloth and quick thinking.

CHAPTER 56

ELIAS

There was a rock stuck in his shoe.

A rock that had to be possessed by a malicious force of some kind, chaotic or otherwise, because it had somehow found a way to wedge itself right in the heel of his boot. And no matter how he swung his foot or wiggled his toes, he couldn't get it loose.

"Just take it off and shake it out," suggested Soren for the fourth time.

"In a cave system that could have gods-know how many snakes and rats and anything else? I'll take the rock over fangs, thanks."

"Rats actually have incisors," Medwenna cut in from the center of their double-file line. "Not fangs. They have to gnaw on tough materials to stave off overgrowth. Wood, brick—"

"Ankles," Everin contributed.

"Heads, if they're hard enough," Matthias chuckled.

"I thought rats ate cheese," said Kessen. "Don't they like cheese?"

"They're not eating the wood, Kess."

"Winnie just said they're chewing on it, Matt, if you were *listening*—"

"Hey, teacher's pet." Everin fell back to cuff Kessen on the ear. "She said they chew on it to trim their teeth. It's different—like sharpening your sword with a whetstone."

Medwenna beamed at Everin. "Exactly."

Everin cleared his throat, nodding before slapping Kessen in the back, shoving him ahead. "Your turn to lead, kid. Matt, shuffle up."

He'd give this to the Triad—even after the distastrous confrontation last night, they moved with the same sinuous connection most battlemate pairs did. Despite having three bodies to coordinate instead of two, none of them fell out of step or tripped into each other as they switched positions; in one smooth trade, Everin matched Medwenna's gait, and Matthias and Kessen took up the front.

After an uneasy night of sleep in a narrow tunnel with no sound except their own breathing—and an awkward check-in over the cookfire the next morning—they'd all agreed to chalk the prior night's confrontations and clashes up to chaos magic. All forgiven…some forgotten.

But not all. Everin kept sneaking side-eyed looks at Soren, a guilty shift to his lips; and Elias only caught them because he kept stealing looks at her, himself.

Her confession, prompted by magic or not, had rattled him. Rattled her, too, judging by how brazenly she'd been bantering this morning. No awkward silence survived longer than a handful of seconds before she made a smartass comment to break it.

As if to prove his theory, Soren leaned into his side, stretching up to mutter in his ear as she fixed her gaze on Everin and Medwenna. "Is this how everyone in the company felt watching us?"

He frowned at the historian and the prince. "We can't have been *that* bad."

"Not a chance. I mean, it's painful to watch."

"Should we say something? Isn't he engaged to your cousin?"

Soren blinked. "Pits, I forgot about that. *Should* we say something?"

"She has to know, right?" Though their meeting had been brief, the Arborian Heir hadn't struck him as a fool, and one would have to be a fool at *least* to call the bond between Medwenna and Everin merely friendship. "Even if they don't?"

"She has to," Soren agreed. "Maybe she's all right with it. I've heard arranged marriages can get a little wibbly-wobbly in that regard."

He couldn't imagine it, but then again, he'd never been the best at sharing…particularly not when it came to Soren. So he just shrugged. "Should we start a betting pool? I heard Jakob made a killing on us."

Soren rolled her eyes. "*I* think he owes us a cut."

"*I* think you two should quit whispering like gossipy schoolgirls and start sharing with the class." Everin scowled over his shoulder, gesturing their way. "You're making my back itch, the way you're talking behind it."

Soren held up her hand, bending her fingers like talons primed to strike. "Want me to scratch it?"

"Anytime you like, Princ—" Medwenna slapped Everin's shoulder, and he quickly amended, "No, thank you."

Elias and Soren shared a meaningful glance.

No, thank you, Soren mouthed, crossing her eyes and contorting her face. Elias snorted into his fist, trying to disguise it as a cough.

"I said stop gossiping!"

"We didn't say anything!" he and Soren protested together.

Everin set his palm to the cave wall, leaning his weight against it while studying his nails. "If you want to run your mouths, we could start by—"

In a shower of dust and gravel, a too-clean cut of stone fell out of the wall like a domino—and Everin tumbled right in after it, so fast he didn't even shout.

Soren cupped her hands around her mouth, yelling, "Start by *what?*" toward the gap.

The three remaining Tallisians all shouted—Medwenna and Matthias *for* Everin, Kessen *at* Soren—before scrambling toward the wall. Kessen wriggled past Medwenna and Matthias, catching himself in the door. "Everin?"

They all held their breath, listening.

"When I get back up there," came the prince's muffled voice, "I am going to kick *all* of your asses." A pause. "Excluding Medwenna, obviously."

"What did *I* do?" Kessen and Matthias cried together.

Medwenna towed Matthias and Kessen back from the door, expression suddenly severe. "Get back—I don't trust that ledge. Everin, are you hurt?"

"Knocked about, but nothing to commit treason for."

"None of us were going to commit treason for you," Matthias assured him.

"Wow, thanks! Feeling the love, Matt."

Already tired of this long-distance shouting match, Elias swung his pack from his shoulder to his back. After a couple tugs to snug it right in the center of his spine, he got down on all fours, inching toward the wall.

Jakob had some of the most out-there methods for training his recruits— and had been accused of abusing his power on multiple occasions—but once again, someone might owe their lives to that slight sadistic streak. Because even though stone and ice weren't quite comparable, Elias's practice with testing the integrity of a frozen lake's surface told him that about one foot out from the door, the floor thinned out to nearly nothing; a trap set to break beneath the first person to unwittingly set their weight atop it.

"Everyone back," he warned. "I'll get him up."

Matthias and Medwenna quickly retreated to the opposite wall; Soren snatched Kessen by the collar when he dithered. "You want to fall through, too? No? Then listen to my husband."

"Fiancé," Elias corrected.

"On second thought, you go right on ahead," Soren said to Kessen. "Just kick him in while you're at it, will you?"

"Smartass," he grunted, spreading his weight as evenly as he could over the precarious floor.

"Jackass," she fired back.

"Dumbass!" Everin's voice again, stringent with scathing temper.

He and Soren exchanged looks.

"He means you," they both said at once.

"I mean *both* of you. All of you." Another pause. "Again, excluding Medwenna."

"Thank you!" the historian called from the other side of the chamber.

"Everybody, *quiet*," Elias gritted out. "Trying to concentrate."

"Maybe you should flash him," he heard Kessen suggest.

Soren coughed—probably choking on her own spit. "How in the pits would that help?"

"It wouldn't, obviously. Didn't you say you wanted him to fall in?"

"Oh." He didn't like the thoughtful silence that followed. "Smart kid. Hey, Elias—"

"Not falling for it." He scooted right up to the edge, peering down into the dark. Gravel crumbled from the lip, raining into the shadows; his stomach tried to throw itself off with them, but he caught it with a hard swallow. "I can't even see him."

"*Him* can see you!" Everin called crossly.

Medwenna groaned. "Everin—grammar. We talked about this. It's important."

A wordless noise of protest from below. "It was for comedic effect. I thought we agreed that—"

"I'm literally begging you two to get a room," Soren moaned.

"Me too," Kessen said.

"Me *flogging* three," Matthias muttered.

Medwenna's brow creased. "How would finding a room help get him out of there?"

"Is she serious?" Soren stage-whispered.

"Medwenna's not great with innuendos," Kessen stage-whispered back.

Conveniently, Medwenna didn't seem to hear that part. And Everin hadn't seemed to hear *any* part.

Elias took a deep, grounding breath. "Soren—toss me the rope in your bag."

"I don't have any rope in my—"

"Yes, you do. I put it in there before we left."

An annoyed sigh; the clatter of a pack being rifled through. "I don't know what you think you did, but if there is even one inch of rope in this pack, I will take my glove off and *eat*—oh. Found it."

The coil of rope smacked down behind him. Nowhere near his hands.

"Where were you aiming?" he demanded.

"I was aiming *not* to throw a twenty-pound bunch of rope at your head!"

He huffed, rearing back to try and reach, sightlessly fishing for the length of rope. "It's not a great idea for me to move this much when—"

Something gave beneath him.

A sharp inhale was all he had time for before the mountain sucked him in.

And he wasn't the only one. Shifting stone above his head suggested something else had gone awry, something that stirred alarmed shouts from the others—then, two by two, they went silent.

The floor hit before the panic did—a full-body blow that emptied his lungs with an ugly hack. He rolled to his stomach, but the aftershocks kept him bent against the floor.

Steel-toed boots overwhelmed his vision. "Impressive rescue."

An equally impressive wheeze was the only retort he could muster. He dropped his head down.

Soren hadn't fallen—that was good. Maybe those shouts were just the rest of the group reacting to his fall a little late.

Or maybe he needed to believe that in order to keep his head on straight.

"The others?" Everin demanded. He cupped his hands around his mouth, aiming his shout toward the ceiling: "Everyone good? Sound off!"

No answer.

Elias rolled onto his back again, squinting upward. "You said you could see me, before—what do you see now?"

"You mean other than your death-loving carcass?" Everin stepped up, standing level with his shoulders; he frowned up at the ceiling, mirth melting into uneasiness. "I don't see the opening anymore."

It was good, he reminded himself—it was good they weren't down here. Good they couldn't see any gaping holes.

"Maybe it's another trial, not a cave-in," he said. "Maybe it closed again, and they're still up there."

"You think the mountain's content just dumping the two of us down here?"

"I'm *hoping* so," Elias muttered. "I don't like the alternative."

Everin scowled. "And I don't like having to guess."

That, they had in common.

Lungs still stiff with shock, Elias stood, sipping air as best he could. He and Everin had fallen into another tunnel—only the fact that they'd fallen at all told him it was actually a different tunnel. It looked identical to the one they'd just left.

"We should start walking," he croaked. "Just until we come across another chamber, or some sign of the next trial. The others will find us there."

Everin crossed his arms with a scoff. "I've heard about *leaps of faith*, but that...that's just a flogging *long* leap."

"Again—do you have a better idea?" Elias spread his arms, shedding cave-dust. "I'm waiting to hear it."

And to his credit, he did wait. A whole minute, while Everin paced and scowled and glared at the ceiling; a whole minute of shallow breaths and a pounding heart and a mounting inability to pretend he wasn't panicking. That his secondary plan was scaling the massive wall and ripping the rock apart with his bare hands to get back to his battlemate's side.

"No," Everin said finally, resignation weighing the word down like a stack of steel. "I just really hate yours."

A second thing they had in common.

Elias shifted his pack off his aching back, balancing it on his shoulder again. "Then a leap of faith it is."

CHAPTER 57

SOREN

All things considered, this could have gone a lot worse.

At least, she and Kessen kept tossing that statement back and forth like a game of Hot Potato (or, as Kessen insisted it was called, Rabid Squirrel Shuffle) while they felt their way down the sloping tunnel they'd tumbled into when the mountain decided to redecorate. Neither of them had been holding a glamour rod, so they had no choice but to fumble ahead in darkness so thick she couldn't see her own fingers if she waved them in front of her face.

"Why do Tallisian games have such terrible names?" Cold, damp rock chilled her palm as she set it to the wall, sliding her hand down its side like she'd seen stablehands do with nervy horses.

"Why do Nyxian games have boring ones?" Kessen didn't seem to fear the mountain's fickle temper; he slapped the wall in time with every game he listed off. "Hot Potato, Sheep Sheep Wolf, Catch the Con…child's play. Literally."

"And Rabid Squirrel Shuffle, Skeet the Goose, and Inquisition's Ire are too terrifying. How many children have to be traumatized before you shape up?"

Kessen laughed, finishing it out with an obnoxious snort. After listening to their own footsteps for a few minutes, he suddenly said, "You think we'll be able to find them?"

"No." Her fingers collided with a clump of moss—at least, what she hoped was moss. Some of it clung to her hand as she yanked it away; she wiped it off on her pants, trying not to gag. "I think we both know we're the idiots of the group."

"Comforting, Princess."

"Elias will figure out how to find me." A belief she had no basis for; yet it stood like a marble wall around her heart, deflecting any doubt that tried to sail over. "And Medwenna was with Matt—between the two of them, they'll find the trail."

Kessen stopped; she copied him a heartbeat later. Not a good idea to fall out of lockstep when they couldn't see each other. "Wouldn't it be easier to find us if we stayed put?"

"Maybe." Almost definitely. "But do you feel like sitting in the dark doing nothing for hours while we wait?"

His footsteps picked back up. "Not even a little."

She kept one hand to the wall, even though it was starting to go numb by now. Without the wall's guiding, the solid obsidian void surrounding them gave her the same panicky jolt as dangling over a plunging cliff—a sensation she hoped she would never experience again.

Her feet might've been planted on solid ground, but to feel and see nothing on all sides…that was a little too much mystery for her. Especially when, if something came upon them in the dark, she was just as likely to hit Kessen as she was an unseen adversary.

Not that it would be the most devastating loss in the world, but she'd certainly feel guilty about it. And it likely wouldn't help her case when it came to Tallis's army, either.

If she still had a shot at earning an alliance at all after last night.

She kicked that thought out as soon as it tried to trespass. Everin had been helpful thus far, in his own annoying way…and this morning, *he'd* been the one to ask *her* whether they were still on good terms after the whole Risk or Ramble situation.

But even if he hadn't written her off just yet, no alliance would survive if Everin's brother-in-arms did not—especially if he was put down by her hand. And while Everin might have been one of the dimmer candles in this candelabra, he wasn't going to buy a lame excuse like *it was just so dark*. Even if it was the truth.

"What're you thinking about so hard?" Kessen demanded. "I can smell your brain smoking."

"Killing you."

A long, long pause. "That's a joke, right? I can't see if you're laughing, so you need to tell me if that's a—"

The sharp *clang* of metal against stone brought everything to a halt—their feet, her breathing, her heart.

They weren't alone.

The sourceless breeze she'd given up trying to figure out by now was blowing toward them—and now that she was paying attention, she realized it no longer smelled crisp and cool, untouched by anything but water and rock. Instead, it carried a bundle of rancid, stagnant smells right to her cringing nose: rotting flesh and stale urine. Old blood and horsehair. Metal and fear.

Again, steel rattled in the distance, just enough to loosen the knot tied between her shoulders—close, yes, but not *directly* in front of them.

"Something's down there," she whispered.

"Thank you, Captain Obvious."

"Oh, you're so welcome, General Jerk—"

A chalky screech silenced their hissy bickering—not metal this time. Sparks scattered across the path ahead; only a blink of light, not enough to make sense of the shape hidden by an impenetrable curtain of shadow, but enough to tell her there *was* a shape.

Enough that she could see that shape move—that she could tell it was large enough to take up the whole span of the tunnel.

"No way around?" Kessen's baleful mutter made no secret of how bleak their situation was.

She teased her sword as far as she could from its sheath without making any sound. "Doesn't seem like it."

A leather tie unsnapped. Too loud—another flurry of movement down the path shoved her back on her heels, battle-stance ready.

When a warm hand brushed against hers, she almost smacked it away.

"All right," Kessen breathed, holding her wrist loosely. Just enough to keep them connected. "What's the plan, Princess?"

The plan. Right. She was good at those—when she could see what she was dealing with.

"We need light," she whispered. "What've you got?"

A quick but quiet shuffle through their things armed them with a flint and steel, a vial of incense-infused oil—Elias needed to keep his grubby hands off her pack—and a single knit sock.

Kessen pressed a thin wooden rod into her hand—an arrow. "You can tie the sock around this."

She closed her fist around the projectile. "Where did you get this?"

"Found it."

"Found it," she echoed scathingly.

"That's what I said."

It wasn't worth prodding at now. She'd circle back around once they were past this.

The arrow felt alarmingly breakable between her fingers as she folded the sock around it, tucking the welt down so it would stay; not her first choice of torch.

Probably not her second, either. But since her first was an *actual* torch—and her second was, well, Elias—it would have to do.

"Be ready," she warned as she primed the flint and steel, hovering the tools over their target. "Once this goes up, gods know what's going to happen."

"I get the gist, yeah." Confident words—but even in the dark, Kessen's nerves gave him away. She could hear him fussing with the leather wrapping on his axe's handle.

Soren held her breath, squinted against the shadow—and struck the flint and steel together.

Limpid drops of scarlet and gold rain plunked onto the soaked sock; a flame gasped into being, small but growing steadily, consuming the sock as it gnawed through yarn and oil. Its glow seemed hungry, too—it devoured the darkness in one quick gnash of its teeth, casting just enough light to reveal the full breadth of the sloping tunnel…

And the misshapen, monstrous hulk of fur and feathers that circled to face them, its hackles bristling like the wooden spokes of a palisade.

At first, she blamed the shadows for her struggle to identify the whole of its parts—then, when each new piece of its body failed to make sense of what she was seeing, dread began to take shape instead.

Moving with sinuous, feline grace, fur-covered and muscle-bound, it paced back and forth with a hunter's stalk, tail whipping side to side as it bared its teeth at them.

No—not teeth.

The creature had a beak—a hooked, calcified beak that snapped the empty air. Its head was feathered and crested; its eyes rolled like black marbles, all pupils and no whites.

And on its back…wings.

Wings coated in sparse coppery feathers; wings that might have been strong, once, but now merely rustled as it twisted and pawed at the ground.

Not horsehair, after all. The stench of this thing's unwashed, patchy fur.

"What," she breathed, "is that?"

"A griffin," Kessen rasped. "The Old Emperor's answer to Mortem's mounts…they were bred to hunt phoenixes."

And considering what Elias had told her of his experience in Artem, they'd *well* fulfilled their purpose.

Now that her mind wasn't so occupied with *what in Tempest's dark, dank depths is that thing,* a trickle of softer emotion infected her fear, her frustration: the griffin's skin hung loose off its sides, revealing racks of ribs that screamed for a meal. Its wings were too large to spread out in the ever-narrowing tunnel—every time it tried, their featherless edges scraped across the ceiling and walls. The exposed skin where the feathers ought to be was scarred, swollen in places…

And around its ankle, she found the source of the rattling shriek that had alerted them to the griffin's presence: an iron fetter, too small for its current size, likely clapped around its ankle in its youth.

Her stomach turned when she caught sight of solder-marks on the fetter's seam…and old scars, bare of fur, above and below the cuff.

Whoever captured this creature fused the fetter closed while it was already wearing it.

Oh, gods. She already hated what they had to do.

"We have to get past it." Kessen sounded just as reluctant as her; even his steps seemed to drag, resignation stamping a frown onto his face.

"I know." No getting around it; the creature was too large to avoid its reach, even with the chain, and it had already spotted them. No hope of sneaking past when it seemed determined to keep them in its sights, its head twitching one way or the other to follow whichever one of them was closest.

They had no choice but to fight their way past.

Didn't mean she had to like it.

"Try not to kill it, if you can," Soren croaked.

Kessen cast her a pitying look. "You're not a hunter, are you?"

Now *her* hackles bristled. "There's no reason to hurt it more than we—"

"Soren, look at it. It's sick and starving—and it's been stuck here for who knows how long." He gestured to the griffin with his axe. "Leaving it like this, that's not…it's not kind."

The look in his eyes…it reminded her of something. Something she didn't want to remember.

Sad, tired smiles. A seaside town. Letters wrapped in twine.

Her shoulders sank, two anchors on one rope.

"We won't hurt it more than we have to," Kessen promised. "You're right about that. But mercy's gonna look a little different here than you're used to, yeah?"

She had to grind the words out of her throat like flecks of sea salt. "Yeah."

"It's ready for us—no point trying to sneak." He echoed her thoughts. "We'll move together, and—"

"No." She studied the creature again, forcing herself to catalogue its weaknesses, its gaps…even if it made her feel dirtier than the soles of her boots. Boots that had tromped through Atlas sand, Nyxian snow, Arborian dirt, shipdeck squalor, and Tallisian gravel without a pause for a good scrub-down.

She'd never been good at puzzles. The fiddly pieces, the jumble of nonsensical color, the fact that only certain bits fit into certain places—the whole process required patience she simply didn't have. All for nothing but the elusive promise of a prettier picture once it was done.

Without knowing what it would look like—*should* look like—in the end, its broken pieces were just that: broken pieces. Something that only had worth as a whole.

And the worst part was, even if she found a different way to put the pieces back together…they didn't make a perfect, pretty picture anymore. Just a jumble of misshapen things that couldn't do the one damned thing they'd been made to do.

But battlefields were different—they were *only* big pictures, puzzles with friendlier edges, fragments that would fit together any way she wanted. The picture would change in the end, yes—but it never stopped being a picture. It never stopped making sense.

It didn't have to be just one thing. It could change, if it had to—if it wanted to.

"That strategy works if there's three bodies," she acquiesced. Two front feet armed with talons, three soldiers—far easier to scramble it, to stop it from landing a blow on any of them. But only two bodies…that meant one for each foot. "But not two. We need battlemate tactics for this."

"Then what do you—?"

"I go first. As soon as it tries to hit me, you go behind it." And hopefully she'd be able to duck those scuffed-up claws long enough to make it count—to make it through, too.

Kessen didn't look keen on the idea. She couldn't blame him. "Why are you the distraction? Shouldn't we draw lots or something?"

She tested the weight of her sword in one hand, the torch in the other—when neither arm twinged or gave, she steadied herself with a huff, flashing him a grim smile. "Because I'm about to prove who's faster."

He didn't get another warning.

She threw herself at the griffin with a scream, forcing the heat in her veins to burn out her reluctance, her guilt—and the griffin screamed back.

The first swipe of its paw, she knocked aside with the flat of her blade; the second she ducked, a chill sweeping across her back as its claws raked the air above her.

A near-decapitation in the first five seconds. That had to be a new record for her.

As she spun into a backward stumble, catching herself before she could crash to her seat—and die, also, since the griffin drove its beak into the space she'd just danced out of, splintering the top layer of hardened sediment—Kessen's thatch of fiery hair streaked toward the slim space between the griffin's tail and the tunnel wall.

Relief tweaked her ribs. She hadn't gotten him killed, after all—good. She didn't think she could carry another death on her conscience…nor was she sure she could have carried his body with her through this death trap of a mountain.

But that distraction cost her.

The griffin's paw swiped out, its blow propelled by a flap of its misshapen wings—and the next thing she knew, her side split down the center, torn open by the very tip of one talon. One just long enough to reach her despite the chain holding the griffin back.

As was the way of battle, when things went bad, they often took a nosedive straight into worse—a principle proved when her scream halted Kessen's flight. He teetered as his gaze shot to her, yelling her name—then yelling something much fouler when the griffin rounded on him, its eardrum-popping shriek dizzying her as she dropped into a crouch, struggling desperately to catch a glimpse of the boy past the griffin's piecemeal body. *"Run!"*

"Trying!" he yelped.

But no matter which way he went, no matter how many blows he dodged, he couldn't seem to get an opening—every time he started to dive, the griffin swiveled, avian head cocking as it tracked its prey.

Its wings flapped again; it tugged fruitlessly on its chain.

And then, an idea.

"Kessen!" she hollered; his eyes, wide to the whites, met hers. "The chain!"

For all they made fun of Kessen's mind, it took him less than a second to understand her meaning; he dodged another swipe of the griffin's claws, readying his axe for his next strike. "Are you *sure?*"

She shouldn't have been. This should have been pure guesswork: unmooring a boat and loosing its sails without testing the wind. Choosing a direction to walk in a blizzard with no sense of where home and hearth might be.

But when she gave the command a second time, she didn't hesitate. Not even a little.

"Do it!" she barked. "Do it *now*, Kessen!"

Sweating, sagging with exhaustion, Kessen shut his eyes. If she hadn't known better, she might've said it looked like a prayer.

Then he barreled forward.

With a hot-blooded roar that set a fire in her own belly—a ferocity that made sense of *why* the future King of Tallis had chosen this goofy, klutzy kid to fight at his side—Kessen dove under the griffin, in easy reach of its claws. The creature reared, its hooked beak separating in a mighty scream, its wasted wings flaring out as it slammed its paws downward—

And Kessen twisted backward, bringing his axe down on the chain with all his strength.

The chain separated with a deafening crack. The tension fled, its links going slack so fast they skated across the stone.

She held her breath. Waited to see which would win out—animal instinct, or broken chains.

The griffin reared back again; for a horrible moment, she feared the fog of battle might overcome the mind she *hoped* was hiding behind those beady, bloodthirsty eyes.

Then it stopped. Shifted. Cocked its head.

She could've sworn she heard it warble in the back of its throat.

Kessen scrabbled to her side, shaking violently, as the griffin spread its tattered wings, let out a ceiling-shaking roar…and launched into a half-flying, half-sprinting dash.

In the opposite direction of them.

Within seconds, it vanished over the top of the slope.

One beat of absolute silence. Two.

Then Kessen guffawed so loudly she almost jumped out of her boots.

"Oh, burn me alive." He tumbled onto his back, almost somersaulting, slapping his hands over his brow as he howled with laughter. "Flog me running, stone me sleeping, that was…"

Soren dropped to her seat, cradling her wounded side, sucking breath back into her aching lungs. "I know. I'm sorry. If I'd been closer—"

"Sorry?" He sat up, grinning like a fool, hair sticking up in bent hanks not unlike the dangly parts of a jester's hat. "*Sorry?* Princess, you just saved my flogging *life*. That was genius. That was…" He fell backward again, letting his arms lay akimbo, waving them like he was making a snow dragon. "It's a damn shame you're going to get wasted on a throne."

Suddenly, she didn't feel like she could sit another minute.

"Come on." She hobbled up, putting all her weight on her uninjured side; even so, pain dragged down the wound like a scalpel lancing the skin.

But it wasn't content with just the wound. It reached further than it ought to, a sting that cut clean down to her hip.

Panic burned like bile in her throat.

It's in your head—it's not a fit.

She tapped her sheath—once, twice, three times—then started walking. "Try to keep up."

"No, you," Kessen wheezed, jogging after her. "If you're ready for that rematch…"

The last thing she actually felt like doing was racing anywhere, for any reason. So when Kessen passed her, she stuck her ankle out.

Her lips ached to smile as he sprawled out, complaining loudly enough that she was sure the others would be able to track them by his whining.

But even that couldn't quite distract her.

Not enough to stop *tap-tap-tapping* on her sore hip.

CHAPTER 58

ELIAS

"Ninety-nine axes up there on the wall, ninety-nine axes up there. Take one down, swing it around…"

If Everin Arden didn't stop belting out bar songs at the top of his lungs, Elias was going to poke holes in them and let all the air out.

He'd grown used to Soren distracting herself with humming and muttering and out-of-key tunes. And yes, she sounded like a yowling cat with laryngitis getting strangled to death—but Everin sounded like the drunken fool at the tavern who believed his voice was the gods' gift to the six kingdoms, and between the two, Elias would rather travel with the cat.

At least the cat didn't love the sound of its own screeching.

He let Everin get down to axe number sixty-four before he finally snapped. "Can you *please* just be quiet?"

"You'd have more fun if you joined in."

"I'm not trying to have fun. I'm trying to get us out of here."

"Will you relax?" Everin pitched himself against the wall, scratching at the arch of his throat and yawning. *Yawning.* "Honestly, our best bet would be to stay put. Medwenna's going to have this all mapped out by midnight, and she'll come find us when she's done."

Midnight couldn't be far off, judging by the moonlight bathing this vein of rock; there was a circular opening in the ceiling, almost perfectly framing the full moon beyond.

"Right." Annoyance sizzled down his throat. "The mountain just shuffled its insides around like a damned deck of cards, but I'm sure she'll have it all sorted in no time."

"See? I knew you'd come around. Optimism's your greatest tool in situations like these."

"Hopeless situations that are probably going to kill us?"

Everin snapped and pointed at him. "Exactly."

Elias tossed down his pack right where he stood, dropping to his seat and crossing his arms. "Fine. You want to sit around and wait? We can do that."

"Sixty-three axes hung—"

Elias pinched the bridge of his nose. "*If* you stop singing that damned *song.*"

Everin grumbled, but considering he couldn't grumble and sing at the same time, Elias would take it. The prince threw himself down next to Elias's pack, setting the glamour rod—this one pink—against the wall, unceremoniously rifling through the contents. "You have any food in here?"

Elias tried to snatch the bag away, but Everin caught a fistful of the lining, bringing them to a stalemate. "What in the pits do you think you're doing?"

"Starving," moaned the prince. "You've got to have something hiding in there. I don't think I've seen you eat any of your rations yet."

That was because the Tallisian rations had the texture of meat that had gotten crushed by a rock, then left out to dry for three days.

Elias tugged harder at the strap. "Just get your hand out of my bag."

"Fine." Everin huffed, removing his hand and tucking it under his arm as he crossed them. "Didn't your mother teach you about sharing?"

"Didn't your mother teach *you* about stealing?"

"Not a thing, actually." He raised an eyebrow. Raised a hand.

Raised a folded piece of paper wrapped in twine.

"Stealing," Everin added with a smirk, "I learned from having a sister."

Red.

Everin's face, the note, the shadows stretching themselves down the cave walls—all of them went red. Like the glamour rod had begun to bleed.

"Give that back." He couldn't hear his own voice over the furious whine building in his head.

Everin studied the paper with another exaggerated yawn. "Let me guess—love note from the princess? She didn't strike me as the sappy sort, but hey, what do I know?"

The prince's fingertip slid beneath the twine.

Death, he could endure. Torture, he'd expected from being trapped in a heathen's company.

This, he couldn't do. This, he couldn't lose.

He exploded like an overheated ember, limbs finding purchase in the prince's open coat, landing solid blows to his exposed chest. A startled grunt of pain rewarded his efforts, but it wasn't enough—Everin just laughed, reeling back, holding the paper above his head as he stumbled out of Elias's reach. "Stones, I thought your girl was the feisty one!"

He'd never dared touch Occassio's worship with a ten-foot pole—had never once been desperate enough to call on her, not even in the face of death. But Finn had mentioned that the goddess liked a good show—and it must have been true. Because as he reeled to snatch up the glamour rod and shattered it against the rock, extinguishing the light, the moon followed suit.

In one gasp, the cavern went from silver-struck and blush-touched to utterly dark.

Magic and moonlight, smothered—but not his fury. Not even close.

Kallias's last words to him were in Prince Everin Arden's hands. And he'd die as many deaths as it took to get them back.

Everin laughed again, this time with an uneasy pitch. "That feels a little dramat—"

Elias plowed into the prince, charging him clean off his feet.

His sanguimancy might have left him to take on this gauntlet alone, but he was Nyxian. He didn't need magic to see in the dark.

Everin's back cracked against the floor; his next groan bubbled over with anger. "Whoa! Are you insane? It's just a—"

Elias pinned his arm over Everin's throat, a dark thrill tantalizing him as it bobbed under his elbow. "*Give it back.*"

"Maybe if you'd asked nicely," Everin coughed. A growl caught on his voice. "But now I'm *pissed.*"

The blow came out of nowhere, tossing stars into Elias's eyes; before he could get his bearings, Everin grabbed him by his shirt and hauled him up and around, slamming him into the rock wall. The sound of steel swinging through the air shot adrenaline through his heart; he closed his eyes instinctively, cringing away—

As Everin's axe cracked straight into the stone, just deep enough that the space between the curve of the blade and the start of the handle pinned Elias's wrist.

No. *No.*

"Better." Everin sounded a bit breathless. "Let's see what all this fuss was about, huh?"

Elias stared up at him, panting, tugging at the axe's handle—to no avail.

He had no fire to burn the axe's handle to ash. No magic to slow the prince's heart; no magic to drop the damned bastard *dead* for daring to touch that, let alone—

With a quiet *snick* that ripped Elias's chest wide open, Everin snapped the twine around the note.

"Stop," he snarled, but the prince ignored him—he just opened the note with a flick of his wrist, irreverent, infuriating.

When the twine tumbled to the floor, Elias's heart tumbled out after it.

"Please." If he could have crawled, he would have. If he could have offered gold or jewels or other fine treasures, he would have. Anything to buy it back.

Anything to not lose Kallias twice.

Everin cleared his throat like a priest about to pontificate through the night, his smug cut of teeth catching the slowly returning moonlight, stinging Elias's eyes. Blurring them. Heat trickled down his face in branching paths.

"Eli," Everin announced, and what was left of Elias's heart powdered to soot, dissolving into the gravel under his feet.

Eli,

By now, you will have discovered that I am a depths-damned coward.

I didn't have to do it like this—I had every chance to look you in the face and give you the proper goodbye you deserve. You could have been sitting here with me, had I been braver.

I didn't do the brave thing. For the same reasons I left this letter for last.

I couldn't bear to let you down.

Had he been able to hear anything but the echoes of Kallias's voice in those words—had he not been fighting the urge to weep so hard he could feel blood vessels bursting beneath the skin—he might have noticed Everin's showmanship falter. Might have noticed the confusion pulling pins out of his voice, its mocking supports beginning to wobble.

"I am…" A cleared throat. "I am…"

I am well-accustomed to that—letting others down. My sisters. My brother. My mother. My people. Myself, for depths' sake.

But after Artem, I swore to myself you would never be one of them. And no amount of courage could make me face you as I broke that vow.

You were my first true friend. The first who came to me not as a soldier under my command, not as a subject to their prince, but as someone who had every reason to treat me like an enemy, like nothing…and instead, you became the first person to treat me like I was something. The first person who told me I had more worth as a man than as an incentive scrawled on a treatise. Even if I lived to see this world's bitter end, I would not have enough time to thank you for that. Not with any semblance of adequacy, anyway.

Gods, Elias, I wish you were here.

A harsh, searing burn preceded a thickening of the mist over his eyes.

Ever since he was a boy, Elias Loch had a fire burning in his chest.

His teachers had named it passion. Had named it purpose.

They were wrong.

Its name was love. And when someone aimed for those he shared that fire with, sometimes it renamed itself *wrath.*

An inferno stormed under his skin. And maybe new magic could not trespass in these halls, but this was not magic—this was not holy.

This was a kind of power that had been born alongside the world, older than the rock they stood on. And no ancient spell or faithless king could douse that.

Trembling in every limb, biting his cheek bloody to hold in his sobs, he poured every bit of that flameless heat out of his heart. Into his hand as he yanked harder and harder on the axe.

Why was Everin still *reading?*

But it's better like this, even if it's not brave. I think we both know I have to do this—and we both know you'd stop me if you could.

I am grateful for you, Elias Loch. Grateful to have had you as a friend—grateful that my sister has you at her back. Grateful you've shown mighty restraint in leaving Finn alive this long. (I know, I know, he's asking for it. But I appreciate you taking the high road, as you always do.)

And I am grateful that I can make this choice without fear for my kingdom, knowing you will one day become its king.

I only wish I could have stayed long enough for you to become my brother.

His grief for Kallias was a weapon.

And the word *brother* seized that weapon without pause, cleaving its serrated edge through his chest, leaving behind a ragged mess of rib and blood and freeing a molten, mighty roar.

A roar that shook the mountain to its roots.

A roar that sent the moon cowering behind a cloud.

A roar that set the Pride of Tallis stumbling back on his heels, the terror-bright whites of his eyes gleaming in the dark as Elias ripped the axe out of the wall, snapped the handle in two, and advanced on him with both halves brandished.

Everin's bravado evaporated in the light of such fury—he thrust back into the obsidian embrace of the cave, but Elias was Nyxian. He walked right into that maw of shadows, pushing in until Tallis's prince had nowhere to hide from the reckoning borne not by a phoenix's blessing, but by the primal piece of Elias that had been born to set the world on fire.

But when Everin's gaze met his again, Elias did not see fear.

Only a familiar weapon held blade-to-blade with his. Forged in a different fire, but beaten by the same tools.

When he cast the axe at Everin's feet and reached for the letter in his hand, the world-consuming blaze went out, casting Elias back into frigid darkness.

And when he snatched that precious paper away, breathing in broken huffs that burned his throat like alcohol over an open wound, he was weeping too hard to see what Everin did next.

He walked out of the tunnel without a word, the letter cradled to his sundered chest.

"Elias."

He ignored the prince's rasping call.

"Elias—Elias, flog me running, will you—stop!"

A hand landed on his shoulder—he ripped away, peeling his lips back from his teeth as he started in on Everin, waving the paper in his face. *"Do you need to see more?"*

Everin stared at him, unblinking. Unfazed.

"I'm an ass," he said—so frankly that Elias's seething sobs actually paused. "I shouldn't have done that. I didn't know what it was."

His heart was a coal, throbbing and hot, flaking apart piece by piece. "Well, now you know. Satisfied?"

Everin scratched his beard, tossing his gaze to the ceiling. "When my best friend was dying, I didn't sleep until he took his last breath. Kept my eyes open for four days straight because I was so flogging scared he'd leave without saying goodbye."

The prince's voice cracked on the word *friend*. The word *goodbye*.

Elias's fire sputtered.

"They did that, him and Winnie—they'd leave everything without saying goodbye. Parties, dinners, whatever. The second no one was looking, they'd be out the door like ghosts in a tailwind, so I talked to that boring bastard every second he was awake—and whenever Medwenna wasn't. I've never talked that gods-damned much. Him, either. We let Medwenna take the floor when she wanted it, but when she slept…Matt and Will and I, we just kept running our mouths. Said every stupid thing we thought of until we were all laughing our asses off."

Were the prince's eyes getting misty?

"I'd kill to do that goodbye all over again," Everin said without shame. "If I carried it around with me, and some mouthy asshole tried to take it…" A shrug. "I didn't know what it was."

The paper rasped lightly as Elias slid it into his pocket. His breath rasped just as lightly as he tried to control the hot blood still pumping through his heart. "Why do you keep doing that?"

"Doing what?"

"Poking at us. Starting fights. I'd think you're trying to sabotage us, but your father already rejected us—it's not like you need to make us look bad in front of anyone. So what're you trying to prove?"

"It's not like that." Everin chewed on the inside of his cheek before he said, "When you grow up like I did, you get good at reading a room…real good, real fast. You learn to spot the tension before it breaks. Gives you time to smooth it over." A grin bled across his face like a split, swollen lip. "Or get out of reach."

"That's the how, not the why."

"I'm getting there, hotshot, relax! Stones, I thought praying men were supposed to be *patient*."

He didn't take that bait. This time, anyway.

"You and the princess got wound up after that run-in with chaos." Everin tapped his ear. "The rest of us eased up after, but not you two. Figured someone had to get you two to talk about it. I meant to poke *that* bear, not..."

Elias almost let his jaw drop. But then the image of some cave insect flying into his open mouth invaded his mind, so he settled for a baffled, "You were trying to get me to *open up?*"

"Look, we have to get on the same page if we're going to survive here. This kind of thing goes bad real fast when there's all this...*stuff* pent up." Everin gestured in the rough direction of Elias's chest, nose crinkled. "People think leaders have to be the peacekeepers. You ask me, leaders are the ones who have to be willing to get people mad enough to tell each other the truth. Fight it out, make up, get back to baseline."

He hated how much sense that made. And that his and Soren's fight had him so off-kilter that a man he'd watched lick a rock yesterday had been able to catch it so easily.

"The letter's not done." Everin shifted on his feet. "I didn't...there's still more for you to read."

A flimsy attempt at comfort, when so much of it had been spilled at his feet against his will. But it did spread a balm over his heart, dulling the ache by pinches and scraps.

"If you want to break my nose," Everin offered, "it's free game. I'll even let you hit it from the prettier side."

His head felt heavy as he wagged it side to side. "My battlemate would get jealous."

Quiet, again.

"You want to..." Everin's words came slow and stumbling, like he'd never used them before; like his tongue didn't know how to hold them. They lurched out in uncertain bursts. "Stones, I don't know. I didn't think it was going to be this heavy. You wanna...talk about it?"

"Gods, no."

"Good," Everin blustered out with a relieved sigh, "because I'm flogging awful at it. You know what my first thought was? *Hey, he's probably better off, considering where we are.* That's a horrible thing to say when someone's dead."

Elias's eyes burned. "He's not..."

Hazy script penned on cheap paper. *I only wish I could have stayed.*

Malicious mist wearing his friend's face. *Elias, give up.*

Raquel, fighting tears of fury, grief punching the air out of her. *Kallias didn't make it.*

His throat closed up around that last and worst word. And this time, he let uncertainty lock it away.

"We should keep going," he said instead. And somehow, even that skirting felt like an admission. A betrayal. "Our best hope is that they'll be there when we hit the next trial."

Everin chuckled ominously in the dark. "*If* we hit the next trial."

CHAPTER 59

ANIMA

"I cannot be blighted. I cannot be hurt by *my* magic!"

Sage let out a longsuffering sigh—his fourth of the morning—as he tugged her eyelid up. "Listen, lass, I know medimancers make the worst patients, but I'm the worst at *patience*. I'm here to give you a diagnosis, not an argument."

Ani bundled her arms around her middle, clenching every muscle against a shiver. Her body temperature had finally steadied after vacillating wildly between boiling fever and nerve-killing cold; unfortunately, it had chosen to stop swinging on one of the extremes rather than settling for equilibrium. "These symptoms could just as easily be magic exhaustion."

"For your run-of-the-mill mortal, maybe. Not a goddess."

"How is that less believable than the Blight?"

"Lass, you know as well as I that magic has a life of its own." Sage ran his thumbs down her arms, pressing into her artery periodically, warmth shooting up her vein every time his thumb lit with magic. "You may have been immune before, but whatever you did to fix Ma..."

"You gave it the opening it needed," Wolf finished grimly. He didn't look like he'd slept all night, either—they hung heavy with folds, the trenches dug beneath them darkening every time he rubbed his eyes. "You didn't fight it."

Her body didn't *feel* like it had stopped fighting. It felt like she'd spent the night wrestling a twenty-foot constrictor snake with one hand tied behind her back.

But Wolf wasn't wrong. To get the Blight out of Genevieve, she'd had to give the parasite a place to go.

So she'd let it in. And now…gods knew if she could get it back out.

"H-How is Genevieve?" An artful swivel between subjects that Soren would've been proud of.

The brothers exchanged looks that answered her even as they silently argued about what that answer *was*.

"She's shaken up," Sage finally said. "But she got her senses back early this morning. Fever broke and all. Da's with her."

"Good." Ani sank into the pillows—they'd brought her back to her borrowed room sometime last night, but she couldn't reach the memory past the throes of her hours-long struggle. "This will pass—the Blight can't feed off me like most. It will die out, and I'll be right as rain."

Sage got off the bed and scooped up his clipboard, uncapping his pen with his teeth and scribbling down shorthand notes.

It had been some time since she'd tried to translate notes just by watching a pen move. But she could pick a few things up—enough to realize, after a couple lines—

"I am not in *denial!*" she cried.

Sage swore; then swore again when Wolf slapped him upside the head, hissing a warning about cursing at goddesses. "Gods *save* me from both of you. Quit eavesdropping on my notes—and you!" He punched his brother in the shoulder. "You're not my ma—quit acting like it."

"When you quit acting out, maybe I will."

"*All* of you can quit whatever this is," Astrid scolded—the three of them turned to face the diplomat as she entered Ani's borrowed room, frowning at them all like a disappointed teacher. "Bickering isn't helpful. Wolf, Sage—go sleep. I'll sit with Ani. If you don't mind the company?"

Ani's cheeks stung. Astrid's displeasure, though never harsh or rageful, had a way of scouring her sore. "I don't mind in the least."

"I mind in the *a lot*," Sage disagreed. "We've seen how contagious the usual sort is, let alone a direct infection. I don't like the idea of you—"

"I don't like the idea of you just now, either." Astrid's prim strike cut him off at the knees. "*You're* sharing my bed, you fool, don't you think I've been exposed plenty?"

Sage blushed and rubbed the back of his neck, gaze askance. "You know I worry."

"I know. And when worry can beat good sense in an argument, I'll be happy to concede."

Sage grumbled under his breath; he went to the bathing room, washed his hands for the third time in the past half hour, then went to Astrid, sliding a hand behind her neck and resting his head on hers. "You'll never be happy to concede, you rotting liar."

Astrid pinched his cheek, smile secretive. "Shh, you. Go rest. You need it."

Ani gathered her blanket-covered knees to her aching chest as she watched the exhausted medimancer kiss his wife goodnight—well, good morning, rather—then hook an arm around his older brother's shoulders, throwing a wave Ani's way with the other as they walked out.

From Wolf, she received nothing—not a word said in farewell, not a look spared for the goddess he'd spent all night talking through her delirious dreams.

She knew how that prince held his anger—he carried a great heap of it now.

But she didn't think Sage was the one who'd saddled him with that burden.

CHAPTER 60

SOREN

"Ow. Ow. Ow. *Owwwww.*"

She hadn't needed to nurse her own wounds in too long; she'd fallen out of practice with the stoic sit required to properly do up her own stitches. Even with the suture thread clamped between her teeth, the *ows* kept wriggling past.

"I can do it for you. I don't mind. I'm trained, I swear."

Didn't mind was an understatement. Kessen had practically been standing over her shoulder the entire time, discomfort bristling off him like lionfish spines. And like lionfish spines, every prick of that anxious energy flooded Soren with venom, ramping up her agitation until her skin ached worse than her freshly-stitched side.

"I've got it," she gritted out, the tip of her tongue teasing the length of thread between her teeth. Not much left, but if she measured carefully, it ought to be enough.

If not, she'd have to resort to unraveling the frayed edge of her torn sleeve. And she'd really prefer not to sew cave dirt into her skin.

"You're sure you didn't sneak any liquor along?" she prompted after spitting out the end of the thread. "I won't tell, I swear on my life."

"I mean, I've looked four times already, but here." Kessen twisted to the side, rifling through his satchel. "Huh, would you look at—"

"All right, lay off." Another *ow* crumbled into a shapeless growl as the needle pierced the most ragged flap of skin, her breath thinning into bracing swallows of air. She knocked her head back against the cave wall, the dull pain just enough to distract her from the small agony of stitching. "What kind of jerk sasses a bleeding woman?"

"What kind of bleeding woman refuses to let someone else stitch her up, then yells at them for not being helpful?"

She dipped her head back down, forcing herself to look at the damage as if it belonged to another person; as if only the hand and needle belonged to her, and the torn-open hole belonged to some other unfortunate girl who'd picked a fight with a giant flying bird-lizard-*thing*. A couple curls tickled her brow; she blew them away with a fierce groan. "Fine, yeah, point made, kid. I was just hoping not to get a raging infection, that's all."

Kessen shuffled behind her, his shoes clipping the stone: toe to heel, toe to heel. Like a tap dancer. Or a very uncomfortable boy in hand-me-down boots. "You're six months younger than me. You're as much of a kid as I am."

A sickening lump rose in her throat, a knot of emotion tied impossibly tight; she cast it aside rather than try to unravel it. "That's pretty exact math for not knowing my birthday."

"You were born on the last day of the year, right?" When she lifted her head to pin him with a reproachful look, he added, "I'm not a creep, so don't look at me like that. You and my older sister shared a birthday. She bragged about it all the time, like it made her special." He snorted, thumbing the tip of his nose as he dropped to his seat in front of her, crossing his legs and leaning over them to watch her work. "Stakes and stones, I can't believe you can do that. I can't even pop my own boils."

All right, *that* made her laugh. "Gross, Kessen."

"What? Like you've never had to pop a boil or two. Or do princesses not get those?"

"We do, thanks. Well, my sister Yvonne never did, but she was born perfect. The rest of us mortals get them plenty." She scowled. "My battlemate still won't let me pop his unless he really can't reach them."

Kessen wrinkled his nose, gagging with his tongue out. "Why would you *want* to?"

"It's satisfying!" She set the needle between her teeth to pinch her fingers toward Kessen, then plucked it back out. "Especially when they—"

"Nope." Kessen covered his ears. "I am setting a boundary. Not talking about this."

A chuckle of her own buzzed through her chest, warm and tired. She finally finished stitching and tied off the end, cutting the thread as close to the knot as possible with her dagger; the second the thread snapped, so did her control over her hands. They began to rattle like chattering teeth; it took her three tries to re-sheath her dagger, and on the fourth, she cursed it until it finally jabbed in. "Damn this thing."

"They have minds of their own, right?" Kessen dropped his hands, rubbing them down his thighs. "Takes me a couple tries every time."

"Mmm." Gods, she was so tired—her eyelids weighed more than a cart full of bricks. "What do you think? Keep going, or stay put?"

"I think if we were going to stay put, we should've done it to start with." He cast a doubtful look at the tear in the side of her shirt as she started to messily stitch that shut, too. "You sure you can walk like this?"

She splayed her hands out. "If you have an alternative, I'd be *thrilled* to hear it."

Kessen grunted in acquiescence. He hauled himself up onto his feet, dancing on his tiptoes for a second or two. "Then we move."

For a girl made of miracles, *moving* felt like the greatest impossibility she had yet to overcome. But she could rally; she would.

Gods knew Elias wasn't out there somewhere sitting on his ass. Honestly, she wouldn't be surprised to hear he'd jogged straight through the last couple trials, gathered the god-killer, and marched back just so he could tell her exactly how much of an idiot she was.

She rubbed the cold spot in the center of her palm as she stood, shaking her head until her eyelids lightened up. "You lead this time."

Kessen ambled forward with a sulky scowl. "Oh, thanks. My turn to take the hit, you mean."

She gestured to her side as she followed on his heels. "I took my turn. It's only fair."

Besides the occasional *ow* from her and the mutters from Kessen warning her about upcoming dips or obstacles, their progression through the tunnels was silent; slow, but uneventful. And oddly, she was grateful Kessen stayed ahead— that he didn't look back every time her pain got the best of her.

Some might have called it inconsiderate. But there was a respect to it, if she said so herself—not a dismissal of her struggle, but an acknowledgment that she had it well in hand.

It made it easier to bear, almost. Knowing she could express her pain without someone rushing to try and fix it. That someone believed she could endure it on her own.

But when they reached the end of the tunnel, their circle of glamour-light washing over a door—not a slab of stone or a pile of rubble, but an actual *door*— not even pain could distract her from the dread that drop-kicked her stomach.

Carved from wood, inlaid with gems, painted purple—this door made no secret of whose trial waited just beyond.

Nor did the riddle carved into it.

Checkers, chess, and card games all,
Are set with rules, perchance to stall
Opponent's victory, by checkmate and chance
You will now join this dastardly dance.
Your burdens removed, your knowledge erased
Name all your pieces and stand them in place
But should you choose wrong, set your gamepiece astray
Three chances you'll have to properly play.
The loss of your players will leave you in grief,
Should you steal their names back from this magical thief
So go carefully friends, test your luck, hold your breath
Thrice tried and thrice failed will end with your death.

"We should wait for the others," she and Kessen said together.

"Jinx," he said, just a breath before she could—with a hissed curse, she dug in her pocket and flipped him a silver coin. He kissed it and shoved it in his own pocket with a beaming grin. "Told you. No one's faster than me."

"Get out of my head. I can't afford to keep getting jinxed."

A grinding sound to their left thrust her heart up into her throat; her stitches screamed as she turned, yanking her dagger back out. She didn't trust her quivering arm to keep her sword aloft right now.

A boulder about half her height rolled down the wall, revealing a small opening: before she could assess whether to pounce or hang back, Matthias's head popped through, braids clacking against the floor.

"Oh, thank the *skies*," he groaned, tumbling out and landing on his back— she couldn't tell if he was injured, but he was certainly *soaked*. His clothes hit the rock with a loud *splat* when he sprawled out. "I thought we'd never find you lot."

"Matt!" For all Kessen's tough talk, palpable relief swelled until his voice went tight; he knelt by his friend, feeling his chest and neck. "Sound off. Any breaks? Any blood?"

"None for none," Matthias wheezed. "Just sick to my soul of *water*."

"Worse than," said Medwenna as she scrambled out of the hole behind Matthias; the historian was shivering, pale, but stood on her own when she slithered into the taller tunnel. She favored her left side as she swung her satchel about, digging around and pulling out a dripping wet scroll. "I've half a notion to peel free of the stuff entirely. I could move to the Onyx Desert—they never have to worry about their parchment getting sopped, I promise you that."

A long, ugly stripe of scarlet measured the length of Medwenna's left forearm; Soren dug around for what little remained of her suture thread. "What got you?"

"Just a sharp rock." Medwenna barely spared the cut a glance. "Looks rougher than it sits. I'll do without the stitching. What about you?"

"Griffin," she and Kessen said together, then: "Jinx!" then: "Damn you!"

"That's a draw," Matthias mumbled from the ground. "No silver exchanged. I don't suppose you two got eyes on Everin?"

Medwenna paused, glancing between them hopefully.

Soren shook her head, hating the anxiety shivering in her stomach. "Nothing. You either?"

Medwenna's eyes dimmed. She cleared her throat, turning toward the door and pulling out one of her books, muttering to herself about old Lapisian riddles.

Matthias shook his head, his gaze mirroring her anxiety nearly to the last inch. "Do we think there's any merit to retracing our steps?"

"Doubt it." Kessen knocked on the wall. "The mountain opened up all those new passages—it probably closed some, too. I don't think we'll find them."

"Not a worry," said a voice from beneath them—yes, *beneath* them, which had her trying to figure out how to break it to the others that she'd lost her mind until something knocked on the ground beneath her sole. "Move over, Princess."

Normally, she didn't care to follow the orders of disembodied voices floating up from what appeared to be solid stone. Still, first time for everything— she shuffled backward, pressing flush against the rock as the knock came again— again—

And a portion of the floor *shattered* in a near-perfect circle, Everin hauling himself up and through a few minutes later, his arms flexing and his jaw grinding with the effort.

"One-way glass fashioned to the stone," he said, though nobody had shaken out of their shock enough to ask. "Clever little trick."

"Stakes and stones, I'm glad to see you." Matthias hauled Everin out and clapped him in a warm embrace. "I had no flogging clue how I was going to tell your father I lost you in a mountain."

Everin laughed, all toothy grins and boisterous confidence like always— until he found Medwenna, who'd actually broken away from her book to slump against the wall, gazing at him with the dazed relief of a woken dreamer. Like she'd been stuck in a nightmare, and he'd shaken her awake.

"What happened?" Everin abandoned them all, shoving through to reach Medwenna; he caught her arm and studied it, the corners of his eyes feathered and tight. His thumb traced a parallel path down the cut. "Do you need—?"

"I'm right as rain." Medwenna patted his chest with her other hand. "And you?"

Everin didn't break from the wound on her arm; the creases in his brow only deepened.

"Everin." Medwenna's eyes rounded in worry. "What is it?"

"Nothing." The single word strained against the prince's voice; he cleared his throat, gently releasing her arm. "Glad you're good."

Finally, Soren's wasting patience couldn't take it anymore. "Where is—?"

"What part of *wait up* wasn't clear?"

Now, she'd recognize *that* grumpy mutter anywhere. She turned back to the hole just in time to see a russet hand clear the top, feeling blindly for a hold; she hurried over and helped Elias through, Matthias scooting over to help when her side spasmed, nearly splitting the stitches.

"Good," huffed Matthias once Elias spilled out onto the floor. "Six bodies? One?"

"Two," Elias muttered, dragging himself up onto his haunches; he twisted to reach for her. "You're all right?"

"Little beat up, but nothing bad." She kissed his knuckles, then looked to Matthias. "Three."

"Four," Kessen and Medwenna said at once—then, after a beat, Kessen sighed, "Five."

"Six," Everin finished off, still sounding distracted. "Does anyone have bandages? Suture thread? We—"

"It's just a scratch!" Medwenna protested. "We can fuss with it later. We're gaining now, there's only two trials left—"

"And if you get separated again?" Soren had never heard Everin take on anger with Medwenna; but as his fingers flexed around her wrist, his voice pulled taut with it, tensed halfway to snapping. "Better we tend it here."

"I really don't think that's—"

"Medwenna, *stop*." Everin grabbed her chin with his other hand, forcing the historian to face him—to abandon her book and the door and *look* at him, her eyes widening behind her spectacles. "Whatever's behind that door, it'll keep until you're seen to. You're more important than a mystery."

Soren leaned into Elias. "We really should've started that betting pool."

"Hm?" Now *he* sounded distracted; she twisted to find him staring down at her side.

"I'm okay," she said, though he hadn't asked.

"Right." He swallowed. "Honest?"

"Honest."

"I vote we take an hour or two." Matthias was watching Everin and Medwenna, but he spoke toward Soren and Elias. "We're all pretty battered; don't want to shove ourselves into another test when we can barely catch our breath."

Though Soren had the same itch as Medwenna, she had to agree—if they ran into another griffin or something worse, she doubted they'd be up to that kind of fight in this state. And knowing whose trial waited on the other side of that door...

They needed all their wits about them for this.

So rest they did; Everin ripping his shirt and bandaging Medwenna's arm, the two of them arguing in hushed tones in the corner; Matthias and Kessen huddled nearby, watching them with the awkward, anxious air of two children listening to their parents bicker; and her and Elias taking turns sharing their tales, though Elias seemed a bit cagey about the details.

When it came time to open the door, they decided to draw lots; Soren and Medwenna excluded, thanks to their injuries. She and Medwenna both argued, but it was no use—they were outnumbered no matter which way they played it, and even Kessen couldn't be swayed to their side.

In the end, Everin drew the short straw. He approached the door without fear; but Soren could just make the cracks and flaws in his bravado. They only showed when he looked toward a certain widow.

"Game faces," he said. "This one's going to be different. I can feel it."

She could, too—the fear no longer lived in her heart, but in her head, a pain beating in time with her pulse.

They filed through the door one by one: Everin first, Elias last. Her battlemate squeezed her hand before releasing it to turn away, shutting the door—

And a flare of blinding, *agonizing* white light exploded around them.

Soren bit back a scream, flinging one arm over her eyes, flinging the other back, but her hand only found empty air. And when the light faded, leaving her blinking away sunspots, dazed and dizzy…

She was surrounded by a host of unfamiliar faces.

CHAPTER 61

ELIAS

When the searing white light finally deposited him into a room he didn't recognize, it didn't take long to realize what had happened:

Firstly, the door had sealed behind him; when he tried to twist the smooth, keyless knob, it stopped short of a full turn.

Secondly, that power had not only left him disoriented, head pounding, eyes aching—it had ripped him away from his companions. Companions he was *sure* he'd had, even if reaching for their names forced him to wander through murky shadows, grasping at mist.

And thirdly, it had left him in the company of strangers…five of them, not even one familiar in the least, each wearing the same confused expression.

Confusion that rapidly shifted to wariness on some, hostility on others.

Elias fell back until he bumped into a boulder; he let the stone guard his back as he dropped his hand to his dagger, squinting against the buzzing in his head. Like a limb that had fallen asleep, the tingling almost hurt—he could think, but not with his usual clarity. Like his mind needed glasses.

Still, a brief assessment pulled out the two greatest threats in rapid succession: the burly man the same size as the boulder Elias now leaned on, and the fire-haired girl coiled like a wildcat prepared to pounce. Her crooked nose and scarred, speckled skin promised she was no stranger to drawing and shedding blood—nor to basking beneath the sun's shining face.

Had he been a gambling man, he would've bet it all on her being the fiercer fighter between the two. Because even though she stood a foot shorter than the mountain of muscle across the way, he couldn't seem to scrape his gaze off of her. Her glare set every prey instinct on edge, the hairs on the back of his neck bristling, his heart sprinting at a breakneck pace.

"Names," demanded the freckled girl, feline green eyes pinning him to the stone like a cluster of claws against his throat. His blood ran hot, climbing the column of his neck like she'd split his throat from ear to ear with that glare alone. "Now."

"How about we start with kingdoms?" One of the others—a blond-haired man with movements as predatory as the freckled girl's eyes—circled wide, finding his own boulder to shield his back. Dove-gray eyes looked down a hawkish nose, seeking each of them in turn. "Names won't do me half as much good as your affiliation."

"Tallis," said two of the group—a redheaded boy and the burly man. Both of them exchanged baffled looks before taking another step away from each other, but unlike Elias and the blond, they didn't dart for cover.

"Tallis as well," spoke the one woman who hadn't made herself known yet—the least of the dangers in this room by his assessment, at least physically. Her gilded-lily eyes spoke of an intelligence sharp enough to slit a throat, but she wore a bow and arrow, no other weapons—suited for distance, not close quarters. And out of everyone, she was the only person who moved without suspicion, studying the room instead of the people inside it. She ran her palm over a carving in the rock, calm curiosity washing over her pretty face. "Well, used to be. Arborius, now."

She tweaked the pendant around her throat: a ring. Instinct brought his hand up to his neck, but his fingers found nothing to hook into; with a shiver of unease, he let them drop.

Something was very wrong.

"I'm Tallisian, too." The blond man studied the distracted woman with a troubled frown of his own, hostility banking—if only by an inch. "But I don't know your faces."

"Well, I'm like her," announced the fire-haired girl, freckles blending as she scrunched her nose and nodded toward the honey-eyed woman. "Atlas-born, but raised in Nyx."

A bell pealed in Elias's head. "I'm Nyxian."

He met the girl's gaze; they studied each other for a long moment. Too long. His cheeks heated the longer she stared.

"I'm Soren," she said finally. "Princess of Nyx, Heir of Atlas. What about you, Sad Eyes? Got a name?"

He scowled. "I do. And it's not *Sad Eyes*."

"Don't care," she said cheerfully. "Share or suck it up."

He swallowed a sigh. "I'm Elias."

"Matthias," the burly man offered, holding up a hand.

"Kessen." The redheaded boy shifted from one foot to the other, looking between them all with nearly wild eyes. "How did we get here?"

"No idea." The blond man rolled one shoulder, hefting a mean-looking axe. "Anyone else?"

"Medwenna." The other woman walked right past the blond man without a care, not even giving him a second look to make sure he wasn't about to attack. He gazed after her in disbelief, axe dipping.

"Everin," he muttered. "Prince of Tallis, if anyone cares to know."

"Shouldn't we know your face, then?" Matthias pointed out. "I know Raini, at least from a distance—why don't I know you?"

Elias had to agree. Soren claimed to be a princess of his kingdom; he should know her name, if not her face. He could picture the other three princesses clear as a calm winter day, but *her*...

No—he couldn't have seen her before. A face like hers...well, people didn't forget faces like hers.

"Your guess is as good as mine," Everin blustered. "So let me get this clear: none of you know how you got here?"

They all traded looks, seeking answers in each other's eyes. Eventually, one by one, they all shook their heads.

"Fantastic." Everin spun in a slow circle, though he stuck close to the wall. "Magic—has to be."

"Occassio," Elias muttered, rubbing the back of his neck. A chill tunneled down his spine.

His tattoo prevented him from getting tricked by illusions, but her stronger magics wouldn't bend to a simple rune. Whatever had rent their minds of their memories—some of them, anyway—and dumped them all in this room, he couldn't reach past it to find any answers.

He knew his name. He knew his home. He knew he had people there...his family, friends.

Something horrible had happened there. He remembered that, too. But when he tried to peel back the curtains, he found nothing behind. Only flashes of blood and screaming and laughter and...music.

Golden-red hair. Sunbright grins. Howling wind.

He'd come here for them. For...for some reason. But why?

"You wear a ring."

He turned, but while Medwenna was standing beside him when she made the observation, she was looking at the fire-haired girl...Soren.

Soren looked down, frowning; she twisted the ring around her finger. "I don't recognize it."

"Well, it's a good start." Medwenna looked around. "Maybe it can tell us something. Who else has rings?"

As the others flashed their hands at each other—resulting in a relieved whistle from the black-braided man and a disappointed *aww* from the redheaded man when theirs were empty—something soft brushed Elias's fingertips. When he looked down, he found his hand had moved of its own accord, fiddling with the tokens hanging around his neck again. A feather and two plaits of cloth…like battlemate braids, but with no hair woven in.

Two. One for Kaia, his first battlemate, and one for…

Another empty wall slammed down in his path when he tried to reach for the grief attached to that second braid.

"Just because we have rings doesn't mean they go together," Soren was arguing when he started paying attention again—she held her hand up beside the lionlike man's, looking between the two rings with a displeased curl of her lips. "No offense. It just doesn't feel right. You're pretty enough, but you're not exactly my type."

"Don't flatter yourself," snorted Everin. "I'm not too keen on you, either."

Soren scowled at him, aggression vanishing all at once into something lighter, pettier; she sheathed her dagger, crossing her arms. She seemed to be favoring her right side. "Well, you better *hope* we're not married, after a comment like that."

"Hey, I don't mean anything by it." Everin put his hands up, mouth bent in a flirtatious smirk. "You're not half bad on the eyes, spitfire. Just not my sort, is all."

For some reason, that made Elias want to throw a punch.

Soren rolled her eyes. "Gee, thanks. I'm swooning."

"She's right. There's no need to be rude," scolded Medwenna, who'd already moved on—out of everyone, she alone seemed to have some sense of purpose, searching along the edges of the room for…something. He couldn't guess what. "Especially when we can't remember who in this room might matter to us. Don't say things you may regret later."

An embarrassed grimace overtook Everin's mocking sneer. He scratched the back of his neck. "Not a bad point."

"Besides, it does make sense." Medwenna flicked her hand between Everin and Soren. "You're the only two royals in the room, and the only two with rings on your fingers—the only logical conclusion would be an arrangement of some sort. Historically, Tallis has pursued Heir-to-Heir matches, though not typical of—"

"Not a chance," Soren scoffed. "The depths-damned *world* would have to be ending for me to agree to that."

"Uh, ouch?" Everin protested. "Who's hurting feelings now?"

Soren smirked. "Sorry. Look, I'm just saying, I'm no queen—there's only so much I'm willing to give up for my kingdom."

A strange pause inserted itself there; one that gave Elias permission to finally look away, following the path of Medwenna's methodical exploration of the chamber.

"What about you, tall, dark, and brooding?"

It took him a bit too long to realize the freckled spitfire was referring to him. "Still not my name."

"Still don't care. Besides, you answered to it."

He flashed his empty fingers. "You're safe. No ring here."

"Hmm." He didn't know what to make of the way Soren's lips knotted, almost a frown. But she turned away, saving him from the arresting power of her gaze—and from staring so hard at her mouth, gods help him. Had this magic blurred his manners, too? "All right, well…we're stuck in here, yeah? Seems to me we must've been looking for a way out, unless we all happen to be passionate about starving to death in creepy caves."

"I agree," called Medwenna—gods, she'd already scaled halfway up the grooved wall, holding on with one hand while she dusted off the surface with her other. "Can someone give me a boost, here? There's something carved on this wall, but I can't tell what it is."

"We should split and look for more," said Matthias. "We'll cover more ground."

And be easier to take out, Elias thought, but he kept quiet. If that was the thought going through Matthias's head, better he played oblivious.

"I've got you, ah…what was it?" asked Everin as he crossed the cavern, axe returned to its sheath. He held a hand out to Medwenna, one brow arched.

She set her hand in his. "Medwenna."

"That's a mouthful. You against a nickname?"

"Not a bit."

"I'll go with Winnie, then." With a polite kiss to her knuckles, Everin released her hand to gesture to the wall. "Let's get you where you need to be."

A warm, solid weight bumped into him—he glared down at the fire-haired girl, Soren, who grinned back. "Guess that leaves us, huh?"

"Oh, joy," he deadpanned.

She pouted. "Who shoved a stalactite up your ass?"

"Probably the same person who screwed your nose on sideways."

"Well, they should've tweaked your attitude on the way out. It could use some adjusting."

Do not take the bait, he told himself. *It's not sportsmanlike to fight an injured woman.*

"Let's do what we need to do so we can get out of here," he gritted out.

"Just follow my lead, jackass." She punched his shoulder a bit too hard to be friendly, whistling as she made for the far end of the chamber.

Maybe we can nibble the bait. Fists clenched, cheeks burning, he tried to breathe through the surge of heat in his chest. *Just a little. Not enough to spring the trap.*

What a smartass. Thank the *gods* he didn't have a matching ring.

The wicked, playful look she tossed over her shoulder snagged him like a thread tied to his middle. "You coming?"

And as if they knew something he didn't, his feet followed her without hesitation.

CHAPTER 62

SOREN

"Do you even know what you're looking for?"

The dark-haired man's disdain—however mild it might be, and definitely flavored with some level of flustered attraction—was really starting to gnaw on her nerves.

"I know exactly as much as you do." She ladled sugary syrup over every word as she turned to meet his uncomfortable frown, walking backwards as she affected a clumsy bow. "Unless you have some new wisdom you'd like to impart, Your Piousness."

He blinked, uncomprehending. "My what?"

"Not the sharpest sword in the sheath, are you?"

"There's only one sword to a sheath."

Damn it. He had her there.

She pointed at the prayer beads around his neck. "I'm just saying, you're literally wearing it on your chest. Mortem, right?"

She didn't know much of anything about the gods, really, but she knew enough to recognize the rose-eyed skull that bounced along with his steps. And even if she hadn't, he had *prude* written all over him. She could practically smell the incense from here.

"Right." His fist closed around the charm. "And what about you? Atlas and Nyx, that's…"

"Weird?" She couldn't get a good grip on *how* she'd come about those two loyalties, the memory slippery as a water snake and half as willing to be held, but she remembered enough to understand his distrust. Bad blood flowed between the two; she just couldn't recall what had dealt the damage. "I'd love to explain it, but unfortunately, it seems I just recently got my brain scrambled."

"It's not really your brain. Occassio's magic works by—"

"*Dooon't* care," she sang, miming a yawn as she stretched out the *O*. "But when I need something to put me to sleep, I'll let you know."

He crossed his arms as they came to a stop at the next marked-up wall…which was completely fine, because the way his biceps strained against his sleeves didn't distract her even a little bit. "Not sure how your husband would feel about you inviting another man back to your bed."

Her turn to blink, to stare—and to laugh, though she would've rather poured boiling oil in her ear than give this stranger the satisfaction. If he started preening, she might be forced to forget why she shouldn't tie a stranger's bootlaces together.

But he didn't get smug or smarmy. He only stared back, looking just as surprised by the outburst as her.

"Was that a joke?" she prompted. "You didn't strike me as the type."

"It didn't—"

"And just for the record, that's *not* how I invite someone to my bed."

All right, she'd admit it: he *did* look kind of cute when he was gaping like a fish. "I did *not* mean to imply—"

"Relax, Pious," she giggled, dropping to her seat—then grimaced, cradling her injured side. She wished she could remember what had torn a chunk out of her…so she could know if she'd finished it off and mounted its stuffed carcass on the wall. She wasn't a fan of hunting, nor those who displayed their victims like trophies, but this singular creature had clearly earned it.

Elias inched forward, dropping into a crouch—still a couple feet back. "You're hurt."

"It's nothing."

"If it hurts, it isn't nothing."

"It doesn't hurt," she lied.

One fathomless eye twitched. "Are you always this stubborn?"

She gestured to her head. "Pits if I know."

To her surprise, he snorted—almost a laugh—before standing up and studying their etching. He smoothed a palm over the lines. "I think it's a chess piece…an older variant of modern sets." He traced the flaming cap atop the piece. "It's labeled 'Cleric.'"

"I have the Empress," Matthias's voice echoed out. He stood by an etching of a similar piece, but grander, capped in a crown.

"I've got the Emperor!" Medwenna's excitement lit up the room better than the glamour-rod in her hand; as she dusted off the last of her design, a mirrored piece to the Empress came into focus. But every place the Empress's edges rounded out, the King jutted in squares, cubed blocks stacked one on top of the other.

"I've got two!" Kessen announced. "One here, and one…" The boy sprinted from one end of the wall to the other, smacking his hand against it. "Right here. Axe and Shield."

"Oh, there's the other one!" Medwenna scrambled down from Everin's hands to brush off the last etching. "The Commander."

Wonderful. Now they could play a round of the most boring game ever invented.

While the rest of the group started lobbing ideas that ranged from sensible to *maybe if we all yell them out at once, it'll open a door. Like a password*, something gurgled low in her stomach.

She'd sell every single soul in this room for a good meal right about now.

She glanced at the others, busy with their fruitless brainstorming; then at her pious partner's bag, abandoned when he'd set himself to task along the wall. The cloth sack had slumped over, contents barely held back from spilling by gravity's lazy grip; with one eye on Elias, she stuck her hand inside, rifling around for anything wrapped in paper or preserving cloth.

"What do you think you're doing?"

Pits burn it, the damned snitch wasn't even *looking*.

"Trying to steal some snacks." Though the lack of crumbs lining the bottom of the bag didn't seem promising. "Do you remember if you're hiding any food?"

He shot her a withering look. Much less attractive than his bashful wince—or his biceps. Not that she'd noticed the biceps, because she hadn't. "Do *you* remember that you're not four years old?"

"Give me a break! I can't remember the last time I ate." Her stomach rumbled again. "*Literally*."

With a lamenting grumble vaguely shaped like *what did I do to deserve this*, Elias turned away from the wall and stomped back to her, hooking one finger under the satchel's leather strap; she reached out to try and catch it, but he yanked it away too fast, tucking it under his arm.

"Jackass," she grumbled.

"Smartass," he shot back.

The flush of heady warmth that dizzied her after that insult probably should've concerned her. Deeply. But for the moment, hunger had her full attention.

While she dragged herself to her feet and made her rounds to each of the other strangers, finally acquiring half a loaf of crusty bread from Medwenna and sitting down to gnaw on it, the others gathered in the center of the chamber. Medwenna tossed down a notebook, its pages now stuffed to the craw with sketches of each chess piece and their names; she knelt before it, hands pressed into the variegated stone. "What do we remember about why we're here?"

"We're looking for something," said Elias, whose jaw twitched when Soren's teeth ground against the bread's craggy crust, trying to break ground.

"We're trying to get out of this cave," Everin added.

Medwenna nodded absently, spectacled gaze fixed on the scratches of charcoal in her book. "*Your burdens removed, your knowledge erased, name all your pieces and stand them in place. But should you choose wrong, set your gamepiece astray...three chances you'll have to properly play.*"

"Why can you remember all that?" Soren demanded. What, she couldn't even remember what she'd had for breakfast—or if she'd had breakfast—and Medwenna could still recall all those self-indulgent rhymes?

The woman blushed, scratching behind her ear. "I couldn't tell you, lass."

"Not her fault she's smarter than you," sniped Everin.

She held up her ring. "You better watch how you're speaking to your wife."

"*Possible* wife," muttered Elias under his breath—delight tingled in her ears. So she *was* getting under his skin, after all.

"So we have three chances to do...whatever this is," said Kessen. He plopped down next to her, hand out—she clutched the bread close to her chest, biting at the air when he tried to take some anyway. He snatched his hand back, eyes wide. "Stones, what are you, a street cat?"

She mimicked a hiss, and he scooted another foot away from her.

Another cough from Elias. "Name all your pieces...we did that. Emperor, Empress, Shield, Axe, Cleric, Commander."

"Aw," Soren said through her next mouthful of stale bread. "They all come in pairs."

Matthias stepped back a few feet, his chin tipping up and down as he eyed the etchings from top to bottom. "I think that's a coincidence."

"It's not," Medwenna said without a shade of doubt. "That's how ancient chess was played—the ranks came in pairs, and if you use the two pieces strategically, each pair comes with an advantage. They mirror each other."

"So maybe we need to find the pieces?" Everin looked around, fussing with the handle of his axe. "It could take *weeks* to turn this whole room over."

Chess, mirrors...strategy. Tricks played in plain sight.

Something about it made her brain feel like a cat being stroked against the grain of its coat. Like every nerve stood on end, bristling in a bad way.

She looked back at the Empress, standing so imposing and tall, the crown not bending her at all. Not wrung to her furthest extremes, so twisted in her center that she might never be made right again; not trying to shove herself into a mold cast in her image, only to find she'd somehow become something so misshapen she could not fit in a thing made to her exact measurements.

Possessed by a sudden thought, she tossed Kessen the bread; he bobbled it, cursing as she hobbled to the wall, fitting her boot against a rock that jutted out just enough to *almost* make a decent foothold.

"What do you think you're doing?"

She looked over her shoulder at Elias, who'd followed on her heels; his severe look turned some crank in her brain, every light flickering to life like a kerosene lamp, the fire in his eyes burning away the dreamlike mist.

"I need a better view," she said.

He is *a better view*, said some disembodied voice in her brain.

Shut up, she replied to herself. *You're a married woman.* Maybe, anyway.

His glare cut to her bloodied side, bared by her tattered shirt. "You're going to climb in that state?"

She sucked in her bottom lip, teasing the hem of her shirt with one hooked finger. "I suppose I could take off the shirt…"

Tension feathered through his jaw; the corners of his eyes tightened. "Now's not the time to be funny."

"I can't really help it."

"You fall from there, and—"

"And a whole bunch of bad things come after, I know." Broken bones being the least of the possibilities. But that didn't change what she'd said: she needed a better vantage point, and unlike Medwenna, she didn't trust any of these people enough to let them boost her. Safer to climb alone than to climb with someone who'd rather see her fall.

She made it up two more footholds before rock scuffed below her; she looked down to see a head of obsidian hair beneath the foothold she'd just abandoned, Elias using it as a handhold instead.

"What are you doing?" she demanded, sticking her leg out and poking his head with the toe of her boot—he grimaced, but bent with it, which was lucky. If he'd shoved her off instead, she might've lost her balance.

"I'm making sure you don't die," he muttered, catching her foot and pushing it back into her foothold. "Gods only know why."

"I've got this, thanks." She tried to push him off again, but he caught her boot by the toe—then caught her gaze with such pinpoint focus that her protest fell straight out of her mouth.

That bristling sense of something being *off* rippled over the surface of her skull again.

"Will you just climb?" he demanded, terse annoyance at odds with the intensity of that depths-damned *look* he was giving her. Like he'd brave something worse than a free climb up this sheer rock wall to keep her in his sights.

And it drove her to such distraction that by the time she remembered she wasn't in the habit of losing arguments, she'd already gone up another foothold.

One by one, they took turns with every shallow chink and flimsy shelf they could find—her footholds became his handholds, her path mapping the way for him to follow.

And then came the time to turn.

Her throat closed up; when she looked down, Elias peered up at her through that fringe of dark hair.

"Turn around," he urged. "I'll brace your ankles."

A sound plan, had she not already been attempting to do so; her body refused to obey, utterly paralyzed by the threatening touch of open air behind her.

Two assessing darts of his midnight eyes across her face, and he said, "I swear on my life, I will not let you fall."

Why did that make her eyes burn like she'd accidentally sprayed perfume in them?

Why did that unstick her muscles from their rigor, allowing her to swivel without hesitation?

And most importantly…

Why did the steady pressure of his calloused hands around her ankles pump giddy, reckless heat directly into her veins?

She didn't thrill like this over strangers. Didn't put mortal trust in them, either.

But when he swore that vow, she believed him. Down to her bones, she believed him.

And that gave her the courage to venture a guess. Another thing she believed without rhyme or reason.

"This ring belongs to you, doesn't it?" Breathless, she bumped her wrist against her temple, wiping away dribbles of cold sweat. She needed to pull herself together.

"*Gods*, I hope so," he muttered fervently, so blunt it startled another laugh out of her. "Otherwise, I'm going to have some serious concerns about my sanity to deal with after this."

"Because you followed me up here?"

"Because you're the most annoying person in this cave, and I'd still rather be up here with you than waiting down there with the others."

"Really? I'm worse than—"

"Yes."

"You didn't even let me fin—"

"Yes."

"*Ugh*." She would've kicked him, but that probably would've ended in both their deaths. So instead, she shored up all her courage with a deep breath of cave air—oddly clean, actually, with a hint of lilac and sugar instead of mildew and damp—and peered past his head to the floor several dozen feet below.

The bread hardened to brick in her stomach.

"Well?" Elias's hands tightened around her ankles. "See any pieces?"

"Actually," she said as she studied the pattern on the stone…not naturally variegated after all, but a pattern of near-perfect squares. Half dark, half light. "I think we *are* the pieces."

CHAPTER 63

ELIAS

This woman, whoever she was, was going to be the death of him.

This chamber might be able to throw impenetrable veils over memories, but it couldn't kill instinct: and instinct told him, as he watched the redheaded princess play a game of hopscotch on a chess board arranged out of their favor, that the chances of them winning in three tries were slim to none.

"All right, so we can all agree I'm the Emperor," said Everin, though none of them had agreed on any such thing. Nor had he given them any reason why they should. "Where does that put the rest of you?"

"Who died and made you Emperor?" Kessen demanded. "Maybe any of us could be any piece."

"Right." Everin watched with pronounced doubt as Kessen joined Soren mid-hop, following a different arrangement of squares. "You do have such regal bearing."

"The riddle implies that there *is* a choice to be made." Medwenna remained crouched over her journal, a frown pinching dimples into her cheeks as she scribbled out notes. Strands of golden-brown hair escaped her bun, tickling her temples; her piece of charcoal flew so fast, he could practically see sparks flying from its tip. "And if we choose wrong, there are consequences."

"Everin *is* descended from emperors, being the Prince of Tallis." Matthias crouched beside Medwenna. "And if Soren is telling the truth about being the Heir of Atlas, she likely lines up with the Empress."

Soren froze on one leg, teetering wildly; she gingerly set her hovering foot back on the ground. "That feels like a leap."

"No, *this* feels like a leap," said Kessen as he thrust off the ground, skipping several rows of squares before landing with one foot on a light square and one on a dark. "Ha! I win."

"That's not how hopscotch works," Soren said.

"What's hopscotch? I'm playing Ram's Romp."

"What in the depths is *Ram's*—?"

"Can we focus, please?" Medwenna's calm dented in, impatience making its debut on her face. "We're mucking with life and death, if you recall."

"Listen to the lady." Everin halted his approach toward the row of squares where Kessen had started his game, backpedaling a step or two. "Let's focus up. We've got Emperor and Empress—what's next?"

Soren pointed back—with a start, Elias realized she'd aimed her finger directly at his chest. "Cleric."

"What makes you think *I'm* the Cleric?" he scoffed.

So many condescending looks piled on him at once, he almost got knocked to the ground.

"Your tattoos," said Medwenna.

"That feather." Matthias knocked over the center of his own chestplate. "Looks phoenix to me."

"The *prayer* beads?" Everin suggested scathingly.

"Have you *looked* at you?" Soren squinted at him; she came over and tapped his forehead. "It's so weird, but someone actually wrote *cleric* in big letters right here—"

"All right, I get it." He swatted her hand away, wishing she wouldn't crinkle her nose when she giggled. It made him want to do insane, terrifying things—like kissing that nose just to make her laugh harder.

Things strangers shouldn't want to do to other strangers.

Things he'd never wanted to do to *anyone*.

"That leaves Axe, Shield, and Commander." Medwenna tapped the tip of her nose. "None of those ring right to me."

Everin aimed a sultry smirk in her direction. "You've been commanding all of us well enough."

Elias had to clear a laugh out of his throat when Medwenna didn't even give Everin the satisfaction of looking up. "I'd call it organizing, not commanding."

"He's not entirely wrong, though," Matthias offered. "I mean, Occassio's a tricky sort—and whatever triggers this trial, it can't be too specific, or it'd never work. It's lucky enough that we came in with six and no more."

"Unless the game adjusts itself according to the invaders." Medwenna's eyes clouded over, troubled and tense.

They all fell silent as one, wrestling privately with that idea.

"I'm a colonel," Matthias said finally. "Can anyone but the royals beat that rank?"

Elias, Medwenna, and Kessen all exchanged looks; none of them spoke up.

"Then we'll call me the Commander for now." Matthias jerked his chin at Medwenna and Kessen. "You two pick Axe and Shield between you, and we'll see what happens."

"I carry an axe," Kessen offered.

"I'm happy to be the Shield," Medwenna agreed.

They all split off, seeking their assigned pieces; when Elias reached the Cleric square, he found it neither dark nor light, but almost…opalescent. It shimmered in the low light, chips of rainbow sprinkled in with a liberal hand.

"On the count of three," Everin's voice echoed out. "One, two—"

On *three*, Elias stepped onto the iridescent square.

Light—all around the cavern, columns of light shot up from the floor, illuminating the etchings of every chess piece.

White light, at first. Then the beam under his feet slowly took on color…the muted shade of the herbs his mother grew in the kitchen window.

Green under his feet. Green under Everin's. Green under Kessen's. The boy's victorious whoop hadn't finished echoing by the time the light began to change under Medwenna's feet…

Blood glossed over the cave wall, and Elias shouted, *"Get off the—"*
Medwenna *screamed.*

Red, red, red—scarlet spilled over the final three etchings, and two more voices joined Medwenna's, all torn by pain he couldn't find the source of.

When he saw Soren drop to her knees, panic poured like acid through his veins.

Everin's triumphant laughter contorted into vicious curses; the prince was pulling at his own leg, almost clawing at it, teeth set in a wrathful snarl. "I can't move!"

Elias's stomach flipped. He tried to take a step off the platform—his shoe snagged in place, like he'd stepped in a bucket of half-dried maple sap. Kessen, too, seemed frozen to his spot.

After a long moment—too damned long—Soren raised her head, blinking slowly, aftershocks still wracking her body. He could see how badly she was shaking from here.

"All right," she called, and his stomach flipped back over into its proper place. "I think we got that one wrong."

"If that's what happens when we get it wrong," gasped Matthias, also on his knees with his head tipped back, "I don't want to know how bad it gets when we get it wrong twice."

"Commander, Shield, Empress." Medwenna stumbled off her platform first, a dizzy sway to her step; Everin's struggles to tear himself off his square renewed. "How do we shift?"

"I'm certainly not the Empress," Matthias chuckled breathlessly, "so I suppose that makes me the Shield."

Medwenna snorted, her smile shocky, complexion pallid beneath the pale light's caress. The vermillion tint had leeched away, leaving it clean white once more. "You ask me, I'm even less Empress than you. Perhaps it assessed us wrong?"

Elias glanced back at Everin; the prince was still trying with all his might to get off the platform. Watching Medwenna with a worry so intense it seemed on the verge of boiling into anger.

"Let's just try it," Soren suggested. "It could be like Matthias said—not so literal."

Medwenna's throat bobbed. "You have to be the Empress, Your Highness—it's all that makes sense."

The princess rubbed her arms like she'd caught a chill, casting a reluctant look at the Empress. "But it—"

"If we're wrong, we only have one try left," Medwenna said; he had no name for the emotion knotting her brow and breaking her voice. "And I...I cannot be the Empress."

One try before they all perished. One try, and they would be dead—no goodbyes given to those they might not remember, either in this chamber or outside of it.

Soren gazed at Medwenna, then at the Empress's platform, now pearlescent and perfect again. Not a shred of scarlet left.

"All right," she acquiesced. "I'll try it again. You be the Commander."

Matthias stepped onto the Shield's platform; Medwenna mounted the Commander's. And after a long second of staring, Soren followed suit, stepping back into the Empress's square with her fists already clenched. Her breath already held.

Matthias's flared green almost immediately—his tight shoulders loosened into a full-bodied sigh of relief, and he mopped his brow shamelessly with the back of his wrist. "Burn me at the stake, that was—"

Crimson columns struck the ceiling, and Medwenna and Soren's screams drowned out even the hum of absolute helplessness in his head.

"Sound off!" Matthias shouted when the lights went out—when neither woman answered, his voice sharpened into a blood-stirring bark. "*Sound off*, ladies!"

"I'm all right," came Soren's dazed groan; Elias fell onto his seat, relief weakening his legs too much to stay standing.

Everin dropped to his knees, stretching as far as he could past the platform's limits, harsh breaths seething through his teeth. Like a rabid wolf on a chain. "*Medwenna?*"

"Present," Medwenna said weakly; Everin's fingers, curled nearly into fists on the stone, loosened into a flat-palmed spread.

"That's only us two left." Soren stumbled off the platform, caught herself, then stumbled again. She dropped to one knee, panting, raising her head to look at the Commander etching.

Her hand fell to the sheath at her side. And while her gaze had already been misty, dampened with pain, the tears that filled them now didn't look like the aftershocks of agony.

"What if it's a trick?" Medwenna sank on her haunches, trails of moisture streaked down her cheeks as she cowered below the Commander. "What if—?"

"Medwenna." Soren rose to her feet; this time, she kept them. "Sometimes the right thing doesn't have to make sense."

Medwenna stared, unblinking, unconvinced—he could see it in the bob of her throat. "How do you know it's the right thing if it doesn't make sense?"

"I *don't* know." Green eyes flashed to him, then away. Too fast—he couldn't take them in, not the way he wanted to. Not long enough to remember. "You just feel it—and then you follow it."

Medwenna's neck jerked back, as if Soren had flung a stone at her face, not a thought; but when she worked herself free of that flinch, determination took its place.

"It doesn't have to make sense," she whispered.

Both women started walking at the same time—Soren to the Commander, Medwenna to the Empress.

Neither hesitated this time when they stepped on the platforms.

What followed was the single longest second of Elias's life…potentially the last before his death.

A flood of perfect, unmarred green light, no scarlet to be seen. And then—

Saltwater-green eyes narrowed in distaste. "I want to see that ring on the shelf back there."

Jakob sealing their fate with a drunken challenge: "I dare you to kiss Soren."

Spat-out whiskey and a horror-stretched set of scarred lips. "Excuse me?"

That same set of lips dancing with his, smokey-sweet and coated with insults. But wherever he faltered, she shifted with him, helping him find his balance in a waltz he'd never practiced.

Her bloodshot gaze piercing into him, thorny branches laden with poison berries. Her finger striking out like a death blow. "I fight with him, or I fight alone."

That damning finger drawing idle patterns down the stitching on his palm, so gentle it didn't even sting. "I mean it this time—together or not at all."

Her sobs gutting him better than the gaping wound in his stomach, their hands twisted together over it. "I would have said yes."

A black diamond set in a silver band, every glittering carat falling far short of the sparkle in her smile. "Elias Tiberius Loch, I'm saying yes."

When he lurched off the platform, gasping Soren's name like it was the first breath he'd ever taken, she'd already cleared half the chamber despite her stitched-up side. And when she leapt into his arms, crashing them both against the rock, he forgot something far less important—their audience—and kissed her until he'd memorized the taste of her lips all over again.

"If you're waiting for me to kiss you like that," he vaguely heard Matthias say, "you're going to be disappointed, Kess."

"Like I'd want your dried beef breath anywhere near me," Kessen gagged. "Wait—hey, you remember me! Does that mean we won?"

"Depends on how you define *winning*," drawled Everin. "I'm not sure I wanted to remember your ugly mugs."

Soren gripped Elias's face in both hands, lips stretching into a grin as she freed herself from his kiss; she ran her thumb under his eye, bringing attention to a tear that hadn't yet fallen. "Oh, that's *right*—Elias Loch! I remember you now. Didn't you kiss me in a closet once?"

He frowned. "Hmm...I don't think so. Must've been a different Elias Loch."

"Then you must be the one who broke my nose." Her eyes narrowed. "Or as you so eloquently put it, *screwed my nose on sideways*."

"That doesn't sound like me."

"Rewriting history is frowned upon, you know." She jerked her chin behind him. "Medwenna says so."

After this particular ordeal, it didn't seem like a fight worth picking. So instead he set her down, hiding his face in her hair, breathing her in until the world finally set itself right again. Until his mind stopped feeling like a patch of quicksand swallowing up everything that set foot inside.

Until he could whisper the thing he was most sickened to have forgotten, and most relieved to remember: "I love you."

She slipped her arm around his waist, rubbing the small of his back as she leaned her weight into him. Her fingers slid upward to cup the brand marking him as Mortem's, cradling his neck from behind. A claim—a tether. "I love you. And I'd love to tell you that as much as you like once we're *out of here*."

"She's right," Everin said; when Elias finally tore himself away from Soren, he found the others had not reunited quite so...enthusiastically. Matthias had an arm around Kessen's shoulders, knuckling the top of his head; but Everin and Medwenna stood further apart than they had this entire journey, Everin fiddling with his claiming ring, Medwenna firmly focused on scribbling notes in her journal...the journal she currently held upside-down. "I heard something move when the light went green—let's find the exit and keep moving."

A sound enough plan, spoken in even enough tones. But as they all split off, testing the walls for shifting plates or fresh gaps, Elias didn't miss how Everin's eyes followed the historian...or how he kept sneaking glances at the

Empress etching, wearing the discomfited look of a man who'd been caught in a lie.

CHAPTER 64

ANIMA

*W*e'll have to wait and see, Sage had said when she'd first come to after opening herself up to the Blight. *Gods know—not even the gods, sorry Ani—what it might do to you. Or not do to you.*

Even when she'd been a girl, patience had not been her virtue. Virtues were taught, after all, not born; and when one was born with the magic of life, the drippings skimmed from the top of a true god's roiling glory, one needn't learn how to wait.

During the harvest season, Brae always brought home baskets of fruit and vegetables for Mora and Peter to pack up and preserve; the only reason their brood made it through the winter as well as they did. The orchard's owner was a stern but fair young man close to Brae's age, one who'd inherited a pair of sisters to raise after his parents had died; every year he told Brae and the other day laborers to take any fallen or overripe fruit that hadn't spoiled, and every year he managed to frame it just enough like a favor to him that Brae didn't refuse. And every spring, the seeds scraped out and carefully dried by her siblings became Ani's charge.

Seeds; ordinarily the foremost teacher of patience. Seconds to bury, weeks to sprout, months to bear fruit.

But not for her. Seconds to bury, certainly; seconds to sprout. Seconds to bear fruit.

Dangerous work done under cover of night, though she hadn't understood why back then. Mora had only told her that if they did not grow and pick every piece before the sun rose, it would wither the magic feeding the plants, and they would have nothing to show for their work.

Now she knew better—an orchard-worthy bounty springing up around their rat-eaten, ramshackle home would have drawn undue interest from their neighbors. Word of it soon would have spread to the city's Clerics, whose pursuit of *serving those in need* put them on a prowling path through the poorer districts…a patrol that tightened Braeden's hands over Ani's shoulders whenever they cast a second look at her.

The one trait every single Medeis sibling shared: they didn't care for charity, not when Old Sanctaviv's idea of it often meant ripping orphans from the loving arms of their caretakers, promising a better life raised in the church's creche rather than providing for the less fortunate families in the heart of the Empire.

So Ani received the best of everything: new clothes and shoes, the fuller plates, the warmest bed, the frequent visits to the bathhouse in the city proper rather than dunking in the stream behind their house like the rest of her siblings…all necessities to keep the Clerics' eyes from picking her out as a destitute child in need of rescue.

All this, she considered while staring at the coat of dirt clinging to her hands. At the crushed acorn sprinkled in with bark and soil, a squirrel's tiny treasure she'd dug up out of the Olivander's private garden.

"Grow," she whispered, stroking its cracked cap with the tip of her finger. "Please, little one. I want to see you live."

A sweet, vibrant warmth zipped through her wrist, traveling up her veins in swirls of shimmering power. It all gathered up in her fingertip, brightening with every dyad of heartbeats, a *thump-thump, thump-thump* that held her breath in with hope…

And extinguished with a mighty *gush* of air as the light guttered out, no sign of a sprout nosing out of its seed.

Heat tingled in the tip of her nose; she set her handful of hope down with a gentle pat, rubbing her nose fiercely until it finally cooled.

"That's all right," she told the shattered seed. "I understand. It's a scary time to try to grow."

Yes—better to think that way.

Better not to think about how her magic had hardly worked since the Blight's strike at the heart of Arborius.

And better not to think about another absence—the absence of Wolf's voice.

Unlike the first time she'd upset him, he had not shirked his duties even once since she'd siphoned the Blight's ravenous magic from his mother's body. Every morning, he arrived precisely at the moment dawn splashed over the rim of the sky, caulking the horizon line in gilt; every evening, he escorted her back to her room when she declared herself ready to retire. And he never commented—not out loud, anyhow—on how that moment came earlier and earlier every day.

In fact, he rarely commented on anything. At all. For four days, she barely heard him speak, and she had to assume it was meant to be a punishment of some kind for…for…well, honestly, she had no rotting *clue* what for.

She'd answered his prayer; she'd saved his mother. And unless he was more upset about the fingernail marks she'd left in his hands afterward than he was grateful for her makeshift miracle, she couldn't imagine what he might be angry about this time.

But the riot of emotion in his eyes when he said goodnight to her the fifth evening brought that all to a close. When he said, breathless, like he couldn't hold it back any longer, "You're not well."

Her stomach churned like he'd dumped a bucket of wriggling worms down her throat. "I'm not sure what you mean by that."

"The first couple weeks you were here, I had to remind you that *I* needed sleep to wrangle you into your rooms before midnight. Now you can barely get through supper without falling asleep in the soup."

"The consequences of my poor sleeping habits, perhaps? Maybe I should have listened to you earlier."

His jaw ticked. "This is not a joke, Anima. You are not merely tired. I have seen you tired. You are *ill*."

As if agreeing with him the only way it could, the inner structures of her body—the veins, the bones, the muscles and nerves—all buckled like sawed-through scaffolding. A malevolent, aching malaise that piled her beneath brick after brick until her knees threatened to splinter under the weight.

She sagged into the doorframe, grinding her forehead against its grain. But no matter how hard she pushed, she couldn't force a believable fib into her head.

Just a sharper edge to the pain thrumming away in her temple. Like she'd caught a woodpecker by using her skull as a net.

"You should be in the infirmary." Strain underlaid his words, like he was in the one in pain. "You should—"

"I know," she interrupted, bashing her brow once against the doorframe—then regretting it immediately. The woodpecker didn't like that one bit.

Wolf waited. A hunter's patience, won by hours upon hours of waiting for a game beast to show itself, tracking its presence by the smallest tells. A bobbing branch. A rustle of leaves out of tune with the wind.

A tear even she hadn't had the skill to spot before it raced down her cheek, trying to outrun its pursuer.

The hunter dashed its hopes with a featherlight knuckle swept across her cheek.

Ani let her head loll the other way, leaning into Wolf instead of the wall; he eyed her closely as he cradled her cheek, brows drawn tighter than bowstrings.

"If I go in there," she whispered, "I feel like I won't come back out."

His gaze softened. "Ani."

"I know it's different. I know *I'm* different. But my magic…"

She lifted her hand. Let him see the *pop-sputter-fizz* of her failing power.

Wolf watched without a word, without expression. Then he said, "Tell me what I can do to help."

At first, she couldn't think of a single thing to ask for except peace and quiet…solitude, so she could sleep. But if she was honest with herself, that wasn't what she wanted at all.

Not when the warmth of his hand against her face was the first thing that hadn't hurt all day.

"There's a place I've been wanting to visit," she whispered. "In the city, close by. Would you take me there?"

An outright refusal would not surprise her. After all, the walls had proven ineffective at keeping the Blight out. And she'd admitted to being exhausted. And—

"Point the way," he said.

Her heart, already off-kilter thanks to the Blight's attempts to stoke frenzy in her blood, went *beserk*.

She cleared her throat hard to try and jostle the misbehaving thing back into place. "Pointing might not be adequate. But I'll show you."

At least the island had given them the boon of a balmy evening. The unseasonable chill had broken earlier in the day with a brief but harrowing rainstorm; Ani had curled up in her window-seat to watch, letting her sore, fever-sensitive body sink into the iris-patterned cushion. Even when the rain had pelted the glass like hail, she hadn't let it drive her back to her bed.

Now, as they slipped into the heavily wooded portion of the city, the darkwood needles shed water like clouds themselves, bathing the sweat from her brow before it could begin to itch; her toes sank inches-deep into the fallow dirt with every step, earthworms flinging curses at her in impressions rather than words as she collapsed their tunnels; the entire city wore petrichor like fine perfume, a scent that cleansed instead of cloyed.

She could have happily forsaken this little mission, settled in a nearby clump of ferns, and let the island sing her to sleep instead. But with her magic rebelling and a monster on the loose, sleeping in the open seemed foolhardy. Even for her.

The narrow, snakelike path where she led Wolf was a gift granted by Ansari's journal. Ansari had been a skilled carpenter, and though much of her knowledge about her craft had passed on with her, muscle memory had proven itself a powerful tool. It hadn't been long before Ani had tested her host's tough, tool-beaten hands and found they felt most comfortable holding a hammer or chisel.

It had taken much longer for the object of her current focus to come into being. But she still remembered, even through the fog of multiple lives, the heady satisfaction of building something with her own two hands.

That memory's glow, dim as it was, led her straight to her quarry: a small treehouse squatting in a sturdy oak, dwarfed by its darkwood neighbors. The centuries had flaked its pastel paint, but somehow, the weather-treated wood remained in good enough repair that she felt confident it was still structurally sound.

It reminded her of Atlas's seaside cottages, in a way—simple, but sweet. Small, but inviting. Leaf-littered instead of sand-blown, its porch decorated with windchimes instead of seashell strings, it still bore a similar charm.

She ran her hand over the oak's trunk.

She'd done her best to convince herself it wouldn't be here anymore. That centuries of wind and winters and woodcutters would surely have done it in by now. But here it was—and so was she.

And she was not alone. Because when she went to climb the ladder, Wolf stopped her, climbing up first without even checking to see if it would hold his weight; and when she crawled through the entrance herself, he assisted her inside.

Odd, that he didn't seem to be a stranger to this place.

Odder, that his presence didn't stifle the cotton caress of homecoming.

She straightened up, brushing her palms off on her skirt. "You've been here before."

For once, one of her guesses landed true; he nodded, a little sheepish. "Sage found it when we were boys. It's a good stargazing spot."

"Stargazing?" She'd built the treehouse with a lovely view of the sky, but surely there had to be better stargazing spots around the island. Even the library at the top of the Olivander's tree had a clearer view.

"In a manner of speaking." He twisted the fastening on the bay window and pushed open the pane, letting the mild breeze in. Then he settled in the corner, propping his legs up on the wide sill and gesturing for her to join him. "I'll show you."

It didn't unnerve her as much as it should have, clambering onto that sill beside him, her bare toes stopping just shy of his silent-soled boots. She tucked her skirt around her ankles, then settled her crossed arms on her knees, seeking the stars he seemed so mesmerized by. "How? The sun hasn't even set yet."

Wordlessly, like he'd done it a thousand times, he reached over and caught her chin between his thumb and forefinger—then tipped her head down.

Startled laughter burst into flight as it left her lungs; she leaned further forward, and he released her chin, letting her marvel without the distraction of his touch.

Not at the sky, but at the sunset shadows beneath them.

Shadows speckled in blinking strobes of yellow light.

"Fireflies," he said. "Throwing a fete in celebration of the warmer weather, it seems."

Ani held one hand out through the open window, murmuring an invitation—and slowly, those little motes of light began to bob upward.

One by one, fireflies alighted on her fingers until she had a handful of blinking brilliance cupped in her palm; she held her other hand out to join, giggling as a constellation of creatures answered her call. When she held her hands out to Wolf, he withdrew at first, a shadow falling over his eyes; then, when she kept offering her hands, he reluctantly reached out.

"You're right. It's like holding the stars," she murmured, watching as a dozen or so fireflies crossed over to Wolf's waiting hands.

"Bored ones," he chuckled—then, when she shot him a questioning glance, he cracked a smile in her direction. "That's what my ma used to say. Fireflies, they're just stars who got bored of the sky. Wanted to see the world so badly that they didn't fear the drop."

Distant creatures made of starstuff and magic, so desperate to taste the earth that they'd let themselves fall back to it. Over and over and over.

"I don't understand," he said, much softer, "how you see the world so differently."

"Differently?"

"Every little thing brings you joy—you laugh when you skin your knees. You say hello to every butterfly you see. You nearly leap out of your skin when you see a new shade of any color." He waved out the window, scattering his stars to the wind. "How can you still love life that way, even when you've lived so much of it?"

How, indeed.

"I died once," she said.

Like lanterns dimmed on a night of mourning, every single firefly's light went out.

"You've died plenty," Wolf said. It could have been a correction—but when she looked up, seeking the intent in his eyes, she found genuine curiosity waiting instead.

"Not the real kind." She battened down her skirt again to fend off the chill; maybe she'd spoken too soon about the weather changing. "That…that I only did once, and never again."

The fireflies took flight as one, returning to their constellation of friends down below. And in their place, Wolf's hand settled over hers.

"You do not have to tell me," he said, "but I will listen if you do."

She covered his hand with her other, absurdly afraid of losing that tether. Like through the story's telling, death might find a way to make her its prisoner again.

But she told it anyway: a tale so lackluster it could only have been the truth. A carriage crash, the result of a bad wheel and a spooked horse; a body broken so fast she did not even know she was dying. A tale that could have been about any girl, in any city, in this century or any other.

A common, everyday death—the last sort she and her siblings had thought to fear.

"I only knew I was dead when I wasn't anymore," she murmured. His hand, like always, was cold—and though she hated it, knowing why, knowing what it meant, she needed it now. Because if a living body felt cold to her, then she had to be alive, too. "It is…my clearest memory. How cold I was when I woke up. How small the coffin was…and dark. Darker than any night I've lived through." She still couldn't sleep without a lantern or candle lit; she still couldn't bear the touch of satin. "My body *broke* in that carriage, but I felt…nothing. No pain."

Nothing to warn her death was coming—nothing to tell her she needed to fight.

Nothing.

"I will never take it for granted again," she said. "Color. Beauty." She dug her heels into the windowsill until they ached. "Pain."

Understanding folded his mouth down like a dog-eared page. "Let it hurt."

There it was again—the relief of being understood, even without words. "Yes."

"Cold. Darkness. They make you remember death." His finger tapped once against her knee. "What reminds you that you're alive?"

A beat of silence so absolute she could only hear her own heartbeat.

"Scraping my knees," she said. "Walking barefoot through thick grass. Finding new freckles. That feeling on the bottom of your feet after you walk on hot sand." Another silence. "What about you, Wolf Olivander? What makes you feel alive?"

Not once had Wolf's gaze drifted—not once had he looked away. But he did now, taking his hand away as he said, "We ought to get back. It will be proper dark soon, and gods know—er, sorry—*who* knows what tomorrow might bring."

Again, that reckless urge to goad him on struck her like a crop to a racing horse's side. A practice she'd always hated, and one Cassi had outlawed upon the conception of Lapis's yearly equestrian games. An impulse she might have blamed on the essence of chaos infecting her body, had she not been fighting it far longer than she'd been fighting the Blight.

"Can we stay?" she asked instead. "Just until the sun sets?"

Gods, that beautiful smile—even tinged with reluctance—was going to be the end of her. "Of course."

So they sat, and they waited, and they watched—because somehow, she'd managed to build this treehouse in just the right place to peer through a long, narrow slice in the mass of trees. A slice that cut from here to the far-off shoreline.

As the last molten line of sunlight sank below the horizon, a cold breeze barreled into Ani so hard it drove a gasp from her; it cut through her clothes like they were sewn from gossamer and tulle, not wool and linen.

Wolf shrugged off his coat so fast she almost missed it, throwing it around her shoulders; but she definitely *didn't* miss that when she started to protest, he stopped her not with words, but with a finger to her lips.

"Not a word out of you," he said gruffly. "Not unless it's *thank you*."

That's two words, she might've said if she was braver. If speaking against his finger wouldn't feel exactly like kissing it. If the thought of *kissing* hadn't spun her thoughts in such a dizzying circle that she…

What wasn't she saying, again?

She blinked at him, thoroughly shushed. And he blinked back at her like he'd somehow startled himself—like his hand no longer belonged to him.

He was looking at her *rotting lips*.

Abruptly, Wolf shoved himself up, abandoning her—and his coat— without a word.

By the time she shook herself out of her flushed stupor, he'd already reached the bottom of the ladder. And by the time her heels hit the ground, chasing after him, he'd nearly disappeared among the growing patches of night hiding beneath the trees.

Oh no you don't—not this time.

She'd had enough.

Enough wondering what she'd done wrong. Enough worrying she'd upset him despite her mighty effort to avoid it. Enough wondering about his hand on her back and the warmth in his smile and the way he'd just looked at her—or rather, *where* he'd looked.

That is, directly at her mouth.

That is, he'd so unmistakably *looked at her mouth* that even her inexperienced mind could not muster up any explanation beyond the obvious. Even though it was obviously *impossible*.

But she had to know.

"Wolf Olivander!" Her shout climbed the trees, leaping between them in echoing bursts. "Do not take another step."

He stopped dead in his tracks.

"I am done chasing you." Yet she took another step. Another. Closer and closer, as quiet as she could. The closest she'd ever come to hunting, afraid that if she so much as snapped a twig, he'd flee her sight for good. "I am done with this silly guessing game. I am done losing sleep over you—" she was going to regret that one later, but she pushed on, because failing to do so would ruin her point, "—and I am done being made to feel as if I am always doing something wrong!"

A muscle in his shoulder jumped. "You have not—"

She cut her hand through the air; he shut his mouth. "I don't know what I did to make you angry this time, but if you would just tell me, maybe I can…you have to at least let me try to fix it."

"I am not angry at you."

"Well, you're *something*!" She threw her hands out to her sides, wishing she could throw her frustration just as easily. Maybe it would make room for some clarity. "Tell me what I'm doing wrong. You're not angry? All right. Are you—are you annoyed with me? Sad? Are you still ashamed, because I told you it's not—"

"I am not ashamed," he croaked, "and I am not *angry*."

"Then *what*?" Her voice cracked. "*What* am I doing wrong? If you're not angry at me, and you're not ashamed, then I don't understand why you keep running away from me!"

"You make everything too hard."

"Make *what* too hard? I haven't asked you to do anything that you haven't—"

Wolf turned in a frightening flash—but the look on his face, the tears in his eyes…the way his hands reached for her, then jerked away, like he had to *remind* himself to stay away…

Those things frightened her, too. And Ani had always been the kind of creature that reacted to fear with flight.

But this time…this time, something made her plant her feet. Something pulled her core taut, ready to take a blow; something held her head high, ready to push back against what had tried to push her away.

"Say it." The dare she'd been trying to make for days now. "Just *say it*, Wolf."

"Ani…" His voice broke. "*You* make me want to live."

Oh.

Her heart split like a lightning-struck tree.

Oh.

Breathless, she stared at him, waiting—he stared back, mouth bent like a broken bone.

"I'm a dying man—I have always been a dying man. I've accepted that. And now you—" He raked a hand down his bearded face, cursing under his breath. "Now *you* come around, with your pebbles and your smiles and that rotting *giggle* you do—"

Righteous indignation replaced her softer stuff, if only for a moment. She braved another step forward, jabbing a finger into his chest. "You *gave* me those pebbles, in case you've forgotten!"

"And now every time I spy one, do you know what happens?" He tugged her closer by the lapels of his coat, still draped over her shoulders. He stuck one hand into the pocket, muttering curses as he rifled through; she hadn't quite figured out what he was doing by the time he stepped back…

Holding out a handful of colorful, misshapen, utterly perfect stones.

"Do you have any idea," he growled, amber eyes burning into hers, "just how *deep* you have to burrow in a hunter's head to have him watching the ground for rocks instead of tracks?"

Ani stared. And stared. And stared some more. "I don't think I understand."

"You make me want…" A bob of his throat. "You make me want everything I can't have, Annelisa."

Annelisa.

Not Goddess. Not Anima. Not even Ani.

Annelisa.

Her name. *Her* name.

He knew *her name.*

And she knew something, too.

She knew why he'd looked at her mouth.

"Wolf," she whispered, "do you want to kiss me?"

He recoiled at first; a folding of his pebble-packed fist against his chest. A shocked, shameful dart of his gaze from her face to the forest floor.

"Yes," he confessed. "I am…I am sorry."

She took a very, very deep breath. Took a moment to accept that she was about to make a dangerous decision.

Dangerous for their hearts. For their pride. For their health, if she had to guess.

But she still whispered, "I'm not."

And she proved it by stretching on her tiptoes and kissing Wolf Olivander like her rotting *life* depended on it.

With the exception of the smattering of kisses between Soren and Elias she'd witnessed from as much of a distance as possible, she had never (to her memory) kissed a man. So it might have been clumsy. It might have been poorly done. It might have been the worst kiss ever witnessed by the mortal world.

But when she broke it to breathe, lips bitter with chicory and petrichor, she didn't even think about apologizing.

For the first time in this life—perhaps for the first time in *any* life—Annelisa Medeis did not apologize for doing what she wanted.

And Wolf—whose look of shock sharpened into something hungry when he cradled her face, thumb teasing down her temple—did not apologize either.

Instead, he kissed her again. And again. And again.

Each one soft, shy, like they might be his first; each one long, lingering, like they might be his last.

"Annelisa," he whispered. Not like a prayer. Not like worship.

Like he was a man she'd met in a rowdy tavern, repeating her name to make sure he'd heard it right.

Like they were two strangers who'd shared a single dance at a ball, and all he'd really carried from the conversation was her name.

Like…

Like maybe, just maybe, he'd stopped seeing her as a goddess long ago. Like she'd always been human to him, but he hadn't known how to say it.

"Wolf," she marveled. Was this what kissing was *supposed* to feel like, all floating and weightless, like a cloud that got turned around on its way up to the sky? Was it supposed to make her so giddy she could dissolve into a giggle fit at any moment? Or were these some odd, offshoot symptoms of the Blight having its way with her even now?

And did it matter if it was *supposed* to feel like this or not, when it might be her new favorite feeling?

Wolf fussed with the folded collar of his coat, staring at it with single-minded determination. He bit his lip, brows crumpling together in the middle of his worry-lined, frown-scoured forehead. "This is a very bad idea."

"No, that's your coat," she joked weakly. *Damn you, Soren.*

He laughed through a groan; he dragged a hand down his face, staring up at the starry sky and muttering a prayer for mercy. "You're going to be the death of me, woman."

Ani did another brave thing—she set her hand to his bearded chin, guiding his face back down to hers, stroking her thumb just beneath his lip. "Does it hurt?"

He shut his eyes. Leaned into her touch. Barely breathed as he murmured, "Yes."

"Then it isn't death." She hesitated. "Do...do you want me to stop?"

His eyes leapt open again, shining like topazine stars. Like fireflies swimming through honey. "No. Let it hurt."

When their lips met again, the pebbles in his other hand clattered to the ground like rainfall; when he coaxed her closer with both hands around her waist, she clung to the exquisite ache in her chest with all her might, sinking into it with a sigh that unwove a thread of longing she hadn't known existed.

And even though the kiss went on so long she forgot how to breathe...she'd never felt so perfectly, unmistakably alive.

CHAPTER 65
SOREN

While everyone else reckoned with the (objectively horrifying) experience of having their minds raided, stripped of their friends' names and faces, Soren set about a different task: finding a place for her and her battlemate to sleep in *private* for once on this claustrophobic cave-fest of a mission.

After all, amnesia was sort of her thing. Didn't seem worth having a crisis over. Not when she had at least three others already lined up in the queue.

And sure, there'd be a toll to pay when the stomach-swirling memory of Elias staring at her like a stranger finally caught up; there'd be nightmares had and reassurances needed and times where she lay awake at night reciting his full name (Elias Tiberius Loch), his favorite food (his mother's molasses bread), his favorite color (black, she was pretty sure—maybe red? This was a bad time to realize she'd never asked) and every other little thing she knew about him until she tired herself out.

But not tonight. Tonight, she had exactly one thing she needed to say to her battlemate.

So when she finally found a small alcove a few dozen feet down the next tunnel, she ignored that it would have been kinder to offer it to Medwenna, who had yet to look Everin in the face since the trial; it would have been smarter to offer it to Kessen and Matthias, both of whom seemed intent on keeping the whole mountain awake with their forced laughter and banter tonight.

Instead, she crept over to Elias, tickled the back of his ear until he looked up from his holy book, and murmured, "Follow me. And bring your bedroll."

For once, even though it was one of those orders he often told her were *"just vague enough to mean that your plan is probably going to get us both killed,"* he didn't argue; in fact, he'd never obeyed a command from her faster. In the span of a second, he'd gathered both his bedroll and her hand, leaning in to stamp a kiss against her cheek. "Lead the way."

Gods, that chess game must've really shaken him up.

They ducked out of the cavern through the cramped, half-crumbled exit she'd discovered while pretending to help Medwenna search for edible plants; the one cluster of fungus she'd pointed out had promptly been identified as highly toxic, dashing her chances of being hailed as a botanical prodigy. But that had always been her elder sister's bag, anyway.

Thinking of Jericho made her sick—in heart and in body. So she kicked her brain back into safer territory.

"If this is your idea of a romantic rendezvous," said Elias, reminding her that she was on a mission of her own, "then I have a few notes."

"Oh, perfect! Do me a favor: find some paper, write them down, and then—"

Elias sighed. "Let me guess—shove them up some unpleasant orifice?"

"I was going to say *eat them raw without salt*, but if you have a preference…"

"*Is* this your idea of a romantic rendezvous?"

"Stop it," she whined. "You're ruining the surprise."

"What surprise?"

"It doesn't—you can't *ask*—" Was he *smirking*? "I'm going to murder you in your sleep."

He was definitely smirking, the jackass. "That's not a very good surprise."

"Would've been better if you hadn't made me tell you."

Shadow bruised the cave walls as they bickered hand-in-hand, brackish blue and soot-gray dappling the dimpled stone. Putting their faith in an offshoot from the main cave system wasn't the wisest idea—even if it was *her* idea—but no nefarious spirits appeared to tempt them away from their goal. No strange plants blew poisonous pollen into their eyes. And the only song that greeted them as they stepped into the alcove was a chorus of sleepy chirps from the bats sleeping just outside its entrance.

"Here." She let go of Elias's hand to dig into her pack; she pulled out one of the Lapisian lamps and cracked its core, shaking it until the alcove blushed with soft pink light. "Well? Is this romantic enough for you?"

On its own, a damp slice of open space surrounded by bats might not have been the ideal place for this sort of evening. But she'd spent nearly an hour sweeping away cave debris so neither stone nor creature would bite into their backs; she'd sacrificed her own bedroll to sop up the groundwater puddling the floor, then abandoned it by the fire Everin had made so it could dry overnight.

And when she set the Lapisian lamp on a shallow shelf in the stone, the enchanted light spilling over their clean, quiet chamber, Elias murmured, "It's perfect."

Warmth chased the mountain chill out of her chest. She kissed his shoulder, rubbing below his shoulder blades. "Almost. Help me finish it?"

In a symphonized rush, they set up their own camp: Elias's bedroll flung across the floor, their packs balled up with spare clothes pushed to the front to make half-decent pillows, and her spare blanket tossed down on top to make up for the extra layer of warmth they were losing by leaving the fire behind.

Soren stepped back and surveyed their handiwork, hands on her hips. It wasn't exactly one of the blanket forts they used to construct in her room or in the barracks some nights, ignoring the hoots and hollers from their fellow soldiers about *getting a room*, but it would do.

"A damned sight better than camping in the snow," Elias said—right on her heels as always, even in the mind.

"Language," she scolded; when he laughed, she elbowed him. "What? I mean it! I think Kallias was a bad influence on you."

"More Raquel, really," he said. "You should've heard the two of them getting into it."

She wished with her whole heart that she had. She'd only caught glimpses of them in the blur of her reunion with her brothers, and by then, they weren't exchanging heated barbs of any sort; only a set of mismatched expressions clashing when their gazes met, troubled scowls from Raquel and tired smiles from Kallias.

She ripped those thoughts from her mind like tearing her tongue from a frozen lamppost. "Well, whoever's responsible, I'm still not sure you should be kissing me with that mouth."

His snort echoed loudly in the small space, and he hooked an arm around her waist, towing her in to try and do exactly that; she bent back so far she nearly lost her balance, arching her neck away.

"No, no, no—don't you dare infect me with your unclean words. I am a holy woman now, if you recall. The vessel of a goddess."

Elias choked on incredulous laughter. "Shut your mouth."

She snapped straight, pushing her fingertips into his chest. "*Make* me."

His eyes narrowed.

Uh oh.

Before she could run, he closed in, hand up—he covered her mouth as he backed her against the wall, a thrill shooting through her from sternum to sole as he pinned her there, a fire of a different sort guttering in his gaze.

"Shut," he drew out, the tip of his nose brushing hers, "Your. Mouth."

She blinked at him, embers popping in her chest…and stuck her tongue out against his palm.

He snatched it away with another curse—one she crushed between their lips as she tugged him down by the collar, cackling as he gripped her wrists and disentangled her arms from around his neck.

"You're a menace," he groaned.

"And you love it."

"I don't. It's pretty irritating, actually."

"You *looove* it."

Just like she loved the exasperated grin that creased the bridge of his nose and deepened the scar on his chin; just like she loved how he always drew her in closer before he kissed her, mapping the shape of her face with his thumb, holding her without having her. Just like she loved how he hesitated for a beat after every shift, watching her face for the slightest suggestion that he'd gone too fast, gone too far.

And she loved that when she breathed, "Make me forget everything *but* you," he did not hesitate *at all* before he lifted her clean off the floor, slipping his hands under her thighs as she wrapped her legs around his waist, and pushed her flush to the wall.

Stone scraped against her bruised back, but the pain barely distracted her; her mind had other things to focus on. Like Elias's hand running up her thigh, her hip, beneath the hem of her shirt; like the small sound he made in the back of his throat when she broke away to kiss the hollow of his throat instead, lazily exploring the column of his neck until she found his lips again.

Every touch lit her up. Every kiss untied a string of tension she'd been carrying for gods-knew how long. Every murmur of her name from his lips made a promise that he'd never have to ask for it again.

But there were other promises they needed to discuss. So with a mighty effort—so mighty she almost gave herself a concussion smacking her head back against the wall—she abandoned the kiss with a gasp, tapping out with a triple-knock of knuckles against his wrist.

He eased her to the ground without complaint, trailing his thumb over her flushed cheek, breathing unevenly; with a dumbfounded shake of his head, he rasped, "*So* much better than a supply closet."

An awful wheezing sound came out of her—not attractive. "Is it?"

"At least it doesn't smell like mop water."

She set her hand over his heart; it thudded beneath her palm, swift but even. Not the same lurching mess as hers, which stumbled over every beat like it had downed a barrel of whiskey in two draws.

Hopefully he wasn't listening to it.

She tucked her head beneath his chin. "Marry me."

His fingertips teased the length of her spine; her skin broke out in goosebumps. "Right now?"

A joke they'd tossed back and forth plenty since his proposal. But she wasn't joking this time. "At your earliest convenience."

"I'm booked up with war-work at the moment, but once that's all over—"

Her throat cinched shut. She could barely squeeze out one whispered word: "No."

Elias frowned. "What?"

She fisted her hands in his shirt, nerves skating across her bones. "No. Not after the war. Not after *anything*, okay?"

Her voice bowed under the weight of unshed tears, the same tension as a bone bent just shy of its breaking point.

There it was—trauma come to see its toll paid. But this fear wasn't about forgetting. It was about remembering.

In forgetting her duty to her kingdom, she'd remembered there was something she was entirely unwilling to give up. Something that had not yet—but could still be—demanded of her, if she did not set it in stone now.

She'd hoped these tears would wait their turn longer; she hadn't wanted to do this weepy. But she meant it…she wasn't waiting for anything. Not even for the lump in her throat to dislodge itself.

Elias's face dropped, alarm flaring in his gaze as he cradled her cheek. "Hey, smartass, wait…what just happened? Where'd you go?"

Nowhere—not this time. But gods knew where she'd go next, and when it happened…

"I'm not waiting for the next goddess or battle or depths-cursed *mind spell* to take you away," she said, slipping her arms around his neck. "Or me. Or both of us. Whatever happens next, wherever we go…I'm going as your wife."

She knew that her sensible, tradition-bound battlemate would argue. That he would remind her they had no officiant or witnesses, that their families weren't here, that they had neither dress nor suit, let alone a set of wedding bands to seal the whole—

"I thought you'd never ask."

The mental pen she'd been using to scribble out her argument paused. "Huh?"

"Only if you're sure, though." Gods, she almost had to *squint* against the joy gleaming in Elias's ebony gaze. "You're sure? Not about *me*, smartass, don't make that face—I mean the wedding."

"We can do that part later." And they *would*, because she'd take any excuse to wear an exorbitantly expensive dress and show her husband off to everyone she knew. "That's only the party. The marriage, that's just making promises to each other, right? We can do that on our own."

His gaze softened; his thumb traced her cheekbone. "Together or not at—"

"No," she interrupted again. His eyebrows shot up nearly to his hairline. "Not that one."

Now those thick brows came together, furrowed with frustration. "Why not?"

"Because we broke it, Elias—both of us." It almost hurt to keep her fingers loose around his neck; to stop herself from bracing the bone. "We need new vows—better ones."

A clean slate. A new start.

His gaze softened. "Whatever vow you ask of me, I'll swear it."

"No more sacrifices," she said immediately. "No more of this *I die to save you, you die to save me* game. We're a gods-damned *team*, and we're going to start acting like it. We're not leaving each other to save each other. We have one goal, us together—nothing takes us apart. Not ever again."

Not a simple vow, to forsake protecting each other at the expense of themselves. But he'd asked—and this was what she needed.

"Never apart," he agreed softly, squeezing her fingers. Lifting her hand. Kissing her ring. "Never again."

"Can you swear it?" Not simple for either of them, but still harder for him than her—he'd always had an unhealthy leaning toward martyrdom, and he made a good one, at that. He had the right face for it, all mournful eyes and stoic jaw and kissable lips. (Maybe not that last one.) But she asked it anyway; she *begged* it anyway, because of all the vows they had once and would now swear to each other, this one mattered the most. "And mean it?"

Elias gazed at her for a long moment, unreadable, unbending.

Then he dropped to his knees, both of them, still holding her hand.

"I swear it," he murmured. "By the bones I broke for your sake. By the breath I thought would be my last. I swear I will never leave you behind—not in death, not in life. Never apart. Never again."

She sucked in her bottom lip before it could quiver—but judging by the saltwater taste, she was too late to hide the tears.

One after the other, her knees hit the floor, cap to cap with his. She lowered their joined hands onto their knees.

"I swear it," she said, "by the soul I nearly sacrificed to save you. By the voice I gave up for the chance to hear yours again." That voice wobbled now, like it was still getting its sea legs back, but she prodded it through the rest of its steps: "I will never leave you behind. Not even to save your pious ass."

"Soren," he laughed.

"I know, I know—" She sniffled sharply, cursing as she tried to dry her tears against her own shoulder. "Let me salvage a bit of my pride, all right?"

"You're the one who wanted this."

Wanted, no—she *needed* this. Before they found out what the last trial might have in store.

Whatever it would demand of her, she could not do it if she feared Elias would sacrifice himself to spare her the blow. Because if she believed that, she would hesitate...

And her kingdom could not afford for her to hesitate. Not this time.

His hand settled over hers. Over the ring he'd carried over borders and battlefields and the shards of a broken vow spilled over a temple floor.

"There is no part of me that isn't already yours," he confessed. "I don't know what else to promise."

When he lifted her hand and bent to kiss her ring, Soren swept aside the hair that fell over his brow. "There is one thing you haven't given me yet."

"If you say something about my socks, smartass, I swear to Mortem—"

"Your name."

Elias looked up at her swiftly. "My—" He caught himself; took a breath. "You're a princess—you're an Heir. I take your name."

"I know." She worried her lip. "But I have two—Atlas and Nyx. And I know I've been using Atlas, but it doesn't sit right, and neither does Nyx. I'm both, but that also makes me neither. I don't want to be reminded of who I'm not when someone says my name—I don't want to hesitate every time I introduce myself. I want my name to be *mine*. So promise me that—promise it's mine."

Out of all the allegiances that laid claim to her heart, this was the only one she had chosen. Had *fought* for. And she didn't give up what was hers.

"Besides," she added, fighting for good humor, "don't tell me you want to share a name with Finnick Atlas."

"It's Kal's name too," he said without blinking. "And yours, if you want it. I'd be honored to take it."

Oh, he had to stop making her cry.

"I love you." She kissed him just to prove it. "But I mean it—I want this for *me*."

If she'd had a name of her own, maybe it would have been different—like Medwenna, who'd chosen to keep her own name when she married her late husband, then had chosen to keep her late husband's name even when he'd passed on. But all she had were two kingdoms, two crowns—two places that would never stop vying for her whole heart. A war she'd never win if she chose to name herself by one or the other.

She'd chosen Atlas for a time, when she'd needed to anchor herself in the life she'd forgotten. And it had served her well enough. But it wasn't Atlas itself that had made the name matter.

What mattered was the choice—and if there was one thing she *knew* she wanted to be, it was this.

Ancient oil and uncomfortable truths aside, the time would come soon when Atlas had to be everything…but that time wasn't here yet. And if she became this *now*, if she became this before she became queen…

They couldn't take it from her then, could they?

"I want to be Soren Loch," she promised. "Can you promise that?"

He didn't at first. At least, not out loud. But the ferocious, utterly breathtaking kiss he crushed against her lips certainly *felt* like some kind of oath.

"You have whatever you want from me," he murmured. "My name's no different."

She shut her eyes. "Say it."

"Soren Loch." His voice broke as he kissed her between her eyes. "I take you as my wife—today and tomorrow and every day after."

"Elias Loch." Joy fizzed in her fingertips as she pulled him down for a better, longer kiss. "I take you as my husband—today and tomorrow and every day after."

"Never apart…"

"Never again," she finished, all laughter gone as even the bats and frogs and other cave creatures fell silent. Only ancient stone to witness the newest tether being forged between her heart and his…a tangle they'd woven themselves.

One not even the gods could break.

CHAPTER 66

ELIAS

"Good mooorning, lovebirds!"

Even Everin's taunting singsong couldn't dampen his spirits this morning—not with his wife tucked under his arm, sleepy-eyed and warm in spite of the stabbing chill in the air, his shirt draping from her shoulders and clinging to her hips. Not with his favorite of her new titles still turning circles in his head, yet to tire of doing backflips through his thoughts.

Soren Loch. His *wife*.

She scowled at Everin, but a yawn ruined it; she twisted to nestle her face into his shoulder. "It's too early for your stupid face."

Elias guided his wife's steps toward the campfire—and the smell of coffee coming from the kettle strung over the flames. "You could always break his nose again. Might make his face look smarter."

"Please don't," chorused Kessen and Matthias—Kessen added, "He complained the entire rest of the voyage about how bad his nose ached. Don't do that to me again. I'm innocent in all this."

Elsewhere in the cavern, the chorus of frogsong rose—like even the slimy creatures cosseted away in crags and puddles and hollow places were laughing in Kessen's face.

More noticeable than their racket was Medwenna's silence; she sat by the fire with the others, a book in her lap and a blanket wrapped around her shoulders, but there was a sleepless crease to her eyes—a tired fog over her face. Even the cadence of her blinks seemed strange, staggered between four rapid and one so long he thought she'd fallen asleep sitting up.

"Were you up all night?" he asked.

"Not *all* night," she and Everin said at once—Medwenna defensive, Everin disparaging, like they'd already had this conversation…and possibly an argument that followed. The air between them smelled of smoke and frost—the kind manifested by heated words and chilly aftermaths.

He traded looks with his wife—who had a name, and maybe one day he'd remember to start using it again—who fussed with her most rebellious curl to guard the dart of her gaze toward Kessen. *I'll ask.*

He scratched the corner of his chin with one finger, then two. *Alone?*

Her lips knotted one way, then the other; she patted his side twice, and he lifted his arm away, leaving her free to swagger over to Kessen. While she distracted him with questions regarding his vision—*So, that tunic with that jerkin…how long have you known you were colorblind?*—he stuck his hands in his pockets and shuffled up to the fire.

"That trial was a beast." He tossed the words over the flames like a spatter of oil, waiting to see where it caught and spread.

"Hardly." Everin brandished his axe as he circled the fire, nudging the logs with its head. "Confusing as it gets, but hey…no blood, no breach, right?"

"Come again?"

"No harm, no foul," Medwenna translated, turning her page. Her spectacles slid down to the tip of her nose; she swore colorfully, shoving them back up.

This time, he accidentally caught Matthias's gaze; the man just put his hands up, standing with a mighty stretch. "I'll go make sure they're not dueling to become the supreme redhead."

Don't leave me to clean up your mess! he wanted to hiss. But Matthias fled, leaving Elias sitting between the pacing prince and the stewing historian.

Fantastic.

Whatever he'd done to get stuck playing liaison to pairs of people on the verge of killing or kissing each other…as soon as he found a passable altar, he'd lie facedown and beg forgiveness until Mortem freed him from it. Raquel and Kallias had been enough of a gauntlet to navigate, and he'd only survived it at all because he was reasonably sure Safi—his Artemisian cousin, a weaponsmith with no willingness to leave things unspoken—had started meddling of her own accord.

"It must have been a difficult weight to balance," he offered to Medwenna, "remembering the loss of your husband all over again."

She flipped another page. "Grief doesn't disappear with memory; only the frame that gives it shape. I never put the weight down."

Everin abruptly cast his axe aside; it clanged against scattered stones as it hit the ground. "I'm going to fill the canteens."

Medwenna flipped another page—she couldn't possibly be reading that fast, genius or not—and said nothing as Everin stormed toward the cave-creek that hemmed the outskirts of the cavern, droplets scattering from his wet hair…taking a swig from a canteen that certainly didn't *look* like it hadn't been filled yet.

Elias knew a thing or two about grief and the guilt that often accompanied it—knew a thing or two about fighting feelings one had no right to feel, as well. One he recognized in Everin's hooded glare and stalking gait; the other lived in Medwenna's pinched lips and misty, bloodshot eyes.

"Medwenna," he ventured, "I don't know what happened with you two during the—"

"You shouldn't, as it is *none* of your business." The anger in her voice was an actor; it mimed the motions of rage, but behind the paint and performance, sadness couldn't hide its true face.

Sometimes grief needed its space. But oftentimes, what grief needed was an outlet—a way to get from the heart to the head. If no one gave grief a place to go, it made one all on its own. And that escape rarely ended prettily.

When he settled cross-legged on the woven mat beside Medwenna, she curled her shoulder away, hunching over her book—hiding behind it.

"Did you say something you regret?" he prompted.

"No." She shut her eyes, dropping her head straight into her book—nose dug into the spine. "Not during the trial. We had…we had a hard night after, both of us. All of us," she amended hastily. "I'm sure Soren has more experience, what with all she went through, but…the fear of mental invasion is hammered into Tallisian minds from the time we're very young."

Elias found Soren across the way as she chatted with Matthias and Kessen, her arms swinging akimbo. Careless ease floated from her like drifting robes of lace, confidence caked into her skin like the expensive Lapisian creams and powders she and some others in the company sometimes splurged on, making each other over in the bathing rooms until they were all giggling like children.

"She's coping," he said, "but nothing prepares you to realize how easily it can all go away…everything that makes up the core of you. How much of it is bound up in memory."

How that realization could spur someone to throw a certain finger toward propriety and sense and long-established understandings. How it could make a princess and a soldier swear marriage vows in the belly of a monstrous mountain…or make Everin say whatever he'd said to upset Medwenna, whose bond with the prince *alone* proved her feathers were nearly impossible to ruffle.

Medwenna peered up from her paper shield, eyes wet and miserable. "I'm afraid I wanted to forget."

"No one can fault you for that." Gods knew he'd wished for such an easy solution to his grief when he was wading through the worst of it. He took one of the chipped mugs Matthias had brought along and poured himself some coffee, trying not to grimace at the watered-down, damp-dirt scent. *Function over taste.* "I think if we were honest, if the chance to forget our deepest agonies dropped into our laps, we'd all take it in a heartbeat."

She sighed, clapping her book shut and setting it aside. "Everin said the same."

Elias grimaced. "I take it back, then. You're a terrible person."

Her laugh was nothing short of miserable. "We fought. We never fight."

How? was his first thought. Luckily, he had great practice waiting to speak until the second thought came rolling in. "A fight isn't worth agonizing over. Trust me—Soren and I fight all the time. Hasn't done any lasting damage."

Medwenna fussed with her braid, twining it through her fingers. "You two make it look so easy."

Hot coffee funneled straight into his lungs; like anything else would when a scalding drink got spilled on it at exactly the worst time, his lungs leapt in the wrong direction, almost splitting his sternum with a laugh that blistered into a racking hack.

"What happened?" Medwenna struck his back as he doubled over, coughing and spluttering, coffee splattering over the ground. "Was it too hot? You—"

"Fine," he wheezed. "Just…picked the worst time to laugh. We were the furthest thing from *easy*—we still are. But—"

A rumbling beneath the skin of the mountain, cracks and divots erupting like goosebumps.

The logs collapsing beneath their own weight, sparks flying like the spittle flung by wrathful screams.

A battle cry that splintered like a bone bent backward, hurtling into the cavern just ahead of its maker; a streak of gold and silver flung to the floor, clawing itself into the cavern before a cloud of slate-gray dust exploded out of the opening, swallowing Everin Arden whole.

Medwenna screamed. Her book—abandoned so swiftly its pages fanned out, the spine cracking—caught the shower of sparks from the destroyed fire, paper penned with timeless knowledge curling into scraps of ashen void. "*Everin!*"

Matthias and Kessen, both closer by half, dove heedlessly into the dust cloud; Soren had hit the ground too, sprawled on her seat, but before his heart could climb too far up his throat, she flipped over and crawled until her heels found traction; she sprang up with a lurch, arrowing straight to him.

"I think the tunnels are collapsing!" she panted.

A brief burst of pain struck the top of his skull; he looked down just in time to watch a scrap of stone clatter to a halt in the dust.

Dread flooded his middle, sweeping his stomach upward, spearing it against his ribs.

"I think it might be worse than that," he croaked—just as the cavern began to quake with a vengeance.

"Time to go!" shouted Matthias; he and Kessen stumbled back into view, dusted in ashen powder from head to toe, hauling Everin with them; the prince was conscious, balancing on one foot. His other leg dragged across the ground, ankle turned just far enough to bring a surge of bile to Elias's throat; simmering scarlet streaked the stone as they hauled him along, bone dust cut with blood.

Medwenna overshot them, running too fast to stop; she backpedaled rapidly, twisting in like a thrust dagger to take Everin herself. She shook her head at Kessen and Matthias's protests. "I have him! Run—don't slow down, don't look up, don't look back, just *run!*"

The men took her order like any good soldiers would. But when they barreled past, neither looking back, Everin tried to writhe out of her grip. "You need to put me—"

"*Don't,*" Medwenna barked—the sternest Elias had ever heard her. The heaviest he'd ever heard her Tallisian twang. "Try and wriggle out and I'll sling your sorry skin over my shoulder!"

"You couldn't."

Medwenna cursed when Everin's weight dragged one of her shoulders down, almost tripping them both, gravity proving a point. But she hauled him back up, bracing her temple against his as she panted, " "Don't you tell me what I can't do."

Everin didn't. Not while Elias was watching, anyway—which wasn't long, because then Soren yanked his arm so hard it nearly dislodged from its socket. "Follow their lead, jackass!"

He obeyed—and not a moment too soon. As they hurtled through the massive cavern, the kind of rain people had nightmares about began to fall; tapered stalactites plunged down like swords raised to stab, one wayward flinch from dealing death in a single blow. Chunks of stone fell like hail cast down by bloodthirsty, bone-craving clouds.

The Sanctum Infidelium was on the warpath. And it had set its sights on the foolish few who'd begun to believe they had a shot at success.

"Where are we going?" he shouted as he and Soren ran.

But the mountain seemed to mistake the question as being directed to it; because with a cacophonic, thunderous roar, a seam in the stone—formerly invisible—separated from the wall, grinding upward like a drawbridge being cranked.

"I think the mountain wants us to go that way." Soren pointed—then jerked her hand back when a stalactite tried to spear through it. "*Pits!*"

He didn't have a great feeling about following the lead of the murderous mountain. But they didn't exactly have a better choice.

He and Soren were first to the exit, hands twined, anchored to each other. But in the exact moment Soren crossed the threshold, him half-running, half-lunging behind her—

Stars spun through his head, a blizzard of silver and white blinding him. And for a moment that felt like forever, he knew nothing but silence.

"Sound off! One!"

The words swam into his ears like salmon wriggling through a silted riverbed, the edges so eroded he could barely make sense of them.

"Two," Medwenna panted.

"Three," Kessen and Soren said at the same time; after a beat, Kessen growled and said, "Gods, I can never have *anything*, just—*four*."

Silence followed. Then a hand on his shoulder, shaking him—a hand on his cheek, gentle at first, then increasing in speed as it slapped at him. "Elias? Elias—open your eyes."

He tried; something gummed them together. He couldn't pry them apart.

"Elias!" Soren's cry thinned, shrill with panic. "Elias, open your damned—"

"Can't," he groaned; as he fumbled for the floor, trying to shove himself up, he could've sworn his elbow creaked like a rusty door hinge. "Tried. Am I still five?"

"You're an *idiot*," she fumed.

He licked his lips—then spat, tongue powdered in the taste of minerals and dirt. "Sorry."

Trickling water. The rough, rapid dab of cloth against his eyes. "Try now," Soren said. "You had dust all over."

He blinked—sneezed—then blinked again. Then sneezed again. Pressure pounded in his head. "Ow."

His wife dropped to her seat in front of him, covering her eyes with one hand; concern cleared his mind like a hand swiped over a foggy window. "You're okay?"

"I'm good," she said unsteadily. "You just...scared me for a minute there."

"Sorry," he repeated.

"Good."

Elias gathered her free hand as he assessed the space; they all sat in a small, cylindrical chamber, its column-like walls cut from volcanic glass. Smokey veins branched through its depths, distracting him just enough that he didn't realize in time that his was the last in the count—that no one had ever said *six*.

But then Matthias made a mistake.

A swivel of his head. A thunderbolt of alarm striking his gaze. No pause to consider the consequences before he opened his mouth and coughed out a single breathless question:

"Where's Ev?"

They all looked between themselves, silently counting. Seeking.

Five faces. Not six.

"He's here," Medwenna stated. She got up, dusting herself off, rotating in a slow circle. "He's here somewhere. Everin?"

None of them dared test that ironclad authority in her voice; nor did emotion seem keen to trespass on her face, frozen over with a clean sheet of calm.

But there was no ignoring the silence that followed her call.

"He's here," she said again—not fact this time. Insistence. *Demand.* "He has to be here, I had him, I had him so he has to be…" She tore her dust-matted hair back from her brow, intelligent gaze clouded, bewildered—like she'd finally come across something she couldn't comprehend. Like Everin's absence made no sense to her. *"Everin?"*

Everin bolted to attention when he heard Medwenna's *footsteps.* If her screaming his name couldn't summon him now…

As if Elias had said the word *run* out loud, as if he'd given it as an order, Medwenna lunged toward the slab of stone that had opened in the wall—the slab that was now sinking, slowly but surely, back to the floor.

Within a minute, maybe less, that slab would fall, closing them all in; closing Everin out. But between his injured leg and whatever had halted his flight with the rest of them, gods knew what state he'd be in. Medwenna would have to haul his greater weight along with her.

She'd never make it back in time.

Even Everin's burly Second and wiry Third wouldn't make it—and Matthias, at least, knew it. Because when Kessen bolted for the exit on Medwenna's heels, Matthias shot his hand out and dragged Kessen back by the collar, thrusting him toward the back of the chamber…then going for Medwenna next.

But she did not stop. Not when Matthias snagged her around the waist, tugging her back—not when Kessen, already sobbing in awful, broken heaves, leapt to block her path as she fought and kicked and writhed to get free. Her single-minded focus had honed into a maddened stare, expression completely detached from the feral frenzy of her movements; that stare stuck on the collapsing cavern, her lips moving rapidly as if reading something aloud.

Or chanting Everin's name, still waiting for him to answer.

Soren moved in, elbowing the two Tallisians out of her way—when Medwenna tried to take the opening, Soren caught her, bending her head against Medwenna's temple and muttering in her ear.

Elias had no idea what she said. But when she pushed Medwenna back into Matthias's arms, the archeress abandoned the fight; she folded against

Matthias like she'd lost all her strength in one blow, befuddled gaze still locked on the falling door.

Then Soren looked at Elias.

Are you with me? her stare asked.

Medwenna wouldn't make it. Matthias and Kessen wouldn't make it.

They wouldn't, either. But Soren was going to try—for whatever reason, for Everin, she was going to try.

No, you reckless, insane woman, was what he wanted to say. *No, absolutely not, don't even think about it.*

But he knew better. And so did she.

So when *she* broke for the tunnel, not even a second wedged between her first step and his.

CHAPTER 67

SOREN

Soren Loch—gods, even about to die, she loved how that sounded—had done plenty of reckless, foolhardy things in her life.

Hiding behind curtains to eavesdrop on important meetings, cloistered away with her brother at her side and hot chocolate in her hands. Tiptoeing into an Atlas general's tent with Jira, holding her breath for so long she'd nearly fainted, painting obscenities on the canvas while the heavy sleeper snored on. Throwing a butterknife at a fickle king's drink-soaked head.

Throwing herself underneath a slab of stone mere inches from pounding into the ground didn't make the top of the list. But it certainly broke the top five, demoting the time she'd gone skinny-dipping in a near-frozen lake to number six.

Rocks sank their teeth into her stomach as she skidded underneath, Elias just slightly behind; she cried out through gritted teeth as the stone lip skimmed the top layer of skin off her back, her nails bending painfully when she clawed herself past the threshold.

A rash of pain spread over her back, inflamed and itchy; still preferable over crushed bones. She rolled to see Elias already scrambling to his feet, wild eyes stretched to the whites, focused on the crumbling ceiling.

"You take me to the nicest places," he deadpanned.

"Shut up." She shoved up on her hands and knees; about twenty feet or so back from the door, a lump of torn cloth and bloodied golden hair lay unnervingly still, coated in dust and debris.

"Everin!" The name tickled her scratchy throat; she coughed it out the second time.

Nothing.

When Soren laid hands on the prince, she lost her own breath as she felt his back rise; shallow, staggered, but definitely a breath.

"Everin!" she barked. "Sound off!"

A low groan. He lifted his head, squinting at her, his glare a haze of silver fog. "Fancy meeting you here, Princess."

Her eyes watered—from all the dust, in case anyone was wondering. "Let me guess—you figured it was better if your empty head took a hit instead of Medwenna's?"

Her name swept a layer of fog from his cloudy gaze; he repeated it silently, mouthing it with no voice. He pushed his palms against the floor, struggling to rise as he panted, "She okay?"

She ducked under his arm, shrugging them both up with a thrust of her legs—and a breathless prayer of thanks to Ani, yet again, for the gift of strength returned. "What do *you* think, dumbass?"

"I think you're *insane*," he choked. "Why'd you come back?"

Because I know how it feels to lose your best friend, and I'm not putting Medwenna through that.

Because I'm definitely not getting an army out of your kingdom if you die.

Because you're my *friend, and I'm not losing you, either.*

"Watch out!"

A slice of core darkness rived above their heads, splitting a falling stone in two.

Her racing heart jumped into her throat belatedly; she held her hand out to Elias, who stood over her and Everin with his scythes crossed above their heads. "It's my turn with the scythes."

"Not the time for jokes!"

Well, good thing it wasn't a joke. The second they dug themselves out of this death trap of a mountain, she was going to get her hands on a rotting *armory* of Artemisian weapons, no matter what it cost.

Everin's head sagged as Soren dragged him up from the ground, flirting with another loss of consciousness; his boots scuffed against the stone, injured ankle trailing limply behind as Soren hoisted him toward…well, she'd figure that out in a moment. Right now, her foremost worry was dodging those falling stalactites.

"Elias!"

"Looking." He threw his gaze up to the ceiling, then across the cavern— he pointed ahead through the haze of dust, shouting, "There! Go!"

Whatever he saw, she didn't. Nor did she dither even a moment before following his direction, because whatever he saw, she *wouldn't*—not with Everin dropping anchor on her own sprint and a cloud of sweat and dust and exertion fogging her eyes up.

The only thing certain to get them killed in here was hesitation. Especially when her next step broke the skin of the stone, sheaves cracked and peeling away in flakes of sediment, revealing ash-veined glass underneath.

And even worse…something molten red far below.

So that was what Medwenna had meant when she'd called this mountain a sister to Mount Igniquit…the damned *Fire-Breathing Mountain.*

"I see it," Elias snapped before she could call out—he shoved her another step ahead, paying no heed to the crumbling floor. "Don't stop!"

Even when she reached the wall, she didn't see the hope he'd promised her until she tumbled to one knee before it: a thin seam in the wall, also glazed with volcanic glass.

Shadows flitted behind its crystal screen—three of them.

With a whoop of relief, she pressed her mouth to the thin glass and shouted, "We've got him! Help me break through!"

A flurry of curses and commands later, an axe plunged through the opening; its wielder shaved loose glass from the sides with keen efficiency, followed by a cliff-beaten hand shoving through the gap. The remaining shards hung like loose teeth barely hanging on to their roots; still, they took some hearty shreds of flesh from Matthias's arm as he reached with all his might.

"I," he seethed when Everin roused enough to take his hand, "am going to *slaughter* you."

"Yeah, yeah," Everin slurred, his grime-coated face contorting in pain as Matt dragged him in, glass raking his shoulders. "Heard it bef—"

"*Everin!*"

At Medwenna's scream, Everin kicked to life, shoving himself the rest of the way through; and though Soren couldn't see what happened next, Medwenna's strangled cry of relief didn't make much of a mystery of it. Nor the snarled, muffled command of a king-to-be that followed: "Kess, help Soren through!"

Kessen crashed down on the other side of the gap; his skinny arm pushed through without a scratch, and he grinned with all his teeth as he said, "You're a badass, you know that?"

She laughed hard enough that her lungs cramped. "I know."

"Grab my hand—you got him, now we've got you."

"Happily."

She'd never know if it was habit that made her look over her shoulder…habit or instinct or some leftover scrap of goddess influence that knew when life had come under threat.

But she did look. And when she did, everything got very, very still inside her.

Because Elias hadn't followed her.

Not of his own choice. Once again, the mountain had chosen their path for them.

He was sprawled across the ground on his stomach, weight spread as evenly as he could get it; the same technique they'd been taught to use on frozen lakes struck with unexpected thaws. The same way he'd tried to save Everin prior to Tenebrae's trial…and had failed, plunging through the broken floor himself.

Even adrenaline-addled and rage-riled, his chest barely rose and fell, like even the air in his lungs might tip the scale too far out of their favor. And even still, the cracks in the floor beneath him continued to spread. To separate.

He couldn't move. Not back, not forward.

"Elias," she called softly. A plea meant only for her husband's ears.

He looked up. Met her stare. Opened his mouth, fight flaring across his face, a wildfire ready to roar through her resolve.

In that fire, she saw it all: her family. Her kingdom. Her crown. All the reasons she could not afford to lay her life down here; all the reasons she needed to take Kessen's hand.

"Never again." She anchored herself in the splintering stone, fingertips stinging, nearly numb with stone-scuff. "You promised."

And so had she.

Promised to get back to her family. Promised to do right by her kingdom. Promised to take back her crown.

Not one of them weighty enough to break the promises they'd made mere hours ago.

She belonged to no kingdom, to no blood, to no throne—to him. Only him.

"You promised." A whisper so heavy it splintered another seam in the stone beneath her. "You *promised.*"

For the second time, fire consumed it all—her family, her kingdom, her crown. The inferno in his gaze blazed hotter and hotter, his gaze branding her with the outline of weaker, wasted vows…

And then it went out.

It didn't dim; it didn't flicker.

It went out. And in its place, bleak understanding wavered like smoke—like tears.

Elias's tears carried an alchemical power to them. One drop, and her resolve thinned to mist, easily blown in the direction he wished it to go.

But not today. Not here, not now, not when they'd come to the edge of another precipice trying to push them apart.

"Never again," he agreed, throat bobbing harshly. He shifted his weight slowly until he could settle on his seat, arms out to his sides.

Waiting for her.

No goodbyes between them. Not this time.

And that made it easy to brave what came next.

"Princess!" Kessen shouted. "My arm's falling asleep, here! Let's go!"

Soren reached out. Wrapped her hand around his. Squeezed it…

And let go.

Confusion contorted his boyish features. "Wait—"

"You're a good kid," she choked. "Don't let this keep you up at night, okay?"

Panic struck confusion down, Kessen's fingers splaying toward her in a futile bid to catch her hand. "Wait, wait, I don't—"

She kicked off the side of the wall, her back crashing against Elias's chest. He hauled her into his lap and crushed her close, his arms tight as a vise around her middle, his face buried between her shoulder blades.

When the world broke beneath them, they did not fear…

Because when it took them, it took them together.

CHAPTER 68

ELIAS

Death didn't smell the same.

The first time…*cinnamon pastries and rose-and-peach shampoo and new yarn.*

But this time…

Dust and blood and molten rock. Adrenaline and leather and hair washed in a freshwater stream.

A shallow breath exhaled against his wrist. A heartbeat stumbling all over itself, drunk on the tangy wine of mortal fear.

Not his heartbeat.

When he tried to speak, a cough came out instead—a cough that sprayed dust and crumbs of rock. Hacking again, he scrubbed at his eyes with one hand, blinking furiously.

He couldn't see a damned thing. But when he tried to lift his other arm, it didn't budge, trapped under something heavy. Something that wasn't moving.

Something with a messy, slurring heartbeat.

Something anchored to him by his numb, tingling arm.

Something that surged awake with a strangled *ack* when he tried to move again, bucking against him.

"Me," he rasped, coughing until he could get his damned voice to work: "Soren! It's me, it's me. Hold still. Are you hurt?"

She rolled off of his arm, coughing so hard it turned into a retch. "Gods, I always thought dying would be *easier.*"

"You do seem to have trouble getting it to stick." The greatest relief of his gods-damned life. "Not for lack of trying, clearly."

"Shut up." A shaky laugh—a shakier breath. "Are you all right?"

He finally blinked hard enough to clear the film over his eyes; Soren lay on her stomach, breathing heavily, her lips parted...glossed with red.

"Just a split," she promised—he must've had one pits-dark look on his face. "You?"

"All right, I think." He looked to see where they'd landed; he sat up, bracing against the tines of fracture-thin pain that forked across his body as the whole picture pieced together.

Unlike the shades of gray they'd been surrounded with through most of the mountain, this small alcove—barely the size of his mother's garden shed back home—was carved from something different. A reddish stone veined in black and...

Light. Streaks of light that branched through the stone, shifting color before his eyes. Like...

"Magic," Soren whispered.

He felt it, too—the air itself had weight to it, putting gentle but insistent pressure on his body.

This magic...whatever it was, it was ancient. He ached from its presence alone. His skin tingled. His head hurt.

...Or maybe that was the very hard fall he'd just taken.

Soren stood, eyes glowing almost white as she stared into the light. Her head nearly brushed the ceiling; she lifted her arm, reaching for one of the veins.

The brand on the back of his neck—which had been cold, dormant, since they'd set foot in the mountain—warmed ever so slightly. "Don't touch it!"

Her finger stopped tantalizingly, terrifyingly close to the vein. "Why not?"

He rubbed at his stinging brand. "Take one guess."

"It's not a trap."

Elias nearly whacked himself in the forehead—then remembered he'd already hit his head pretty hard, and should probably avoid self-inflicted concussions for a bit. "You don't think the shiny magic cave in a mountain where magic doesn't work is a trap?"

She looked up once more. Set her jaw. "I think it's a trial."

When she poked the pulsing light, the entire cave went dark.

"Oops," came Soren's voice in the darkness.

Then again, maybe a concussion would help him cope with all this. "Good going."

"Hey, at least I did something. What's *your* plan, start drawing up plans for a cave house and coming up with recipes for rat stew? Because I'm not—"

Beneath his feet, movement caught his eye: a sleepy flutter of crimson, ember-like light. Not veins, but sparks.

"Shh," he hissed, waving in Soren's general direction—not that she could see it.

"I will not be *shhh*ed, thank you, not when I'm—"

"Shhh!"

The embers whirled together, their combined light flaring like a struck match; that cluster of brightness shot out sharp a crossbow bolt, whizzing into the darkness, leaving a trail of slightly dimmer light behind.

Just enough to see the stalactite-fanged mouth of a gaping tunnel ahead.

He and Soren found each other again in the dark.

She held out her hand, forcing a smile. He hated that—he hated when she lied to him, even without words. "Coming, lover?"

"Do I have a choice?"

Her eyes twinkled. "Have you ever?"

He had. When Jakob had dared him to kiss her on that whiskey-laden night, he could have taken the consequences for squirming out of it; when Soren demanded he become her new battlemate after Jira, he could have refused, could have retired his sword early; when she'd asked him to swear their vows again, the first vulnerability she'd willingly given, he could have told her once was enough.

When she'd vanished on that Ursa battlefield, he could have chosen to believe she was dead, like so many others had.

When she'd told him her true name, he could have left her in the Atlas palace and gone straight back home to die in peace.

When Tallisian mercenaries had taken her and Anima, he could have let them have the goddess, believing his battlemate dead already.

Every battle, every trial, he'd had a choice. He always could have chosen to walk away.

But he hadn't.

And he never would.

"I'm coming," he sighed; then called out in protest when she started to jog after the ember without him. "Wait for me!"

"Keep up!" she retorted, already barely more than an echo, a shadow. Like the cave meant to swallow her whole.

He picked up his pace. And the second his wife got in reach of his other arm, he held her hand so tightly he couldn't tell where his ended and hers began.

CHAPTER 69

SOREN

Someone was watching them.

Not some*thing*; the eyes stabbing holes into her head didn't feel predatory. She didn't feel hunted, nor threatened…just watched.

That didn't make it any less eerie.

Though the shooting star guiding them had vanished around the next turn, its sanguine trail glittered beneath their feet; she walked it like a tightrope, imagination taking the black stone to either side and convincing her she balanced over an endless abyss instead.

Elias crowded closer to her, half-behind, half-beside. "We're not alone."

She didn't look over her shoulder. "I know."

"Should we turn back?"

Maybe. It might have been safer, or at least less of a mystery—maybe she could get used to living life as a ratmonger's wife, since *she* certainly wouldn't be going anywhere near those disease-riddled flesh-bags, and the two of them could live out their days in blessed solitude.

Not exactly what she'd imagined for their blissful life of matrimony, but…

"Life of *rat*rimony," she mumbled under her breath.

"What?"

"Nothing." He wouldn't appreciate the joke enough to make it worth explaining her whole path of thought. "We made it this far. If someone's watching, they should know better than to try anything."

Yes, surely anyone surviving down here in the bowels of a mountain would be *far* too intimidated by a dusty, dehydrated, thoroughly lost pair of travelers.

A twinkle caught her eye from above.

Another glimmer had appeared in the ceiling…not a vein this time, but a speck. A starburst. A silver shimmer that winked coyly her way.

Keep up, the star seemed to say before it raced down the tunnel after its crimson cousin.

Urgency grabbed her hand and yanked her forward; she dug one heel into the rock under her foot, holding herself back.

She didn't need to run. She didn't need to keep that light in her sight; they could follow its trail just as easily.

So why did she feel like she'd burst out of her skin if she didn't try to chase it?

She couldn't trust her mind in this place; Occassio's trial had seen to that.

"Trap," she whispered.

Elias's shoulder brushed against hers. "Yeah."

"We can't turn back."

"No." Resigned. Knowing.

She turned to look at him; he looked back, crimson starlight blazing through his scorch-black gaze.

"Why does it have to be us?" she whispered.

Elias lifted her hand. Kissed her ring. Never broke eye contact with her.

He gave no other answer. Maybe there wasn't one to give.

So she turned her eyes back to the stars. And even though a thousand wishes crowded in her mind and heart, she gathered them up and clutched them to her chest, refusing to let a single drop of starlight shine on them.

She didn't trust these stars. Not to carry her wishes; not even to look on them kindly.

But they had no choice but to follow them.

Together, they broke into a measured jog; enough of a run to satisfy the urgency beating in her blood, but not such a hard sprint that their bruised-up bodies gave out. Every corner they turned, they were just in time to see the stars disappear around the next; each time they crossed a fork, the stars had stopped to wait for them, only zooming off into the darkness once they could tell which path to take.

She felt a little too much like a fish with its eye caught on a lure, too pretty a promise to be real. But she couldn't fight what she couldn't see; if something wicked was after them, they'd have to let it reel them in.

Just as she started to grow sick of the chase, they broke out of the tunnel and into a wider chamber. Not a forking path this time.

Worse: a dead end.

A cave that, upon first sight, she thought might have been carved from opaque black stone; but as they stepped inside, more stars joined their guides, sailing through the rock like flicker-fish through dark water. As if they stared into a glass bowl filled with living light.

And in the very center of the cavern, so clearly staged that even Medwenna herself could not have convinced Soren it was naturally occurring, was a spire of gleaming stone.

It was shaped like an upside-down icicle with the sharp end sliced off at an angle; its flat pane faced them, held distinctly like a hand held up in greeting.

This time, they did not even need to share a look. It was obvious what was expected of them.

They didn't say a word as they walked up to the spire.

One hand, she twined so tightly with Elias's that he grunted under his breath; the other, she pressed to the ice-slick surface.

When he followed suit, those moonbright flecks swarmed around their hands—an undulating cloud of gray to silver to white against her palm, a swarm of red and orange and gold around his. A shiver took root in the center of her palm; as it spread, coating her arm in sparkling frost, she tried to tug free. But no matter how hard she pulled—even when she planted her heel against the spire and tried to pry herself off—her hand wouldn't budge.

Elias didn't even try—when she looked at him, she realized with a pang of panic that his eyes were closed, his features slack as if in sleep.

Thank the gods no one else was seeing this. *Sprang a clear and obvious trap because it looked sparkly* was about the most embarrassing way to die that she could imagine.

The last thought she had before starlight devoured her.

CHAPTER 70

SOREN

When she opened her eyes again, she met the squinting glare of her own reflection.

She ripped her hand away from the wall; it came free without resistance, throwing her so off-balance that she staggered backward several paces before falling to her seat. Pride and ass smarting, she did her best to soothe both as she stood, rubbing her haunch while she took stock of her surroundings.

Still in the crystal cave—but no longer bathed in crimson and silver glory. Instead, a twilight sky stared back at her from behind faceted glass. The silver speckles that had overwhelmed her now winked in clusters across a silken sheet of midnight blue, forming unfamiliar constellations.

No—not unfamiliar. When she drew invisible lines between them, marking them out in her mind's eye, she *could* put names to shapes…if she imagined them flipped the other way.

The constellations of home, but reversed. As if viewed in a mirror, not through a window.

"It took me time to get used to it, too."

A new swarm of starlight came together within the wall…a swarm that took on a familiar shape. One that stepped into the cavern as if walking straight from Soren's last memory of her: stoic, smiling, set on her course.

Mama.

Not a thought; a spear hurled through her sternum. A little girl's keening cry as she wandered a crowded market, getting more lost with every step. An accusation of betrayal, because how *dare* this mountain use her grief against her twice, how dare it think her so foolish as to fall for it *again*, how…

How dare it cast Enna's smile in this sinister starlight, shaded so precisely to Soren's memory that it could not possibly be false?

But she would not, could not, fall for it again.

So instead, she took this weapon meant for her downfall and set it in the hands of her rage, her oldest and most trusted friend; in its smelting grip, that weapon took the shape of a shield, stripped of its vulnerabilities, dripped clean of all its dross.

When she took it back, it felt right in her hand. Balanced just so. Measured exactly to the span of her body. No more blows would strike past its protective wall around her battered heart.

No more. She could take *no more.*

Only when she could heft that shield without her grip wobbling did she say, with no emotion at all, "Whatever I need to do here, just say it. I'm sick of your tricks."

Enna sighed, a longsuffering but fond sound, the ghost of a thousand others echoing out behind it. "You just won me a bet, so thank you for that. But if you are waiting on a test, I'm afraid I don't have one to offer."

Right. And she was a hundred rats stacked up in a very long coat. "You already used this trick, remember? The lake, the drowning? I did this whole thing already. So unless you're going to poison me out of my mind again—"

Enna's gaze sharpened, from misty starlight to a moonbeam cutting through glass. "You were *poisoned?*"

Soren paused.

That wasn't the reaction she'd expected from a puppet of light and memory.

"I'm fine," she said, fumbling her conviction; she tightened her grip on it again, steeling herself against the plea of her poor, pleading heart. The busted-up thing that couldn't stop begging for just one loss to be undone. "I mean it. Tell me what I have to do."

"You have nothing left to do." Enna's footsteps didn't echo as she crossed the cave; another tell that clad her bones with the conviction that this was not real, this was not right.

She drew her sword and pointed it out—like steel could hold back a figment of dust and a daughter's desperate dreams. "Don't."

Don't come any closer, was what she'd meant to say, to *command*—but the words crumbled away sharply after *don't,* tumbling down her tight throat like a rockslide.

Because Enna *did* stop—and though she still smiled, a new luminescence twinkled in her eyes. Like mercurial tears.

"Tell me what I can say to make you see me, sweetheart," she whispered.

I'm staying, sweetheart…this is what it means to be queen.

She blinked furiously against the burn in her own eyes. This cursed mountain could dig into her head to find the means of making its puppets; she couldn't trust any mimicry it constructed from her own memory. "I...you can't. You're not real. And I'm not going to *help* you trick me."

Enna gazed at her for so long, the constellations around them began to shift. Night crawling ever-so-slowly toward an inevitable dawn.

Maybe that was the trick—maybe the sun would burn away this ghost like morning dew. Maybe if she only kept her at bay long enough, she would win.

"You do not have to believe me," Enna said eventually, dashing away a gleaming drop from her cheek. "But I wish you would let me help."

Help.

Disbelief, so strong it actually dizzied her, made her laugh. "Help me with what?"

"Making your choice."

"I have no *choice* to make."

"That's what you keep telling yourself, yes."

She squeezed the grip of her sword, straining the color from her knuckles until they went white as the false moon. "I don't know what you're implying."

"Do you remember the gift I gave you before I sent you away?"

Sent you away was a very delicate way to describe ordering Elias to drag her kicking and screaming out of the castle. "Yes."

"You haven't opened it."

She refused to so much as glance toward the pack resting on her hip. "Haven't had time."

"Of course." Enna's eyes glimmered. A mother always knew better. "Well, if you have no choice to make, you must have made it…you've decided you'll go back to Atlas and be its Heir. One day, its queen."

Frigid understanding put out the fiery anger she kept stoking in her stomach.

"I told you," she whispered, "I cannot let them down again. And now…"

Now she might be the only Heir left, anyway.

Enna raised a brow. "If that's what you want."

Soren's hackles went up at that carefully neutral tone. "Is that what this is about? Trying to get me to change my mind?"

Mortem was the Goddess of *Death*. Why would her trial have anything to do with how Soren intended to live her *life?*

"If there is one thing I learned about death," said Enna, as if she read Soren's mind—which made sense, of course, because she was a figment of Soren's imagination— "it is that much of it relies on the choices we make in life. The names they will one day write on our gravestones, the way we live on in people's memory…" Enna's hand smoothed down her skirt. "The way we haunt them after. Much of death is bound up in life."

"I don't follow," Soren ground out.

"I am well aware." Enna's gaze twinkled brighter than any stars. "Open the gift, sweetheart."

She didn't lower her sword. "I think I won't."

"What could be hiding in that bag that could possibly cause you harm?"

She didn't know; she didn't *want* to know. "I don't want to open it."

"Soren—"

"I'm not ready."

Gods *damn* it. Her voice broke like an overplayed fiddle string.

Enna took another step forward—close enough that Soren's blade slid into her torso. She didn't even look down as she held out her arms.

"Come here," she whispered.

Soren's whole body quaked. "I can't."

"Soren Andromeda Nyx." Not the name she went by any longer, but one that squeezed her heart until it begged for mercy; one that flooded the banks of her eyes, tears streaming down her cheeks, so warm against her ice-cold skin that they stung. "Not in any life would I let anything harm you. I know what you saw earlier—but you're clear-headed now. You're cleverer than you give yourself credit for. Look at me—am I going to hurt you?"

She knew the answer. Even before she met Enna's gaze, she knew—but it was so much easier to keep pretending she didn't. So much easier to scoff at the ghost stories Everin and the others had shared along the way; easier to believe this haunting was a trick, a trap.

"No," she whispered.

She let her mother's arms close around her. And in that embrace…

The lies she'd been telling herself this whole time fell to pieces. As if a drop of that damned confessional oil had waited for just the right moment to seep all the way through her skin.

"My brothers are dead, Mama," she whispered.

The word echoed off the crystal, off her inner shield, off the pieces of her heart that had refused to collapse in on themselves: *dead.*

And not just dead, but *sacrificed*—a downfall they'd chosen.

They had chosen to break their promises to her.

They had chosen…they had chosen to…

"Tell me," Enna said softly.

"They *left* me," she sobbed. "*You* left me. It's not fair."

It's not fair. Like a child throwing a tantrum; like they'd cheated at some silly game.

"What isn't fair?" Enna's hand felt utterly real as it cradled her head, bracing her by the curls.

Soren buried her face in her mother's shoulder, hating that she could only smell ice and stone…no roses, no spices, none of the things that reminded her of Enna. But with her face safely hidden, the truth felt brave enough to creep out of its hiding place.

"That you all got to stop fighting, and *I can't.*"

The truth she could tell no one. Not Elias; not Anima; not her family; not even her newest allies, who had no stake in her survival.

"It isn't fair. I've been fighting so much longer. Why do you all get to stop?" She dashed her hand beneath her running nose, grief—grief unmasked as anger, as resentment, as a sickening bramble of emotions she should be *ashamed* to feel—overwhelming her in a torrent of heat. Of fire.

For ten years, she'd fought so hard that the Goddess of Time had to come back again and again and again, forcing her to forget her born family.

When Ani took her—a fate that should have been permanent—she'd fought again. All alone, abandoned by everyone—even Elias—she'd fought to stay alive. To come back to them.

Even when she'd shared her body with Ani, she'd had to fight. When the weight of divinity tried to crush her under its heel, she'd refused to give up, because Nyx was under siege…Nyx needed her. Atlas was under a false queen's rule, her parents imprisoned, if she was *lucky*—they needed her, too.

So many battles. So many little wars she'd fought nearly or entirely alone. And when it was their turn to fight, to endure, to hold the line…

"I fought for you. I fought for *them.*" She wasn't weeping anymore. She was shouting—lionlike roars that ripped out of her in painful surges as she tore back from Enna, pounding a fist over her heart. Everything burned. "Why didn't any of you fight for *me?*"

That *me* strafed her throat like broken glass.

Selfish. A selfish, wrathful, furious demand that she'd tried so hard to bury.

But buried things only grew beneath the surface.

"I wouldn't have chosen this." Another confession. She was going to overtake Elias at this rate. "Not at that cost."

"What would you choose," Enna whispered, "if you could?"

Soren's chin quivered. Her shield fell with a mighty clatter. Her heart took its final blow.

"I want to stop."

She had survived what should not have been survived. And now, she couldn't *stop* surviving—the fate that had felled her brothers and sister had not claimed her. She had slipped away from a siege intended for her, swept away on a tide of her mother's blood. She'd plunged into the core of this mountain, ready to die alongside her battlemate, only to end up here instead, and…

And she was tired.

Tired in her bones. Tired in her soul. Tired of outrunning a grave that sated itself on her loved ones every time she evaded its clutches.

Tired of miracles.

No, she was *sick* of miracles—sick of what they made of her, sick of them always picking her to save—and not even for her own sake. Why did she always have to be the miracle, and everyone else the sacrifices made to manifest it? Where was Kallias's miracle—where was Finn's?

Where had *Enna's* been, the night Andromeda fell?

"Why do I always have to be the miracle, and everyone else gets to be the sacrifice?" she whispered. "Why do you all get to stop fighting, and *I don't*?"

She shut her eyes against the starlit glow of her mother's ghost, misery pooling like blood shed from her broken heart. And she waited.

Waited for the lecture. Waited for the reminder that she should be grateful for her survival; that she should not be angry at her loved ones for loving her back.

Her mother's hand slid under her chin, cradling it; she tipped Soren's head back, studying her face with solemn sorrow.

"You're right," Enna whispered. "We all made choices to save you or spare you…but that's the trouble with sacrificing yourself, isn't it? You can only do it once, and never again. The people you die to save, you can't save them anymore…they have to save themselves. And they have to do it without you."

She'd spent all her words, all her truth; she could only nod against her mother's gentle hand.

"We left you to carry a heavy burden. And you're right—that isn't fair." A kiss to her brow. "But I know my daughter, and I've never seen her say no to a fight. So tell me…do you really want to stop?"

Soren shut her eyes.

It *sounded* like such a relief…to finally let someone else carry the weight, the responsibility, of being the survivor. To let someone else fight this fight. To finally take the rest she had earned.

But in the center of all that exhaustion, all that despair…a kernel of something brighter shimmered in the dark.

Something that riled and roared against the idea of setting down her sword. Of setting her loved ones, however few remained, in someone else's hands. Of trusting anyone else to fight for them.

No one else would raise up sword and shield for so long; no one else would fight to as bitter of an end. Not like she would. Like she *had*, over and over again.

"I just…" Her very soul shook with hopeless longing. "Gods, Mama, I don't know. I just don't want to do this alone."

Enna let go of her face; she held Soren by the shoulders instead, limpid gaze catching with silver starfire.

"You are not alone," she said. "You are *never* alone."

A finger poked playfully at her side—the same spot Jira used to jab to get her to jump out of her skin.

A hand mussed her hair—broad and rope-roughened, a sailor's hand. The same hand her brother had used to teach her how to guide their sailboat home.

The memory of a brown-eyed stare rose from watery depths, a vision conjured within haunted waters: *Can you keep it up, kid? Just for a little while longer?*

She twisted her engagement ring—her *wedding* ring—around her finger, closing her fist around it, letting the stone cut into her palm.

Never apart. Never again.

"Open the gift," Enna said softly. "Trust me."

And against all reason, against all good sense...she did.

She stepped back so she could flip open her satchel, digging through until her hand brushed against the garment box.

It had not fared so well through these trials, if she was being honest—it had been banged around and soaked through and stepped on so much that whatever lay inside might well be ruined by now.

But maybe it wouldn't hurt to get one last little miracle.

Dragging the moment out would only make it worse—she tore the box open without even holding her breath, a thousand guesses at what it might be hurtling through her mind in that last second before...

Before the lid fell away, and her heart fell with it.

Tentatively, half-afraid it would vanish—half-afraid it wouldn't—Soren eased her fingers into the box, thumbing the stiff, perfect folds of black fabric. Tracing the row of silver buttons, still shiny despite the beating they'd endured. Lifting the silver-stitched shoulder, counting the stars.

One. Two. Three. Four. Five.

Then counting again, because she had to be seeing things: *One. Two. Three. Four. Five.*

"Mama," she whispered, "this is a general's uniform."

Enna said nothing. Soren looked up, still clutching the stitched shoulder, to find the crystal-caged sky shifting toward the gray-gold of dawn...to find the stars winking out one by one.

And Enna's form thinning, vanishing, indeed evaporating like dew beneath the morning sun.

Panic clutched her heart in both hands. "Mama—"

"Your story has such a beautiful beginning," Enna interrupted. "People are telling it across the kingdoms even now...a lost princess who found her way home." She looked up to the sky, a strange longing overcoming all other emotion. "Do you know what the ending should be?"

"What should it be?"

A soft chuckle. Another layer of her form shimmered away, leaving her barely visible against the cave wall. "I'm not telling you, sweetheart—I'm asking you."

Soren looked down at the box in her hands. The invisible weight of the crown on her head seemed to double as she dipped her chin. "I don't...I don't know."

But maybe that wasn't true.

She knew what the answer *should* be, *needed* to be...and she knew what she *wanted* it to be.

The two were not the same.

"This is the trial, Soren—this is where you need to decide. What happens next...that all depends on what you choose here." Barely a wisp now, Enna floated forward—but her fingers were still warm as they settled over Soren's. "You were born to be one thing—you were raised to be another. This miracle of yours, it isn't a shackle...it's a second chance. You get to decide what the world will remember you as."

Soren's eyes burned. "How do I decide?"

Her mother took her chin again—tipped it upward, to where the last handful of silver stars remained. Where the others were fading, winking out with every surge of the sun, these few seemed to glow ever-brighter. Fighting the force that wanted so badly to erase them.

"The stars are listening," Enna whispered. "Now make a wish."

CHAPTER 71

ELIAS

It was not the first time Elias Loch had been visited by ghosts.

Back in Artem—when he'd been little more than a ghost himself, adrift in a state halfway between life and death—he had often been "visited." In memories and dreams they came to him—Soren, at first, then later his father. Evan Loch had been a frequent visitor of his when he'd gone through the trials…the trials his father had also taken.

So when a torrent of crimson swept him away to a cave wreathed in fire, its heat a welcome comfort after so long remembering the cold, he wasn't as shocked as he should have been.

Not even when he turned to find Evan Loch standing in the center of the inferno, somber as a priest standing over a funeral pyre.

"You're not surprised," said his father by way of greeting. It had never taken him long to see straight into Elias's head—or his heart.

"Is this a trial," he said, "or a nightmare?"

Evan snorted—not the most ghost-like thing to do. But then again, what did Elias know? "I shudder to imagine what you've been through if those are your only two options. Couldn't it be a blessing?"

"Not here." Not in this godless, faith-killing cage. "Are you here to challenge me? To question me? To make me call my faith into question? Whatever you have to say to me, say it—the god-killer will not be mine to wield. If you must be faithless to claim it, you will not find that in me."

Pride, muted by sadness, glowed in Evan's deep blue eyes. "You're my son, all right." Those eyes traveled down, taking in the measure of him…filling with tears as they came back up to his face. "Gods, you've grown so much. You were barely over my shoulder when I saw you last."

The emotion in Elias's throat would have to stay there, where he could easily swallow it—he couldn't let it travel up to his face, where it would give him away; he couldn't let it burrow down into his heart, where it would weaken his resolve. "Time will do that."

"Time and trouble." He didn't move when his father approached, hands out; nor did he flinch when those hands, oddly warm, framed his face. Evan chuckled. "Look at this beard."

"My battlemate refuses to let me shave it."

"Soren." Evan nodded knowingly. "That girl's trouble in two helpings— you'd *have* to add some length to your legs to keep up with her." A rueful grin. "She's perfect for you. I wish I could have known her."

The mention of Soren brought his attention to her absence—and rubbed his nerves the wrong way. He stepped back. "Tell me what I have to do."

Evan's smile vanished. "The god-killer, you said."

"Yes."

He didn't understand the grief shrouding his father's gaze. "The answer is not what you want, son—nor will it be easy to hear. And once you do, there is no going back to before."

No turning back.

"I am ready," he said quietly. "Tell me."

Evan set his hand to Elias's face again, bending their brows together. "It's easier if I show you."

Even in the shaded halls of this seaside palace, the air burdened Evan's back like he'd stuffed his shirt with bricks.

The dead of winter, yet Atlas remained balmy and blooming…and the fire chewing through the walls didn't do a thing to lift the oppressive heat.

A monstrous deed King Byron had chosen to commit tonight.

Evan's mission perhaps more monstrous for the fact that he had not stopped it.

He was not here on the King's orders; he was here at the behest of someone far greater, in both power and in heart.

But even she had told him in no uncertain terms: he had no part to play in favor of or against the King's machinations. He had only to use his ambition as an opportunity.

She had given him no more than that. Orders to trail the King's company, sent to slip through a seam in Atlas's security and set fire to their beautiful palace—and orders not to involve himself in their scheme.

The rest, she'd promised, would come when required. And he had faith it would.

"Evan."

He froze as that pyreside voice whispered in his ear, so cold it raised the hairs on the back of his neck—a whisper of home on the wrong side of the Atlas border.

"I'm listening," he murmured to Mortem. "Where would you have me go?"

The smoke curling through the air swirled of its own accord, tendrils of ink drifting into shape…the vague sketch of his goddess's grim, ageless face.

"There is an enemy nearby," she said.

"There are many enemies nearby."

"Not like this one." A ribbon of smoke rippled into a warning scowl. "If their life does not come to an end today, something worse than war will soon come to your door. But it is not too late."

A rush thrilled through his blood…dread and excitement as one. He gripped the hilt of his sword, the sheath warming as his pyromancy bled into the blade. "Explain."

"You will know when you see them." A flicker in the fast-approaching flames, a trick of the light; a flash of her real face, eyes dark and sorrowful, mouth pursed in displeasure. "I will warn you, it will not sit kindly on your soul… your conscience will feel as if it stands on unsteady ground. But on my word as a goddess, this death must be dealt."

For her to do so much convincing, when he had never raised a protest against her orders—and did not raise one now—blew new air onto an ember of caution in his chest, fanning it into a full flame.

But he was not afraid of fire.

He bowed his head. "As you will it, Goddess."

"Do not falter, Phoenix Priest." For a moment, the smoke encircled him, clinging to his skin like watered-down tar. "Or far more blood will coat your hands."

When he drew his sword from its sheath, the heat against his leg too much to bear, it glowed brighter than the inferno rapidly consuming this hallway. And when he looked again, Mortem's visage had disappeared, leaving only lifeless smoke behind.

With the screams of innocents ringing in his ears, the Phoenix Priest hunted in the dark.

He'd crossed into one corridor the fire had not yet reached; beyond drapeless windows, the moon was hidden, but he had no need of its light to guide him. The purring fire ever-burning in his chest led him just fine, its flames rearing or banking depending on which direction he turned.

Hot and Cold. It was a little silly, a goddess using a game he played with his children to lead him to his next mission…but he didn't mind it. In fact, it made him miss home a little less.

That blaze burned hotter and hotter the further it pulled him; when he approached a door where the screaming rose in pitch and volume, the fire in his chest exploded, flooding his body with scalding blood. Heart in his throat, he reached for the knob—

Only for it to twist of its own accord.

He staggered backwards, pressing himself flat to the wall as a lanky silhouette hurtled into the hall. Whoever it was, they did not shout over their shoulder that they'd found a safer path; perhaps because they were already wheezing, weaving on their feet, smoke robbing them of strength. They carried a rolled-up blanket; judging by the acrid scent of burned fibers, they'd used it to beat out flames on their way here.

The molten heat in his core ignited with a roar of power. He only just managed to smother it before it flared in his sword, his armor—his eye.

The silhouetted figure did not seem to sense him there in the shadows. They broke into an unsteady run, calling out something Evan couldn't understand at first; a name, he thought.

"Soleil!" A cracked, almost shrill cry; a cough followed it.

Whoever they searched for, they would not find them.

Evan peeled away from the wall, brandishing his blade…letting his power seep into it until even the shadows flinched away from its heat.

The figure whirled with a caught breath; and as holy fire washed away the dark, Evan's breath caught, too.

First confusion—then something worse.

He was just a boy—*a boy no older than fifteen or sixteen, a thatch of red hair grown to his nape, a freckled face only just beginning to shed its childish softness. His pale green eyes were bloodshot, bleary with tears.*

She'd warned him. She'd known—and she had still given her orders.

Do not falter, Phoenix Priest.

He's just a child. *He could barely even* think *a prayer past his horror.*

Not merely a child. *Mortem's voice manifested so quickly he nearly jumped; she rarely came to him so fast when he spoke.* A scion—a mortal born with the strength to hold one of us as a host. There are four of them in this palace…four we can fell in one stroke, if you work quickly. Such kismet is rarely granted. We must not waste it.

He could not imagine what great harm could be wrought by a teenaged boy who was running *toward* danger, *not away from it—no matter what he was capable of.* I…I don't understand.

Faith does not require understanding. Only action.

A mantra he himself had recited before. But this…

How do you know he will pursue that path? There must be another way.

Dangerous, to ask so many questions—he had never asked any *before. Her word was as law; she spoke, and he acted. A battlemate pair in their own right.*

But in this boy's terrified face, he saw his eldest boy, Elias, and the teary-eyed way he pled to sleep in Evan and Sera's bed when he had one of his night terrors. In the way this boy clutched that soot-stained blanket against his chest like a shield, he saw the way his son snuggled his cat while he slept—as much a ward against the wicked things that stirred in the dark as the incense Evan burned every night.

Displeasure poured over his back in the form of a bone-deep chill. You question the knowledge of a goddess?

No. I merely—

If this prince and the others are allowed to live, not only Nyx will suffer—Atlas will, too. *A hint of smoke drifted under his nose, clearing his senses like a smelling salt.* Which will weigh heavier on your conscience—his life, or his kingdom?

A prince of Atlas—the First Prince, judging by his age. Kallias.

Even his name reminded Evan of his eldest boy.

Heart sinking, heavier than the iron his wife hauled in her forge, he sheathed his sword and stalked forward. With no sound, he pulled off his black leather glove…let the frigid, breathless cold of mortemancy frostbite his fingers instead.

It would be painless. The boy would feel nothing—he would simply be gone.

First Prince Kallias did not retreat from Death's approach. He squared his shoulders and his jaw, dropping the blanket; he fell into a passable swordsman's stance, though he had no such weapon to wield.

"I'm not looking for a fight," croaked the boy. His cry before hadn't been cracked through from smoke inhalation, after all—he was just at the age where his voice began to drop, suffering some fractures on the way down. "My baby sister, we lost track of her…she's just a little kid." The Prince's lips trembled—fear, but not for himself. "We're just kids."

Faith did not require understanding—only action.

He reached for Kallias's shoulder. Gripped it tightly when the boy tried to rear back.

Evan raised his other hand, his fingertips frosted over with death.

For a moment, they only stared at each other, scion and priest.

Then he whispered, "I'm sorry."

"You *defied* my orders."

Evan slouched in his tent, staring at the wall—still breathing hard from his mad dash back to his makeshift camp outside Port Atlas proper, chased all the way by the sound of the boy falling to the ground…struck unconscious by a blow to the head. "I'm not a murderer."

"This would not have changed that."

"This would have been worse *than that." He rocked up to his feet, pacing—ignoring how her shadowy form did the same, flickering furiously in the light of his lantern. "The fire might take him anyway."*

"It will not."

"And I could not."

"You *could* not?" *Her shadow halted, wavering against the tent wall like a heat haze.* "Or you *would* not?"

His mouth dried out—but his conviction did not. "I would not. Killing in cold blood—killing children—that is not something we do. It is not something we have ever *done."*

"My word is not for you to question."

"Because you need not answer to a mortal?" Dangerous, dangerous. "Or because you do not have a good answer to give?"

They stared at each other in silence. Goddess beheld man; man beheld goddess.

"I chose you," said Mortem, hushed as a graveside prayer, "because your faith is beyond any I have held in my many, many centuries. Tell me, Evan Loch—has that faith reached its limit?"

"My faith knows no boundaries." He clenched his fists. "But my conscience does. Forgive me, Goddess…but I am not above such things like you. I am still a mortal."

"I understand."

The shadow peeled off the tent wall—as it stepped into the space, it also stepped into true form. No longer wisps of smoke and darkness, but a woman—a woman with fire in her eyes and death in her scowl.

"But I have no need for a mortal," she said softly. "I have need of a weapon."

"You will be hard-pressed to find a person of faith who can be the latter, but not the former."

She settled her hand over the feather dangling over his heart.

"I am patient," she murmured. "I will keep looking."

When she ripped the feather away, he lost all warmth in his body…so cold he could have been a corpse.

"I revoke my blessing," she said. "May you find peace in the choice you made today, Evan Loch…you have doomed us in more ways than you know."

Elias gasped like he'd been punched in the chest—he doubled over with a cough, his father catching him with murmured reassurances. Apologies.

"I don't understand," he choked. "I don't…"

"Kallias Atlas should have died that night…but I spared him, at the cost of my blessing." His father's bereaved gaze trailed down to Elias's chest—to the phoenix feather. "I know now what Mortem meant…why she commanded me to kill him. But I couldn't, even knowing something of the damage it would cause one day." He looked up at Elias. "She has asked you to perform a similar deed."

Killing Anima. But he'd refused, as well—and had not been so thoroughly punished.

"Why didn't she take it from me?"

Evan's frown turned sorrowful. "I suspect because you have not defied her quite so soundly…or, if I flatter myself, because the loss of my blessing meant the loss of my life, albeit some years later."

A life that had been protected by mortemancy. A wound dealt by an Atlas blade—a wound that would have burned shut, had Mortem not…

Understanding, caustic and bitter, almost choked him. "She abandoned you to die."

"I doubt she intended for her punishment to be so thorough—I was not yet a soldier, after all." His father did not sound particularly sure. "Though I cannot say how far her sight might have extended…if she knew what shape my fate would take."

Oh, gods. Oh gods.

His father was dead because of her.

He'd become a soldier in his father's name—had been set on the path to that Atlas temple, to his eventual deathbed—because of her.

Kallias…and *Soren*…

Soren had not been saved that night because of her. And Kallias had carried that blame…carried it so long and so close that he'd started looking for some way, any way, to atone for it. Some price he could pay to wipe out his failure.

A failure his father had caused.

Elias was going to be sick.

"I do not tell you this to rob you of convinction," Evan said when he'd been quiet too long. "I say it because you will have to make a choice very soon…your heart, or your faith. I made my choice—I cannot make yours. But I would have you understand the consequences before you choose."

"Papa…"

"There is more, but we are out of time." His father clasped his hands, pressing a fierce kiss to his forehead. "No matter what you become, no matter what you choose, I am proud of you, Elias. Do not falter. No path that lies before you now is easy."

"Wait!" Panic had him grasping for his father, but he only caught empty air—already that crimson cast to him had faded, his smile only barely visible. "What about the god-killer?"

His father gave him the most loving look he ever had. And the words he spoke next…the last words Elias might ever hear from his father…

They broke him. In ways he had never been broken before.

CHAPTER 72

SOREN

Gods, she was sick to death of *rock*.

Sleeping on it. Walking on it. Staring at it. Smelling it. Waking up kneeling on it, her knees scraped bloody through her pants, white-knuckling a black-and-silver uniform like someone was about to try and snatch it from her.

A blink after she came to, Elias—who knelt across from her, forehead scoured with lines so deep he was *absolutely* going to have permanent wrinkles left behind—surged awake with a wrench, his back snapping straight as he sucked in a noisy, strangled breath.

"Whoa, whoa!" She forced her stiff, claw-bent fingers to release the uniform, letting it settle in her lap; she reached out for him instead as he sagged, hands braced on his knees, breathing like he'd just sprinted a mile. "Easy, jackass."

No *smartass* in return; only a strangled sob that made her blood boil.

"Talk." She slipped one hand behind his back, wishing there was a more subtle way to feel for a break—wishing she didn't have to settle her fear by treading the paths of his trauma. But the way he'd spasmed… "Does something hurt?"

Dust showered from his hair as he shook his head, drifting down to coat his knees; he brushed it away with trembling fingers as his tears fell, streaking mud down his face. "I'm…"

In her defense, she did wait patiently—for a whole five seconds, actually, if anyone cared to count—for him to get the end of that sentence out. A *fine*, or an *all right*…she would have even accepted an *I'm not sure*, if it proved he could get all the way to the end of a thought.

But fear couldn't wait its turn longer than five seconds. "You're *what?* Fine, terrible, dying—?"

More tears; more muddy streaks; more ghosts living in his eyes, a haunted absence of feeling that chilled her to the bone.

"You're *what?*" She jostled his shoulders. "Spit it out, jackass, you're scaring me. Who'd you see? Did they tell you how to get the god-killer?"

But what happened next scared her more than anything. Because instead of speaking, or crying, or even shivering some more…

Elias laughed.

He laughed—so raspy and crackling it could have been a cough if not for the humorless gnash of his teeth, a grin calligraphed in a script she couldn't read.

Elias's expressions, however minute or strange, never were *so* misshapen she couldn't wrest some kind of meaning out of them.

"You're scaring me," she whispered again. "Who did you see? What did they say about the weapon?"

When her hand slipped from his cheek, he caught it—held onto it so tightly her knuckles scraped against each other, a painful crush that told her he was beyond soothing with sense.

"She wanted a weapon," he muttered.

"Still not an answer!"

I'm fine, was what she'd hoped for. *I'm hurt* or *I'm afraid* she could have done something to solve.

But when he finally reached the end of his stammering sentence…she wished to the gods she'd let him hold his silence.

"I think *I'm* the god-killer."

CHAPTER 73

ELIAS

The confession fell so heavily from his lips that even the cave's greedy echoes couldn't get a grip on it. It dropped like a stone, clattering between him and his battlemate like a gauntlet thrown.

Soren fell back on her seat; she stared at him, unblinking. He stared back.

"I don't understand," she rasped. "It's—you're not—it's a weapon, Elias, everything we've heard—"

"She *wanted* a weapon. She said—"

"Tell me what that *means*—"

"I'm trying! I'm trying, just…give me a second." He dug the heels of his hands into his eyes, forcing darkness on them, wishing he could shove *himself* back in the dark. "I saw…I saw my father."

When he ripped his hands down, Soren met him there—she'd crossed the space between them, her knees only an inch from his. She held his gaze, nodding for him to go on.

He didn't hold anything back—he took her with him as he walked back to the Port Atlas palace. A fire, a mission…a prince spared only by the slip of a hesitant hand.

To the Nyxian barracks, and a princess who had no idea she fought beside the son of a man who'd nearly murdered her brother—who might have killed his way through all four Atlas children, had he obeyed his orders.

A man whose faith had never faltered. A man who had never questioned his goddess—save once—and had been sentenced to death for it.

A price demanded, a price paid.

And he didn't stop there. He confessed—with only a flicker of reluctance—how Mortem had given him similar orders to dispatch Anima. How she'd commanded him to try and put an end to her before her magic settled.

A lie, he realized now—a lie of omission, perhaps, but still a lie.

"She was testing my father," he said, ignoring how Soren tightened up her fists like she planned on picking a fight with Mortem bare-handed. "Weapons don't question their wielder."

"She wanted him to kill us." Soren's voice utterly *seethed.* "To see if he would hesitate."

"And slow down Tenebrae's plans in the process."

"How did she know what we were?"

Elias shrugged. "Occassio would be my guess."

"But she's on Tenebrae's side."

"Knowing what we know of her, it wouldn't surprise me if she played both sides for as long as she could." All guesswork; but then again, did it matter how Mortem knew? Did *any* of it matter, knowing she'd consigned his father—and one day, Elias himself—to death?

Quiet, for a time. Then: "Elias?"

"Yes?"

"How does this make you the god-killer?"

He shook his head. "It's not a weapon. It's magic…mortemancy."

A magic only gifted to one goddess, and from her, one mortal…a weapon indeed, forged by her own hand.

No less a tool than the scythes strapped to his back.

Soren was quiet for a moment.

"So what you're saying is," she said flatly, "we had the god-killer this *whole damned time?*"

"Seems so."

"We came in here for nothing?"

"I'm not any happier about it than you are."

Soren stared straight ahead—too calm. For a moment, he feared she might be about to start screaming.

"I hate her," she said. "I'm allowed to say that now, right? I've always *hated* her. What, she couldn't have just *told* you that mortemancy worked on gods? Why didn't *we* try that?"

Because by the time he'd had this magic, only one god had been in reach—and she'd been inextricably tied with Soren.

Because they'd been told nothing they possessed could do the job—and they'd blindly believed it.

He'd blindly believed it. And look what it had cost them.

Blood. Pain. Time.

Time they could have used to try and help Kallias. Time that might have doomed him, had he not been doomed from the start.

"The legend comes from somewhere," he rasped. "This Sanctum wasn't built to protect nothing."

"Then we need to figure out what. Because otherwise, we're not going to get out of here."

He blinked at her. "What do you mean?"

"Every time we passed a trial before, it led us to the exit—or made one." She looped her finger in a wide circle, encompassing the round-roofed cave around them. "I don't see anything that looks like an exit in here, do you?"

Now that she mentioned it… "No."

"So we haven't triggered it yet. Whatever we're here to find, we haven't found it."

"Or we failed the trial." Whatever the trial had been. He'd only listened to a story. And Soren…

Soren's hand sank to her lap, clutching a pile of cloth he hadn't noticed until now—a familiar folded garment.

"Is that a uniform?" Had she been holding that the whole time? "Where'd you get that?"

"I…" She looked down at her lap, brushing her hand over the shoulder…stitched with five gleaming stars. "I saw my mother."

Her explanation was far swifter, far sadder…and in some places, the emotion in her voice pulled back just enough to leave space for secrets. A distance that told him she was holding a few details close to her chest.

That was all right. Sometimes, a loved one's last words were a gift that belonged only to whom they'd been given.

Like the letter in his own pack.

"And did you?" he prompted when she stopped speaking for a time, long enough that he knew no more revelations were coming.

She looked up as if startled out of a daydream, dropping the uniform back into her lap. "Did I what?"

"Decide."

"Honestly?"

"No," he deadpanned, "I actually prefer it when you lie to me."

A brief bob of her shoulders, an attempt to laugh—but her chapped, blood-scabbed lips stayed stoic. "I don't think it was about deciding. I think I already knew." She rubbed her wrist under her eye, streaking damp stone-dust across her cheekbone. "I want to go home."

His heart sank—but only a short ways before it caught itself. This was what he'd been preparing for—what he'd been doing his best to accept for himself. "I know. We'll be back in Atlas soon—"

"No."

He stared at her, and she stared at the uniform in her lap—a tear-washed but steady glare. "No?"

"No. I want—" A sudden sob. She cleared her throat fiercely, but the tears kept falling; her breath kept hitching. She hugged the uniform to her chest, squeezing her eyes shut. "I want Nyx. I want home—I want *our* home, with the skating pond and the fireplace and the orange door. I don't want to be Queen. I want to go *home.*"

It was *painful,* the way his heart leapt from one extreme to another—how it soared back into his chest on wings of fire, scorching everything inside him with the sting of hope. He leaned forward, grasping her hand. "What are you saying?"

Because if she was saying what he *thought* she was saying...

He almost didn't care if they ever got out of this cave.

CHAPTER 74

SOREN

"What are you saying?"

What *was* she saying?

The longer she held that beautiful uniform in her hands, the less she felt like she could let it go—like the stitching had undone itself only to thread itself into her skin, sewing her hands into its folds.

It said something that she almost wished it would. That she wished it would become so inextricably part of her that no one could take it away.

Her crown had always felt similar…like it had been nailed into her head with iron stakes. A birthright no one could take away; a burden she could never be freed from.

But Enna was right. She'd been born for one burden…she'd been built for another. And she knew which one she wished to—*longed* to—carry.

"I'm saying I don't…" Her body locked up, determination squaring her jaw. "I won't be Queen. I don't want it. I know it's the selfish choice—I don't care. I can't do it. I'm not Kallias—I'm not Finn."

Not Kallias, who could lay his every want and need as a sacrifice at Atlas's altar, spilling his own hopes and wishes like blood paid for answered prayers. Not Finn, who could play any part to perfection, tailoring any skin to fit snugly atop his own.

She was Soren. Not a martyr; not a con; not a queen.

She was a soldier. She wore a sword, not a crown. She fought to protect what she loved.

And that included herself.

She was no stranger to loss. But she'd lost enough.

"I have earned selfishness," she whispered. "And selfishly, I love Atlas— but it's not mine anymore."

Really, it never had been. If anything, it had only been hers to give away when the time came.

She had never been a woman of faith. But the current of irrational *knowing* that flowed into her heart, pumped into her blood as reckless conviction…she had no other name for it.

She had faith. In herself. In her kingdom. In her family.

Even her brothers.

Maybe they hadn't been given a miracle—maybe they wouldn't be, no matter how much they deserved one.

But maybe they didn't need to be given a miracle. Maybe she could make one.

Elias held one hand toward her chin, then waited—she nodded, and he pulled her in for a kiss. Possibly the worst they'd ever had—at least their klutzy, dare-driven first kiss hadn't tasted like mountain mud—but still welcome.

"I love you," he croaked.

"I love you back," she said.

I would love for you two to shut your sappy mouths, said the mountain.

Well. Not in those exact words. But it did start to quake underneath them, which basically translated to the same thing.

Elias cursed against her mouth and grabbed her around the waist, dragging her with him against the wall. "*Please* let that be the exit opening up."

As if on cue, a single rock clattered down from the ceiling. Then another.

Soren glared up at the ceiling, cupping her hands around her mouth and yelling, "*Will you stop that?*"

"Soren—" Elias began.

"No, no, I'm gods-damned tired of the ironic timing, the mountain does not get to almost kill us and also have a sense of *humor* about—"

Another rumble, much harder than the first, dropped them both on all fours.

Cursing to herself, Soren snatched up the rusted old lantern, its flame swelling as she swung it around to the far wall. "Look for an opening—a gap, a lever, anything!"

Elias joined her in her frantic exploration of the wall, practically clawing at the immovable facets. "You think there's a *lever* to open the door to a magical—"

"It's this or *die*, jackass!"

He stopped arguing after that.

Behind them, the quake got louder and louder, faster and faster—a rapid rainfall of stone that made it almost impossible to keep her eyes fixed on the task at hand.

One rock struck her shoe, and she twisted to check that it hadn't done any real damage, swearing again—then pausing, drawing the lantern in her hand closer to her face.

The flame barely shivered when she moved the lantern, as if the air had no effect on it. But she could have sworn…

She held it out toward the center of the room, away from the wall; the lantern's flame guttered, pulling in on itself, clinging so tightly to the wick it barely shed light past its own frame.

She held it out to the back wall; the flame loosened up, swelling back to its former size, flickering merrily in the face of their inevitable demise.

"Keep looking," she said, getting up and taking a few steps to the right. The flame shrank again, though not as much as before.

"Soren, what're you—"

She sidled back to the left, skirting around Elias. "Pardon my step."

"We don't have time for this!"

The flame expanded with a burst of light and heat—so sudden she almost jumped hard enough to trip and fall on her ass.

Weird. But not the weirdest thing she'd seen in her life—pits, not the weirdest thing she'd seen in this *mountain.*

"Cover me," she snapped, dropping to her knees in the far left corner.

No matter how thoroughly things shifted, both around and between them, one thing stayed the same: when your battlemate asked you to cover their back, you did it. No questions asked.

Elias's shadow fell over her. "Whatever you're doing," he hissed, "do it fast."

If they'd been in a slightly less deadly situation, she might have been tempted to take her time, just to spite him. But even her pettiness had limits.

Just to be sure, she held the lantern up as high as her arm would go—the flame dimmed, if only a touch. She lowered it again—it brightened up immediately.

She skimmed the ground with her eyes, heart crawling up her throat with every beat, until—

There.

A symbol scratched into the stone…a circle surrounding a lantern. A lantern that looked awfully close to the one in her hand.

With a prayer pointed to no one at all, she shoved the lantern over that circle.

A sound like all the air sucking out of the room; like the first desperate breath after drowning.

The soft golden glow behind the crystalline walls brightened all at once—like daybreak spilling through the cavern, forcing them both to cover their eyes to avoid being blinded.

And then…a voice.

A voice she couldn't describe, not in the way most could be described—not as masculine or feminine, not as deep or high, not as rough or smooth.

This voice was the reverberation of a struck gong, a vibration that struck in the bones. A choir hitting a perfect harmony, the music falling away until only singing held silence at bay. A mourning dove's call on a drowsy summer morning.

A voice that called her by name.

"Elias and Soren Loch," it said.

She couldn't help herself—she peeked through her fingers.

The light no longer glowed behind a crystal case, shapeless and slumbering.

The crystal had gone dark. And stepping from it—through it—was a figure.

A figure only just holding the shape of a human; a silhouette in reverse, a form of light outlined against a background of shadow. Not fire, but *light*, brilliance tinted oh-so-slightly in the richest of gold.

It had no face. Yet, she could have sworn it smiled.

"Come," it said, bending its fingers in the simplest command. "You have earned the answers you ask for. I will give them to you."

It was only because she was halfway convinced she was already dead that she was able to say: "And who are you?"

A world-weary sigh. It brimmed with an exhaustion so potent she felt it push on her own shoulders; she could only call it ancient.

"My true name is mine to protect," the being of light said. "But once upon a time, humanity named me Sancta."

CHAPTER 75

ELIAS

There could be no more doubt.

Those they called gods…they *were* humans, playing make-believe with throwaway scraps of banal magic. Children who sometimes saw fit to share with those younger and weaker.

The glory he beheld now…

This was matter and heat and the water that made up blood and sinew and leaves and rivers. The stardust that shed from the tails of comets and shimmered in the terrestrial ripples of a fingerprint. The might of an earthquake and a mother and a kiss between the eyes. Things that shook the earth and the sky and what came before the earth and the sky and what would one day rip the earth and sky from their binding, splitting the seams of mist and dust, nothingness and somethingness. The rage of a daughter. The tears of a son.

Godhood unmistakable.

He could not feel the knees he fell to.

Even more telling than the sheer *presence* of this being was the fact that Soren *also* knelt—and did so without rolling her eyes or poking fun at him for offering deference.

"Stand, please," Sancta said. "We do not have much time. I would see you out of the mountain before daybreak."

Soren stood immediately. Elias could not.

"Elias."

He couldn't open his eyes.

A warm hand settled on his head. "When a god asks you to stand, boy," said a voice made of all voices, a voice of rock and water and earth, a voice like the world itself had chosen to speak, "it is best to listen."

Boy. It could have been deprecating. It wasn't. More fond than anything.

He forced himself up, knees quaking in protest. "I don't...I don't understand."

"Why are you here?" Soren demanded.

"I am many places. Anywhere light shines, there I can be found." Sancta walked ahead of them without looking back; his cloak shone behind him like rippling rays of sunlight. "You have questions."

"How'd you guess?" Soren muttered.

"My ears bend under their weight. You—" A pause. "Ah. Sarcasm. I always forget—so human, to say one thing and mean the opposite. I never understood why you needed another kind of lying—especially one that wasn't meant to be believed."

"It's kind of supposed to be a joke."

"I see." Faceless light shone in her direction. "Ask your questions, Soren. They need not wait."

"Are you here to help us or hurt us?"

"Help you, if you will allow it."

"Why? Because you're the reason we're in this mess?"

"Soren," Elias hissed.

Soren didn't look at him. "What? He knows."

"If you mean to blame me for the Medeis siblings and their actions," said Sancta, "you are right—I gifted them with their magic. They had been mistreated greatly, and they loved greatly...they had the potential to become what you might call heroes. And in some lives, they were." Sancta's light dimmed a touch, sickened with shadow. "But one reached too far. One who saw mortality itself as another shackle placed on him."

A melody itched at Elias's ear. "Tenebrae."

"I did not fear much to do with his schemes...Mora, as you now know, had all she needed to end it." Another layer of darkness draped over Sancta, a shroud of transparent black chiffon. "But when the moment came, she refused."

Refused?

Disbelief already frothed at the brim of his brain; another drop, and it was bound to overflow.

"I did not grant her power over death without *much* consideration…and it was not gifted free of duty. She knew what I expected of her. She defied me." Sancta's fist closed; shadow peeled away, light brightening again. Though Sancta had no eyes Elias could see, he felt it when that eyeless gaze fell on him. "The truth to the legend of the god-killer, as such things often are, is…smudged. You are right—there is no weapon here. Mora was given her directive…it will remain hers until she completes it, whether by her own hand or by proxy. Your mortemancy makes you capable, Elias…but to kill this *god*, not his host body, you have need of one last thing."

Soren groaned. "If we have to go on *another* mountain crawl…"

Sancta chuckled; he reached over to muss Soren's hair, almost affectionate. "No, Soren—you've done enough. This one piece of the puzzle, I will give you myself."

"What is it?" Elias dared ask.

"I believe you have been calling them *relics*. Objects imbued with powerful magics."

He and Soren exchanged looks.

"We have them all," he confessed, heart sinking. "Or rather, the gods—er—I mean—"

"I know what you mean, Elias." Again, good humor sparked from Sancta. "Yes, the Medeis family has collected their relics, with the exception of the one you carry. I don't speak of their relics—I speak of *mine*."

Elias hadn't realized they'd reached the end of the tunnel until Sancta set his hand to the wall—light poured through cracks in the surface, lighting up an invisible symbol cut through the stone. A lantern held aloft by a featureless figure.

When Sancta pushed, the round stone bearing the symbol rotated with a mighty groan; and when the slab moved aside as if pushed by an invisible hand, he nearly wept at the sight beyond.

Darkness, still…but not the smothering darkness found in halls of stone.

Fresh air swept into the tunnel, filling his lungs with their first breath that *wasn't* stale in gods-knew how many days—and when he looked up, he was greeted by thousands of winking stars.

They'd made it. They'd *made it*.

Behind him, he heard Soren's sharp intake of breath—he turned to find her gazing up at Sancta, wearing a childlike uncertainty as he tapped the lantern in her hands.

"When its light shines on all your enemies, throw it down on the ground as hard as you can. If they are too far from its light or you don't manage to shatter it, it will not work, do you understand?"

"Yes." Such a soft response it couldn't possibly have come out of his battlemate.

"Good." Sancta set one hand to Elias's shoulder, the other on Soren's. "You two may save this broken world yet—and what a miracle it will be if you do."

Sancta's form flared, forcing him to shield his eyes—when he lowered his arm, only he and Soren remained.

Soren blinked at the lantern in her hand. "What," she said slowly, "in Mortem's dank, dark, sulfur-scented, tar-tainted—"

He covered her mouth to stop the stream of profanity in the wake of a holy gift. And as they waded out into a world sparkling with familiar stars and new snow, he let the haze of shock and exhaustion roll over his mind like a fog, his emotions vanishing into the gray.

CHAPTER 76

SOREN

She didn't remember most of the trek down the mountain.

Like she'd fallen asleep standing up, her awareness drifted shortly after they exited the Sanctum. A drifting that let her stop thinking for a while; a drifting that ended when, just as they started to trade empty rock for straggling trees, a familiar shout nearly scared both her *and* Elias out of their shoes:

"Soren? *Soren!*"

Next thing she knew, she was snugly, impossibly, wrapped up in Kessen Drake's arms; he was trying to hug her, but he was doing a far better job of choking the life out of her.

"How," she wheezed, pushing herself up in his arms to try and free her lungs, "did you get—"

"Oh, thank the *flogging* skies," Kessen rambled, squeezing tighter—her ribs quivered, so close to fracturing she could feel tiny bits flaking off. "We thought you were *so* dead. We backtracked and followed the trail that griffin left when it broke out—I guess they can dig through stone?—but you guys never showed up. We had to get Everin's head dealt with, and his leg—"

"Kessen!" Speak of the prince—Everin Arden himself limped past the treeline with a scowl sharp enough to stab her through. "You're going to pop the freckles off the poor girl's face. Put her down."

"Oh." Kessen set her down gently; his sheepish smile, paired with the misty touch to his eyes, made it difficult to stay annoyed. "Sorry. Excited."

"Yeah, we got that." Everin limped the full distance to them—he clapped Elias on the shoulder, then gave Soren a nod. "Glad to see you alive, Princess."

"I'm happy to see you, too." Oddly enough, it was true; if someone had told her at the start of this journey that the sight of Everin Arden's pretentious face would almost bring her to tears, she wouldn't have expected the cause to be *relief*.

Nor would she have expected him to give her a firm, fast hug, patting her on the back once.

"Thank you," he muttered in her ear. "For...you know what it's for."

She awkwardly reciprocated the back pat. "You all right?"

"Fine. Looked worse than it was, but if you hadn't gotten me out of there..." Everin shook his head, letting her go with a cough, rasping a hand over his beard. "Well, we were going to start looking for a way in, but you just saved us a few hours, so...allow me to show you to our magnificent abode."

The *magnificent abode* turned out to be a clearing a couple miles into the forest.

Frankly, it could have been a mud pit infested with foot-long worms, and Soren might've gotten on her knees and kissed it just because it wasn't gods-damned *rock*.

By the time Soren finished getting bullied—lovingly—into letting Matthias patch up her bumps and scrapes, Medwenna had already cornered Elias by the fire, the two of them taking turns piecing together the new information they'd received in the tunnel.

The lantern, Soren still held. The idea of letting anyone else carry it...she didn't know why, but it made her stomach queasy.

So she held it, ignoring the Tallisian triad when they gave her looks and mumbled amongst themselves about her hugging a lantern to her chest like it might try to run away.

Its light slumbered now. But it would return when she had need of it. She didn't know how she knew...but she did.

Faith.

She snorted softly. Figured, that the end of days would make a believer out of her.

Matthias sat down beside her, snipping the last length of bandaging material and rolling it up. "Glad you didn't die in there. Kess couldn't stop wailing about it—cried like a baby the whole night."

"I did *not*," Kessen protested as he carried a stack of fresh-cut firewood in. "Stop it. Soren, I did not. He's just trying to—"

"He did, he cried," Everin agreed; he stood beside the fire, most of his weight resting on his uninjured leg. His gray eyes gleamed with amusement as he nudged the logs around with his axe. "Real snotty stuff, too. Ruined his shirt. You owe him a new one."

"I hate you all," Kessen whined, pretending to kick Everin's leg as he walked behind him, setting the firewood next to the log Soren and Matthias had chosen as their perch. "I wish *all* of you got stuck in there, actually—Medwenna excluded."

"He did cry," Medwenna called. "It was very sweet."

Kessen scowled. "Medwenna no longer excluded."

"So." Everin limped away from the fire, dropping down on Soren's other side just as Kessen tried to take the same seat—Kessen ended up on Everin's lap, and Everin shoved him off, all three men bursting into laughter as Kessen propped himself against the log. "You two got out, great—but how? And what about the god-killer? I mean, I don't know about you all, but I'm not keen on going back in there."

Soren looked over to Elias, still getting his ear rambled off by Medwenna; he worried his lip for a moment, then dipped his head. Permission.

"Long story," she said. "We'll tell you on the way."

Everin frowned. "On the way where?"

"Castle Craghaven." She tightened the strap of her satchel. "I owe your father another chat."

"He won't change his mind," Everin warned. "He refused you already, remember?"

"He was dealing with the princess then."

Everin threw a look over to Kessen and Matthias; both men shrugged, and Everin turned back to her, raising his brow nearly to his hairline. "Fine, I'll snap the snare. Who exactly is he going to be dealing with this time?"

She smiled. "It's a surprise."

CHAPTER 77

SOREN

"Wait—stop! You can't just walk in here and—*someone stop that woman!*"

Oh, yes—she liked that introduction *much* better than her first.

The first time she'd entered Castle Craghaven, she'd done it head-down and heartsick, so afraid to shame her kingdom that she'd barely looked any of the castle guards in the eye. She'd let them whisk her away to some stuffy sitting room in the bowels of the castle where they'd forced her to change her outfit, relieve herself of her weapons…even her hair hadn't been "suitable" for an audience with the King of Tallis.

This entrance was far better suited to her tastes: having Everin dismiss the initial guard at the front entrance, then storming ahead to conquer these halls herself. Each door she reached, she blew by, ignoring the guards' commands to *halt*—she didn't even look back over her shoulder, trusting Everin would handle any pursuers attempting to block off her warpath. And trusting that either her battlemate or Everin's triad would tackle any guards who leveled weapons her way, intent on creating a more permanent solution to the problem of Soren Loch.

She would not submit herself to pampering and primping and pretty dresses today.

No. When she threw open the doors to the Tallisian king's throne room, giving a handful of guards heart attacks—and likely most of the lords seated throughout, as well—she did so with the full authority of the quintet of stars she carried on her shoulder.

She'd expected her shoulder to grow sore from the new responsibility she carried. Instead, she flew through that door like she weighed nothing at all; they could have been shooting stars streaking through the sky, letting her catch a ride on their twinkling tails.

King Denali didn't seem too invested in the matters of his kingdom at the moment, regardless—he slumped in his throne, face heavily lined with bad-tempered crags, a multitude of scowls stamped with a generous hand anywhere his skin hung loose. His head drooped in his hand, resting so heavily against it that when he jerked from his bored stupor, nail-marks remained embedded in his chin.

"What is *she* doing back here?" he snarled, flagrant blue gaze darting amongst the men gathered around him—clearly not noticing they all wore a slap of shock across their faces, too.

"I do apologize, Your Majesty," she said, breezing straight to the center of the room and planting herself over his self-adulating mosaic. Planting her heel right into its eye so it couldn't look down its nose at her. "I don't think I gave you a fair shake before. See, when I presented you with the offer for an alliance—"

"A request I *denied*, and you should hope I don't—"

"Not a request," she interrupted. "An *offer*."

King Denali sat forward, glassy eyes rolling like loose marbles. She half expected one to drop out. "You offered nothing in exchange for everything."

"I offered you the opportunity to go to war against the gods—something your ancestors would have *killed* to do, would they have had a chance in the pits to succeed—and I offered you the chance to win back something you have lost."

"Oh?" A dangerous, lazy purr in the mountain king's voice. "And what is that?"

"The loyalty of your people."

Denali blinked at her, then threw his head back—an uproarious fit of laughter she'd won more than once from his son. But Everin's laugh rarely took on the cruel edge his father's did; it didn't aim a low blow, trying to cut her off at the knees.

She stood strong. And she waited.

In that waiting, scattered footsteps punctuated the King's laughter—Elias, standing just shy of her heels, her loyal second shadow. Matthias and Kessen, splitting off to stand on either side of him.

Everin, who didn't ascend the dais to join his father this time; instead, he stood shoulder to shoulder with her, steady as her own heartbeat. An occasional tick on the left side of his jaw was the only sign his leg still pained him.

"Adorable," Denali chuckled—*bide your time,* she chanted to herself, ignoring the prickle of her rising hackles. He stood and swept his arms out to either side, turning in a slow half-circle. "Any one of my people would tell you otherwise."

"You think so?" Soren tapped her chin, frowning as she turned a deliberate circle of her own. She let her gaze wander lazily over every man in the room, making sure Denali could track her path of thought. "That's pretty funny. I don't think you know your kingdom like you think you do."

"You will swallow those words, or—"

"Let me tell you what I see." She turned her back on him, allowing herself the slightest smirk when she caught his jaw dropping out of the corner of her eye. "I walked through four checkpoints on my way here, sword on my belt—" she pulled it two inches out of its scabbard to prove it, then let it slide back in, clasping her hands to her chest as she continued her rotation, "—and not one of them detained me. I beelined straight for this room, where their King is holding court, my weapon on full display…and they didn't chase me. Do you know why?"

"I'm on the edge of my seat," Denali gritted out.

She'd take his word for it—no need to give him the satisfaction of her attention. "Prince Everin here stepped in and told them to leave it be—and they did. Without question. Isn't that interesting?"

"Oh, thanks," Everin hissed out of the corner of his mouth. "Way to throw me under the cart, there."

"Relax, I'm making a point." Once she completed her circle—pausing briefly to bask in the glow of pride in Elias's gaze as he watched her play with her prey—she jerked one thumb over her shoulder, smiling plainly at Denali. "I'm making a fool out of you in front of your court. I'm a foreign royal standing ten feet from your throne. I'm wearing almost as many weapons as I have fingers. And do you see what your guards are doing?"

Denali's jaw clenched, a snowstorm blowing over his gaze as he swept it across his throne room, taking in what Soren had already clocked:

The guards, the lords…none of them were watching the King, ready to leap to his defense or obey his orders. Nor were they watching her to see what she'd do or say next. She'd started to draw her sword, for gods' sakes, and none of them had even taken a step in her direction.

Because instead, they all had their eyes on Everin. Taking their cues from him. He kept his hand away from his weapon, so they did not reach for theirs.

"You," Soren said softly, taking one more step forward, "do not have the power in this castle, Your Majesty. Your son's just letting you play pretend a little while longer."

Denali rose with a thunderous growl, lurching down two of the dais steps as he drew his own weapon: an *unfairly* beautiful blade of unidentifiable make, its hilt decorated in silver and gold—both white and yellow gold—reinforced with some tougher material beneath. When he raised it to point at her, its blade wavering between her heart and her stomach, the light caught on the design etched into the crossguard: a lantern carrying an undying light.

"I have entertained your tantrum long enough." King Denali jerked his head in her direction. "Guards, take the girl and—"

"What did you just call me?"

Nothing had ever thrilled her the way saying those words did—not just that she'd said them, a threat scorched cold with starfire, but that she *felt* the air rush out of the room when she did. Hands finally grasped for hidden hilts; feet shifted toward the door, poised to run.

"I say what I see—and I see a little girl who thinks she can cow me into joining her hopeless cause by puffing out her chest and showing off how loudly she can lie." He stomped down another step, so off-balance her head spun just watching him.

"Are you sure?" So soft she could barely hear herself over the ring of Denali's wheedling insults in her ear. "I don't know many kings who have to face *little girls* with their swords drawn."

"Take this *girl*," he repeated, seething like a teakettle, face so flushed she almost expected steam to roar out of his nose, "and throw her in the stocks. We'll see how much she mouths off after she's spent a night in the cold."

Breathe in.

Soren breathed in deeply through her nose, refusing to let her muscles lock up as guards began to shuffle closer, darting nervous glances at their prince all the while.

Breathe out.

She exhaled through rounded lips.

Control what you can.

"General," she said.

The guards halted; the King rolled his eyes. "I am done listening to—"

"You will address me by my *title*," she interrupted, "and by my *name*. You will show me the respect I am due as an Heir and as a soldier. You will stop speaking *around* me. And when I ask you if Tallis will fight alongside us, you will agree—or you will regret it. This I vow."

And she kept her rotting vows.

"I am General Soren Loch," she said, "Daughter of queens, sister to tricksters and kings-at-heart, wife and battlemate of the Phoenix Priest, and friend to the Goddess of Life. I am impossible. I am a miracle. I am a smartass. And I am not leaving here without your *gods-damned* army!"

She and the King stared at each other, four dais steps and a sword all that stood between them.

He regarded her the same way he had that first time: with the cold, careless boredom of a tyrant.

A king who let fear rule in his stead. A king who had good people killed according to the whims of his pride and prejudices. A king who only let women into his throne room to serve him wine and shove broken glass into their hands.

A man who had done such terrible things to brave, brilliant Medwenna she could not *speak* of them all, let alone stomach being in the same room as him.

And he said, without any thought at all, "No."

So she turned to look at Everin.

"What you said before, about hating him," she said.

The prince's dagger-dark glare met hers. "Yes?"

"I really hope you were telling the truth."

And then she moved.

Two steps, and she'd reached the dais stairs.

One more, and she'd drawn her sword.

One more when the King stumbled up a stair himself, spittle flying with the force of his shout; he swung wildly at her, all strength and no form, the heft of his sword dragging him to the side.

"What are you *doing?*" he roared past her, sword careening the other way; she dodged with a backstep and an affected yawn, rewarded by Kessen's fox-bark laughter—shriller than usual, strung a few notes too high with stress, but still worth it. "Help me—*help me!*"

A couple of guards did start to step forward, to their credit. But Everin raised a hand, balling it into a fist; he watched the scene on the dais with as much emotion as the stone-faced mountains beheld a budding sunrise.

"Anyone thinking of climbing those stairs," he said, "notice I'm not standing in her way."

A threat even the Lion of Tallis chose to leave alone…that wasn't something any old castle guard was willing to test their luck on. They stayed put.

"Traitors!" Denali threw his whole weight at her, driving for her legs—an attempt to knock her over. "*Trait—*"

She swung her elbow around, slamming his sword arm aside; in her other hand, she gripped a handful of his tunic, letting his weight do what he'd wanted it to do.

But when she went down, she took him with her.

Teeth gritted, shoulders and wrists smarting, she wrenched around and landed on top of him—when they tumbled to a bruising halt at the bottom of the dais steps, she had one hand fisted in his tunic, the other holding her sword to his throat.

Vessels had burst in his eyes, stained glass windows painted crimson; he bared his teeth at her behind thin, foam-flecked lips. "You wouldn't *dare.*"

"Actually," she said, conscious of Elias's eyes on her face, "I've never turned down a dare."

When she dragged her sword across King Denali's neck, not a single voice cried out—no grief, no horror, no fury.

The only sound was the King's sword crashing to the ground, the impact pealing through the silent room…and a second impact after, bone against stone, the dull impact of someone's knee striking the floor.

But her display wasn't done.

She cleaned her sword on the King's tunic. Sheathed it. Stood up as slowly as she could, her own knees holding as steady as she could have hoped for.

The crown stuck when she tried to tug it off Denali's head—not a good fit. It took two more tries to pry it off, stopping just short of planting her boot on his shoulder for leverage. The last thing she needed right now was a famous Elias Loch lecture about disrespecting the dead.

Everin hadn't said a word yet; when she turned to face the room, she found him on one knee, arms limp at his sides. He seemed rooted to the spot, staring at his father's body.

Soren knew grief well enough to recognize it on others. She saw it nowhere on Everin's face now.

The wary way he watched his father's lifeblood slip into the crevices between stone tiles, blinking fiercely, his fingers digging mercilessly into the side of his leg…it was like he half expected the man to find his feet, slit throat and all, and start screaming in their faces all over again.

When she approached with the crown, Everin rocked back to his feet, his throat bobbing as he shifted his sights from his father to his crown. Barely anything—it could have been a twitch, for all she knew.

Except that she did know—she knew better than she had any right to.

But Everin wasn't like her. Everin had been born *and* built for this—he had earned what she had not. All he needed was someone to finally give him what he deserved.

"King Everin." She held the crown out to him, not bothering to wipe his predecessor's blood from her fingers. "Wanna help us kill a god?"

He took the crown without a second's hesitation. Set it on his brow without blinking. Let the blood drip down his temple, down his neck, slipping beneath his collar.

"Princess…" A feral, lion-hearted grin. "I thought you'd never flogging ask."

CHAPTER 78

ANIMA

The artists of the world—poets and bards, storytellers and songwriters—often wrote about the wonder of first love.

Their songs were penned in wistful ink, striking a longing note in every listener's ear; they were composed to call out the dreamer in someone, the romantic, the piece of them—however small or hidden—that believed in the stuff of fables and fairytales.

But the more sensible sorts—the people who explored the method behind the machinations of the world, people who studied and spoke the language of logic alone—they spoke of love as an affliction. A thing one came down with. A thing one suffered from.

Lovesick.

That was the diagnosis Ani assigned to herself as she drifted through the motions of making her breakfast without consciously participating in the task, swaying to the melody of malaise.

She did not know what else to call it. While her hands set to work cutting up fruit, softening oats in a mixture of milk and warm spices and tossing her cuttings into the compost bin at the end of the butcher-block counter, her mind slipped away from her body, skulking back through the sparse hours of sleep she'd gotten. Stealing back down that path of sparkling dew and fading sunlight. Returning to the scene of her crime.

And the longer her mind floated past reality, the stranger her symptoms became.

At first, she hardly noticed them: they came in sprinklings, a sourceless smile here, an idle hum there. All her thoughts losing their shape before they came to a definitive end, replaced by the honeyed notes of an old Sanctan love song.

Where she'd heard it, she only vaguely remembered…Cassi, maybe. For a short while before a stake and a secret had broken everything, she'd come home from the tailor's shop most afternoons singing—singing *so* much, and so often love songs, that Peter had demanded to know what lucky person had managed to rob the best pickpocket in Sanctaviv of her heart…and her good sense.

She'd teased, and lied, and danced around the subject with a ballerina's grace—but she'd never told. After receiving her magic, she rarely used her voice for any performance other than her prophecies…and after suffering something even worse, a horror none of them had been able to save her from, she never sang at all.

Cassandra Medeis, so head-spun she couldn't stop singing love songs. Such a mind-boggling idea now, she almost wondered if she'd made up the memory.

Heart aching, she crumpled a fistful of her apron just above it…wishing she could reach right through and tug that pointless pain right out.

Nostalgia. Another symptom.

She set the knife down and stepped back, wiping her hands on her apron while she forced herself to focus on her breakfast fixings. Oatmeal and cut fruit; not her heartiest of choices, but with her stomach fluttering like it was, so bubbly she could barely keep it from floating clean up to her sternum…

Butterflies in the stomach. She flipped a notepad open in her mind, jotting it down with the others.

The whole morning had been like this, not to mention the evening prior. No matter how well she plumped her pillows or how kindly the trees outside followed her request to rustle their leaves to create a thrum of soothing noise, sleep had dodged her like a rabbit in the path of a carriage race. She'd had to pace herself into exhaustion just to get a wink or two in—and this morning, she'd woken with the same uncomfortable energy skating beneath her skin, a restless itch she couldn't scratch.

It wasn't until the love songs started to sound more like a familiar lullaby that she realized, with a strike of fear, that these symptoms might not be *lovesickness* at all.

Nothing could calm her spiraling thoughts after that. Not her breakfast, which she only managed to swallow a few pasty bites of before the butterflies made it impossible; not her journals, which she'd carried to the royal library and cracked open only to find herself skimming the same sentence over and over without actually *reading* it; not even sipping the sweet chamomile tea she'd taken from the kitchen downstairs.

She scowled down at her journal. At her barely-dented bowl of cold oatmeal and the lukewarm tea beside it. At her useless, sickened heart.

"Not so fond of the tale?"

The cream-colored journal flew out of her hands, landing facedown, performing a painful skid across the floor; she slammed her hand over her pounding heart as Wolf bent down to rescue the tome, grimacing at the carnage she'd made of paper and ink. "Not fond of it *at all,* then."

"You startled me," she accused—a tone that might've kept a sharper edge if it hadn't come hand in hand with a smile sillier than a goose. "And you're late."

"My apologies. It took me some time to find rest last night, and I fear I made up for it this morning."

A circumstance he hadn't chosen willingly, judging by his embarrassed grimace. "So you couldn't sleep either?"

An infinitesimal twitch of his brows. "Either?"

Her cheeks went pinker than the bubblegum so many Lapisian confectionaries were famous for. "I meant—oh, forget it. I meant either."

He tapped a knuckle under her chin, a playful twinkle dancing through his eyes, even with exhaustion trampling circles around them. "Not a fair comparison. You're as radiant as ever."

In the back of her mind, she started tabulating the titles on the shelves nearby, wondering if any of them could inform her of the commonality of a compliment melting a woman into a puddle of pinkish goo.

The rest of her mind was making a sound remarkably like a mockingbird's screech.

"Wolf Olivander, a shameless flirt," she squeaked. "Who knew?"

A scoff. "Shameless, hardly. You did have to order me to stop apologizing, if you recall."

"You're doing quite well." She glanced at the cuckoo clock ticking merrily on the wall. "It's been nearly a whole minute already."

"Imagine if I make it to two."

She giggled. "I'll make you a plaque celebrating your accomplishment."

When he actually *laughed,* the bonfire-bright chortle that rumbled all the way into his chest, she squeezed her knee just to make sure it hadn't actually turned to jelly. "An honor beyond words, Goddess."

She wrinkled her nose. Giddiness slammed into sour temper, falling flat on its back—like a bird hurtling itself into a dangerously clean window. "No."

"No…what?"

"You *know* what."

His nose wrinkled this time. "No, I'm confused."

"Wolf," she half-whined, half-laughed. "*Goddess?*"

"Ach, that's right—my apologies, love." He set one hand to each arm of the chaise, leaning in so close the tip of his nose brushed hers. "An honor beyond words…Annelisa."

One quick, petulant glance at the clock. Both to make her point and to keep herself from swooning outright. "Just under two minutes. No plaque for you."

"Mm. A pity. I was so looking forward to lording that over Sage…" His fingers crept up into her hair, gripping the base of her braid like the arch of a bow, taking aim as he spoke toward her mouth. "Might've even moved my pebble collection to make room…"

Her giggles softened into a sigh as he drew her into a kiss; as she drew him down to the chaise beside her, dragging her fingertips lightly down his leather jerkin.

Fresh grass ground to a pulp, fresh air never further than the next breath, the lowing of the herd never further than—

Irritation sprouted like a weed; she dug it up with a groan, abandoning her exploration of Wolf's lips to tug at the leather strings tying his jerkin shut.

"Whoa—loosen your bootlaces, lass—" He chuckled, catching her by the wrists, tipping his head with a quizzical smirk. "What do you think you're doing down there?"

Again, twin suns of mortified heat rose in her cheeks. Her fingers froze midway through untangling the middle knot; she'd already bared a sizable portion of the knit brown tunic underneath.

"It's being loud," she explained.

He glanced downward; when his gaze met hers again, he only looked more bemused. "What is?"

She tapped the leather. "This."

"I didn't hear a peep." Still smiling, but starting to take on a concerned sort of caution. He pressed the back of his hand to her forehead. "You feeling all right?"

"It's the leather." Rot her bones, she *did* sound mad. "The cow, actually."

"The cow."

If she didn't get this explanation in order, he was going to whisk her off to the infirmary faster than a mosquito drank up its favorite meal.

"It takes time for dead things to let go." She shrugged sheepishly, her fingers giving in to an old nervous habit: twirling her hair. *Just* a nervous habit, she insisted to herself—nothing more frightening than that. "Leather, furniture built from trees, feather pillows…it's the same soulstuff that necromancy feeds on. I'm the only one that can hear them, so…sometimes they want to tell me their stories."

Wolf leaned into the chaise cushion, tucking one hand behind his head, the other reaching up to toy with the same strand of hair she kept twirling. His lips paled around the edges as he pressed them together—a tell she finally understood. A tell that no longer made her brace for an angry word or cold look. "Well, I'll give you this—that's the oddest excuse for trying to take my clothes off I've *ever* heard."

She slapped his chest. "*Wolf?*"

Another laugh, and the hunter-prince bent forward, stealing a kiss as he shrugged off his jerkin. He worked it down to his bicep, then shook it the rest of the way off his arm, flinging it somewhere amongst the shelves. He spread his arms wide. "There. No more cows trying to horn in."

Ani scowled at him. "You're *teasing* me."

His smile softened. He reached out to brush a strand of hair from where it had caught on the corner of her lip. "A little. Forgive me if it's too much—I'm a tad rusty."

She checked the clock again. "You made it three minutes that time."

A playful growl of "Oh, you think you're *funny*, do you—" was her only warning before Wolf dug his fingers into her sides, expertly prodding into every dimple and dip in her ribs that happened to be outrageously, *stupendously* ticklish.

She'd never screamed so loud and shrill—nor had she laughed so hard, nearly hard enough to break one of those ribs, than when she somersaulted off the chaise and took flight through the library.

Shelved books flew by, her speed muddying them into watercolor smudges. Stifling her laughter with all her might—and with her teeth firmly clamped over the heel of her hand, since she'd never actually achieved the self-control it took to stop laughter or tears once they'd started—she dove into a nook where the corners of two shelves met, an L-shaped shadow she fit into like a mushroom tentatively taking up residence in a tree's wayward root.

Don't mind me, she thought, giving the wood a soothing pat. *Just a friend sharing some space, if you don't mind.*

Wood so well-worked over didn't carry as much lingering life in its sanded layers; still, it mustered up *something* for its maker, a memory of gentle breezes plucking old leaves from its branches, helping them find a safe space to settle on the ground.

She gifted it a tender kiss in return, the nutty aroma of darkwood melding with the chisel-sharp scent of wood polish. *Thank you, little one.*

Either her shoeless feet had managed to muffle her steps, or this prince secretly enjoyed the thrill of the hunt—here and there, a creaking floorboard told her he was circling nearby, but he had yet to step into her path.

"All right, where'd you go, you wily little beast?" he called; gruff as always, but the undercurrent of glee in it, the swell of laughter always hidden just beneath the dry brush above...

He sounded...happy.

Gods, she couldn't remember the last time she'd made someone sound so happy.

Not a happiness she'd bought with magic in hand and a miracle in tow, every benevolent smile teetering on the edge of desperation. Waiting with bated breath for night to burst into day in their eyes; for the moment that skepticism and despair were chased out by joy and wonder.

This happiness, she'd earned...this happiness, she shared.

And the last thing she wanted was to hide from it.

She crawled out from her hiding place on all fours, peeking out—Wolf wasn't waiting down this row of shelves, so she swung her feet underneath her and pushed off her palms to stand, doing her best impression of Cassi's tiptoed ballerina stride as she danced down to the end of the row.

She paused, setting her ear to the edge of the shelf first; nothing to her right, but to her left, she definitely heard rustling. The weak groan of wood bearing the weight of someone's toes.

Doing a poor job of muffling her laughter now, she curled around the shelf, anticipation bubbling over in her stomach.

She came face to face with scleral eyes and a smile like the pale belly scales of a washed-up fish.

"You," snarled the Blight, its voice layered with the roars of prowling predators…feline, canine, avian, more. This monster sang with the voices of beasts.

Horror strangled that seedling of happiness before it could even bud, could even bloom—she backed away as the monster consumed her one chance at escape, seizing vines braiding through the gaps in the shelves to bear it aloft.

"You hurt me." A vine slithered between two books, scratching Ani's cheek with a loving caress. It retracted with a *snap* like a cracked whip; the vine offered itself up to the monster's mouth, and it stuck out its tongue, taking a tentative lick of Ani's blood.

The sheen of its gaze shifted from pebble-gray to rust-red.

"*I hurt you*," growled the voice of beasts.

The vines slung the monster forward, its jaw unhinging like a constrictor snake's.

Ani did not scream so loud and shrill this time; her soul had leapt clean out of her body, so getting enough breath to scream *at all* would have been a feat. Instead, she threw herself under the monster, the floorboards tearing at her stomach through her dress; she crawled for her life, begging breath to return, as she looked around wildly for Wolf.

There; he'd crouched behind a nearby armchair. He held two hunting knives, his back pressed to the back of the chair; when he saw her, he sagged to one side, like he'd been holding his breath and had lost it all at the sight of her.

He gestured for her to crawl to him; she shook her head.

"It wants me," she mouthed.

The Blight prowled out on all fours now, half-lupine, half-human; its head wagged back and forth like it sought a scent, though it had no proper nose. Its back was to them; it hadn't spotted them yet.

Wolf widened his eyes, pointing *hard* at the floor in front of him. "*Now*," he mouthed back.

She swallowed hard, rooting her fingers in the wood. She could do nothing but whisper his name under her breath, too terrified to defy, too terrified to obey.

Anguished eyes, wet with fear, held hers in an unbreakable grip.

"Ani," he begged without a voice. His knuckles were *white* where he held the dagger, like his bones were about to break through his skin. *"Please—"*

The Blight's head snapped around.

And just like that, the time for quiet was over.

"Run!" she screamed to Wolf—and as one, they bolted for the window.

Wolf flipped one of his knives, stabbing the hilt into the window; the glass shattered, defeated in one blow by the density of darkwood.

The snake-like hiss of vines slithering across the library floor came to an abrupt halt.

So did Ani's heart.

Luckily, that venomous quiet failed to paralyze Wolf; after sheathing his knives, his warm arm wrapped around her waist, kicking her heart back into motion as his hand snugged over her chest. He swung her up and propped her on the windowsill, releasing her to reach over her shoulder. "We could use a ride, friend!"

When a darkwood branch drifted to the window, leaves spread like a helping hand, Wolf pushed her by the small of her back. "Get on!"

She shoved her palms against either side of the windowpane, pushing back fruitlessly against his hand. "You go first, you go—"

"This is not up for debate, Goddess!"

She hated that damned title.

She flipped onto her back, driving her heel into the wall, begging him without words. Pleading for her gaze to show everything she couldn't say. "And if your goddess commanded you?"

No pain compared to watching Wolf look at her with such tender, terrible devotion; no agony compared to the backhanded sweep of his fingers against her cheek, the gentlest touch she'd been given in centuries.

"Then I fear my days of asking for forgiveness are not yet behind me," he said.

A sudden impact to both her shoulders. The whistle of wind in her ears. The theft of breath from her lungs.

She didn't realize she was falling—that she'd been *pushed*—until spindly branches caught her in their grasp.

No fury compared to realizing she'd been defied outright; no rage compared to scrabbling to her feet on this darkwood branch, looking back to see Wolf lingering behind, head turned to seek their pursuer.

Ani twisted on her toes, her skirts tangling around her calves as she strained back toward the window. *"Hurry!"*

It seemed he could not stomach defying her twice; he climbed up on the sill, boots teetering as he reached back, a frustrated groan scraping through his teeth as he strained for her hand.

A groan that cut off with a soft, glottal gasp.

A knife stuck out through Wolf's side, its tip glazed morning-glory red. A knife from his own bandolier.

A thorn-riddled vine slapped over Wolf's shoulder, sinking its claws in; a disjointed arm wrapped around his waist, yanking the blade out with such force that the serrated blade *ripped* through his body without catching, tearing the wound wide open.

Frayed flesh; sprayed blood.

Trapped in the in-between place where only unmoored spirits lurked—the miasmic kaleidoscope of almost-living where she existed (not lived) between hosts—she could only watch the world go by, her hands and nose pressed to the glass. She could offer miracles, she could answer prayers, she could whisper in her believers' ears…but she could not reach out with her own hands. Neither to help nor hold them through their pain.

She kept little when she left that place. But that helpless ache in her empty hands…she never forgot that.

This was worse.

There was no glass, no separation, nothing—*nothing* to shield her from the shock ripping her open from sternum to ribs, like she'd taken the blow herself.

But the screaming didn't start until Wolf's head slumped toward his chest. Until she cried out for him, and he did not answer her summons.

Ani's scream tore in half, drifting uselessly to the ground; she reached for the wounded prince, sobbing his name over and over, her soul shrieking for the tree to stretch further, to move faster, to take her back to him—to bring him back to her.

It should have been easy; it should have been *nothing.*

As effortless as the monster's *snap* of the knife, a clean break right through steel. The monster let it fall, watching it go with a beastly grin.

A *grin,* while Wolf bled in its arms.

"Put him down!" she screamed.

The monster actually *recoiled;* the vines winding lazily around Wolf's body reared back, seized with a strange rigor.

Letting Wolf's limp body tumble out of the window.

"*No!*"

Ani thrust her hands into the darkest wells of her blessed power. The hidden pockets even she rarely dared peek into.

This Blight knew her too well—had sipped every other wellspring dry, siphoning her magic until it feared its own mistress's touch, not knowing the difference between her and her corrupted shadow.

But there had to be something. She had to have *something.*

For a prince whose prayers she'd forgotten, whose pockets were full to bursting with pebbles, whose lips were the first to call her by *her* name in so long…

Something. *Anything.*

Her fingertips met only dead, dry sand. Even her deepest wells of power drained dry.

A blur of movement by the window.

The monster plunged from the sill in jerky, shuddering lurches of movement; it slid down the tree with terrifying speed, vines unraveling like spiraling crepe paper streamers.

On the hunt for its next kill. Not sated by spilling Wolf's blood.

And Ani couldn't move.

Her legs gave out, and she fell to her seat against the trunk, staring at the spot where Wolf had vanished beneath the treetops.

Once, she could have reached out for the shining light of his life, a brilliant flare burning inside every mortal—she would have seen it, known it, when it extinguished. She would have been able to tell if he still lived.

But every time she tried to pour power into her veins, it ached. It ached like her bloodpaths would burst, flooding her body with putrescent chaos.

The leaves started rustling again.

Threshing-floor hair appeared first. Then a pitted set of eyes; eyes that no longer shone red. Bone-shard teeth clamped around a scarred arm.

Disbelief slapped Ani between the shoulder blades, shoving her onto all fours; she crawled dangerously far out onto the tapered branch, heart hammering like a woodpecker's beak as she screamed Wolf's name.

The prince did not raise his head; he hung in the monster's jaw like a brace of rabbits caught in a snare, unmoving. But he was there—not falling, not broken on the forest floor.

When the monster halted in front of Ani, it did not snarl or babble or hiss familiar threats.

It simply draped Wolf over the thickest portion of the branch, then drifted backward, its unblinking stare almost…stricken.

"I hurt him," it said. "He helped me. I hurt him. I cannot stop."

Ani dragged Wolf into her lap, then pressed two fingertips to his jaw. *Please. Please, please, please, please, please…*

A throbbing, uneven heartbeat lurched beneath her touch.

"Fix him," said the beast. "Fix me."

Ani couldn't speak. Her lungs prickled with nettle-stings, swelling against her breastbone like she'd opened her chest and invited a horde of wasps inside; panic like she'd never known chilled her down to her marrow, her bones hollowed out to house a horror bigger than her body.

Her island was dying. Her people were dying.

Wolf was dying.

Her fault.

Her fault.

All her fault.

She made a shadow box of her body, framing him in with her fragile grip. Her bottom lip split as she hurled the only words she could think of, begging them to do the wounding her magic could not. *"Leave us alone!"*

Pathetic. A little girl flinging words at bullies armed with rocks.

Something squirmed in her stomach, a worm burrowing into the meat of a shiny apple. The infestation festering at the heart of something so deceivingly shiny and sweet.

She had nothing to pluck it out. No way to stop it from coring the potency from her power.

But in the monster's mind, it seemed parchment-thin words somehow beat rock-hard might; when Wolf coughed, his chest gurgling under Ani's ear, she opened her eyes to find only boughs bristling with evergreen needles surrounding them.

"Hang on." An order to herself as much as a plea to him. "Help can't be far."

As long as she lived, she would never forget the way Sage howled his brother's name when she dragged Wolf through the infirmary door, sobbing so hard she couldn't catch her rotting breath.

The medimantically gifted ranger thrust everything weighing him down—an armful of bandages, a bottle of clotting poultices, his precious bow, *everything*—into another medimancer's arms before bolting, clearing the infirmary's beautiful tile floor in two seconds flat.

Ani didn't realize how heavily she'd been leaning on the fairytale she'd spun for herself—the one where she reached the infirmary in time, medimancers greeted her with calm reassurances that Wolf would be right as rain in minutes, and she could sink into the relief of an overreaction put to rest—until Sage's shout swept that yarn right out from under her. Until he hauled Wolf's shivering body away, and she toppled like a storm-struck tree, her fingers streaking blood across the tiles.

"What happened?" Sage swung himself over his unconscious brother, corkscrewing two fingers into the wound; to stop the bleeding at the source, she knew, but she gagged anyway; whimpered anyway.

She'd seen worse. She'd *done* worse. In this infirmary and hundreds, thousands, of others.

But never to someone she…never when it was…

"Anima!" A pitiless, commanding bark. "Tie yourself together and tell me what did this!"

Ani stared down at her splayed fingers, soaked in sap—the sort bled from trees and the sort spiled from mortal veins.

One finger twitched.

Her arm spasmed.

"I tried," she said, voice so small she couldn't have made it out under a magnifying glass. "It's…I told him…"

An ear-splittingly foul curse. "Forget it, lass, you'll be gods-damned useless until you're out of shock." Then—softer, shaken, but wrapped up in a fearsome wrath she hadn't thought the easygoing ranger capable of—he muttered, "I swear on the roots of this wretched island, Wolf, if a hole in your hide's what does you in, I'm going to spit in your grave as many times as it takes to soak your rotting coffin."

Scarlet sap dripping from her hands. Withered, worm-eaten glory, so pocked and picked clean she could barely summon a seedling, let alone the kind of divine retribution required to run off a living, breathing blaspheme against her name.

Somehow she ended up standing, even though she couldn't feel her legs. Somehow she didn't realize that her own nails were scratching furrows into her arms, sight fixed on the bloodied scratches down Wolf's wrists. And somehow, when she turned to flee—

Somehow, she ran right into a familiar embrace. An embrace that, as usual, refused to let her flee from the truth of what she'd done.

"Ani?" Soren's voice had never sounded more like a stranger's. Like the thin mountain air had not yet left her lungs. "What in the *pits* is going on?"

A fist of emotion closed around her windpipe, choking out her words. Instead, she collapsed into her friend's arms, losing the last of her breath to weeping…

And the cracked hum of an ancient lullaby she couldn't seem to get out of her head.

CHAPTER 79

SOREN

"**Y**ou had *one job*!"

She really hadn't thought it too much to hope for an uneventful return to Arborius. Or at least to find a relatively unscathed Goddess of Life waiting for them.

Judging by the hour it had just taken her to talk Ani down from her tearful, frantic explanation—and to get her to stop humming that damned song so Elias could come back in the room without his hands stuck to his ears—she'd been wrong.

Thoroughly, infuriatingly wrong.

"Actually," said Sage, tone far too casual for someone in the middle of strapping a thrashing man down to an infirmary bed, "I have quite a few jobs, all of which I've kept up with swimmingly—and none of which involved babysitting a goddess. That was Wolf's bag."

Soren gestured to Wolf—the aforementioned thrashing man. "Well, I can't exactly take that up with him, now can I?"

"I can *hear* you," seethed Wolf through his teeth; he tore his arm free from Sage's grip for the fourth time, and both of them swore together, followed by Wolf's rasping, "Sorry."

"If you think I'm actually buying that you're throwing this little fit against your will, you've got another thing coming." A joke, she thought—but devoid of Sage's usual good humor. Not that she could blame him. He finally tugged the last strap tight, then let himself sway back into the wall, his arms falling limp at his sides. "Gods, I'm going to be sore as a plucked pigeon tomorrow. Aren't dying men supposed to be frail?"

"Dying?" Soren demanded. "He just got infected—don't you think that's a bit of a leap?"

Sage waved her off with a feeble jerk of his arm. "Inside joke, lass. I'm not a horse, so get off my back, will you?"

Wolf's chattering teeth made it difficult to tell if he was grinning or grimacing. "N-no, you're a—a horse's *a-arse*."

"And I suppose you'll tell me name-calling's a symptom, too." Sage rolled his eyes, leaning in to pat his brother's shoulder…then doubling down, squeezing it till his knuckles paled. "Hang in there, yeah?"

Wolf shut his eyes. "Don't tell Ma."

Sage rolled his misty eyes. "About the names, or about the hole in your hide?"

"Both."

"Oh, so you want me *dead* dead."

Wolf's throat bobbed. "Promise. Don't tell Ma."

"I'll tell whoever I like whatever I like." Sage's hard swallow, visible even from the other side of the room, belied his sass. "Rest, fool. You're in the best hands I've got."

"Always am," Wolf mumbled…a slow, drifting slur that ended in a congested cough.

A grim, awful knot tied up her insides as she looked from Wolf to Ani…from Ani back to Wolf. Then to Sage, who stared at nothing, wearing the thousand-yard look of a soldier coming off a battlefield for the first time in days.

"Sorry," she mumbled. "You're right—I don't need to get on your back."

"I get it—if I'd gone off on a world-saving quest and come back to this mess, I would've doled out a tongue-lash or two, myself." Sage sank down against the wall, propping his arms on his knees. "We're mired in quite the mud slick here, lass. I won't lie to you. Illness, assault, we put up our best defenses against it all…that thing, this Blight, it treated them like a playground." A sharp gesture to Ani and Wolf. "They were in our rotting *library,* for gods' sakes. Top of the damned tree."

Soren exchanged a look with Elias; he still hovered near the door, ready to duck out if Ani got to humming again. She'd argued that the song itself didn't hold any power, but…well, there were risks her battlemate was willing to take, and this wasn't one of them.

She couldn't muster much of an argument. Not when she still did her best to dress every morning with her back facing him so he wouldn't catch sight of the cauterized scythe-scars marring her middle.

"Nothing's helped?" she croaked. "Medimancy, sanguimancy…?"

"Not even good old-fashioned physician work." Sage shook his head. "We've done our best to slow the spread, to ease the pain, but it's a losing battle. It's not like an illness or injury…or a poison. The closest we can compare it to is a parasite, but one we can't excise…and one we can't starve out."

The slightest rousing from her battlemate. A blink; a downshift of his brow.

"Elias just had an idea," she said.

"It's a bad one," he warned—but he didn't deny it.

"Better than *none*." Sage spread his arms. "I'm all ears, lad."

Elias looped one finger through his prayer beads—since he'd donned them in the mountain, he hadn't taken them back off. He looked at her first, reluctance in the shift of his jaw…then he looked to Ani.

"Parasites can't survive on their own," he said. "The host dies, they die."

"Knew that," Sage and Soren said together.

Not even a shade of annoyance flickered over Elias's troubled frown. An idea bad enough that she couldn't distract him by being obnoxious?

Her heart sank. "Rip out the stitch, jackass."

"The god-killer," he said carefully; her heart jumped up to her throat this time. "Legend says it can kill the god without killing the mortal. Kill the parasite…"

"Without killing the host." Sage frowned. "But the Blight's not a god."

"No, but in theory, the solution might be similar." Elias held up his hand, frostbite-black crowning his fingertips. "Kill the parasite with mortemancy…heal the host with medimancy. If we work fast enough, we might be able to eradicate the Blight without killing the host."

"I don't like it," Soren said immediately.

"I agree," Sage said…but slowly. The sort of slow that suggested he wasn't willing to dismiss it as quickly as her. "Mortemancy, that's a host-level magic…one mortals aren't born with. Even our most talented medimancers and biomancers wouldn't be able to keep up with power like that. You'd end up killing the whole island to kill the Blight."

"Mortals couldn't keep up," Elias agreed. "But Anima could."

"You heard Sage," Soren protested. "Her magic isn't working." Even the shallow scratches she'd dealt to herself earlier had barely scabbed over by now.

"Which is why I brought up the god-killer." Elias held her gaze. "Easiest way to kill the parasite is to kill the host."

"Which we just agreed is not an option."

"Not for the rest…but Ani's come back to life before. Even when she was human."

Like a clockhand forced to move forward by rusted gears, comprehension tried to dig its heels in, refusing to get close enough to make sense of the picture Elias was painting; but her mind, still Sanctum-primed for puzzle-solving, shoved ahead into understanding's harsh light.

"You want to kill Ani," she said.

Elias nodded—no hesitation, no apology. Honest as ever. "To try and save her…and the rest of them. Yes."

"But the stories said the god-killer is supposed to kill the soul, not the body."

Elias gestured at his own chest—a demonstration that made sense to no one but her. "Most of what we were told about it was wrong. Maybe intention matters, too—maybe it depends on what you're aiming for."

"Hearing a whole lot of *maybes*," Sage muttered.

Her thoughts exactly. "Okay, fine—let's say you're right. Her magic still isn't working." She raked a hand through her hair. "Am I talking to the wall, here, or what? It's moot—she can't heal!"

"It's not working because of the Blight," Elias argued. "But if the Blight is gone, it should be able to—"

"And if you're wrong, she doesn't *come back*, Elias!"

"We should do it."

Petal-soft, that voice barely floated past the line between audible and not. But when a goddess spoke, even softly, mortals couldn't help but lend an ear—all three of their heads swiveled toward Anima.

Unseen by Soren, Ani had curled up from her sickbed, kneeling on the mattress instead; she regarded them with placid, pond-still eyes, but her fingers still spasmed—no matter how tightly she curled them into the quilt cast over her lap, they kept leaping out of formation.

"Ani, we're not there yet," Soren argued. "We can try—"

"We *are* there—you just haven't walked the whole path with us." Ani's smile, hesitant though it was, showed no malice. No blame. "I can't heal the Blight. I've tried. But *killing* it…that might work."

"By killing you." She couldn't seriously be the only one who saw the massive flaws in this leap of logic. "And hoping you come back after."

"Do you have a better idea?" Ani's tone took on a rare note of steel.

"Any idea is better than this one!"

Ani's gaze wrenched away from hers, her lips set in a set-minded line. "When can you be ready, Elias?"

Elias hesitated, looking toward Soren; she shook her head adamantly, and he said, "I…maybe we should—"

"*When?*"

Elias flashed her an unhappy look, mouthing an apology; he turned back to Ani, running his hands down his thighs to grasp his knees. Maybe to stop himself from kneeling, if Ani's commanding tone had triggered his pious habits. "When you are ready, I will be, too."

"No one is ever ready to die, are they?" A bat of Ani's lashes; a swift glance at Wolf. A swifter trading of looks between her and Sage. "I'm as ready as I'll ever be…and the Blight will not wait."

"Best not do it here," Sage murmured. "In case anything goes wrong."

"While we're *killing you*," Soren added scathingly. Just in case she hadn't said it clearly enough; just in case another reminder would make them all realize how unbelievably foolish this was.

But Ani simply squared her jaw and said, "I know a place."

CHAPTER 80

ANIMA

When they arrived at the shrine, Ani asked for a moment alone.

Stoicism was a well-known façade, one she could just about get her hands around despite her lack of talent for lies. But even familiar masks did not fit so well on Ani's *earnest face*.

That was what Tempest had called it when she'd proven entirely inept at stopping the truth from bleeding over her face…*earnest*.

"It's not a flaw, being a bad liar," he'd comforted her. *"You'll just have to practice."*

Centuries later, and she still had not practiced enough to lie about this…not well enough to fool the eyes she'd once lived behind.

She could fool the others. She could not fool Soren.

And as she blindly forded her path into the Crownless Queen's shrine, batting aside willow branches and ivy strings with sobbed little *sorrys*, she could not fool herself, either.

Elias's idea was the best they had—that much was true. One she was willing to try, if it meant saving her people…saving Wolf.

The lie, she'd told no one but herself: that she was at all ready to say goodbye.

That her magic would bring her back, like it always had, because she had tried—because she had done her best. Because she deserved to come back.

But even a talented liar struggled to lie to themselves. And Ani was not that.

The Blight was her doing. Her people's suffering, *Wolf's* suffering…she had caused it. Created it.

She did not deserve *anything*.

She crashed to her knees, blinded by tears; her fingers anchored around the first solid thing they found, and she bent into it, pressing her brow to the unyielding wall and finally, finally letting herself break.

Letting herself *shatter*.

Her jaw cracked open in a wounded animal wail; she screamed silently at the stones, at the water, at her own misshapen reflection.

She raised her head to glare at the silent spectator standing over her, fingers aching to rip the paper prayer chains from its unworthy shoulders.

"*Why?*" Shouting in a whisper so Soren and the others could not overhear, she struck the water with the flat of her palm, scattering ruddy droplets across its surface. "What was the *point* of it all? Why bless me at all if you knew it would lead here? Why—*why*—"

She crumbled across the Crownless Queen's basin, forehead pressed so hard into the stones that it ached, her hair tugged gently by the fountain's subtle current.

"Why did you make me?" she sobbed. "Why did you *make me* like this?"

Capable of incredible feats of creation—cursed to manifest calamity wherever she went.

Desperately in love with life and all its little wonders—doomed to lose it too early no matter what form she took, stolen or not.

Doomed, always, to lose that which dared love her in return.

"Whoever you're praying to, I'm afraid I cannot speak for them. But I can make a guess of my own, whatever good it might do."

Sniffling, sick of the sight of her own face, she raised her head to meet the Guardian's watchful gaze. "You should go. Something terrible is about to happen."

"I made a vow. I am exactly where I need to be."

"And if I release you from it?"

A strangely fond smile. He sighed heavily as he sank to his knees beside her, grimacing at their groans and pops. "It wouldn't be the first time you tried…nor the first time you failed."

Confusion spilled down her throat, cooling the acid-like shame eating away at her. "I don't recall—"

"I know." His hand slid into his coat—he withdrew a journal from it, offering it to her. A cream-colored, plush-covered journal.

A journal she'd dropped in the library…and had not recovered.

"How did you—?"

"I hope you will forgive an old man's sentiment. The rest of the journals *are* yours, written by your hand, but there was one forgery. Not a word changed between them, you have my word." When she didn't reach for it, he opened it himself, flipping through only a handful of pages before using his thumb to mark his place. "It's…an old favorite. I only wanted to read it one last time."

He held it out again, thumb resting beside a line scrawled in frustrated chicken-scratch script:

Alder Finch will not let me dismiss him.

"*Oh.*" The word broke into three jagged pieces. "Oh, no…"

"How is your orchid?"

"Exactly as I remember."

His orchid.

His *Orchid.*

When she looked up, there it was again—that smile that didn't make sense. Not from a stranger to a stranger—not even a stranger to a goddess.

"Hello, Ani," Alder murmured.

"No," she said again. Then: "*How?*"

Centuries had passed since she'd been Orchid—*centuries.* Even notoriously long-lived Arborians couldn't cling to life that long…and certainly not looking so young, no older than fifty, raven-feather hair only half-grayed.

"You swore a vow of your own the day I lost you." Grief crusted over those words like old blood. "You promised I would see you again."

Something possessed her trembling hand—something lifted it to follow the paths of those creases in his face. Proof life had handled him harshly, to deal those wounds—or proof it had carried him too gently, forcing him to endure past any natural end?

"How long?" she choked.

"It is a gift and a curse," he hedged, "being loved by the Goddess of Life."

"That is not an answer."

A tired smile. "I stopped counting after a while."

"Why didn't anyone *tell*—?"

"I went away," he interrupted. "After you passed. Wandered for quite a long time. By the time I came back here, I'd already stopped tallying the years."

A guard without his charge. A husband without his wife.

So devoted to his cause that he had taken up arms to protect this place in her absence.

Yet, no matter which way she tipped her head…no matter which angle she searched from, or how closely she squinted…

Her eyes began to burn again, misery and shame a cocktail mixed to burn. "I don't remember you."

"As you shouldn't—and you shouldn't want to." Alder gently pulled her hand away from his face, settling it atop her journal instead. "It was a different life. A beautiful one...but no longer yours."

"I'm so sorry."

"Not for this—not for us. Don't you dare." Steel rang in that stern command—the ghost of a younger, fiercer man.

New sobs ached in her throat; she set one hand to it, cradling that pain. "But you've waited so *long*."

"And I would wait again—a hundred lifetimes, if I had to. If that is the price for the little eternity I got to love you."

Such beautiful, precious words...but they rang hollow in her heart. A heart that didn't belong to him.

A heart that longed to turn back time, but only to this afternoon. Only far enough to take Wolf's hand and drag him out of the library before the monster came to call.

"None of that," Alder said softly—he scooped up a tear she hadn't meant to let fall, wiping it on his coat. "Nobody gets the privilege of experiencing first love a second time, Ani. It's a gift. One you deserve."

First love.

"I don't know how to save him," she confessed. "To save you all."

Alder raised his eyes to the sky. "May I ask who told you that you had to?"

She blinked at him. "I...what? Of course I—"

"Who told you," he interrupted, "that you have a duty to do the impossible, Ani? Who told you that this world is yours to carry—that you must carry it alone?"

And indeed, the burden that sloped her back felt heavy as an island—heavy as a continent. Heavy as a crown.

No one had needed to *tell* her to shoulder that burden—how could she do otherwise, knowing the power rooted inside her? If she had the ability to help, how could she choose not to?

Yes, it cost her something—sometimes, it had cost her everything.

But how could she live with herself otherwise? How could she bear to hold a full cup, knowing so many others were empty?

She had no answer for him. She had no answers at all.

"Perhaps," he said like a sidestep, like a feint, "you might try asking for help."

She stared, speechless, as he got up from the makeshift altar, patting the basin twice. But when he turned to walk away...

As if by its own mind, her hand shot out, catching his before he could slip away.

"I'm about to do something terrible," she said, "and I am so afraid."

Alder looked down at her, expression pivoting from serene to severe. He dropped to one knee on the moss-mortared stone. "What do you need from me?"

"Stay." Her fingers spasmed around his—half chaos, half plea. "Don't try to fight it. Don't try to save me from it. But…stay. If you're willing."

She could not remember him. But the body remembered what the mind could not—and while the mind could not get ahold of him, the body could not let him go.

Alder set his hand over hers. "I am at your command, milady."

"It will not be easy to—"

"Nothing in my life has been easy," he interrupted. "I care not for ease— I care for what is right. I am meant to be here…as are you." His forget-me-not gaze glimmered. "I have faith."

She did not know if she could live up to that faith…nor if what she was about to do was right as well as difficult. But there was only one way to find out.

Now that the choice had been made, the minutes seemed to fly by as if swept up in a funnel cloud; before she could truly root herself back to the ground, the arrangements had been made around her.

Soren, posted against the wall, fists clenched so tightly her knuckles were liable to pop right through her skin.

Sage, kneeling beside Wolf, who had woken on the way—lost to delirium, he clawed at the dirt, towing up furrows of earth and boot-flattened moss as he seethed through gritted teeth. She had spoken to him, or tried—but he had only looked at her like he could see through her, no recognition registering in his rabid gaze.

"I'll fix it," she'd whispered to him anyway, planting a kiss on his forehead more tenderly than she planted a new seed into fallow dirt. "I won't let it hurt you."

Then there was Alder, who stood guard in the shadows to the side of the fountain—none of the others had spared him more than a cursory glance. Though he wore no helmet today, only armor, that was how most guards tended to be…faceless. Voiceless. Walls between their quarries and danger, nothing more.

But not to her.

According to Orchid's journal, it was customary for Anima's host to be brought here for the ritual to take place…the body set at the feet of the statue like another kind of offering. A last breath given to the sky…a first breath gasped in through water. From the tomb to the womb.

It seemed as good a deathbed as any.

The water was surprisingly warm when she slipped her bare feet into it. Like the sun-warmed tide pools Tempest used to let her fill with minnows and marine foliage, but filled with lily pads instead of seaweed. Sunfish flittered past her ankles, bumping her with far more force than any minnow could manage; a brave, curious few stopped to nibble at her toe-tips, gentle as any goodbye kisses she could hope for.

But when she lowered herself into the water, bracing her arm against the basin's lip to keep her blighted body from clawing its way back out, something seized her around the wrist with startling ferocity.

She looked up to meet the dazed, delirious gaze of Wolf.

"Wolf!" Sage advanced, ready to tussle his brother back to the ground. Ani halted him with a flash of her other hand.

"Wolf?" she prompted softly, utterly arrested by the intensity of his stare, cognizant or not. "What is it?"

For the first time, he'd grabbed her hard enough to bruise. But the fervor lighting the amber in his gaze near to gold, terror so pure it bordered on divine...

This was not rage. This was his best try at a rescue.

"No," he said, like he'd just now heard the promise she'd made minutes ago. His voice dropped, a growl too weak to warn her off this path. "Let it hurt— let it hurt, *let it hurt.*"

Not enough words. But even so, she understood.

A new feeling dug its roots into her heart, knife-sharp and nettle-stung. She clutched his wrist in return, squeezing as hard as she could...fighting a flinch when his bones shifted tangibly under her thumbs.

"I'm sorry," she whispered. "I'm sorry."

But this was one pain she could not stand. Even if ending it meant her death.

When Sage gently towed his brother back to the ground, Wolf stayed there, wide-eyed—his hand still outstretched, grasping for her.

They could have been muscle spasms...the Blight driving him to find a fight wherever he could. But she knew the difference between panic and frenzy, and too much fear wallowed in Wolf's eyes to call it the latter.

"Let it hurt," he growled again, voice crackling with tears. "*Please.*"

If she looked at him a second longer, she'd lose her nerve.

With a gulp of breath, she settled herself on her back in the basin, letting the water make her weightless. She floated just above the stones, fingertips brushing the frost of algae around their edges; when she looked up, she found Elias looking back at her, grave-dark eyes solemn and...sweetly, surprisingly, a little scared.

"I don't want to hurt you," he said. "That's not why I said it."

"I know." She trusted that, if only because she trusted Soren's love for her—had felt it herself—and knew Elias would never harm something Soren loved. "I trust you, Elias. It will be all right."

He blinked, looking stricken. "I—"

"Will it hurt?" Her voice trembled—she hated that it trembled. Especially because it made Soren surge from her spot against the wall like she planned on picking a fight.

"No," Elias promised. "Not at all."

He sounded so *sure*. But then again, a man of faith would. "The god-killer...what is it?"

There were no new sheaths strapped to his body. No quiver hung across his back. No oddities dangling from his belt. No hint at the weapon shaped by mortal hands to kill the unkillable.

Elias's mouth twisted to one side. She couldn't tell if it was deprecating or sorrowful.

"It turns out," he said very softly, "mortemancy has more reach than I might have been led to believe."

Not a weapon shaped by mortal hands—mortal hands shaped *into* a weapon.

"Oh." She sounded so small, even to herself. "It really won't hurt."

Elias held out his hand.

"This is your choice," he said quietly. "Whenever you're ready, take my hand."

"Just like that?"

"Just like that."

She tipped her head back. Found the Crownless Queen's eyes, staring into lifeless stone.

In a moment, they would look more alike than ever.

But like the statue, she had a guardian waiting nearby...a handful of friends standing guard, their love a bastion against the cowardly parts of her that wanted to change her mind.

A man who held her heart in his hands. Hands that would never be steady enough to shoot a bow or pluck a pebble from the dirt again if she did not act fast...did not act now.

With a last breath so deep she felt it down to her toes, she reached out and took the Godkiller's hand.

And as her eyes shut, Annelisa Medeis began to pray.

CHAPTER 81

ANIMA

Death greeted her clothed in blinding brilliance.

Not dark like the coffin, not this time. Shining like the sun—pulsing like the stars.

Just like before, it had taken her so swiftly she had not noticed it until it was already there…nor did she think to stop praying when it arrived.

Sancta. When I asked you to help me save my friend, you gave me the strength I needed. I asked you for a chance to make it right…to give back what I took. I am asking again: will you help me save my people?

A voice nearly as vibrant as the light. **What help do you ask from me, Annelisa Medeis?**

My magic…it is gone.

It is gone?

Not gone, but…corrupted. Trapped. To free it, I was sent to death—but if it does not come back to me, I cannot come back, either.

What help do you ask from me, Annelisa Medeis?

I…

Ask it.

I ask for one last miracle. These people should not bear the price for my mistakes; they should not take the punishment meant for me.

One last *miracle?*

If you are willing.

You ask if I am willing to give you what I have already given. You need no help from me.

Wait—wait! I don't understand. My magic—

Your magic has not left you. You have hidden it yourself.

But I...

The others stole their divinity. I gave it to you of my own accord. Do you truly believe magics younger and weaker could steal what I have given? The boundary you fear to cross was not placed by me. If it is a miracle you want, you can make it—if you are willing.

But how?

It will not come without cost—but you can choose to pay it, if you truly wish to repent. To redeem. To fix it.

Redemption? Even for me?

For anyone who seeks it. For anyone who earns it.

What would you have me do?

One last miracle.

Make it count.

CHAPTER 82

ANIMA

In a sanctuary filled with stone, Annelisa Medeis asked for a miracle.

A goddess, praying at her own altar.

A force of nature, rising to redeem her own failings.

A lost little girl, found at last.

In a sanctuary filled with stone, a garden bloomed; a garden that, to this very day, has never wilted or withered. Even when the harshest of winters or the swiftest of storms come to call, they leave with appetites unsated, defied by even the daintiest of petals.

Emerald light exploded through the darkness, and she braced herself for the telltale sign of life returned.

But it wasn't pain that flooded her body—wasn't agony that swept all that she had been, all that she was, all she would ever be out of its skintight cell.

Not pain at all, but power.

Power that sizzled and sang; power that ruptured the thin membrane between Real and Unreal. A frisson of static-pop pressure crashing over her skin in a riptide rush, erasing every blemish of mortality.

An exultant, ecstatic chorus of voices warbled through her head like birdsong, and something stretched inside her mind—a long, leisurely sensation, like a cat arching its back, like a snake uncurling, like a bird spreading its wings.

It started in her head. Then went lower, and further, spreading through every vein, every muscle, every hair and nail and bone…

For her people, for her island, for her friends…Annelisa Medeis set aside her mortal skin.

Skin and bone and hard-won muscle. Scars and wounds and sundust freckles. Sweat and blood and lovelorn tears.

Humanity was not a shackle. But she broke free of it regardless.

And underneath…

Real and not real. Here and not here. Alive and more.

Ani and Isa and Lilibet. Lotus, Viola, Fearne. Venetia, Ansari, Orchid…

Soren.

She could remember *all* of her names. *All* of her lives.

And…

When she surged out of the water and looked back over her shoulder, there he was.

Alder Finch, her Guardian, watching her with the kind of faith the divine hungered for: unshaken and unshakeable.

A faith that had stood for centuries, waiting on the fulfilment of her promise.

She met his blue-jay gaze, and his back straightened. His mouth jerked down at the corners—once, twice. A brief but vicious battle against emotion.

She touched her fingertips to her lips, then blew him a kiss. *Thank you for waiting.*

He caught the kiss and pressed it to his heart. *My pleasure, milady.*

And then her attention turned to Wolf.

He lay so still now, though his eyes were still open. But like this, able to see beyond the real and the here, she could see the infection eating through his body …the gangrenous rot of Blight's insatiable appetite.

In a dozen lives, she had not been able to heal it.

But she had been human then. At least in part.

She was more than that today…or less than. But whatever that made her, she knew one thing for certain.

She had made the Blight. And in this moment, veins aglow with magic unmatched…

She could *un*make it.

In the end, it took laughably little. Her hand over Wolf's wound; the Godkiller's hand over Wolf's heart. A kiss between his brows not half as gentle as the last she'd given him.

With a thrust of Elias's hand, a forced beat of Wolf's heart, their magic swept through Wolf, cleaning out the corruption like one might swipe cobwebs out of dusty corners.

When his chest lifted with a clean, steady breath, the human piece of her heart cried out in relief.

When she sought his wound to make sure it had healed, the sight of her own hands arrested her in place; she lifted them, marveling at their gilded creases, the green glow pulsing like twin hearts in both her palms.

One life saved was miracle enough…but she had more miracle left to give.

She stood up. Looked around at her friends—her family, or the closest she had to it.

"I'm ending this," she said in a dozen voices. "Be ready…it will fight back."

She found the Godkiller's gaze—he gazed back with grim understanding, offering a nod. "I know what to do."

"Ani." Soren's eyes rounded in worry. "Hold on, wait—"

No. Her people had waited long enough.

She glanced at Alder.

They had *all* waited for her long enough.

She turned her back on her precious few and walked out of the shrine.

Wolf, she knew—in the way waking conversations sometimes drifted into dreams, the real world invading the sleeping—was shouting her name. Or…he was shouting one of them. The one that mattered most; the one she couldn't answer to today.

Anima, Goddess of Life, paid him no heed as she abandoned them all. Wolf, held back by Alder…Soren, held back by Elias.

She did not look back as she went to save her island, her home…her people.

It was time to put her very last miracle to use. And she knew exactly where to start.

CHAPTER 83

ANIMA

When the door to the Arboretum Absolute shut behind her, it sucked all sound out of the tree.

Like fluid rushing to cushion a break, swelling the skin and numbing the nerves, that silence packed in tightly around Ani as she strode into the center of the main chamber. Dark, like before; peppered throughout with lifeless lumps, like before.

But this time, she did not waste time debating before she raised one hand, breaking the silence—and the shadows—with a snap of her fingers.

Light.

It did not web out through the corrugated walls of the tree this time. It simply *became;* one moment, it was dark, and the next, it was not.

Which allowed her to see that she was the only living creature in this room. No sign of the Blight.

But it was here. She knew it in the simple, effortless way those of divine ilk knew things.

"You can't hide from me," Anima seethed, arcing toward the stairs. "Not here. Not in my home!"

Her home, infected at the very core; her home, the beating heart of the Blight.

Midnight purple roots were embedded in the supple wood; she walked past pile after pile of sawdust and splinters, gore strewn around the wounds dealt by this creature's footsteps.

Malicious invaders in holy temples were not treated with much mercy. Especially not *her* temples, where the neediest and most vulnerable people often gathered to pray for help.

Her feet barely touched the stairs as she climbed; what had been an insurmountable obstacle only weeks ago now barely warranted her notice. And when she reached the shrine at the very top, she would waste no time with—

A soft creak to her left halted her in her tracks.

Step by step, she walked backwards to the landing she'd hopped over; the one sitting before the lime-green door painted with an arching rainbow of blooming flowers. Dahlias and hibiscus and daffodils; spire-bells and forget-me-nots and globe thistles.

Roots burrowed beneath the door, hunched up under it like they were trying to carry it on their shoulders.

Found you.

She gripped the roots and hissed a command to the life inside them:

FLEE.

The roots collapsed in on themselves, withering like plump, fresh fruit set out to dry in the sun.

Someone screamed in the next room. A scream so terribly human Anima almost forgot herself.

Without the corrupted roots holding it up, the door buckled into its damaged hinges; it scraped the floor as it swung open, hanging there like a broken jaw.

Beyond, her bedchambers remained much the same as she remembered…a grand four-poster bed in the very center, its frame built from a variety of dwarf darkwood she'd rooted into the floor, burying its roots in substrate piled beneath the floorboards by a helpful horde of rodents.

A carnation-pink bedspread, its edges still tucked under the mattress; a lace bedskirt torn to shreds, stained with syrupy black ichor.

It had been a millennium or more since she'd asked her older siblings to check under her bed for monsters; she'd decided she was too old for that little routine before they'd even gotten their magic. But that didn't mean she'd stopped believing in such things…it just meant she'd had to get brave enough to look for the monster herself.

Even childish fears could make a goddess's heart quail.

But she got down on her hands and knees anyway, staring into the shadows without allowing herself a second thought.

The monster under the bed stared back at her, its thorny talons gripping the wood for dear life, its pale cheeks streaked in the same foul liquid that had stained Ani's old bedskirt, the stairs, the rug…the deathbeds of far, far too many people, Arborians and others alike.

"You *hurt* me," it snarled. "That *hurt*."

Fury would not allow sympathy any space…not for this mockery of creation. Not even for its pain. "Do you know how many *you* have hurt here?"

"I *am* here." It gathered one of the dead roots in its hands, clutching it like a precious toy. "Fix me!"

Why was she arguing with this thing like it was a person—like it wasn't a piecemeal puppet of magic that drove innocents to create their own destruction? Magics that shuffled organs like plants being repotted into smaller vessels, cramming tangles of viscera where they couldn't possibly function? Where they had no choice but to die?

"I'm sorry," whispered her gentler, better self. "It's my fault you're here, I know. But you need to go."

To rip out a weed—to make sure it never grew back—you could leave no piece of it behind. Even a single root left behind could cause a new infestation.

When another root seized up, wrenched out of the wood against its will, the forest wailed with the monster.

Bellowing bears. Howling wolves. Groaning trees. Even the rivers babbled through their pain as it recoiled, its roots bunching inward like a flinch.

"Stop!" the Blight screamed.

Cries for mercy…unheeded. Unheard.

Another piece of Anima withered away, too. A terrible, hollow ache replaced it, the sliver of pain left embedded in the skin even after a splinter had been removed. A pain from the absence of something.

The mortal wept for that loss.

The goddess did not.

If this fight cost her everything for everything, it would be a price well paid.

Tether after tether shriveled and snapped, life obeying its mistress's call. Only a handful more, and then—

"*STOP!*"

The monstrous scream came only half a heartbeat before the agony: a writhing, thorny thrust of its hand into the meat of her shoulder, ripping whatever flesh it could from bone as it fled.

Screaming out her agony, Anima coiled to the side, the healing heat of sun-warmed stone pulsing through her shoulder as it knit itself back together.

No more dead friends. No more mercy held in an open hand.

Her softness was a strength in so many ways—but Brae had learned how to turn it back on her through gentle manipulations and careful staging. This weapon might be dressed up like something innocent, but it was a weapon like any other—a weapon aimed for her heart.

So she did not let the monster go. She gave chase—and when she sprinted back outside the tree, plunging into a patch of moss, the path shuddered under her feet.

The Goddess of Life, for the first time in history, was on the hunt.

But judging by the raucous chorus of roars, bellows, and screeches that rose across the island's face...she was not the only one.

CHAPTER 84

SOREN

If Kessen didn't learn how to keep his gods-damned feet planted, he was going to die sitting on his ass, and she had half a mind to let him.

After Ani had gotten all glowy and strange and *stupid*, leaving them all to gape after her without actually telling them where she was *going*, it hadn't taken long for her warning to come true. They'd barely made it back to Elderwood proper—running into Everin, Matthias, and Kessen on the way, Everin swearing he'd felt his ancestors backflip in their graves mere minutes before—when a collective scream had risen above the trees in all directions, bestial battle cries setting her hackles on end.

Sage and Wolf—the latter with his senses regained, though a different kind of frenetic emotion had claimed him now—had sent them to the edges of the city when she'd asked where they could make themselves useful. Everin had followed suit, and now—

Well, now she was about to stick her nose where it didn't belong again, because Kessen couldn't hold a stance properly to save his life.

"Kess!" she barked, kicking aside a blighted weasel—yes, a blighted *weasel*, which she'd found hilarious until it had lunged for her ankle with a strangled scream that didn't belong in such a fluffy little creature—and dropping into a crouch just before Elias's flaming scythe swung above her in a powerful arc, slicing the creature clean down the middle. When she caught Kessen's eyes between blows, she smacked the ground with her open palm. "*Both* heels in the gods-damned dirt!"

"Eyes on your own boy, Princess!" Everin hollered over Kessen's curse-riddled apology; the King of Heretics and his pair of warriors were taking turns at the toothy end of a blighted bear, keeping its frenzied focus on them while the other two sought to drop it from another angle.

She'd known bears were big. She hadn't realized they were quite *so* big, big enough to dwarf even the largest wolves she'd seen wandering the Nyxian woods. As disturbing as it was to see a weasel gnash its teeth while straining for her leg, she'd happily take it over the furry behemoth holding its own against three sizable fighters.

"He's got a point," Elias said when she lurched back up; he twisted in toward her, breathing hard, sweat trickling from his hair. He wiped it away with his cuff, leaving behind a streak of blight-blackened blood. "There's three of them and only two of us, so I'd prefer if—"

"I'm sorry, are you agreeing with him now?"

"It's just, he's almost always wrong, so when he *is* right…"

Everin grinned in their direction—while surfing precariously on the bear's back, trying to line his axe up with its spine. "Told you I'd win you over!"

"You have to be joking," she fumed, twirling her finger in the air—Elias turned in sync with her, their backs colliding as she skimmed the treeline around the city for emerging threats. "You spent the whole trip ready to call the sky red if he said it was blue, and now—"

Elias groaned. "Why do you always try to pick fights with me in the middle of a battle?"

"Why do you always *interrupt me* when I'm trying to pick a fight?"

"Huh, I *wonder*—"

Swish. Thunk. A guttural bellow that petered off into a rumbling moan.

When she turned her attention back to the Tallisians, she expected to find them already bickering over who got to claim the kill; instead, Everin and Kessen stood off to the side, catching their breath while Matthias knelt by the bear's head, giving its ears an affectionate ruffle.

"Sorry, friend," he murmured, shutting its eyes. "You fought hard. Get your rest."

Eyes stinging, Soren cleared her throat, turning to Everin instead. "Strange custom for hunters."

Everin shrugged, all amusement gone; he watched the bear with his jaw set. "This isn't a hunt."

"Everin! Soren!"

The two of them turned toward the summons; Sage stood at the crest of the hill, Medwenna half a step behind him. Neither looked to be carrying good news.

"Big Blight's on its way," Sage said. "Rangers sent word—they spotted it bolting our way like its arse was on fire. Anima's after it, but—"

"It's heading for the city," Medwenna interrupted. "We appreciate the support, but you both have to go—the boats are ferrying people out, but not many are left."

"She's right." Sage kept his bow aimed behind him; without looking, he released the string, and a death rattle followed shortly after. "I hate to see you two pains in my arse leave so soon, but someone has to think about the bigger picture here. Can't have two Heirs getting roach-stomped on our shores. Not good for our reputation."

Soren and Everin met each other's gaze.

"Over my stake-burnt skin," Everin said.

"What he said," Soren agreed.

Medwenna slung her bow onto her back, sliding down the hill and approaching Everin with her hand out. Everin wrenched his mouth into a deeper scowl, crossing his arms as she advanced. "Whatever reasons you're pulling off the shelves in your head right now, you can take them and shove them right back—"

Medwenna covered his mouth with one hand. "You're not my flogging king," she said sharply, accent bending into its trace of Tallisian twang, "and this is not your kingdom. Go home."

Everin ripped her hand off his mouth, but didn't release it; he held it between them like a challenge, glaring Medwenna down. "And you're not my mother, so what says I have to listen to you?"

Medwenna's breath staggered; Soren couldn't tell if it was anger or anguish that broke her voice when she said, "Ev, this is *not* your fight—"

"We're not staying for the flogging *fight*." Everin threw his thumb over his shoulder, where Matthias and Kessen both mirrored his cross-armed pose, nodding their agreement. "We're staying for the fool who thinks she can get the three biggest idiots under the sun to do something sensible."

Medwenna turned a pleading look on Matthias. "Matt—"

"Sorry, Winnie. We're all walking the same trail." Matthias walked up and gripped her by the back of her head, planting a brotherly kiss on her hair. "Promised Will. You'll have to take it up with him."

"Send Kessen, at least—"

Kessen's soles settled firmly on the ground. And though he said nothing, that rare silence spoke volumes.

"We're staying too." Elias's shoulder bumped Soren's as he fell in beside her.

"This *is* our fight," Soren agreed. "And we're not running."

"Then get ready," Sage ordered…after taking a moment to curse the gods for burdening him with a *"gaggle of fools more stubborn than a cat on its tenth life."* He turned back toward his city, setting another arrow to his string. "And if you're the praying sort…I'd get to it, if I were you."

"Is that our plan?" A protest she hadn't expected to hear from Elias, of all people. "Praying for the best?"

"You have a better one, lad?"

The ground suddenly jolted; a sharp, powerful shift to the left that sent them stumbling like a shove. Soren snagged Elias's elbow, stopping him from falling on his own scythe; Everin did the same with Medwenna, but he grabbed her by the shoulders, hauling her against him and anchoring her there as the island rocked in the other direction. "What in the flogging—"

Above the treeline—the *darkwood* treeline, which rose hundreds of feet high—something reared up into the sky.

Something—that was all she could call it, because she had no name at *all* for whatever loomed above them now. Ani had called it a beast, a monster.

This was no beast.

This was a *behemoth.*

Almost human-shaped, but just wrong enough in places to make her shiver. Too many arms on one side; its head was misshapen, dented in on one side, swollen out on the other. It had no skin or hair or features, only trees and earth and bone; and when its mangled jaws parted to bellow out a war cry, her blood ran cold.

And as for the plan…

Before she could push herself stumbling into *that* impossible task, primed like a snare and aiming for her newfound sense of purpose, a second impossibility rose to meet it.

A darkwood more massive than even the tallest among the terrestrial spread…one she recognized from a similarly dire day.

The Arboretum Absolute rose up to defy the twisted mass of corruption. And it did so at the behest of the golden, gleaming star at its heart.

Soren had to cough up the words, almost choking on the fear wedged in her windpipe: "I think Ani's taking care of it."

"You need to go," Medwenna said, wrestling out of Everin's arms; he started protesting, but she pushed him into Matt with one hand on his chest. Her gaze had already fogged over, her focus stolen entirely by the behemoth heading for the shore, dragging a sickening portion of the forest with it. "Take him and go, Matt!"

"He already told you—"

"He's the flogging *king*," Medwenna snarled, "and he cannot die here, do you understand?"

Matthias stared at her for a beat too long. "Winnie…"

"You know why he can't." Medwenna's hand twisted into her tunic, just over her sternum. "You *know*."

Matthias sniffed—hard. Nodded her way, with the stiff understanding of a salute. And with a new glint in his eye, he patted Everin twice on the shoulder. "You heard our girl, Ev. Time to go."

"I'll stick out my tongue and let you flog it with a stakes-burnt *fire-poker* before I even think about—Winnie! *Medwenna*!"

Everin's frustrated shout could have stood in Medwenna's path with two flaming blades in its hands, and it wouldn't have stopped her—Soren knew, because Elias did exactly that, and Medwenna sprinted past him without taking her eyes off the two forces of nature going to war miles away. Not enough miles away.

A historical first; she'd bet all her coin on it. Which meant nothing short of a brick wall was going to keep Medwenna from finding a better view.

"Whoa!" Matthias caught Everin when he tried to barrel after Medwenna. "You're not catching her on that leg—"

"I can damn well try!"

The Lion of Tallis had a roar to shake even the staunchest of soldiers. And ordinarily, she would have stayed to see if it won him his way. But she didn't have time to watch Everin and his triad argue over their next move—she had a friend out there who needed her help.

"What are you thinking?" Elias drew her attention by rubbing the nape of her neck, just under her curls—when she turned her attention back to the conflict, his hand moved to the tangle of muscle between her shoulder and neck. Unraveling the knot. Helping her think.

"They're heading for the harbor," she said. "Someone has to help those ships."

He made a face at her new Tallisian curse. "You think we can fight it?"

"No—but we can defend the boats from any of the creatures it sics on them." She was reckless, yes, but not stupid—that thing could crush an army with one swipe of its massive arm. "And worst comes to worst…"

"We'll be the distraction," he finished grimly.

"You don't like it."

"I never like your plans." He rolled his shoulders; a moment later, the fire coating his scythes did the same, the flames lowering and rising again like a cresting wave sputtering before it could curl into something surf-worthy. "But you're right—some set of fools has to do it, and we're the best fools I know."

Affection seized her by the heart, squeezing until she lost her breath; she pulled Elias in to steal that breath back from him.

A sweaty, battle-bloodied kiss was probably not the kind of method most thieves employed. But even if that breath she was looking for slipped her grasp thanks to unconventional technique…that was all right. She liked how war tasted on his mouth.

"What's that for?" If anything, she'd at least robbed the breath out of his lungs; he stared at her, dazed, lips still parted.

She rubbed the wrinkles out of his furrowed brow. "Just glad you're here, jackass."

Gods, she loved that dangerous, war-wolf smile of his. "Couldn't get rid of me if you wanted to, smartass."

One last kiss, faster and sweeter—then the two of them sprinted toward the fray, a shared battle cry on their tingling lips.

CHAPTER 85

SOREN

The boats were not moving fast enough.

By the time they'd reached the beaches, Wolf and Sparrow had already arrived, wading through the throngs of panicked people and calmly directing them to the vessels that still had room; and those were few in number. It wouldn't be enough to save everyone.

They needed a backup plan.

"Get to the bottleneck and start directing people to the other side of the island," she told a trio of rangers. "The numbers out here will already overwhelm the boats, and if we keep letting people gather, they'll be one massive—"

"Whoa, there—who died and put you in charge?" Sage held out a hand to the three rangers, who paused in their tracks; then, with a sigh, he let it drop. "Fine, yeah, that's what I was going to say. Get moving before you grow roots, will you?"

"And spread the word!" Soren shouted after them before turning back to her cousin. "Ani told me about a way you keep sharks out of the harbor here…something about kelp forests under the water?"

"Medwenna's on it." He pointed with his bow toward the far end of the half-moon dock, where Medwenna had gathered a handful of rangers whose regalia showed off more shades of green than others. "They'll try and tie it up from below, but it's mostly made of plants—not likely it'll work for long."

"Any time we can buy Ani is worth it." Even if she could barely comprehend the glistering humanoid form riding in the heart of a walking forest as *Ani*. "Aunt Gen and Uncle Cy?"

Sage's mouth bent unhappily. "What do you think?"

Right. *A queen doesn't abandon her people.*

She swallowed the lump in her throat, rolling her shoulder; the stars she wore suddenly seemed stitched in heavy steel, not silk. "The blighted patients?"

"Under guard. But we can't move them."

Soren looked out at the water; the last of the boats was leaving, a cluster of hysterical people left behind; one mother shouldered through the throng just in time to hold her child out toward the boat, sobbing for someone to *take her, take her, please.*

A man nearly dove off the edge of the boat himself, stretching as far as he could; swiping the girl up in one arm, he drew back to safety, his other hand wrapped firmly around a young boy's. And before Soren could see what happened next, the mother was swallowed by the shrill, terrified crush of people with no hope of escape.

Something cold as ice, crystal-clear, froze into focus in Soren's head.

She didn't ask; she just moved, knowing Elias would follow. "Get some fire in your hand, but don't let anyone see."

He did as she asked; when they reached the dock, she cupped her hands around her mouth and screamed, "Fire! Off the dock!"

In the split second he had to follow her line of thinking, Elias managed a small groan of, "I *hate* your plans."

By the time panicked eyes found the blaze—a tiny one only just beginning to gnaw at the rope slung between the posts as a handrail—Elias had already neatly stepped behind her, patting his hand out on his pants and shouting vague warnings with her.

It didn't matter that the rope would likely fizzle out before actually causing damage to the well-treated wood; the people saw fire, and instinct did the rest.

"Head for the other side of the island!" she yelled after them as they stampeded off the dock, a couple getting shoved into the water in all the commotion; but they made it safely to the shore before Soren had to think about jumping in after them.

If they tried it again, even panicked people might get wise to the game. But at least one dock spoke was clear.

"Now what?" Elias panted beside her, nodding to the gargantuan beast dead-set on the water. "If it steps out there before they make open water—"

"I know." Capsized boats, easy pickings, hundreds of people drowned. "I'm thinking."

"We're out of time to think," Sage shouted. "Anima's got her own ideas!"

Ideas shaped like one of the older, broader darkwoods twisting around itself like a ribbon of taffy; bark split and flaked off the trunk as it bent, raining thousands of projectiles down on the forest. Ani raised an arm, and the tree groaned as its branches folded to its trunk, Ani's magic whittling it into the shape of a crude spear.

"Everyone, *off the docks!*" Sage bellowed.

The spear flew.

The spear struck.

The Blight's scream lanced into her ears; pressure crushed in on her skull, twin pops of agony burst in her ear canals, and vertigo struck her down to one knee in the sand, the world shifting above and below.

She cursed—then cursed again, because she could barely hear the first one. She pulled her hands away from her ears and found them bloody.

Fantastic.

"…ren. Soren!" Elias jostled her shoulders, shouting right into her bleeding ear; she flinched away, but caught his shoulder, letting him haul her to her feet. "Can you hear me?"

"Barely," she yelled back.

He flashed a thumbs up, then pointed to the blighted behemoth; it had staggered into the water, but the darkwood had pierced its center. When it tried to pull itself off, the tree's branches unfurled in a sharp snap, catching on its back— holding the beast in place.

Elias tapped her on the shoulder; she twisted in that direction, and her stomach flipped.

The blighted creatures had found their way to the harbor.

Between the horde of beasts and the beast-shaped Blight, her attention frayed at the edges, close to tearing.

Where did they go? Where could they help?

The Blight's mouth was still open; still screaming, maybe. She couldn't hear it anymore.

But she certainly saw when its arm reared back, its head turning toward the people still fleeing the docks.

Her attention focused with a sharp tug and a shout of her battlemate's name; when he looked at her, she pointed up, wriggling her fingers.

His gaze flicked upward. "On it," he mouthed.

All she got before he made a break for it, running right underneath the beast's plummeting arm.

"How?" she muttered, not even able to hear herself as she caught up to her battlemate, twirling on her toes to cover his back, tracking the beasts flinging themselves into the fight. "How does my life keep getting *weirder*?"

No answer came; none but a fist of wood and vine and bone falling from the sky, aiming to crush the life out of anything it could.

Elias stopped in the center of one of the dock spokes; she crashed against him, back-to-back, and he reached back to shove her into a crouch before flinging his hands upward.

The roar he unleashed…she didn't hear it, but she felt it. The boards under her feet chattered like teeth; their iron nails trembled in their fastenings, trying to jump ship and bolt for safety.

When she dared a peek over her shoulder…there was only fire.

Fire in her battlemate's hands. Fire streaming down his arms, following the paths of his tattoos. Fire from his *mouth*, a mimicry of fabled dragon-breath she and Finn used to pretend to wield, screaming their heads off at each other until they'd frayed their mother's last nerve.

Fire incinerating the beast's fist before it could wipe them out in one blow.

It recoiled, hugging its limb close, wailing again; Elias dropped his arms and staggered backward, almost tripping over her. She spun up to catch him, steadying him on his feet; the heat still sizzling through his skin scalded her, but it only stung, not a true burn.

"Good, jackass?" she panted.

"Good, smartass." He tapped out against her wrist, and she released him. "It'll think twice about trying that again."

Maybe, at least for the moment. But they couldn't count on it.

Without warning, someone else's hands clapped over her ears with a rush of heat; she started, whirling with her sword out, but Sage stumbled back with his hands up. "Whoa, lass! Only me—just fixing those ears."

"Don't scare a girl like that!" Even if it was a relief to have her hearing back. She rubbed her ear. "That tickled."

"You can thank me later." A blighted wildcat prowled toward them, fangs dripping black, scleral eyes unblinking; in the time it took to take one stride, Sage drew and nocked his arrow, sighted down the shaft, and let it fly.

The cat fell, the arrow buried up to the fletching in its eye.

"You're too good," Soren said. "You know you're too good?"

Sage grinned through dried specks of blighted blood freckling his face. "Oh, yeah. I know." He jerked his chin toward the beasts. "Good thought with the fire—let's hope Ani can handle it from here."

"*Put it out!*"

Soren froze mid-step.

Another scream—mind-numbingly loud, layered in unearthly shrieks and roars.

"Put it out, put it out, *put it out!*"

Put it out!

Is the fire out?

Oh yeah, kid—the fire's long out.

For one second—a second that kicked and screamed and clawed as time tried to make it move on, refusing to go any faster—Soren stared at the beast instead of the battle.

The Blight was writhing at the end of the darkwood spear, bashing its smoking arm wildly into the water; massive waves sloshed back into the harbor before lunging forward, crashing too far past the docks. The back ranks of the rangers kept getting knocked off their feet, washed right into the claws and teeth of their adversaries.

"Soren!"

Elias and Sage's melded shouts gripped her by the hair, yanking her viciously back into the fight—she tore back around just in time for hot, sulfuric blood to spatter across her face, the blighted buck that had been charging for her with antlers down crashing to the sand with an arrow in its throat, fire licking down its back.

She searched out Sage through the throng. "Thanks!"

He winked at her as he nocked another arrow. "It's what I'm—"

That wink stuttered into a startled blink—a warning shout as he swiveled away from her. "*Medwenna*, look—"

It happened too fast.

By the time she found Medwenna in the fray, a bristle-backed blur had leapt onto Medwenna's back, sinking its fangs into her shoulder; the historian's agonized shout rose over the muddled din of battle, over the blood-beat of shock in Soren's skull. Over the howls of the Arborian wolves that flocked to the scent of spilled blood, snarling as Medwenna thrust a hunting knife into the spider that had mounted her back and shoved its twitching body off of her.

Elias was already heading that way, brandishing his scythes, he and the wolves circling Medwenna wearing matching snarls; he mirrored their predatory rotation, keeping their attention on him rather than Medwenna, whose arm hung limp and bloody.

Pack tactics.

She let him take their attention, pulling it off Medwenna; when she saw an opening, she arrowed toward it—

And skidded to a halt when that gap filled with another frenzied, fur-coated adversary.

This forest cat lifted its head, jaws dripping scarlet and ebony; it lurched toward her, stumbling, drunk on blood and blight. Its snarl skidded through three shrill pitches, saliva trailing through the sand as it pounced toward her.

Teeth and steel flashed; claws and blade slashed through the air.

The sword won.

"Hey!" Elias almost fell into her as she lurched past the cat's sundered corpse, his stance unbalanced by Medwenna; the archeress was shivering, gaze glassy, shock setting in. Her shoulder was already soaked in blood. "I think it's like that bite Ani took before—she's losing her senses fast. Losing blood faster."

Ani.

Soren swiveled once more, dizzied with battle-rush. She had to focus on one battlefield, she knew that, but Ani…

They couldn't leave Ani.

"Right," Elias said, though she didn't say a word. He shifted more of Medwenna's weight onto his shoulder; her head lolled a bit, another shiver rattling her as her eyes rolled. Cursing, he passed her off to Sage, who wasted no time barking for a couple rangers to cover them; when Elias turned back to her, his goddess eye was nearly all fire. "What's the plan?"

Soren pointed to the two palace-sized combatants. "We need to get closer."

Elias shut his eyes for a moment, a moment of potent longsuffering they simply didn't have time for. "I know we do."

"You with me?"

"Where else would I go?"

CHAPTER 86

ANIMA

She did not how long a miracle was meant to last.

It had not been all that long—half an hour, at most, since the shrine—but every blow she threw seemed to cause less and less damage. For every portion of the beast she sheared away, seeking the altered core beneath, twice as much grew back, padding the monster with more fodder to defend its center.

Or maybe that was her pulling her punches subconsciously. Because with every blow the Blight took…

It took part of Arborius to patch up the wound.

She could not wither its living parts fast enough; she could not puppet its dead parts away before it could gather new ones. All necromancy really required was bone, and this island had more bones than most.

She struck out with one hand, showing her magic where to go as she dragged her bent fingers through the air; where she aimed, vines and leaves crumbled.

Not enough of them. Fresh ones slithered into place, green blotched with blighted black, by the time she raised her other hand for her next strike.

Either she was growing weaker…or the Blight was getting stronger.

Her darkwood spear remained rooted in the ground; now that she'd released it, the striations in its bark had stiffened once more, leaving it twisted into the shape of a spinning wheel's spindle. And thanks to its branches—branches with a girth equal to most mature trees in other, more ordinary forests—the Blight could not free itself.

For now. But its frenzied writhing, slowed but also strengthened by its size, had begun to use those branches like a chisel, cutting through its own heart to escape. Like an animal gnawing off its own leg to free itself from a snare.

It twisted her heart in two. But she did not let it go. Not when it moaned and screamed; not when it staggered back from her, great waves sloshing so powerfully into the docks that several boards snapped clean off, doomed to the fate of driftwood.

But then its cry took a new shape.

"Stop *hurting me*," it begged. "I cannot stop. I am *here*."

That plea struck the back of her skull.

Its other cries hadn't touched her…not like this. They'd been mimicry, manipulations of magic…nothing but noise.

This plea was different.

This plea was a *prayer*.

"Say that again," she whispered.

It whimpered. Collapsed on what might have been its attempt to mimic knees. Crawled toward her, bleeding a trail of ichor and sap in the sea behind it.

"I am here." Pebble-gray eyes caught hers, wide, shimmering with primal fear. "I cannot stop. Fix me."

I am here.

She looked back down at those roots…the roots that wound beneath earth and sand and sea. Roots that spread like veins under the forest's skin.

I am here.

You made me.

Not nonsense after all.

An introduction.

If you truly wish to repent. To redeem. To fix it.

Understanding burst through her mind like the dawn reclaiming the sky.

"Fix it," she whispered.

She could rip at the plant all she wanted, but it would not stop the spread. Not when the infection still festered under the ground.

Why did you make me like this?

She had not been made to destroy.

She had been made to *heal*.

And with all her magic and might straining at her skin, begging to be set free…

Maybe. Maybe. If she didn't hold back. If she didn't hold on.

"You are *Here*," she whispered. "You're not hurting the island—you are the island."

It held out a massive, gnarled hand. Bone-white and bark-black.

"Fix it," pled her island, sundered and sickened with chaos. "Fix me."

Wrath washed away. Without it, she felt…cleaner. Calmer.

With the Arboretum Absolute as her proxy, she took that hand of bone and branch and held it tight.

Miracles do not come without cost.

"Whatever the cost," she whispered to Sancta, "I will pay it."

When Anima, Goddess of Life, bid her power to trickle into her island like groundwater, the world shifted to make room for it.

Gild and green found all the small, secret places beneath the earth's skin—rabbit warrens and fox dens, worm tunnels and molehills, root clusters and acorn caches—and steeped them all in gentle, giving glory. It took nothing but what did not belong; it gave only what should have been there in the first place.

And then she who feared Death above all else called out for its aid.

"Elias, now!"

She couldn't see him in the tumult below. But she didn't have to.

When the corrupted portions of the world began to scream, it sounded like music.

With the finesse of a scalpel and the might of a sword, Anima excised decay and mayhem from growth and order; with one-minded focus rare for a girl so mesmerized by everything she saw, she cut and cut and cut and *cut* until she was satisfied that not even a spore of blight remained.

Until there was nothing but gild and green and glory.

And where she cut, Elias cauterized—what she excised, he eliminated. His magic attacked what hers could not heal, a scarlet beast that devoured with no teeth.

She healed and she healed and she healed.

He killed and he killed and he *killed.*

And then, like the final gasping beat of a dying heart…it was over.

In the quiet, Ani closed her eyes, savoring the sensation of the *new,* a feeling in her body she had never experienced before.

A cicada shell left behind on a stump. A dandelion that had just been wished on, its seeds scattered to the fickle wind. A sky-blue eggshell half-hidden by the fresh grasses of the spring season.

A thing emptied to set something else free.

The behemoth bent on the destruction of her people—its people—emptied itself, too. Foliage and decay and whatever else it had scraped together to build a body tumbled into the sea, no magic left to bind it; and though she should have been, she was not surprised when her shell forsook her, too.

Empty. Empty sky—empty air. Nothing above or around or below her.

Cold. Wet. Quiet.

Peace. If only for a moment.

She thought someone shouted her name—thought she might have fallen, too, but only when she was picked up again, a warm hand cradling the nape of her neck. A blur of amber and sable and onyx; a pair of lips shaping her name again and again.

Annelisa. Annelisa.

If Wolf felt warm to her, she must've been awfully cold.

"It's all right," she heard herself say, startled by the wafer-thin wisp of her own voice. "It doesn't hurt."

Even the raindrops kissing her face felt warm; when one changed course to seep between her lips, she tasted salt.

There you are. There you are.

You're not alone, love. Don't be afraid.

She'd feared this for so long. But now...

She wasn't alone. And if she wasn't alone, it was already better.

Exhaustion, pure and thick as fresh molasses, drizzled over her eyes until everything became very, very dark.

Until she could feel nothing at all.

CHAPTER 87

SOREN

Ani was not dead. But when she woke up, Soren was considering changing that outcome.

When she'd tipped forward out of the tree, utterly boneless, Soren had nearly popped her own eyes with the force of her scream. And when none of them had been able to reach her before she plunged into the water with a *crack* like a thousand necks snapping as one, Soren had stopped—because she could not do it again.

She could not wade out there and find Ani floating lifeless, broken in ways no one could fix, stare gilded and glassy as an antique mirror.

And that had been before Elias had collapsed, too, cold as a corpse and nearly as still.

Maybe that made her a coward. Maybe she should have ripped the stars off her shoulder when she dropped to her seat in the sand, shaking, clinging to

Elias's hands and sobbing hysterically as she searched for the pulse in his wrist without looking; as she watched the waves roll in and out, refusing to look down and see her most loyal nightmare come to life.

As she watched Wolf ford those depths like he wasn't the only Arborian royal without any trace of Atlas in his lineage, stopping at nothing to reach his fallen goddess.

Not dead, he'd shouted when he'd stumbled back onto the shore—almost perfectly in time with the steady thump of Elias's pulse strangled beneath her fingers. *Not dead, she's not dead.*

Soren didn't remember much between then and now, but she knew someone else had carried both Elias and Ani here—knew she'd threatened her way through the dockside infirmary's door when rangers tried to make her get stitched before she could follow her battlemate—knew Elias had regained enough consciousness at some point to mumble for her to stop causing a ruckus.

When she finally pushed off the last ranger in her way and joined Wolf in the space between Ani and Elias's cots, he gave her what most might consider a good report on Ani: no injuries, no trace of lingering Blight…but she wouldn't wake when shaken or spoken to. Even when Soren called her a couple names choice enough to get her whacked on the head with the balled-up jacket Wolf was wringing like a towel, she'd just…slept.

She might have tried harder, Wolf's sensitivities be damned, if her attention hadn't been startled elsewhere by the black-powder *bang* of a door being thrown against a wall not even fifteen minutes after her own arrival.

"Medwenna Sigrid Reydis-Harald," Everin drawled as he limped into the infirmary wing, bloodied furs shifting on his broad shoulders as he batted the door aside, "you better have one fantastic explanation for why I had to find out from flogging *Kessen* that my favorite historian is lazing about in the—"

Even with her heart hammering and her eyes blurred with battle-strain, she knew the exact moment when Everin found Medwenna across the room— the exact moment he took in the overspill of blood, the crimson pile of saturated and discarded stanches, and the muzzy, listless glaze to the overeager historian's eyes as she muttered something about Sanctan customs for proper disposal of medical waste.

And she knew with abrupt, chilling certainty that someone was going to die for what had been done to Medwenna.

Since the guilty party was gone, she had to assume it would be whoever happened to be nearest to Everin when the dark, predatory thing claiming his countenance slipped its collar.

"Talk," he commanded the physician as he crossed the room, no longer beaming with false bravado, his stalking steps eating up the distance in three long strides.

The physician blinked at him, his blood-soaked hands pinning yet another stanch to Medwenna's shoulder. Not a good sign, bleeding this much even with all that gauze jammed into her. "What?"

"Talk." Fury seethed in Everin's voice as he leaned over Medwenna, roughly shoving the physician aside and moving the stanch to look at the injury himself—at the same time, his other hand gently pushed the sweat-soaked fringe of hair from Medwenna's brow. Such an odd collision of rough edges and tender touches. "What did this? What happened?"

"Blighted creature," Soren called—when Everin swung around to meet her gaze, she didn't flinch back. "One of those overgrown spiders. The venom stops clotting."

The wrathful flush drained from Everin's face as his gaze snapped back to Medwenna's shoulder. To the brackish green tint staining the borders of the wound. To the wild edge in her dull eyes. Her shocky mutters had taken on a frantic quality, like educating them on—well, Soren had lost the thread of it now, but something too ancient for anyone but Medwenna to care about—was more important than their efforts to save her life.

"Captain," said the physician, reaching back in—Everin's head snapped toward him, and whatever look he leveled at the physician, the man slid a good two steps back. But he continued speaking to Medwenna. "Captain Reydis-Harald, take a deep breath for me."

"N-no, you need to—it's dangerous." The words slurred, fuzzy at the edges, like Medwenna spoke through a mouthful of cotton. Her eyes darted, her chest shuddering as she fought for breath, fingers twitching spasmodically at the tips. "When plague tore through the Sanctan empire, they had to…they invented the—"

"Captain, please, try to—"

"You're not *listening!*" Terror cracked Medwenna's voice—a violent shudder seized her, pitching her to the side like a tossing sea. At the first physician's call, two more ran to help, one with medimancy glowing in their hands; but Medwenna only writhed harder, sobbing, "You aren't listening, you have to—"

"Medwenna. Look here." Everin left tending her shoulder to the physicians now; he snapped his fingers in front of her eyes, then tapped right between his, never breaking her gaze. "I'm listening—look at me. I'm listening. Tell me more. What happened after the—the plague, the plague in Old Sanctaviv? What changed?"

Her brows furrowed, warm-honey gaze fixing on his finger. But when he lowered it, she didn't follow; she stayed locked on his eyes, the frenzied edge to her voice softening. "They, um…after the plague burned through to the empire's core, they were vulnerable…th-the Medeis siblings saw an opportunity, so they—"

Her body seized up as the medimancer plunged their magic into the wound, her dazed lecture buckling into a cry. Everin snatched her hand when it flailed toward her shoulder, cradling it close to his bearded mouth and shushing her. "I know it hurts, I know, I know—hey, can you remind me of their names, again? The human ones?"

Medwenna glared blearily at him, vague understanding flickering across her pallid face. "You're trying to distract me."

"Who, me? Never." Everin gave her a broad grin, too smug, too taunting to match the intensity of his gaze…or the worry and distrust hiding behind it as he stole glances at the medimancer's shining hands. "C'mon, you know I'm terrible with names."

Medwenna Sigrid Reydis-Harald, he'd called her when he'd waltzed into the room. Terrible with names, but he'd rattled hers off like he'd been born knowing it.

"I…" Medwenna squinted, brow wrinkling; her eyes flitted back and forth, back and forth, like she was trying to read a language she didn't understand. "I don't know."

"Not a good time to mess around with me." Everin squeezed her hand. "Come on, almost got it."

"I *can't*." Medwenna's brow smoothed in defeat, eyes glazing over. She tugged her hand back from Everin, shoving her palm against her forehead with a sob. "I can't remember. I can't *think*, it hurts to—"

When the medimancer's magic split like a popped stitch, another gush of blood bathing Medwenna's arm, she didn't scream again; her chin dipped toward her chest, her hand weaving briefly toward Everin as she slurred, "Hurts to…hurts…"

"*Medwenna*," Everin barked over the medimancer's curses, snatching that hand back like it belonged to him—the shift from coaxing murmurs to a general giving orders set Soren back on her heels. She almost stood at attention without thinking. "Get that head up, you can't go to sleep."

Medwenna's whole body shuddered. She blinked, a funny squint to her eyes—Soren knew that exact look intimately. The look of someone fighting a losing battle against the heavy hand of unconsciousness. A tear rolled down her cheek, picking up traces of blood on the way. "I can't—I can't. I'm trying. Don't be angry." A breathless sob. "I don't want to fight again. W-we never fight."

Everin's gaze followed the path of her tear, his jaw flexing. All at once, the brutal bearing of the would-be King of Tallis softened into a bewildered fear— like he didn't know what to do when a joke and a taunting wink couldn't fix the problem in front of him. When the world did not salute and snap its heels together at his command, his will made manifest by his word alone.

Soren knew that feeling, too.

"I'm not fighting," he croaked. "Winnie, hey…I'm not angry. I didn't…I know you're trying, I see you. I'm sorry—don't cry, I'm sorry." He brushed a streak of blood from the corner of her mouth with his thumb, bracing her there, forcing her to stay level with his eyes. Forcing a wobbly smile. "You're breaking my heart, here, you know that? Please don't cry."

The medimancer had stopped trying to stitch the wound; a creak from behind warned her Elias had pushed himself up from his cot to join them. He ignored her hissed command to *get back in bed, jackass* as he hobbled around her; he went to lean over Medwenna's shoulder, the medimancer nodding along as he murmured questions. Something about removing the venom.

"Keep talking," Everin demanded when Medwenna's eyes closed again. He folded his hands over hers...a heathen bent in prayer. "Keep talking to me. You can't remember their names, that's fine—tell me something else. Anything you *can* remember."

Perhaps the first time anyone had needed to beg words from Medwenna.

Medwenna's eyelids gave one last valiant effort, struggling bit by bit to reveal the faintest sheen of amber brown.

"I love you," she said, with the same certainty she identified bird calls and spun historical lectures from thin air. A truth carved in stone, scribed in ink—a fact as indelible as any other.

Everin's throat strained as he swallowed—he looked over his shoulder to the empty space behind him. "Who's here—is it Will? If it is, tell him to he can kiss my ass. He's the one who cut out early, so he can wait his stake-scorched—"

Medwenna's hand cupped his cheek, turning his face back to her. "Everin." Her bloodless lips turned up at the corners. "I love you."

Three words.

It took three words to break the Lion of Tallis.

"You shouldn't have said that," Everin whispered; he broke down on his knees, crushing a kiss into her hand. "You *really* shouldn't have flogging said that."

A twinkle pierced through the haze in Medwenna's eyes, a star peeking through the clouds—then blinked out.

"Medwenna." Everin's face dropped; he rocked forward when Medwenna's eyelids lost their battle, dropping her hand to reach for her face instead, wiping away her bloodied tears with his thumbs. "I'm sorry. I'm sorry, that was stupid. Say it again."

But only blood spilled from Medwenna's lips now.

"Say it again." Everin traced his knuckles over her cheekbone, her temple, her jaw—kept pausing to wipe more blood away, like he thought it was the only thing stopping Medwenna from doing what he asked. "C'mon, baby, please, please just say it one more time, *please.*"

Nausea churned in Soren's empty stomach; but she couldn't look away as watched Elias and the medimancer press in together, both pairs of hands prodding Medwenna's wound—one glowing a faint, sputtering red, the other glowing green.

When Everin's gaze landed on those flaring magics, he went another shade paler. And when he shoved back from the bed with the back of his hand pressed to his mouth, blindly thrusting his way back out of the room, she only hesitated long enough to catch her battlemate's eye.

"I'm good," Elias promised. "You got him?"

"Yeah." Too many people who needed her; too many bleeds that needed stanching. Her sinking heart tried to anchor her here, with Elias, with Ani—but strategy had to win over sentiment. Everin was the only one she could actually help. "I got him."

Everin didn't make it far. Only to the end of the hallway before he doubled over, clutching his chest and heaving like a man about to be violently sick.

Nothing came up; this sickness was all shock, all terror. But the body barely knew the difference; he retched one more time before falling to his seat, shoving the heels of his hands against his forehead, staring at the opposite wall.

Soren padded down the hall and slid to her seat next to him.

"If you're going to call me an ass," he said, "you can save your breath. I already know."

"Actually, I was going to ask how you got put in charge of Tallis's army if you vomit at the sight of blood."

A sharp intake of breath—then he laughed. Too loudly for this silent, solemn hall. A cackle so brittle it crumbled to pieces when it hit her ears.

"Stakes, Princess," he muttered. "How do you do that?"

"What, mock people having the worst day of their life? They usually make it easy, it's low-hanging fruit—"

"How do you make the worst jokes at the worst times without making me want to punch you in the nose again?"

She decided to let that one go. She bumped his shoulder with hers. "Telling people you're sorry for what they're going through never actually makes them feel better. An awful joke is usually better."

"Or it makes them want to punch you."

"Or it makes them want to punch me, but either way, it feels better than what they were doing."

Everin grunted, then sniffed sharply, grinding the heels of his hands into his eyes. "Damn it."

Soren rested her hand on his shoulder. "I know."

Another thing that never made anyone feel better: *I know how you're feeling.*

Which was why she only said it when she really, truly did. And with her hands forever stained by the memory of Elias bleeding out in her arms, forcing out deathbed confessions with all his strength…

Yeah. She really, truly did.

"She thinks she was the last one to talk to Will," he rasped. "Her husband. She wasn't. She was sleeping when he started to go…I went to wake her, and he told me not to. Made me swear on his deathbed I'd take care of her."

"You have."

"Not like I should have. And why—because I was too flogging scared of my *father* to tell him off when he decided to solder a ring on my finger? Because I was too flogging scared she'd tell me to go jump off a cliff if I told her the truth?"

"A lot of things feel impossible until it's life or death," she hedged. "That's the worst part—when something like this happens, it makes everything else feel so silly. So small. But it wasn't silly or small—not until now."

Everin just stared straight ahead, misery painting a glaze over his eyes. "I've been in love with that girl for two damned decades, Princess. Nothing's bigger than that."

"Do you want me to find Matt and Kess?"

"No. Not until I've got better news. I told them to report to Brook and make themselves useful." He rolled his eyes, forcing another laugh. "Besides, Kess is too good…if he sees me crying, he'll go too, and Matt will end up with two blubbering idiots to wrangle."

"Isn't he used to that by now?"

Everin pointed a warning finger in her face—but he only poked her forehead, an almost affectionate gesture. "Watch it, Princess. You're starting to look pretty punchable."

"I always look pretty."

"I said pretty *punchable*."

"I don't really hear anything people say if it's not a compliment."

Everin smiled this time; so much smaller than his usual grins. He dragged in a ragged breath, knuckling his tears away, shaking out his fingers like he'd driven them into someone's jaw. "Don't know why I'm such a mess. She's tougher than the rest of us. Toughest there is."

"I know."

His throat bobbed. He set a hand over it, rolling his eyes to stare at the ceiling—or to keep more tears from falling.

"Why didn't I say it back?" he rasped. "Why didn't I flogging *say it back*?"

Soren rested her head on his shoulder this time; a familiarity she wasn't sure she'd earned. But he didn't push her off; in fact, after another shaky breath, he rested his head on top of hers.

Maybe he just needed someone to lean on, and she happened to be the closest someone. But it warmed her all the same.

"Elias waited until he was bleeding out to ask me to marry him," she said. "I didn't answer the right way, either—but we did all right."

Everin turned to look at her; when she didn't let on to a joke, he snorted, "He did *not*. You're serious?"

"He did. Kind of. I think the exact words were 'I was *going to* ask you to marry me.'"

"Dramatic bastard."

Her turn for an obnoxious, too-loud laugh. "Damn it, Arden—I really didn't want to like you."

"Yeah, well…tough." Everin shrugged. "Don't think you can go through a gauntlet like Sanctum and not be friends after."

She tapped her chin. "So what you're saying is—"

"Don't—"

"Maybe the real god-killer is the friends we made along the—"

"Shut *up*," Everin groaned, shoving her off his shoulder while she cackled. "Don't ruin it. Gods, you're like the sister I never wanted."

"You have a sister."

"Didn't want her, either."

Soren just snorted, out of clever comebacks—she was too tired to try for another. Instead, she said, "Do you want me to go check on her for you?"

"In…in a minute," he said gruffly.

Soldier-speak for *I'm not ready to know yet.*

So they just sat, staring at the wall together…Heirs, generals, and cowards in their own right, pretending neither of them were hiding from what came next.

CHAPTER 88

ANIMA

She couldn't figure out why everyone was staring.

Sure, she'd woken up with a gasp loud enough to startle a bear out of hibernation. And she'd fallen flat on her face while trying to escape the sheets someone had tucked around her so tightly she'd had to wriggle around for a good five minutes before she loosened them enough to pop an arm out. And yes, the soft cotton gown she was currently wandering around in only came down to her knees, which made it fairly obvious she wasn't strictly *supposed* to be out of her sickbed yet...

Well. Maybe she *did* know why they were all staring.

The strange part was that they were all staring at her face—not her outfit.

An open window somewhere must have let a breeze or two in, though none were open in this stuffy intensive care ward. The intrusive zephyrs wound around her ankles like ribbon-dancers; warmer than before, damp and seasoned with the scent of new growth as summer poked its nose out of its den, making its tentative journey back across the island. It seemed the unseasonable cold snap was over.

Still, when those breezes teased the hem of her thin gown, she shivered; that playful nudge buffeted her like a hurricane gale, her body so oddly frail she almost feared the wind would sweep her straight into the sky.

Just to be sure, she ran a hand over her front, then used her eyes to check the rest—no bandages, no stitches, no scabs or bruises or breaks. No injuries to explain the disorienting lightness.

In her dreams, her exhausted mind had spun up a fistful of fable-worthy explanations. In one, a well-meaning witch had turned her into a dandelion seed, granting her wish to see the world without the tedium of carriage rides or weeks-long walks; in another, she woke up as a bird, hollow-boned and full-feathered, a song of joy warbling through her chest as she took off into the clouds.

Sleeping, this emptiness had been a boon, a gift. Waking…

In wakefulness, she'd never felt so untethered.

Instinct screamed to drop to her knees, to press her body into the ground and root her fingers into something solid—a rock, a tree, anything with weight—to keep herself from flying away like a kite with a cut string.

But she was not a kite, nor a bird, nor a dandelion seed. And she had someone she needed to find.

Grief tied a new string onto her windswept heart, towing it back down to earth.

When she'd asked where she could find the Crownless Queen's guardian. the medimancer had gazed at her with the gentlest sorrow before breaking the news. And when she'd asked to be taken to him anyway, the woman had insisted on seeing to Ani first—a sensibility she had neither time nor patience for.

She hadn't waited for the suggested summoning of Prince Wolf, the promised change of clothes, or the insisted-upon exit examination. The second her medimancer's back had turned, she'd tiptoed to the door, paused just long enough to swipe a rose-pink knit shawl from the hooks where the medimancers kept their coats and cloaks, and fled for her life to find the intensive care ward closest to the infirmary's entrance.

The place where they took those closest to death.

But despite beelining straight to this crowded but quiet chamber, each bed filled with a body so still she couldn't tell if they were dying or dead already, she had yet to find Alder.

This pervasive emptiness in her body had caught in her mind, too. Her brief possession of all her lives, all her memories, had ended alongside the fight…she could no longer remember him, not with the clarity she'd had when she abandoned the shrine for the battlefield.

But just like before, in the shrine…the body remembered what the mind could not. And she could not rest until she found him.

And when she succeeded at last with a medimancer's assistance, her heart needed no memory to help it shatter.

Alder Finch, the medimancer said, had chosen his deathbed himself—he had marched straight to the furthest cot in the furthest row at the furthest end of the room, allowed them to realize his wounds had been dealt too long ago now for their magic to drag his body back from the brink, and asked to be left alone. He had even refused the clean infirmary gown offered to him; he still wore his torn-up uniform, and it did nothing to hide the damage done by the Blighted beasts he'd struck down.

Dozens, the medimancer had whispered before they'd left Ani to her business. Maybe hundreds. They'd found him in a circle of corpses, kneeling at its center, ichor-soaked blade resting across his knees. Like he'd been happy to sit and wait there for death to find him.

Yes, Ani had choked through tears. *He's quite good at waiting.*

But Ani had made him wait long enough.

She sat carefully on the side of the bed, not bothering with the chair pulled up beside it; she pulled the curtain strung between Alder's cot and the next closed, despite no one sleeping in the next cot over. "Alder. Can you hear me?"

A sharp blink; his blue eyes pierced the dusky gloom in this windowless chamber. Before, they'd shone clear as the sky, clear as polished glass—now, she looked out into a haze of frost-blue fog.

"I told them not to summon you." Not even a *hello.*

"They didn't. I came looking, I—"

"No, you leave me," he rasped. "Do you hear me? Don't stay, don't watch this. You have a new life—do not carry me into it with you."

Her throat was so rotting tight she couldn't speak. But when she put her hand over the mess of split skin and torn muscle and so much blood it stopped making sense to her as blood and she tried—she tried *so* hard to coax it to close, and it refused—

That tightness snapped, loosening the lock on her vault of tears.

She dropped her head against him and cried. And though he muttered her name like he might have been frustrated, even that frustration held her with gentleness.

"I'm *so* sorry," she sobbed into his shoulder. "I can't help you. I—" A heave that felt like it tore something in *her* center. "I don't have any miracles left."

"Shhh." His hand settled over the back of her head. "It's all right, love. I don't fear it. I have someone waiting for me." When she lifted her head, sniffling, drying her tears with her hand instead of his sleeve, his gaze drifted behind her. "And so do you."

When she followed that look, she didn't see anyone. But after a moment, she heard it: a deep, grim, beautiful voice not quite as low as propriety demanded in a place of deathbeds. An anxious line of questioning that led to whether or not anyone here had seen a golden-eyed woman wandering around in an infirmary gown.

Oh, Wolf.

It would have been simple enough to kiss Alder's hand, murmur her final farewell, and leave him to pass on in peace while she went to put Wolf's worries to rest. As Alder had requested. As Alder had commanded.

Instead, she gripped his hand in both of hers, crushing a kiss to his weathered knuckles. And with a teasing glare through her tears, she said, "I will not allow you to dismiss me, Alder Finch. Not after all you put me through."

Those cloudy blue eyes twinkled. Good humor—perhaps tears of his own. "I should never have let you read that rotting journal."

"Too late for all that, now." Ani laid her cheek to his cold hand, allowing a silly, girlish grin to spread across her damp cheeks. One she didn't think she'd worn in this life, not precisely…but familiar, all the same. "No use picking up new regrets to carry off with you. You ought to focus on putting the old ones to rest."

A gentle snort. A breathless cough. Alder shook his head, resting his free hand over his heart.

"I have no regrets, milady," he murmured. "Certainly none to do with you."

If it hurt this much now, with only fragile strands of memory tied to his name, how much would it have hurt the version of her who loved him?

She didn't know the woman she'd once been. But after so many years…so many lives…she had come to know enough about the unchangeable, steadfast parts of her soul to guess. To imagine how that woman would want to say farewell to her husband.

"Alder." Ani blinked, loosing another volley of tears. "I have known people who treat promises like pocket change, spending them without a care, never giving them a second thought…and I have known people who swear vows as if bound to them by life or death. You have outdone them all."

Alder's throat bobbed; his eyes tracked her tears. "Milady, please—"

"That is not my name." She sniffled sharply. "And I suspect you are one of the very few who know the real one."

Now, at last, his tears overflowed; with a tired smile, so tired it broke her rotting heart, he kissed her hand with trembling lips. "Oh, Annelisa. I wish you would go."

She had suspected. But she hadn't been sure. And if he had not known it, maybe it would have softened this.

But to have trusted him with her true name…

He had *loved* her. The kind of love she had not yet known in this life, and had not thought she had known in others.

But a kind of love she had witnessed through someone else's eyes. The vow-keeping, blood-shedding, world-damning kind.

A love that, if she was very very lucky, she might yet have again.

A second chance. Once given to him, now given in turn to her.

She owed that love something. Something more than she could give.

"This isn't the goodbye you deserve," she whispered. "I wish she could be here instead of me."

"She is here…and it is not a goodbye." Alder's eyes drifted closed…then flared open one more time, a valiant last look. One that regarded her with no wistfulness or sorrow…only devotion. "I will see you again, Annelisa. I swear it."

"I won't make you wait so long this time."

When his eyes closed, they did not open again—but his smile was full of peace.

"Take your time," he said. "I don't mind waiting."

CHAPTER 89

ANIMA

She could not bring herself to leave Alder until the medimancers came and took him away themselves.

After she had wept herself weak and made them promise on their very lives that they would give him the best and most honorable care—and that she would be the one they came to when it was time to finalize his arrangements— she honored Alder's wish at last.

She dried her tears. She washed her face. She held herself until her heart stopped feeling as though it would fall out of her chest.

And then she went to find Wolf.

Sparrow was the one she found first, the princess's features set in a mask of calm plastered poorly over exhaustion; when Ani had asked after Wolf, the princess had pointed upward.

"He was checking the library for you," she'd said by way of explanation. "Lifted every book just in case, I bet. I heard his door close a bit back—it latches odd, what with all those plants crawling about. If you hurry, you might catch him before he starts organizing his drawers to see if you're hiding in his skivvies."

"Hiding in his *what?*"

Sparrow chuckled. "Ach, forget it—joke isn't funny when you have to explain it. If you hear me tell it to Sage later, act like it's new material, will you? I don't get good ones that often."

Still confused, she left Sparrow to her work. But as she left, she thought Sparrow's humor broke a bit when she met Ani's gaze—a slight furrow of the brow, a brief parting of her lips. But the princess didn't say anything else, and by now, Ani was almost afraid to ask.

When she reached Wolf's door, little had changed—he hadn't regrown the plants she'd untangled during her last visit, so the knob still stuck out, waiting to be turned. But when she tried it, it stopped short, jammed against the lock.

She set her cheek to the door and shut her eyes. Just listening.

He didn't make her wait long.

"Whoever's out there," he said, voice scraping like a rake being dragged over gravel, "you'll not change my mind, so beat it."

"I'm not here to change your mind." Whatever exactly it was made up on. "But if you won't let me in, would you mind if I rested out here? I don't know if I'll make it back to the lift, and—"

The door swung open so fast, it would have smacked her in the face if it swung outward rather than inward.

She had no time to assess how Wolf looked—he opened the door and enveloped her in his arms in one smooth motion, her still-dazed awareness jumping straight from *closed door wood polish ivy leaves* to *woodsmoke chicory spilled tonic racing heart.*

"Annelisa." A mutter so broken with relief, drowned in unshed tears, the tension drained right out of her tired body. Her muscles eased with such swiftness it must have shocked her limbs a bit, because when she lifted them to wrap snugly around his middle, they shook.

"Wolf," she whispered into his shirt. "Are you all right?"

His beard scratched her scalp as he nodded. "I am now."

She craned her head back, seeking his face; when he tried to duck away, she caught him by the chin, firmly lifting his head until she found his eyes.

A ragged man stared back at her, hollow-cheeked and sleepless, clearly *not* all right. But even he blinked, briefly startled out of his abject exhaustion by whatever he saw on her face.

"What?" she demanded. "What's wrong? Is there something on my face?"

Now that she'd had the thought, it struck her she hadn't actually checked her face to ensure all was in order; she lifted her hand, but Wolf caught it, a throaty laugh sticking in his chest.

"No, no, it's just..." He swallowed, something like wonder softening his expression as he ran his thumb over the arch of her brow. "Your eyes."

"What about them? Are they still there? Oh, of course they're there, I can see, but—"

"They're fine," he said—then hastily amended, "They're beautiful. They're just..." He frowned, gaze drifting—looking *at* her eyes, not *into* them. "They're brown."

Ani blinked.

Without a thought in her head, she pushed past him, hurrying into his chambers; when he called out, "Up the stairs, to the right of the bed," she followed his instructions, fatigue forgotten. She was so preoccupied she didn't even spare a thought that the upstairs level—furnished with a huge bed outfitted with an absurd number of pillows, a reading chair with a knit blanket draped over its back, and shelves piled with just as many plants as books—was obviously Wolf's bedroom. She went straight for the long mirror propped up next to a door that had been left open, revealing a closet behind.

...Fine. Maybe she spared a single thought, however poorly timed and terribly insensitive, that she was currently standing in Wolf's bedroom.

But that thought flitted out of her head the second she found her own gaze in the mirror.

As slow, heavy footsteps ascended the curved staircase after her, she leaned closer, then back—then closer again, tracing her fingers underneath her eyes, stopping just short of actually poking the irises to test for truth.

No matter how closely she looked, no matter which way she leaned, trying to let the light catch on every fleck of color...

No gold in her eyes.

No gold at all.

Only soft, doe-eyed brown...the color of melted chocolate and tavern bartops and the hair of her first real doll.

It changed a bit when she blinked...tears altered the exact shade, turning them the color of muddied riverbanks and freshly dug-up clay and a puddle of whiskey spilled across a wooden floor.

No fine jewelry or blinding sunlight or coins tossed on altar steps.

Just...brown.

Wolf's hands fastened to her shoulders. "Are *you* all right?"

"Yes." The break in her voice wasn't the most convincing. She didn't care. "I am. I actually...I actually think I am."

A cost, Sancta had promised—a cost for one last miracle. Her final miracle.

The emptiness in her body, the feeling that her insides had been stripped clean of something she'd never been without...

She looked down at her palms and pictured a simple, perfect daisy in her mind's eye. Nothing special; not even a stem. Just the golden-hearted bloom, its mane of snow-white petals unfurling in the middle of her hand.

Nothing.

Nothing but the lines in her palm, fine as quill-tip scratches, branching like the lines cartographers used to demarcate the boundaries of a river.

Ani's heart cracked right in half. And while one half sank into sorrow, grieving a gift she'd given away…

The other soared, as if freed from a burden it hadn't realized it was carrying.

"I am," she repeated decisively, turning in Wolf's arms to set her hands on his chest. "But you are not. Sit down."

Wolf avoided her gaze. "We should let Soren know you're—"

She pointed to the bed. "Sit. Down."

Wolf sat down.

She almost smiled. Instead, she sat beside him, lacing her fingers through his and settling their joined hands in her lap.

"What happened?" she murmured, tracing the scabbed-over scratches down his arm…wounds, she realized with a stab of unease, she could no longer heal.

Wolf stared at their hands; his eyes glazed over, a frost of exhaustion and tears.

"You fell out of the sky," he whispered, letting go of her hand to wring his together. "I wasn't fast enough."

"Wolf."

"I heard you hit the water, and I thought…" He scrubbed the back of his wrist over his eyes. "I pulled you out, but you were so quiet. I kept saying your name, and you just…" He pushed his fingers through his hair and braced the heels of his hands against his forehead, curling over his knees, staring at the floor. "You were so rotting quiet."

She remembered the fall—a little. Less so the landing. It hadn't hurt.

A lump like a peach pit lodged in her throat. She set her brow to his shoulder, shutting her eyes…listening to his controlled, slightly ragged breathing.

"I am so sorry I scared you," she whispered. "It won't happen again."

A promise she could actually keep…if she applied it with specificity. Her days of playing falling star were over. Neither a mother's fairytales or her own wistful whimsy could make her anything more than what she was: a firefly with no light left.

She would never soar quite that high again. So he would never have to watch her fall that far again, either.

She could live with that.

"It had better not." Wolf turned to bury his face against her hair; his long fingers slipped into the tangled tresses, worrying them loose. She hadn't taken the time to brush it after waking up; what a sight she must have been. "I have quite the array of ailments to carry without my heart going, too."

The peach-pit in her throat roughened into pumice stone. "Don't talk like that."

That, she couldn't bear. Not fresh from her Guardian's deathbed.

Maybe not ever. She couldn't imagine a day when she might be capable of considering Wolf's demise with acceptance. So little time she'd known him, in the grand scheme of her life—but the idea of his absence reinstating itself, now that she knew what it was to have him? Intolerable.

"I'm sor—" A pause. A gruff cough. "I won't."

Despite herself, she giggled. A sound so off and airy it reminded her of her lightheadedness.

A shame, that such a malady demanded she keep her head on Wolf's shoulder. But without her magic to heal it, alas, there was nothing she could do.

A smile tickled the edges of her lips as she tucked herself into the safety of his side, tipping her dizzy head back to find his face. "You might earn that plaque yet."

His chest rose and fell in a deliberate, steady breath. She couldn't see his expression from this angle, but she could see the way his jaw worked before he said, a bit hushed, "I think you'll find I'm quite finished apologizing for wanting you in my life."

Well, that was not helping the dizziness *at all*.

"Wolf." She reached up and took his chin, tipping it downward. "Kiss me?"

Predictably, he hesitated. "Are you sure you're in good condition to—"

"*Wolf.*" A whine this time, hardly goddess-like. But then again…

Then again, she wasn't a goddess anymore.

She was human. Fully, dangerously, beautifully human—and she'd never been more delightfully sure of it than when Wolf Olivander shook his head fondly, murmured her name, and leaned down to kiss her utterly, absurdly senseless.

CHAPTER 90

SOREN

Arborian funerals were not half so somber as Nyxian or Atlas ones. The order of events was different, to start—the body or bodies were buried long before the wake even began, and that alone lifted the shroud of grief some. Wakes had always seemed awkward to her, trying to mingle and comfort and share stories with each other, pretending you weren't avoiding looking directly at the open casket.

Not to mention the expectation to eventually go up to that casket, stare into it, and pretend it wasn't whisking your body straight into fight or flight. To pretend it was somehow a comfort to look at a loved one's slack face, frozen forever in death's icy rigor. To pretend it wasn't making you unbearably queasy.

Or maybe Soren was just strange that way.

Regardless, the pyre-burning part in Nyx had always been easier. Her heart never really eased into mourning until the flames kicked up, and it was always a strange relief when she finally was able to *feel*; when she was no longer the odd woman out in a sea of broken hearts, fiddling with her fingers in the corner and biting her tongue to keep from impulsively spitting out dark jokes.

Instead, Arborian wakes could have been mistaken for a festival or birthday celebration; after the families held private burials at sunset, the entire city lit lanterns and hung them from the branches of their family trees, dousing the dark in a fuzzy golden glow. In the circular city center, a bonfire was built, more massive than any she'd seen before; big enough that she had to hang back in the shadows at the edge of the circle just to keep breathing. To avoid losing herself in girlhood fear.

As she watched the mourners milling throughout the circle of painted stone pavers, trading jokes and gossip and fond stories of the fallen, a warm arm wrapped around her waist. Spiced smoke and weapon polish tickled her nose as a familiar weight settled on her shoulder, followed by a familiar pair of lips against her neck. "Wondered where you wandered off to."

"A girl can only take so much religious debate." If anything, she was surprised Elias had noticed her absence at all. At dinner, he'd been deeper in his argument with Wolf over the origination of tattoos as a form of worship than most of these people were in their cups. And considering it was an open bar—her favorite sort—that was saying something.

She took another sip of her own drink as Elias settled his chin on her shoulder; she'd never been a fan of the mulled wine some street vendors sold in Nyx, but mulled cider was a revelation. The blend of spices and fresh apples and Arborian rum warmed her from inside to outside.

"Did you speak with your aunt?" Elias's other arm came around her waist, and she sank gratefully into his steady hold. This far from the fire, even with the help of her drink and her thick sweater, the evening chill had a way of creeping in wherever it could. It was nice, having her own personal bonfire at her back.

"And Everin, once I wrestled him away from Medwenna." The historian was still sleeping off her ordeal; the first day and night had been touch-and-go, but thanks to Elias, Cypress, and a handful of medimancers—an intervention watched closely by the magic-wary Triad—they were cautiously optimistic about her recovery.

Elias's throat bobbed against her shoulder before he rasped, "Numbers?"

The giddy flutter in her chest had less to do with the fact that this was her third mug of mulled cider and far more to do with the fact that, for once, she could give him good news. "A full battalion from Arborius. Four from Tallis; possibly more if Everin can get his pelicans in a row."

No reaction from Elias; not what she'd been expecting.

"You awake?" she prompted, reaching back to poke him in the ribs.

"I'm awake, smartass, just…what in the pits is a *pelican*?"

Soren completely lost it.

Laughing so hard she thought she might break a rib, she doubled over to try and cushion them, wheezing, "Oh my *gods*, Elias, you've never seen a *pelican*?"

"No, I've never even *heard* of a pelican. It's not a real thing, is it? You're making fun of me. That's not a real—"

"Pelicans are *absolutely real,* jackass, they're—they're birds, these birds with long beaks they use to scoop fish out of—"

"Oh." He rolled his eyes. "It's an Atlas thing. No wonder."

"You were there for long enough, you must have seen—"

"Why are we laughing?" chirped Ani, skipping up to them with a smile leaning far into tipsy territory; she held an empty mug in one hand and dragged Wolf behind her with the other, who watched her with a more reserved smile of his own.

"You know what a pelican is, right?"

Ani's mouth screwed up, her eyes narrowing to a suspicious squint as she glanced between the two of them. Like she was searching for a sign she might be about to become the new victim of their joke. "The bird?"

Elias flung his hands to the sky; Soren lost it again, wheezing, "Stop, *stop,* I'm going to snap a rib."

"You're all in rare form tonight," sighed Wolf. "You do remember you have a meeting first thing in the morning, don't you?"

"Oh, leave them alone," Ani cajoled, twirling against his side to plant a kiss on his cheek; her sage-green skirts spun out and back in, like a flower blooming and shutting again in the span of a second. Her gown had to be custom-made; it fit her like a glove, layers of tulle floating over a slip of silk, a corset belt embroidered with yellow and white wildflowers cinching around her narrow waist. "They deserve a good laugh."

Soren looked up at Elias, who looked down at her; together, they looked to Wolf and Ani.

"When did that happen?" they chorused, Elias pointing between them, Soren tapping her own cheek.

She never thought she'd see Ani look so gods-damned *smug.*

"That," Ani said primly, glossy lips pursed, "is *none* of your business."

"None of my *business?*" Soren squawked, pushing out of Elias's arms and diving for Ani; the goddess-turned-girl screamed like a boiling kettle, shrieking with laughter as she ducked out of Wolf's arms and fled, shoving Elias into Soren's path like it would buy her any time.

Elias yelped as Soren pushed him out of her way, diving after Ani. "You get *back* here and you tell me right *now* when you started kissing my cousin!"

"It's none of your—"

"You stole my body for *four months—*"

"It was less than that," Elias called unhelpfully from the sidelines.

"—and peeked into my memories—"

"Of which you had very few," Wolf reminded her.

"—shut *up,* both of you—and you think you get to pull that *not your business* nonsense? Nuh-uh, I don't think so!"

Finally, the universe offered her a boon—a crooked paver stone painted in chrysanthemums, its left end sticking out just enough to catch Ani's slipper. She stumbled with a dismayed cry; Soren caught her, lifting her fully off the ground, cursing as Ani started kicking her feet, straining for the ground. "Put me down!"

"Tell me when you started kissing my cousin!"

"Never!"

"You just kissed him on the cheek!"

"I meant I'll never *tell*," Ani groaned through her giggles.

"Oh, you're going to tell, or *I'll* tell Wolf you liked it when Elias tried to strangle—"

"Two days before you got back, right around sunset, in the woods by my old treehouse," Ani squeaked, frozen mid-wriggle, mortified heat splashing her cheeks.

"Much better." Soren dropped her friend on her feet—then pulled her back in for a tight hug.

Ani hugged her back, hiding her face in Soren's shoulder; when she spoke again, her voice strained with emotion. "What's this for?"

"Nothing." Soren buried her face in Ani's coiffed hair. "Missed you."

A soft sniffle. "I missed *you*. I didn't think I'd miss having a—a—"

"Smartass?" Elias offered, still unhelpful.

Soren glared at him. "Will you stop it?"

He smiled banally back at her. "No."

Ani raised her head, smiling in his direction, though her eyes—gods, it was still weird seeing brown instead of gold—shone with damp rather than delight. "Sure. I didn't think I'd miss having a smartass talking back in my head all the time."

"Well, I didn't think I'd miss having a nervous, flighty, goody-two-shoes know-it-all—"

Ani pouted. "I only did one, you don't have to keep going—"

"But," Soren finished, putting a hand over Ani's mouth, "I did. And I'm so *rotting* glad you're still here."

"Me too." Ani hesitated. "What...what do we do now?"

A fantastic question. If only she had a better answer.

"I'm meeting with my aunt and Everin again tomorrow to talk transport," she hedged. "But the Arborian battalion needs training, which means at least one Tallisian battalion will need to stay behind as well, and they still have to get here first. The timing is...up in the air."

Possibly her least favorite place for timing to be.

"Princess?"

She and Ani both turned—followed by Ani flashing an apologetic smile and mouthing *Sorry, habit*—to find a page waiting behind them, nervously shifting his weight between his feet.

"I apologize for the interruption," he said, "but you're needed in the Queen's study."

She caught Wolf's eye first; he frowned, shrugging, so she looked to Elias, who also looked puzzled.

"Did she say why?" Now that she thought about it, she hadn't seen her aunt among the rest of the mourners.

The page worried his lip with his top teeth. "It seems a missive has arrived for you…word from Port Atlas."

Her heart did not skip a beat—it stopped utterly in its tracks. Frozen. Not knowing whether to fight or flee.

Like she'd stumbled upon a more familiar wake…but the body had sat up and stretched, asking why everyone looked so startled.

When she blinked, she found herself running—dashing past blurs that might have been buildings or people or gods-knew what else, running faster than she ever had through this city.

And her heart wasn't beating—it was *racing*, running faster than she was, a dead sprint toward something she'd lost in the Sanctum of the Faithless:

Hope.

CHAPTER 91

ELIAS

ord from Port Atlas.

It had been some time since he'd struggled to keep up with his battlemate—and while the ease with which she stayed ahead of him was no doubt a blessing, it also left him wheezing by the time he stumbled after her into Genevieve's study.

Not the state he would have preferred to arrive in. Because the second he set foot in the room, the smell of lilac and pipesmoke and visceral fear nearly bowled him over.

Occassio's blessing hung heavy over this room, wreathing the air like effervescent fog.

Tension trickled down his limbs like kerosene, ready to catch at the first sign of trouble; and it didn't take long for that sign to show itself.

A stranger sat in one of the chairs across from Genevieve herself; a stranger wearing a plain gray cloak, hood up, ring-adorned hands folded on the edge of the desk. Beneath those folded hands was a letter.

A letter whose seal shimmered in the candlelight, rippling with ethereal magic.

Astrid sat in the chair beside her, but Sage was notably absent—likely finishing out the arrangements for his fallen rangers. The diplomat sat straight and poised, hands folded in her lap, keen gaze tracking the stranger with a pleasant smile held in place.

"Princess Soren." The stranger rose when they entered, directing a curtsy toward Soren; to Elias, she merely nodded. "Captain Loch."

She knew his name. With no introduction made.

No. Nope. He didn't like that one little bit.

He drew one scythe out, baring just an inch of the blade. He set a spark free in that current of kerosene, catching it aflame, letting his tattoos do the rest of the talking.

"Hmm." The amusement in the stranger's purr set his hackles on edge. "Jumpy, isn't he?"

"Well, you're clearly doing your best to creep him out, so. Can't blame him, can you?" Soren scowled at the stranger, crossing her arms—and, for once, letting him edge just slightly in front of her. "Start talking."

The stranger threw off her hood, letting it slump back over her shoulders; a mane of corkscrew curls waited beneath, static-teased and lightning-struck. She wore miniature mirrors lashed to her wrists—typical of most Occassio-blessed, to focus and amplify their finicky magic—along with pants that climbed to the top of her waist and a draping top, both dyed a vivid shade of violet. A jeweled belt wrapped around her middle, but from the way the light bounced off the gems…probably all fake.

"My name is Luisa," introduced the seer, "and I have something I think you'll want to see."

She held the letter out to Soren; before he could utter a word of caution, his battlemate took it, frowning as she poked the terrifying magic seal.

Typical.

He palmed his face as she said, "How am I supposed to open it?"

Luisa shrugged, hands perched on her hips. "Beats me, Your Highness. He said it would only open for you."

Soren's gaze snapped back to Luisa's face, and for a moment, *every* emotion played out plainly through her eyes…suspicion, worry, anger, but most prominently—and perhaps most dangerously—hope.

She slid her thumb under the lip of the envelope, pushing toward the seal—and with a soft, simple *snick*, the seal gave.

He'd never seen someone struggle so much to retrieve a letter from an open envelope—her fingers were shaking so badly she practically had to shred the envelope from around the missive, shaking it open rather than unfolding it. Her eyes darted over the text, devouring it; then they leapt back to the top of the page, skimming through again, and again, and again. She clutched the paper so tightly he worried she might tear it right in half.

Then, without a word—without a twitch or a gasp or even a blink—she walked right out of the room.

"Sor—hey! Soren, wait—" He rushed out after her, only glancing back at the seer once; she gazed back, impassive, but her eyes drilled straight into his soul. He turned aside, struggling not to shudder as he chased his battlemate to the room they'd been staying in. "Soren, what in the pits does it—?"

"Here." She shoved the letter at him without a backward glance; with her other hand, she dragged her pack out, tossing it on top of the unmade bed and beelining for the dresser. They hadn't unpacked much; everything they *had* unpacked, she started tossing onto the bed, eyes unfocused as she set to work.

His battlemate hated folding anything; he usually tackled the packing, because otherwise, she'd shove everything in as one big lump and call it good enough. But here she was, folding like a gods-damned maniac.

Whatever was in this letter, it had obviously caused her to finally crack.

He opened it slowly, almost afraid to peek.

Kid,
Playing a game. Need you on my team.
Hope you remember how to swim.

There was no name at the bottom—no signature, no indication of who could have penned it.

Elias held the note back out to her. "So?"

Soren now stood on her knees on the bed, dropping the last piece of clothing in—she dove off the mattress, snatching the letter from him in passing, rushing into the bathing room. A moment later, a bar of soap came flying out; he dodged, cursing as it landed neatly on the bed. "Soren, will you slow down? What's the big—"

"It's Finn's handwriting."

Oh.

His heart sank, sympathy twisting it like a wet rag; he went to the bathing room door, leaning against the frame, watching her throw together the bag of cosmetics she'd left behind when they went to Tallis. "Soren…"

She put up one finger in warning. "Don't."

"I know you want to believe it's—"

"I said *don't*. I know what you're thinking, but just look at it." She thrust the letter back into his hands, then halfway crawled into the cabinet under the sink, voice muffled, a series of clatters and crashes announcing she was rifling through belongings. "It's his handwriting, and he didn't sign it—Occassio would have signed it—"

"Soren, I really don't think—hey!"

With a growl of frustration, she scooted back out of the cabinet and snatched the letter back—he hadn't even opened it again—and marched out of the room.

When he chased her back into the Queen's office, calves burning, breathing a bit heavily, he could only watch in confusion as she handed the letter off to Astrid, who still sat in her chair.

Not a word passed between the diplomat and the princess; Astrid merely unfolded the letter, read it once, and went worryingly pale.

Then she pushed her chair aside, hurrying to her own desk across the room—smaller than Genevieve's, tucked into the corner, but clearly well-loved. She tugged open one of the smaller drawers in the hutch and withdrew a stack of envelopes—all opened, all tied together with a yellow hair ribbon stained with something dark and muddy. Maybe coffee? He couldn't be sure.

Astrid brought the envelopes over and untied the ribbon, letting them fan out over Genevieve's desk; she plucked one letter after the other from their envelopes, holding them next to the one in her hand. With every comparison, her hand rattled harder and harder.

Finally, the diplomat fell back into her chair, nodding as she handed the new letter back to Soren. "It's him."

Soren gave him a wide-eyed look, a silent *told-you-so*; but he shook his head. "Occassio could have *easily* forged that."

"It's Finn," Luisa spoke up—she hovered by the door, one hand on the knob, like she was getting ready to run. Not exactly convincing, in his opinion. "I spoke with him myself."

"How…" Soren tugged a hand through her curls, taking the letter back, running her thumb over the neat rows of text. "How is this possible?"

Luisa's mouth quirked up; she almost, almost looked proud. "It's Finn," she repeated, like that was all the answer they needed.

And for Soren, maybe it was. Because when she found his gaze again across the room, the desperate hope in her eyes crushed his skepticism like a bug meeting a steel-toed boot.

"I know." She hugged the letter to her chest. "Elias, I know it might be a trap. But if it's not, he's out there—and he needs me. If there's *any* chance he's alive—"

"We have to go." Resignation signed his fate in indelible ink. "I know, Soren. Of course we're going to go."

If that letter had come penned by Kallias's hand, he would already be sailing off on any pits-scorched ship he could find, seasickness be damned.

Soren spread the note out on the table, pinning it with one thumb at the bottom and the other at the top; she squinted at it like it might be hiding something, scouring it up and down.

"How are we going to get in there?" she muttered, seemingly to herself.

Elias leaned over her shoulder, skimming the text again himself. He set his fingertip to the second paragraph. "That part about swimming."

"Yeah, I know." She waved distractedly at him. "He's telling me where to go."

He didn't ask how she knew.

"The drowning dungeon, maybe?" There were plenty of cracks in that horrid place—he wouldn't be surprised if there was some opening a body could swim through at high tide. But the idea of having to force himself underwater again…

He put a hand over his chest, willing his stomach to settle back into its proper place.

"No." Soren slapped the tabletop with a hiss of satisfaction; she took the letter and folded it up, tucking it back into her pocket. "I know what he means."

"Great." Not great. This was definitively not great. "What's the plan?"

"Well, we can't show up empty-handed, so I'll have to talk to—"

"Your Majesty?" The same nervous page's head poked into the room. "I am deeply sorry, but…"

"Just tell me," Genevieve sighed, kneading her temple with her fingertips. From what they'd been told, the Queen had suffered from a brief touch of Blight herself before Ani had taken the ailment into her own body; though she looked no worse for the wear, the steadfast cheer she'd radiated when they'd first arrived had not shown itself since they'd returned.

The page cleared his throat, nodding once. "I'm afraid there's been a problematic arrival at the harbor."

"What do you mean, problematic?" Astrid prompted.

The page glanced at Soren and Elias, then back to his queen and diplomat. He tugged on his collar with a hard swallow. "Do you recall the ship that set off its cannons in the harbor?"

Soren and Elias exchanged looks again.

It couldn't be. That kind of coincidence, it just…

Luisa's restrained, smug smirk caught his eye. Just a flash; a wink of hidden steel from inside an open coat.

Right. Not a coincidence at all—good fortune guided by foresight's cheating hand.

"Sounds like you should go sort out our passage back," he said to Soren.

She frowned. "Where are you going to be?"

"Someone should warn Everin our timetable just moved up." And if he was honest, the notion of letters penned by princes had woken a ghost first stirred in the Sanctum…one he needed to put to rest before he could step into this next trial. "I'll meet you at the docks."

Soren's squint didn't set its suspicion aside; but she nodded, blowing a kiss to him as she made her exit. "Tell Medwenna she's got till morning before I start sketching in all her books. If she's not awake to stop me—"

"I'm sure Everin's already tried that."

"Still." She caught herself on the doorframe and swung back his way, the excitement in her eyes holding strong. "Finn's alive, a bunch of pirates kept their promises…it's a good night for miracles. Why not try for one more?"

CHAPTER 92

ELIAS

A duet of snores greeted him when he slipped into Medwenna's private sickroom.

Kessen and Matthias sat in chairs on either side of the bed, holding Medwenna's hands. They'd both propped their legs on the mattress, sprawled over Medwenna's; neither stirred when he shut the door, though he wasn't quiet about it. The worst it could do was startle Medwenna awake, and somehow, he didn't think Everin would go after him for it.

Not when the prince neither sat nor slept; instead, he stood by the window, leaning his whole weight into the wall, a book open and turned to face the watery cast of moonlight filtered through the glass.

"You're going to strain your eyes like that," he said. "Moonlight's no good for reading."

"Nothing for it." Everin's gaze didn't lift from the page.

"No lanterns?"

"No lighter. Matt and Kess were out by the time I realized, and…"

And he hadn't wanted to leave Medwenna without someone keeping watch.

Elias strode to the lantern on the bedside table. He felt it when Everin's gaze lifted from the page, sticking to him instead as he opened the lantern and strafed his fingertip over the wick.

Everin's heavy sigh when the wick leapt to life spoke volumes. But the fact that he held his tongue when Elias set the lantern on a nearby shelf and leaned against the wall beside him…that said a lot, too.

"I hate reading," Everin said frankly; his eyes had fallen back to the page. "Couldn't get through lessons to save my flogging life in school. My teachers thought I had an attitude because of my title."

"You didn't?"

"No, I did—that's just not why I couldn't read." Everin smirked, but even in the stronger light of the lantern, it seemed…ghostly. Liable to vanish with the next shift of shadow. "Sitting still *hurt*. I used to tell my mother it made my bones itch."

"Soren says the same thing." He tried to peek at the book's cover, but the shadows fell just thickly enough to hide it. "If you hate it, what's with the book?"

Everin lifted the tome in answer, holding the cover to the light. Raised golden letters spelled out the title: *An Altered State.*

"Flogging useless," Everin grumbled, clapping the book shut, running his thumb over the textured cover. "Thought I'd give Winnie's method a go, but it just says the same thing all the medimancers did: we'll only know for sure if the magic took when she wakes up. Or when she…doesn't."

"Give her time. This is probably the best sleep she's gotten since Soren and I showed up."

"Yeah." The skin around Everin's eyes had gone nearly purple, bruised with sleeplessness of his own. He tossed the book onto the bedside table; it landed with a *snap*, both Kessen and Matthias jerking and mumbling in their sleep—but not Medwenna. "Saw what you did for her, with the…you know. Your magic. Thank you."

"You can use manners now? When'd you learn that trick?"

"Shut your flogging mouth, zealot." No real bite in that bark—in fact, he could've sworn the prince was smiling. "What're you doing up here, anyway? Your wife *strongly* implied she had every intention of booking up your entire evening."

He decided he didn't want to know what that meant. Instead, he gave a hasty explanation: the soothsayer, the letter, the ship—then said, "I don't think Soren will wait long past daybreak."

"Don't blame her." Everin snugged his crossed arms over his chest. "This you trying to say your goodbyes and good riddances?"

"It's me asking a favor."

Everin blinked. "You're yanking my chain."

He wished he was—he'd already started regretting this decision. But now that he'd said it, he couldn't walk it back.

Like the anchor that had trapped them in the center of a storm inside the Sanctum, the lump in his throat refused to be moved; no matter how hard he swallowed, no matter how hard he cleared his throat, he couldn't dislodge it. It held his request fast, refusing to let it sail free or sail home. To advance or retreat.

But Soren had taught him how to tread those waters.

"I have to finish that goodbye." One stroke forward. A kick toward the shore. "But I can't do it with her, not now…and I don't want to do it alone."

The anchor in his throat tore at his voice, leaving it embarrassingly small; but Everin just nodded. No mocking; no laughter.

"Heard." Everin tilted his head toward his injured leg. "You got me; I've got you."

No more, no less—but it was enough.

For the first time, when he retrieved Kallias's note, his hand didn't rattle. And when he unfolded it, forcing himself to take in the words instead of letting his gaze leap away…

He actually thought he might be able to survive it.

Eli,

By now, you will have discovered that I am a depths-damned coward.

I didn't have to do it like this—I had every chance to look you in the face and give you the proper goodbye you deserve. You could have been sitting here with me, had I been braver.

I didn't do the brave thing. For the same reasons I left this letter for last.

I couldn't bear to let you down.

I am well-accustomed to that—letting others down. My sisters. My brother. My mother. My people. Myself, for depths' sake.

But after Artem, I swore to myself you would never be one of them. And no amount of courage could make me face you as I broke that vow.

You were my first true friend. The first who came to me not as a soldier under my command, not as a subject to their prince, but as someone who had every reason to treat me like an enemy, like nothing…and instead, you became the first person to treat me like I was something. The first person who told me I had more worth as a man than as an incentive scrawled on a treatise. Even if I lived to see this world's bitter end, I would not have enough time to thank you for that. Not with any semblance of adequacy, anyway.

Gods, Elias, I wish you were here.

But it's better like this, even if it's not brave. I think we both know I have to do this— and we both know you'd stop me if you could.

I am grateful for you, Elias Loch. Grateful to have had you as a friend—grateful that my sister has you at her back. Grateful you've shown mighty restraint in leaving Finn alive this long. (I know, I know, he's asking for it. But I appreciate you taking the high road, as you always do.)

And I am grateful that I can make this choice without fear for my kingdom, knowing you will one day become its king.

I only wish I could have stayed long enough for you to become my brother.

I know Atlas is not your home. But if you give it the same chances you gave me, I think you'll find it will pledge itself to you all the same. And should you ever need to look up at the stars and pretend you're back in that frigid tundra you call a kingdom, go dig around in the locked closet in our private beach entryway. The spare key's in the top drawer of my desk. There's a telescope in there, a pretty fancy one…some impressive model I can't remember the name of. A hybrid of Lapisian and Nyxian craft. You can see the craters in the moon so clearly you'll think you can step right into them.

Show Raquel, too, will you? I promised her once I'd take her to see an Atlas sunset, do some stargazing after. I want her to see that, at least once…how the sky and the sea become one.

I've already almost soaked this page with ink, so I'll spare you more sentiment, but I will leave you with this: I trust you. With my kingdom and with my family.

You earned that trust. Remember that.

Love,

Kal

P.S. If your sorry carcass washes up in whatever afterlife I find on the other side of this before you're gray as a gull and wrinkled as a dried-out jellyfish, you will wish you'd fallen into one of Mortem's pits instead when I'm through with you.

Live, Eli. As long and as well as you can. You earned that, too.

Death can wait her gods-damned turn.

He'd read the letter twice—was halfway through his third go—when Everin grabbed him by the shoulder.

"Hey." A firm but gentle shake. "Breathe, Elias."

Elias dragged in a sharp breath—then expelled it in a harsh, guttural sob.

"Yeah." Everin turned away, didn't look at him—but he kept his grip on Elias's shoulder as he wept for his friend. Held him steady. "Just breathe."

It didn't feel like he could. But he tried—and every time he tried, Everin's hand tightened the same amount the pressure in his chest eased.

"You handled that better than me," Everin said offhandedly. "I cried so hard after Will's last breath that it gave me the hiccups. Trust me, *not* the ideal way discuss arrangements over your best friend's deathbed."

At the image of Everin bent in mourning, slumped shoulders bouncing with every ill-timed hiccup, Elias's next sob mutated into an ugly, ragged burst of laughter. He shoved the heels of his hands against his eyes, falling back on what he knew: applying pressure to the open wound. But even that couldn't stanch the flow of tears. "Oh, gods, that's *horrible.*"

"Yeah, I thought so too. Kept apologizing every time I got a breath in. Made Winnie laugh, though." A beat. "For what it's worth, from what I could tell, Kallias was a good man. Always liked him. Be a shame if he was the only one of them not to get a miracle."

"I never thought I'd see the day, the Prince of Heretics praying for a miracle."

"Not praying. Call it a wish, if you need to name it." Everin cracked his neck, then took his hand away—but oddly, that made Elias feel steadier, too. If a faithless prince believed in his strength enough to take away that support, it had to be close to true. "Finnick's alive, maybe. Soren lived. What do you think, Phoenix Priest? Did Death get a better grip on the First Prince?"

No one had asked him outright yet. A relief, up until now…because he hated the answer.

"I think Kallias has been looking for a fight to lose for a long time," he admitted. "And I'm terrified he finally found it."

And there it was—the truth he couldn't allow Soren to see.

"But I hope I'm wrong," he added fervently. "Gods, I hope I'm wrong."

"And if you're not?" Everin's brow cocked. "What're you going to do about it, Godkiller?"

When he finally swallowed that immovable weight in his throat, the lantern light guttered. A kernel of cold wound through his body, settling in his center…a pebble of reckless *something* he'd picked up during their gauntlet within the Sanctum Infidelium.

"I don't know," he whispered.

And that terrified him more than all the rest of it.

CHAPTER 93

SOREN

"**Y**ou have the *best* timing of *any* pirate I have *ever met*!"

Still riding the thrill of knowing her brother was alive—*alive, he's alive, he's alive*—she practically threw herself at Captain Patch as he walked down the gangplank. He caught her with a grunt, laughing as he set her down…but something about it rang differently. Less carefree, maybe, than it used to be. Or maybe it was just the moonlight washing him out.

"Maybe keep the whole pirate thing under your breath, lass," Patch teased, rumpling her hair with one hand. "Gods, you're a whole different woman than last I saw you. Give me a spin?"

She cocked one eyebrow. "I'm a bit too tipsy to take that risk. Besides, if you're looking to ogle my backside, I'm afraid my husband might take issue with it."

"*Husband!*" Patch's face split into a grin; he turned back toward the boat, cupped his hands around his mouth, and hollered, "*Half you lot owe me some gold!* She said *husband!*"

A chorus of complaints and groans and curses on her and Elias's marriage went up around and below the deck. Patch just chortled, turning back and clapping her on the shoulder. "I mean it—you look well." His gaze fell to her shoulder, and something in his gaze…softened, oddly. She didn't know what to make of it. "Can't say it doesn't give me the willies, former prisoner of war and all, but the uniform's a good fit."

"Thanks. Wait, what did you—"

"Long story. Tell you later, love." Patch thumbed his chin, frowning at the harbor—most of which was still in shambles. "Not to be rude or anything, but this place is looking a bit, ah…" He gestured vaguely at the mess. "What in the depths happened to you?"

She shrugged. "Tenebrae set a trap, we sprung it, and we accidentally created a living plague that tried to destroy the entire island."

Patch pursed his lips, nodding slowly. "Aye, well—that's about as sharkshit crazy as I thought it'd be. I suppose you're looking for a ride?"

"If you're willing."

"You're sweet," he snorted. "Trust me, lass—I've got even less of a choice than you think I do."

She frowned. "What's that supposed to mean?"

Another strange smile—was he *sad?* Did he even know what *sad* felt like?

He turned and whistled sharply, waving down one of the crew; she recognized Aabria, the navigator. "Get the girls up from belowdeck, yeah? They've had enough beauty sleep to last them the bloody week, I think they can manage a midnight docking without turning crone."

"Oh, you're one to *talk,*" sniped a cross voice—a *Nyxian* voice. "You can barely drag your backside out of bed before noon on a good day."

Her jaw dropped straight into the sand as a young woman stepped out on the gangplank—older than Soren by a handful of years, starlight hair grown out just enough to show her dark roots, a leather belt hanging from her waist with a—

No. That couldn't be her—that couldn't be Yvonne Nyx striding off a *ship* like it had her name on its hull, a gods-damned *rapier* dangling from the belt lashed around her thick waist, leather trousers clinging to her hips. It couldn't be Yvonne who ran for Soren with a grin that showed off a bruised lip and cheekbone, like Princess Perfect-Manners had gotten into a brawl, of all things.

Not only that, but suddenly, the man before her couldn't be Patch, either—because she'd sailed with him for weeks, watched him banter and flirt and command his crew, and never once had he really stopped smiling. Never once had he dropped the look of a man daring the world to throw whatever it liked in his direction.

But when Yvonne sailed past to wrap her arms around Soren, his eyes fastened to her—to the bruises on her face—and the darker emotion in him caught the wind, flaring out like a sail buffeted by a stiff summer breeze.

Difficult to be sure what that emotion *was*, what with her head swimming through a pool of spiced—and spiked—cider. But still…good to tuck away for consideration later.

"I'll go set the course for the crew," he said gruffly. "You two catch up— I'm sure Auralee's just digging out that satchel of shells to show off."

Yvonne twisted back to catch his wrist as he turned away. "Thank you."

Patch's fingers spasmed out—then closed around her wrist, a halfhearted squeeze. "Yeah, yeah. Don't get weepy on me, Majesty."

With a cleared throat and a two-fingered wave her way, Patch sauntered off, shoving his hands in his pockets and whistling his way up the gangplank—a whistle that went off-pitch more than once.

Soren turned wide eyes on her sister, who frowned at her. "What?"

"What do you mean, *what?* Yvonne, what in the *pits* are you doing here? Did he say Auralee? I thought you two—you were supposed to be—" She leaned in, dropping her voice to a hiss. "What did you do to that poor pirate?"

Yvonne's eyes gleamed—part mischief, part sorrow. "It is a very long story. One I'll tell you once we're safely aboard." She squeezed Soren's hands, peering past her shoulder. "In the meantime, tell me yours…start with why that Tallisian prick of a prince is here. And why he and his triad are watching me like they'll eat me alive if I do anything they don't like to you."

Soren turned to see a small audience had gathered—Wolf and Ani, who must have heard the news about the cannon-happy ship sailing back into port in the dead of night; Elias, of course, though he hung back, watching her and Yvonne with a smile; and coming up the path, flanked as always by his men, was Everin Arden. He, Matthias, and Kessen were all uncharacteristically quiet, clothes and hair sleep-rumpled like they'd all rushed here from Medwenna's bedside…and, with a surge of warmth that knocked her heart sideways, she realized they *were* watching her and Yvonne with assessing frowns, Kessen already casually resting his hand on his axe.

"Come on." Soren tugged Yvonne toward the others. "Let me introduce you to my family—and my friends."

CHAPTER 94

ANIMA

So far, the trickiest part of being human was determining when an unpleasant physical sensation crossed the line from *uncomfortable* to *concerning.*

The pounding pain in her head she'd woken up to after meeting Soren's sisters and getting some real sleep, for example…uncomfortable, but not concerning. Or at least, that was what Soren told her after she shook her awake in a panic, insisting she'd somehow taken on a concussion in her sleep.

"Ani," Soren said, with the most patience she'd ever received from the princess, "it's just a hangover. You drank too much cider."

Ani stared at her blankly, the throbbing in her brain making it difficult to push those words through. "Huh?"

"A *hangover,*" Soren enunciated; Elias mumbled something under his breath, rolling on his side and jamming a pillow over his head. Soren rubbed the small of his back, her jaw cracking open in an impressive yawn. "Which we also have, or at least *I* do, and I'd like the chance to sleep it off before we set sail. Go drink some water and eat something greasy. I recommend literally any form of potato."

So this dizziness pushing her back and forth like a pair of schoolyard bullies pulling one pigtail, then the other…she couldn't decide if she needed to tell someone about it. But if she recalled the symptoms of a hangover properly—something she'd treated enough times, but never experienced, thanks to her magic—dizziness was somewhere on the list.

So instead, she sat on the edge of the one intact dock spoke, trailing her bare toes in the water, slowly sipping from her canteen while she watched Soren and Elias load their things on the ship.

Last time, she'd hardly been able to bear it. But knowing she was going with them this time—that no one was leaving her behind—made it easier.

She just hadn't expected that the ache of leaving someone *else* behind hurt almost as badly.

She hadn't seen Wolf yet this morning, but he'd promised he'd be there to see her off. He and the other Reapers had endured a long night and early morning to assist with the repairs to the island, but—

"Goddess."

Anxiety unhinged its jaw, sinking inch-long teeth into her chest; terror bled into her lungs as she swiveled on her seat, looking up at Prince Everin Arden.

He'd dressed down for the warmer weather; no furs, only dark trousers and a cream-colored tunic, a thin leather pauldron strapped to his shoulder. He gazed down at her without expression, arms crossed, boot tapping on the dock.

"You tagging along this time?" he asked, nodding toward the ship.

A splinter burrowed under her nail as she dug her fingertips into the dock, forcing a smile. "It's Ani, actually. And yes, I'll be going. Is that a problem?"

"No. Soren told us as much." He rolled the shoulder capped with the pauldron. "I get it. You're part of her triad—a lesser part than Loch, maybe, but still part of it. Like Kessen."

"I heard that!" shouted the younger boy; despite standing enough paces away that he should have been out of earshot, he'd stopped loading his own things onto the ship to flash Everin two rudely posed fingers.

"How does he do that?" grumbled Everin; then he sighed, pointing downward. "This spot taken?"

Ani glanced at the spot, then back up at him. "Pardon me?"

Instead of repeating himself, Everin just dropped to his seat beside her; his sleeve came so close to brushing her bare arm, the hairs on her shoulder stood straight up.

"So," he said, kicking through the water, the minnows scattering from his steel-capped boot, "no more goddess powers?"

She gestured to her eyes. "Not a one."

His dove-gray gaze dropped to her hand. "Nothing at all?"

A shiver of apprehension raised goosebumps on her arms. But she kept her head up, forcing it to shake again. "Nothing."

She'd tried it all: growing flowers and vines and grasses, healing little scratches and bumps, inviting dead things to dance.

Not one spark of green.

A grief she had yet to reckon with, really; and a relief she wasn't sure she deserved to feel. But most of all, as much as it ached, as much as it scared her…it still felt right.

She had done the right thing. Had paid the price to set her wrongs straight again.

Redemption.

It did not come for free. But it could be earned, sometimes, if one did their best to repair what they'd broken. If they sacrificed in equal measure to what they'd taken.

"You're good," Everin said suddenly.

"Huh?"

"You and I, we're good." He shrugged, casually scratching behind his ear. "You gods and goddesses, you only do miracles when you get something out of them. That's what I told your friends, and I meant it. For the most part, I still believe it." He glanced at her sidelong, flashing his teeth in an almost sheepish smile. "This miracle didn't give you anything—actually, it took everything. And you did it anyway."

She frowned. "What other choice did I have?"

He slapped the dock, snapped his fingers, then pointed at her. "And that's why we're good."

That didn't make anything clearer. "But I—"

"Be seeing you, Ani." With a pat on her shoulder and a jaunty whistle, the Prince of Tallis stood and strode back down the dock, heading for the pile of cargo at the end.

"What was that about?"

Ani swore, swiveling to Soren, who cackled—she scooped up a handful of water, flinging it at the princess's legs. "Will you all *stop that?*"

"Sorry, sorry." Soren stole Everin's spot, drawing one knee up and resting her chin on it. "Was he bothering you? 'Cause I'll kick his ass."

"No, I…" Ani frowned in Everin's direction. "I think he struck a truce."

Soren dropped her leg, her boot splashing into the water. The minnows, who'd begun tentatively flitting back to her toes, fled once again. "You're joking."

"I'm really not."

Soren squinted up at the sky. After a moment, she shielded her eyes against the sun.

"What are you looking for?"

"Flying wolves."

"What?"

"You've never heard that saying? *It'll happen when wolves fly?* It's a—never mind." Soren leaned back on her elbows, scowling out at the water. "My humor is wasted on you."

Ani studied her friend: the sparkle in her eyes, the lightness present even in her scowl, the impatient bounce in her leg. "You're…happier."

"Finn is still out there." Soren gazed up at the sky, the clouds sailing through the green in her gaze. "And if he is, Kal might be, too."

Hope against all odds—another uniquely human trait.

Ani took Soren's hand. "I pray that they are."

Soren turned her head to smile up at her—then her face dropped. She clapped her hands against the dock, shoving up to her seat, staring over Ani's shoulder. "No rotting way."

"What?" She followed Soren's gaping look, braced for something awful, something dangerous…

And instead, she turned just in time to see Everin Arden drop everything he was holding. No, not drop—he *threw* everything he was holding aside, rocking forward like he might launch into a run—but instead, he dropped to one knee, his gaze fixed on the treeline.

On a woman sitting astride a horse, a satchel looped over one shoulder and a look of almighty wrath painted across her pretty face.

"Medwenna," Soren breathed in relief.

"Where, exactly," the woman said crossly, dropping down from the horse with a wince when she reached the dock, "do you get off, Everin Arden, thinking you're going to stay for the dangerous bit and then sod right off to the *next* dangerous bit without me?"

"Winnie—"

"Don't you *Winnie* me, you enormous ass's arse, I am *talking* to you."

"Is that redundant?" Ani whispered to Soren out of the corner of her mouth.

"I don't know what that means," Soren whispered back.

"Winnie," Everin repeated, lurching up to his feet again, swaying like a man who'd downed five too many drinks, "I need—"

"Oh, I don't give a flying *flog* what you need right now." Medwenna marched up to him, dropping her satchel to poke him in the chest. "Not only did I wake up with an arrow hole in my shoulder, I then found out you've been sitting around at my bedside for days, only to up and leave without even telling me goodbye! If you think just because you're *unofficially* King of Tallis now that you can pull that kind of nonsense on me, you have got another thing coming, you spoiled, selfish—"

"I flogging love you."

Ani might not be a goddess anymore, but she knew a confession of sins when she heard one—and Everin's rasping, tear-roughened whisper was absolutely *soaked* in shame.

In stark opposition, his friends Matthias and Kessen—who had both frozen mid-haul, staring open-mouthed after their prince—silently set their burdens down, mouthed a triumphant *Yes!* toward each other, and mimed out a high-five without actually slapping their palms together. Kessen actually went as far as to perform a brief, graceless victory dance.

She couldn't see Everin's face, not at the angle he stood at; but Medwenna's told her enough. The historian stared up at him, mouth frozen mid-lecture, honey-brown eyes utterly devastated with an emotion Ani had *never* seen. One that had no name.

"Come on, not with the big eyes. You must've known that." Scathing, almost—like he couldn't believe he had to say this out loud at all. He rocked to the side, scrubbing a hand over his beard, coughing a laugh into his palm before whirling back toward her, hands folded behind his neck. "You're too damned smart not to, so I don't know why I'm bothering, but—yeah, all right? Yeah. I love you, too. Happy?"

Now Medwenna's eyes were devastated with tears. "You're angry at me."

"No. Stone me and stake me, *no.*" The last word cracked like a fractured wrist; he ran his hands up and down her upper arms, pulling her in.

"Not you," he muttered with an idle, reassuring kiss to her temple. With a distracted stroke of his thumb over her bandaged shoulder before shoving his hand against his heart. "It's me. I can't even tell you how long I've…but after Will, and you were here, and this wretched *ring,* and it just…the timing, the reasons, they were all awful. And I was…" His jaw worked, like he had to grind his voice into the right shape for the next word, "*afraid* you wouldn't feel that way. That it would…I mean, you're my best friend, you know?" Another fracture through his voice. "I didn't want to ruin it."

Matthias and Kessen exchanged looks again, this time vaguely offended. *Best friend?* they mouthed to each other.

Medwenna's jaw twitched, a mimicry of Everin's struggle to spit out his words; then she struck his hand down from her shoulder, crossing her arms. "Did you ever consider asking me what *I* wanted?"

Everin's throat bobbed. But he nodded; took a breath like he was preparing to dive into waters of unknown depth, unknown cold.

"What do you want, Medwenna?" he asked, low and lilting and so in love it burned her ears roasted red.

Medwenna fisted her hand around his open collar, glaring at him like a historical tome with a ghastly error she'd just discovered.

"To ruin it," she said. "To flogging *wreck* it."

Whatever the prince was going to say, the historian didn't give him a chance. Because instead, she kissed him.

And Sancta save them, did that prince kiss her *back.*

When he broke off to whoop in a gasp of air, Medwenna started to step back, uncertainty claiming a face clearly unused to not being *sure.* But Everin shook his head, a cocky grin spreading across his features.

"Oh, no, no, no," he growled, stalking forward, wagging his finger with a *tsk-tsk* click of his tongue. "I'm not flogging done with you, Grand Historian."

Medwenna's nose crinkled in giddy glee as he snared the back of her neck with one hand; he took his time, trailing his nose down hers, grazing kisses against her cheekbone and her top lip before—

"Ani." Soren elbowed her with a hiss. "You're staring."

Gods, she had to get better about that.

She threw her gaze to the ground, but not before she saw Prince Everin kiss Medwenna like he'd waited a hundred rotting years to do it; and even then, Medwenna's giggly reminders that they had an audience needed no sight. Nor did the creak of leather and Prince Everin's departing footsteps as he literally swept the historian off her feet and carried her onto to the ship.

"Coast is clear," Soren said after a moment; when Ani looked up, Yvonne and Patch had appeared on the dock beside them. Annoyance flared when she realized despite Soren's scolding, the other three were all staring after the Tallisian pair: Patch biting his thumbnail, Yvonne shamelessly fanning her face, Soren a little glassy-eyed.

"That was bloody *hot*," Patch announced; when the ladies all turned on him, voices raised in a chorus of scolding cries, he threw his hands in the air. "We were all thinking it! What'm I getting shoved out on the plank for? Viv was about to faint!"

Soren cast a raised eyebrow toward Yvonne. "Viv, huh?"

Yvonne scowled at Patch. "You better watch it, or I'm going to start using a certain name myself, Captain *Patch*."

"Wait—you know his real name?" Soren shared a wide-eyed look at Elias, who'd promptly fled the ship after Everin and Medwenna boarded; when Patch took off after Yvonne, already bickering about why nicknames were different, Soren and Elias went running after him. "Yvonne! Yvonne, I'll give you *so* much money if you tell me his name, I swear I will!"

"You told me your purse was empty, Princess!" Patch called crossly.

"I will scrounge up something if it gets me your name. Is it Patchouli? I'm going to laugh so hard if it's…"

As Soren's pleas faded, stolen by the sea breeze, a low chuckle came from somewhere behind and above Ani's head. "Well…this is going to be an interesting journey."

Her heart tripped, falling flat on its face; she twisted to look up at Wolf, who smiled down at her, a hint of shyness darkening his amber gaze. He wasn't wearing his robes—today he wore a mix of hunter's garb and ranger armor, mottled greens and browns mimicking the tones of the forest past the darkwood gates.

And on his shoulder, he carried a pack.

"Are you…" The words stuck in her throat; she was almost afraid to ask, to hope. "What's in the bag?"

"Oh, this?" He cast a disinterested look at the satchel. "Well, it didn't make sense to pack *too* heavy, but gods know what we'll be getting into when we get to Atlas. Figured I could use some—"

He broke off with a grunt when she flung herself into his arms; that grunt softened into a chuckle as she kissed him, barely stopping herself from bouncing on her tiptoes.

Hardly the same sort of skill Everin had just demonstrated, but she was new—she'd have to practice.

She dropped back on the flats of her feet, beaming up at him. "You're coming with us?"

Wolf smoothed her hair back from her forehead, kissing above her right eyebrow. "Someone has to keep an eye on you, don't they?"

"I thought Sage was supposed to—"

"He was. We agreed it would be better if he stayed to start arranging for the Tallisian troops' arrival."

She squinted at him.

Wolf's bashful smile broke a jar of butterflies in her stomach. "Fine. We wrestled for it, and I kicked his arse."

Her joy sputtered some. "Are you sure? It will be dangerous."

"Well, that's the good thing about being a dying man." His gaze twinkled, a defiance of his solemn words. "Everything is dangerous...so it's up to me to decide which risks are worth taking. And you're a risk I'll take every time."

She covered her cheeks, willing them to stop with all the easy blushes.

"Besides," he added, digging into his pocket and pulling out a handful of rocks, "what am I going to do with all these pebbles if you're not around?"

Oh, Sancta save her from this wonderful, wonderful man.

She kissed him again, and again—and the third time, she gently nipped his bottom lip.

Wolf hissed, lifting a hand to his mouth; he stared at her, bemused. "What was that for?"

"Did it hurt?"

"Yes!"

"Then you're not dead." She gripped the sides of his jerkin, pulling herself up on her tiptoes to meet him at eye level. "And if I have any say, you're not dying anytime soon. So stop acting like it. Understand?"

He smiled. The innocent, beautiful smile that outdid even fables and holy relics of old.

"As you command, Annelisa," he murmured.

They walked hand-in-hand onto the ship; Wolf's grip was a little too tight, a little too fierce, like he feared she might slip away if he let go.

It hurt...but she didn't mind.

It meant she was alive.

It meant she was human.

She squeezed his hand back, closing her eyes and whispering one little prayer.

Let it hurt.

Let it hurt for a long, long time.

EPILOGUE

SOREN

"I still can't believe you and Elias got married without me."

Soren leaned against the Starsinger's railing, tipping her face back to bathe in the sun. She'd missed this part of sailing…the easy access to light and warmth. In the forest, even the strongest sunlight came through in dapples…and in the Sanctum, there'd been none at all.

Even Yvonne seemed to be basking in it, though her sister had always treated the sun a bit like an unpleasant but overly doting relative; one who beamed when she saw you, then wasted no time scorching your self-worth under her pinpoint rays. Her white-gold hair was tied back in a patterned bandana, a kaleidoscope tumble of dusty blue and dusty rose and the color of leather-bound spines holding dusty books together; despite the tie, the knot of hair itself seemed determined to slip its pins, decorating her shoulders in pale silk streamers that draped this way and that, a long-forgotten birthday display forced to take itself down. Her skin turned a shade pinker every day, despite Elowyn and a handful of other crew members taking turns reminding her to reapply her sunblock every couple hours…and one incident in the early afternoon involving a hammock nap, Yvonne (the champion of sleeping through anything, even storms deadly and dreadfully loud enough to wake the entire kingdom), and a self-proclaimed, self-centered pirate captain who spent a good twenty minutes smoothing the coconut-scented cream over Yvonne's exposed skin, muttering to himself about sunsickness and blisters and *the things I do for this spoiled seabird. Should let your feathers scorch and shrivel, that'd teach you.*

Though she hardly would've compared her sister to the obnoxious gulls that wheeled above in greater and greater numbers the closer they came to shore, Yvonne certainly preened like one—she looked entirely unruly, a perfect addition to this matching set of pirate figurines, yet she held herself with the air of someone who *knew* the way her presence alone could alter a room…or a ship.

Or a self-centered pirate captain who needed to set his wandering eyes back on course just as often as he needed to guide the drifting wheel.

Which was why Soren replied to her sister's play on hurt feelings with, "I can't believe you slept with a pirate."

Yvonne smacked her on the arm with a huff, adjusting the lacy cuff of her elbow-length sleeve. "You say the worst things."

"So you *did* sleep with him!"

"Yes, Soren. I slept with him. We had a torrid love affair, and now I'm carrying his child. But I shan't breathe a word of it to him, lest he chain himself to the land to care for us and grow to resent me in time."

That was…far too much detail. "Wait, did you actually—?"

Yvonne rolled her eyes. "No, Soren, I did not sleep with a pirate. I'm a Queen, for gods' sakes."

Pain—and, selfishly, relief—twisted her heart around her ribs, her fingers around the railing. "So you do know."

"We came across an Atlas town shortly after the news arrived." Hate glimmered in her gaze. "Three days of celebration before we got there. Gods know how many they had after we left."

And Yvonne had seen it all. Heard it all. Kept her head low as they gave thanks for the death of her mother.

"Patch shoved us all back on the boat when he realized…" The thought faded off into the distance as Yvonne's hand slipped down to her signet ring instead, spinning it around the knuckle of her middle finger. It would need to be resized.

"When he realized he brought the new Queen of Nyx into a town that would chum the waters with her if they found out?"

"He was crasser about it, but yes." Her smile tipped her hand, flashing a little fondness. "He realized it faster than I did…I should have been the one to insist we leave. Instead, I almost wiped the town clean off the map. What kind of Queen thinks about that first—vengeance over her kingdom's safety?"

Soren took her older sister's hand. "One who also happens to be a grieving daughter."

Adriata's face flickered in her mind.

Or a grieving mother.

Perhaps they were two sides of the same coin, her grief and her birth mother's…but tonight was not the night to ponder that too closely.

Yvonne fastened both hands around Soren's, holding to it like she feared to lose her mooring. And though she said nothing else, the tears in her eyes— mirror to Soren's—said it all.

Not the other side of the coin, but the same side.

To hold grief in perfect sameness with another person was entirely rare— and entirely precious. To sit with someone who understood the exact breadth of your pain gave you permission to feel it utterly.

So together, they grieved, these two daughters. And they let the sun and sea breeze dry their tears before one of them dared speak another word.

"I'm glad she gave it to you." Yvonne released her hand to pinch Soren's sleeve, tugging gently at the crinkled fabric.

"I don't know that I earned it."

"Experience counts for something. After all you went through in Atlas and after…" Yvonne shrugged. "I'm sure she would've given you Captain first, if things were different, just to keep people from crying favoritism. But I think we both know she didn't give it to you because of what you've already done."

No. It took years—a decade, sometimes, if not more—of service to earn a sleeve stitched with five stars.

It was the role she would *have* to play in the coming weeks, months…possibly years. This uniform was meant to be grown into, whether by necessity or by choice.

"I don't know how she knew," she admitted.

Nor did she know how she just kept *crying*, when she ought to have run out of tears some time ago.

Yvonne squeezed her arm. "Mothers always know."

Soren breathed in deeply; her voice snagged, caught in her throat. "It's so annoying."

A tearful giggle; Yvonne set her head on Soren's shoulder, taking her hand again. "It's the worst."

Another long silence; another shared ache.

"You really believe that letter is from your brother?" Yvonne asked once their eyes had run dry again. "Proof that he survived?"

She didn't let go of Soren's hand—or maybe Soren didn't let go of hers as she said, "I don't believe it. I *know* it."

A vision of a balmy winter day had told her so, long before she had any sort of proof.

Can you keep it up, kid? Just a little while longer?

She'd keep it up as long as she needed to. As long as Finn asked her to. Because she'd promised.

Playing a game. Need you on my team.

Because *he'd* promised, and kept it—because he hadn't left her.

One fathomless grief set free, transforming into a winged sort of hope—the kind that carried her on a sea-borne breeze, sailing ceaselessly toward home.

Toward bone-aching cold and glittering snow-swept porches and mornings filled to the brim with knit blankets and strong coffee and dragging her weak-willed husband back into bed for *just five more minutes, for real this time, I'll be good I swear.*

Atlas, first…then to war. Then *home.*

One calling, one purpose…a guiding star that never flickered.

She set her sights on that star and made a wish.

THE END

ACKNOWLEDGMENTS

Firstly, I'd like to acknowledge me, for getting through the drafting of this monstrously big book while burned out beyond belief. Good job, me. We did the thing.

But in all seriousness…

Thank you to God, first and foremost, who answered my prayers when I feared I would never find the "right" story to tell. If I wrote solely by my own strength, this book would not be here.

Thank you to my family, as always, who keep me afloat with their endless enthusiasm, make me cry when they brag about my books to their friends and coworkers, and help me lug all my stuff around when I attend events. You're the real MVPs—even those who aren't caught up on the series. (They're huge books. It's okay.)

Renee, thanks for kicking my ass. XOXO.

Thank you to Savannah Goins, who listened to me lament how absurdly long Book 4 was going to be with all five POVs added in, then earnestly said, "So are you going to split it into two books?" when I finally finished. Thank you for being a voice of reason in a time of great despair—and thank you for always welcoming me when I crash your writing dates with Renee. You saved this series in more ways than you know!

Okay, now for the REAL thank you, Renee: thanks for kicking my ass, yes, but also thank you for being the staunchest supporter of this series from day one. Thank you for the insane amount of work you put into editing and CPing even when you had so much on your own plate. Thanks for slogging through the drafting trenches with me and dangling Kilgrave in front of me like a poisoned carrot to get me to the finish line. Thanks for teaching me to prioritize my capacity, even when I didn't want to. And most of all, thanks for inviting me to share your release date. Now, let's celebrate—because we FLOGGING EARNED IT.

Thank you to Kristin Ardis, who ALSO listened to me lament the length of this book a few times and always had something encouraging to say…or offered solidarity as we both trudged through the editing process across a coffee shop table. Thank you for also letting me crash your writing dates with Renee,   for introducing me to your amazing laptop riser, and for always showing up to writing sessions with a dedication and professionalism that inspires me actually buckle down and do the work instead of goofing off on Pinterest. (And thank you in advance for giving Gage aall the happiness and love and never hurting him ever, right? RIGHT?

Thank you to Caitlan Honer for trading funny reels and heart-wrenching snippets alike, for always being up for an adventure, for taking stunning sunset pictures, and for being patient when I forget to answer your texts for a couple ~~hours~~ ~~days~~ ~~weeks~~ uh, a little while. You're one of my favorite people in the universe, and it's the universe's worst joke that we live almost an entire country apart. (What if we just take Oregon and push it somewhere else?) Here's to writing unhinged redheads and their dark-haired scowly love interests.

Thank you to Julia Martel, who introduced me to the beauty of California's desert, who made me feel for the first time like I wasn't the weird kid trying to sit at the cool kids' table, who is perhaps the most fiercely authentic and welcoming woman I've ever met. You and Caitlan have created a truly life-changing space in Intrepid, and I'm literally counting down the seconds until Raleigh.

And as always, thank YOU, reader. For loving these characters as much as I do. For asking when the next one is coming. (Much sooner this time, I promise!). For your patience and your enthusiasm and your tearful rage. (It fuels me.)

I hope you all had as much fun reading this story as I did writing it. But now that Soren, Ani, and Elias are on their way back to Atlas, it's time to buckle up and brace yourself for what comes next.

Because while they've been off collecting pebbles, battling a sentient plague, and solving puzzles in a magic-proof mountain…the Trickster Prince has been playing a *very* different game.

INTRODUCING BOOK FIVE OF THE
BLOOD & WATER SAGA…

THE MIRROR GAME

COMING WINTER 2025

ABOUT THE AUTHOR

Cassidy Clarke is a proud Michigander, barista, and Hallmark movie expert who loves all things fantasy, from Disney movies to Dungeons & Dragons. Her debut series THE BLOOD AND WATER SAGA is a high fantasy love letter to the lost princess daydreams of her childhood and an attempt to put her experience growing up with three younger siblings (all of whom are cooler than her) to good use. She spends her days writing like she's running out of time, binging Critical Role campaigns, hoarding pretty dice like a dragon, and baking the world's best chocolate chip cookies.